# A
# JOHN DICKSON
# CARR TRIO

# A
# JOHN
# DICKSON
# CARR
# TRIO

*including*

THE THREE COFFINS

THE CROOKED HINGE

THE CASE OF THE CONSTANT SUICIDES

Harper & Brothers Publishers New York

A JOHN DICKSON CARR TRIO

Copyright © 1957 by John Dickson Carr

THE THREE COFFINS: Copyright 1935 by John Dickson Carr

THE CROOKED HINGE: Copyright 1938 by John Dickson Carr

THE CASE OF THE CONSTANT SUICIDES: Copyright 1941 by
John Dickson Carr

Printed in the United States of America

# CONTENTS

THE THREE COFFINS                                    1

THE CROOKED HINGE                                  175

THE CASE OF THE
CONSTANT SUICIDES                                  339

# FOREWORD

John Dickson Carr has become known with justification as one of the masters of detection, with emphasis on the locked room and the impossible murder.

His famous detective, Dr. Gideon Fell, has become legendary.

For readers of recent vintage, who are not acquainted with the early career of the fabulous Dr. Fell, and for those who once enjoyed the stories, but would like a chance to reread them, we have chosen three of John Dickson Carr's best detective stories featuring Dr. Fell—ones that have been long unavailable in their original editions.

In recent years the detective story has moved on the whole from the true art of detection into the suspense field, where the crime and its detection are often subordinated and the characterization of the individuals involved in the story has become of primary interest.

Suspense novels today have reached a plateau of fine craftsmanship and genuine excitement, but many of us have missed the puzzle and the mystery that the earlier novels in the field of detection supplied.

John Dickson Carr's characters are fully and expertly realized; his books are never only puzzles, built around people who are paper-thin. He supplies, as few other writers ever have, the sleight-of-hand, the wonder of how could it have happened, and the absolute fair play of planting every clue so that the reader can, if he is very alert, solve the puzzle successfully, along with the detective.

In this trio, Carr's skill is splendidly revealed, and the reissue of these early novels in one volume should delight a large audience, new or old.

J. K.

*August,* 1957

# THE THREE COFFINS

# THE PROBLEM OF THE SAVANT'S STUDY

## I

### The Threat

To THE murder of Professor Grimaud, and later the equally incredible crime in Cagliostro Street, many fantastic terms could be applied—with reason. Those of Dr. Fell's friends who like impossible situations will not find in his casebook any puzzle more baffling or more terrifying. Thus: two murders were committed, in such fashion that the murderer must not only have been invisible, but lighter than air. According to the evidence, this person killed his first victim and literally disappeared. Again according to the evidence, he killed his second victim in the middle of an empty street, with watchers at either end; yet not a soul saw him, and no footprint appeared in the snow.

Naturally, Superintendent Hadley never for a moment believed in goblins or wizardry. And he was quite right—unless you believe in a magic that will be explained naturally in this narrative at the proper time. But several people began to wonder whether the figure which stalked through this case might not be a hollow shell. They began to wonder whether, if you took away the cap and the black coat and the child's false-face, you might not reveal nothing inside, like a man in a certain famous romance by Mr. H. G. Wells. The figure was grisly enough, anyhow.

The words "according to the evidence" have been used. We must be very careful about the evidence when it is not given at first-hand. And in this case the reader must be told at the outset, to avoid useless confusion, on whose evidence he can absolutely rely. That is to say, it must be assumed that *somebody* is telling the truth—else there is no legitimate mystery and, in fact, no story at all.

Therefore it must be stated that Mr. Stuart Mills at Professor Grimaud's house was not lying, was not omitting or adding anything, but telling the whole business exactly as he saw it in every case. Also it must be stated that the three independent witnesses of Cagliostro Street (Messrs. Short and Blackwin, and Police-constable Withers) were telling the exact truth.

Under these circumstances, one of the events which led up to the crime must be outlined more fully than is possible in retrospect. It was the keynote, the whip-lash, the challenge. And it is retold from Dr. Fell's notes, in essential details exactly as Stuart Mills later told it to Dr. Fell and Superintendent Hadley. It occurred on the night of Wednesday, February 6th, three days before the murder, in the back parlour of the Warwick Tavern in Museum Street.

Dr. Charles Vernet Grimaud had lived in England for nearly thirty years, and spoke English without accent. Except for a few curt mannerisms when he was excited, and his habit of wearing an old-fashioned square-topped bowler hat and black string tie, he was even more British than his friends. Nobody knew much about his earlier years. He was of independent means, but he had chosen to be "occupied" and made a good thing of it financially. Professor Grimaud had been a teacher, a popular lecturer and writer. But he had done little of late, and occupied some vague unsalaried post at the British Museum which gave him access to what he called the low-magic manuscripts. Low magic was the hobby of which he had made capital: any form of picturesque supernatural devilry from vampirism to the Black Mass, over which he nodded and chuckled with childlike amusement—and got a bullet through the lung for his pains.

A sound common-sense fellow, Grimaud, with a quizzical twinkle in his eye. He spoke in rapid, gruff bursts, from deep down in his throat; and he had a trick of chuckling behind closed teeth. He was of middle size, but he had a powerful chest and enormous physical stamina. Everybody in the neighbourhood of the Museum knew his black beard, trimmed so closely that it looked only like greying stubble, his shells of eye-glasses, his upright walk as he moved along in quick short steps, raising his hat curtly or making a semaphore gesture with his umbrella.

He lived, in fact, just round the corner at a solid old house on the west side of Russell Square. The other occupants of the house were his daughter Rosette, his housekeeper, Mme Dumont, his secretary, Stuart Mills, and a broken-down ex-teacher named Drayman, whom he kept as a sort of hanger-on to look after his books.

But his few real cronies were to be found at a sort of club they had instituted at the Warwick Tavern in Museum Street. They met four or five nights in a week, an unofficial conclave, in the snug back room reserved for that purpose. Although it was not officially a private room, few outsiders from the bar ever blundered in there, or were made welcome if they did. The most regular attendants of the club were fussy bald-headed little Pettis, the authority on ghost stories; Mangan, the newspaperman; and Burnaby, the artist; but Professor Grimaud was its undisputed Dr. Johnson.

He ruled. Nearly every night in the year (except Saturdays and Sundays, which he reserved for work), he would set out for the Warwick, accompanied by Stuart Mills. He would sit in his favourite cane armchair before a blazing fire, with a glass of hot rum and water, and hold forth autocratically in the fashion he enjoyed. The discussions, Mills says, were often brilliant, although nobody except Pettis or Burnaby ever gave Professor Grimaud serious battle. Despite his affability, he had a violent temper. As a rule they were content to listen to his storehouse of knowledge about witchcraft and sham witchcraft, wherein trickery hoaxed the credulous; his childlike love of mystification and drama, wherein he would tell a story of mediæval sorcery, and, at the end, abruptly explain all the puzzles in the fashion of a detective story. They were amusing evenings, with something of the rural-inn flavour about them, though they were tucked away behind the gas-lamps of Bloomsbury. They were amusing evenings—until the night of February 6th, when the premonition of terror entered as suddenly as the wind blowing open a door.

The wind was blowing shrewdly that night, Mills says, with a threat of snow in the air. Besides himself and Grimaud, there were present at the fireside only Pettis and Mangan and Burnaby. Professor Grimaud had been speaking, with pointed gestures of his cigar, about the legend of vampirism.

"Frankly, what puzzles me," said Pettis, "is your attitude towards the whole business. Now, I study only fiction; only ghost stories that never happened. Yet in a way I believe in ghosts. But you're an authority on attested happenings—things that we're forced to call facts unless we can refute 'em. Yet you don't believe a word of what you've made the most important thing in your life. It's as though Bradshaw wrote a treatise to prove that steam-locomotion was impossible, or the editor of the Encyclopædia Britannica inserted a preface saying that there wasn't a reliable article in the whole edition."

"Well, and why not?" said Grimaud, with that quick, gruff bark of his wherein he hardly seemed to open his mouth. "You see the moral, don't you?"

" 'Much study hath made him mad,' perhaps?" suggested Burnaby.

Grimaud continued to stare at the fire. Mills says that he seemed more angry than the casual gibe would have warranted. He sat with the cigar exactly in the middle of his mouth, drawing at it in the manner of a child sucking a peppermint-stick.

"I am the man who knew too much," he said, after a pause. "And it is not recorded that the temple priest was ever a very devout believer. However, that is beside the point. I am interested in the causes behind these superstitions. How did the superstition start? What gave it impetus, so that the gullible could believe? For example! We are speaking of the vampire legend. Now, that is a belief which prevails in Slavonic lands. Agreed? It got its firm grip on Europe when it swept in a blast out of Hungary between 1730 and 1735. Well, how did Hungary get its proof that dead men could leave their coffins, and float in the air in the form of straw or fluff until they took human shape for an attack?"

"Was there proof?" asked Burnaby.

Grimaud lifted his shoulders in a broad gesture.

"They exhumed bodies from the churchyards. They found some corpses in twisted positions, with blood on their faces and hands and shrouds. That was their proof. . . . But why not? Those were plague years. Think of all the poor devils who were buried alive though believed to be dead. Think how they struggled to get out of the coffin before they really died. You see, gentlemen? That's what I mean by the causes behind superstitions. That's what I am interested in."

"*I also*," said a new voice, "*am interested in it.*"

Mills says that he had not heard the man come in, although he thought he felt a current of air from the opened door. Possibly they were startled by the mere intrusion of a stranger, in a room where a stranger seldom intruded and never spoke. Or it may have been the man's voice, which was harsh, husky, and faintly foreign, with a sly triumph croaking in it. Anyhow, the suddenness of it made them all switch round.

There was nothing remarkable about him, Mills says. He stood back from the firelight, with the collar of his shabby black overcoat turned up and the brim of his shabby soft hat pulled down. And what little they could see of his face was shaded by the gloved hand with which he was stroking his chin. Beyond the fact that he was tall and shabby and of gaunt build, Mills could tell nothing. But in his voice or bearing, or maybe a trick of gesture, there was something vaguely familiar while it remained foreign.

He spoke again. And his speech had a stiff, pedantic quality, as though it were a burlesque of Grimaud.

"You must forgive me, gentlemen," he said, and the triumph grew, "for intruding into your conversation. But I should like to ask the famous Professor Grimaud a question."

Nobody thought of snubbing him, Mills says. They were all intent; there was a kind of wintry power about the man, which disturbed the snug firelit room. Even Grimaud, who sat dark and solid and ugly as an Epstein figure, with his cigar halfway to his mouth and his eyes glittering behind the thin glasses, was intent. He only barked:

"Well?"

"You do not believe, then," the other went on, turning his gloved hand round from his chin only far enough to point with one finger, "that a man can get up out of his coffin; that he can move anywhere invisibly; that four walls are nothing to him; and that he is as dangerous as anything out of hell?"

"I do not," Grimaud answered, harshly. "Do you?"

"Yes. I have done it. But more! I have a brother who can do much more than I can, and is very dangerous to you. *I* don't want your life; he does. But if *he* calls on you. . . ."

The climax of this wild talk snapped like a piece of slate exploding in the fire. Young Mangan, an ex-footballer, jumped to his feet. Little Pettis peered round nervously.

"Look here, Grimaud," said Pettis, "this fellow's stark mad. Shall I—" He made an uneasy gesture in the direction of the bell, but the stranger interposed.

"Look at Professor Grimaud," he said, "before you decide."

Grimaud was regarding him with a heavy, graven contempt. "No, no, no! You hear me? Let him alone. Let him talk about his brother and his coffins—"

"Three coffins," interposed the stranger.

"Three coffins," agreed Grimaud, with bristling suavity, "if you like. As many as you like, in God's name! Now perhaps you'll tell us who you are?"

The stranger's left hand came out of his pocket and laid a grubby card on the table. Somehow the sight of that prosaic visiting-card seemed to restore sane values; to whirl the whole delusion up the chimney as a joke; and to make of this harsh-voiced visitor nothing but a scarecrow of an actor with a bee under his shabby hat. For Mills saw that the card read: *Pierre Fley. Illusionist.* In one corner was printed *2B Cagliostro Street*, W.C. 1., and over it was scribbled *Or c/o Academy Theatre.* Grimaud laughed. Pettis swore and rang the bell for the waiter.

"So," remarked Grimaud, and ticked the card against his thumb. "I thought we should come to something like that. You are a conjuror, then?"

"Does the card say so?"

"Well, well, if it's a lower professional grade, I beg your pardon," nodded Grimaud. A sort of asthmatic mirth whistled in his nostrils. "I don't suppose we might see one of your illusions?"

"With pleasure," said Fley, unexpectedly.

His movement was so quick that nobody anticipated it. It looked like an attack, and was nothing of the kind—in a physical sense. He bent across the table towards Grimaud, his gloved hands twitching down the collar of his coat, and twitching it back up again before anybody else could get a glimpse of him. But Mills had an impression that he was grinning. Grimaud remained motionless and hard. Only his jaw seemed to jut and rise, so that the mouth was like a contemptuous arc in the clipped beard. And his colour was a little darker, though he continued to tick the card quietly against his thumb.

"And now, before I go," said Fley, curtly, "I have a last question for the famous professor. Some one will call on you one evening soon. I also am in danger when I associate with my brother, but I am prepared to run that risk. Some one, I repeat, will call on you. Would you rather I did—or shall I send my brother?"

"Send your brother," snarled Grimaud, getting up suddenly, "and be damned!"

The door had closed behind Fley before anybody moved or spoke. And the door also closes on the only clear view we have of the events leading up to the night of Saturday, February 9th. The rest lies in flashes and glimpses, to be interpreted in jig-saw fashion as Dr. Fell later fitted together the charred fragments between the sheets of glass. The first deadly walking of the hollow man took place on that last-named night, when the side streets of London were quiet with snow and the three coffins of the prophecy were filled at last.

## II

### *The Door*

THERE was roaring good-humour that night round the fire in Dr. Fell's library at Number 1 Adelphi Terrace. The doctor sat ruddy-faced and enthroned in his largest, most comfortable, and decrepit chair, which had sagged and cracked across the padding in the only way a chair can be made comfortable, but which for some reason makes wives go frantic. Dr. Fell beamed with all his vastness behind the eye-glasses on the black ribbon, and hammered his cane on the hearth rug as he chuckled. He was celebrating. Dr. Fell likes to celebrate the arrival of his friends; or, in fact, anything else. And tonight there was double cause for revelry.

For one thing, his young friends, Ted and Dorothy Rampole, had arrived from America in the most exuberant of good spirits. For another, his friend Hadley—now Superintendent Hadley of the C.I.D., remember—had just concluded a brilliant piece of work on the Bayswater forgery case, and was relaxing. Ted Rampole sat at one side of the hearth, and Hadley at the other, with the doctor presiding between over a steaming bowl of punch. Upstairs the Mesdames Fell, Hadley, and Rampole were conferring about something, and down here the Messieurs Fell and Hadley were already engaged in a violent argument about something else, so Ted Rampole felt at home.

Sitting back lazily in the deep chair, he remembered old days. Across from him Superintendent Hadley, with his clipped moustache and his hair the colour of dull steel, was smiling and making satiric remarks to his pipe. Dr. Fell flourished the punch ladle in thunder.

They seemed to be arguing about scientific criminology, and photography in particular. Rampole remembered hearing echoes of this, which had roused the ribald mirth of the C.I.D. During one of his absent-minded intervals of pottering about after a hobby, Dr. Fell had been snared by his friend the Bishop of Mappleham into reading Gross, Jesserich, and Mitchell. He had been bitten. Now Dr. Fell has not, it may be thankfully stated, what is called the scientific brain. But his chemical researches left the roof on the house, since, fortunately, he always managed to smash the apparatus before the experiment had begun; and, beyond setting fire to the curtains with a Bunsen burner, he did little damage. His photographic work (he said) had been very successful. He had bought a Davontel microscopic camera, with an achromatic lens, and littered the place with what resembled X-ray prints of a particularly dyspeptic stomach. Also, he claimed to have perfected Dr. Gross' method of deciphering the writing on burnt paper.

Listening to Hadley jeer at this, Rampole let his mind drift drowsily. He could see the firelight moving on crooked walls of books, and hear fine snow ticking the window panes behind drawn curtains. He grinned to himself in sheer amiability. He had nothing in the excellent world to irk him—or had he? Shifting, he stared at the fire. Little things popped up like a jack-in-the-box to jab you when you were most comfortable.

Criminal cases! Of course there was nothing to it. It had been Mangan's ghoulish eagerness to enrich a good story. All the same—

"I don't give a hoot *what* Gross says," Hadley was declaring, with a flap of his hand on the chair-arm. "You people always seem to think a man is accurate just because he's thorough. In most cases the letters against burnt paper don't show up at all. . . ."

Rampole cleared his throat pacifically. "By the way," he said, "do the words 'three coffins' mean anything to you?"

There was an abrupt silence, as he had hoped there would be. Hadley regarded him suspiciously. Dr. Fell blinked over the ladle with a puzzled air, as though he vaguely associated the words with a cigarette or a pub. Then a twinkle appeared in his eye.

"Heh," he said, and rubbed his hands. "Heh-heh-heh! Making peace, hey? Or do you by any chance mean it? What coffins?"

"Well," said Rampole, "I shouldn't exactly call it a criminal case—"

Hadley whistled.

"—but it's a queer business, unless Mangan was stretching things. I know Boyd Mangan quite well; he lived on the other side for a couple of years. He's a damned good fellow who's knocked about the world a lot and has a too-Celtic imagination." He paused, remembering Mangan's dark, slovenly, rather dissipated good looks; his slow-moving ways despite his excitable temperament; his quick generosity and homely grin. "Anyhow, he's here in London working for the *Evening Banner* now. I ran into him this morning in the Haymarket. He dragged me into a bar and poured out the whole story. Then," said Rampole, laying it on with a trowel, "when he learned I knew the great Dr. Fell—"

"Rats," said Hadley, looking at him in that sharp, watchful way of his. "Get down to cases."

"Heh-heh-heh," said Dr. Fell, highly delighted. "Shut up, will you, Hadley? This sounds interesting, my boy. Well?"

"Well, it seems that he's a great admirer of a lecturer or writer named

Grimaud. Also he has fallen hard for Grimaud's daughter, and that makes
him a still greater admirer of the old man. The old man and some of his
friends have a habit of visiting a pub near the British Museum, and a few
nights ago something happened which seems to have shaken up Mangan
more than the antics of a casual lunatic would warrant. While the old man
was talking about corpses getting up out of their graves, or some such cheerful
subject, in walked a tall queer-looking bird who began babbling some nonsense about himself and his brother really being able to leave their graves
and float in the air like straw." (Here Hadley made a disgusted noise and
relaxed his attention, but Dr. Fell continued to look curiously at Rampole.)
"Actually, it seems to have been some sort of threat against this Professor
Grimaud. At the end this stranger made a threat that his brother would call
on Grimaud before long. The odd part was that, though Grimaud didn't turn
a hair, Mangan swears he was actually scared green."

Hadley grunted. "That's Bloomsbury for you. But what of it? Somebody
with a scary old-womanish mind—"

"That's the point," growled Dr. Fell, scowling. "He isn't. I know Grimaud quite well. I say, Hadley, you don't know how queer it is unless you
know Grimaud. H'mf. Ha. Go on, son. How did it end?"

"Grimaud didn't say anything. In fact, he turned it into a joke and an
anti-climax that punctured the lunacy pretty well. Just after this stranger
had gone, a street musician came up against the door of the pub and struck
up 'The Daring Young Man on the Flying Trapeze.' The whole crowd of
them burst out laughing, and sanity was restored. Grimaud smiled and said,
'Well, gentlemen, our revived corpse will have to be even nimbler than that
if he expects to float down from *my* study window.'

"They dismissed it at that. But Mangan was curious to find out who this
visitor, this 'Pierre Fley,' was. Fley had given Grimaud a card with the name
of a theatre on it. So the next day Mangan followed it up in the guise of getting a newspaper story. The theatre turned out to be a rather broken-down
and disreputable music-hall in the East End, staging nightly variety. Mangan
didn't want to run into Fley. He got into talk with the stage-door keeper,
who introduced him to an acrobat in the turn before Fley. This acrobat calls
himself—Lord knows why—'Pagliacci the Great,' although he's actually an
Irishman and a shrewd one. He told Mangan what he knew.

"Fley is known at the theatre as 'Loony.' They know nothing about him;
he speaks to nobody and ducks out after every show. But—this is the point—
he is *good*. The acrobat said he didn't understand why some West End
manager hadn't tumbled to it long before, unless Fley was simply unam-
bitious. It's a sort of super-conjuring, with a specialty in vanishing-
tricks. . . ."

Hadley grunted again, derisively.

"No," insisted Rampole, "so far as I can gather it isn't just the old, old stuff. Mangan says he works without an assistant, and that all his props together can go into a box the size of a coffin. If you know anything about magicians, you'll know what a whale of an incredible thing that is. In fact, the man seems hipped on the subject of coffins. Pagliacci the Great once asked him why, and got a jump he didn't expect. Fley turned round with a broad grin and said: 'Three of us were once buried alive. Only one escaped.' Pagliacci said: 'And how did you escape?' To which Fley answered, calmly: 'I didn't, you see. I was one of the two who did not escape.' "

Hadley was tugging at the lobe of his ear. He was serious now.

"Look here," he said, rather uneasily, "this may be a little more important than I'd thought. The fellow's crazy, right enough. If he's got any imaginary grudge— You say he's an alien? I might give the Home Office a call and have him looked up. Then, if he tries to make trouble for your friend . . ."

"*Has* he tried to make trouble?" asked Dr. Fell.

Rampole shifted. "Some sort of letter has come for Professor Grimaud in every post since Wednesday. He has torn 'em up without saying anything, but somebody told his daughter about the affair at the pub, and she has begun to worry. Finally, to cap the whole business, yesterday Grimaud himself began to act queerly."

"How?" asked Dr. Fell. He took away the hand with which he had been shading his eyes. His little eyes blinked at Rampole in startling sharpness.

"He phoned Mangan yesterday, and said: 'I want you to be at the house on Saturday evening. Somebody threatens to pay me a visit.' Naturally, Mangan advised warning the police, which Grimaud wouldn't hear of. Then Mangan said: 'But hang it, sir, this fellow's stark mad and he may be dangerous. Aren't you going to take *any* precautions to defend yourself?' To which the professor answered: 'Oh yes, by all means. I am going to buy a painting.' "

"A what?" demanded Hadley, sitting up.

"A painting to hang on the wall. No, I'm not joking. It seems he did buy it: it was a landscape of some sort, weird business showing trees and gravestones, and a devil of a huge landscape that it took two workmen to carry upstairs. I say 'devil of a landscape' advisedly; I haven't seen it. It was painted by an artist named Burnaby, who's a member of the club and an amateur criminologist. . . . Anyhow, that's Grimaud's idea of defending himself."

To Hadley, who was again eyeing him suspiciously, he repeated his words with some violence. They both turned to look at Dr. Fell. The doctor sat wheezing over his double chins, his big mop of hair rumpled and his hands folded on his cane. He nodded, staring at the fire. When he spoke, the room seemed to grow less comfortable.

"Have you got the address of the place, my boy?" he asked, in a colourless voice. . . . "Good. Better warm up your car, Hadley."

"Yes, but look here—!"

"When an alleged lunatic threatens a sane man," said Dr. Fell, nodding again, "then you may or may not be disturbed. But when a sane man begins to act exactly like the lunatic, then I know *I'm* jolly well disturbed. It may be nothing at all. But I don't like it." Wheezing, he hoisted himself up. "Come on, Hadley. We'll go and have a look at the place, even if we only cruise past."

A sharp wind bit through the narrow streets of the Adelphi; the snow had stopped. It lay white and unreal on the terrace, and in the Embankment gardens below. In the Strand, bright and deserted during the theatre hour, it was churned to dirty ruts. A clock said five minutes past ten as they turned up into Aldwych. Hadley sat quiet at the wheel, his collar turned up. At Dr. Fell's roar for more speed, Hadley looked first at Rampole and then at the doctor piled into the rear seat.

"This is a lot of nonsense, you know," he snapped. "And it's none of our business. Besides, if there has been a visitor, he's probably gone by now."

"I know," said Dr. Fell. "That's what I'm afraid of."

The car shot into Southampton Row. Hadley kept hooting the horn as though to express his own feelings—but they gathered speed. The street was a bleak canyon, opening into the bleaker canyon of Russell Square. On the west side ran few foot-tracks and even fewer wheel-marks. If you know the telephone box at the north end, just after you pass Keppel Street, you will have seen the house opposite even if you have not noticed it. Rampole saw a plain, broad, three-storied front, the ground floor of stone blocks painted dun, and red brick above. Six steps led up to a big front door with a brass-edged letter-slot and brass knob. Except for two windows glowing behind drawn blinds on the ground floor over the areaway, the whole place was dark. It seemed the most prosaic house in a prosaic neighbourhood. But it did not remain so.

A blind was torn aside. One of the lighted windows went up with a bang just as they idled past. A figure climbed on the sill, outlined against the crackling blind, hesitated, and leaped. The leap carried him far over beyond the spiked area rails. He struck the pavement on one leg, slipped in the snow, and pitched out across the kerb nearly under the wheels of the car.

Hadley jammed on his brakes. He was out of the car as it skidded against the kerb, and had the man by the arm before the latter had got to his feet. But Rampole had caught a glimpse of the man's face in the headlights.

"Mangan!" he said. "What the devil—!"

Mangan was without a hat or overcoat. His eyes glittered in the light like the glassy bits of snow streaking his arms and hands.

"Who's that?" he demanded, hoarsely. "No, no, I'm all right! Let go, damn it!" He yanked loose from Hadley and began to wipe his hands on his coat. "Who— *Ted!* Listen. Get somebody. Come along yourself. Hurry! He locked us in—there was a shot upstairs; we just heard it. He'd locked us in, you see. . . ."

Looking behind him, Rampole could see a woman's figure silhouetted against the window. Hadley cut through these incoherent words.

"Steady on. Who locked you in?"

"*He* did. Fley. He's still in there. We heard the shot, and the door's too thick to break. Well, are you coming on?"

He was already running for the front steps, with Hadley and Rampole after him. Neither of the latter had expected the front door to be unlocked, but it swung open when Mangan wrenched the knob. The high hallway inside was dark except for a lamp burning on a table far at the rear. Something seemed to be standing back there, looking at them, with a face more grotesque than any they might have imagined on Pierre Fley; and then Rampole saw it was only a suit of Japanese armour decked out in its devil mask. Mangan hurried to a door at the right, and turned the key that was in the lock. The door was opened from inside by the girl whose silhouette they had seen at the window, but Mangan held her back with his arm extended. From upstairs they could hear a heavy banging noise.

"It's all right, Boyd!" cried Rampole, feeling his heart rise in his throat. "This is Superintendent Hadley—I told you about him. Where is it? What is it?"

Mangan pointed at the staircase. "Carry on. I'll take care of Rosette. He's still upstairs. He can't get out. For God's sake be careful!"

He was reaching after a clumsy weapon on the wall as they went up thick-carpeted stairs. The floor above was dark and seemed deserted. But a light shone down from a niche in the staircase to the next floor, and the banging had changed to a series of thuds.

"Dr. Grimaud!" a voice was crying. "Dr. *Grimaud!* Answer me, will you?"

Rampole had no time to analyze what seemed the exotic, thick atmosphere of this place. He hurried after Hadley up the second staircase, under an open archway at its top, and into a broad hallway which ran the breadth of the house instead of the length. It was panelled to the ceiling in oak, with three curtained windows in the long side of this oblong opposite the staircase, and its thick black carpet deadened every footstep. There were two doors—facing each other from the narrow ends of the oblong. The door far down at their left was open; the door at their right, only about ten feet from the staircase, remained closed despite the man who was beating on it with his fists.

This man whirled round at their approach. Although there was no illumination in the hallway itself, a yellow light streamed through the arch from the niche on the staircase—from the stomach of a great brass Buddha in the niche—and they could see everything clearly. Full in the glow stood a breath-

less little man who was gesturing uncertainly. He had a big goblinlike shock
of hair on his big head, and peered behind big spectacles.

"Boyd?" he cried. "Drayman? I say, is that you? Who's there?"

"Police," said Hadley, and strode past him as he jumped back.

"You can't get in there," said the little man, cracking the joints of his
fingers. "But we've got to get in. The door's locked on the inside. Somebody's
in there with Grimaud. A gun went off— He won't answer. Where's Madame
Dumont? Get Madame Dumont! That fellow's still in there, I tell you!"

Hadley turned round snappishly.

"Stop dancing and see if you can find a pair of pliers. The key's in the lock;
we'll turn it from the outside. I want a pair of *pliers*. Have you got 'em?"

"I—I really don't know where—"

Hadley looked at Rampole. "Hop down to the tool-box in my car. It's
under the back seat. Get the smallest pliers you can find, and you might
bring along a couple of heavy spanners. If this fellow is armed—"

Rampole turned round to see Dr. Fell emerge through the arch, wheezing
heavily. The doctor did not speak, but his face was not so ruddy as before.
Going downstairs three at a time, Rampole blundered for what seemed hours
before he found the pliers. As he returned he could hear Mangan's voice
behind the closed door in the downstairs room, and the hysterical tones of a
girl. . . .

Hadley, still impassive, eased the pliers gently into the keyhole. His powerful hands clamped, and began to turn towards the left.

"There's something moving in there—" said the little man.

"Got it," said Hadley. "Stand back!"

He drew on a pair of gloves, braced himself, and threw the door inward.
It flapped back against the wall with a crash that shook tinglings from the
chandelier inside. Nothing came out, although something was trying to come
out. Except for that, the bright room was empty. Something, on which Rampole saw a good deal of blood, was painfully trying to drag itself on hands
and knees across the black carpet. It choked, rolled over on its side, and lay
still.

## III

### The False Face

"Stay in the door, two of you," Hadley said, curtly. "And if anybody's got
weak nerves, don't look."

Dr. Fell lumbered in after him, and Rampole remained in the doorway
with his arm extended across it. Professor Grimaud was heavy, but Hadley
did not dare wrench. In that effort to crawl to the door there had been a

hemorrhage which was not altogether internal, although Grimaud kept his teeth clenched against the blood. Hadley raised him up against one knee. His face had a bluish tinge under the mask of blackish-grey stubble; his eyes were closed and sunken; and he was still trying to press a sodden handkerchief to the bullet hole in his chest. They heard his breath sink thinly. Despite a draught, there was still a sharp mist of powder-smoke.

"Dead?" muttered Dr. Fell.

"Dying," said Hadley. "See the colour? He got it through the lung." He whirled round towards the little man in the doorway. "Phone for an ambulance. Quick! There's not a chance, but he may be able to say something before—"

"Yes," said Dr. Fell, with a kind of fierce sombreness; "that's the thing we're most interested in, isn't it?"

"If it's the only thing we can do," Hadley answered, coolly, "yes. Get me some sofa pillows from over there. Make him as comfortable as we can." When Grimaud's head lolled on one pillow, Hadley bent close. "Dr. Grimaud! *Dr. Grimaud!* Can you hear me?"

The waxy eyelids fluttered. Grimaud's eyes, only half open, moved in a queer, helpless, puzzled way, like a small child's in a face that you would have described as "knowing" or "civilized." He could not seem to understand what had happened. His glasses hung down on a cord from the dressing-gown; he made a weak twitching of his fingers as though he would try to raise them. His barrel chest still rose and fell slightly.

"I am from the police, Dr. Grimaud. Who did this? Don't try to answer if you can't. Nod your head. Was it the man Pierre Fley?"

A faint look of comprehension was succeeded by an even more puzzled expression. Then, distinctly Grimaud shook his head.

"Who was it, then?"

Grimaud was eager; too eager, for it defeated him. He spoke for the first and last time. His lips stuttered in those words whose interpretation, and even the exact wording itself, was so puzzling afterwards. Then he fainted.

The window in the left-hand wall was a few inches up, and a chill draught blew through. Rampole shivered. What had been a brilliant man lay inert on a couple of pillows, spilled and torn like a sack; with something rattling like clockwork inside it to show that it lived, but no more. There was too much blood in the bright, quiet room.

"My God!" Rampole said, uncontrollably, "isn't there anything we can *do*?"

Hadley was bitter. "Nothing, except get to work. 'Still in the house?' Fine lot of dummies!—oh, myself included." He pointed to the partly open window. "Of course the fellow was out of there before we were even inside the house. He certainly isn't here now."

Rampole looked round. The sharp tang of powder-smoke was blowing away, from his vision as well as from the room. He saw the place for the first time in focus.

It was a room some fifteen feet square, with walls panelled in oak and thick black carpet on the floor. In the left-hand wall (as you stood at the door) was the window with its brown velvet draperies blowing. On either side of the window stretched high bookshelves with marble busts along the top. Just out from the window, so as to get the light from the left, stood a great flat-topped desk heavy in claw-footed carving. A padded chair was pushed back from it; at the extreme left was a lamp of mosaic glass, and a bronze ash-tray over which a dead cigar had smouldered to long ash. The blotter, on which a closed calfskin book had been put down, was clean except for a tray of pens and a pile of note-slips held down by a curious little figure —a buffalo carved in yellow jade.

Rampole looked across the room at the side directly opposite the window. In that wall was a great stone fireplace, flanked also by shelves and busts. Above the fireplace, two fencing-foils hung crossed behind a blazoned shield of arms which Rampole did not (then) examine. Only on that side of the room had furniture been disarranged. Just before the fire, a long brown-leather sofa had been knocked awry, and a leather chair rolled back in a twisted-up hearth rug. There was blood on the sofa.

And finally, towards the rear wall of the room facing the door, Rampole saw the painting. Between the bookshelves in this wall there was a vast cleared space where cases had recently been removed; removed within the last few days, for the marks of their bases were still indented in the carpet. A place on the wall had been made for the painting which Grimaud would now never hang. The painting itself lay face upwards on the floor not far from where Grimaud himself lay—and it had been slashed across twice with a knife. In its frame it was fully seven feet broad by four feet high: a thing so big that Hadley had to trundle it out and switch it round in the cleared space down the centre of the room before he could prop it up for a look.

"And that," said Hadley, propping it against the back of the sofa, "is the painting he bought to 'defend himself' with, is it? Look here, Fell, do you think Grimaud was just as mad as this fellow Fley?"

Dr. Fell, who had been owlishly contemplating the window, lumbered round. "As Pierre Fley," he rumbled, and pushed back his shovel-hat, "who *didn't* commit the crime. H'm. I say, Hadley, do you see any weapon?"

"I do not. First there isn't any gun—a high-calibre automatic is what we want—and now there isn't any knife with which this thing was cut to blazes. Look at it! It looks like an ordinary landscape to me."

It was not, Rampole thought, exactly ordinary. There was a sort of blowing power about it, as though the artist had painted in a fury and caught in oils the wind that whipped those crooked trees. You felt bleakness and terror. Its motif was sombre, with a greenish tint underlying greys and blacks, except for low white mountains rising in the background. In the foreground, through the branches of a crooked tree, you could see three headstones in rank grass. Somehow it had an atmosphere like this room, subtly foreign, but as hard to identify as a faint odour. The headstones were toppling; in one way you looked at it, there was an illusion that this was because the grave mounds had begun to heave and crack across. Even the slashes did not seem to disfigure it.

Rampole started a little as he heard a trampling of feet up the staircase in the hall. Boyd Mangan burst in, thinner and more dishevelled than Rampole remembered. Even his black hair, which clung to his head in wirelike scrolls, looked rumpled. He took a quick look at the man on the floor, the heavy brows shading his eyes, and then began to rub a parchmentlike cheek. Actually he was about Rampole's age, but the slanting lines drawn under his eyes made him look ten years older.

"Mills told me," he said. "Is he—?" He nodded quickly at Grimaud.

Hadley ignored this. "Did you get the ambulance?"

"Chaps with a stretcher—coming now. The whole neighbourhood's filthy with hospitals, and nobody knew where to telephone. I remembered a friend of the professor's who's got a nursing-home round the corner. They're—" He stood aside to admit two uniformed attendants, and behind them a placid little clean-shaven man with a bald head. "This is Dr. Peterson—er—the police. And that's your—patient."

Dr. Peterson sucked in his cheek and hurried over. "Stretcher, boys," he said, after a brief look. "I won't dig for it here. Take him easy." He scowled and stared curiously round as the stretcher was carried out.

"Any chance?" asked Hadley.

"He might last a couple of hours; not more, and probably less. If he hadn't the constitution of a bull he'd be dead already. Looks as though he's made a further lesion in the lung trying to exert himself—torn it across." Dr. Peterson dived into his pocket. "You'll want to send your police surgeon round, won't you? Here's my card. I'll keep the bullet when I get it. I should guess a thirty-eight bullet, fired from about ten feet off. May I ask what happened?"

"Murder," said Hadley. "Keep a nurse with him, and if he says anything have it taken down word for word." As the doctor hurried out, Hadley scribbled on a leaf of his notebook and handed it to Mangan. "Got your head about you? Good. I wish you'd phone the Hunter Street police station with these instructions; they'll get in touch with the Yard. Tell 'em what happened if they ask. Dr. Watson is to go to the address of this nursing-home, and the rest are to come on here. . . . Who's that at the door?"

The man at the door was the small, thin, top-heavy youth who had been pounding there to begin with. In full light Rampole saw a big goblin-like shock of dark red hair. He saw dull brown eyes magnified behind thick gold-rimmed glasses, and a bony face sloping outwards to a large and loose mouth.

This mouth wriggled with a sonorous precision of utterance, showing wide-spaced teeth with an upward movement of the lip like a fish. The mouth looked flexible from much speaking. Every time he spoke, in fact, he had the appearance of thinly addressing an audience, raising and lowering his head as though from notes, and speaking in a penetrating singsong towards a point over his listeners' heads. You would have diagnosed a Physics B.Sc. with Socialist platform tendencies, and you would have been right. His clothes were of a reddish-check pattern, and his fingers were laced together before him. His earlier terror had changed to inscrutable calm. He bowed a little, and replied without expression:

"I am Stuart Mills. I am, or was, Dr. Grimaud's secretary." His big eyes moved round. "May I ask what has happened to the—culprit?"

"Presumably," said Hadley, "he escaped through the window while we were all so sure he couldn't get out. Now, Mr. Mills—"

"Pardon me," the sing-song voice interposed, with a sort of aerial detachment about it. "He must have been a very extraordinary man if he did that. Have you examined the window?"

"He's right, Hadley," said Dr. Fell, wheezing heavily. "Take a look! This business is beginning to worry me. I tell you in all sincerity that, if our man didn't leave here by way of the door . . ."

"He did not. I am not," announced Mills, and smiled, "the only witness to that. I saw it all from start to finish."

". . . then he must have been lighter than air to leave by the window. Open the window and have a look. H'mf, wait! We'd better search the room first."

There was nobody hidden in the room. Afterwards, growling under his breath, Hadley eased the window up. Unbroken snow—stretching flat up to the window-frame itself—covered all the wide sill outside. Rampole bent out and looked round.

There was a bright moon in the west, and every detail stood out sharp as a wood-cut. It was a good fifty feet to the ground; the wall fell away in a drop of smooth, wet stone. Just below there was a back yard, like that of all the houses in this row, surrounded by a low wall. The snow lay unbroken in this courtyard, or any other as far as they could look, and along the tops of the walls. Below in the whole side of the house there were no windows whatever. The only windows were on this top floor; and the nearest one to this room was in the hallway to the left, a good thirty feet away. To the right, the nearest window would have been in the adjoining house, an equal distance away. Ahead there lay a vast chessboard of adjoining back yards from houses lining the square, so that the nearest house was several hundred yards away. Finally, there stretched above this window a smooth upward run of stone for some fifteen feet to the roof—whose slope afforded neither hold for the fingers nor for the attaching of a rope.

But Hadley, craning his neck out, pointed malevolently.

"All the same, that's it," he declared. "Look there! Suppose he first hitched a rope to a chimney or something, and had it dangling outside the window when he paid his visit. Then he kills Grimaud, swings out, climbs up over the edge of the roof, crawls up to untie the rope from the chimney, and gets away. There will be plenty of tracks of *that*, right enough. So—"

"Yes," said Mills' voice. "That is why I must tell you that there aren't any."

Hadley looked round. Mills had been examining the fireplace, but now he regarded them with his wide-spaced teeth showing in an impassive smile, though his eyes looked nervous and there was sweat on his forehead.

"You see," he continued, lifting his hand with the forefinger raised, "as soon as I perceived that the man in the false face had disappeared—"

"The *what?*" said Hadley.

"The false face. Do I make myself clear?"

"No. We must see whether we can't extract some sense presently, Mr. Mills. In the meantime, what is this business about the roof?"

"There are no tracks or marks of any nature on it, you see," the other answered, with a bright expression of his eyes as he opened them wide. This was another trick of his, smiling and staring as though with inspiration, even if it sometimes seemed rather a half-witted inspiration. He raised his forefinger again. "I repeat, gentlemen: when I saw that the man in the false face had evidently disappeared, I foresaw difficulties for myself—"

"Why?"

"Because I myself had this door under observation, and I should have been compelled to asseverate that the man had not come out. Very well. It was therefore deducible that he must have left (a) by way of a rope to the roof, or (b) by means of climbing up inside the chimney to the roof. This was a simple mathematical certainty. If $PQ = pq$, it is therefore quite obvious that $PQ = pq + p\beta + qa + a\beta$."

"Is it indeed?" said Hadley, with restraint. "Well?"

"At the end of this hallway which you see—that is to say, which you could see if the door were open," pursued Mills, with unshakable exactitude, "I have my workroom. From there a door leads to the attic, and thence to a trap-door opening out on the roof. By raising the trap-door I could see clearly both sides of the roof over this room. The snow was not marked in any fashion."

"You didn't go out there?" demanded Hadley.

"No. I could not have kept my footing if I had. In fact, I do not at the moment see how this could be done even in dry weather."

Dr. Fell turned a radiant face. He seemed to resist a desire to pick up this phenomenon and dangle him in the air like an ingenious toy.

"And what then, my boy?" he enquired, affably. "I mean, what did you think when your equation was shot to blazes?"

Mills remained smiling and inflexibly profound. "Ah, that remains to be seen. I am a mathematician, sir. I never permit myself to think." He folded his arms. "But I wished to call this to your attention, gentlemen, in spite of my firm statement that he did not leave by the door."

"Suppose you tell us exactly what did happen here tonight," urged Hadley, passing a hand across his forehead. He sat down at the desk and took out his notebook. "Easy, now! We'll lead up to it gradually. How long have you worked for Professor Grimaud?"

"For three years and eight months," said Mills, clicking his teeth. Rampole saw that, in the legal atmosphere of the notebook, he was compressing himself to give brief answers.

"What are your duties?"

"Partly correspondence and general secretarial duties. In greater ratio to assist him in preparing his new work, *The Origin and History of Middle-European Superstitions, Together with . . .*"

"Quite so. How many people live in this house?"

"Besides Dr. Grimaud and myself, four."

"Yes, yes, well?"

"Ah, I see! You wish their names. Rosette Grimaud, his daughter. Madame Dumont, who is housekeeper. An elderly friend of Dr. Grimaud, named Drayman. A general maid whose last name I have never yet been told, but whose first name is Annie."

"How many were here tonight when this happened?"

Mills brought the toe of his shoe forward, balanced himself, and studied it, another trick of his. "That, obviously, I cannot say with certainty. I will tell you what I know." He rocked back and forth. "At the conclusion of dinner, at seven-thirty, Dr. Grimaud came up here to work. This is his custom on Saturday evenings. He told me he did not wish to be disturbed until eleven o'clock; that is also the inviolable custom. He said, however,"—quite suddenly beads of sweat appeared on the young man's forehead again, though he remained impassive—"he said, however, that he might have a visitor about half-past nine."

"Did he say who this visitor might be?"

"He did not."

Hadley leaned forward. "Come, now, Mr. Mills! Haven't you heard of any threat to him? Didn't you hear what happened on Wednesday evening?"

"I—er—I had previous information of it, certainly. In fact, I was at the Warwick Tavern myself. I suppose Mangan told you?"

Uneasily, but with startling vividness, he sketched out the story. Meantime, Dr. Fell had stumped away and was going through an examination he several times made that night. He seemed most interested in the fireplace.

Since Rampole had already heard an outline of the tavern incident, he did not listen to Mills; he watched Dr. Fell. The doctor inspected the bloodstains splashing the top and right arm of the disarranged sofa. There were more blood-stains on the hearth, though they were difficult to follow against the black carpet. A struggle there? Yet, Rampole saw, the fire-irons were upright in their rack, in such a position that a struggle before the hearth must have sent them clattering. A very small coal fire had been nearly smothered under a drift of charred papers.

Dr. Fell was muttering to himself. He reared up to examine the escutcheon. To Rampole, no student of heraldry, this presented itself as a divided shield in red and blue and silver: a black eagle and crescent moon in the upper part, and in the lower a wedge of what looked like rooks on a chessboard. Though its colours were darkened, it glowed with barbaric richness in a queerly barbaric room. Dr. Fell grunted.

But he did not speak until he began to examine the books in the shelves at the left of the fireplace. After the fashion of bibliophiles, he pounced. Then he began to yank out book after book, glance at the title-page, and shoot it back in again. Also, he seemed to have pounced on the most disreputable-looking volumes in the shelves. He was raising some dust, and making so much noise that it jarred across Mills' sing-song recital. Then he rose up and waved books at them in excited intentness.

"I say, Hadley, I don't want to interrupt, but this is very rummy and very revealing. Gabriel Dobrentei, '*Yorick és Eliza levelei*,' two volumes. '*Shakspere Minden Munkái*,' nine volumes in different editions. And here's a name—" He stopped. "H'mf. Ha. Do you know anything about these, Mr. Mills? They're the only books in the lot that haven't been dusted."

Mills was startled out of his recital. "I—I don't know. I believe they are from a batch that Dr. Grimaud meant for the attic. Mr. Drayman found them put away behind others when we removed some bookcases from the room last night to make room for the painting to be hung. . . . Where was I, Mr. Hadley? Ah yes! Well, when Dr. Grimaud told me that he might have a visitor tonight, I had no reason to assume it was the man of the Warwick Tavern. He did not say so."

"What, exactly, did he say?"

"I—you see, after dinner I was working in the big library downstairs. He suggested that I should come upstairs to my workroom at half-past nine, sit with my door open, and—and 'keep an eye on' this room, in case . . ."

"In case?"

Mills cleared his throat. "He was not specific."

"He told you all this," snapped Hadley, "and you still did not suspect who might be coming?"

"I think," interposed Dr. Fell, wheezing gently, "that I may be able to explain what our young friend means. It must have been rather a struggle.

He means that in spite of the sternest convictions of the youngest B.Sc., in spite of the stoutest buckler emblazoned with $x^2 + 2xy + y^2$, he still had enough imagination to get the wind up over that scene at the Warwick Tavern. And he didn't want to know any more than it was his duty to know. Is that it, hey?"

"I do not admit it, sir," Mills returned, with relief, nevertheless. "My motives have nothing to do with the facts. You will observe that I carried out my orders exactly. I came up here at precisely half-past nine—"

"Where were the others then? Steady, now!" urged Hadley. "Don't say you can't reply with certainty; just tell us where you *think* they were."

"To the best of my knowledge, Miss Rosette Grimaud and Mangan were in the drawing-room, playing cards. Drayman had told me that he was going out; I did not see him."

"And Madame Dumont?"

"I met her as I came up here. She was coming out with Dr. Grimaud's after-dinner coffee; that is to say, with the remnants of it. . . . I went to my workroom, left my door open, and drew out the typewriter desk so that I could face the hallway while I worked. At exactly"—he shut his eyes, and opened them again—"at exactly fifteen minutes to ten I heard the front-door bell ring. The electric bell is on the second floor, and I heard it plainly.

"Two minutes later, Madame Dumont came up from the staircase. She was carrying one of those trays on which it is customary to place visiting-cards. She was about to knock at the door when I was startled to see the—er—the tall man come upstairs directly after her. She turned round and saw him. She then exclaimed certain words which I am unable to repeat verbatim, but whose purport was to ask why he had not waited downstairs; and she seemed agitated. The—er—tall man made no reply. He walked to the door, and without haste turned down the collar of his coat and removed his cap which he placed in his overcoat pocket. I think that he laughed, and that Madame Dumont cried out something, shrank back against the wall, and hurried to open the door. Dr. Grimaud appeared on the threshold in some evident annoyance; his exact words were, 'What the devil is all this row about?' Then he stood stock-still, looking up at the tall man; and his exact words were, 'In God's name, who are *you?*'"

Mills' sing-song voice was hurling the words faster; his smile had become rather ghastly, although he tried to make it merely bright.

"Steady, Mr. Mills. Did you get a good look at this tall man?"

"A fairly good look. As he came up under the arch from the staircase, he glanced down in my direction."

"Well?"

"The collar of his overcoat was turned up, and he wore a peaked cap. But I am endowed with what is called 'long sight,' gentlemen, and I could distinctly observe the conformation and colour of the nose and mouth. He was wearing a child's false face, a species of mask in papier-mâché. I have an impression that it was long, of a pinkish colour, and had a wide-open mouth. And, so far as my observation went, he did not remove it. I think I am safe in asserting—"

"You are generally right, are you not?" asked a cold voice from the doorway. "It was a false face. And, unfortunately, he did not remove it."


## IV

### *The Impossible*

SHE stood in the doorway, looking from one to the other of them. Rampole received the impression of an extraordinary woman without knowing why he felt it. There was nothing remarkable about her, except a certain brilliance and vividness of the black eyes, which had a sanded, reddish look as though of smart without tears. She seemed all contradiction. She was short, and of sturdy figure, with a broad face, rather high cheekbones, and a shiny skin: yet Rampole had a curious impression that she could have been beautiful if she had tried. Her dark brown hair was coiled loosely over her ears, and she wore the plainest of dark dresses slashed with white across the breast: yet she did not look dowdy.

Poise, strength, carriage, what? The word "electric" is meaningless, yet it conveys the wave that came with her; something of crackle and heat and power, like a blow. She moved towards them, her shoes creaking. The prominent dark eyes, turned a little upwards at the outer corner, sought Hadley. She was rubbing the palms of her hands together before her, up and down. Rampole was conscious of two things—that the killing of Professor Grimaud had struck her with a hurt from which she would never recover, and would have left her stunned and crying if it had not been for one other wish.

"I am Ernestine Dumont," she said, as though interpreting the thought. "I have come to help you find the man who shot Charles."

She spoke almost without accent, but with a certain slur and deadness. The palms of her hands continued to brush up and down.

"When I heard, I could not come up—at first. Then I wished to go with him in the ambulance to the nursing-home, but the doctor would not let me. He said the police would wish to speak with me. Yes, I suppose that was wise."

Hadley rose and moved out for her the chair in which he had been sitting.

"Please sit down, madame. We should like to hear your own statement in a moment. I must ask you to listen carefully to what Mr. Mills is saying, in case you should be required to corroborate . . ."

She shivered in the cold from the open window, and Dr. Fell, who had

been watching her sharply, lumbered over to close it. Then she glanced at
the fireplace, where the fire had smouldered nearly out under the mass of
burnt papers. Realizing Hadley's words over the gap, she nodded. She looked
at Mills absent-mindedly, with a sort of vacant affection which showed almost
in a smile.

"Yes, of course. He is a nice poor fool boy, and he means well. Do you
not, Stuart? You must go on, by all means. I will—look."

Mills showed no anger, if he felt any. His eyelids flickered a few times,
and he folded his arms.

"If it gives the Pythoness any pleasure to think so," he sang, imperturbably,
"I have no objection. But perhaps I had better continue. Er—where was I?"

"Dr. Grimaud's words when he saw the visitor, you told us, were, 'In God's
name, who are *you?*' Then?"

"Ah yes! He was not wearing his eye-glasses, which were hanging down
by their cord; his sight is not good without them, and I am under the impression that he mistook the mask for a real face. But before he could raise the
glasses, the stranger made so quick a movement that I was rather confused,
and he darted in at the door. Dr. Grimaud made a movement to get in front
of him, but he was too quick, and I heard him laughing. When he got inside—" Mills stopped, apparently puzzled. "This is most extraordinary. I am
under the impression that Madame Dumont, although she was shrinking back
against the wall, closed the door after him. I recall that she had her hand on
the knob."

Ernestine Dumont blazed.

"What do you wish to be understood by that, little boy?" she asked. "You
fool, be sure you know what you are saying. Do you think I would willingly
have had that man alone with Charles?—He kicked the door shut behind him.
Then he turned the key in the lock."

"One moment, madame. . . . Is that true, Mr. Mills?"

"I wish it clearly understood," Mills sang, "that I am merely trying to give
*every* fact and even every impression. I meant nothing. I accept the correction.
He did, as the Pythoness says, turn the key in the lock."

"That is what he calls his little joke, 'the Pythoness,'" Mme Dumont said,
savagely. "Ah, bah!"

Mills smiled. "To resume, gentlemen: I can well believe that the Pythoness
was agitated. She began to call Dr. Grimaud's Christian name, and to shake
the knob of the door. I heard voices inside, but I was some distance away,
and you will perceive that the door is thick." He pointed. "I could distinguish
nothing until, after an interval of about thirty seconds, during which it is
deducible that the tall man removed his mask, Dr. Grimaud called out, to
the Pythoness, rather angrily: 'Go away, you fool. I can handle this.'"

"I see. Did he seem—afraid, or anything of the sort?"

The secretary reflected. "On the contrary, I should have said that he sounded in a sense relieved."

"And you, madame: you obeyed and went away without further—?"

"Yes."

"Even though," said Hadley, suavely, "I presume it is not usual for practical jokers to call at the house in false faces and act in such a wild way? You knew, I suppose, of the threat to your employer?"

"I have obeyed Charles Grimaud for over twenty years," said the woman, very quietly. The word "employer" had stung her hard. Her reddish, sanded eyes were intent. "And I have never known a situation which he could *not* handle. Obey! Of course I did; I would always obey. Besides, you do not understand. You have asked me nothing." The contempt changed to a half-smile. "But this is interesting—psychologically, as Charles would say. You have not asked Stuart why *he* obeyed, and caused no fuss. That is merely because you think he would have been afraid. I thank you for the implied compliment. Please go on."

Rampole had a sensation of watching a supple wrist on a swordsman. Hadley seemed to feel this, too, although he addressed the secretary.

"Do you remember, Mr. Mills, the time at which this tall man went into the room?"

"It was at ten minutes to ten. There is a clock on my typewriter desk, you see."

"And when did you hear the shot?"

"At exactly ten minutes past ten."

"You mean to say that you watched the door all that time?"

"I did, most assuredly." He cleared his throat. "In spite of what the Pythoness describes as my timidity, I was the first to reach the door when the shot was fired. It was still locked on the inside, as you gentlemen saw—you yourselves arrived very shortly afterwards."

"During the twenty minutes while these two were together, did you hear any voices, movements, sounds of any kind?"

"At one point I was under the impression that I heard voices raised, and something which I can only describe as resembling a bumping sound. But I was some distance away. . . ." He began to rock again, and stare, as he met Hadley's cold eye. The sweat broke out again. "Now I am aware, of course, that I am under the necessity of telling what must seem an absolutely incredible story. Yet, gentlemen, I *swear* . . . !" Quite suddenly he lifted a plump fist and his voice went high.

"That is all right, Stuart," the woman said, gently. "I can confirm you."

Hadley was suavely grim. "That would be just as well, I think. One last question, Mr. Mills. Can you give an exact outward description of this caller you saw? . . . In a moment, madame!" he broke off, turning quickly. "In good time. Well, Mr. Mills?"

"I can state accurately that he wore a long black overcoat, and a peaked cap of some brownish material. His trousers were darkish. I did not observe his shoes. His hair, when he took off the cap—" Mills stopped. "This is extraordinary. I do not wish to be fanciful, but now that I recall it, his hair had a dark, painted, *shiny* look, if you understand me, almost as though his whole head were made of papier-mâché."

Hadley, who had been pacing up and down past the big picture, turned on him in a way that brought a squeak from Mills.

"Gentlemen," cried the latter, "you asked me to tell you what I saw. And that is what I saw. It is true."

"Go on," said Hadley, grimly.

"I believe he was wearing gloves, although he put his hands in his pockets and I cannot be absolutely certain. He was tall, a good three or four inches taller than Dr. Grimaud, and of a medium—er—anatomical structure. That is all I can definitely assert."

"Did he look like the man Pierre Fley?"

"Well—yes. That is to say, in one way yes, and another no. I should have said this man was even taller than Fley, and not quite so thin, but I would not be prepared to swear it."

During this questioning, Rampole had been watching Dr. Fell out of the tail of his eye. The doctor, his big cloak humped and his shovel-hat under one arm, had been lumbering about the room with annoyed digs of his cane at the carpet. He bent down to blink at things until his eye-glasses tumbled off his nose. He looked at the painting, along the rows of books, at the jade buffalo on the desk. He went down wheezingly to look at the fireplace, and hoisted himself up again to study the coat of arms over it. Towards the last he seemed to become blankly amiable—and yet always, Rampole saw, he was watching Mme Dumont. She seemed to fascinate him. There was something rather terrible in that small bright eye, which would swing round the second he had finished looking at something. And the woman knew it. Her hands were clenched in her lap. She tried to ignore him, but her glance would come round again. It was as though they were fighting an intangible battle.

"There are other questions, Mr. Mills," said Hadley, "particularly about this Warwick Tavern affair and that painting. But they can wait until we get things in order. . . . Would you mind going down and asking Miss Grimaud and Mr. Mangan to come up here? Also Mr. Drayman, if he has returned? . . . Thanks. Stop a bit! Er—any questions, Fell?"

Dr. Fell shook his head with broad amiability. Rampole could see the woman's white knuckles tighten.

"*Must* your friend walk about in that way?" she cried, abruptly, and in the shrillness of the voice she pronounced the *w* as *v*. "It is maddening. It is—"

Hadley studied her. "I understand, madame. Unfortunately, that is his way."

"Who are you, then? You walk into my house—"

"I had better explain. I am the superintendent of the Criminal Investigation Department. This is Mr. Rampole. And the other man, of whom you may have heard, is Dr. Gideon Fell."

"Yes. Yes, I thought so." She nodded, and then slapped the desk beside her. "Well, well, well! Even so, must you forget your manners? Must you make the room freezing with your open windows, even? May we not at least have a fire to warm us?"

"I don't advise it, you know," said Dr. Fell. "That is, until we see what papers have already been burnt there. It must have been rather a bonfire."

Ernestine Dumont said, wearily: "Oh, why must you be such fools? Why do you sit here? You know quite well who did this. It was the fellow Fley, and you know it. Well, well, well? Why don't you go after him? Why do you sit here when I tell you he did it?"

There was a look about her, a trance-like and gypsyish look of hatred. She seemed to see Fley go down a trap on a gallows.

"Do you know Fley?" Hadley snapped.

"No, no, I never saw him! I mean, before this. But I know what Charles told me."

"Which was what?"

"Ah, zut! This Fley is a lunatic. Charles never knew him, but the man had some insane idea that he made fun of the occult, you understand. He has a brother who is"—she gestured—"the same, you understand? Well, Charles told me that he might call here tonight at half-past nine. If he did, I was to admit him. But when I took down Charles's coffee-tray at half-past nine, Charles laughed and said that if the man had not arrived by then he would not come at all. Charles said: 'People with a grudge are prompt.'" She sat back, squaring her shoulders. "Well, he was wrong. The door-bell rang at a quarter to ten. I answered it. There was a man standing on the step. He held out a visiting-card, and said, 'Will you take this to Professor Grimaud and ask if he will see me?'"

Hadley leaned against the edge of the leather sofa and studied her.

"What about the false face, madame? Didn't you think that a little odd?"

"I did not see the false face! Have you noticed there is only one light in the downstairs hall? Well! There was a street lamp behind him, and all I could see was his shape. He spoke so courteously, you understand, and handed in the card, that for a second I did not realize . . ."

"One moment, please. Would you recognize that voice if you heard it again?"

She moved her shoulders as though she were shifting a weight on her back. "Yes! I don't know—yes, yes! But it did not sound right, you see; muffled up in that mask, I think now. Ah, why are men such—!" She leaned back in the chair, and for no apparent reason tears brimmed over her eyes. "I do not see such things! I am real, I am honest! If some one does you a hurt, good. You lie in wait for him and kill him. Then your friends go into court and swear you were somewhere else. You do not put on a painted mask, like old Drayman with the children on Guy Fawkes night; you do not hand in visiting-cards like this horror of a man, and go upstairs and kill a man and then vanish out of a window. It is like the legends they told us when I was a girl. . . ." Her cynical poise cracked across in hysteria. "Oh, my God, Charles! My poor Charles!"

Hadley waited, very quietly. She had herself in hand in a moment; she also was as still, and as foreign and inexplicable, as the big painting which faced her in tortured sombreness across the room. The gust of emotion left her relieved and watchful, though she breathed hard. They could hear the scraping noise of her finger nails on the chair-arms.

"The man said," Hadley prompted, "'Will you take this to Professor Grimaud and ask if he will see me?' Very well. Now at this time, we understand, Miss Grimaud and Mr. Mangan were downstairs in the drawing-room near the front door?"

She looked at him curiously.

"Now that is a strange thing to ask. I wonder why you ask it? Yes—yes, I suppose they were. I did not notice."

"Do you remember whether the drawing-room door was open or shut?"

"I don't know. But I should think it was shut, or I should have seen more light in the hall."

"Go on, please."

"Well, when the man gave me the card, I was going to say, 'Step in, please, and I will see,' when I did see. I could not be faced with him alone—a lunatic? I wished to go up and get Charles to come down. So I said, 'Wait there and I will see.' And I very quickly slammed the door in his face, so that the spring-lock caught and he could not get in. Then I went back to the lamp and looked at the card. I still have it; I had no chance to deliver it. And it was blank."

"Blank?"

"There was no writing or printing on it at all. I went up to show it to Charles, and plead with him to come down. But the poor little Mills has told you what happened. I was going to knock at the door, when I heard somebody come upstairs behind me. I looked round, and there he was coming big and thin behind me. But I will swear, I will swear on the Cross, that I had locked that door downstairs. Well, I was not afraid of him! No! I asked him what he meant by coming upstairs.

"And still, you understand, I could not see the false face, because his back was to that bright light on the stairs, which shows up all this end of the hall

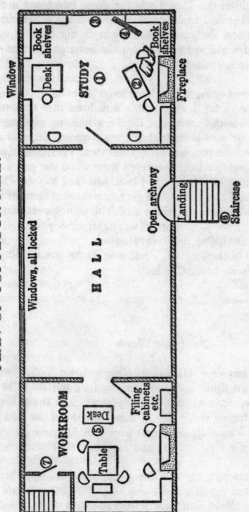

PLAN OF TOP-FLOOR REAR

1. Where Grimaud's body was found.
2. Disarranged sofa, chairs, and hearth rug.
3. Cleared space against wall, where painting was to have been hung.
4. Painting itself, propped up lengthwise against bookshelves.
5. Where Mills sat.
6. Where Mme Dumont stood.
7. Door leading to staircase communicating with trap in roof.

and Charles's door. But he said, in French, '*Madame, you cannot keep me out like that,*' and turned down his collar and put his cap in his pocket. I opened the door because I knew he would not dare face Charles, just as Charles opened it from inside. Then I saw the mask, which was a pinkish colour like flesh. And before I could do anything he made a horrible jump inside, and kicked the door shut, and turned the key in the lock."

She paused, as though she had got through the worst part of the recital, and could breathe more easily now.

"And then?"

She said, dully: "I went away, as Charles ordered me to do. I made no fuss or scene. But I did not go far. I went a little way down the stairs, where I could still see the door to this room, and I did not leave my post any more than poor Stuart did. It was—horrible. I am not a young girl, you understand. I was there when the shot was fired; I was there when Stuart ran forward and began to pound the door; I was even there when you people began to come upstairs. But I could not stand it. I *knew* what had happened. When I felt myself going faint, I had just time to get to my room at the foot of that flight when I was—ill. Women sometimes are." The pale lips cracked across her oily face in a smile, shakily. "But Stuart was right; nobody left that room. God help us both, we are telling the truth. However else that horror left the room, he did not leave by the door. . . . And now please, please, will you let me go to the nursing-home to see Charles?"

## V

### The Jig-saw Words

It was Dr. Fell who answered. He was standing with his back to the fireplace, a vast black-caped figure under the fencing foils and shield of arms. He seemed to fit there, like a baron out of feudalism, with the bookshelves and white busts towering on either side of him. But he did not look like a very terrible Front de Bœuf. His eye-glasses were coming askew on his nose as he bit off the end of a cigar, turned, and expectorated it neatly into the fireplace.

"Ma'am," he said, turning back with a long challenging sound in his nose, like a battle cry, "we shall not detain you very long. And it is only fair to say that I don't in the least doubt your story, any more than I doubt Mills's. Before getting down to business, I will prove that I believe you. . . . Ma'am, do you remember what time tonight it stopped snowing?"

She was looking at him with hard, bright, defensive eyes. She had evidently heard of Dr. Fell.

"Does it matter? I think it was about half-past nine. Yes! I remember, because when I came up to collect Charles's coffee tray I looked out of the window and I noticed that it had stopped. Does it matter?"

"Oh, very much, ma'am. Otherwise we have only half an impossible situation. . . . And you are quite right. H'mf. Remember, Hadley? Half-past nine is about the time it stopped. Right, Hadley?"

"Yes," admitted the superintendent. He also looked at Dr. Fell suspiciously. He had learned to distrust that blank stare over the several chins. "Granting that it was half-past nine, what then?"

"Not only had it stopped snowing a full forty minutes before the visitor made his escape from this room," pursued the doctor, with a meditative air, "but it had stopped fifteen minutes before the visitor even arrived at this house. That's true, ma'am? Eh? He rang the door-bell at a quarter to ten? Good. . . . Now, Hadley, do you remember when *we* arrived at this house? Did you notice that, before you and Rampole and young Mangan went charging in, *there wasn't a single footprint on the flight of steps leading up to the front door, or even the pavement leading up to the steps?* You see, I did. I remained behind to make sure."

Hadley straightened up with a kind of muffled roar. "By God! that's right! The whole pavement was clean. It—" He stopped, and swung slowly round to Mme Dumont. "So this, you say, is your evidence of why you believe madame's story? Fell, have you gone mad, too? We hear a story of how a man rang the door-bell and walked through a locked door fifteen minutes after the snow had stopped, and yet—"

Dr. Fell opened his eyes. Then a series of chuckles ran up the ridges of his waistcoat.

"I say, son, why are you so flabbergasted? Apparently he sailed out of here without leaving a footprint. Why should it upset you to learn that he also sailed in?"

"I don't know," the other admitted, stubbornly. "But, hang it, it does! In my experience with locked-room murders, getting in and getting out are two very different things. It would throw my universe off balance if I found an impossible situation that worked sensibly both ways. Never mind! You say—"

"Please listen. I say," Mme Dumont interposed, pale but with the bunched muscles standing out at the corners of her jaws, "that I am telling the absolute truth, so help me God!"

"And I believe you," said Dr. Fell. "You mustn't let Hadley's stern Scotch common-sense overawe you. He will believe it, too, before I'm through with him. But my point is this. I have shown you, haven't I, that I have strong faith in you—if I can credit what you have said? Very well. I only want to warn you not to upset that faith. I should not dream of doubting what you have already told me. But I fancy I shall very strongly doubt what you are going to tell me in a moment."

Hadley half-closed one eye. "I was afraid of that. I always dread the time when you begin to trot out your damned paradoxes. Seriously, now—"

"Please go on," the woman said, stolidly.

"Humph. Harrumph. Thanks. Now, ma'am, how long have you been Grimaud's housekeeper? No, I'll change that. How long have you been with him?"

"For over twenty-five years," she answered. "I was more than his house-keeper—once."

She had been looking at her interlocked fingers, which she moved in and out; but now she lifted her head. Her eyes had a fierce, steady glaze, as though she wondered how much she dared tell. It was the expression of one peering round a corner at an enemy, ready for instant flight.

"I tell you that," she went on, quietly, "in the hope that you will give me your word to keep silent. You will find it in your alien records at Bow Street, and you may make unnecessary trouble that has nothing to do with this matter. It is not for myself, you understand. Rosette Grimaud is my daughter. She was born here, and there had to be a record. But she does not know it—nobody knows it. Please, please, can I trust you to keep silent?"

The glaze over her eyes was changing to a different one. She had not raised her voice, but there was a terrible urgency in it.

"Why, ma'am," said Dr. Fell, a wrinkle in his forehead, "I can't see that it's any of our business. Can you? We shall certainly say nothing about it."

"You mean that?"

"Ma'am," the doctor said, gently, "I don't know the young lady, but I'll bet you a tanner you're worrying yourself unnecessarily, and that you've both been worrying yourselves unnecessarily for years. She probably knows already. Children do. And she's trying to keep it from *you*. And the whole world goes skew-wiff because we like to pretend that people under twenty will never have any emotions, and people over forty never had. Humph. Let's forget it. Shall we?" He beamed. "What I wanted to ask you, Where did you first meet Grimaud? Before you came to England?"

She breathed hard. She answered, but vacantly, as though she were thinking of something else.

"Yes. In Paris."

"You are a Parisienne?"

"Er—what—? No, no, not by birth! I am of the provinces. But I worked there when I met him. I was a costumier."

Hadley looked up from jotting in his notebook. " 'Costumier'?" he repeated. "Do you mean a dressmaker, or what?"

"No, no, I mean what I say. I was one of the women who made costumes for the opera and the ballet. We worked in the Opéra itself. You can find record of that! And, if it will save you time, I will tell you that I was never married and my maiden name was Ernestine Dumont."

"And Grimaud?" Dr. Fell asked, sharply. "Where was he from?"

"From the south of France, I think. But he studied at Paris. His family are all dead, so that will not help you. He inherited their money."

There was an air of tension which these casual questions did not seem to warrant. Dr. Fell's next three questions were so extraordinary that Hadley stared up from his notebook, and Ernestine Dumont, who had recovered herself, shifted uneasily, with a wary brilliance in her eyes.

"What is your religious faith, ma'am?"

"I am a Unitarian. Why?"

"H'm, yes. Did Grimaud ever visit the United States, or has he any friends there?"

"Never. And he has no friends that I know of there."

"Do the words 'seven towers' mean anything to you, ma'am?"

"No!" cried Ernestine Dumont, and went oily white.

Dr. Fell, who had finished lighting his cigar, blinked at her out of the smoke. He lumbered out from the hearth and round the sofa, so that she shrank back. But he only indicated the big painting with his cane, tracing out the line of the white mountains in the background of the picture.

"I won't ask you whether you know what this represents," he continued, "but I will ask you whether Grimaud told you why he bought it. What sort of charm was it supposed to contain, anyhow? What power did it have to ward off the bullet or the evil eye? What sort of weight could its influ . . ." He stopped, as though recalling something rather startling. Then he reached out, wheezing, to lift the picture off the floor with one hand and turn it curiously from side to side. "Oh, my hat!" said Dr. Fell, with explosive absent-mindedness. "O Lord! O Bacchus! Wow!"

"What is it?" demanded Hadley, jumping forward. "Do you see anything?"

"No, I don't see anything," said Dr. Fell argumentatively. "That's just the point. Well, madame?"

"I think," said the woman, in a shaky voice, "that you are the strangest man I ever met. No. I do not know what that thing is. Charles would not tell me. He only grunted and laughed in his throat. Why don't you ask the artist? Burnaby painted it. He should know. But you people will never do anything sensible. It looks like a picture of a country that does not exist."

Dr. Fell nodded sombrely. "I am afraid you are right, ma'am. I don't think it does exist. And if three people were buried there, it might be difficult to find them—mightn't it?"

"Will you stop talking this gibberish?" shouted Hadley; and then Hadley was taken aback by the fact that this gibberish had struck Ernestine Dumont like a blow. She got to her feet to conceal the effect of those meaningless words.

"I am going," she said. "You cannot stop me. You are all crazy. You sit here raving while—while you let Pierre Fley escape. Why don't you go after him? Why don't you *do* something?"

"Because you see, ma'am . . . Grimaud himself said that Pierre Fley did not do this thing." While she was still staring at him, he let the painting fall back with a thump against the sofa. The scene out of a country which did not exist, and yet where three gravestones stood among crooked trees, brought Rampole's mind to an edge of terror. He was still looking at the painting when they heard footsteps on the stairs.

It was a heartening thing to see the prosaic, earnest, hatchet face of Sergeant Betts, whom Rampole remembered from the Tower of London case. Behind him came two cheerful plain-clothes men carrying the photographic and fingerprint apparatus. A uniformed policeman stood behind Mills, Boyd Mangan, and the girl who had been in the drawing-room. She pushed through this group into the room.

"Boyd told me you wanted me," she said, in a quiet but very unsteady voice. "But I insisted on going over with the ambulance, you see. You'd better get over there as quick as you can, Aunt Ernestine. They say he's—going."

She tried to be efficient and peremptory, even in the way she drew off her gloves; but she could not manage it. She had those decided manners which come in the early twenties from lack of experience and lack of opposition. Rampole was rather startled to see that her hair was a heavy blond colour, bobbed and drawn behind the ears. Her face was squarish, with somewhat high cheekbones; not beautiful, but disturbing and vivid in the way that makes you think of old times even when you do not know what times. Her rather broad mouth was painted dark red, but in contrast to this, and to the firm shape of the whole face, the long hazel eyes were of an uneasy gentleness. She looked round quickly, and shrank back towards Mangan with her fur coat drawn tightly round. She was not far from sheer hysteria.

"Will you please hurry and tell me what you want?" she cried. "Don't you realize he's *dying*? Aunt Ernestine . . ."

"If these gentlemen are through with me," the woman said, stolidly, "I will go. I meant to go, as you know."

She was docile all of a sudden. But it was a heavy docility, with a half challenge in it—as though there were limits. Something bristled between these two women, something like the uneasiness in Rosette Grimaud's eyes. They looked at each other quickly, without a direct glance; they seemed to burlesque each other's movements, to become abruptly conscious of it, and stop. Hadley prolonged the silence, as though he were confronting two suspects with each other at Scotland Yard. Then:

"Mr. Mangan," he said, briskly, "will you take Miss Grimaud down to Mr. Mills's room at the end of the hall? Thank you. We shall be with you in a moment. Mr. Mills, just a second! Wait. . . . . Betts!"

"Sir?"

"I want you to do some important work. Did Mangan tell you to bring ropes and a flashlight? . . . Good. I want you to go up on the roof of this place and search every inch of it for a footprint or a mark of any kind, especially over this room. Then go down to the yard behind this place, and both adjoining yards, and see if you can find any marks there. Mr. Mills will show you how to get to the roof. . . . Preston! Is Preston here?"

A sharp-nosed young man bustled in from the hall—the Sergeant Preston whose business it was to poke for secret places and who had discovered the evidence behind the panel in the Death Watch case.

"Go over this room for any secret entrance whatever, understand? Tear the place to bits if you like. See if anybody could get up the chimney. . . . You fellows carry on with the prints and pictures. Mark out every bloodstain in chalk before you photograph. But don't disturb that burnt paper in the fireplace. . . . Constable! Where the hell's that constable?"

"Here, sir."

"Did Bow Street phone through the address of a man named Fley—Pierre Fley? . . . Right. Go to wherever he lives and pick him up. Bring him here. If he's not there, wait. Have they sent a man to the theatre where he works? . . . All right. That's all. Hop to it, everybody."

He strode out into the hall, muttering to himself. Dr. Fell, lumbering after him, was for the first time imbued with a ghoulish eagerness. He poked at the superintendent's arm with his shovel-hat.

"Look here, Hadley," he urged, "you go down and attend to the questioning, hey? I think I can be of much more service if I stay behind and assist those duffers with their photographs . . ."

"No, I'm hanged if you spoil any more plates!" said the other, with heat. "Those film packs cost money, and, besides, we need the evidence. Now, I want to talk to you privately and plainly. What's all this wild mumbo-jumbo about seven towers, and people buried in countries that never existed? I've seen you in these fits of mystification before, but never quite so bad. Let's compare notes. What did you . . . yes, yes. What is it?"

He turned irascibly as Stuart Mills plucked at his arm.

"Er—before I conduct the sergeant up to the roof," said Mills, imperturbably, "I think I had better tell you that in case you wish to see Mr. Drayman, he is here in the house."

"Drayman? Oh yes! When did he get back?"

Mills frowned. "So far as I am able to deduce, he did not get back. I should say he had never left. A short time ago I had occasion to look into his room . . ."

"Why?" enquired Dr. Fell, with sudden interest.

The secretary blinked impassively. "I was curious, sir. I discovered him asleep there, and it will be difficult to rouse him; I believe he has taken a sleeping draught. Mr. Drayman is fond of taking them. I do not mean that he is an inebriate or a drug-user, but quite literally that he is very fond of taking sleeping draughts."

"Rummiest household I ever heard of," declared Hadley, after a pause, to nobody in particular. "Anything else?"

"Yes, sir. There is a friend of Dr. Grimaud's downstairs. He has just arrived, and he would like to see you. I do not think it is anything of immediate importance, but he is a member of the circle at the Warwick Tavern. His name is Pettis—Mr. Anthony Pettis."

"Pettis, eh?" repeated Dr. Fell, rubbing his chin. "I wonder if that's the Pettis who collects the ghost stories and writes those excellent prefaces? H'm, yes. I dare say. Now, how would he fit into this?"

"I'm asking you how anything fits into it," insisted Hadley. "Look here. I can't see this fellow now, unless he's got something important to tell. Get his address, will you, and say I'll call on him in the morning? Thanks." He turned to Dr. Fell. "Now carry on about the seven towers and the country that never existed."

The doctor waited until Mills had led Sergeant Betts down the big hall to the door at the opposite end. A subdued mutter of voices from Grimaud's room was the only noise. The bright yellow light still streamed from the great arch of the staircase, illuminating the whole hall. Dr. Fell took a few lumbering steps round the hall, looking up and down and then across at the three brown-draped windows. He pulled back the drapes and made certain that these three windows were all firmly locked on the inside. Then he beckoned Hadley and Rampole towards the staircase.

"Scrum," he said. "A little comparing of notes, I admit, will be advisable before we tackle the next witnesses. But not for a second about the seven towers. I'll lead up to those gradually, like Childe Roland. Hadley, a few disjointed words—the only real evidence we have, because it comes from the victim—may be the most important clue of all. I mean those few mutterings from Grimaud just before he fainted. I hope to heaven we all heard 'em. Remember, you asked him whether Fley had shot him. He shook his head. Then you asked him who had done it. What did he say?—I want to ask each of you in turn what you thought you heard."

He looked at Rampole. The American's wits were muddled. He had a strong recollection of certain words, but the whole was confused by a too-vivid picture of a blood-soaked chest and a writhing neck. He hesitated.

"The first thing he said," Rampole answered, "sounded to me like *hover—*"

"Nonsense," interrupted Hadley. "I jotted it all down right away. The first thing he said was *Bath* or 'the bath,' though I'm hanged if I see—"

"Steady now. Your own gibberish," said Dr. Fell, "is a little worse than mine. Go on, Ted."

"Well, I wouldn't swear to any of it. But then I did hear the words *not suicide,* and *he couldn't use rope.* Next there was some reference to a *roof* and to *snow* and to a *fox*. The last thing I heard sounded like *too much light*. Again, I wouldn't swear it was all in consecutive order."

Hadley was indulgent. "You've got it all twisted, even if you have got one or two of the points." He seemed uneasy, nevertheless. "All the same, I'm bound to admit that my notes don't make much better sense. After the word *bath*, he said *salt and wine*. You're right about the rope, although I heard nothing about suicide. Roof and snow are correct; '*too much light*' came afterwards; then '*got gun.*' Finally, he did say something about a fox, and the last thing—I barely heard it because of that blood—was something like *Don't blame poor . . .* And that's all."

"O Lord!" groaned Dr. Fell. He stared from one to the other. "This is terrible. Gents, I was going to be very triumphant over you. I was going to explain what he said. But I am beaten by the staggering size of your respective ears. I never heard all that out of the gabble, although I dare say you're within some distance of the truth. Wow!"

"Well, what's your version?" demanded Hadley.

The doctor stumped up and down, rumbling. "I heard only the first few words. They make tolerably good sense if I'm right—*if* I'm right. But the rest is a nightmare. I have visions of foxes running across roofs in the snow, or—"

"Lycanthropy?" suggested Rampole. "Did anybody mention werewolves?"

"No, and nobody's going to!" roared Hadley. He struck his notebook. "To put everything in order, Rampole, I'll write down what you thought you heard for comparison. . . . So. We now have:

"Your list. *Hover. Not suicide. He couldn't use rope. Roof. Snow. Fox. Too much light.*

"My list. *Bath. Salt. Wine. He couldn't use rope. Roof. Snow. Too much light. Got gun. Don't blame poor—*

"There we are. And, as usual, with your own brand of cussedness, Fell, you're most confident about the most senseless part. I might rig up an explanation that could fit together all the latter part, but how the devil does a dying man give us a clue by talking about baths and salt and wine?"

Dr. Fell stared at his cigar, which had gone out.

"H'mf, yes. We'd better clear up a little of that. There are puzzles enough as it is. Let's go gently along the road. . . . First, my lad, what happened in that room after Grimaud was shot?"

"How the hell should I know? That's what I'm asking you. If there's no secret entrance—"

"No, no, I don't mean how the vanishing-trick was worked. You're obsessed with that business, Hadley; so obsessed that you don't stop to ask yourself what *else* happened. First let's get clear the obvious things for which we can find an explanation, and go on from there. Humph. Now, then, what clearly did happen in that room after the man was shot? First, all the marks centred round the fireplace—"

"You mean the fellow climbed up the chimney?"

"I am absolutely certain he didn't," said Dr. Fell, testily. "That flue is so narrow that you can barely get your fist through. Control yourself and think. First, a heavy sofa was pushed away from in front of the fireplace; there was a good deal of blood on the top, as though Grimaud had slipped or leaned against it. The hearth rug was pulled or kicked away; there was blood on that; and a fireside chair was shoved away. Finally, I found spots of blood on the hearth and even in the fireplace. They led us to a huge mass of burnt papers that had nearly smothered the fire.

"Now, consider the behaviour of the faithful Madame Dumont. As soon as she came into that room, she was very terribly concerned about that fireplace. She kept looking at it all the time, and nearly grew hysterical when she saw I was doing so, too. She even, you recall, made the foolish blunder of asking us to light a fire—even though she must have known that the police wouldn't go fooling about with coals and kindling to make witnesses comfortable on the very scene of a crime. No, no, my boy. Somebody had tried to burn letters or documents there. She wanted to be certain they had been destroyed."

Hadley said, heavily: "So she knew about it, then? And yet you said you believed her story?"

"Yes. I did and do believe her story—about the visitor and the crime. What I don't believe is the information she gave us about herself and Grimaud. . . . Now think again what happened! The intruder shot Grimaud. Yet Grimaud, although he is still conscious, does not shout for help, try to stop the killer, make a row of any kind, or even open the door when Mills is pounding there. But he does do something. He does do something, with such a violent exertion that he tears wide open the wound in his lung: as you heard the doctor say.

"And I'll tell you what he did do. He knew he was a goner and that the police would be in. He had in his possession a mass of things that *must be* destroyed. It was more vital to destroy them than to catch the man who shot him or even save his own life. He lurched back and forth from that fireplace, burning this evidence. Hence the sofa knocked away, the hearth rug, the stains of blood. . . . You understand now?"

There was a silence in the bright bleak hall.

"And the Dumont woman?" Hadley asked, heavily.

"She knew it, of course. It was their joint secret. And she happens to love him."

"If this is true, it must have been something pretty damned important that he destroyed," said Hadley, staring. "How the devil do you know all this? What secret could they have had, anyway? And what makes you think they had any dangerous secret at all?"

Dr. Fell pressed his hands to his temples and ruffled his big mop of hair. He spoke argumentatively.

"I may be able to tell you a little of it," he said, "although there are parts that puzzle me beyond hope. You see, neither Grimaud nor Dumont is any more French than I am. A woman with those cheekbones, a woman who pronounces the silent 'h' in honest, never came from a Latin race. But that's not important. They're both Magyar. To be precise: Grimaud came originally from Hungary. His real name is Károly, or Charles, Grimaud Horváth. He probably had a French mother. He came from the principality of Transylvania, formerly a part of the Hungarian kingdom but annexed by Rumania since the war. In the late 'nineties or early nineteen hundreds, Károly Grimaud Horváth and his two brothers were all sent to prison. Did I tell you he had two brothers? One we haven't seen, but the other now calls himself Pierre Fley.

"I don't know what crime the three brothers Horváth had committed, but they were sent to the prison of Siebenturmen, to work in the salt-mines near Tradj in the Carpathian Mountains. Charles probably escaped. Now, the rather deadly 'secret' in his life can't concern the fact that he was sent to prison or even that he escaped before finishing the sentence; the Hungarian kingdom is broken up, and its authority no longer exists. More probably he did some black devilry that concerned the other two brothers; something pretty horrible concerning those three coffins, and people buried alive, that would hang him even now if it were discovered. . . . That's all I can hazard at the moment. Has anybody got a match?"

## VI

### The Seven Towers

IN THE long pause after this recital, Hadley tossed a matchbox to the doctor and eyed him malevolently.

"Are you joking?" he asked. "Or is this black magic?"

"Not about a thing like this. I wish I could. Those three coffins . . . Dammit, Hadley!" muttered Dr. Fell, knocking his fists against his temples, "I wish I could see a glimmer—something. . . ."

"You seem to have done pretty well. Have you been holding out information, or how do you know all that? Stop a bit!" He looked at his notebook. " 'Hover.' 'Bath.' 'Salt.' 'Wine.' In other words, you're trying to tell us that what Grimaud really said was, 'Horváth,' and 'salt-mine'? Take it easy, now!

If that's your basis, we're going to have a lot of star-gazing on our hands to twist round the rest of those words."

"This assumption of rage," said Dr. Fell, "shows that you agree with me. Thankee. As you yourself shrewdly pointed out, dying men do not commonly mention bath salts. If your version is correct, we might as well all retire to a padded cell. He really said it, Hadley. I heard him. You asked him for a name, didn't you? Was it Fley? No. Who was it, then? And he answered, Horváth."

"Which *you* say is his own name."

"Yes. Look here," said Dr. Fell. "If it will salve your wounds, I will cheerfully admit that it wasn't fair detective work, and that I didn't show you the sources of my information from that room. I'll show you them presently, although Lord knows I tried to show them to you at the time.

"It's like this. We hear from Ted Rampole about a queer customer who threatens Grimaud, and significantly talks about people 'buried alive.' Grimaud takes this seriously; he has known that man before and knows what he is talking about, since for some reason he buys a picture depicting three graves. When you ask Grimaud who shot him, he answers with the name 'Horváth' and says something about salt-mines. Whether or not you think that's odd of a French professor, it is rather odd to find up over his mantelpiece the device of a shield graven thus: *coupé, a demi-eagle issuant sable, in chief a moon argent . . .*"

"I think we may omit the heraldry," said Hadley, with a sort of evil dignity. "What is it?"

"It's the arms of Transylvania. Dead since the war, of course, and hardly very well known in England (or France) even before that. First a Slavic name, and then Slavic arms. Next those books I showed you. Know what they were? They were English books translated into the Magyar. I couldn't pretend to read 'em—"

"Thank God."

"—but I could at least recognize the complete works of Shakespeare, and Sterne's *Letters from Yorick to Eliza*, and Pope's *Essay on Man*. That was so startling that I examined 'em all."

"Why startling?" asked Rampole. "There are all sorts of funny books in anybody's library. There are in your own."

"Certainly. But suppose a scholarly Frenchman wants to read English. Well, he reads it in English, or he gets it translated into French. But he very seldom insists on getting its full flavour by first having it translated into Hungarian. In other words, they weren't *Hungarian* books; they weren't even French books on which a Frenchman might have been practising his Magyar; they were English. It meant that whoever owned those books, his native language was Hungarian. I went through all of 'em, hoping to find a name. When I found *Károly Grimaud Horváth,* 1898 faded out on one flyleaf, it seemed to put the tin hat on it.

"If Horváth was his real name, why had he kept up this pretence for so long? Think of the words 'buried alive,' and 'salt-mines,' and there is a gleam. But, when you asked him who shot him, he said Horváth. A moment like that is probably the only time when a man isn't willing to talk about himself; he didn't mean himself, but somebody else named Horváth. While I was thinking of that, our excellent Mills was telling you about the man called Fley at the public house. Mills said that there seemed something very familiar about Fley, although he had never seen him before, and that his speech sounded like a burlesque of Grimaud's. Was it Grimaud he suggested? Brother, brother, brother! You see, there were three coffins, but Fley mentioned only two brothers. It sounded like a third.

"While I was thinking about this, there entered the obviously Slavic Madame Dumont. If I could establish Grimaud as coming from Transylvania, it would narrow down our search when we tried to find out his history. But it had to be done delicately. Notice that carved figure of a buffalo on Grimaud's desk? What does that suggest to you?"

"It doesn't suggest Transylvania, I can tell you that," the superintendent growled. "It's more like the Wild West—Buffalo Bill—Indians. Hold on! Was that why you asked her whether Grimaud had ever been in the United States?"

Dr. Fell nodded guiltily. "It seemed an innocent question, and she answered. You see, if he'd got that figure in an American curio shop— H'm. Hadley, I've been in Hungary. I went in my younger and lither days, when I'd just read *Dracula*. Transylvania was the only European country where buffaloes were bred; they used 'em like oxen. Hungary was full of mixed religious beliefs; but Transylvania was Unitarian. I asked Madame Ernestine, and she qualified. Then I threw my hand grenade. If Grimaud had been innocently associated with salt-mines, it wouldn't matter. But I named the only prison in Transylvania where convicts were used to work the salt-mines. I named the Siebenturmen—or the Seven Towers—without even saying it was a prison. It almost finished her. Now perhaps you will understand my remark about the seven towers and the country that does not now exist. And for God's sake will somebody give me a match?"

"You've got 'em," said Hadley. He took a few strides round the hall, accepted a cigar from the now bland and beaming Dr. Fell, and muttered to himself: "Yes—so far as it goes, it seems reasonable enough. Your long shot about the prison worked. But the whole basis of your case, that these three people are brothers, is pure surmise. In fact, I think it's the weakest part of the case. . . ."

"Oh, admitted. But what then?"

"Only that it's the crucial point. Suppose Grimaud didn't mean that a person named Horváth had shot him, but was only referring to himself in some way? Then the murderer might be anybody. But if there are three brothers, and he did mean that, the thing is simple. We come back to the belief that Pierre Fley *did* shoot him, after all, or Fley's brother did. We can put our hands on Fley at any time, and as for the brother—"

"Are you sure you'd recognize the brother," said Dr. Fell, reflectively, "if you met him?"

"How do you mean?"

"I was thinking of Grimaud. He spoke English perfectly, and also passed perfectly for a Frenchman. I don't doubt he did study at Paris, and that the Dumont woman did make costumes at the Opéra. Anyhow, there he went stumping round Bloomsbury for nearly thirty years, gruff, good-natured, harmless, with his clipped beard and his square bowler, keeping a check on a savage temper and placidly lecturing in public. Nobody ever saw a devil in him—though somehow I fancy it must have been a wily, brilliant devil. Nobody ever suspected. He could have shaved, cultivated tweeds and a port-wine complexion, and passed for a British squire, or anything else he liked. . . . Then what about this third brother? He's the one who intrigues me. Suppose he's right here somewhere in our midst, in some guise or other, and nobody knows him for what he really is?"

"Possibly. But we don't know anything about the brother."

Dr. Fell, struggling to light his cigar, peered up with extraordinary intentness.

"I know. That's what bothers me, Hadley." He rumbled for a moment, and then blew out the match with a vast puff. "We have two theoretical brothers who have taken French names: Charles and Pierre. Then there's a third. For the sake of clearness and argument, let's call him Henri—"

"Look here. You're not going to tell me you know something about him also?"

"On the contrary," returned Dr. Fell, with a sort of ferocity, "I'm going to emphasize just how little we know about him. We know about Charles and Pierre. But we haven't even the merest hint about Henri, *although* Pierre appears to be forever talking about him and using him as a threat. It is, 'My brother who can do much more than I can.' 'My brother who wants your life.' 'I am in danger when I associate with him.' And so on. But no shape comes out of the smoke, neither man nor goblin. Son, it worries me. I think that ugly presence is behind the whole business, controlling it, using poor half-crazy Pierre for his own ends, and probably as dangerous to Pierre as to Charles. I can't help feeling that this presence staged the whole scene at the Warwick Tavern; that he's somewhere close at hand and watchful; that—" Dr. Fell stared round, as though he expected to see something move or speak in the empty hall. Then he added: "You know, I hope your constable gets hold of Pierre and keeps hold of him. Maybe his usefulness is over."

Hadley made a vague gesture. He bit at the end of his clipped moustache.

"Yes, I know," he said; "but let's stick to the facts. The facts will be difficult enough to dig out, I warn you. I'll cable the Rumanian police tonight. But if Transylvania's been annexed, in the fuss and uproar there may be few official records left. The Bolshies were storming through there just after the war, weren't they? Um. Anyhow, we want facts! Come on and let's get after Mangan and Grimaud's daughter. I'm not entirely satisfied with *their* behaviour, by the way. . . ."

"Eh? Why?"

"I mean, always provided the Dumont woman is telling the truth," Hadley amended. "You seem to think she is. But, as I've heard the thing, wasn't Mangan here tonight at Grimaud's request, in case the visitor should drop in? Yes. Then he seems to have been rather a tame watch-dog. He was sitting in a room near the front door. The door-bell rings—if Dumont's not lying—and enter the mysterious visitor. All this time Mangan doesn't show any curiosity; he sits in the room with the door shut, pays no attention to the visitor, and only kicks up a row when he hears a shot and suddenly finds that the door has been locked. Is that logical?"

"Nothing is logical," said Dr. Fell. "Not even— But that can wait."

They went down the long hall, and Hadley assumed his most tactful and impassive manner when he opened the door. It was a room somewhat smaller than the other, lined with orderly books and wooden filing cabinets. It had a plain rag carpet on the floor, hard businesslike chairs, and a sickly fire. Under a green-shaded hanging-lamp, Mills's typewriter desk was drawn up directly facing the door. On one side of the machine neat manuscript sheets lay clipped in a wire basket; on the other side stood a glass of milk, a dish of dried prunes, and a copy of Williamson's *Differential and Integral Calculus.*

"I'll bet he drinks mineral water, too," said Dr. Fell, in some agitation. "I'll swear by all my gods he drinks mineral water and reads that sort of thing for fun. I'll bet—" He stopped at a violent nudge from Hadley, who was speaking to Rosette Grimaud across the room. Hadley introduced the three of them.

"Naturally, Miss Grimaud, I don't wish to distress you at this time—"

"Please don't say anything," she said. She was sitting before the fire, so tense that she jumped a little. "I mean—just don't say anything about *that.* You see, I'm fond of him, but not so fond that it hurts terribly unless somebody begins to talk about it. Then I begin to think."

She pressed her hands against her temples. In the firelight, with her fur coat thrown back, there was again a contrast between eyes and face. But it was a changing contrast. She had her mother's intense personality shaped into blond, square-faced, rather barbaric Slavic beauty. Yet in one moment the face would be hard and the long hazel eyes gentle and uneasy, like the curate's daughter. And in the next moment the face would be softened and the eyes brilliantly hard, like the devil's daughter. Her thin eyebrows turned a little upwards at the outer corners, but she had a broad humorous mouth. She was restless, sleek, and puzzling. Behind her stood Mangan in gloomy helplessness.

"One thing, though," she went on, pounding her fist slowly on the arm of the chair—"one thing I've got to know, though, before you start your third degree." She nodded towards a little door across the room, and spoke breathlessly. "Stuart's—showing that detective of yours up to the roof. Is it true, *is* it true what we hear about a man getting in—and out—and killing my father—without—without—?"

"Better let me handle this, Hadley," said Dr. Fell, very quietly.

The doctor, Rampole knew, was firmly under the impression that he was a model of tact. Very often this tact resembled a load of bricks coming through a skylight. But his utter conviction that he was doing the thing handsomely, his vast good-nature and complete naïveté, had an effect that the most skilled tact could never have produced. It was as though he had slid down on the bricks himself to offer sympathy or shake hands. And people instantly began to tell him all about themselves.

"Harrumph!" he snorted. "Of course it's not true, Miss Grimaud. We know all about how the blighter worked his trick, even if it was done by somebody you never heard of." She looked up quickly. "Furthermore, there'll be no third degree, and your father has a fighting chance to pull through. Look here, Miss Grimaud, haven't I met you somewhere before?"

"Oh, I know you're trying to make me feel better," she said, with a faint smile. "Boyd has told me about you, but—"

"No, I mean it," wheezed Dr. Fell, seriously. He squinted at memory. "H'm, yes. Got it! You're at London University, aren't you? Of course. And you're in a debating circle or something? It seems to me I officiated as chairman when your team debated Woman's Rights in the World, wasn't it?"

"That's Rosette," assented Mangan, gloomily. "She's a strong feminist. She says—"

"Heh-heh-heh," said Dr. Fell. "I remember now." He was radiant, and pointed with a vast flipper. "She may be a feminist, my boy, but she has startling lapses. In fact, I remember that debate as ending in the most beautiful and appalling row I ever heard outside a Pacifist meeting. You were on the side for Woman's Rights, Miss Grimaud, and against the Tyranny of Man. Yes, yes. You entered very pale and serious and solemn, and stayed like that until your own side began to present their case. They went on something awful, but you didn't look pleased. Then one lean female carried on for twenty minutes about what woman needed for an ideal state of existence, but you only seemed to get madder and madder. So when your turn came, all you did was rise to proclaim in silvery ringing tones that what woman needed for an ideal existence was less talking and more copulation."

"Good God!" said Mangan, and jumped.

"Well, I felt like it—then," said Rosette, hotly. "But you don't need to think . . ."

"Or perhaps you didn't say copulation," ruminated Dr. Fell. "Anyway, the effect of that terrible word was beyond description. It was as though you had whispered, 'Asbestos!' to a gang of pyromaniacs. Unfortunately, I tried to keep a straight face by swallowing water. This, my friends, is a practice to which I am unaccustomed. The result had the general aspect, to eye and ear, of a bomb exploding in an aquarium. But I was wondering whether you and Mr. Mangan often discussed these subjects. They must be enlightening talks. What was the argument about this evening, for instance?"

Both of them began to speak at once, chaotically. Dr. Fell beamed, and they both stopped with a startled expression.

"Yes," nodded the doctor. "You understand now, don't you, that there's nothing to be afraid of in talking to the police? And that you can speak as freely as you like? It'll be better, you know. Let's face the thing and clear it up sensibly now, among ourselves, hey?"

"Right," said Rosette. "Has somebody got a cigarette?"

Hadley looked at Rampole. "The old blighter's done it," he said.

The old blighter was again lighting his cigar while Mangan fumbled in his haste to produce cigarettes. Then Dr. Fell pointed.

"Now, I want to know about a very rummy thing," he continued. "Were you two kids so engrossed in each other that you didn't notice anything to-night until the rumpus started? As I understand it, Mangan, Professor Grimaud asked you here tonight to be on the lookout for possible trouble. Why didn't you? Didn't you hear the door-bell?"

Mangan's swarthy face was clouded. He made a fierce gesture.

"Oh, I admit it's my fault. But at the time I never gave it a thought. How was I going to know? Of course I heard the door-bell. In fact, we both spoke to the fellow—"

"You *what?*" interrupted Hadley, striding past Dr. Fell.

"Certainly. Otherwise you don't think I'd have let him get past me and upstairs, do you? But he said he was old Pettis—Anthony Pettis, you know."

## VII

### The Guy Fawkes Visitor

"OF COURSE we know now that it wasn't Pettis," Mangan pursued, lighting the girl's cigarette with an angry snap of his lighter, "Pettis must be all of five feet four inches tall. Besides, now that I think back on it, it wasn't even a very exact imitation of his voice. But he sang out and spoke in words Pettis always uses. . . ."

Dr. Fell scowled. "But didn't it strike you as queer that even a collector of ghost stories should walk about dressed up like a Fifth of November Guy? Is he addicted to pranks?"

Rosette Grimaud looked up with a startled expression. She held out her cigarette level and motionless, as though she were pointing, and then twitched round to look at Mangan. When she turned back again there was a narrow flash of those long eyes, a deepness of breathing like anger or cruelty, or enlightenment. They had shared a thought—and Mangan was much the more disturbed by it. He had the air of one who is trying to be a good fellow and at peace with the world, if the world would only let him. Rampole had a feeling that this secret thought did not concern Pettis at all, for Mangan stumbled before he could recapture Dr. Fell's question.

"Pranks?" he repeated, and passed a hand nervously over his wiry black hair. "Oh! Pettis? Good Lord, no! He's as correct and fussy as they make 'em. But, you understand, we didn't see his face. It was like this:

"We'd been sitting in that front room since just after dinner—"

"Stop a bit," interrupted Hadley. "Was the door to the hall open?"

"No. Hang it all," said Mangan in a defensive tone, and shifted, "you don't sit in a draughty room on a snowy night with the door standing open; not without central heating, you don't. I knew we could hear the bell ring if it did ring. Besides—well, honestly, I didn't expect anything to happen. The professor gave us the impression at dinner that it was a hoax, or that it had been adjusted somehow; anyway, that he had been inclined to get the wind up over nothing. . . ."

Hadley was looking at him with hard, bright eyes. "You got that impression, too, Miss Grimaud?"

"Yes, in a way. . . . I don't know! It's always hard to tell," she answered, with a faint anger (or rebellion?), "whether he's annoyed or amused or just pretending both. My father has a queer sense of humour, and he loves dramatic effects. He treats me as a child. I don't think I ever in my life saw him frightened, so I don't know. But for the past three days, he's been acting so dashed queerly that when Boyd told me about the man in that pub—" She lifted her shoulders.

"In what way was he acting queerly?"

"Well, muttering to himself, for instance. And suddenly roaring out over trifles, which he seldom does. And then again he would laugh too much. But most of all it was those letters. He began to get them in every post. Don't ask me what was in them; he burnt all of them. They were in plain penny envelopes. . . . I shouldn't have noticed at all if it hadn't been for a habit of his." She hesitated. "Maybe you'll understand. My father is one of those people who can never get a letter in your presence without your instantly knowing what it's about or even who it's from. He'll explode, 'Damned swindler!' or, 'Now, there's impudence for you!' or, genially, 'Well, well, here's a letter from old So-and-so!'—in rather a surprised tone, as though he expected somebody in Liverpool or Birmingham to be at the other side of the moon. I don't know if you understand . . . ?"

"We understand. Please go on."

"But when he got these notes, or whatever they were, he didn't say anything at all. He didn't move a muscle. Yet, you see, he never openly destroyed one except yesterday morning at the breakfast table. After he'd glanced at it he crumpled it up, got up from his chair, and went over in a thoughtful sort of way and threw it in the fire. Just at that second Au—" Rosette glanced quickly at Hadley, seemed to discover her own hesitation, and blundered into confusion. "Mrs.—Madame—oh, I mean Aunt Ernestine! Just at that second she asked him if he would have some more bacon. Suddenly he whirled round from the fire and yelled, 'Go to hell!' It was so unexpected that before we had recovered our wits he'd stamped out of the room, muttering that a man couldn't have any peace. He looked devilish. That was the day he came back with that painting. He was good-humoured again; he banged about, chuckling, and helped the cabman and somebody else cart it upstairs. I—I don't want you to think—" Evidently the memories were crowding back again to this complex Rosette; she began to think, and that was bad. She added, shakily, "I don't want you to think I don't like him."

Hadley ignored the personal. "Did he ever mention this man at the public house?"

"Off-handedly, when I asked him. He said it was one of the quacks who often threatened him for jeering at—the history of magic. Of course I knew it wasn't merely that."

"Why, Miss Grimaud?"

During a pause she looked at him unwinkingly.

"Because I felt that this was the real thing. And because I have often wondered whether there was anything in my father's past life which might bring something like that on him."

It was a direct challenge. During a long silence they could hear muffled creakings and flat, heavy footsteps shaking on the roof. Some change moved and played like firelight on her face—fear, or hatred, or pain, or doubt. That illusion of the barbaric had returned—as though the mink coat should have been a leopard-skin coat. Crossing her legs, she leaned back voluptuously, wriggling into the chair. She tilted her head against the back of the chair, so that the firelight gleamed on her throat and in her half-shut eyes. She regarded them with a faint, fixed smile; the cheekbones were outlined in shadow. All the same, Rampole saw that she was trembling. Why, incidentally, should her face seem broader than it was long?

"Well?" she prompted.

Hadley appeared mildly surprised. "Bring something on him? I don't quite understand. Had you any reason to think so?"

"Oh, no reason! I don't think so, really. Just these fancies—" The denial was quick, but the sharp rise and fall of her breast had quietened. "Probably it's living with my father's hobby. And then my mother—she's dead, you know; died when I was quite a kid—my mother was supposed to have second-sight." Rosette raised her cigarette again. "But you were asking me . . . ?"

"About tonight, first of all. If you think it would be helpful to go into your father's past, the Yard will certainly act on your suggestion."

She jerked the cigarette away from her lips.

"But," pursued Hadley in the same colourless voice, "let's get on with the story Mr. Mangan was telling. You two went to the drawing-room after dinner, and the door to the hall was shut. Now, did Professor Grimaud tell you what time he expected a dangerous visitor?"

"Er—yes," said Mangan. He had taken out a handkerchief and was mopping his forehead. Seen sideways in the firelight, there were many small wrinkles across the forehead of the thin, hollowed, sharp-angled face. "That was another reason why I didn't tumble to who it might be. He was too early. The professor said ten o'clock, and this fellow arrived at a quarter to."

"Ten o'clock. I see. You're sure he said that?"

"Well—yes! At least, I think so. About ten o'clock. Wasn't it, Rosette?"

"I don't know. He didn't say anything to me."

"I—see. Go on, Mr. Mangan."

"We had the radio on. That was bad, because the music was loud. And we were playing cards in front of the fire. All the same, I heard the door-bell, I looked up at the clock on the mantel, and it said a quarter to ten. I was getting up when I heard the front door open. Then I heard Mrs. Dumont's voice saying something like, 'Wait, I'll see,' and a sound as though the door slammed. I called out, 'Ahoy there! Who is it?' But the radio was making such a row that I naturally stepped over and shut it off. And just afterwards we heard Pettis—naturally we both thought it was Pettis—call out: 'Hullo, children! It's Pettis. What's all this formality about seeing the Governor? I'm going up and break in on him.'"

"Those were his exact words?"

"Yes. He always called Dr. Grimaud the Governor; nobody else had the nerve to; except Burnaby, and he calls him Pop. . . . So we said, 'Righto,' as you do, and didn't bother any more about it. We both sat down again. But I noticed that it was getting near ten o'clock and I began to be watchful and jumpy, now that it was coming towards ten o'clock . . ."

Hadley drew a design on the margin of his notebook.

"So the man who called himself Pettis," he mused, "spoke to you through the door without seeing you? How did he know you two were there, do you think?"

Mangan frowned. "He saw us through the window, I suppose. As you come up the front steps you can see straight into the front room through the nearest window. I always notice it myself. In fact, if I see anybody in the front room I usually lean across and tap on the window instead of ringing the bell."

The superintendent was still drawing designs, meditatively. He seemed about to ask a question, but checked himself. Rosette regarded him with a sharp, unwinking gaze. Hadley merely said:

"Go on. You were waiting for ten o'clock—"

"And nothing happened," Mangan insisted. "But, a funny thing, every minute past ten o'clock I got more nervous instead of more relieved. I told you I didn't really expect the man would come, or that there would be any trouble. But I kept picturing that dark hall, and the queer suit of armour with the mask out there, and the more I thought of it the less I liked it. . . ."

"I know exactly what you mean," said Rosette. She looked at him in a strange, rather startled manner. "I was thinking the same thing. But I didn't want to talk about it in case you called me a fool."

"Oh, I have these psychic fits, too. That," Mangan said bitterly, "is why I get the sack so often, and why I shall probably get the sack for not phoning in this story tonight. News editor be damned. I'm no Judas." He shifted. "Anyway, it was nearly ten past ten when I felt I couldn't stand it any longer. I slammed down the cards and said to Rosette, 'Look here, let's get a drink and turn on all the lights in the hall—or do something.' I was going to ring for Annie, when I remembered it was Saturday and her night out. . . ."

"Annie? That's the maid? Yes. I'd forgotten her. Well?"

"So I went over to open the door, and it was locked on the outside. It was like . . . like this! You have some conspicuous object in your bedroom, like a picture or an ornament, that's so common you never fully notice it. Then one day you walk in and have a vague feeling that there's something wrong with the room. It irritates and disturbs you, because you can't imagine why. Then all of a sudden a gap jumps up, and you see with a shock that the object has been removed. Understand? I felt just like that. I *knew* something was wrong, I felt it ever since that fellow had sung out from the hall, but it never hit me with a smash until I found that door locked. Just as I began idiotically yanking at the knob, we heard the shot.

"A firearm indoors makes a devil of a noise, and we heard it even up at the top of the house. Rosette screamed—"

"I did not!"

"Then she pointed at me and said what I'd been thinking, too. She said, 'That wasn't Pettis at all. He's got in.'"

"Can you fix the time of that?"

"Yes. It was just ten minutes past ten. Well, I tried to break the door down." In spite of staring at that memory, a wry and mocking gleam of mirth twinkled in Mangan's eyes. It was as though he hated to speak, but could not help commenting. "I say, have you ever noticed how easy it is to break down doors in the stories? Those stories are a carpenter's paradise. They're an endless trail of doors smashed down on the slightest pretext, even when somebody inside won't answer a casual question. But try it on one of these doors! . . . That's about all. I banged my shoulder-bone against it for a while, and then I thought about getting out through the window and in again through the front door or the area door. I ran into you, and you know what happened."

Hadley tapped the notebook with his pencil. "Was it customary for the front door to be unlocked, Mr. Mangan?"

"O Lord! I don't know! But it was the only thing I could think of. Anyhow, it *was* unlocked."

"Yes, it was unlocked. Have you anything to add to that, Miss Grimaud?"

Her eyelids drooped. "Nothing—that is, not exactly. Boyd has told you everything that happened just as it happened. But you people always want all kinds of queer things, don't you? Even if they don't seem to bear on the matter? This probably has nothing to do with the matter at all, but I'll tell you. . . . A little while before the door-bell rang, I was going over to get some cigarettes from a table between the windows. The radio was on, as Boyd says. But I heard from somewhere out in the street, or on the pavement in front of the door, a loud sound like—like a thud, as though a heavy object had fallen from a big height. It wasn't an ordinary street noise, you see. Like a man falling."

Rampole felt himself stirring uneasily. Hadley asked:

"A thud, you say? H'm. Did you look out to see what it was?"

"Yes. But I couldn't see anything. Of course, I only pulled the blind back and peeped round the side of it, but I can swear the street was empt—" She stopped in full flight. Her lips fell open a little, and her eyes were suddenly fixed. "Oh, my *God!*" she said.

"Yes, Miss Grimaud," said Hadley without inflection, "the blinds were all down, as you say. I especially noticed that, because Mr. Mangan got entangled with one when he jumped out. That was why I wondered how the visitor could have seen you through any window in that room. But possibly they weren't drawn down all the time?"

There was a silence, except for faint noises on the roof. Rampole glanced at Dr. Fell, who was propped back against one of the unbreakable doors with his chin in his hand and his shovel-hat tilted over his eyes. Then Rampole looked at the impassive Hadley, and back to the girl.

"He thinks we're lying, Boyd," said Rosette Grimaud, coolly. "I don't think we'd better say anything more."

And then Hadley smiled. "I don't think anything of the kind, Miss Grimaud. I'm going to tell you why, because you're the only person who can help us. I'm even going to tell you what did happen. —Fell!"

"Eh?" boomed Dr. Fell, looking up with a start.

"I want you to listen to this," the superintendent pursued, grimly. "A while ago you were having a lot of pleasure and mystification out of saying that you believed the stories—apparently incredible—told by Mills and Mrs. Dumont; without giving any reasons why you believed them. I'll return the compliment. I'll say that I believe not only their story, but the story told by these two also. And, in explaining why, I'll also explain the impossible situation."

This time Dr. Fell did come out of his abstraction with a jerk. He puffed out his cheeks and peered at Hadley as though prepared to leap into battle.

"Not all of it, I admit," pursued Hadley, "but enough to narrow down the field of suspects to a few people, and to explain why there were no footprints in the snow."

"Oh, *that!*" said Dr. Fell, contemptuously. He relaxed with a grunt. "You know, for a second I hoped you had something. But that part is obvious."

Hadley kept his temper with a violent effort. "The man we want," he went on, "made no footprints on the pavement or up the steps because he never walked on the pavement or up the steps—after the snow had stopped. He was in the house all the time. He had been in the house for some time. He was either (a) an inmate; or (b) more probably somebody who had concealed himself there, using a key to the front door earlier in the evening. This would explain all the inconsistencies in everybody's story. At the proper time he put on his fancy rig, stepped outside the front door on the swept doorstep, and rang the door-bell. It explains how he knew Miss Grimaud and Mr. Mangan were in the front room when the blinds were drawn—he had seen them go in. It explains how, when the door was slammed in his face and he was told to wait outside, he could simply walk in—he had a key."

Dr. Fell was slowly shaking his head and rumbling to himself. He folded his arms argumentatively.

"H'mf, yes. But why should even a slightly cracked person indulge in all that elaborate hocus-pocus? If he lived in the house, the argument isn't bad: he wanted to make the visitor seem an outsider. But if he really came from outside, why take the dangerous risk of hanging about inside long before he was ready to act? Why not march straight up at the right time?"

"First," said the methodical Hadley, checking it off on his fingers, "he had to know where people were, so as to have no interference. Second, and more important, he wanted to put the finishing touches on his vanishing trick by having no footprints whatever, anywhere, in the snow. The vanishing trick would be everything to the crazy mind of—brother Henri, let's say. So he got in while it was snowing heavily, and waited until it had stopped."

"Who," Rosette asked in a sharp voice, "is brother Henri?"

"He's a name, my dear," Dr. Fell returned, affably. "I told you that you didn't know him. . . . Now, Hadley, here's where I enter a mild, firm objection to this whole rummy affair. We've talked glibly about snow starting and stopping, as though you could regulate it like a tap. But I want to know how in blazes a man can tell WHEN snow is going to start or stop? That is, a man seldom says to himself, 'Aha! On Saturday night I will commit a crime. On that night, I think, it will commence to snow at exactly 5:00 P.M., and leave off at exactly 9:30 P.M. This will afford me ample time to get into the house, and be prepared with my trick when the snowfall ends.' Tut, tut! Your explanation is rather more staggering than your problem. It's much easier to believe that a man walked on snow without leaving a footprint than to believe he knew precisely when he would have it to walk on."

The superintendent was irritable. "I am trying," he said, "to get to the main point of all this. But if you must fight about that— Don't you see it explains away the last problem?"

"What problem?"

"Our friend Mangan here says that the visitor threatened to pay his visit at ten o'clock. Mrs. Dumont and Mills say nine-thirty. Wait!" He checked Mangan's outburst. "Was A lying, or B? First, what sane reason could either have for lying *afterwards* about the time he *threatened* to come? Second, if A says ten o'clock and B says nine-thirty, then, innocent or guilty, one of the two should have learned beforehand the time at which the visitor really would arrive. And which was right about the time he did arrive?"

"Neither," said Mangan, staring. "It was between 'em. At 9:45."

"Yes. That's a sign that neither lied. It's a sign that the visitor's threat to Grimaud was not definite; it was 'nine-thirty or ten o'clock or thereabouts.' And Grimaud, who was trying pretty desperately to act as though the threat hadn't scared him, nevertheless took very good care to mention both times in order to make sure everybody was there. My wife does the same thing with invitations to bridge parties. . . . Well, but *why* couldn't brother Henri be definite? Because, as Fell says, he couldn't turn off the snow like a tap. He could risk a long gamble on there being snow tonight, as there's been for several nights; but he had to wait until it stopped even if he waited until midnight. He didn't have to wait so long. It stopped at half-past nine. And then he acted exactly as such a lunatic would—he waited fifteen minutes so that there could be no argument afterwards, and rang the bell."

Dr. Fell opened his mouth to speak, looked shrewdly at the intent faces of Rosette and Mangan, and stopped.

"Now, then!" said Hadley, squaring his shoulders. "I've shown you two that I believe everything you say, because I want your help on the most important thing this tells us. . . . The man we want is no casual acquaintance. He knows this house inside out—the rooms, the routine, the habits of the occupants. He knows your phrases and nicknames. He knows how this Mr. Pettis is accustomed to address not only Dr. Grimaud, but *you*; hence he's no casual business friend of the professor whom you haven't seen. So I want to know all about everybody who's a frequent enough visitor to this house, everybody who is close enough to Dr. Grimaud, to answer the description."

She moved uneasily, startled. "You think—somebody like that. . . . Oh, it's impossible! No, no, no!" (It was a queer echo of her mother's voice.) "Not anybody like that, anyhow!"

"Why do you say that?" Hadley asked, sharply. "Do you know who shot your father?"

The sudden crack of the words made her jump. "No, of course not!"

"Or have any suspicion?"

"No. Except," her teeth gleamed, "I don't see why you should keep looking outside the house. That was a very nice little lesson in deduction you gave, and thanks awfully. But if the person had come from *inside* the house, and acted as you said, then it would really be reasonable, wouldn't it? It would apply much better."

"To whom?"

"Let's see! Well . . . that's your business, isn't it?" (He had somehow stirred a sleek tiger cat, and she was enjoying it.) "Of course, you haven't met the whole household. You haven't met Annie—or Mr. Drayman, come to think of it. But your other idea is utterly ridiculous. In the first place, my father has very few friends. Outside of the people in this house, there are only two who fit the qualifications, and neither of them could possibly be the man you want. They couldn't be in the mere matter of their physical characteristics. One is Anthony Pettis himself; he's no taller than I am, and I'm no Amazon. The other is Jerome Burnaby, the artist who did that queer picture. He has a deformity; a slight one, but it couldn't be disguised and anybody could spot it a mile away. Aunt Ernestine or Stuart would have known him instantly."

"All the same, what do you know about them?"

She lifted her shoulders. "Both are middle-aged, well-to-do, and potter after their hobbies. Pettis is bald-headed and fastidious. . . . I don't mean he's old-womanish: he's what the men call a good fellow, and he's clever as sin. Bah! Why won't they *do* something with themselves!" She clenched her hands. Then she glanced up at Mangan, and a slow, calculating, drowsily pleasant expression came into her look. "Burnaby—yes, Jerome has done something with himself, in a way. He's fairly well known as an artist, though he'd rather be known as a criminologist. He's big and bluff; he likes to talk about crime and brag about his athletic prowess of old. Jerome is attractive in his way. He's very fond of me, and Boyd is horribly jealous." Her smile widened.

"I don't like the fellow," said Mangan, quietly. "In fact, I hate him like poison—and we both know it. But at least Rosette's right about one thing. He'd never do a thing like that."

Hadley scribbled again. "What is this deformity of his?"

"A club foot. You can see how he couldn't possibly conceal it."

"Thank you. For the moment," said Hadley, shutting up his notebook, "that will be all. I should suggest that you go along to the nursing-home. Unless . . . er—any questions, Fell?"

The doctor stumped forward. He towered over the girl, peering down at her with his head a little on one side.

"Just one last question," he said, brushing aside the black ribbon of his eye-glasses as he would a fly. "Harrumph! Ha! Now! Miss Grimaud, why are you so certain that the guilty person is this Mr. Drayman?"

## VIII

### The Bullet

HE NEVER received any answer to that question, although he received some illumination. It was all over before Rampole realized what had happened. Since the doctor had spoken with the greatest casualness, the name "Drayman" had made no impression on Rampole, and he was not even looking at Rosette. Uneasily, he had been wondering for some time what had happened to change the gusty, garrulous, beaming Mangan he used to know into this shuffling figure who backed and deprecated and talked like a fool. In the past Mangan had never talked like a fool, even when he talked like an idiot. But now—

"You *devil!*" cried Rosette Grimaud.

It was like a screech of chalk on a blackboard. Rampole whirled round to see high cheekbones gone still higher as her mouth widened, and a blaze that seemed to take the colour from her eyes. It was only a glimpse; she had flung herself past Dr. Fell, the mink coat flying, and out into the hall, with Mangan after her. The door slammed. Mangan reappeared for a moment, said to them, "Er—sorry!" and quickly closed the door once more. He looked almost grotesque in the doorway, his back bent and his head lowered, so that it seemed all wrinkled forehead and nervous dark eyes shining intensely. His hands were extended, with palms turned down, as though he were trying to quiet an audience. "Er—sorry!" he said, and closed the door.

Dr. Fell remained blinking at it.

"She's her father's daughter, Hadley," he wheezed, and shook his head slowly. "Harrumph, yes. She goes just so far under hard emotional pressure; very quiet, powder packed into a cartridge; then some little thing jars the hair trigger, and—h'm. I'm afraid she's morbid in the real sense, but maybe she thinks she has reason to be. I wonder how much she knows?"

"Oh, well, she's a foreigner. But that's not the point. It seems to me," said Hadley, with some asperity, "that you're always making a wild shot like a trick rifleman and knocking the cigarette out of somebody's mouth. What was that business about Drayman, anyhow?"

Dr. Fell seemed bothered.

"In a minute, in a minute. . . . What did you think of her, Hadley? And Mangan?" He turned to Rampole. "My ideas are a little mixed. I'd got the impression, from what you said, that Mangan was a wild Irishman of the type I know and like."

"He was," said Rampole. "Understand?"

"As to what I think of her," Hadley said, "I think she could sit here as cool as you please, analyzing her father's life (she's got a damned good head on her, by the way); and yet at this moment I'll bet she's in tears and hysterics, rushing across there, because she didn't show him enough consideration. I think she's fundamentally sound. But she's got the Old Nick in her, Fell. She wants a master in both senses. She and Mangan will never hit it off until he has sense enough to punch her head or take her own advice at the London University debate."

"Ever since you have become superintendent of the C.I.D.," declared Dr. Fell, squinting at him, "I have detected in you a certain raffish air which pains and surprises me. Listen, you old satyr. Did you honestly believe all that rubbish you talked, about the murderer sneaking into this house to wait until the snowstorm had stopped?"

Hadley permitted himself a broad grin. "It's as good an explanation as any," he said, "until I can think of a better. And it keeps their minds occupied. Always keep witnesses' minds occupied. At least I believe their story. . . . We're going to find something in the way of footprints on that roof, don't you worry. But we'll talk about that later. What about Drayman?"

"To begin with, I had stuck in my mind an odd remark made by Madame Dumont. It was so odd that it jumped out of the sentence. Not a calculated remark; she cried it out at the time she was most hysterical, when she could not understand why even murderers acted out so silly a charade. She said (if you wish to kill somebody), 'You do not put on a painted mask, like old Drayman with the children on Guy Fawkes night.' I filed away the suggestion of this Guy Fawkes spectre, wondering what it meant. Then, all unintentionally, I phrased a question about Pettis—when speaking to Rosette—with the words, 'dressed up like a Fifth of November Guy?' Did you notice her expression, Hadley? Just my suggestion that the visitor was dressed like that gave her the hint, but it startled her as much as it pleased her. She didn't say anything; she was thinking. She hated the person she was thinking of. What person?"

Hadley stared across the room. "Yes, I remember. I could see she was hinting at somebody she suspected or wanted us to suspect; that was why I asked her flat out. She practically made me see it was somebody in this house. But to tell you the truth,"—he rubbed his hand across his forehead—"this is such a rum crowd that for a second I thought she was hinting at her own mother."

"Not by the way she dragged in Drayman. 'You haven't met Annie—or Mr. Drayman, come to think of it.' The important news was in the postscript. . . ." Dr. Fell stumped round the typewriter desk, peering malevolently at the glass of milk. "We must rout him out. He interests me. Who is this Drayman, this old friend and hanger-on of Grimaud, who takes sleeping draughts and wears Fifth of November masks? What's his place in the household; what's he doing here, anyway?"

"You mean—blackmail?"

"Rubbish, my boy. Did you ever hear of a schoolmaster being a blackmailer? No, no. They're much too worried about what people might find out about *them*. The academic profession has its faults, as I know for my sins; but it doesn't produce blackmailers. . . . No, it was probably only a kindly impulse of Grimaud to take him in, but—"

He paused as a rush of cold air blew his cloak. A door across the room, evidently communicating with a staircase to the attic and the roof, opened and shut. Mills popped in. His mouth was bluish and a large wool muffler was wound round his neck; but he looked warm with satisfaction. After refreshing himself with a pull at the glass of milk (impassively, with head thrown back in a way which somehow suggested a sword-swallower), he put out his hands to the fire.

He chattered: "I have been watching your detective, gentlemen, from a point of vantage at the top of the trap-door. He has caused a few landslides, but. . . . Excuse me! Didn't you have a commission of some description for me to execute? Ah yes. I am anxious to lend assistance, but I fear I forgot—"

"Wake up Mr. Drayman," the superintendent said, "if you have to slosh him with water. And . . . Hullo! Pettis! If Mr. Pettis is still here, tell him I want to see him. What did Sergeant Betts discover up there?"

Betts answered for himself. He looked as though he had taken a header in a ski-jump; he breathed hard, stamped and slapped the snow from his clothes as he shook his way towards the fire.

"Sir," he announced, "you can take my word for it that not even a bird's lit on that roof anywhere. There's no mark of any kind in any place. I've covered every foot of it." He stripped off his sodden gloves. "I had myself tied on a rope to each of the chimneys, so I could get down and crawl straight along the gutters. Nothing round the edges, nothing round the chimneys, nothing anywhere. If anybody got up on that roof tonight, he must have

been lighter than air. Now I'll go down and have a look at the back garden . . ."

"But—!" cried Hadley.

"Quite so," said Dr. Fell. "Look here, we'd better go down and see what
your bloodhounds are doing in the other room. If the good Preston—"

Sergeant Preston, fuming a little, pulled open the door to the hall as
though he had been summoned. He looked at Betts and back to Hadley.

"It's taken me a little time, sir," he reported, "because we had to pull
out all those bookcases and shove 'em back again. The answer is nothing! No
secret entrance of any kind. Chimney's solid and no funny business about it;
flue's only about two or three inches wide, and goes up on an angle at that.
. . . Is that all, sir? The boys have finished."

"Fingerprints?"

"Plenty of prints, except— You raised and lowered that window yourself,
didn't you, sir? With your fingers on the glass up near the top of the frame?
I recognized your prints."

"I am generally careful about things like that," snapped Hadley. "Well?"

"Nothing else on the glass. And all the woodwork of that window, frame
and sill, is high-gloss varnish that'd take a glove-smudge as clear as a print.
There's nothing, not even a smudge. If anybody went out there, he must have
stood back and dived out head first without touching anything."

"That's enough, thanks," said Hadley. "Wait downstairs. Get after that
back garden, Betts. . . . No, wait, Mr. Mills. Preston will fetch Mr. Pettis,
if he's still there. I should like to speak to you."

"It would seem," said Mills, rather shrilly, when the other two had gone,
"that we return to doubts about my own story. I assure you I am telling the
truth. Here is where I sat. See for yourself."

Hadley opened the door. Ahead of them the high, sombre hallway ran
thirty feet to the door opposite—a door brilliantly illuminated by the glow
from under the archway.

"I don't suppose there's any possibility of a mistake?" muttered the superintendent. "That he really didn't go in, or something like that? A lot of
funny business might go on in a shuffle at the doorway; I've heard of its
being done. I don't suppose the woman was up to any funny business, dressing
up in a mask herself, or— No, you saw them together, and anyway. . . .
Hell!"

"There was absolutely none of what you describe as funny business," said
Mills. Even in his perspiring earnestness he handled the last two words with
distaste. "I saw all three of them clearly and wide apart. Madame Dumont
was in front of the door, yes; but towards the right. The tall man was towards
the left, and Dr. Grimaud separating them. The tall man really did go in; he
closed the door behind him; and he did not come out. It is not as though

the occurrence took place in half-light. There was no possibility of ever mistaking that man's gigantic stature."

"I don't see how we can doubt it, Hadley," said Dr. Fell, after a pause. "We've got to eliminate the door also." He wheeled round. "What do you know about this man Drayman?"

Mills' eyes narrowed. His sing-song voice had a guarded quality.

"It is true, sir, that he offers a subject for intelligent curiosity. Hurrum! But I know very little. He has been here some years, I am informed; in any event, before I arrived. He was forced to give up his academic work because he had gone almost blind. He is still almost blind, in spite of treatment, although you would not deduce this from the—er—aspect of his eyes. He appealed to Dr. Grimaud for help."

"Had he some sort of claim on Dr. Grimaud?"

The secretary frowned. "I cannot say. I have heard it mentioned that Dr. Grimaud knew him at Paris, where he studied. That is the only bit of information I have, except one remark which Dr. Grimaud made when he had, let us say, imbibed a convivial glass." A superior kind of smile curved round Mills's mouth without opening it; his eyes narrowed, and gleamed in drowsy satire. "Hum! He stated that Mr. Drayman had once saved his life, and described him as the best damned good fellow in the world. Of course, under the circumstances . . ."

Mills had a jerky trick of putting one foot before the other, rocking, and tapping the toe of one shoe with the heel of the other. With his jerky movements, tiny figure, and big shock of hair, he was like a caricature of Swinburne. Dr. Fell looked at him curiously. But Dr. Fell only said:

"So? And why don't *you* like him?"

"I neither like nor dislike him. But he does nothing."

"Is that why Miss Grimaud doesn't like him, either?"

"Miss Grimaud does not like him?" said Mills, opening his eyes and then narrowing them. "Yes, I had fancied that. I watched, but I could not be certain."

"H'mf. And why is he so interested in Guy Fawkes night?"

"Guy Fa— Ah!" Mills broke off in his surprise, and uttered a flat bleat of laughter. "I see! I did not follow. You see, he is very fond of children. He had two children of his own, who were killed—by the falling of a roof, I believe, some years ago. It was one of those foolish, petty tragedies which we shall eliminate when we build the bigger, greater, more spacious world of the future." At this point in the recital Dr. Fell's face was murderous, but Mills went on: "His wife did not survive long. Then he began to lose his sight. . . . He likes to help the children in all their games, and has himself a somewhat childish mind in spite of certain mental qualities." The fish lip lifted a little. "His favourite occasion seems to be the Fifth of November, which was the birthday of one of his unfortunate progeny. He saves up throughout the year to buy illuminations and trappings, and builds a Guy for a procession to—"

A sharp knocking at the door was followed by the appearance of Sergeant Preston.

"There's nobody downstairs, sir," he reported. "That gentleman you wanted to see must have left. . . . A chap from the nursing-home just brought this over for you."

He handed over an envelope and a square cardboard box like a jeweller's box. Hadley ripped open the letter, glanced down it, and swore.

"He's gone," snapped Hadley, "and not a word. . . . Here, read this!"

Rampole looked over Dr. Fell's shoulder as the latter read.

For Superintendent Hadley:

Poor Grimaud died at 11:30. I am sending you the bullet. It's a thirty-eight, as I thought. I tried to get in touch with your police surgeon, but he was out on another case, and so I am sending it to you.

He was conscious just before the end. He said certain things which can be attested by two of my nurses and myself; but he might have been wandering and I should be careful of them. I knew him pretty well, but I certainly never knew he had a brother.

First he said he wished to tell me about it; then he spoke exactly as follows:

"It was my brother who did it. I never thought he would shoot. God knows how he got out of that room. One second he was there, and the next he wasn't. Get a pencil and paper, quick! I want to tell you who my brother is, so that you won't think I'm raving."

His shouting brought on the final hemorrhage, and he died without saying anything else. I am holding the body subject to your orders. If there is any help I can give, let me know.

                                                            E. H. PETERSON, M.D.

They all looked at each other. The puzzle stood rounded and complete; the facts stood confirmed and the witnesses vindicated; but the terror of the hollow man remained. After a pause the superintendent spoke in a heavy voice.

" 'God knows,' " repeated Hadley, " 'how he got out of that room.' "

# THE PROBLEM OF CAGLIOSTRO STREET

## IX

### *The Breaking Grave*

DR. FELL walked over aimlessly, sighed, and settled himself down in the largest chair. "Brother Henri—" he rumbled. "H'mf, yes. I was afraid we should get back to Brother Henri."

"Damn Brother Henri," said Hadley in a flat voice. "We're going after Brother Pierre first. He knows! Why haven't I had any message from that constable? Where's the man who was to pick him up at that theatre? Have the whole blasted lot of them gone to sleep and—"

"We mustn't get the wind up about this thing," interposed the other, as Hadley began to stamp and declaim rather wildly. "That's exactly what Brother Henri would want us to do. Now that we've got Grimaud's last statement, we've at least got one clue. . . ."

"To what?"

"To the words he spoke to *us*, the ones we couldn't make any sense of. The unfortunate point is that they may not help us now that we can hazard a theory as to what they mean. With this new evidence, I'm afraid we were listening to Grimaud running up a blind alley. He wasn't telling us anything; he was only trying to ask us a question."

"What's all this?"

"Don't you see that's exactly what he must have been doing? Last statement: 'God knows how he got out of that room. One second he was there and the next he wasn't.' Now let's try to sort out the words from that invaluable notebook of yours. You and friend Ted have slightly different versions; but we'll begin with the words on which you both agree and which we must assume to be correct. Put aside the first puzzlers—I think we can now feel safe in saying that the words were 'Horváth' and 'salt-mine.' Put aside also the terms on which you do not agree. What words are found in both lists?"

Hadley snapped his fingers. "I begin to— Yes! The words are, 'He couldn't use rope. Roof. Snow. Fox. Too much light.' Well, then! If we try to make a composite statement; fit together the words and the sense of both statements; we have his meaning as something like this: 'God knows how he got out. He couldn't use a rope, either up to the roof or down in the snow. One second he was there, and the next he wasn't. There was too much light for me to miss any move he made—' Stop a bit, though! What about. . . ."

"And now," said Dr. Fell, with a disgusted grunt, "you can begin to fit in the differences. Ted heard, 'not suicide.' That goes into the picture as an assurance to accord with the other expressions. 'This isn't suicide; I didn't kill myself.' You heard, 'Got gun'; which isn't difficult to tie up with the sentence out of the other statement, 'I never thought he would shoot.' BAH! All the clues whirl straight round in a circle and become questions. It's the first case I ever heard of in which the murdered man was just as inquisitive as everybody else."

"But what about the word 'fox'? That doesn't fit anywhere."

Dr. Fell regarded him with a sour twinkle in his eye.

"Oh, yes, it does. It's the easiest part of all—though it may be the trickiest, and we mustn't jump to conclusions about applying it. It's a matter of how words strike the ear when they're not spelled out. If I'm using the word-association test (that damned thing) on various people, and I suddenly whisper, 'Fox!' to a horseman, he will probably answer, 'Hounds!' But if I use the same word on a historian, he is likely to yell . . . quick! What?"

"Guy," said Hadley, and swore. After a lurid interval he demanded: "Do you mean that we come back to some babbling about a Guy Fawkes mask, or the resemblance to a Guy Fawkes mask?"

"Well, everybody else has been doing a tall amount of babbling about it," the doctor pointed out, scratching his forehead. "And I'm not surprised it struck the eye of somebody who saw it at somewhat closer quarters. Does that tell you anything?"

"It tells me to have a little talk with Mr. Drayman," said the superintendent, grimly. He strode towards the door, and was startled to find the bony face of Mills poked out in eager listening against the thick glasses.

"Steady, Hadley," Dr. Fell interposed as the superintendent gave indications of an explosion. "It's a queer thing about you: you can be steady as the Guards when riddles are flying, but you never seem able to keep your shirt on when we get within sight of the truth. Let our young friend stop. He should hear all this, if only to hear the end of it." He chuckled. "Does that make you suspicious of Drayman? Pfaa! On the contrary, it should be just the opposite. Remember, we haven't quite finished putting the pieces in our jig saw. There's one last bit we haven't accounted for, and it was a bit you heard yourself. That pink mask suggested Drayman to Grimaud, just as he seems to have been suggested to several others. But Grimaud knew whose face was behind the mask. Therefore we have a fairly sensible explanation of those final words you noted down, 'Don't blame poor—' He seems to have had a great liking for Drayman, you know." After a silence, Dr. Fell turned to Mills, "Now go and fetch him up here, son."

When the door had closed, Hadley sat down wearily and took from his breast pocket the frayed cigar he had not yet lighted. Then he ran a finger round under his collar with that malevolent, broken-necked expression which people have when worry makes them think the collar is too tight.

"More trick marksmanship, eh?" he suggested. "More deductive tight-rope work, and the daring young man on the—um!" He stared at the floor, and then grunted with annoyance. "I must be losing my grip! It's no good getting fantastic notions like the one I just had. Have you got any concrete suggestions?"

"Yes. Later, if you'll permit it, I am going to apply Gross's test."

"Apply what?"

"Gross's test. Don't you remember? We were arguing about it tonight. I'm going to collect very carefully all the mass of burnt and half-burnt paper in that fireplace, to see whether Gross's test will bring out the writing. Be quiet, will you?" he roared, as Hadley made scornful noises. "I don't say all of it, or even half of it, will come out. But I should get a line here and there to give me a hint about what was more important to Grimaud than saving his own life. Purph! Hah! Yes."

"And how do you work this trick?"

"You'll see. Mind, I don't say that thoroughly burnt paper will come out satisfactorily. But there'll be something, especially in the charred parts sandwiched in and only scorched black, that *will* come out. . . . Aside from that, I haven't a suggestion, unless we ask—yes, what is it?"

Sergeant Betts, not quite so plastered with snow this time, made his report woodenly. He looked out the door behind him before he closed it.

"I've been all over that back-garden, sir. And the two adjoining ones, and the tops of all the walls. There's no footprint or any kind of mark. . . . But I believe we've caught a fish, Preston and I. As I was coming back through the house, down the stairs comes running a tallish old bloke, plunging away with his hand on the banister rail. He ran over to a clothes closet, and banged about as though he wasn't familiar with the place, until he got on his overcoat and hat, and then made for the door. He says his name's Drayman and that he lives here, but we thought—"

"I think you'll find that his sight isn't any too good," said Dr. Fell. "Send him in."

The man who entered was, in his own way, an impressive figure. His long, quiet face was hollowed at the temples; his grey hair grew far back on the skull, giving him a great height of narrow and wrinkled forehead. His bright blue eyes, which did not seem at all dimmed despite the wrinkles round them, looked gentle and puzzled. He had a hooked nose, and deep furrows running down to a kindly, uncertain mouth; and his trick of wrinkling the forehead, so that one eyebrow was slightly raised, made him look more uncertain still. Despite his stoop he was still tall; despite his bony frailty he was still powerful. He looked like a military man gone senile, a well-brushed man gone slovenly. There was nothing of humour in the face, but a great deal of muddled and apologetic good nature. He wore a dark overcoat buttoned up to the chin. Standing in the doorway, peering hard at them from under tangled eyebrows, he held a bowler hat pressed against his chest, and hesitated.

"I am sorry, gentlemen. I am honestly very sorry," he said. His deep voice had a curious quality as though the man were unused to speech. "I know I should have come to see you before going over there. But young Mr. Mangan woke me up to tell me what had happened. I felt I had to go over and see Grimaud, to see whether there might be anything I could do—"

Rampole had a feeling that he was still dull-witted and uncertain from sleep or sleeping-drugs; that the bright stare of his eyes might have been so much glass. He moved over, and one hand found the back of a chair. But he did not sit down until Hadley asked him to do so.

"Mr. Mangan told me—" he said, "Dr. Grimaud—"

"Dr. Grimaud is dead," said Hadley.

Drayman remained sitting as bolt upright as his stoop would allow, his hands folded across his hat. There was a heavy silence in the room, while Drayman shut his eyes and opened them again. Then he seemed to stare a long way off, and to breathe with heavy, whistling sluggishness.

"God rest his soul," Drayman said, very quietly. "Charles Grimaud was a good friend."

"Do you know how he died?"

"Yes. Mr. Mangan told me."

Hadley studied him. "Then you will understand that to tell everything, *everything* you might happen to know, will be the only way to help us catch the murderer of your friend?"

"I— Yes, of course."

"Be very certain of that, Mr. Drayman! More certain than you are. We wish to know something of his past life. You knew him well. Where did you first know him?"

The other's long face looked muddled; an illusion as though the features had got out of line. "In Paris. He took his doctorate at the university in 1905, the same year I . . . the same year I knew him." Facts seem to elude Drayman; he shaded his eyes with his hand, and his voice had a querulous note like a man asking where somebody has hidden his collar studs. "Grimaud was very brilliant. He obtained an associate professorship at Dijon the year afterwards. But a relative died, or something of the sort, and left him well provided for. He—he gave up his work and came to England shortly afterwards. Or so I understand. I did not see him until years afterwards. Was that what you wished to know?"

"Did you ever know him before 1905?"

"No."

Hadley leaned forward. "Where did you save his life?" he asked, sharply. "Save his life? I don't understand."

"Ever visit Hungary, Mr. Drayman?"

"I—I have travelled on the Continent, and I may have been in Hungary. But that was years ago, when I was young. I don't remember."

And now it was Hadley's turn to pull the trigger in trick marksmanship.

"You saved his life," he stated, "near the prison of Siebenturmen, in the Carpathian Mountains, when he was escaping. *Didn't you?*"

The other sat upright, his bony hands clenched across the bowler. Rampole had a feeling that there was more dogged strength in him now than there had been for a dozen years.

"Did I?" he said.

"There's no use going on with this. We know everything—even to dates, now that you've supplied them. Károly Horváth, as a free man, wrote the date in a book in 1898. With full academic preparation behind, it would have taken him four years at least to get his doctorate at Paris. We can narrow down the time of his conviction and escape to three years. With that information," said Hadley, coolly, "I can cable to Bucharest and get the full details within twelve hours. You had better tell the truth, you see. I want to know all you know of Károly Horváth—and his two brothers. One of those two brothers killed him. Finally, I'll remind you that withholding information of this kind is a serious offence. Well?"

Drayman remained for a little time with his hand shading his eyes, his foot tapping the carpet. Then he looked up. They were startled to see that, though his puckered eyes kept their blue glassiness, the man was gently smiling.

"A serious offence," he repeated, and nodded. "Is it, indeed? Now, frankly, sir, I don't give a damn for your threats. There are very few things which can move or anger or terrify a man who can see you only in outline, as he sees a poached egg on his plate. Nearly all the fears of the world (and its ambitions, too) are caused by shapes—eyes and gestures and figures. Young people can't understand this, but I had hoped you would. You see, I am not precisely blind. I can see faces and the morning sky, and all those objects which the poets insist blind men should rave about. But I cannot *read*, and the faces I cared most to see have been for eight years blinder than mine. Wait until your whole life is built on those two things, and you will learn that not much can move you when they go." He nodded again, staring across the room. His forehead wrinkled. "Sir, I am perfectly willing to give you any information you wish, if it will help Charles Grimaud. But I don't see the sense of raking up old scandal."

"Not even to find the brother who killed him?"

Drayman made a slight gesture, frowning. "Look here, if it will help you,

I can honestly tell you to forget such an idea. I don't know how you learned it. He did have two brothers. And they were imprisoned." He smiled again. "There was nothing terrible about it. They were imprisoned for a political offence. I imagine half the young fire-eaters of the time must have been concerned in it. . . . Forget the two brothers. They have both been dead a good many years."

It was so quiet in the room that Rampole heard the last collapsing rattle of the fire and the wheezing breaths of Dr. Fell. Hadley glanced at Dr. Fell, whose eyes were closed. Then Hadley regarded Drayman as impassively as though the latter's sight had been sharp.

"How do you know that?"

"Grimaud told me," said the other, accentuating the name. "Besides, all the newspapers from Budapest to Brasso were shouting about it at the time. You can easily verify all this." He spoke simply. "They died of bubonic plague."

Hadley was suave. "If, of course, you could prove this beyond any doubt . . ."

"You promise that there would be no old scandal raked up?" (That bright blue stare was difficult to meet. Drayman twisted and untwisted his bony hands.) "If I tell you exactly, and you receive the proof, you will let the dead rest?"

"It depends on your information."

"Very well. I will tell you what I saw myself." He reflected—rather uneasily, Rampole thought. "It was in its own way a horrible business. Grimaud and I never spoke of it afterwards. That was agreed. But I don't intend to lie to you and say I've forgotten it—any detail of it."

He was silent for so long a time, tapping his fingers at his temple, that even the patient Hadley was about to prompt him. Then he went on:

"Excuse me, gentlemen. I was trying to remember the exact date, so that you can verify everything. The best I can do is to say it was in August or September of nineteen hundred . . . or was it nineteen one? Anyhow, it occurs to me that I might begin, with perfect truth, exactly in the style of the contemporary French romances. I might begin, 'Towards dusk of a cool September day in the year 19— a solitary horseman might have been seen hurrying along a road,' and what a devil of a road!—'in a rugged valley below the southeastern Carpathians.' Then I should launch into a description of the wild scenery and so on. I was the horseman; it was coming on to rain, and I was trying to reach Tradj before dark."

He smiled. Hadley stirred in some impatience, though Dr. Fell opened his eyes; and Drayman was quick to take it up.

"I must insist on that sort of novelesque atmosphere, because it fitted into my mood and explains so much. I was at the romantic Byronic age, fired with ideas of political liberty. I rode horseback instead of walking because I thought I cut a good figure; I even took pleasure in carrying a pistol against (mythical) brigands, and a rosary as a charm against ghosts. But if there weren't either ghosts or brigands, there should have been. I know that I several times got the wind up about both. There was a sort of fairy-tale wildness and darkness about those cold forests and gorges. Even about the cultivated parts there was something queer. Transylvania, you see, is shadowed in on three sides by mountains. It startles an English eye to see a rye-field or a vineyard going straight up the side of a steep hill; the red-and-yellow costumes, the garlicky inns, and even, in the bleaker parts, hills made of pure salt.

"Anyhow, there I was going along a snaky road in the bleakest part, with a storm blowing up and no inn for miles. People saw the devil lurking behind every hedge in a way that gave me the creeps, but I had a worse cause for the creeps. Plague had broken out after a hot summer, and was over the whole area like a cloud of gnats, even in the chilly weather. In the last village I passed through—I've forgotten its name—they told me it was raging at the salt-mines in the mountains ahead. But I was hoping to meet an English friend of mine, also a tourist, at Tradj. Also I wanted a look at the prison, which got its name after seven white hills, like a low range of mountains, just behind. So I said I meant to go on.

"I knew I must be getting near the prison, for I could see the white hills ahead. But, just as it was getting too dark to see at all, and the wind seemed to be tearing the trees to pieces, I came down into a hollow past the three graves. They had been freshly dug, for there were still footmarks round them; but no living person was in sight."

Hadley broke across the queer atmosphere which that dreaming voice was beginning to create.

"A place," he said, "just like the one in the painting Dr. Grimaud bought from Mr. Burnaby."

"I—I don't know," answered Drayman, evidently startled. "Is it? I didn't notice."

"Didn't notice? Didn't you see the picture?"

"Not very well. Just a general outline—trees, ordinary landscape—"

"And three headstones . . . ?"

"I don't know where Burnaby got his inspiration," the other said, dully, and rubbed his forehead. "God knows I never told him. It's probably a coincidence; there were no headstones over these graves. They wouldn't have bothered. There were simply three crosses made of sticks.

"But I was telling you. I sat there on my horse, looking at those graves, and with a not very pleasant feeling. They looked wild enough, with the greenish-black landscape around and the white hills beyond. But it wasn't that. If they were prison graves, I wondered why they had been dug so far away. The next thing I knew my horse reared and nearly threw me. I slewed round against a tree; and, when I looked back, I saw what was wrong with the horse. The mound of one grave was upheaving and sliding. There was a cracking noise; something began to twist and wriggle; and a dark-coloured thing came groping up out of the mound. It was only a hand moving the fingers—but I don't think I have ever seen anything more horrible."

## X

### The Blood on the Coat

"By THAT time," Drayman went on, "there was something wrong with me as well. I didn't dare dismount, for fear the horse would bolt; and I was ashamed to bolt, myself. I thought of vampires and all the legends of hell coming up out of the twilight. Frankly, the thing scared me silly. I remember battering round on that horse like a teetotum, trying to curb it with one hand while I got out my revolver. When I looked back again, the thing had climbed clear out of the grave and was coming towards me.

"That, gentlemen, was how I met one of my best friends. The man reached down and seized a spade, which somebody who dug the grave must have left there and forgotten. And still he came on. I yelled in English, 'What do you want?'—because I was so fuddled that I couldn't remember a word in any other language. The man stopped. After a second he answered in English, but with an outlandish accent. 'Help,' he said, 'help, milord; don't be afraid,' or something of the sort, and threw down the spade. The horse was quieter, but I wasn't. The man was not tall, but very powerful; his face was dark and swollen, with little scaly spots which gave it a pinkish look in the twilight. And down came the rain while he was still standing there waving his arms.

"He stood in the rain, crying out to me. I won't try to reproduce it, but he said something like, 'Look, milord, I am not dead of plague like those two poor devils,' and pointed at the graves. 'I am not infected at all. See how the rain washes it off. It is my own blood which I have pricked out of my skin.' He even stuck out his tongue to show how it was blackened with soot, and the rain made it clean. It was as mad a sight as the figure and the place. Then he went on to say that he was not a criminal, but a political offender, and was making his escape from the prison."

Drayman's forehead wrinkled. He smiled again.

"Help him? Naturally I did. I was fired by the idea. He explained things to me while we laid plans. He was one of three brothers, students at the University of Klausenburg, who had been arrested in an insurrection for an independent Transylvania under the protection of Austria; as it was before 1860. The three of them were in the same cell, and two had died of the pestilence. With the help of the prison doctor, also a convict, he had faked the same symptoms—and died. It wasn't likely that anybody would go very close to test the doctor's judgment; the whole prison was mad with fear. Even the people who buried those three would keep their heads turned away when they threw the bodies into pine coffins and nailed on the lids. They would bury the bodies at some distance from the prison. Most of all, they would do a quick job of nailing the lids. The doctor had smuggled in a pair of nail-cutters, which my resurrected friend showed me. A powerful man, if he kept his nerve and didn't use up too much air after he had been buried, could force up the lid with his head enough to wedge the nail-cutters into the loose space. Afterwards a powerful man could dig up through loose ground.

"Very well. When he found I was a student at Paris, conversation became easy. His mother had been French, and he spoke the language perfectly. We decided that he had better make for France, where he could set up a new identity without suspicion. He had a little money hidden away, and there was a girl in his native town who—"

Drayman stopped abruptly, like one who remembers that he has gone too far. Hadley merely nodded.

"I think we know who the girl was," he said. "For the moment, we can leave 'Madame Dumont' out of this. What then?"

"She could be trusted to bring the money and follow him to Paris. It wasn't likely that there would be a hue and cry—in fact, there wasn't any. He passed as dead; even if Grimaud was frightened enough to tear away from that neighbourhood before he would even shave or put on a suit of my clothes. We excited no suspicion. There were no passports in those days, and he posed on the way out of Hungary as the English friend of mine I had been expecting to meet at Tradj. Once into France . . . you know all the rest. Now, gentlemen!" Drayman drew a curiously shuddering breath, stiffened, and faced them with his hard blank eyes. "You can verify everything I have said—"

"What about that cracking sound?" interjected Dr. Fell, in an argumentative tone.

The question was so quiet, and yet so startling, that Hadley whirled round. Even Drayman's gaze groped towards him. Dr. Fell's red face was screwed up absently, and he wheezed as he poked at the carpet with his stick.

"I think it's very important," he announced to the fire, as though somebody had contradicted him. "Very important indeed. H'mf. Ha. Look here, Mr. Drayman, I've got only two questions to ask you. You heard a cracking sound—of the lid wrenching on the coffin, hey? Yes. Then that would mean it was a fairly shallow grave Grimaud climbed out of?"

"Quite shallow, yes, or he might never have got out."

"Second question. That prison, now . . . was it a well or badly managed place?"

Drayman was puzzled, but his jaw set grimly. "I do not know, sir. But I do know it was under fire at that time from a number of officials. I think they were bitter against the prison authorities for letting the disease get started—it interfered with the usefulness of the workmen at the mines. By the way, the dead men's names were published; I saw them. And I ask you again, what's the good of raking up old scandals? It can't help you. You can see that it's not any particular discredit to Grimaud, but—"

"Yes, that's the point," rumbled Dr. Fell, peering at him curiously. "That's the thing I want to emphasize. It's not discreditable at all. Is it anything to make a man bury all traces of his past life?"

"—but it might become a discredit to Ernestine Dumont," said Drayman, raising his voice on a fiercer note. "Can't you see what I'm implying? What about Grimaud's daughter? And all this digging into the mess rests on some wild guess that one or both of his brothers might be alive. They're dead, and the dead don't get out of their graves. May I ask where you got such a notion as that one of Grimaud's brothers killed him?"

"From Grimaud himself," said Hadley.

For a second Rampole thought Drayman had not understood. Then the man shakily got up from his chair, as though he could not breathe. He fumbled to open his coat, felt at his throat, and sat down again. Only the glassy look of his eyes did not alter.

"Are you lying to me?" he asked—and it was with a shaky, querulous, childish tone coming through his gravity. "Why do you lie to me?"

"It happens to be the truth. Read this!"

Very quickly he thrust out the note from Dr. Peterson. Drayman made a movement to take it; then he drew back and shook his head.

"It would tell me nothing, sir. I—I— You mean he said something before he . . . ?"

"He said that the murderer was his brother."

"Did he say anything else?" asked Drayman, hesitating. Hadley let the man's imagination work, and did not reply. Presently Drayman went on: "But I tell you it's fantastic! Are you implying that this mountebank who threatened him, this fellow he had never seen before in his life, was one of his brothers? I suppose you are. I still don't understand. From the first moment I learned he had been stabbed . . ."

"*Stabbed?*"

"Yes. As I say, I—"

"He was shot," said Hadley. "What gave you the idea that he had been stabbed?"

Drayman lifted his shoulders. A wry, sardonic, rather despairing expression crept over his wrinkled face.

"I seem to be a very bad witness, gentlemen," he said in an even tone. "I persist with the best intentions, in telling you things you don't believe.

Possibly I jumped to conclusions. Mr. Mangan said that Grimaud had been attacked and was dying; that the murderer had disappeared after slashing that painting to pieces. So I assumed—" He rubbed the bridge of his nose. "Was there anything else you wished to ask me?"

"How did you spend the evening?"

"I was asleep. I— You see, there are pains. Here, behind the eyeballs. I had them so badly at dinner that instead of going out (I was to go to a concert at the Albert Hall), I took a sleeping-tablet and lay down. Unfortunately, I don't remember anything from about half-past seven to the time Mr. Mangan woke me."

Hadley was studying his open overcoat, keeping himself very quiet, but with a dangerous expression like a man about to pounce.

"I see. Did you undress when you went to bed, Mr. Drayman?"

"I beg your—Undress? No. I took off my shoes, that's all. Why?"

"Did you leave your room at any time?"

"No."

"Then how did you get that blood on your jacket? . . . Yes, that's it. Get up! Don't run away, now. Stand where you are. Now take off your overcoat."

Rampole saw it when Drayman, standing uncertainly beside his chair and pulling off the overcoat, moved his hand across his own chest with the motions of a man groping on a floor. He was wearing a light grey suit, against which the stain splashed vividly. It was a darkish smear running from the side of the coat down across the right pocket. Drayman's fingers found it and stopped. The fingers rubbed it, then brushed together.

"It can't be blood," he muttered, with the same querulous noise rising in his voice. "I don't know what it is, but it can't be blood, I tell you!"

"We shall have to see about that. Take off the coat, please. I'm afraid I must ask you to leave it with us. Is there anything in the pockets you want to take out?"

"But—"

"Where did you get that stain?"

"I don't know. I swear to God I don't know, and I can't imagine. It isn't blood. What makes you think it is?"

"Give me the coat, please. Good!" He watched sharply while Drayman with unsteady fingers removed from the pockets a few coppers, a concert ticket, a handkerchief, a paper of Woodbine cigarettes, and a box of matches. Then Hadley took the coat and spread it across his knees. "Do you have any objection to your room being searched?—It's only fair to tell you I have no authority to do it, if you refuse."

"No objection at all," said the other, dully. He was rubbing his forehead. "If you'd only tell me how it happened, Inspector! I don't know. I've tried to do the right thing . . . yes. The right thing. . . . I didn't have anything to do with this business." He stopped, and smiled with such sardonic bitterness that Rampole felt more puzzled than suspicious. "Am I under arrest? I have no objection to that, either, you know."

Now, there was something wrong here: and yet not wrong in the proper way. Rampole saw that Hadley shared his own irrational doubts. Here was a man who had made several erratic misstatements. He had told a lurid tale which might or might not be true, but which had a vaguely theatrical, pasteboard flimsiness about it. Finally, there was blood on his coat. And yet, for a reason he could not determine, Rampole was inclined to believe his story— or, at least, the man's own belief in his story. It might have been his complete (apparent) lack of shrewdness; his utter simplicity. There he stood, looking taller, more shrunken and bony in his shirt sleeves, the blue shirt itself faded to a dingy white, the sleeves tucked up on corded arms, his tie askew and the overcoat trailing from one hand. And he was smiling.

Hadley swore under his breath. "Betts!" he called, "Betts! Preston!" and tapped his heel impatiently on the floor until they answered. "Betts, get this coat to the pathologist for analysis of this stain. See it? Report in the morning. That's all for tonight. Preston, go down with Mr. Drayman and have a look round his room. You have a good idea what to look for; also keep an eye out for something in the mask line. I'll join you in a moment. . . . Think it over, Mr. Drayman. I'm going to ask you to come down to the Yard in the morning. That's all."

Drayman paid no attention. He blundered out in his batlike way, shaking his head and trailing the overcoat behind him. He even plucked Preston by the sleeve. "Where could I have got that blood?" he asked, eagerly. "It's a queer thing, you know, but where could I have got that blood?"

"Dunno, sir," said Preston. "Mind that doorpost!"

Presently the bleak room was quiet. Hadley shook his head slowly.

"It's got me, Fell," he admitted. "I don't know whether I'm coming or going. What do you make of the fellow? He seems gentle and pliable and easy enough; but you can keep pounding him like a punching-bag, and at the end of it he's still swinging gently in the same old place. He doesn't seem to care a rap *what* you think of him. Or what you do to him, for that matter. Maybe that's why the young people don't like him."

"H'm, yes. When I gather up those papers from the fireplace," grunted Dr. Fell, "I'm going home to think. Because what I think now . . ."

"Yes?"

"Is plain horrible."

With a gust of energy Dr. Fell surged up out of the chair, jammed his shovel-hat down over his eyes, and flourished his stick.

"I don't want to go jumping at theories. You'll have to cable for the real truth. Ha! Yes. But it's the story about the three coffins I don't believe—although Drayman may believe it, God knows! Unless our whole theory is blown to blazes, we've got to assume that the two Horváth brothers aren't dead. Hey?"

"The question being . . ."

"What happened to them. Harrumph, yes. What I think might have happened is based on the assumption that Drayman believes he's telling the truth. First point! I don't believe for a second that those brothers were sent to prison for a political offence. Grimaud, with his 'little money saved,' escapes from prison. He lies low for five years or more, and then suddenly 'inherits' a substantial fortune, under an entirely different name, from somebody we haven't heard of. But he slides out of France to enjoy it without comment. Second point, supporting! Where's the dangerous secret in Grimaud's life, if all this is true? Most people would consider that Monte Cristo escape as merely exciting and romantic; and, as for his offence, it would sound to English ears about as hideous and blasting an infamy as pinching a Belisha beacon or pasting a policeman in the eye on boat-race night. Dammit, Hadley, it won't do!"

"You mean—?"

"I mean," said Dr. Fell in a very quiet voice, "Grimaud was alive when he was nailed up in his coffin. Suppose the other two were alive, too? Suppose all three 'deaths' were faked exactly as Grimaud's was faked? Suppose there were two living people in those other coffins when Grimaud climbed out of his? But they couldn't come out . . . because he had the nail-cutters and didn't choose to use 'em. It wasn't likely that there would be more than one pair of cutters. Grimaud had 'em, because he was the strongest. Once he got out, it would have been easy for him to let the others out, as they had arranged. But he prudently decided to let them lie buried, because then there would be nobody to share the money that all three had stolen. A brilliant crime, you see. A brilliant crime."

Nobody spoke. Hadley muttered something under his breath; his face was incredulous and rather wild as he got up.

"Oh, I know it's a black business!" rumbled Dr. Fell; "a black, unholy business that would turn a man's dreams sick if he'd done it. But it's the only thing that will explain this unholy case, and why a man *would* be hounded if those brothers ever climbed up out of their graves. . . . Why was Grimaud so desperately anxious to rush Drayman away from that spot without getting rid of his convict garb as soon as he could? Why would he run the risk of being seen from the road, when a hideaway near a plague grave would be the last place any native would venture? Well, those graves were very shallow. If, as time went on, the brothers found themselves choking to death . . . and still nobody had come to let them out . . . they might begin to shriek and batter and pound in their coffins. It was just possible Drayman might have seen the loose earth trembling or heard the last scream from inside."

Hadley got out a handkerchief and mopped his face.

"Would any swine—" he said in an incredulous voice, which trailed away. "No. We're running off the rails, Fell. It's all imagination. It can't be! Besides, in that case they wouldn't have climbed up out of their graves. They'd be dead."

"Would they?" said Dr. Fell, vacantly. "You're forgetting the spade."

"What spade?"

"The spade that some poor devil in his fear or hurry left behind when he'd dug the grave. Prisons, even the worst prisons, don't permit *that* sort of negligence. They would send back after it. Man, I can see that business in every detail, even if I haven't one shred of proof to support it! Think of every word that crazy Pierre Fley said to Grimaud at the Warwick Tavern, and see if it doesn't fit. . . . Back come a couple of armed, hard-headed warders looking for that discarded spade. They see or hear what Grimaud was afraid Drayman would see or hear. They either tumble to the trick or else they act in common humanity. The coffins are smashed open; the two brothers are rolled out, fainting and bloody, but alive."

"And no hue and cry after Grimaud? Why, they'd have torn Hungary apart looking for the man who had escaped and—"

"H'mf, yes. I thought of that too, and asked about it. The prison authorities would have done just that . . . if they weren't being so bitterly attacked that their heads were in danger at the time. What do you think the attackers would have said if it became known that, through carelessness, they allowed a thing like that to happen? Much better to keep quiet about it, hey? Much better to shove those two brothers into close confinement and keep quiet about the third."

"It's all theory," said Hadley, after a pause. "But, if it's true, I could come close to believing in evil spirits. God knows Grimaud got exactly what he deserved. And we've got to go on trying to find his murderer just the same. If that's the whole story—"

"Of course it's not the whole story!" said Dr. Fell. "It's not the whole story even if it's true, and that's the worst part. You talk of evil spirits. I tell you that in some way I can't fathom there's a worse evil spirit than Grimaud; and that's X, that's the hollow man, that's brother Henri." He pointed out with his stick. "Why? Why does Pierre Fley admit he fears him? It would be reasonable for Grimaud to fear his enemy; but why does Fley even fear his brother and his ally against the common antagonist? Why is a skilled illusionist afraid of illusion, unless this gentle brother Henri is as rattle-brained as a criminal lunatic and as clever as Satan?"

Hadley put his notebook in his pocket and buttoned up his coat.

"*You* go home if you like," he said. "We've finished here. But I'm going after Fley. Whoever the other brother is, Fley knows. And he's going to tell, I can promise you that. I'll have a look round Drayman's room, but I don't anticipate much. Fley is the key to this cipher, and he's going to lead us to the murderer. Ready?"

They did not learn it until the next morning; but Fley, as a matter of fact, was already dead. He had been shot down with the same pistol that killed Grimaud. And the murderer was invisible before the eyes of witnesses, and still he had left no footprint in the snow.

# XI

## *The Murder by Magic*

WHEN Dr. Fell hammered on the door at nine o'clock next morning, both his guests were in a drowsy state. Rampole had got very little sleep the night before. When he and the doctor returned at half-past one, Dorothy had been hopping with eagerness to hear all the details, and her husband was not at all unwilling to tell them. They equipped themselves with cigarettes and beer, and retired to their room, where Dorothy piled a heap of sofa pillows on the floor like Sherlock Holmes, and sat there with a glass of beer and a sinister expression of wisdom while her husband stalked about the room, declaiming. Her views were vigorous but hazy. She rather liked the descriptions of Mme Dumont and Drayman, but took a violent dislike to Rosette Grimaud. Even when Rampole quoted Rosette's remarks to the debating society, a motto of which they both approved, she was not mollified.

"All the same, you mark my words," said Dorothy, pointing her cigarette at him wisely, "that funny-faced blonde is mixed up in it somehow. She's a wrong un, old boy. I mean she wants ber-lud. Bah! I'll bet she wouldn't even make a good—um—courtesan, to use her own terms. And if I had ever treated you the way she treats Boyd Mangan, and you hadn't landed me a sock under the jaw, I'd never have spoken to either of us again . . . if you see my meaning?"

"Let's omit the personal," said Rampole. "Besides, what's she done to Mangan? Nothing that I can see. And you don't seriously think she would kill her father, even if she hadn't been locked in the front room?"

"N-no, because I don't see how she could have put on that fancy costume and fooled Mrs. Dumont," said Dorothy, with an expression of great profundity in her bright dark eyes. "But I'll tell you how it is. Mrs. Dumont and Drayman are both innocent. As for Mills—well, Mills does sound rather a prig, but then your view is highly coloured because you don't like science or the Vision of the Future. And you'll admit he does sound as though he's telling the truth?"

"Yes."

She smoked reflectively. "'M. I'm getting tremendous ideas. The people

I'm most suspicious of, and the ones against whom it'd be easiest to make out a case, are the two you haven't seen—Pettis and Burnaby."

"What?"

"Like this. The objection to Pettis is that he's too small, isn't it? I should have thought Dr. Fell's erudition would have got it like a shot. I was thinking of a story. . . . I can't remember where I've read it, but it comes in one shape or another into several mediæval tales. J'you remember? There's always an enormous figure in armour, with its vizor down, who rides in a tournament and smacks everybody flat. Then along comes ye mightiest knight to joust against it. Down he rides with a bang, hits the tall champion's helmet squarely in the middle of the vizor, and to everybody's horror knocks the head clean off. Then up pipes a voice from inside the shell, and they discover it belongs to a handsome young lad who's not tall enough to fill up the suit of armour. . . ."

Rampole looked at her. "Beloved," said he, with dignity, "this is pure drivelling. This is beyond all question the looniest idea which . . . Look here, are you seriously trying to tell me Pettis might walk about with a dummy head and shoulders rigged up on him?"

"You're too conservative," she said, wrinkling her nose. "I think it's a jolly-good idea. And do you want confirmation? Right! Didn't Mills himself comment on the shiny look about the back of the head, and say it looked as though the whole head were made of papier-mâché? What have you got to say to that?"

"I say it's a nightmare. Haven't you any more practical idea?"

"Yes!" said Dorothy, wriggling. She had obviously just been struck with the inspiration, but she passed it off as an old one. "It's about the impossible situation. Why didn't the murderer want to leave any footprints? You're all going after the most horribly complicated reasons. And, anyway, they generally end in your thinking that the murderer just wants to have some fun with the police. Rats, darling! What's the only real reason, the first reason anybody would think of outside a murder case, why a man mightn't want to leave any footprints? Why, because the footprints would be so distinctive that they'd lead straight to him! Because he had a deformity or something which would hang him if he left a footprint. . . ."

"And—?"

"And, you tell me," she said, "this chap Burnaby has a club foot."

When, towards daylight, Rampole at last fell asleep, he was haunted by images in which Burnaby's club foot seemed even more sinister than the man who wore a dummy head. It was all nonsense; but it was a disturbing kind of nonsense to mingle in a dream with the puzzle of the three graves.

He struggled out of bed when Dr. Fell knocked at the door towards nine o'clock on Sunday morning; he shaved and dressed hastily, and stumbled down through a silent house. It was an unearthly hour for Dr. Fell (or any-

body else) to be stirring, and Rampole knew some fresh deviltry had broken
overnight. The hallways were chilly; even the great library, where a roaring
fire had been lighted, had that unreal look which all things assume when
you get up at daybreak to catch a train. Breakfast—for three—was set out in
the embrasure of the bay window overlooking the terrace. It was a leaden
day, the sky already moving with snow. Dr. Fell, fully dressed, sat at the
table with his head in his hands and stared at a newspaper.

"Brother Henri—" he rumbled, and struck the paper. "Oh yes. He's at it
again. Hadley just phoned with more details, and he'll be here any minute.
Look at this for a starter. If we thought we'd got a hard problem on our
hands last night—oh, Bacchus, look at *this* one! I'm like Drayman—I cán't
believe it. It's crowded Grimaud's murder clean off the front page. Fortunately, they haven't spotted the connection between 'em, or else Hadley's
given 'em the word to keep off. Here!"

Rampole, as coffee was poured out for him, saw the headlines. "MA-
GICIAN MURDERED BY MAGIC!" said one, which must have given
great pleasure to the writer. "RIDDLE OF CAGLIOSTRO STREET."
" 'THE SECOND BULLET IS FOR YOU!' "

"Cagliostro Street?" the American repeated. "Where in the name of sanity
is Cagliostro Street? I thought I'd heard of some funny street names, but
this one—"

"You'd never hear of it ordinarily," grunted Dr. Fell. "It's one of those
streets hidden behind streets, that you only stumble on by accident when
you're looking for a short-cut, and you're startled to find a whole community
lost in the middle of London. . . . Anyway, Cagliostro Street is not more
than three minutes' walk from Grimaud's house. It's a little cul-de-sac behind Guilford Street, on the other side of Russell Square. So far as I remember, it has a lot of tradesmen's shops overflowing from Lamb's Conduit
Street, and the rest lodging-houses. . . . Brother Henri left Grimaud's place
after the shooting, walked over there, hung about for a little time, and then
completed his work."

Rampole ran his eye down the story:

The body of the man found murdered last night in Cagliostro Street,
W. C. 1, has been identified as that of Pierre Fley, a French conjuror and
illusionist. Although he had been performing for some months at a music-
hall in Commercial Road, E.C., he took lodgings two weeks ago in Cagliostro
Street. About half-past ten last night, he was found shot to death under circumstances which seem to indicate that a magician was murdered by magic.
Nothing was seen and no trace left—three witnesses testify—although they all
distinctly heard a voice say, *The second bullet is for you.*

Cagliostro Street is two hundred yards long, and ends in a blank brick
wall. There are a few shops at the beginning of the street, closed at that time,
although a few night lights were burning, and the pavements were swept

in front of them. But, beginning some twenty yards on, there was unbroken snow on the pavement and the street.

Mr. Jesse Short and Mr. R. G. Blackwin, Birmingham visitors to London, were on their way to visit a friend with lodgings near the end of the street. They were walking on the right-hand pavement, and had their backs to the mouth of the street. Mr. Blackwin, who was turning round to make sure of the numbers on the doors, noticed a man walking some distance behind them. This man was walking slowly and rather nervously, looking round him as though he expected to see some one near. He was walking in the middle of the street. But the light was dim, and, aside from seeing that he was tall and wore a slouch-hat, neither Mr. Short nor Mr. Blackwin noticed anything else. At the same time, P. C. Henry Withers—whose beat was along Lamb's Conduit Street—reached the entrance to Cagliostro Street. He saw the man walking in the snow, but glanced back again without noticing him. And in the space of three or four seconds the thing happened.

Mr. Short and Mr. Blackwin heard behind them a cry that was nearer a scream. They then heard some one distinctly say the words, "The second bullet is for you," and a laugh followed by a muffled pistol-shot. As they whirled round, the man behind staggered, screamed again, and pitched forward on his face.

The street, they could see, was absolutely empty from end to end. Moreover, the man was walking in the middle of it, and both state that there were no footprints in the snow but his own. This is confirmed by P. C. Withers, who came running from the mouth of the street. In the light from a jeweller's window, they could see the victim lying face downward, his arms spread out, and blood jetting from a bullet-hole under his left shoulder blade. The weapon—a long-barrelled .38 Colt revolver, of a pattern thirty years out of date—had been thrown away some ten feet behind.

Despite the words they had all heard, and the gun lying at some distance, the witnesses thought because of the empty street that he must have shot himself. They saw that the man was still breathing, and carried him to the office of Dr. M. R. Jenkins near the end of the street, while the constable made certain there were no footprints anywhere. The victim, however, died, without speaking, not long afterwards.

Then occurred the most startling disclosures. The man's overcoat round the wound was burnt and singed black, showing that the weapon must have been pressed against his back or held only a few inches away. But Dr. Jenkins gave it as his opinion—later confirmed by the police—that suicide was not possible. No man, he stated, could have held any pistol in such a way as to shoot himself through the back at that angle, and more especially with the long-barrelled weapon which was used. It was murder, but an incredible murder. If the man had been shot from some distance away, from a window or door, the absence of a murderer and even the absence of footprints would mean nothing. But he was shot by some one who stood beside him, spoke to him, and vanished.

No papers or marks of identification could be found in the man's clothes, and nobody seemed to know him. After some delay he was sent to the mortuary—

"But what about the officer Hadley sent round to pick him up?" Rampole asked. "Couldn't he identify the man?"

"He did identify him, later," growled Dr. Fell. "But the whole hullabaloo was over by the time he got there. He ran into the policeman, Hadley says, when Withers was still making inquiries from door to door. Then he put two and two together. Meantime, the man Hadley had sent to the music-hall also in quest of Fley had phoned through that Fley wasn't there. Fley had coolly told the theatre manager he had no intention of doing his turn that night, and walked out with some sort of cryptic remark. . . . Well, to identify the body at the mortuary they got hold of Fley's landlord in Cagliostro Street. And, to make sure it was the same person, they asked for somebody from the music-hall to come along. An Irishman with an Italian name, who was also on the bill but couldn't do his turn that night because of some sort of injury, volunteered. Harrumph, yes. It was Fley, and he's dead, and we're in a hell of a mess. Bah!"

"And this story," cried Rampole, "is actually true?"

He was answered by Hadley, whose ring at the bell was belligerent. Hadley stamped in, carrying his briefcase like a tomahawk, and released some of his grievances before he would even touch bacon and eggs.

"It's true, right enough," he said, grimly, stamping his heels before the fire. "I let the papers splash it out so we could broadcast an appeal for information from anybody who knew Pierre Fley or his —— —— —— brother Henri. By God! Fell, I'm losing my mind! That damned nickname of yours sticks in my head, and I can't get rid of it. I find myself referring to brother Henri as though I knew that was his real name. I find myself getting imaginary pictures of brother Henri. At least we soon ought to know what his real name is. I've cabled to Bucharest. Brother Henri! Brother Henri! We've picked up his trail again, and lost it again. Bro—"

"For Lord's sake go easy!" urged Dr. Fell, puffing uneasily. "Don't rave; it's bad enough now. I suppose you've been at it nearly all night? And got some more information? H'mf, yes. Now sit down and console the inner man. Then we can approach in—humph—a philosophic spirit, hey?"

Hadley said he wanted nothing to eat. But, after he had finished two helpings, drunk several cups of coffee, and lighted a cigar, he mellowed into a more normal mood.

"Now; then! Let's begin," he said, squaring himself determinedly as he took papers from the briefcase, "by checking over this newspaper account point by point—as well as what it doesn't say. Hum! First, as to these chaps Blackwin and Short. They're reliable; besides, it's certain neither of them is brother Henri. We wired Birmingham, and found they've been well known in their district all their lives. They're prosperous, sound people who wouldn't go off the handle as witnesses in a thing like this. The constable, Withers, is a thoroughly reliable man; in fact, he's painstaking to the extent of a vice. If those people say they didn't see anybody, they may have been deceived, but at least they were telling the truth as they knew it."

"Deceived . . . how?"

"I don't know," growled Hadley, drawing a deep breath and shaking his head grimly, "except that they must have been. I had a brief look at the street, although I didn't go through Fley's room. It's no Piccadilly Circus for illumination, but at least it's not dark enough for any man in his five wits to be mistaken about what he saw. Shadows—I don't know! As to footprints, if Withers swears there weren't any, I'll take his word for it. And there we are."

Dr. Fell only grunted, and Hadley went on:

"Now, about the weapon. Fley was shot with a bullet from that Colt .38, and so was Grimaud. There were two exploded cartridge-cases in the magazine, only two bullets, and bro—and the murderer scored with each. The modern revolver, you see, ejects its shells like an automatic; but this gun is so old that we haven't a ghost of a chance of being able to trace it. It's in good working order, it fires modern steel-jacket ammunition, but somebody has kept it hidden away for years."

"He didn't forget anything, Harry didn't. Well. Did you trace Fley's movements?"

"Yes. He was going to call on Henri."

Dr. Fell's eyes snapped open. "*Eh?* Look here, you mean you've got a lead about—"

"It's the only lead we have got. And," said Hadley, with bitter satisfaction, "if it doesn't produce results within a couple of hours I'll eat that briefcase. You remember, I told you over the phone that Fley had refused to perform and walked out of the theatre last night? Yes. My plain-clothes officer got the story both from the theatre-manager, fellow named Isaacstein, and from an acrobat named O'Rourke, who was friendlier with Fley than anybody else and identified the body later.

"Saturday, naturally, is the big night down Limehouse way. The theatre runs continuous variety from one in the afternoon until eleven at night. Business was booming in the evening, and Fley's first night turn was to begin at eight-fifteen. About five minutes before then, O'Rourke—who had broken his wrist and couldn't go on that night—sneaked down into the cellar for a smoke. They have a coal furnace for hot-water pipes there."

Hadley unfolded a closely written sheet.

"Here is what O'Rourke said, just as Somers took it down and O'Rourke later initialled.

"The minute I got through the asbestos door and downstairs, I heard a noise like somebody smashing up kindling-wood. Then I did get a jump. The furnace door was open, and there was old Loony with a hatchet in his hand, busting hell out of the few properties he owned and shoving them all in the fire. I said, 'For cat's sake, Loony, what are you doing?' He said, in that queer way of his, 'I am destroying my equipment, Signor Pagliacci.' (I use the name of Pagliacci the Great, you understand, but then he always talked like that, so help me!) Well, he said, 'My work is finished; I shall not need them any longer'—and, zingo! in went his faked ropes and the hollow bamboo rods for his cabinet. I said, 'Loony, great goddelmighty, pull yourself together.' I said, 'You go on in a few minutes, and you're not even dressed.' He said: 'Didn't I tell you? I am going to see my brother. He will do something that will settle an old affair for both of us.'

"Well, he walked over to the stairs and then turned around sharp. Loony's got a face like a white horse, Lord pity me for saying it, and it had a queer creepy look with the fire from the furnace shining on it. He said, 'In case anything happens to me after he has done the business, you will find my brother in the same street where I myself live. That is not where he really resides, but he has taken a room there.' Just then down comes old Isaacstein, looking for him. He couldn't believe his ears when he heard Loony refuse to go on. There was a row. Isaacstein bawled, 'You know what'll happen if you don't go on?' And Loony says, as pleasant as a three-card man, 'Yes, I know what will happen.' Then he lifts his hat very courteously, and says, 'Good night, gentlemen. I am going back to my grave.' And up the stairs this lunatic walks without another word."

Hadley folded up the sheet and replaced it in his briefcase.

"Yes, he was a good showman," said Dr. Fell, struggling to light his pipe. "It seems a pity brother Henri had to . . . what then?"

"Now, it may or may not mean anything to track Henri down in Cagliostro Street, but we're sure to get his temporary hideout," Hadley went on. "The question occurred to me, where was Fley *going* when he was shot? Where was he walking to? Not to his own room. He lived at number 2B, at the beginning of the street, and he was going in the other direction. When he was shot he was a little over halfway down, between number 18 on his right and number 21 on his left—but in the middle of the street, of course. That's a good trail, and I've sent Somers out on it. He's to turn out every house past the middle, looking for *any* new or suspicious or otherwise noticeable lodger. Landladies being what they are, we shall probably get dozens, but that doesn't matter."

Dr. Fell, who was slouched as far down in the big chair as the bulk of his weight would allow, ruffled his hair.

"Yes, but I shouldn't concentrate too much on any end of the street. Rip 'em all up, say I. You see, suppose Fley was running from somebody, trying to get away from somebody, when he was shot?"

"Running away into a blind alley?"

"It's *wrong!* I tell you it's all wrong!" roared the doctor, hoisting himself up in the chair. "Not merely because I can't see anywhere a chink or glimmer of reason (which I freely admit), but because the simplicity of the thing is so maddening. It's no matter of hocus-pocus within four walls. There's a street. There's a man walking along it in the snow. Scream, whispered words, bang! Witnesses turn, and murderer gone. Where? Did the pistol come flying through the air like a thrown knife, explode against Fley's back, and spin away?"

"Rubbish!"

"I know it's rubbish. But I still ask the question," nodded Dr. Fell. He let his eye-glasses drop and pressed his hands over his eyes. "I say, how does this new development affect the Russell Square group? I mean, considering that everybody is officially under suspicion, can't we eliminate a few of those? Even if they were telling us lies at Grimaud's house, they still weren't out hurling Colt revolvers in the middle of Cagliostro Street."

The superintendent's face was ugly with sarcasm. "Now there's another bit of luck for us, kindly notice. I forgot that! We could eliminate one or two—if the Cagliostro Street business had occurred a little later, or even a little earlier. It didn't. Fley was shot at just ten-twenty-five. In other words, about fifteen minutes after Grimaud. Brother Henri took no chances. He anticipated exactly what we would do: send out a man to pick up Fley as soon as the alarm was given. Only brother Henri (or somebody) anticipated us in both ways. He was there with his little vanishing-trick."

" 'Or somebody'?" repeated Dr. Fell. "Your mental processes are interesting. Why 'or somebody'?"

"That's what I'm getting at—the unfortunate, unobserved fifteen minutes just after Grimaud's murder. I'm learning new wrinkles in crime, Fell. If you want to commit a couple of shrewd murders, don't commit one and then hang about waiting for the dramatic moment to pull off the other. Hit once—and then hit again instantly, while the watchers are still so muddled by the first that nobody, including the police, can definitely remember who was where at a given time. Can we?"

"Now, now," growled Dr. Fell, to conceal the fact that he couldn't. "It ought to be easy to work out a time-table. Let's see. We arrived at Grimaud's . . . when?"

Hadley was jotting on a slip of paper. "Just as Mangan jumped out the window, which couldn't have been more than two minutes after the shot. Say ten-twelve. We ran upstairs, found the door locked, got the pliers, and opened the door. Say three minutes more."

"Isn't that allowing a small margin of time?" Rampole interposed. "It seemed to me we were doing a good deal of tearing around."

"People often think so. In fact," said Hadley, "I thought so myself until

I handled that Kynaston knifing case (remember, Fell?), where a damned
clever killer depended for his alibi on the tendency of witnesses always to
*over*-estimate time. That's because we think in minutes rather than seconds.
Try it yourself. Put a watch on the table, shut your eyes, and look again
when you think a minute is up. You'll probably look thirty seconds too soon.
No, say three minutes here!" He scowled. "Mangan phoned, and the ambulance was round very quickly. Did you notice the address of that nursing-
home, Fell?"

"No. I leave these sordid details to you," said Dr. Fell, with dignity.
"Somebody said it was just round the corner, I remember. Humph. Ha."

"In Guilford Street, next to the Children's Hospital. In fact," said Hadley,
"backed up against Cagliostro Street so closely that the back gardens must
be in line. . . . Well, say five minutes to get the ambulance to Russell
Square. That's ten-twenty. And what about the next five minutes, the time
just before the second murder, and the equally important five or ten or
fifteen minutes afterwards? Rosette Grimaud, alone, rode over in the ambulance with her father, and didn't return for some time. Mangan, alone, was
downstairs doing some telephoning for me, and didn't come upstairs until
Rosette returned. I don't seriously consider either of 'em, but take it all for
the sake of argument. Drayman? Nobody saw Drayman all this time and for
a long while afterwards. As to Mills and the Dumont woman—h'm. Well,
yes; I'm afraid it does clear them. Mills was talking to us all the earlier part
of the time, until at least ten-thirty anyhow, and Madame Dumont joined
him very shortly; they both stayed with us for a while. That tears it."

Dr. Fell chuckled.

"In fact," he said, reflectively, "we know exactly what we did before, no
more and no less. The only people it clears are the ones we were sure were
innocent, and who had to be telling the truth if we made any sanity of the
story. Hadley, it's the cussedness of things in general which makes me raise
my hat. By the way, did you get anything last night out of searching Drayman's room? And what about that blood?"

"Oh, it's human blood, right enough, but there was nothing in Drayman's
room that gave a clue to it—or to anything else. There were several of those
pasteboard masks, yes. But they were all elaborate affairs with whiskers and
goggle eyes: more the sort of thing that would appeal to a kid. Nothing,
anyway, in the—the plain pink style. There was a lot of stuff for kids' amateur theatricals, some old sparklers and pinwheels and the like, and a toy
theatre. . . ."

"Penny plain and twopence coloured," said Dr. Fell, with a wheeze of
reminiscent pleasure. "Gone forever the glory of childhood. Wow! The gran-
deur of a toy theatre! In my innocent childhood days, Hadley, when I came
trailing clouds of glory to the view (a thesis, by the way, which might have
been open to considerable debate on the part of my parents); in my child-

hood days, I say, I owned a toy theatre with sixteen changes of scenery. Half of 'em, I am pleased to say, were jail scenes. Why does the young imagination run so strongly to jail scenes, I wonder? Why—"

"What the hell's the matter with you?" demanded Hadley, staring. "Why the sentimentality?"

"Because I have suddenly got an idea," said Dr. Fell, gently. "And, oh, my sacred hat, what an idea!" He remained blinking at Hadley. "What about Drayman? Are you going to arrest him?"

"No. In the first place, I don't see how he could have done it, and I couldn't even get a warrant. In the second place—"

"You don't believe he's guilty?"

"H'm," grunted Hadley, with an innate caution about doubting anybody's innocence. "I don't say that, but I think he's likely to be less culpable than anybody else. Anyhow, we've got to get a move on! Cagliostro Street first, then to interview several people. Finally—"

They heard the door-bell ring, and a sleepy maidservant tumbled down to answer it.

"There's a gentleman downstairs, sir," said Vida, poking her head into the room, "who says he wants to see either you or the superintendent. A Mr. Anthony Pettis, sir."

## XII

### The Picture

DR. FELL, rumbling and chuckling and spilling ashes from his pipe like the Spirit of the Volcano, surged up to greet the visitor with a cordiality which seemed to put Mr. Anthony Pettis much more at his ease. Mr. Pettis bowed slightly to each of them.

"You must excuse me, gentlemen, for intruding so early," he said. "But I had to get it off my mind, and couldn't feel easy until I did. I understand you were—um—looking for me last night. And I had an unpleasant night of it, I can tell you." He smiled. "My one criminal adventure was when I forgot to renew a dog license, and my guilty conscience was all over me. Every time I went out with that confounded dog I thought every policeman in London was eyeing me in a sinister way. I began to slink. So in this case I thought I'd better hunt you out. They gave me this address at Scotland Yard."

Dr. Fell was already stripping off his guest's overcoat, with a gesture that nearly upset Mr. Pettis, and hurling him into a chair. Mr. Pettis grinned. He was a small, neat, starched man with a shiny bald head and a startlingly booming voice. He had prominent eyes, looking more shrewd with a wrinkle of concentration between them, a humorous mouth and a square cleft chin.

It was a bony face—imaginative, ascetic, rather nervous. When he spoke he had a trick of sitting forward in his chair, clasping his hands, and frowning at the floor.

"It's a bad business about Grimaud," he said, and hesitated. "Naturally I'll follow the formula of saying I wish to do everything I can to help. In this case it happens to be true." He smiled again. "Er—do you want me sitting with my face to the light, or what? Outside novels, this is my first experience with the police."

"Nonsense," said Dr. Fell, introducing everybody. "I've been wanting to meet you for some time; we've written a few things on the same lines. What'll you drink? Whisky? Brandy and soda?"

"It's rather early," said Pettis, doubtfully. "Still, if you insist—thanks! I'm very familiar with your book on the supernatural in English fiction, Doctor; you're a great deal more popular than I shall ever be. And it's sound." He frowned. "It's very sound. But I don't entirely agree with you (or Dr. James) that a ghost in a story should always be malignant. . . ."

"Of course it should always be malignant. The more malignant," thundered Dr. Fell, screwing his own face up into a tolerably hideous leer, "then the better. I want no sighing of gentle airs round *my* couch. I want no sweet whispers o'er Eden. I want BLOOD!" He looked at Pettis in a way which seemed to give the latter an uncomfortable idea that it was his blood. "Harrumph. Ha. I will give you rules, sir. The ghost should be malignant. It should never speak. It should never be transparent, but solid. It should never hold the stage for long, but appear in brief vivid flashes like the poking of a face round a corner. It should never appear in too much light. It should have an old, an academic or ecclesiastical background; a flavour of cloisters or Latin manuscripts. There is an unfortunate tendency nowadays to sneer at old libraries or ancient ruins; to say that the really horrible phantom would appear in a confectioner's shop or at a lemonade stand. This is what they call applying the 'modern test.' Very well; apply the test of real life. Now, people in real life honestly *have* been frightened out of their five wits in old ruins or churchyards. Nobody would deny that. But, until somebody in actual life really does scream out and faint at the sight of something at a lemonade stand (other, of course, than that beverage itself), then there is nothing to be said for this theory except that it is rubbish."

"Some people would say," observed Pettis, cocking one eyebrow, "that the old ruins were rubbish. Don't you believe that good ghost stories can be written nowadays?"

"Of course they can be written nowadays, and there are more brilliant people to write 'em . . . if they would. The point is, they are afraid of the thing called Melodrama. So, if they can't eliminate the melodrama, they try to hide it by writing in such an oblique, upside-down way that nobody under heaven can understand what they are talking about. Instead of saying flat out what the character saw or heard, they try to give Impressions. It's as though a butler, in announcing guests at a ball, were to throw open the drawing-room doors and cry: 'Flicker of a top-hat, vacantly seen, or is it my complex fixed on the umbrella stand faintly gleaming?' Now, his employer might not find this satisfactory. He might want to know who in blazes was calling on him. Terror ceases to be terror if it has to be worked out like an algebra problem. It may be deplorable if a man is told a joke on Saturday night and suddenly bursts out laughing in church next morning. But it is much more deplorable if a man reads a terrifying ghost story on Saturday night, and two weeks later suddenly snaps his fingers and realizes that he ought to have been scared. Sir, I say now—"

For some time an irritated superintendent of the C.I.D. had been fuming and clearing his throat in the background. Now Hadley settled matters by slamming his fist down on the table.

"Easy on, will you?" he demanded. "We don't want to hear any lecture now. And it's Mr. Pettis who wants to do the talking. So—" When he saw Dr. Fell's puffings subside into a grin, he went on, smoothly, "As a matter of fact, it is a Saturday night I want to talk about; last night."

"And about a ghost?" Pettis inquired, whimsically. Dr. Fell's outburst had put him entirely at his ease. "The ghost who called on poor Grimaud?"

"Yes. . . . First, just as a matter of form, I must ask you to give an account of your movements last night. Especially between, say, nine-thirty and ten-thirty?"

Pettis put down his glass. His face had grown troubled again. "Then you mean, Mr. Hadley—after all, I *am* under suspicion?"

"The ghost said he was you. Didn't you know that?"

"Said he was. . . . Good God, no!" cried Pettis, springing up like a bald-headed jack-in-the-box. "Said he was me? I mean—er—said he was—hang the grammar! I want to know what you're talking about? What do you mean?" He sat down quietly and stared as Hadley explained. But he fussed with his cuffs, fussed with his tie, and several times nearly interrupted.

"Therefore, if you'll disprove it by giving an account of your movements last night . . ." Hadley took out his notebook.

"Nobody told me about this last night. I was at Grimaud's after he was shot, but nobody told me," said Pettis, troubled. "As for last night, I went to the theatre: to His Majesty's Theatre."

"You can establish that, of course."

Pettis frowned. "I don't know. I sincerely hope so. I can tell you about the play, although I don't suppose that's much good. Oh yes; and I think I've still got my ticket stub somewhere, or my program. But you'll want to know if I met anybody I knew. Eh? No, I'm afraid not—unless I could find somebody who remembered me. I went alone. You see, every one of the few friends I have runs in a set groove. We know exactly where he is at most

times, especially Saturday evenings, and we don't try to change the orbit."
There was a wry twinkle in his eye. "It's—it's a kind of respectable Bohemianism, not to say stodgy Bohemianism."

"That," said Hadley, "would interest the murderer. What are these orbits?"

"Grimaud always works . . . excuse me; I can't get used to the idea that
he's dead . . . always works until eleven. Afterwards you could disturb him
as much as you liked; he's a night owl; but not before. Burnaby always plays
poker at his club. Mangan, who's a sort of acolyte, is with Grimaud's daughter. He's with her most evenings, for that matter. I go to the theatre or the
films, but not always. I'm the exception."

"I see. And after the theatre last night? What time did you get out?"

"Near enough to eleven or a little past. I was restless. I thought I might
drop in on Grimaud and have a drink with him. And—well, you know what
happened. Mills told me. I asked to see you, or whoever was in charge. After
I had waited downstairs for a long time, without anybody paying any attention to me,"—he spoke rather snappishly—"I went across to the nursing-home
to see how Grimaud was getting on. I got there just as he died. Now, Mr.
Hadley, I know this is a terrible business, but I will swear to you—"

"Why did you ask to see me?"

"I was at the public house when this man Fley uttered his threat, and I
thought I might be of some help. Of course I supposed at the time it was
Fley who had shot him; but this morning I see in the paper—"

"Just a minute! Before we go on to that, I understand that whoever imitated you used all your tricks of address, and so on, correctly? Good! Then
who in your circle (or out of it) would you suspect of being able to do that?"

"Or wanting to do it," the other said, sharply.

He sat back, being careful about the knife-crease of his trousers. His nerv-
ousness was clearly giving way before the twistings of a dry, curious, insatia-
ble brain; an abstract problem intrigued him. Putting his fingertips together,
he stared out of the long windows.

"Don't think I'm trying to evade your question, Mr. Hadley," he said, with
an abrupt little cough. "Frankly, I can't think of anybody. But this puzzle
bothers me apart from the danger, in a way, to myself. If you think my
ideas suffer from too much subtlety, or from too much plain damned nonsense, I'll put it up to Dr. Fell. Let's suppose, for the sake of argument,
that I am the murderer."

He looked mockingly at Hadley, who had straightened up.

"Hold on! I am not the murderer, but let's suppose it. I go to kill Grimaud
in some outlandish disguise (which, by the way, I *would* rather commit a
murder than be seen wearing). Hum! I indulge in all the rest of the tomfoolery. Is it likely that, after all these things, I would blatantly sing out
my real name to those young people?"

He paused, tapping his fingers.

"That's the first view, the short-sighted view. But the very shrewd investigator would answer: 'Yes, a clever murderer might do just that. It would be the most effective way of bamboozling all the people who had jumped to the first conclusion. He changed his voice a very little, just enough so that people would remember it afterwards. He spoke as Pettis because he wanted people to think it *wasn't* Pettis.' Had you thought of that?"

"Oh yes," said Dr. Fell, beaming broadly. "It was the first thing I did think of."

Pettis nodded. "Then you will have thought of the answer to that, which clears me either way. If I were to do a thing like that, it isn't my voice I should have altered slightly. If the hearers accepted it to begin with, they might not later have the doubts I wanted them to have. *But*," he said, pointing, "what I should have done was to make one slip in my speech. I should have said something unusual, something wrong and obviously not like myself, which later they would have remembered. And this the visitor didn't do. His imitation was too thorough, which seems to excuse me. Whether you take the forthright view or the subtle one, I can plead not guilty either because I'm not a fool or because I am."

Hadley laughed. His amused gaze travelled from Pettis to Dr. Fell, and he could keep his worried expression no longer.

"You two are birds of a feather," he said. "I like these gyrations. But I'll tell you from practical experience, Mr. Pettis, that a criminal who tried anything like that would find himself in the soup. The police wouldn't stop to consider whether he was a fool or whether he wasn't. The police would take the forthright view—and hang him."

"As you would hang me," said Pettis, "if you could find contributory evidence?"

"Exactly."

"Well—er—that's frank, anyhow," said Pettis, though he seemed acutely uneasy and startled at the reply. "Er—shall I go on? You've rather taken the wind out of my sails."

"Go on, certainly," urged the superintendent, with an affable gesture. "We can get ideas even from a clever man. What else have you to suggest?"

Whether or not that was a deliberate sting, it had a result nobody had expected. Pettis smiled, but his eyes had a fixed quality and his face seemed to become more bony.

"Yes, I think you can," he agreed. "Even ideas you should have had yourselves. Let me take one instance. You—or somebody—got himself quoted at some length in all the papers this morning, about Grimaud's murder. You showed how the murderer was careful to ensure unbroken snow for his vanishing-trick, whatever it was. He could be sure that it would snow last night, lay all his plans accordingly, and gamble on waiting until the snow stopped

for the working of his scheme. In any event, he could reasonably depend on
there being some snow. Is that correct?"

"I said something of the sort, yes. What of it?"

"Then I think you should have remembered," Pettis answered, evenly,
"that the weather forecast said he could do nothing of the kind. Yesterday's
weather forecast announced that there would be no snow at all."

"Oh, Bacchus!" boomed Dr. Fell, and brought his fist down on the table
after a pause in which he blinked at Pettis. "Well done! I never thought of
it. Hadley, this changes things altogether! This—"

Pettis relaxed. He took out a cigarette-case and opened it. "Of course,
there is an objection. I mean, you can make the obvious retort that the murderer knew it was bound to snow because the weather forecast said it
wouldn't. But in that case *you'd* be the one who took subtlety to the edge
of comedy. I can't follow it so far. Fact is, I think the weather forecast comes
in for as many untrue jeers as the telephone service. It dropped a brick in
this instance, yes . . . but that doesn't matter. Don't you believe me? Look
up last night's papers and see."

Hadley swore, and then grinned.

"Sorry," he said. "I didn't mean to touch you on the raw, but I'm glad I
did. Yes, it does seem to alter matters. Blast it, if a man intended to commit a crime that depended on snow, he'd certainly treat the forecast with
some sort of consideration." Hadley drummed on the table. "Never mind;
we'll come back to that. I seriously ask for ideas now."

"That's all, I'm afraid. Criminology is more in Burnaby's line than in
mine. I only happened to notice," Pettis admitted, with a jeering look at his
own clothes, "so as to decide whether I ought to wear overshoes. Habit! . . .
As to the person who imitated my voice, why try to implicate *me*? I'm a
harmless enough old codger, I assure you. I don't fit into the rôle of gigantic
nemesis. The only reason I can think of is that I'm the only one of the
group who has no definite orbit on Saturday night and might not be able
to prove an alibi. But as to who could have done it . . . Any good mimic
could have pulled it off; still, who knew just how I addressed those people?"

"What about the circle at the Warwick Tavern? There were others besides
the ones we've heard about, weren't there?"

"Oh yes. There were two other irregulars. But I can't see either as a candidate. There's old Mornington, who has had a post at the Museum for over
fifty years; he's got a cracked tenor that would never pass for me. There's
Swayle, but I believe he was speaking on the wireless last night, about ant
life or something, and should have an alibi. . . ."

"Speaking at what time?"

"Nine forty-five or thereabouts, I believe, although I wouldn't swear to it.
Besides, neither of them ever visited Grimaud's house.—And casual drifters
at the pub? Well, some may have listened or sat down at the back of the

room, though nobody ever joined the conversation. I suppose that's your best lead, even if it's a very thin one." Pettis took out a cigarette and closed the case with a snap. "Yes. We'd better *decide* it was an unknown quantity, or we shall be in all kinds of quicksand, eh? Burnaby and I were Grimaud's only close friends. But I didn't do it, and Burnaby was playing cards."

Hadley looked at him. "I suppose Mr. Burnaby really was playing cards?"

"I don't know," the other admitted, with flat candour. "But I'll give you odds he was, all the same. Burnaby's no fool. And a man would have to be rather an outstanding fathead to commit a murder on the one night when his absence from a certain group would be certain to be noticed."

Clearly this impressed the superintendent more than anything Pettis had yet said. He continued to drum on the table, scowling. Dr. Fell was occupied with some obscure, cross-eyed meditation of his own. Pettis looked curiously from one to the other of them.

"If I have given you food for thought, gentlemen—?" he suggested, and Hadley became brisk.

"Yes, yes! No end! Now, about Burnaby: you know he painted the picture which Dr. Grimaud bought to defend himself?"

"To defend himself? How? From what?"

"We don't know. I was hoping you might be able to explain it." Hadley studied him. "The taste for making cryptic remarks seems to run in his family. Do you know anything about his family, by the way?"

Pettis was evidently puzzled. "Well, Rosette is a very charming girl. Er—though I shouldn't say she had a taste for making cryptic remarks. Quite the contrary. She's a little too modern for my taste." His forehead wrinkled. "I never knew Grimaud's wife; she's been dead some years. But I still don't see—"

"Never mind. What do you think of Drayman?"

Pettis chuckled. "Old Hubert Drayman is the most unsuspicious man I ever met. So unsuspicious that some people think it hides a deep and devilish cunning. Excuse me, but have you got him on the carpet? If you have, I should forget it."

"We'll go back to Burnaby, then. Do you know how he came to paint that picture, or when he did it, or anything about it?"

"I think he did it a year or two ago. I remember it particularly, because it was the biggest canvas at his studio; he used it as a screen or a partition, turned up endways, whenever he needed one. I asked him once what it was intended to represent. He said, 'An imaginative conception of something I never saw.' It had some French name, *Dans l'Ombre des Montagnes du Sel*, or something of the sort." He stopped tapping the still unlighted cigarette on the case. His curious, restless brain was probing again. "Hullo! Now that I remember it, Burnaby said, 'Don't you like it? It gave Grimaud a hell of a turn when he saw it.'"

"Why?"

"I paid no attention. I naturally supposed it was some joke or piece of bragging; he laughed when he said it, and Burnaby's like that. But the thing had been lying about the studio, collecting dust, for such a long time that I was surprised when Grimaud came charging in on Friday morning and asked for it."

Hadley leaned forward sharply. "You were there, then?"

"At the studio? Yes. I'd dropped in early for some reason or other—I forget what. Grimaud came stumping in . . ."

"Upset?"

"Yes. N-no. Say excited." Pettis reflected, studying Hadley covertly. "Grimaud said, with that machine-gun snap of his, 'Burnaby, where's your salt-mountain picture? I want it. What's your price?' Burnaby looked at him in a queer way. He came hobbling over and pointed to the picture and said, 'The thing's yours, man, if you want it; take it.' Grimaud said, 'No, I have a use for it and I insist on buying it.' Well, when Burnaby named some fool price like ten shillings, Grimaud quite solemnly got out a cheque-book and wrote a cheque for ten shillings. He would say nothing except that he had a place on the wall where it ought to go, in his study. That's all. He took the picture downstairs, and I got him a cab to take it away in. . . ."

"Was it wrapped up?" asked Dr. Fell, sharply; so sharply that Pettis jumped a little.

Dr. Fell had been showing more interest, not to say fierce concentration, in this recital than in anything Pettis had yet said. The doctor was bending forward with his hands clasped over his stick, and Pettis regarded him curiously.

"I wonder why you ask that?" he said. "It's what I was just going to mention—the fuss Grimaud made about wrapping it. He asked for paper, and Burnaby said, 'Where do you think I'd get a sheet of paper big enough to go round that? Why be ashamed of it? Take it as it is.' But Grimaud insisted on going downstairs and getting yards of brown paper off one of those rolls in somebody's shop. It seemed to annoy Burnaby a good deal."

"You don't know whether Grimaud went straight home with it?"

"No . . . I think he was going to have it framed, but I'm not sure."

Dr. Fell sat back with a grunt and let the subject go without more questions, in spite of Pettis's hints. Although Hadley kept on questioning for some time, nothing of importance was elicited so far as Rampole could see. On the personal side Pettis spoke guardedly; but there was, he said, little to conceal. There had been no friction in Grimaud's household, and none in the immediate circle except an antagonism between Mangan and Burnaby. Burnaby, although nearly thirty years older, had a strong interest in Rosette Grimaud, at once lazy and jealous. Dr. Grimaud had said nothing about this;

if anything, he encouraged it, although so far as Pettis could observe he made no objection to Mangan.

"But I think you'll find, gentlemen," concluded Pettis, as he rose to go when Big Ben was striking ten, "that all these are side issues. It would be difficult to associate the *crime passionel* with any of our group. As to the financial side of affairs, I can't tell you much, either. Grimaud was fairly well-to-do, I should think. His solicitors, I happen to know, are Tennant and Williams of Gray's Inn. . . . By the way, I wonder if you'd all have lunch with me on a dreary Sunday? I'm just at the other side of Russell Square, you know; I've had a suite of rooms at the Imperial for fifteen years. You're investigating in that neighbourhood, and it might be handy; besides, if Dr. Fell feels inclined to discuss ghost stories—?"

He smiled. The doctor cut in to accept before Hadley could refuse, and Pettis left with a much more jaunty air than he had worn at his entrance. Afterwards they all looked at each other.

"Well?" growled Hadley. "Straightforward enough, it seemed to me. Of course we'll check it up. The point, the impressive point, is: why should *any* of them commit a crime on the one night when absence would be bound to be noticed? We'll go after this chap Burnaby, but he sounds out of it, too, if only for that reason. . . ."

"And the weather forecast said it wouldn't snow," said Dr. Fell, with a kind of obstinacy. "Hadley, that shoots everything to blazes! It turns the whole case upside down somehow, but I don't see . . . Cagliostro Street! Let's go on to Cagliostro Street. Anywhere is better than this darkness."

Fuming, he stumped over after his cloak and shovel-hat.

## XIII

### The Secret Flat

LONDON, on the morning of a grey winter Sunday, was deserted to the point of ghostliness along miles of streets. And Cagliostro Street, into which Hadley's car presently turned, looked as though it would never wake up.

Cagliostro Street, as Dr. Fell had said, contained a thin dingy overflow of both shops and rooming-houses. It was a backwater of Lamb's Conduit Street —which itself is a long and narrow thoroughfare, a shopping centre of its own, stretching north to the barrack-windowed quiet of Guilford Street, and south to the main artery of traffic along Theobald's Road. Towards the Guilford Street end on the west side, the entrance to Cagliostro Street is tucked between a stationer's and a butcher's. It looks so much like an alley that you would miss it altogether if you were not watching for the sign. Past these

two buildings, it suddenly widens to an unexpected breadth, and runs straight
for two hundred yards to a blank brick wall at the end.

This eerie feeling of streets in hiding, or whole rows of houses created by
illusory magic to trick you, had never deserted Rampole in his prowlings
through London. It was like wondering whether, if you walked out your own
front door, you might not find the whole street mysteriously changed overnight, and strange faces grinning out of houses you had never seen before.
He stood with Hadley and Dr. Fell at the entrance, staring down. The overflow of shops stretched only a little way on either side. They were all shut-
tered, or had their windows covered with a folding steel fretwork, with an
air of defying customers as a fort would defy attackers. Even the gilt signs
had an air of defiance. The windows were at all stages of cleanliness, from the
bright gloss of a jeweller's farthest down on the right, to the grey murkiness of
a tobacconist's nearest on the right: a tobacconist's that seemed to have
dried up worse than ancient tobacco, shrunk together, and hidden itself behind news placards headlining news you never remembered having heard of.
Beyond there were two rows of flat three-story houses in dark red brick, with
window-frames in white or yellow, and drawn curtains of which a few (on the
ground floor) showed a sportive bit of lace. They had darkened to the same
hue with soot; they looked like one house except where iron railings went
to the front doors from the lone line of area rails; they sprouted with hopeful
signs announcing furnished rooms. Over them the chimney-pots stood up
dark against a heavy grey sky. The snow had melted to patches of grey slush,
despite a sharp wind that was swooping through the entrance and chasing a
discarded newspaper with flaps and rustlings round a lamp-post.

"Cheerful," grunted Dr. Fell. He lumbered forward, and there were echoes
of his footsteps. "Now, let's get this all straight before we attract attention.
Show me where Fley was when he was hit. Stop a bit! Where did he live,
by the way?"

Hadley pointed at the tobacconist's near which they were standing.

"Up over that place; just at the beginning of the street, as I told you.
We'll go up presently—although Somers has been there, and says there's
nothing at all. Now, come along and get roughly the middle point of the
street . . ." He went ahead, pacing off a yard at a stride. "The swept pavements and the marked street ended somewhere about here; say, more or less,
a hundred and fifty feet. Then unmarked snow. A good distance beyond that,
nearer to another hundred and fifty . . . *here*."

He stopped and turned round slowly.

"Halfway up, centre of the roadway. You can see how broad the road is;
walking there, he was a good thirty feet from any house on *either* side. If he'd
been walking on the pavement, we might have constructed some wild theory
of a person leaning out of a window or an areaway, with the gun fastened to
the end of a pole or something, and—"

"Nonsense!"

"All right, nonsense; but what else can we think?" demanded Hadley, with some violence, and made a broad gesture with his briefcase. "As you said, yourself, here's the street; it's plain, simple, and impossible! I know there was no hanky-panky like that, but what *was* there? Also, the witnesses didn't see anything; and, if there had been anything, they must have seen it. Look here! Stay where you are, now, and keep facing the same direction." He paced again to a point some distance farther on, and turned after inspecting the numbers. Then he moved over to the right-hand pavement. "Here's where Blackwin and Short were when they heard the scream. You're walking along there in the middle of the street. I'm ahead of you. I whirl around—so. How far am I from you now?"

Rampole, who had drawn off from both of them, saw Dr. Fell standing big and alone in the middle of an empty rectangle.

"Shorter distance this time. Those two chaps," said the doctor, pushing back his shovel-hat, "were not much more than thirty feet ahead! Hadley, this is even rummier than I thought. He was in the middle of a snow desert. Yet they whirl round when they hear the shot . . . h'm . . . h'mf. . . ."

"Exactly. Next, as to lights. You're taking the part of Fley. On your right— a little distance ahead, and just beyond the door of number 18—you see a street lamp. A little distance behind, also on the right, you see that jeweller's window? Right. There was a light burning in that; not a bright one, but still it was there. Now, can you explain to me how two people, standing where I'm standing now, could possibly be mistaken about whether they saw anybody near Fley?"

His voice rose, and the street gave it a satiric echo. The discarded newspaper, caught again by an eddy of the wind, scuttled along with a sudden rush; and the wind tore with a hollow roar among chimney-pots as though it blew through a tunnel. Dr. Fell's black cloak flapped about him, and the ribbon on his eye-glasses danced wildly.

"Jeweller's—" he repeated, and stared. "Jeweller's! And a light in it. . . . Was there anybody there?"

"No. Withers thought of that and went to see. It was a show-light. The wire fretwork was stretched across both the window and the door; just as it is now. Nobody could have got in or out of there. Besides, it's much too far away from Fley."

Dr. Fell craned his neck round, and then went over to look owlishly into the protected window. Inside were displayed velvet trays of cheap rings and watches, an array of candlesticks, and in the middle a big round-hooded German clock with moving eyes in its sun of a face, which began to tinkle eleven. Dr. Fell stared at the moving eyes, which had an unpleasant effect of seeming to watch with idiot amusement the place where a man had been killed.

It lent a touch of the horrible to Cagliostro Street. Then Dr. Fell stumped back to the middle of the street.

"But that," he said—obstinately, as though he were continuing an argument—"that is on the right-hand side of the street. And Fley was shot through the back from the *left* side. If we assume, as apparently we must assume, that the attacker approached from the left . . . or at least the flying pistol travelled over from the left . . . I don't know! Even granting that the murderer could walk on snow without leaving a footprint, can we at least decide where he came from?"

*"He came from here,"* said a voice.

The rising of the wind seemed to whirl the words about them, as though they came from empty air. For one second in that gusty half-light Rampole experienced a worse shock than he had known even in the days of the Chatterham Prison case. He had a mad vision of flying things, and of hearing words from an invisible man exactly as the two witnesses had heard the hollow murderer whisper the night before. For one second, then, something took him by the throat—before he turned and, with a drop of anti-climax, saw the explanation. A thick-set young man with a reddish face and a bowler pulled down on his forehead (which gave him a somewhat sinister air) was coming down the steps from the open door of number 18. The young man grinned broadly as he saluted Hadley.

"He came from here, sir. I'm Somers, sir. You remember, you asked me to find out where the dead one, the Frenchie, was going when he was killed? And to find out what landlady had any sort of rum lodger that might be the man we're looking for? . . . Well, I've found out about the rum lodger, and it oughtn't to be difficult to find him. He came from *here*. Excuse my interrupting you."

Hadley, trying not to show that the interruption had been unpleasantly startling, growled a pleased word. His eyes travelled up to the doorway, where another figure stood hesitating. Somers followed the glance.

"Oh no, sir. That's not the lodger," he said, and grinned again. "That's Mr. O'Rourke; chap from the music-hall, you know, who identified the Frenchie last night. He's been giving me a bit of help this morning."

The figure detached itself from the gloom and came down the steps. He looked thin despite his heavy overcoat; thin and powerful, with the quick smooth steps carried on the ball of the foot which mark the trapeze or high-wire man. He was affable, easy, and bent slightly backwards as he spoke, like a man who wants room for his gestures. In looks he was rather swarthily reminiscent of the Italian: an effect that was heightened by a luxuriant black moustache with waxed ends, which curled under his hooked nose. Beneath this a large curved pipe hung from one corner of his mouth, and he was puffing with evident enjoyment. His wrinkled eyes had a humorous blue gleam; and he pushed back an elaborate fawn-coloured hat as he introduced himself. This was the Irishman with the Italian pseudonym; he spoke like an American, and in point of fact was, he explained, a Canadian.

"O'Rourke's the name, yes," he said. "John L. Sullivan O'Rourke. Does anybody know what my middle name is? You know, the name of the—" He squared back and took a hard right-hander at the empty air—"the greatest of 'em all? I don't. My old man didn't, when he named me. L. is all I know. I hope you don't mind my butting in. You see, I knew old Loony—" He paused, grinned, and twisted his moustache. "I see, gents! You're all looking at this soup-strainer of mine. Everybody does. It's on account of that goddam song. You know. The management thought it'd be a good idea if I got myself up like the fellow in the song. Oh, it's real! Look"—he pulled—"nothing phony about it, see? But I was telling you, excuse my butting in. I'm damn sorry for old Loony. . . ." His face clouded.

"That's all right," said Hadley. "Thanks for all the help as it is. It saves me seeing you at the theatre—"

"I'm not working, anyway," said O'Rourke, gloomily. He thrust his left hand out of a long overcoat sleeve. The wrist was wound into a cast and bandaged. "If I'd had any sense I'd have followed Loony last night. But here! Don't let me interrupt. . . ."

"Yes. If you'll come along, sir," Somers interposed, grimly, "I've got something pretty important to show you. As well as tell you. The landlady's downstairs getting dressed up, and she'll tell you about the lodger. There's no doubt he's the man you want. But first I'd like you to see his rooms."

"What's in his rooms?"

"Well, sir, there's blood, for one thing," replied Somers. "And also a very queer sort of rope. . . ." He assumed an expression of satisfaction as he saw Hadley's face. "You'll be interested in that rope, and in other things. The fellow's a burglar—at least a crook of some sort, by the look of his outfit. He's put a special lock on the door, so that Miss Hake (that's the landlady) couldn't get in. But I used one of my keys—there's nothing illegal about that, sir; the fellow's evidently cleared out. Miss Hake says he's had the rooms for some time, but he's only used them one or two times since . . ."

"Come on," said Hadley.

Somers, closing the door behind, led them into a gloomy hallway and up three flights of stairs. The house was narrow, and had on each floor one furnished flat which ran the whole depth from back to front. The door of the top floor—close up near a ladder which led to the roof—stood open, its extra lock gleaming above the ordinary keyhole. Somers took them into a darkish passage with three doors.

"In here first, sir," he said, indicating the first on the left. "It's the bathroom. I had to put a shilling in the electric meter to get any light—now!"

He pressed a switch. The bathroom was a dingy converted box-room, with glazed paper on the wall in imitation of tile, worn oilcloth on the floor, a top-heavy geyser bath whose tank had gone to rust, and a wavy mirror hung over a washstand with bowl and pitcher on the floor.

"Effort made to clean the place up, you see, sir," Somers went on. "But you'll still see reddish traces in the bath where the water was poured out. That was where he washed his hands. And over behind this clothes-hamper, now—"

With dramatic satisfaction he swung the hamper to one side, reached into the dust behind, and produced a still-damp face-cloth with sodden patches that had turned to dull pink.

"—he sponged his clothes with that," said Somers, nodding.

"Well done," said Hadley, softly. He juggled the face-cloth, glanced at Dr. Fell, smiled, and put down the find. "The other rooms, now. I'm curious about that rope."

Somebody's personality permeated those rooms like the sickly yellow of the electric lights; like the chilly chemical smell which was not quite obliterated by the strong tobacco O'Rourke smoked. It was a den in more senses than one. Heavy curtains were drawn across the windows in a fairly large front room. Under a powerful light on a broad table lay an assortment of little steel or wire tools with rounded heads and curved ends, (Hadley said, "Lock-picks, eh?" and whistled), an assortment of detached locks, and a sheaf of notes. There was a powerful microscope, a box fitted with glass slides, a bench of chemicals on which six labelled test-tubes were arranged in a rack, a wall of books, and in one corner a small iron safe at the sight of which Hadley uttered an exclamation.

"If he's a burglar," said the superintendent, "he's the most modern and scientific burglar I've seen in a long time. I didn't know this trick was known in England. You've been dipping into this, Fell. Recognize it?"

"There's a big hole cut right out of the iron in the top, sir," put in Somers. "If he used a blow-pipe, it's the neatest acetylene-cutting job I ever saw. He—"

"He didn't use a blow-pipe," said Hadley. "It's neater and easier than that. This is the Krupp preparation. I'm not strong on chemistry, but I think this is powdered aluminum and ferrous oxide. You mix the powder on top of the safe, you add—what is it?—powdered magnesium, and set a match to it. It doesn't explode. It simply generates a heat of several thousand degrees and melts a hole straight through the metal. . . . See that metal tube on the table? We have one at the Black Museum. It's a detectascope, or what they call a fish-eye lens, with a refraction over half a sphere like the eye of a fish. You can put it to a hole in the wall and see everything that's going on in the next room. What do you think of this, Fell?"

"Yes, yes," said the doctor, with a vacant stare as though all this were of no importance; "I hope you see what it suggests. The mystery, the— But where's that rope? I'm very much interested in that rope."

"Other room, sir. Back room," said Somers. "It's got up in rather grand style, like an Eastern . . . you know."

Presumably he meant divan; or even harem. There was a spurious Turkish floridity and mysteriousness about the rich-coloured couches and hangings; the tassels, gimcracks, and weapon-groups; yet your eye was almost startled into belief by finding such things in such a place. Hadley flung back the curtains. Bloomsbury intruded with winter daylight, making sickly the illusion. They looked out on the backs of the houses along Guilford Street, on paved yards below, and an alley winding up towards the back of the Children's Hospital. But Hadley did not consider that for long. He pounced on the coil of rope that lay across a divan.

It was thin but very strong, knotted at intervals of two feet apart; an ordinary rope except for the curious device hooked to one end. This looked like a black rubber cup, something larger than a coffee-cup, of great toughness and with a grip edge like a car tire.

"Wow!" said Dr. Fell. "Look here, is that—"

Hadley nodded. "I've heard of them, but I never saw one before and I didn't believe they existed. See here! It's an air-suction cup. You've probably seen the same sort of thing in a child's toy. A spring toy-pistol fires at a smooth card a little rod with a miniature suction-cup in soft rubber on the end. It strikes the card, and the suction of the air holds it."

"You mean," said Rampole, "that a burglar could force that thing against the side of a wall, and its pressure would hold him on the rope?"

Hadley hesitated. "That's how they *say* it works. Of course, I don't—"

"But how would he get it loose again? That is, would he just walk away and leave it hanging there?"

"He'd need a confederate, naturally. If you pressed the edges of this thing at the bottom, they would let the air in and destroy the grip. Even so, I don't see how the devil it could have been used for—"

O'Rourke, who had been eyeing the rope in a bothered way, cleared his throat. He took the pipe out of his mouth and cleared his throat again for attention.

"Look, gents," he said in his hoarse, confidential voice. "I don't want to butt in, but I think that's all bunk."

Hadley swung round. "How so? Do you know anything about it?"

"I'll make you a little bet," nodded the other, and poked at the air with his pipe-stem for emphasis, "that this thing belonged to Loony Fley. Give it to me for a second and I'll see. Mind, I don't *swear* it belonged to Loony. There are plenty of queer things in this joint. But—"

He took the rope, and ran his fingers gently along it until he reached the middle. Then he winked and nodded with satisfaction. He twirled his fingers, and then suddenly held his hands apart with the air of a conjuror. The rope came in two pieces.

"Uh-huh. Yes. I thought it was one of Loony's trick ropes. See this? The rope's tapped. It's fitted with a screw in one side and a thread in the other, and you can twist it together just like a screw in wood. You can't see the joint; you can examine the rope all you like, and yet it won't come apart under any pressure. Get the idea? Members of the audience tie the illusionist, or whatdyecallum—tie him up tight in his cabinet. This joint of the rope goes across his hands. The watchers outside can hold the ends of the rope tight to make sure he don't try to get out of it. See? But he unscrews the thing with his teeth, holds the rope taut with his knees, and all kinds of hell start to pop inside the cabinet. Wonder! Mystification! Greatest show on earth!" said O'Rourke, hoarsely. He regarded them amiably, put the pipe back in his mouth, and inhaled deeply. "Yes. That was one of Loony's ropes, I'll bet anything."

"I don't doubt that," said Hadley. "But what about the suction-cup?"

Again O'Rourke bent slightly backwards to give room for his gestures.

"We-el, Loony was as secretive as they make 'em, of course. But I haven't been around with magic acts and the rest of that stuff without keeping my eyes peeled. . . . Wait a minute; don't get me wrong! Loony had tricks that were GOOD, and I mean good. This was just routine stuff that everybody knew about. Well. He was working on one. . . . You've heard of the Indian rope trick, haven't you? Fakir throws a rope up in the air; it stands upright; boy climbs up it—whoosh! he disappears. Eh?"

A cloud of smoke whirled up and vanished before his broad gesture.

"I've also heard," said Dr. Fell, blinking at him, "that nobody has ever yet seen it performed."

"Sure! Exactly! That's just it," O'Rourke returned, with a sort of pounce. "That's why Loony was trying to dope out a means of doing it. God knows whether he did. I think that suction-cup was to catch the rope somewhere when it was thrown up. But don't ask me how."

"And somebody was to climb up," said Hadley, in a heavy voice; "climb up, and disappear?"

"We-el, a kid—!" O'Rourke brushed the idea away. "But I'll tell you this much: that thing you've got won't support a full-grown man's weight. Look, gents! I'd try it for you, and swing out the window, only I don't want to break my goddam neck; and besides, my wrist is out of kilter."

"I think we've got enough evidence just the same," said Hadley. "You say this fellow's bolted, Somers? Any description of him?"

Somers nodded with great satisfaction.

"We shouldn't have any difficulty in pulling him in, sir. He goes under the name of 'Jerome Burnaby,' which is probably a fake; but he's got a pretty distinctive appearance—and he has a club foot."

## XIV

### *The Clue of the Church Bells*

THE next sound was the vast, dust-shaking noise of Dr. Fell's mirth. The doctor did not only chuckle; he roared. Sitting down on a red-and-yellow divan, which sagged and creaked alarmingly, he chortled away and pounded his stick on the floor.

"Stung!" said Dr. Fell. "Stung, me bonny boys! Heh-heh-heh. Bang goes the ghost. Bang goes the evidence. Oh, my eye!"

"What do you mean, stung?" demanded Hadley. "I don't see anything funny in getting our man dead to rights. Doesn't this pretty well convince you that Burnaby's guilty?"

"It convinces me absolutely that he's innocent," said Dr. Fell. He got out a red bandana and wiped his eyes as the amusement subsided. "I was afraid we should find just this sort of thing when we saw the other room. It was a little too good to be true. Burnaby is the Sphinx without a secret; the criminal without a crime—or at least this particular sort of crime."

"If you would mind explaining . . . ?"

"Not at all," said the doctor, affably. "Hadley, take a look around and tell me what this whole place reminds you of. Did you ever know of any burglar, any criminal at all, who ever had his secret hideaway arranged with such atmospheric effect, with such romantic setting? With the lockpicks arranged on the table, the brooding microscope, the sinister chemicals and so on? The real burglar, the real criminal of any kind, takes care to have his haunt looking a little more respectable than a churchwarden's. This display doesn't even remind me of somebody playing at being a burglar. But if you'll think for a second you'll see what it does remind you of, out of a hundred stories and films. I know that," the doctor explained, "because I'm so fond of the atmosphere, even the theatrical atmosphere, myself. . . . It sounds like somebody playing detective."

Hadley stopped, rubbing his chin thoughtfully. He peered round.

"When you were a kid," pursued Dr. Fell, with relish, "didn't you ever wish for a secret passage in your house?—and pretend that some hole in the attic *was* a secret passage, and go crawling through it with a candle, and nearly burn the place down? Didn't you ever play the Great Detective, and wish for a secret lair in some secret street, where you could pursue your deadly studies under an assumed name? Didn't somebody say Burnaby was a fierce amateur criminologist? Maybe he's writing a book. Anyhow, he has the time and the money to do, in rather a sophisticated way, just what a lot of other grown-up children have wished to do. He's created an *alter ego*. He's done it on the quiet, because his circle would have roared with laughter if they had known. Relentlessly the bloodhounds of Scotland Yard have tracked down his deadly secret; and his deadly secret is a joke."

"But, sir—!" protested Somers, in a kind of yelp.

"Stop a bit," said Hadley, meditatively, and gestured him to silence. The superintendent again examined the place with a half-angry doubt. "I admit there's an unconvincing look about the place, yes. I admit it has a movie-ish appearance. But what about that blood and this rope? This rope is Fley's, remember. And the blood . . ."

Dr. Fell nodded.

"H'mf, yes. Don't misunderstand. I don't say these rooms mightn't play a part in the business; I'm only warning you not to believe too much in Burnaby's evil double-life."

"We'll soon find out about that. And," growled Hadley, "if the fellow's a murderer I don't care how innocent his double-life as a burglar may be. Somers!"

"Sir?"

"Go over to Mr. Jerome Burnaby's flat—yes, I know you don't understand, but I mean his other flat. I've got the address. H'm. 13A Bloomsbury Square, second floor. Got it? Bring him here; use any pretext you like, but see that he comes. Don't answer any questions about this place, or ask any. Got that? And when you go downstairs, see if you can hurry up that landlady."

He stalked about the room, kicking at the edges of the furniture, as a bewildered and crestfallen Somers hurried out. O'Rourke, who had sat down and was regarding them with amiable interest, waved his pipe.

"Well, gents," he said, "I like to see the bloodhounds on the trail, at that. I don't know who this Burnaby is, but he seems to be somebody you already know. Is there anything you'd like to ask *me*? I told what I knew about Loony to Sergeant, or whatever he is, Somers. But if there's anything else . . . ?"

Hadley drew a deep breath and set his shoulder back to work again. He went through the papers in his briefcase.

"This is your statement—right?" The superintendent read it briefly. "Have you anything to add to that? I mean, are you positive he said his brother had taken lodgings in this street?"

"That's what he said, yes, sir. He said he'd seen him hanging around here."

Hadley glanced up sharply. "That's not the same thing, is it? Which did he say?"

O'Rourke seemed to think this a quibble. He shifted. "Oh, well, he said that just afterwards. He said, 'He's got a room there; I've seen him hanging around.' Or something. That's the honest truth, now!"

"But not very definite, is it?" demanded Hadley. "Think again!"

"Well, hell's bells, I *am* thinking!" protested O'Rourke in an aggrieved tone. "Take it easy. Somebody reels off a lot of stuff like that; and then afterwards they ask you questions about it and seem to think you're lying if you can't repeat every word. Sorry, partner, but that's the best I can do."

"What do you know about this brother of his? Since you've known Fley, what has he told you?"

"Not a thing! Not one word! I don't want you to get the wrong idea. When I say I knew Loony better than most people, that don't mean I know anything about him. Nobody did. If you ever saw him, you'd know he was the last person you could get confidential with over a few drinks, and tell about yourself. It would be like treating Dracula to a couple of beers. Wait a minute!—I mean somebody who looked like Dracula, that's all. Loony was a pretty good sport in his own way."

Hadley reflected, and then decided on a course.

"The biggest problem we have now—you'll have guessed that—is an impossible situation. I suppose you've seen the newspapers?"

"Yes." O'Rourke's eyes narrowed. "Why ask me about that?"

"Some sort of illusion, or stage trick, must have been used to kill both those men. You say you've known magicians and escape artists. Can you think of any trick that would explain how it was done?"

O'Rourke laughed, showing gleaming teeth under the elaborate moustache. The wrinkles of amusement deepened round his eyes.

"Oh, well! That's different! That's a lot different. Look, I'll tell you straight. When I offered to swing out the window on that rope, I noticed you. I was afraid you were getting ideas. Get me? I mean about me." He chuckled. "Forget it! It'd take a miracle man to work any stunt like that with a rope, even if he had a rope and could walk without leaving any tracks. But as for the other business . . ." Frowningly O'Rourke brushed up his moustache with the stem of his pipe. He stared across the room. "It's this way. I'm no authority. I don't know very much about it, and what I do know I generally keep mum about. Kind of"—he gestured—"kind of professional etiquette, if you get me. Also, for things like escapes from locked boxes, and disappearances, and the rest of it . . . well, I've given up even talking about 'em."

"Why?"

"Because," said O'Rourke, with great emphasis, "most people are so damned disappointed when they know the secret. Either, in the first place, the thing is so smart and simple—so simple it's funny—that they won't believe they could have been fooled by it. They'll say, 'Oh, hell! don't tell us that stuff! I'd have seen it in a second.' Or, in the second place, it's a trick worked with a confederate. That disappoints 'em even more. They say, 'Oh, well, if you're going to have somebody to help—!' as though anything was possible then."

He smoked reflectively.

"It's a funny thing about people. They go to see an illusion; you tell 'em it's an illusion; they pay their money to see an illusion. And yet for some funny reason they get sore because it isn't *real* magic. When they hear an explanation of how somebody got out of a locked box or a roped sack that they've examined, they get sore because it *was* a trick. They say it's far-fetched when they know how they were deceived. Now, it takes BRAINS, I'm telling you, to work out one of those simple tricks. And, to be a good escape-artist, a man's got to be cool, strong, experienced, and quick as greased light-ning. But they never think of the cleverness it takes just to fool 'em under their noses. I think they'd like the secret of an escape to be some unholy business like real magic; something that nobody on God's earth could ever do. Now, no man who ever lived can make himself as thin as a post-card and slide out through a crack. No man ever crawled out through a key-hole, or pushed himself through a piece of wood. Want me to give you an example?"

"Go on," said Hadley, who was looking at him curiously.

"All right. Take the second sort first! Take the roped and sealed sack trick: one way of doing it."* O'Rourke was enjoying himself. "Out comes the performer—in the middle of a group of people, if you want him to—with a light sack made out of black muslin or sateen, and big enough for him to stand up in. He gets inside. His assistant draws it up, holds the sack about six inches below the mouth, and ties it round tightly with a long handkerchief. Then the people watching can add more knots if they want to, and seal his knots and theirs with wax, and stamp 'em with signets . . . anything at all. Bang! Up goes a screen round the performer. Thirty seconds later out he walks, with the knots still tied and sealed and stamped, and the sack over his arm. Heigh-ho!"

"Well?"

O'Rourke grinned, made the usual play with his moustache (he could not seem to leave off twisting it), and rolled on the divan.

"Now, gents, here's where you take a poke at me. There's duplicate sacks, exactly alike. One of 'em the performer's got all folded up and stuck inside his vest. When he gets into the sack, and he's moving and jerking it around, and the assistant is pulling it up over his head—why, out comes the duplicate. The mouth of the other black sack is pushed up through the mouth of the first, six inches or so; it *looks* like the mouth of the first. The assistant grabs it round, and what he honest-to-God ties is the mouth of the duplicate sack, with such a thin edge of the real one included so that you can't see the join-ing. Bang! On go the knots and seals. When the performer gets behind his screen, all he does is shove loose the tied sack, drop the one he's standing in, stick the loose sack under his vest, and walk out holding the duplicate sack roped and sealed. Get it? See? It's simple, it's easy, and yet people go

* See the admirable and startling book by Mr. J. C. Cannell.

nuts trying to figure out how it was done. But when they hear how it *was* done, they say, 'Oh, well, with a confederate—!' " He gestured.

Hadley was interested in spite of his professional manner, and Dr. Fell was listening with a childlike gaping.

"Yes, I know," said the superintendent, as though urging an argument, "but the man we're after, the man who committed these two murders, couldn't have had a confederate! Besides, that's not a vanishing-trick. . . ."

"All right," said O'Rourke, and pushed his hat to one side of his head. "I'll give you an example of a whopping-big vanishing-trick. This is a stage illusion, mind. All very fancy. But you can work it in an outdoor theatre, if you want to, where there's no trap-doors, no wires from the flies, no props or funny business at all. Just a stretch of ground. Out rides the illusionist, in a grand blue uniform, on a grand white horse. Out come his gang of attendants, in white uniforms, with the usual hoop-la like a circus. They go round in a circle once, and then two attendants whisk up a great big fan which—just for a moment, see?—hides the man on the horse. Down comes the fan, which is tossed out in the audience to show it's O.K.; but the man on the horse has vanished. He's vanished straight from the middle of a ten-acre field. Heigh-ho!"

"And how do you get out of that one?" demanded Dr. Fell.

"Easy! The man's never left the field. But you don't see him. You don't see him because that grand blue uniform is made of paper—*over* a real white one. As soon as the fan goes up, he tears off the blue one and stuffs it under the white. He jumps down off the horse, and just joins in the gang of white-uniformed attendants. Point is, nobody ever takes the trouble to *count* them attendants beforehand, and they all exit without anybody ever seeing. That's the basis of most tricks. You're looking at something you don't see, or you'll swear you've seen something that's not there. Hey presto! Bang! Greatest show on earth!"

The stuffy, gaudily coloured room was quiet. Wind rattled at the windows. Distantly there was a noise of church bells, and the honking of a taxi that passed and died. Hadley shook his notebook.

"We're getting off the track," he said. "It's clever enough, yes; but how does it apply to this problem?"

"It don't," admitted O'Rourke, who seemed convulsed by a noiseless mirth. "I'm telling you—well, because you asked. And to show you what you're up against. I'm giving you the straight dope, Mr. Superintendent: I don't want to discourage you, but if you're up against a smart illusionist, you haven't got the chance of a snowball in hell; you haven't got the chance of *that*." He snapped his fingers. "They're trained to it. It's their business. And there ain't a prison on earth that can hold 'em."

Hadley's jaw tightened. "We'll see about that when the time comes. What bothers me, and what's been bothering me for some time, is why Fley sent his brother to do the killing. Fley was the illusionist. Fley would have been the man to do it. But he didn't. Was his brother in the same line?"

"Dunno. At least, I never saw his name billed anywhere. But—"

Dr. Fell interrupted. With a heavy wheeze, he lumbered up from the couch and spoke sharply.

"Clear the decks for action, Hadley. We're going to have visitors in about two minutes. Look out there!—but keep back from the window."

He was pointing with his stick. Below them, where the alley curved out between the blank windows of houses, two figures shouldered against the wind. They had turned in from Guilford Street; and, fortunately, had their heads down. One Rampole recognized as that of Rosette Grimaud. The other was a tall man whose shoulder lunged and swung as he walked with the aid of a cane; a man whose leg had a crooked twist and whose right boot was of abnormal thickness.

"Get the lights out in those other rooms," said Hadley, swiftly. He turned to O'Rourke. "I'll ask you a big favour. Get downstairs as quickly as you can; stop that landlady from coming up and saying anything; keep her there until you hear from me. Pull the door shut after you!"

He was already out into the narrow passage, snapping off the lights. Dr. Fell looked mildly harassed.

"Look here, you don't mean we're going to hide and overhear terrible secrets, do you?" he demanded. "I've not got what Mills would call the anatomical structure for such tomfoolery. Besides, they'll spot us in a second. This place is full of smoke—O'Rourke's shag."

Hadley muttered profanities. He drew the curtains so that only a pencil of light slanted into the room.

"Can't be helped; we've got to chance it. We'll sit here quietly. If they've got anything on their minds, they may blurt it out as soon as they get inside the flat and the door is shut. People do. What do you think of O'Rourke, by the way?"

"I think," stated Dr. Fell, with energy, "that O'Rourke is the most stimulating, enlightening, and suggestive witness we have heard so far in this nightmare. He has saved my intellectual self-respect. He is, in fact, almost as enlightening as the church bells."

Hadley, who was peering through the crack between the curtains, turned his head round. The line of light across his eyes showed a certain wildness.

"Church bells? What church bells?"

"Any church bells," said Dr. Fell's voice out of the gloom. "I tell you that to me in my heathen blindness the thought of those bells has brought light and balm. It may save me from making an awful mistake. . . . Yes, I'm quite sane." The ferrule of a stick rapped the floor and his voice became tense. "Light, Hadley! Light at last, and glorious messages in the belfry."

"Are you sure it's not something else in the belfry? Yes? Then for God's

sake will you stop this mystification and tell me what you mean? I suppose
the church bells tell you how the vanishing-trick was worked?"

"Oh no," said Dr. Fell. "Unfortunately not. They only tell me the name
of the murderer."

There was a palpable stillness in the room, a physical heaviness, as of
breath restrained to bursting. Dr. Fell spoke in a blank, almost an incredulous
voice which carried conviction in its mere incredulity. Downstairs a back door
closed. Faintly through the quiet house they heard footsteps on the staircase.
One set of footsteps was sharp, light, and impatient. The other had a drag
and then a heavy stamp; there was the noise of a cane knocking the banisters.
The noises grew louder, but no word was spoken. A key scraped into the lock
of the outer door, which opened and closed again with a click of the spring-
lock. There was another click as the light in the hallway was snapped on.
Then—evidently when they could see each other—the two burst out as though
they had been the ones who held in breath to suffocation.

"So you've lost the key I gave you," a man's thin, harsh, quiet voice spoke.
It was mocking and yet repressed. "And you say you didn't come here last
night, after all?"

"Not last night," said Rosette Grimaud's voice, which had a flat and yet
furious tone; "not last night or any other night." She laughed. "I never had
any intention of coming at all. You frightened me a little. Well, what of it?
And now that I *am* here, I don't think so much of your hideout. Did you have
a pleasant time waiting last night?"

There was a movement as though she had stepped forward, and been restrained. The man's voice rose.

"Now, you little devil," said the man, with equal quietness, "I'm going to
tell you something for the good of your soul. I wasn't here. I had no intention
of coming. If you think all you have to do is crack the whip to send people
through hoops—well, I wasn't here, do you see? You can go through the hoops
yourself. I wasn't here."

"That's a lie, Jerome," said Rosette, calmly.

"You think so, eh? Why?"

Two figures appeared against the light of the partly opened door. Hadley
reached out and drew back the curtains with a rattle of rings.

"We also would like to know the answer to that, Mr. Burnaby," he said.

The flood of murky daylight in their faces caught them off-guard; so much
off-guard that expressions were hollowed out as though snapped by a camera.
Rosette Grimaud cried out, making a movement of her raised arm as though
she would dodge under it, but the flash of the previous look had been bitter,
watchful, dangerously triumphant. Jerome Burnaby stood motionless, his
chest rising and falling. Silhouetted against the sickly electric light behind,
and wearing an old-fashioned broad-brimmed black hat, he bore a curious
resemblance to the lean Sandeman figure in the advertisement. But he was

more than a silhouette. He had a strong, furrowed face, that ordinarily might have been bluff and amiable like his gestures; an underhung jaw, and eyes which seemed to have lost their colour with anger. Taking off his hat, he tossed it on a divan with a swash-buckling air that struck Rampole as rather theatrical. His wiry brown hair, patched with grey round the temples, stood up as though released from pressure like a jack-in-the-box.

"Well?" he said with a sort of thin, bluff jocularity, and took a lurching step forward, on the club foot. "Is this a hold-up, or what? Three to one, I see. I happen to have a sword-stick, though—"

"It won't be needed, Jerome," said the girl. "They're the police."

Burnaby stopped; stopped and rubbed his mouth with a big hand. He seemed nervous, though he went on with ironical jocularity. "Oh! The police, eh? I'm honoured. Breaking and entering, I see."

"You are the tenant of this flat," said Hadley, returning an equal suavity, "not the owner or landlord of the house. If suspicious behaviour is seen. . . . I don't know about suspicious, Mr. Burnaby, but I think your friends would be amused at these—Oriental surroundings. Wouldn't they?"

That smile, that tone of voice, struck through to a raw place. Burnaby's face became a muddy colour.

"Damn you," he said, and half-raised the cane, "what do you want here?"

"First of all, before we forget it, about what you were saying when you came in here. . . ."

"You overheard it, eh?"

"Yes. It's unfortunate," said Hadley, composedly, "that we couldn't have overheard more. Miss Grimaud said that you were in this flat last night. Were you?"

"I was not."

"You were not. . . . Was he, Miss Grimaud?"

Her colour had come back; come back strongly, for she was angry with a quiet, smiling poise. She spoke in a breathless way, and her long hazel eyes had that fixity, that luminous strained expression, of one who determines to show no emotion. She was pressing her gloves between the fingers, and in the jerkiness of her breathing there was less anger than fear.

"Since you overheard it," she answered, after a speculative pause while she glanced from one to the other, "it's no good my denying it, is there? I don't see why you're interested. It can't have anything to do with—my father's death. That's certain. Whatever else Jerome is," she showed her teeth in an unsteady smile, "he's not a murderer. But since for some reason you *are* interested, I've a good mind to have the whole thing thrashed out now. Some version of this, I can see, is going to get back to Boyd. It might as well be the true one. . . . I'll begin by saying, yes, Jerome was in this flat last night."

"How do you know that, Miss Grimaud? Were you here?"

"No. But I saw a light in this room at half-past ten."

## XV

### The Lighted Window

BURNABY, still rubbing his chin, looked down at her in dull blankness. Rampole could have sworn that the man was genuinely startled; so startled that he could not quite understand her words, and peered at her as though he had never seen her before. Then he spoke in a quiet, common-sense tone which contrasted with his earlier one.

"I say, Rosette," he observed, "be careful now. Are you sure you know what you're talking about?"

"Yes. Quite sure."

Hadley cut in briskly. "At half-past ten? How did you happen to see this light, Miss Grimaud, when you were at your own home with us?"

"Oh no, I wasn't—if you remember. Not at that time. I was at the nursing-home, with the doctor in the room where my father was dying. I don't know whether you know it, but the back of the nursing-home faces the back of this house. I happened to be near a window, and I noticed. There was a light in this room; and, I think, the bathroom, too, though I'm not positive of that . . ."

"How do you know the rooms," said Hadley, sharply, "if you've never been here before?"

"I took jolly good care to observe when we came in just now," she answered, with a serene and imperturbable smile which somehow reminded Rampole of Mills. "I *didn't* know the rooms last night; I only knew he had this flat, and where the windows were. The curtains weren't quite drawn. That's how I came to notice the light."

Burnaby was still contemplating her with the same heavy curiosity.

"Just a moment, Mr.—Inspector—er—!" He humped his shoulder. "Are you sure you couldn't have been mistaken about the rooms, Rosette?"

"Positive, my dear. This is the house on the left-hand side at the corner of the alley, and you have the top floor."

"And you say you saw *me?*"

"No, I say I saw a light. But you and I are the only ones who know about this flat. And, since you'd invited me here, and said you would be here . . ."

"By God!" said Burnaby, "I'm curious to see how far you'll go." He hobbled over, with a trick of pulling down the corner of his mouth each time he lunged on the cane; he sat down heavily in a chair, and continued to study her out of his pale eyes. That upstanding hair gave him somehow a queerly alert look. "Please go on! You interest me. Yes. I'm curious to see how far you have the nerve to go."

"Are you really," said Rosette, in a flat voice. She whirled round; but her resolution seemed to crack and she succeeded in looking only miserable to the point of tears. "I wish I knew myself! I—I wish I knew about *you!* . . . I said we'd have this out," she appealed to Hadley, "but now I don't know whether I want to have it out. If I could decide about him, whether he's really sympathetic, and just a nice bluff old—old—"

"Don't say friend of the family," snapped Burnaby. "For Lord's sake don't say friend of the family. Personally, I wish I could decide about you. I wish I could decide whether you think you're telling the truth, or whether you're (excuse me for forgetting my chivalry for a moment!) a lying little vixen."

She went on steadily: "—or whether he's a sort of polite blackmailer. Oh, not for money!" She blazed again. "Vixen? Yes. Bitch if you like. I admit it. I've been both—but why? Because you've poisoned everything with all the hints you've dropped . . . if I could be sure they were hints and not just my imagination; if I could even be sure you were an honest blackmailer! . . ."

Hadley intervened. "Hints about what?"

"Oh, about my father's past life, if you must know." She clenched her hands. "About my birth, for one thing, and whether we mightn't add another nice term to bitch. But that's not important. That doesn't bother me at all. It's this business about some horrible thing—about my father—I don't know! Maybe they're not even hints. But . . . I've got it in my head somehow that old Drayman is a blackmailer. . . . Then, last night, Jerome asked me to come over here—why, why? I thought: well, is it because that's the night Boyd always sees me, and it will tickle Jerome's vanity no end to choose just that night? But I don't and I didn't—please understand me!—want to think Jerome was trying a little blackmail himself. I do like him; I can't help it; and that's what makes it so awful. . . ."

"We might clear it up, then," said Hadley. "Were you 'hinting,' Mr. Burnaby?"

There was a long silence while Burnaby examined his hands. Something in the posture of his bent head, in his slow heavy breathing, as though he were bewilderedly trying to make up his mind, kept Hadley from prompting him until he raised his head.

"I never thought—" he said. "Hinting. Yes. Yes, in strict accuracy, I suppose I was. But never intentionally, I'll swear. I never thought—" He stared at Rosette. "Those things slip out. Maybe you mean only what you think is a subtle question. . . ." He puffed out his breath in a sort of despairing hiss, and shrugged his shoulders. "To me it was an interesting deductive game, that's all. I didn't even think of it as prying. I swear I never thought anybody noticed, let alone taking it to heart. Rosette, if that's the only reason for your interest in me—thinking I was a blackmailer, and afraid of me—then I'm sorry I learned. Or am I?" He looked down at his hands again, opened and shut them, and then looked slowly round the room. "Take a look at this place, gentlemen. The front room especially . . . but you'll have seen that. Then you know the answer. The Great Detective. The poor ass with the deformed foot, dreaming."

For a second Hadley hesitated.

"And did the Great Detective find out anything about Dr. Grimaud's past?"

"No. . . . If I had, do you think I'd be apt to tell you?"

"We'll see if we can't persuade you. Do you know that there are blood-stains in that bathroom of yours, where Miss Grimaud says she saw a light last night? Do you know that Pierre Fley was murdered outside your door not long before half-past ten?"

Rosette Grimaud cried out, and Burnaby jerked up his head.

"Fley mur . . . Blood-stains! No! Where? Man, what do you mean?"

"Fley had a room in this street. We think he was coming here when he died. Anyhow, he was shot in the street outside here by the same man who killed Dr. Grimaud. Can you prove who you are, Mr. Burnaby? Can you prove, for instance, that you are not actually Dr. Grimaud's and Fley's brother?"

The other stared at him. He hoisted himself up shakily from the chair.

"Good God! man, are you mad?" he asked, in a quiet voice. "Brother! Now I see! . . . No, I'm not his brother. Do you think if I were his brother I should be interested in . . ." He checked himself, glanced at Rosette, and his expression became rather wild. "Certainly I can prove it. I ought to have a birth certificate somewhere. I—I can produce people who've known me all my life. Brother!"

Hadley reached round to the divan and held up the coil of rope.

"What about this rope? Is it a part of your Great Detective scheme, too?"

"That thing? No. What is it? I never saw it before. Brother!"

Rampole glanced at Rosette Grimaud, and saw that she was crying. She stood motionless, her hands at her sides and her face set; but the tears brimmed over her eyes.

"And can you prove," Hadley continued, "that you were not in this flat last night?"

Burnaby drew a deep breath. Relief lightened his heavy face.

"Yes, fortunately I can. I was at my club last night from eight o'clock—or thereabouts; maybe a little earlier—until past eleven. Dozens of people will tell you that. If you want me to be specific, ask the three I played poker with the whole of that time. Do you want an alibi? Right! There's as strong an alibi as you're ever likely to get. I wasn't here. I didn't leave any blood-stains, wherever the devil you say you found some. I didn't kill Fley, or Grimaud, or anybody else." His heavy jaw came out. "Now, then, what do you think of *that?*"

The superintendent swung his batteries so quickly that Burnaby had hardly finished speaking before Hadley had turned to Rosette.

"You still insist that you saw a light here at half-past ten?"

"Yes! . . . But, Jerome, truly, I never meant—!"

"Even though, when my man arrived here this morning, the electric meter was cut off and the lights would not work?"

"I . . . Yes, it's still true! But what I wanted to say—"

"Let's suppose Mr. Burnaby is telling the truth about last night. You say he invited you here. Is it likely that he invited you here when he intended to be at his club?"

Burnaby lurched forward and put a hand on Hadley's arm. "Steady! Let's get this straightened out, Inspector. That's what I did. It was a swine's trick, but—I did it. Look here, have I *got* to explain?"

"Now, now, now!" struck in the quiet, rumbling, deprecating tones of Dr. Fell. He took out the red bandana and blew his nose with a loud honking noise, to attract attention. Then he blinked at them, mildly disturbed. "Hadley, we're confused enough as it is. Let me put in a soothing word. Mr. Burnaby did that, as he expressed it himself, to make her jump through a hoop. Hurrum! Excuse my bluntness, ma'am, but then it's all right because that particular leopard wouldn't jump, eh?— About the question of the light not working, that's not nearly so ominous as it sounds. It's a shilling meter, d'ye see. Somebody was here. Somebody left the lights burning, possibly all night. Well, the meter used up a bob's worth of electricity, and then the lights went out. We don't know which way the switches were turned, because Somers got here first. Blast it, Hadley, we've got ample proof that there *was* somebody here last night. The question is, who?" He looked at the others. "H'm. You two say that nobody else knew of this place. But—assuming your story to be straight, Mr. Burnaby; and you'd be a first-class fathead to lie about a thing so easily checked up as that story—then somebody else must have known of it."

"I can only tell you I wasn't likely to speak of it," insisted Burnaby, rubbing his chin. "Unless somebody noticed me coming here . . . unless . . ."

"Unless, in other words, I told somebody about it?" Rosette flared again. Her sharp teeth bit at her under lip. "But I didn't. I—I don't know why I didn't"—she seemed fiercely puzzled—"but I never mentioned it to anybody. There!"

"But you have a key to the place?" asked Dr. Fell.

"I had a key to the place. I lost it."

"When?"

"Oh, how should I know? I never noticed." She had folded her arms and was walking round the room with excited little movements of her head. "I kept it in my bag, and I only noticed this morning, when we were coming over here, that it was gone. But one thing I insist on knowing." She stopped, facing Burnaby. "I—I don't know whether I'm fond of you or whether I hate you. If it was only a nasty little fondness for detective work, if that's all it really was and you didn't mean anything, then speak up. What do you know about my father? Tell me! I don't mind. They're the police, and they'll find out anyway. Now, now, don't act! I hate your acting. Tell me. What's this about brothers?"

"That's good advice, Mr. Burnaby. You painted a picture," said Hadley, "that I was going to ask about next. What did you know about Dr. Grimaud?"

Burnaby, leaning back against the window with an unconsciously swaggering gesture, shrugged his shoulders. His pale grey eyes, with their pin-point black pupils, shifted and gleamed sardonically.

He said: "Rosette, if I had ever known, if I had ever suspected, that my detective efforts were being interpreted as . . . Very well! I'll tell you in a few words what I'd have told you long ago, if I had known it worried you at all. Your father was once imprisoned at the salt-mines in Hungary, and he escaped. Not very terrible, is it?"

"In prison! What for?"

"For trying to start a revolution, I was told. . . . My own guess is for theft. You see, I'm being frank."

Hadley cut in quickly. "Where did you learn that? From Drayman?"

"So Drayman knows, does he?" Burnaby stiffened, and his eyes narrowed. "Yes, I rather thought he did. Ah! Yes. That was another thing I tried to find out, and it seems to have been construed into . . . And, come to think of it, what do *you* fellows know about it, anyhow?" Then he burst out. "Look here, I'm no busybody! I'd better tell you if only to prove it. I was dragged into the thing; Grimaud wouldn't let me alone. You talk about that picture. The picture was the cause rather than the effect. It was all accident—though I had a bad time persuading Grimaud of that. It was all on account of a damned magic-lantern lecture."

"A what?"

"Fact! A magic-lantern lecture. I ducked into the thing to get out of the rain one night; it was out in North London somewhere, a parish hall, about eighteen months ago." Wryly Burnaby twiddled his thumbs. "For the first time there was an honest and homely expression on his face. "I'd like to make a romantic story out of this. But you asked for the truth. Right! Chap was lecturing on Hungary: lantern-slides and plenty of ghostly atmosphere to thrill the church-goers. But it caught my imagination; by George, it did!" His eyes gleamed. "There was one slide—something like what I painted. Nothing effective about it; but the story that went with it, about the three lonely graves in an unhallowed place, gave me a good idea for a nightmare. The lecturer inferred that they were vampires' graves, you see? I came home and worked like fury on the idea. Well, I frankly told everybody it was an imagi-

native conception of something I never saw. But for some reason nobody
believed me. Then Grimaud saw it . . ."

"Mr. Pettis told us," Hadley remarked, woodenly, "that it gave him a turn.
Or that you said it did."

"Gave him a turn? I should say it did! He hunched his head down into
his shoulders and stood as quiet as a mummy, looking at it. I took it as a
tribute. And then, in my sinister innocence," said Burnaby, with a kind of
leer, "out I came with the remark, 'You'll notice how the earth is cracking on
one grave. He's just getting out.' My mind was still running on vampires, of
course. But he didn't know that. For a second I thought he was coming at
me with a palette knife."

It was a straightforward story Burnaby told. Grimaud, he said, had questioned him about that picture; questioned, watched, questioned again, until
even a less imaginative man would have been suspicious. The uneasy tension
of being always under surveillance had set him to solve the puzzle in ordinary
self-defence. A few pieces of handwriting in books in Grimaud's library; the
shield of arms over the mantelpiece; a casual word dropped . . . Burnaby
looked at Rosette with a grim smile. Then, he continued, about three months
before the murder Grimaud had collared him and, under an oath of secrecy,
told him the truth. The "truth" was exactly the story Drayman had told
Hadley and Dr. Fell last night: the plague, the two dead brothers, the escape.

During this time Rosette had been staring out of the window with an
incredulous, half-witted blankness which ended in something like a tearful-
ness of relief.

"And that's *all*?" she cried, breathing hard. "That's all there is to it? That's
what I've been worrying about all this time?"

"That's all, my dear," Burnaby answered, folding his arms. "I told you it
wasn't very terrible. But I didn't want to tell it to the police. Now, however,
that you've insisted . . ."

"Be careful, Hadley," grunted Dr. Fell in a low voice, and knocked
against the superintendent's arm. He cleared his throat. "Harrumph! Yes.
We have some reason to believe the story, too, Miss Grimaud."

Hadley took a new line. "Supposing all this to be true, Mr. Burnaby: you
were at the Warwick Tavern the night Fley came in first?"

"Yes."

"Well, then? Knowing what you did, didn't you connect him with that
business in the past? Especially after his remarks about the three coffins?"

Burnaby hesitated, and then gestured. "Frankly, yes. I walked home with
Grimaud on that night—the Wednesday night. I didn't say anything, but I
thought he was going to tell me something. We sat down on either side of
the fire in his study, and he took an extra large whisky, a thing he seldom
does. I noticed he seemed to be looking very hard at the fireplace. . . ."

"By the way," Dr. Fell put in, with such casualness that Rampole jumped, "where did he keep his private and personal papers? Do you know?"

The other darted a sharp glance at him.

"Mills would be better able to tell you that than I," he returned. (Something veiled, something guarded, some cloud of dust here?) "He may have had a safe. So far as I know, he kept them in a locked drawer at the side of that big desk."

"Go on."

"For a long time neither of us said anything. There was one of those uncomfortable strains when each person wants to introduce a subject, but wonders whether the other is thinking about it, too. Well, I took the plunge, and said, 'Who was it?' He made one of those noises of his, like a dog just before it barks, and shifted round in the chair. Finally he said: 'I don't know. It's been a long time. It may have been the doctor; it looked like the doctor.'"

"Doctor? You mean the one who certified him as dead of plague at the prison?" asked Hadley. Rosette Grimaud shivered, and suddenly sat down with her face in her hands. Burnaby grew uncomfortable.

"Yes. Look here, must I go on with this? . . . All right, all right! 'Back for a little blackmail,' he said. You know the look of the stoutish opera stars, who sing Mephistopheles in 'Faust'? He looked just like that when he turned round towards me, with his hands on the arms of the chair, and his elbows hooked as though he were going to get up. Face reddish with the firelight, clipped beard, raised eyebrows—everything. I said, 'Yes, but actually what can he do?' You see, I was trying to draw him out. I thought it must be more serious than a political offence, or it wouldn't carry any weight after so long. He said, 'Oh, *he* won't do anything. He never had the nerve. *He* won't do anything.'

"Now," snapped Burnaby, looking round, "you asked for everything, and here it is. I don't mind. Everybody knows it. Grimaud said, with that barking directness of his, 'You want to marry Rosette, don't you?' I admitted it. He said, 'Very well; you shall,' and began nodding and drumming on the arm of the chair. I laughed and said . . . Well! I said something about Rosette's having a preference in another direction. He said: 'Bah! the young one! I'll fix that.'"

Rosette was looking at him with a hard, luminous, inscrutable stare, her eyes nearly closed. She spoke in a tone too puzzling to identify. She said:

"So you had it all arranged, did you?"

"O Lord, don't fly off the handle! You know better than that. I was asked what happened, and here it is. The last thing he said was that, whatever happened to him, I was to keep my mouth shut about what I knew—"

"Which you didn't . . ."

"At your express orders, no." He turned back to the others. "Well, gentlemen, that's all I can tell you. When he came hurrying in on Friday morning to get that picture, I was a good deal puzzled. But I had been told to keep out of it entirely, and I did."

Hadley, who had been writing in his notebook, went on without speaking until he came to the end of the page. Then he looked at Rosette, who was sitting back on the divan with a pillow under her elbow. Under the fur coat she wore a dark dress, but her head was bare as usual; so that the heavy blond hair and square face seemed to fit with the gaudy red-and-yellow divan. She turned her hand outward from the wrist, shakily.

"I know. You're going to ask me what *I* think of all this. About my father . . . and all." She stared at the ceiling. "I don't know. It takes such a load off my mind, it's so much too good to be true, that I'm afraid somebody's not telling the truth. Why, I'd have admired the old boy for a thing like that! It's—it's awful and terrible, and I'm glad he had so much of the devil in him! Of course if it was because he was a thief"—she smiled in some pleasure at the idea—"you can't blame him for keeping it quiet, can you?"

"That was not what I was going to ask," said Hadley, who seemed a good deal taken aback by this frankly broad-minded attitude. "I do want to know why, if you always refused to come over here with Mr. Burnaby, you suddenly decided on coming this morning?"

"To have it out with him, of course. And I—I wanted to get drunk or something. Then things were so unpleasant, you see, when we found that coat with the blood on it hanging in the closet. . . ."

She stopped as she saw faces change, and jerked back a little.

"When you found *what?*" said Hadley, in the midst of a heavy silence.

"The coat with blood inside it, all stained down the inside of the front," she answered, with something of a gulp. "I—er—I didn't mention it, did I? Well, you didn't give me any chance! The minute we walked in here, you leaped out at us like . . . like . . . Yes, that's it! The coat was hanging up in the coat-closet in the hall. Jerome found it when he was hanging up his own."

"Whose coat?"

"Nobody's! That's the odd part! I never saw it before. It wouldn't have fitted anybody at our house. It was too big for father—and it's a flashy tweed overcoat of the kind he'd have shuddered at, anyway; it would have swallowed Stuart Mills, and yet it isn't quite big enough for old Drayman. It's a new coat. It looks as though it had never been worn before . . ."

"*I see,*" said Dr. Fell, and puffed out his cheeks.

"You see what?" snapped Hadley. "This is a fine state of affairs now! You told Pettis you wanted blood. Well, you're getting blood—too infernally much blood!—and all in the wrong places. What's on your mind now?"

"I see," replied Dr. Fell, pointing with his stick, "where Drayman got the blood on him last night."

"You mean he wore the coat?"

"No, no! Think back. Remember what your sergeant said. He said that Drayman, half-blind, came blundering and rushing downstairs; blundered round in the clothes-closet getting his hat and coat. Hadley, he brushed close up against that coat when the blood was fresh. And it's no wonder he couldn't understand afterwards how it got there. Doesn't that clear up a good deal?"

"No, I'm damned if it does! It clears up one point by substituting another twice as bad. An extra coat! Come along. We're going over there at once. If you will go with us, Miss Grimaud, and you, Mr. . . ."

Dr. Fell shook his head. "You go along, Hadley. There's something I must see now. Something that changes the whole twist of the case; something that has become the most vitally important thing in it."

"What?"

"Pierre Fley's lodgings," said Dr. Fell, and shouldered out with his cape whirling behind him.

*Third Coffin:*

## THE PROBLEM OF SEVEN TOWERS

## XVI

### The Chameleon Overcoat

BETWEEN that discovery and the time they were to meet Pettis for lunch, Dr. Fell's spirits sank to a depth of gloom Rampole would not have believed possible, and which he certainly could not understand.

To begin with, the doctor refused to go straight back to Russell Square with Hadley, although he insisted Hadley should go. He said the essential clue must be at Fley's room. He said he would keep Rampole behind for some "dirty work of a strenuous pattern." Finally, he swore at himself with such heart-felt violence that even Hadley, sometimes sharing the views he expressed, was moved to remonstrate.

"But what do you expect to find there?" insisted Hadley. "Somers has already been through the place!"

"I don't expect anything. I can only say I hope," grumbled the doctor, "to find certain traces of brother Henri. His trademark, so to speak. His whiskers. His . . . oh, my hat, brother Henri, damn you!"

Hadley said that they could forego the Soliloquy in a Spanish Cloister, and could not understand why his friend's rage at the elusive Henri seemed to have grown to the status of a mania. There appeared nothing fresh to inspire it. Besides, the doctor, before leaving Burnaby's lodging-house, held up everybody for some time with a searching examination of Miss Hake, the landlady. O'Rourke had been gallantly keeping her downstairs with reminiscences of his trouping days; but both of them were tall talkers, and it is to be doubted whether he reminisced any more than Miss Hake did.

The questioning of Miss Hake, Dr. Fell admitted, was not productive. Miss Hake was a faded, agreeable spinster with good intentions but somewhat wandering wits, and a tendency to confuse erratic lodgers with burglars or murderers. When she was at last persuaded out of her belief that Burnaby was a burglar, she could give little information. She had not been at home last night. She had been at the moving pictures from eight o'clock until eleven, and at a friend's house in Gray's Inn Road until nearly midnight. She could not tell who might have used Burnaby's room; she had not even known of the murder until that morning. As to her other lodgers, there were three: an American student and his wife on the ground floor, and a veterinary surgeon on the floor above. All three had been out on the night before.

Somers, who had returned from his futile errand to Bloomsbury Square, was put to work on this lead; Hadley set out for Grimaud's house with Rosette and Burnaby, and Dr. Fell, who was doggedly intent on tackling another communicative landlady, found instead an uncommunicative landlord.

The premises over and under the tobacconist's shop at number 2 looked as flimsy as one of those half-houses which stand out from the side of the stage in a musical comedy. But they were bleak, dark-painted, and filled with the mustiness of the shop itself. Energy at a clanking bell at last brought James Dolberman, tobacconist and news agent, materializing slowly from the shadows at the back of his shop. He was a small, tight-lipped old man with large knuckles and a black muslin coat that shone like armour in a cave of fly-blown novelettes and mummified peppermints. His view of the whole matter was that it was no business of his.

Staring past them at the shop window, as though he were waiting for some one to come and give him an excuse to leave off talking, he bit off a few grudging answers. Yes, he had a lodger; yes, it was a man named Fley—a foreigner. Fley occupied a bed-sitting-room on the top floor. He had been there two weeks, paying in advance. No, the landlord didn't know anything about him, and didn't want to, except that he gave no trouble. He had a habit of talking to himself in a foreign language, that was all. The landlord didn't know anything about him, because he hardly ever saw him. There were no other lodgers; he (James Dolberman) wasn't carrying hot water upstairs for anybody. Why did Fley choose the top floor? How should he know? They had better ask Fley.

Didn't he know Fley was dead? Yes, he did; there had been a policeman here asking fool questions already, and taking him to identify the body. But it wasn't any business of his. What about the shooting at twenty-five minutes past ten last night? James Dolberman looked as though he might say something, but snapped his jaws shut and stared even harder at the window. He had been belowstairs in his kitchen with the radio on; he knew nothing about it, and wouldn't have come out to see if he had.

Had Fley ever had any visitors? No. Were there ever any suspicious-looking strangers, any people associated with Fley, hereabouts?

This had an unexpected result: the landlord's jaws still moved in a somnambulistic way, but he grew almost voluble. Yes, there was something the police ought to see to, instead of wasting taxpayers' money! He had seen somebody dodging round this place, watching it, once even speaking to Fley and then darting up the street. Nasty-looking customer. Criminal most likely! He didn't like people who dodged. No, he couldn't give any description of him—that was the police's business. Besides, it was always at night.

"But isn't there anything," said Dr. Fell, who was nearly at the limit of his affability and was wiping his face with the bandana, "you can give as description? Any clothes, anything of that sort? Hey?"

"He might," Dolberman conceded, after a tight-lipped struggle with the window, "he *might* have been wearing a kind of fancy overcoat, or the like. Of a light yellow tweed; with red spots in it, maybe. That's your business. You wish to go upstairs? Here is the key. The door is outside."

As they were stamping up a dark and narrow stairway, through a house surprisingly solid despite its flimsy appearance, Rampole fumed.

"You're right, sir," he said, "in saying that the whole case has been turned upside down. It has been—on a matter of overcoats—and it makes less sense than anything else. We've been looking for the sinister figure in the long black overcoat. And now along comes another figure in a bloodstained tweed coat that you can at least call gay in colour. Which is which, and does the whole business turn on a matter of overcoats?"

Dr. Fell puffed as he hauled himself up. "Well, I wasn't thinking of that," he said, doubtfully, "when I said that the case had been turned upside down—or perhaps I should say wrong way round. But in a way it may depend on overcoats. H'm. The Man with Two Overcoats. Yes, I think it's the same murderer, even if he doesn't happen to be sartorially consistent."

"You said you had an idea as to who the murderer might be?"

"I know who he is!" roared Dr. Fell. "And do you know why I feel an urge to kick myself? Not only because he's been right under my nose all the time, but *because he's been practically telling me the truth the whole time,* and yet I've never had the sense to see it. He's been so truthful that it hurts me to think of how I disbelieved him and thought he was innocent!"

"But the vanishing-trick?"

"No, I don't know how it was done. Here we are."

There was only one room on the top floor, to which a grimy skylight admitted a faint glow on the landing. The room had a door of plain boards painted green; it stood ajar, and opened on a low cave of a room whose window had evidently not been opened in some time. After fumbling round in the gloom, Dr. Fell found a gas-mantle in a tipsy globe. The ragged light showed a neat, but very grimy, room with blue cabbages on the wall-paper and a white iron bed. On the bureau lay a folded note under a bottle of ink. Only one touch remained of Pierre Fley's weird and twisted brain: it was as though they saw Fley himself, in his rusty evening clothes and top-hat, standing by the bureau for a performance. Over the mirror hung framed an old-fashioned motto in curly script of gilt and black and red. The spidery scrollwork read, "*Vengeance is Mine, Saith the Lord; I Will Repay.*" But it was hung upside down.

Wheezing in the quiet, Dr. Fell lumbered over to the bureau and picked up the folded note. The handwriting was flowery, Rampole saw, and the short message had almost the air of a proclamation.

James Dolberman, Esq.

I am leaving you my few belongings, such as they are, in lieu of a week's notice. I shall not need them again. I am going back to my grave.

PIERRE FLEY.

"Why," said Rampole, "this insistent harping on 'I am going back to my grave'? It sounds as though it ought to have a meaning, even if it doesn't. . . . I suppose there really was such a person as Fley? He existed; he wasn't somebody else pretending to be Fley, or the like?"

Dr. Fell did not answer that. He was at the beginning of a mood of gloom which sank lower and lower as he inspected the tattered grey carpet on the floor.

"Not a trace," he groaned. "Not a trace or a bus ticket or anything. Serene and unswept and traceless. His possessions? No, I don't want to see his possessions. I suppose Somers had a look through those. Come on; we'll go back and join Hadley."

They walked to Russell Square through a gloom of mind as well as overcast sky. As they went up the steps, Hadley saw them through the drawing-room window and came to open the front door. Making sure the drawing-room door was closed—there was a mutter of voices beyond—Hadley faced them in the dimness of the ornate hallway. Behind him the devil mask on the suit of Japanese armour gave a fair caricature of his face.

"More trouble, I perceive," said Dr. Fell, almost genially. "Well, out with it. I have nothing to report. I was afraid my expedition would be a failure, but I have no consolation merely from being a good prophet. What's up?"

"That overcoat—" Hadley stopped. He was in such a state that wrath could go no farther; he touched the other side, and ended with a sour grin. "Come in and listen to it, Fell. Maybe it'll make sense to you. If Mangan is lying, I don't see any good reason why he should be lying. But that overcoat . . . we've got it right enough. A new coat, brand new. Nothing in the pockets, not even the usual grit and fluff and tobacco ash that you get when you've worn a coat a little while. But first we were faced with the problem of two overcoats. Now we have what you would probably call the Mystery of the Chameleon Overcoat. . . ."

"What's the matter with the overcoat?"

"It's changed colour," said Hadley.

Dr. Fell blinked. He examined the superintendent with an air of refreshed interest. "I don't imagine by any chance," he said, "that this business has turned your brain, has it? Changed colour, hey? Are you about to tell me that the overcoat is now a bright emerald green?"

"I mean it's changed colour since . . . Come on!"

Tension was thick in the air when he threw open the door on a drawing-room furnished in heavy old-fashioned luxury, with bronze groups holding lights, gilt cornices, and curtains stiff with such an overdose of lace that they looked like frozen waterfalls. All the lights were on. Burnaby lounged on a sofa. Rosette was walking about with quick, angry steps. In the corner by the radio stood Ernestine Dumont, her hands on her hips and her lower lip folded across the upper, amused, or satiric, or both. Finally, Boyd Mangan stood with his back to the fire, hopping a little and moving from one side to the other as though it burnt him. But it was excitement, or something else, that burnt him.

". . . I know the damn thing fits me!" he was saying, with an air of fierce repetition. "I know it. I admit it. The overcoat fits me, but it's not my coat. In the first place, I always wear a waterproof; it's hanging up in the hall now. In the second place, I could never afford a coat like that; the thing must have cost twenty guineas if it cost a penny. In the third place—"

Hadley figuratively rapped for attention. The entrance of Dr. Fell and Rampole seemed to soothe Mangan.

"Would you mind repeating," said Hadley, "what you've just been telling us?"

Mangan lit a cigarette. The match-flame gleamed in dark eyes that were a little bloodshot. He twitched out the match, inhaled, and expelled smoke with the air of one who is determined to be convicted in a good cause.

"Personally, I don't see why everybody should want to jump all over me," he said. "It may have been another overcoat, although I don't see why anybody should want to strew his wardrobe all over the place. . . . Look here, Ted, I'll put it up to you." He seized Rampole's arm and dragged him over in front of the fire as though he were setting up an exhibit. "When I got here for dinner last night, I went to hang up my coat—my waterproof, mind you— in the clothes-closet in the hall. Generally you don't bother to turn on the light in there. You just grope round and stick your coat on the first convenient hook. I wouldn't have bothered then, but I was carrying a parcel of books I wanted to put on the shelf. So I switched on the light. And I saw an overcoat, an extra coat, hanging by itself over in the far corner. It was about the same size as the yellow tweed one you've got; just the same, I should have said, only it was black."

"An extra coat," repeated Dr. Fell. He drew in his chins and looked curiously at Mangan. "Why do you say an extra coat, my boy? If you see a line of coats in somebody's house, does the idea of an extra one ever enter your head? My experience is that the least noticed things in a house are coats hanging on a peg; you have a vague idea that one of 'em must be your own, but you're not even sure which it is. Eh?"

"I knew the coats people have here, all the same. *And*," replied Mangan,

"I particularly noticed this one, because I thought it must be Burnaby's. They hadn't told me he was here, and I wondered if he was. . . ."

Burnaby had adopted a very bluff, indulgent air towards Mangan. He was not now the thin-skinned figure they had seen sitting on the divan in Cagliostro Street; he was an elder chiding youth with a theatrical wave of his hand.

"Mangan," he said, "is very observant, Dr. Fell. A very observant young man. Ha-ha-ha! Especially where I am concerned."

"Got any objections?" asked Mangan, lowering his voice to a calm note.

". . . But let him tell you the story. Rosette, my dear, may I offer you a cigarette? By the way, I may say that it wasn't my coat."

Mangan's anger grew without his seeming to know exactly why. But he turned back to Dr. Fell. "Anyway, I noticed it. Then, when Burnaby came here this morning and found that coat with the blood inside it . . . well, the light one was hanging in the same place. Of course, the only explanation is that there were two overcoats. But what kind of crazy business is it? I'll swear that coat last night didn't belong to anybody here. You can see for yourself that the tweed one doesn't. Did the murderer wear one coat, or both, or neither? Besides, that black coat had a queer look about it—"

"Queer?" interrupted Dr. Fell, so sharply that Mangan turned round. "How do you mean, queer?"

Ernestine Dumont came forward from beside the radio, her flat-heeled shoes creaking a little. She looked more withered this morning; the high cheekbones more accentuated, the nose more flat, the eyes so puffed round the lids that they gave her a hooded, furtive appearance. Yet, despite the gritty look, her black eyes still had their glitter.

"Ah, bah!" she said, and made a sharp, somehow wooden gesture. "What is the reason to go on with all this foolishness? Why do you not ask me? I would know more about such things than he. Would I not?" She looked at Mangan and her forehead wrinkled. "No, no, I think you are trying to tell the truth, you understand. But I think you have mixed it up a little. That is easy, as the Dr. Fell says. . . . The yellow coat was there last night, yes. Early in the evening, before dinner. It was hanging on the hook where he says he saw the black one. I saw it myself."

"But—" cried Mangan.

"Now, now," boomed Dr. Fell, soothingly. "Let's see if we can't straighten this out. If you saw the coat there, ma'am, didn't it strike you as unusual? A little queer, hey, if you knew it didn't belong to anybody here?"

"No, not at all." She nodded towards Mangan. "I did not see him arrive. I supposed it was his."

"Who did let you in, by the way?" Dr. Fell asked Mangan, sleepily.

"Annie. But I hung up my things myself. I'll swear—"

"Better ring the bell and have Annie up, if she's here, Hadley," said Dr. Fell. "This problem of the chameleon overcoat intrigues me. Oh, Bacchus, it intrigues me! Now, ma'am, I'm not saying you're not telling the truth, any more than you say it of our friend Mangan. I was telling Ted Rampole a while ago how unfortunately truthful a certain person has been. Hah! Incidentally, have you spoken to Annie?"

"Oh yes," Hadley answered, as Rosette Grimaud strode past him and rang a bell. "She tells a straight story. She was out last night, and didn't get back until past twelve. But I haven't asked her about this."

"I don't see what all the fuss is about!" cried Rosette. "What difference does it make? Haven't you better things to do than go fooling about trying to decide whether an overcoat was yellow or black?"

Mangan turned on her. "It makes a lot of difference, and you know it. I wasn't seeing things. No, and I don't think she was, either! But somebody's got to be right. Though I admit Annie probably won't know. God! I don't know anything!"

"Quite right," said Burnaby.

"Go to hell," said Mangan. "Do you mind?"

Hadley strode over between them and spoke quietly but to the point. Burnaby, who looked rather white, sat down on the couch again. The fray and strain of nerves showed raw in that room; everybody seemed eager to be quiet when Annie answered the bell. Annie was a quiet, long-nosed serious-minded girl who showed none of that quality which is called nonsense. She looked capable; she also looked hard-worked. Standing rather bent at the doorway, her cap so precise on her head that it seemed to have been stamped there, she regarded Hadley with level brown eyes. She was a little upset, but not in the least nervous.

"One thing I neglected to ask you about last night—er," said the superintendent, not too easy himself. "Hum! You let Mr. Mangan in, did you?"

"Yes, sir."

"About what time was that?"

"Couldn't say, sir." She seemed puzzled. "Might have been half an hour before dinner. Couldn't say exactly."

"Did you see him hang up hat and coat?"

"Yes, sir! He never gives them to me, or of course I'd have—"

"But did you look into the clothes-closet?"

"Oh, I see. . . . Yes, sir, I did! You see, when I'd let him in, I went straight back to the dining-room, but then I discovered I had to go down-stairs to the kitchen. So I went back through the front hall. And I noticed he'd gone away and left the light on in the clothes-closet, so I went down and turned it out. . . ."

Hadley leaned forward. "Now be careful! You know the light tweed over-coat that was found in that closet this morning? You knew about that, did you? Good! Do you remember the hook it was hanging from?"

"Yes, sir, I do." Her lips closed tightly. "I was in the front hall this morning when Mr. Burnaby found it, and the rest came round. Mr. Mills said we must leave it where it was, with that blood on it and all, because the police . . ."

"Exactly. The question, Annie, is about the colour of that coat. When you looked into that closet last night, was the coat a light brown or a black? Can you remember?"

She stared at him. "Yes, sir, I can re— light brown or black, sir? Do you mean it? Well, sir, strictly speaking, it wasn't either. *Because there was no coat hanging from that hook at all*."

A babble of voices crossed and clashed: Mangan furious, Rosette almost hysterically mocking, Burnaby amused. Only Ernestine Dumont remained wearily and contemptuously silent. For a full minute Hadley studied the set, now fighting-earnest face of the witness: Annie had her hands clenched and her neck thrust out. Hadley moved over towards the window, saying nothing in a markedly violent fashion.

Then Dr. Fell chuckled.

"Well, cheer up," he urged. "At least it hasn't turned another colour on us. And I must insist it's a very revealing fact, although I shall be in some danger of having that chair chucked at my head. H'mf. Hah! Yes. Come along, Hadley. Lunch is what we want. Lunch!"

## XVII

### The Locked-Room Lecture

THE coffee was on the table, the wine-bottles were empty, cigars lighted. Hadley, Pettis, Rampole, and Dr. Fell sat round the glow of a red-shaded table lamp in the vast, dusky dining-room at Pettis's hotel. They had stayed on beyond most, and only a few people remained at other tables in that lazy, replete hour of a winter afternoon when the fire is most comfortable and snowflakes begin to sift past the windows. Under the dark gleam of armour and armorial bearings, Dr. Fell looked more than ever like a feudal baron. He glanced with contempt at the demi-tasse, which he seemed in danger of swallowing cup and all. He made an expansive, settling gesture with his cigar. He cleared his throat.

"I will now lecture," announced the doctor, with amiable firmness, "on the general mechanics and development of that situation which is known in detective fiction as the 'hermetically sealed chamber.' "

Hadley groaned. "Some other time," he suggested. "We don't want to hear any lecture after this excellent lunch, and especially when there's work to be done. Now, as I was saying a moment ago—"

"I will now lecture," said Dr. Fell, inexorably, "on the general mechanics and development of the situation which is known in detective fiction as the 'hermetically sealed chamber.' Harrumph. All those opposing can skip this chapter. Harrumph. To begin with, gentlemen! Having been improving my mind with sensational fiction for the last forty years, I can say—"

"But, if you're going to analyze impossible situations," interrupted Pettis, "why discuss detective fiction?"

"Because," said the doctor, frankly, "we're in a detective story, and we don't fool the reader by pretending we're not. Let's not invent elaborate excuses to drag in a discussion of detective stories. Let's candidly glory in the noblest pursuits possible to characters in a book.

"But to continue: In discussing 'em, gentlemen, I am not going to start an argument by attempting to lay down rules. I mean to speak solely of personal tastes and preferences. We can tamper with Kipling thus: 'There are nine and sixty ways to construct a murder maze, and every single one of them is right.' Now, if I said that to me every single one of them was equally interesting, then I should be—to put the matter as civilly as possible—a cockeyed liar. But that is not the point. When I say that a story about a hermetically sealed chamber is more interesting than anything else in detective fiction, that's merely a prejudice. I like my murders to be frequent, gory, and grotesque. I like some vividness of colour and imagination flashing out of my plot, since I cannot find a story enthralling solely on the grounds that it sounds as though it might really have happened. All these things, I admit, are happy, cheerful, rational prejudices, and entail no criticism of more tepid (or more able) work.

"But this point must be made, because a few people who do not like the slightly lurid insist on treating their preferences as rules. They use, as a stamp of condemnation, the word 'improbable.' And thereby they gull the unwary into their own belief that 'improbable' simply means 'bad.'

"Now, it seems reasonable to point out that the word 'improbable' is the very last which should ever be used to curse detective fiction in any case. A great part of our liking for detective fiction is *based* on a liking for improbability. When A is murdered, and B and C are under strong suspicion, it is improbable that the innocent-looking D can be guilty. But he is. If G has a perfect alibi, sworn to at every point by every other letter in the alphabet, it is improbable that G can have committed the crime. But he has. When the detective picks up a fleck of coal dust at the seashore, it is improbable that such an insignificant thing can have any importance. But it will. In short, you come to a point where the word 'improbable' grows meaningless as a jeer. There can be no such thing as any probability until the end of the story. And then, if you wish the murder to be fastened on an unlikely person (as some of us old fogies do), you can hardly complain because he acted from motives less likely or necessarily less apparent than those of the person first suspected.

"When the cry of 'This-sort-of-thing-wouldn't-happen!' goes up, when you complain about half-faced fiends and hooded phantoms and blond hypnotic sirens, you are merely saying, 'I don't like this sort of story.' That's fair enough. If you do not like it, you are howlingly right to say so. But when you twist this matter of taste into a rule for judging the merit or even the probability of the story, you are merely saying, 'This series of events couldn't happen, because I shouldn't enjoy it if it did.'

"What would seem to be the truth of the matter? We might test it out by taking the hermetically-sealed-chamber as an example, because this situation has been under a hotter fire than any other on the grounds of being unconvincing.

"Most people, I am delighted to say, are fond of the locked room. But—here's the damned rub—even its friends are often dubious. I cheerfully admit that I frequently am. So, for the moment, we'll all side together on this score and see what we can discover. Why are we dubious when we hear the explanation of the locked room? Not in the least because we are incredulous, but simply because in some vague way we are *disappointed*. And from that feeling it is only natural to take an unfair step farther, and call the whole business incredible or impossible or flatly ridiculous.

"Precisely, in short," boomed Dr. Fell, pointing his cigar, "what O'Rourke was telling us today about illusions that are performed *in real life*. Lord! gents, what chance has a story got when we even jeer at real occurrences? The very fact that they do happen, and that the illusionist gets away with it, seems to make the deception worse. When it occurs in a detective story, we call it incredible. When it happens in real life, and we are forced to credit it, we merely call the explanation disappointing. And the secret of both disappointments is the same—we expect too much.

"You see, the effect is so magical that we somehow expect the cause to be magical also. When we see that it isn't wizardry, we call it tomfoolery. Which is hardly fair play. The last thing we should complain about with regard to the murderer is his erratic conduct. The whole test is, *can* the thing be done? If so, the question of whether it *would* be done does not enter into it. A man escapes from a locked room—well? Since apparently he has violated the laws of nature for our entertainment, then heaven knows he is entitled to violate the laws of Probable Behaviour! If a man offers to stand on his head, we can hardly make the stipulation that he must keep his feet on the ground while he does it. Bear that in mind, gents, when you judge. Call the result uninteresting, if you like, or anything else that is a matter of personal taste. But be very careful about making the nonsensical statement that it is improbable or farfetched."

"All right, all right," said Hadley, shifting in his chair. "I don't feel very strongly on the matter myself. But if you insist on lecturing—apparently with some application to this case—?"

"Yes."

"Then why take the hermetically sealed room? You yourself said that Grimaud's murder wasn't our biggest problem. The main puzzle is the business of a man shot in the middle of an empty street. . . ."

"Oh, that?" said Dr. Fell, with such a contemptuous wave of his hand that Hadley stared at him. "That part of it? I knew the explanation of that as soon as I heard the church bells. —Tut, tut, such language! I'm quite serious. It's the escape from the room that bothers me. And, to see if we can't get a lead, I am going to outline roughly some of the various means of committing murders in locked rooms, under separate classifications. This crime belongs under one of them. It's got to! No matter how wide the variation may be, it's *only* a variation of a few central methods.

"H'mf! Ha! Now, here is your box with one door, one window, and solid walls. In discussing ways of escaping when both door and window are sealed, I shall not mention the low (and nowadays very rare) trick of having a secret passage to a locked room. This so puts a story beyond the pale that a self-respecting author scarcely needs even to mention that there is no such thing. We don't need to discuss minor variations of this outrage: the panel which is only large enough to admit a hand; or the plugged hole in the ceiling through which a knife is dropped, the plug replaced undetectably, and the floor of the attic above sprayed with dust so that no one seems to have walked there. This is only the same foul in miniature. The principle remains the same whether the secret opening is as small as a thimble or as big as a barn door. . . . As to legitimate classification, you might jot some of these down, Mr. Pettis. . . ."

"Right," said Pettis, who was grinning. "Go on."

"First! There is the crime committed in a hermetically sealed room which really is hermetically sealed, and from which no murderer has escaped because no murderer was actually in the room. Explanations:

"1. It is not murder, but a series of coincidences ending in an accident which looks like murder. At an earlier time, before the room was locked, there has been a robbery, an attack, a wound, or a breaking of furniture which suggests a murder struggle. Later the victim is either accidentally killed or stunned in a locked room, and all these incidents are assumed to have taken place at the same time. In this case the means of death is usually a crack on the head—presumably by a bludgeon, but really from some piece of furniture. It may be from the corner of a table or the sharp edge of a chair, but the most popular object is an iron fender. The murderous fender, by the way, has been killing people in a way that looks like murder ever since Sherlock Holmes' adventure with the Crooked Man. The most thoroughly satisfying solution of this type of plot, which includes a murderer, is in Gaston Leroux's *The Mystery of the Yellow Room*—the best detective tale ever written.

"2. It is murder, but the victim is impelled to kill himself or crash into an accidental death. This may be by the effect of a haunted room, by suggestion, or more usually by a gas introduced from outside the room. This gas or poison makes the victim go berserk, smash up the room as though there had been a struggle, and die of a knife-slash inflicted on himself. In other variations he drives the spike of the chandelier through his head, is hanged on a loop of wire, or even strangles himself with his own hands.

"3. It is murder, by a mechanical device already planted in the room, and hidden undetectably in some innocent-looking piece of furniture. It may be a trap set by somebody long dead, and work either automatically or be set anew by the modern killer. It may be some fresh quirk of devilry from present-day science. We have, for instance, the gun-mechanism concealed in the telephone receiver, which fires a bullet into the victim's head as he lifts the receiver. We have the pistol with a string to the trigger, which is pulled by the expansion of water as it freezes. We have the clock that fires a bullet when you wind it; and (clocks being popular) we have the ingenious grandfather clock which sets ringing a hideously clanging bell on its top, so that when you reach up to shut off the din your own touch releases a blade that slashes open your stomach. We have the weight that swings down from the ceiling, and the weight that crashes out on your skull from the high back of a chair. There is the bed that exhales a deadly gas when your body warms it, the poisoned needle that leaves no trace, the—

"You see," said Dr. Fell, stabbing out with his cigar at each point, "when we become involved with these mechanical devices we are rather in the sphere of the general 'impossible situation' than the narrower one of the locked room. It would be possible to go on forever, even on mechanical devices for electrocuting people. A cord in front of a row of pictures is electrified. A chess-board is electrified. Even a glove is electrified. There is death in every article of furniture, including a tea-urn. But these things seem to have no present application, so we go on to:

"4. It is suicide, which is intended to look like murder. A man stabs himself with an icicle; the icicle melts; and, no weapon being found in the locked room, murder is presumed. A man shoots himself with a gun fastened on the end of an elastic—the gun, as he releases it, being carried up out of sight into the chimney. Variations of this trick (not locked-room affairs) have been the pistol with a string attached to a weight, which is whisked over the parapet of a bridge into the water after the shot; and, in the same style, the pistol jerked out of a window into a snowdrift.

"5. It is a murder which derives its problem from illusion and impersonation. Thus: the victim, still thought to be alive, is already lying murdered inside a room, of which the door is under observation. The murderer, either dressed as his victim or mistaken from behind for the victim, hurries in at the door. He whirls round, gets rid of his disguise, and instantly comes out of the room *as himself*. The illusion is that he has merely passed the other man in coming out. In any event, he has an alibi; since, when the body is discovered later, the murder is presumed to have taken place some time after the impersonated 'victim' entered the room.

"6. It is a murder which, although committed by somebody outside the room at the time, nevertheless seems to have been committed by somebody who must have been inside.

"In explaining this," said Dr. Fell, breaking off, "I will classify this type of murder under the general name of the Long-Distance or Icicle Crime, since it is usually a variation of that principle. I've spoken of icicles; you understand what I mean. The door is locked, the window too small to admit a murderer; yet the victim has apparently been stabbed from inside the room and the weapon is missing. Well, the icicle has been fired as a bullet from outside—we will not discuss whether this is practical, any more than we have discussed the mysterious gases previously mentioned—and it melts without a trace. I believe Anna Katherine Green was the first to use this trick in detective fiction, in a novel called *Initials Only*.

"(By the way, she was responsible for starting a number of traditions. In her first detective novel, over fifty years ago, she founded the legend of the murderous secretary killing his employer, and I think present-day statistics would prove that the secretary is still the commonest murderer in fiction. Butlers have long gone out of fashion; the invalid in the wheel-chair is too suspect; and the placid middle-aged spinster has long ago given up homicidal mania in order to become a detective. Doctors, too, are better behaved nowadays, unless, of course, they grow eminent and turn into Mad Scientists. Lawyers, while they remain persistently crooked, are only in some cases actively dangerous. But cycles return! Edgar Allan Poe, eighty years ago, blew the gaff by calling his murderer Goodfellow; and the most popular modern mystery-writer does precisely the same thing by calling his arch-villain Goodman. Meanwhile, those secretaries are still the most dangerous people to have about the house.)

"To continue with regard to the icicle: Its actual use has been attributed to the Medici, and in one of the admirable Fleming Stone stories an epigram of Martial is quoted to show that it had its deadly origin in Rome in the first century A.D. Well, it has been fired, thrown, or shot from a crossbow as in one adventure of Hamilton Cleek (that magnificent character of the *Forty Faces*). Variants of the same theme, a soluble missile, have been rock-salt bullets and even bullets made of frozen blood.

"But it illustrates what I mean in crimes committed inside a room by somebody who was outside. There are other methods. The victim may be stabbed by a thin swordstick blade, passed between the twinings of a summer-house and withdrawn; or he may be stabbed with a blade so thin that he does not know he is hurt at all, and walks into another room before he suddenly collapses in death. Or he is lured into looking out of a window inaccessible from below; yet from above our old friend ice smashes down on his head, leaving him with a smashed skull but no weapon because the weapon has melted.

"Under this heading (although it might equally well go under head number 3) we might list murders committed by means of poisonous snakes or insects. Snakes can be concealed not only in chests and safes, but also deftly hidden in flowerpots, books, chandeliers, and walking-sticks. I even remember one cheerful little item in which the amber stem of a pipe, grotesquely carven as a scorpion, comes to life a real scorpion as the victim is about to put it into his mouth. But for the greatest long-range murder ever committed in a locked room, gents, I commend you to one of the most brilliant short detective stories in the history of detective fiction. (In fact, it shares the honours for supreme untouchable top-notch excellence with Thomas Burke's, *The Hands of Mr. Ottermole*, Chesterton's, *The Man in the Passage*, and Jacques Futrelle's, *The Problem of Cell 13*.) This is Melville Davisson Post's, *The Doomdorf Mystery*—and the long-range assassin is the sun. The sun strikes through the window of the locked room, makes a burning-glass of a bottle of Doomdorf's own raw white wood-alcohol liquor on the table, and ignites through it the percussion cap of a gun hanging on the wall: so that the breast of the hated one is blown open as he lies in his bed. Then, again, we have . . .

"Steady! Harrumph. Ha. I'd better not meander; I'll round off this classification with the final heading:

"7. This is a murder depending on an effect exactly the reverse of number 5. That is, the victim is presumed to be dead long before he actually is. The victim lies asleep (drugged but unharmed) in a locked room. Knockings on the door fail to rouse him. The murderer starts a foul-play scare; forces the door; gets in ahead and kills by stabbing or throat-cutting, while suggesting to other watchers that they have seen something they have not seen. The honour of inventing this device belongs to Israel Zangwill, and it has since been used in many forms. It has been done (usually by stabbing) on a ship, in a ruined house, in a conservatory, in an attic, and even in the open air—where the victim has first stumbled and stunned himself before the assassin bends over him. So—"

"Steady! Wait a minute!" interposed Hadley, pounding on the table for attention. Dr. Fell, the muscles of whose eloquence were oiling up in a satisfactory way, turned agreeably and beamed on him. Hadley went on: "This may be all very well. You've dealt with all the locked-room situations—"

"All of them?" snorted Dr. Fell, opening his eyes wide. "Of course I haven't. That doesn't even deal comprehensively with the methods under that particular classification; it's only a rough offhand outline; but I'll let it stand. I was going to speak of the other classification: the various means of hocussing doors and windows so that they can be locked on the inside. H'mf! Hah! So, gentlemen, I continue—"

"Not yet you don't," said the superintendent, doggedly. "I'll argue the thing on your own grounds. You say we can get a lead from stating the various ways in which the stunt has been worked. You've stated seven points; but, applied to *this* case, each one must be ruled out according to your own classification-head. You head the whole list, 'No murderer escaped from the room because no murderer was ever actually in it at the time of the crime.' Out goes everything! The one thing we definitely do know, unless we presume Mills and Dumont to be liars, is that the murderer really was in the room! What about that?"

Pettis was sitting forward, his bald head gleaming by the glow of the red-shaded lamp as he bent over an envelope. He was making neat notes with a neat gold pencil. Now he raised his prominent eyes, which seemed more prominent and rather froglike as he studied Dr. Fell.

"Er—yes," he said, with a short cough. "But that point number 5 is suggestive, I should think. Illusion! What if Mills and Mrs. Dumont really didn't see somebody go in that door; that they were hoaxed somehow or that the whole thing was an illusion like a magic-lantern?"

"Illusion me foot," said Hadley. "Sorry! I thought of that, too. I hammered Mills about it last night, and I had another word or two with him this morning. Whatever else the murderer was, he wasn't an illusion and he did go in that door. He was solid enough to cast a shadow and make the hall vibrate when he walked. He was solid enough to talk and slam a door. You agree with that, Fell?"

The doctor nodded disconsolately. He drew in absent puffs on his dead cigar.

"Oh yes, I agree to that. He was solid enough, and he did go in."

"And even," Hadley pursued, while Pettis summoned the waiter to get more coffee, "granting what we know is untrue. Even granting a magic-lantern shadow did all that, a magic-lantern shadow didn't kill Grimaud. It was a solid pistol in a solid hand. And for the rest of the points, Lord knows Grimaud didn't get shot by a mechanical device. What's more, he didn't shoot himself—and have the gun whisk up the chimney like the one in your example. In the first place, a man can't shoot himself from some feet away. And in the second place, the gun can't whisk up the chimney and sail across the roofs to Cagliostro Street, shoot Fley, and tumble down with its work finished. Blast it, Fell, my conversation is getting like yours! It's too much exposure to your habits of thought. I'm expecting a call from the office any minute, and I want to get back to sanity. What's the matter with you?"

Dr. Fell, his little eyes opened wide, was staring at the lamp, and his fist came down slowly on the table.

"Chimney!" he said. "Chimney! Wow! I wonder if—? Lord! Hadley, what an ass I've been!"

"What about the chimney?" asked the superintendent. "We've proved the murderer couldn't have got out like that: getting up the chimney."

"Yes, of course; but I didn't mean that. I begin to get a glimmer, even if it may be a glimmer of moonshine. I must have another look at that chimney."

Pettis chuckled, tapping the gold pencil on his notes. "Anyhow," he suggested, "you may as well round out this discussion. I agree with the superintendent about one thing. You might do better to outline ways of tampering with doors, windows, or chimneys."

"Chimneys, I regret to say," Dr. Fell pursued, his gusto returning as his abstraction left him, "chimneys, I regret to say, are not favoured as a means of escape in detective fiction—except, of course, for secret passages. There they are supreme. There is the hollow chimney with the secret room behind; the back of the fireplace opening like a curtain; the fireplace that swings out; even the room under the hearthstone. Moreover, all kinds of things can be dropped *down* chimneys, chiefly poisonous things. But the murderer who makes his escape by climbing up is very rare. Besides being next to impossible, it is a much grimier business than monkeying with doors or windows. Of the two chief classifications, doors and windows, the door is by far the more popular, and we may list thus a few means of tampering with it so that it seems to be locked on the inside:

"1. Tampering with the key which is still in the lock. This was the favourite old-fashioned method, but its variations are too well-known nowadays for anybody to use it seriously. The stem of the key can be gripped and turned with pliers from outside; we did this ourselves to *open* the door of Grimaud's study. One practical little mechanism consists of a thin metal bar about two inches long, to which is attached a length of stout string. Before leaving the room, this bar is thrust into the hole at the head of the key, one end under and one end over, so that it acts as a lever; the string is dropped down and run under the door to the outside. The door is closed from outside. You have only to pull on the string, and the lever turns the lock; you then shake or pull out the loose bar by means of the string, and, when it drops, draw it under the door to you. There are various applications of this same principle, all entailing the use of string.

"2. Simply removing the hinges of the door without disturbing lock or bolt. This is a neat trick, known to most schoolboys when they want to burgle a locked cupboard; but of course the hinges must be on the outside of the door.

"3. Tampering with the bolt. String again: this time with a mechanism of pins and darning-needles, by which the bolt is shot from the outside by leverage of a pin stuck on the inside of the door, and the string is worked through the keyhole. Philo Vance, to whom my hat is lifted, has shown us this best application of the stunt. There are simpler, but not so effective, variations using one piece of string. A 'tomfool' knot, which a sharp jerk will straighten out, is looped in one end of a long piece of cord. This loop is passed round the knob of the bolt, down, and under the door. The door is then closed, and, by drawing the string along to the left or right, the bolt is shot. A jerk releases the knot from the knob, and the string drawn out. Ellery Queen has shown us still another method, entailing the use of the dead man himself—but a bald statement of this, taken out of its context, would sound so wild as to be unfair to that brilliant gentleman.

"4. Tampering with a falling bar or latch. This usually consists in propping something under the latch, which can be pulled away after the door is closed from the outside, and let the bar drop. The best method by far is by the use of the ever-helpful ice, a cube of which is propped under the latch; and, when it melts, the latch falls. There is one case in which the mere slam of the door suffices to drop the bar inside.

"5. An illusion, simple but effective. The murderer, after committing his crime, has locked the door from the outside and kept the key. It is assumed, however, that the key is still in the lock on the inside. The murderer, who is first to raise a scare and find the body, smashes the upper glass panel of the door, puts his hand through with the key concealed in it, and 'finds' the key in the lock inside, by which he opens the door. This device has also been used with the breaking of a panel out of an ordinary wooden door.

"There are miscellaneous methods, such as locking a door from the outside and returning the key to the room by means of string again, but you can see for yourselves that in this case none of them can have any application. We found the door locked on the inside. Well, there are many ways by which it could have been done—but it was *not* done, because Mills was watching the door the whole time. This room was only locked in a technical sense. It was watched, and that shoots us all to blazes."

"I don't like to drag in famous platitudes," said Pettis, his forehead wrinkled, "but it would seem pretty sound to say exclude the impossible and whatever remains, however improbable, must be the truth. You've excluded the door; I presume you also exclude the chimney?"

"I do," grunted Dr. Fell.

"Then we come back in a circle to the window, don't we?" demanded Hadley. "You've gone on and on about ways that obviously couldn't have been used. But in this catalogue of sensationalism you've omitted all mention of the only means of exit the murderer *could* have used. . . ."

"Because it wasn't a locked window, don't you see?" cried Dr. Fell. "I can tell you several brands of funny business with windows if they're only locked.

It can be traced down from the earliest dummy nail-heads to the latest hocus-pocus with steel shutters. You can smash a window, carefully turn its catch to lock it, and then, when you leave, simply replace the whole pane with a new pane of glass and putty it round; so that the new pane looks like the original and the window is locked inside. But this window wasn't locked or even closed—it was only inaccessible."

"I seem to have read somewhere of human flies . . ." Pettis suggested.

Dr. Fell shook his head. "We won't debate whether a human fly can walk on a sheer smooth wall. Since I've cheerfully accepted so much, I might believe that if the fly had any place to light. That is, he would have to start from somewhere and end somewhere. But he didn't; not on the roof, not on the ground below. . . ." Dr. Fell hammered his fists against his temples. "However, if you want a suggestion or two in that respect, I will tell you—"

He stopped, raising his head. At the end of the quiet, now deserted dining-room a line of windows showed pale light now flickering with snow. A figure had darted in silhouette against them, hesitating, peering from side to side, and then hurrying down towards them. Hadley uttered a muffled exclamation as they saw it was Mangan. Mangan was pale.

"Not something else?" asked Hadley, as coolly as he could. He pushed back his chair. "Not something else about coats changing colour or—"

"No," said Mangan. He stood by the table, drawing his breath in gasps. "But you'd better get over there. Something's happened to Drayman; apoplectic stroke or something like that. No, he's not dead or anything. But he's in a bad way. He was trying to get in touch with you when he had the stroke. . . . He keeps talking wildly about somebody in his room, and fireworks, and chimneys."

## XVIII

### The Chimney

AGAIN there were three people—three people strained and with frayed nerves —waiting in the drawing-room. Even Stuart Mills, who stood with his back to the fireplace, kept clearing his throat in a way that seemed to drive Rosette half frantic. Ernestine Dumont sat quietly by the fire when Mangan led in Dr. Fell, Hadley, Pettis, and Rampole. The lights had been turned off; only the bleakness of the snow-shadowed afternoon penetrated through heavy lace curtains, and Mills' shadow blocked the tired gleam of the fire. Burnaby had gone.

"You cannot see him," said the woman, with her eyes fixed on that shadow. "The doctor is with him now. Things all come at once. Probably he is mad."

Rosette, her arms folded, had been pacing about with her own feline grace. She faced the newcomers and spoke with harsh suddenness.

"I can't stand this, you know. It can go on just so long, and then— *Have* you any idea of what happened? Do you know how my father was killed, or who killed him? For God's sake say something, even if you only accuse me!"

"Suppose you tell us exactly what happened to Mr. Drayman," Hadley said, quietly, "and when it happened. Is he in any grave danger?"

Mme Dumont shrugged. "That is possible. His heart . . . I do not know. He collapsed. He is unconscious now. As to whether he will ever come alive again, that I do not know, either. About what happened to him, we have no idea what caused it. . . ."

Again Mills cleared his throat. His head was in the air, and his fixed smile looked rather ghastly. He said:

"If, sir, you have any idea of—um—foul play, or any suspicion that he was murderously set upon, you may dismiss it. And, strangely enough, you will receive confirmation of it from us in—what shall I say—pairs? I mean that the same people were together this afternoon who were together last night. The Pythoness and I," he bowed gravely towards Ernestine Dumont, "were together upstairs in my little workroom. I am given to understand that Miss Grimaud and our friend Mangan were down here. . . ."

Rosette jerked her head. "You had better hear it from the beginning. Did Boyd tell you about Drayman coming down here first?"

"No, I didn't tell 'em anything," Mangan answered, with some bitterness. "After that business of the overcoat, I wanted somebody to give me a little confirmation." He swung round, the muscles tightening at his temples. "It was about half an hour ago, you see. Rosette and I were here alone. I'd had a row with Burnaby—well, the usual thing. Everybody was yelling and fighting about that overcoat affair, and we'd all separated. Burnaby had gone. I hadn't seen Drayman at all; he'd kept to his room this morning. Anyhow, Drayman walked in here and asked me how he could get in touch with you."

"You mean he had discovered something?"

Rosette sniffed. "Or wanted us to think he had. Very mysterious! He came in with that doddering way of his, and as Boyd says, asked where he could find you. Boyd asked him what was up. . . ."

"Did he act as though he might have—well, found something important?"

"Yes, he did. We both nearly jumped out of our shoes. . . ."

"Why?"

"So would you," said Rosette, coolly, "if you were innocent." She twitched her shoulders, her arms still folded, as though she were cold. "So we said, 'What is it, anyhow?' He doddered a little, and said, 'I've found something missing from my room, and it makes me remember something I'd forgotten about last night.' It was all a lot of nonsense about some subconscious memory, though he wasn't very clear on the point. It came down to some hallucination that, while he was lying down last night after he'd taken the sleeping-powder, somebody had come into his room."

"Before the—crime?"

"Yes."

"Who came into his room?"

"That's it! He either didn't know, or wouldn't say, or else the whole thing was a plain dream. Of course that's probably what it was. I won't suggest," said Rosette, still coolly, "the other alternative. When we asked him, he simply tapped his head, and hedged, and said, 'I really can't say,' in that infuriating way of his. . . . Lord! how I hate these people who won't come out and say what they mean! We both got rather annoyed—"

"Oh, he's all right," said Mangan, whose discomfort appeared to be growing. "Only, damn it all, if I hadn't said what I did . . ."

"Said what?" asked Hadley, quickly.

Mangan hunched his shoulders and looked moodily at the fire. "I said, 'Well, if you've discovered so much, why don't you go up to the scene of the 'orrid murder and see if you can't discover some more?' Yes, I was sore. He took me seriously. He looked at me for a minute and said: 'Yes, I believe I will. I had better make sure.' And with that out he went! It was maybe twenty minutes later that we heard a noise like somebody banging downstairs. . . . You see, we hadn't left the room, although—" He checked himself suddenly.

"You might as well go on and say it," Rosette told him, with an air of surprised indifference. "I don't mind who knows it. I wanted to sneak up after him and watch him. But we didn't. After that twenty minutes, we heard him blundering downstairs. Then, apparently when he'd just got to the last step, we heard a choking sound and a thud—*flap*, like that. Boyd opened the door, and there he was lying doubled up. His face was all congested, and the veins up round the forehead were standing out in a blue colour; horrible business! Of course we sent for the doctor. He hasn't said anything except to rave about 'chimneys' and 'fireworks.'"

Ernestine Dumont still remained stolid, her eyes not moving from the fire. Mills took a little hopping step forward.

"If you will allow me to take up the story," he said, inclining his head, "I think it probable that I can fill the gap. That is, of course, with the Pythoness' permission. . . ."

"Ah, bah!" the woman cried. Her face was in shadow as she looked up, there was about her a rigidity as of whalebone, but Rampole was startled to see that her eyes blazed. "You must always act the fool, must you not? The Pythoness this, the Pythoness that. Very well, I must tell you. I am Pythoness enough to know that you did not like poor Drayman, and that

my little Rosette does not like him, either. God! what do you know of human
men or sympathy or . . . Drayman is a good man, even if he may be a little
mad. He may be mistaken. He may be full of drugs. But he is a good man
at the heart, and if he dies I shall pray for his soul."

"Shall I—er—go on?" observed Mills, imperturbably.

"Yes, you shall go on," the woman mimicked, and was silent.

"The Pythoness and I were in my workroom on the top floor; opposite
the study, as you know. And again the door was open. I was shifting some
papers, and I noticed Mr. Drayman come up and go into the study . . ."

"Do you know what he did there?" asked Hadley.

"Unfortunately, no. He closed the door. I could not even venture a deduction as to what he might be doing, since I could hear nothing. After
some time he came out, in what I can only describe as a panting and unsteady condition—"

"What do you mean by that?"

Mills frowned. "I regret, sir, that it is impossible to be more precise. I
can only say that I received an impression as though he had been indulging
in violent exercise. This, I have no doubt, caused or hastened the collapse,
since there were clear evidences of an apoplectic stroke. If I may correct
the Pythoness, it had nothing to do with his heart. Er—I might add something which has not yet been mentioned. When he was picked up after the
stroke, I observed that his hands and sleeves were covered with soot."

"The chimney again," Pettis murmured, very softly, and Hadley turned
round towards Dr. Fell. It gave Rampole a shock to see that the doctor was
no longer in the room. A person of his weight and girth can, as a rule, make
small success of an effort to fade mysteriously away; but he was gone, and
Rampole thought he knew where.

"Follow him up there," Hadley said quickly to the American. "And see
that he doesn't work any of his blasted mystification. Now, Mr. Mills—"

Rampole heard Hadley's questions probing and crackling as he went out
into the sombre hall. The house was very quiet; so quiet that, as he mounted
the stairs, the sudden shrilling of the telephone bell in the lower hall made
him jump a little. Passing Drayman's door upstairs, he heard hoarse breathing
inside, and quiet footfalls tiptoeing about the room: through the door he
could see the doctor's medicine-case and hat on a chair. No lights burned
on the top floor; again such a stillness that he could distinctly hear Annie's
voice answering the telephone far below.

The study was dusky. Despite the few snowflakes, some faint lurid light,
dull red-and-orange with sunset, glimmered through the window. It made a
stormy glow across the room; it kindled the colours of the shield of arms,
glittered on the crossed fencing-foils above the fireplace, and made vast and
shadowy the white busts on the bookshelves. The shape of Charles Grimaud,
half-studious, half-barbaric like the room, seemed to move and chuckle here

after Charles Grimaud was dead. That vast blank space in the panelled wall, where the picture was to have hung, faced Rampole in mockery. And, standing motionless in his black cloak before the window, Dr. Fell leaned on his cane and stared out into the sunset.

The creaking of the door did not rouse him. Rampole, his voice seeming to make echoes, said:

"Did you—?"

Dr. Fell blinked round. His breath, when he puffed it out with a sort of weary explosiveness, turned to smoke in the sharp air.

"Eh? Oh! Did I what?"

"Find anything."

"Well, I think I know the truth. I think I know the truth," he answered, with a sort of reflective stubbornness, "and tonight I shall probably be able to prove it. H'mf. Hah. Yes. D'ye see, I've been standing here wondering what to do about it. It's the old problem, son, and it becomes more difficult each year I live: when the sky grows nobler, and the old chair more comfortable, and maybe the human heart—" He brushed his hand across his forehead. "What is justice? I've asked it at the end of nearly every case I ever handled. I see faces rise, and sick souls and bad dreams. . . . No matter. Shall we go downstairs?"

"But what about the fireplace?" insisted Rampole. He went over, peered at it, hammered it, and still he could see nothing out of the way. A little soot had been scattered on the hearth, and there was a crooked streak in the coating of soot on the back of the fireplace. "What's wrong with it? Is there a secret passage, after all?"

"Oh no. There's nothing wrong with it in the way you mean. Nobody got up there. No," he added, as Rampole put his hand into the long opening of the flue and groped round. "I'm afraid you're wasting your time; there's nothing up there to find."

"But," said Rampole, desperately, "if this brother Henri—"

"Yes," said a heavy voice from the doorway, "brother Henri."

The voice was so unlike Hadley's that at the moment they did not recognize it. Hadley stood in the doorway, a sheet of paper crumpled in his hand; his face was in shadow, but there was such a dull quietness in his tones that Rampole recognized something like despair. Closing the door softly behind him, Hadley stood in the darkening and went on calmly:

"It was our own fault, I know, for being hypnotized by a theory. It ran away with us—and now we've got to start the whole case afresh. Fell, when you said this morning that the case had been turned upside down, I don't believe you knew just how true it was. It's not only upside down; it's nonexistent. Our chief prop is knocked to blazes. Damn the rotten, impossible . . . !" He stared at the sheet of paper as though he meant to crush it into a ball. "A phone-call just came through from the Yard. They've heard from Bucharest."

"I'm afraid I know what you're going to say," Dr. Fell nodded. "You're going to say that brother Henri—"

"*There is no brother Henri,*" said Hadley. "*The third of the three Horváth brothers died over thirty years ago.*"

.    .    .    .    .    .    .    .    .    .    .

The faint reddish light had grown muddy; in the cold, quiet study they could hear from far away the mutter of London awaking towards nightfall. Walking over to the broad desk, Hadley spread out the crumpled sheet on the desk so that the others could read. The shadow of the yellow jade buffalo lay across it sardonically. Across the room they could see the slashes gaping in the picture of the three graves.

"There's no possibility of a mistake," Hadley went on. "The case is a very well-known one, it seems. The whole cablegram they sent was very long, but I've copied the important parts verbatim from what they read over the phone. Take a look."

No difficulty about information desired [it ran]. Two men now in my personal service were at Siebenturmen as warders in 1900, and confirm record. Facts: Károly Grimaud Horváth, Pierre Fley Horváth, and Nicholas Revéi Horváth were sons of Professor Károly Horváth (of Klausenburg University) and Cécile Fley Horváth (French) his wife. For robbery of Kunar Bank at Brasso, November, 1898, the three brothers were sentenced, January, 1899, to twenty years' penal servitude. Bank watchman died of injuries inflicted, and loot never recovered; believed to have been hidden. All three, with aid of prison doctor during plague scare of August, 1900, made daring attempt at escape by being certified as dead, and buried in plague-ground. J. Lahner and R. Görgei, warders, returning to graves an hour later with wooden crosses for marking, noticed disturbance had taken place on earth at grave of Károly Horváth. Investigation showed coffin open and empty. Digging into other two graves, warders found Pierre Horváth bloody and insensible, but still alive. Nicholas Horváth had already suffocated to death. Nicholas reburied after absolute certainty made the man was dead; Pierre returned to prison. Scandal hushed up, no chase of fugitive, and story never discovered until end of war. Pierre Fley Horváth never mentally responsible afterwards. Released January, 1919, having served full term. Assure you no doubt whatever third brother dead.

                                        —ALEXANDER CUZA, Policedirector, Bucharest.

"Oh yes," said Hadley, when they had finished reading. "It confirms the reconstruction right enough, except for the little point that we've been chasing a ghost as the murderer. Brother Henri (or brother Nicholas, to be exact) never did leave his grave. He's there yet. And the whole case . . ."

Dr. Fell rapped his knuckles slowly on the paper.

"It's my fault, Hadley," he admitted. "I told you this morning that I'd come close to making the biggest mistake of my life. I was hypnotized by brother Henri! I couldn't think of anything else. You see now why we knew so remarkably little about that third brother, so little that with my cursed cocksuredness I put all kinds of fantastic interpretations on it?"

"Well, it won't do us any good just to admit the mistake. How the devil are we going to explain all those crazy remarks of Fley's now? Private vendetta! Vengeance! Now that that's swept away, we haven't a lead to work on. Not one lead! And, if you exclude the motive of vengeance on Grimaud and Fley, what is there left?"

Dr. Fell pointed rather malevolently with his stick.

"Don't you see what's left?" he roared. "Don't you see the explanation of those two murders that we've got to accept now or retire to the madhouse?"

"You mean that somebody cooked up the whole thing to make it look like the work of an avenger?—I'm at the state now," explained the superintendent, "where I could believe nearly anything. But that strikes me as being a good bit too subtle. How would the real murderer ever know we could dig so far into the past? We'd never have done it if it hadn't been, saving your presence, for a few lucky shots. How would the real murderer know we should ever connect Professor Grimaud with a Hungarian criminal, or connect him with Fley or any of the rest of it? It strikes me as a false trail far *too* well concealed." He paced up and down, driving his fist into his palm. "Besides, the more I think of it the more confusing it gets! We had damned good reason to think it was the third brother who killed those two . . . and, the more I think of that possibility, the more I'm inclined to doubt that Nicholas is dead. Grimaud *said* his third brother shot him!—and when a man's dying, and knows he's dying, what earthly reason would he have for lying? Or . . . Stop a bit! Do you suppose he might have meant *Fley*? Do you suppose Fley came here, shot Grimaud, and then afterwards somebody else shot Fley? It would explain a lot of the puzzles—"

"But," said Rampole, "excuse the interruption, I mean, but it wouldn't explain why Fley kept talking about a third brother as well! Either brother Henri is dead or he isn't. Still, if he is dead, what reason have both victims got to lie about him all the time? If he's really dead, he must be one hell of a live ghost."

Hadley shook the briefcase. "I know. That's exactly what I'm kicking about! We've got to take somebody's word for it, and it seems more reasonable to take the word of two people who were shot by him, rather than this cablegram which might be influenced or mistaken for several reasons. Or—h'm! Suppose he really is dead, but the murderer is pretending to be that dead brother come to life?" He stopped, nodded, and stared out of the window. "Now I think we're getting warm. That would explain all the inconsistencies, wouldn't it? The real murderer assumes the rôle of a man neither of the other brothers has seen for nearly thirty years; well? When the murders are committed, and we get on his track—if we do get on his track—we put it all down to vengeance. How's that, Fell?"

Dr. Fell, scowling heavily, stumped round the table.

"Not bad . . . no, not bad, as a disguise. But what about the motive for which Grimaud and Fley were really killed?"

"How do you mean?"

"There has to be a connecting thread, hasn't there? There might be any number of motives, plain or obscure, why a person would kill Grimaud. Mills or Dumont or Burnaby or—yes, anybody *might* have killed Grimaud. Also, anybody might have killed Fley: but not, I must point out, anybody in the same circle or group of people. Why should Fley be killed by a member of Grimaud's group, none of whom had presumably ever seen him before? If these murders are the work of one person, where is the connecting link? A respected professor in Bloomsbury and a tramp actor with a prison record. Where's the human motive that ties those two together in the murderer's mind, unless it is a link that goes back into the past?"

"I can think of one person who is associated with both from the past," Hadley pointed out.

"Who? You mean the Dumont woman?"

"Yes."

"Then what becomes of somebody impersonating brother Henri? Whatever else you decide on, you must decide that she's not doing that. No, my lad. Dumont is not only a bad suspect; she's an impossible suspect."

"I don't see that. Look here, you're basing your whole belief that Dumont didn't kill Grimaud on the grounds that you think she loved Grimaud. No defence, Fell—no defence at all! Remember that she told the whole fantastic story to begin with . . ."

"In coöperation with—Mills," boomed Dr. Fell, with a sardonic leer. He was puffing again. "Can you think of any two less likely conspirators to band together at the dark of the moon and hoodwink the police with their imaginative fairy-tales? She might wear a mask; I mean a figurative mask in life. Mills might wear a mask. But the combination of those two masks, and their activities, is too much. I prefer the one literal false face. Besides, bear in mind that as the double killer Ernestine D. is absolutely O-U-T. Why? Because, at the time of Fley's death sworn to by three good men and true, she was here in this room, talking to us." He pondered, and a twinkle began to appear in his eye. "Or will you drag in the second generation? Rosette is Grimaud's daughter; suppose the mysterious Stuart Mills is really the son of the dead brother Henri?"

About to reply, Hadley checked himself and studied Dr. Fell. He sat down on the edge of the desk.

"I know this mood. I know it very well," he asserted, with the air of one who confirms a sinister suspicion. "It's the beginning of some more blasted mystification, and there's no use arguing with you now. Why are you so anxious for me to believe the story?"

"First," said Dr. Fell, "because I wish to force it into your head that Mills told the truth. . . ."

"You mean, as a point in the mystification, in order to prove later that he didn't? The sort of low trick you played me in that Death Watch case?"

The doctor ignored this with a testy grunt. "And, second, because I know the real murderer."

"Who is somebody we've seen and talked to?"

"Oh yes; very much so."

"And have we got a chance of—?"

Dr. Fell, an absent, fierce, almost pitying expression on his red face, stared for some time at the desk.

"Yes, Lord help us all," he said, in a curious tone, "I suppose you've got to. In the meantime, I'm going home. . . ."

"Home?"

"To apply Gross's test," said Dr. Fell.

He turned away, but he did not immediately go. As the muddy light deepened to purple, and dust-coloured shadows swallowed up the room, he remained for a long time staring at the slashed picture which caught the last glow with its turbulent power, and the three coffins that were filled at last.

XIX

*The Hollow Man*

THAT night Dr. Fell shut himself up in the small cubbyhole off the library which was reserved for what he called his scientific experiments and what Mrs. Fell called "that horrible messing about." Now, a liking for messing about is one of the best of human traits, and Rampole and Dorothy both offered to assist. But the doctor was so serious, and so unwontedly troubled, that they left off with an uncomfortable feeling that to make a joke would be bad taste. The tireless Hadley had already gone off to check alibis. Rampole left the matter with only one question.

"I know you're going to try to read those burnt letters," he said, "and I know you think they're important. But what do you expect to find?"

"The worst possible thing," replied Dr. Fell. "The thing that last night could have made a fool of me."

And with a sleepy shake of his head he closed the door.

Rampole and Dorothy sat on opposite sides of the fireplace, looking at each other. The snow was whirling outside, and it was not a night to venture far. Rampole at first had an idea that he ought to invite Mangan out to dinner, to renew old times; but Mangan, when he telephoned, said that obviously Rosette could not go, and he had better remain with her. So the other two, Mrs. Fell being at church, had the library to themselves for argument.

"Ever since last night," commented her husband, "I've been hearing about Gross's method for reading burnt letters. But nobody seems to know what it is. I suppose you mix chemicals or something?"

"I know what it is," she told him, with an air of triumph. "I looked it up while you people were dashing about this afternoon. And what's more, I bet you it won't work even if it is simple. I bet you *anything* it won't work!"

"You read Gross?"

"Well, I read it in English. It's simple enough. It says something like this. It says that anybody who has thrown letters on the fire will have noticed that the writing on the charred fragments stands out quite clearly, usually white or grey against a black background, but sometimes with the colours reversed. Did you ever notice that?"

"Can't say I have. But then I've seen very few open fires before I came to England. Is it true?"

She frowned. "It works with cardboard boxes that have printing on them, boxes of soap flakes or things like that. But regular writing. . . . Anyway, here's what you're supposed to do. You get a lot of transparent tracing-paper and pin it to a board with drawing-pins. As you pick up each of the charred pieces of paper you cover a place on the tracing-paper with gum, press the charred paper down on it. . . ."

"When it's crumpled up like that? It'll break, won't it?"

"Aha! That's the trick, Gross says. You have to soften the fragments. You arrange over and around the tracing-paper a frame two or three inches high, with all the bits under it. Then you stretch across a damp cloth folded several times. That puts the papers in a damp atmosphere, and they straighten out. When they're all flattened out and fixed, you cut out the tracing-paper round each separate fragment. Then you reconstruct them on a sheet of glass. Like a jig-saw puzzle. Afterwards you press a second sheet of glass over the first, and bind the edges, and look through both against the light. But I'll bet you anything you like—"

"We'll try it," said Rampole, impressed and afire with the idea.

The experiments at burning paper were not a complete success. First he got an old letter out of his pocket and touched a match to it. Despite his frantic manœuvring, it soared up into flame, twitched round, sailed out of his hand, and shrank to rest on the hearth as not more than two inches of shrivelled blackness rolled up like an umbrella. Though they got down on their knees and scrutinized it from every angle, no writing was visible. Rampole burnt several more pieces, which sailed apart like gentle skyrockets and powdered the hearth. Then he began to get mad and burn everything within reach. And, the madder he got, the more convinced he grew that the trick could be worked somehow if he did it properly. Typewriting was tried; he tapped out "Now is the time for all good men to come to the aid of the party" a number of times on Dr. Fell's machine; and presently the carpet was littered with floating fragments.

"Besides," he argued, with his cheek against the floor and one eye closed as he studied them, "these aren't charred—they're burnt to hell. They're too far gone to fulfill the conditions. Aha! Got it! I can see 'party' as plain as day. It's much smaller than the actual typing; it seems to be indented on the black; but here it is. Have you got anything out of that handwritten letter?"

Her own excitement was growing as she made a discovery. The words "East 11th Street" stood out in dirty grey letters. With some care, but much powdering of the brittle pieces, they at last deciphered plainly the words, "Saturday night," "ginch," "hangover," and "gin." Rampole got up with satisfaction.

"If those pieces can be straightened out by dampness, then it works!" he declared. "The only thing is whether you could get enough words out of any letter to make sense of it. Besides, we're only amateurs; Gross could get the whole thing. But what does Dr. Fell expect to find?"

This was the subject of an argument which was carried on far into the night.

"And with the case turned upside down," Rampole pointed out, "where do we go now for a motive? That's the crux of the whole business. There's no motive that could connect both Grimaud and Fley with the murderer! By the way, what's become of your wild theories last night, that the guilty person must be either Pettis or Burnaby?"

"Or the funny-faced blonde," she corrected, with a certain emphasis on the term. "I say, you know, what bothers me most is that overcoat changing colour and disappearing and all the rest of it. It seems to lead straight back to that house, or does it?" She brooded. "No, I've changed my mind altogether. I don't think Pettis or Burnaby can be implicated. I don't even think the blonde is. The possible murderer, I'm certain now, can be narrowed down to two other people."

"Well?"

"It's either Drayman or O'Rourke," she said, firmly, and nodded. "You mark my words."

Rampole stifled a strong protest. "Yes, I'd thought of O'Rourke," he admitted. "But you're picking him for just two reasons. First because he's a trapeze man, and you associate a flying escape of some sort with the way this thing was done. But, so far as I can see, it's impossible. Second and more

important, you're picking him for the reason that he doesn't seem to have
any connection with this case at all; that he's standing around for no good
reason, and that's always a suspicious sign. Isn't that so?"

"Maybe."

"Then Drayman . . . yes, Drayman might have been the only one who
could now be associated with both Grimaud and Fley in the past. That's a
point! H'm. Also, nobody saw him during the whole evening from dinner
time until a much later hour—eleven o'clock, anyhow. But I don't believe he's
guilty. Tell you what: let's make a rough time-table of last night's events
to get this thing straightened out. We'll put in everything, from before dinner
on. It'll have to be a very rough time-table, with a lot of guessing on smaller
points. We don't know much definitely except the time of the actual murders
and a few statements leading up to them, but we can make a stab at it. Our
times before dinner are vague too. But let's say . . ."

He took out an envelope and wrote rapidly.

(About)  6:45  Mangan arrives, hangs his coat in the hall closet, and sees a
                black overcoat hanging there.
(About)  6:48  (give her three minutes) Annie comes from the dining-
                room, switches off the light in the hall closet left burning
                by Mangan, and sees no overcoat at all.
(About)  6:55  (this is not specified, but we know it was before dinner),
                Mme Dumont looks into the hall closet and sees a yellow
                overcoat.

"I arrange it like that," said Rampole, "because presumably in the very
brief time between Mangan's hanging up his own coat and going away
with the light left on, Dumont didn't rush out to look in there before Annie
came to turn the light off."

The girl's eyes narrowed. "Oo, wait! How do you know that? I mean, if
the light wasn't on, how did she see a yellow coat at all?"

There was a pause while they looked at each other. Rampole said:

"This is getting interesting. And, if it comes to that, why did she look
in there, anyhow? The point is this: If the sequence of times can be established at what I've written, that's reasonable. First, there's a black coat,
which Mangan sees. Well, then somebody swipes the black coat just after
Mangan goes—for what reason we don't know—and Annie sees nothing. Later
the coat is replaced with a light tweed one. That sounds all right. *But*," he
cried, stabbing out with his pencil, "if it worked the other way around, then
either somebody is lying or the whole thing is impossible. In that case it
doesn't matter what time Mangan arrived, because the whole business must
have taken place in a matter of minutes or even seconds. See it? Boyd gets
there, hangs his coat up, and walks away. Out comes Dumont, looks in, and
walks away. Along comes Annie immediately afterwards, turns out the light,

and *she* goes. In that short flash a black overcoat has first turned yellow
and then disappeared. Which is impossible."

"Well done!" said the other, beaming. "Then which one was lying? I
suppose you'll insist it wasn't your friend—"

"I certainly will. It's the Dumont woman, I'll bet you anything you like!"

"But she's not guilty. That's been proved. Besides, I like her."

"Don't mix me up, now," Rampole urged. "Let's go on with this time-
table and see if we can discover anything else. Haa! Where were we?
Yes. Dinner we'll put at seven o'clock, because we know it was over at
seven-thirty. Hence—

"7:30 Rosette G. and Mangan go to drawing-room.
7:30 Drayman goes upstairs to his room.
7:30 E. Dumont—where she goes is not known, except that she remains
        in the house.
7:30 Mills goes to downstairs library.
7:30 Grimaud joins Mills in downstairs library, tells him to come up-
        stairs about 9:30, since he expects a visitor then.

"Whoa! Here's a snag. I was just going to write that then Grimaud goes
on to the drawing-room, and tells Mangan the visitor is expected at ten
o'clock. But that won't do, because Rosette knew nothing about it, and yet
she was with Mangan! The trouble is, Boyd didn't say exactly when he was
told that. But it isn't important—Grimaud might have taken him aside or
something like that. Similarly, we don't know when Madame Dumont was
told to expect the visitor at nine-thirty; probably earlier. It amounts to the
same thing."

"Are you sure it does?" enquired Dorothy, searching after cigarettes.
"H'm! Well, carry on."

"(About) 7:35 Grimaud goes up to his study.
            7:35 to 9:30 no developments. Nobody moves. Heavy snow.
(About) 9:30 snow stops.
(About) 9:30 E. Dumont collects coffee-tray from Grimaud's study.
            Grimaud remarks that visitor will probably not come that
            night. E. Dumont leaves study just as—
            9:30 Mills comes upstairs.

"I don't think anything noticeable happened in the next interval. Mills
was upstairs, Drayman in his room, and Rosette and Boyd in the front room
with the radio on. . . . Wait! I'm forgetting something. A little while before the door-bell rang, Rosette heard a thud from somewhere out in the
street, as though somebody had fallen off a high place. . . ."

"How did she hear that if they had the radio on?"

"Apparently it wasn't playing loudly enough to— Yes, it was, though. It made such a racket they could hardly hear the fake 'Pettis's' voice. But put that in order:

> "9:45 Door-bell rings.
> 9:45 to 9:50. E. Dumont goes to answer door; speaks to visitor (failing to recognize voice). She receives card, shuts the door on him, examines card and finds it blank, hesitates, and starts upstairs. . . .
> 9:45 to 9:50. Visitor, after E. D. has started upstairs, gets inside somehow, locks Rosette G. and Boyd M. in front room, answers their hail by imitating the voice of Pettis—"

"I don't like to keep on interrupting you," cut in Dorothy. "But doesn't it seem to have taken them a terribly long time to sing out and ask who the caller was? I mean, would anybody wait so long? If I were expecting a visitor like that, I know I should have piped up, 'Hullo! who is it?' as soon as I heard the door open."

"What are you trying to prove? Nothing? Sure of that? Don't be so hard on the blonde! It was some time before they expected anybody, remember —and that sniff of yours indicates prejudice. Let's continue, with the still inclusive times of nine forty-five to nine-fifty, the interval between the moment X entered the house and the moment he entered Grimaud's study:

> "9:45 to 9:50. Visitor follows E. Dumont upstairs, overtakes her in upper hall. He takes off cap and pulls down coat collar, but does not remove mask. Grimaud comes to the door, but does not recognize visitor. Visitor leaps inside and door is slammed. (This is attested by both E. Dumont and S. Mills.)
> 9:50 to 10:10. Mills watches door from end of hall; Dumont watches same door from staircase landing.
> 10:10 Shot is fired.
> 10:10 to 10:12. Mangan in front room finds door to hall locked, on the inside.
> 10:10 to 10:12. E. Dumont faints or is sick, and gets to her room. (N. B. Drayman, asleep in his room, does not hear shot.)
> 10:10 to 10:12. Mangan in front room finds door to hall locked, attempts to break it and fails. He then jumps out window, just as—
> 10:12 We arrive outside; front door unlocked; we go up to study.
> 10:12 to 10:15. Door is opened with pliers, Grimaud found shot.
> 10:15 to 10:20. Investigation, ambulance sent for.
> 10:20 Ambulance arrives. Grimaud removed. Rosette goes with him in ambulance. Boyd M., at orders from Hadley, goes downstairs to telephone police.

"Which," Rampole pointed out with some satisfaction, "absolutely clears both Rosette and Boyd. I don't even need to set down minute times there. The ambulance-men coming upstairs, the doctor's examination, the body taken down to the ambulance—all that in itself would have taken at least five minutes if they'd moved fast enough to slide down the banisters with that stretcher. By God! it's as plain as print when you write it out! It would have taken a good deal longer before they could get to the nursing-home . . . and yet Fley was shot in Cagliostro Street at just ten twenty-five! Now, Rosette did ride over with the ambulance. Boyd was in the house when the ambulance-men arrived, because he came upstairs with them and went down after them. There's a fairly perfect alibi."

"Oh, you don't need to think I'm so anxious to convict them!—especially Boyd, who's rather nice what little I've seen of him." She frowned. "That's always granting your guess that the ambulance didn't arrive at Grimaud's before ten-twenty."

Rampole shrugged. "If it did," he pointed out, "then it flew over from Guilford Street. It wasn't sent for before ten-fifteen, and even so it's something like a miracle that they had it at Grimaud's in five minutes. No, Boyd and Rosette are out of it. Besides, now that I remember, she was at the nursing-home—in the presence of witnesses—when she saw the light in the window of Burnaby's flat at ten-thirty. Let's put the rest into the record and exonerate anyone else we can.

"10:20 to 10:25. Arrival and departure of ambulance with Grimaud.
    10:25 Fley shot in Cagliostro Street.
    10:20 to (at least) 10:30. Stuart Mills remains with us in study, answering questions.
    10:25 Madame Dumont comes into study.
    10:30 Rosette, at nursing-home, sees a light in the window of Burnaby's flat.
    10:25 to 10:40. Madame Dumont remains with us in the study.
    10:40 Rosette returns from nursing-home.
    10:40 Arrival of police at Hadley's call."

Rampole, sitting back to run his eye down the scrawl, drew a long flourish under the last item.

"That not only completes our time-table as far as we need to go," he said, "but it unquestionably adds two more to our list of innocents. Mills and Dumont are out. Rosette and Boyd are out. Which accounts for everybody in the house except Drayman."

"But," protested Dorothy, after a pause, "it's getting even worse tangled up. What happens to your brilliant inspiration about the overcoat? You suggested somebody was lying. It could only have been either Boyd Mangan or Ernestine Dumont; and both are exonerated. Unless that girl Annie— But that won't do, will it? Or it shouldn't."

Again they looked at each other. Wryly he folded up his list and put it into his pocket. Outside, the night wind whirled by in a long blast, and they could hear Dr. Fell blundering round his cubbyhole behind the closed door.

Rampole overslept the next morning, partly from exhaustion and partly because the following day was so overcast that he did not open his eyes until past ten o'clock. It was not only so dark that the lights were on, but a day of numbing cold. He had not seen Dr. Fell again last night, and, when he went downstairs to breakfast in the little back dining-room, the maid was indignant as she set out bacon and eggs.

"The doctor's just gone up to have a wash, sir," Vida informed him. "He was up all night on them scientific things, and I found him asleep in the chair in there at eight o'clock this morning. I don't know what Mrs. Fell will say, indeed I don't. Superintendent Hadley's just got here, too. He's in the library."

Hadley, who was impatiently knocking his heels against the fender as though he were pawing the floor, asked for news with some eagerness.

"Have you seen Fell?" he demanded. "Did he go after those letters? And if so—?"

Rampole explained. "Any news from you?"

"Yes, and important news. Both Pettis and Burnaby are out. They've got cast-iron alibis."

Wind whooped past along Adelphi Terrace, and the long window-frames rattled. Hadley continued to paw the hearth rug. He went on: "I saw Burnaby's three card-playing friends last night. One, by the way, is an Old Bailey judge; it'd be pretty difficult to drag a man into court when the judge on the bench can testify to his innocence. Burnaby was playing poker on Saturday night from eight o'clock to nearly half-past eleven. —And this morning Betts has been round to the theatre where Pettis said he saw the play that night. Well, he did. One of the bar-attendants at the theatre knows him quite well by sight. It seems that the second act of the show ends at five minutes past ten. A few minutes afterwards, during the interval, this attendant is willing to swear he served Pettis with a whisky-and-soda in the bar. In other words, he was having a drink at just about the exact moment Grimaud was shot nearly a mile away."

"I expected something like that," said Rampole, after a silence. "And yet, to hear it confirmed. . . . I wish you'd look at this."

He handed over the time-table he had made last night. Hadley glanced over it.

"Oh yes. I sketched out one of my own. This is fairly sound; especially the point about the girl and Mangan, although we can't swear too closely to time in that respect. But I think it would hold." He tapped the envelope against his palm. "Narrows it down, I admit. We'll have another go at Drayman. I phoned the house this morning. Everybody was a bit hysterical because they've brought the old man's body back to the house, and I couldn't get much out of Rosette except that Drayman was still only half-conscious and under morphia. We—"

He stopped as they heard the familiar, lumbering step with the tap of the cane, which seemed to have hesitated just outside the door as though at Hadley's words. Then Dr. Fell pushed open the door. There was no twinkle in his eye when he wheezed in. He seemed a part of the heavy morning, and a sense of doom pervading that leaden air.

"Well?" prompted Hadley. "Did you find out what you wanted to know from those papers?"

Dr. Fell fumbled after, found, and lit his black pipe. Before he answered he waddled over to toss the match into the fire. Then he chuckled at last, but very wryly.

"Yes, I found out what I wanted to know. —Hadley, twice in my theories on Saturday night I unintentionally led you wrong. So wrong, with such a monstrous and dizzying stupidity, that if I hadn't saved my self-respect by seeing the truth of this thing yesterday, I should have deserved the last punishment reserved for fools. Still, mine wasn't the only blunder. Chance and circumstance made an even worse blunder, and they've combined to make a terrifying, inexplicable puzzle out of what is really only a commonplace and ugly and petty murder-case. Oh, there was shrewdness to the murderer; I admit that. But—yes, I've found out what I wanted to know."

"Well? What about the writing on those papers? What was on those papers?"

"Nothing," said Dr. Fell.

There was something eerie in the slow, heavy way he spoke the word.

"You mean," cried Hadley, "that the experiment didn't work?"

"No, I mean that the experiment did work. I mean that there was *nothing* on those papers," boomed Dr. Fell. "Not so much as a single line or scrap or shred of handwriting, not so much as a whisper or pothook of the deadly secrets I told you on Saturday night we might find. That's what I mean. Except—well, yes. There were a few bits of heavier paper, rather like thick cardboard, with one or two letters printed there."

"But why burn letters unless—?"

"Because they weren't letters. That's just it; that's where we went wrong. Don't you see even yet what they were? . . . Well, Hadley, we'd better finish this up and get the whole mess off our minds. You want to meet the Invisible Murderer, do you? You want to meet the damned ghoul and hollow man who's been walking through our dreams? Very well; I'll introduce you. Got your car? Then come along. *I'm going to see if I can't extract a confession.*"

"From—?"

"From somebody at Grimaud's house. Come on."

Rampole saw the end looming, and was afraid of it, without an idea in his whirling head as to what it might be. Hadley had to spin a half-frozen engine before the car would start. They were caught in several traffic blocks on the way up, but Hadley did not even curse. And the quietest of all was Dr. Fell.

All the blinds were drawn on the house in Russell Square. It looked even more dead than yesterday, because death had come inside. And it was so quiet that even from outside they could hear the ringing of the bell when Dr. Fell pressed it. After a long interval Annie, without her cap or apron, answered it. She looked pale and strained, but still calm.

"We should like to see Madame Dumont," said Dr. Fell.

Hadley jerked his head round to look, even though he remained impassive. Annie seemed to speak out of the darkness in the hall as she moved back.

"She is in with the—she's in there," the girl answered, and pointed towards the drawing-room door. "I'll call—" She swallowed.

Dr. Fell shook his head. He moved over with surprising quietness and softly opened the drawing-room door.

The dull brown blinds were drawn, and the thick lace curtains muffled what little light filtered through. Although the room looked vaster, its furniture was lost in shadow; except for one piece of furniture, of gleaming black metal lined with white satin. It was an open coffin. Thin candles were burning around it. Of the dead face Rampole afterwards remembered that from where he stood he could see only the tip of a nose. But those candles alone, or the faint thickness of flowers and incense in the air, moved the scene weirdly from dun London to some place of crags and blasts among the Hungarian mountains: where the gold cross loomed guard against devils, and garlic wreaths kept off the prowling vampire.

Yet this was not the thing they first noticed. Ernestine Dumont stood beside the coffin, one hand gripping its edge. The high, thin candle-light above turned her greying hair to gold; it softened and subdued even the crumpled posture of her bent shoulders. When she turned her head slowly round, they saw that her eyes were sunken and smeared—though she still could not weep. Her breast heaved jerkily. Yet round her shoulders she had wound a gay, heavy, long-fringed yellow shawl, with red brocade and bead embroidery that burnt with a shifting glitter under the light. It was the last touch of the barbaric.

And then she saw them. Both hands suddenly gripped the edge of the coffin, as though she would shield the dead. She remained a silhouette, one hand outspread on either side, under the unsteady candles.

"It will do you good, madame, to confess," said Dr. Fell, very gently. "Believe me, it will do you good."

For a second Rampole thought she had stopped breathing, so easy was every motion to follow in the unearthliness of that light. Then she made a sound as though she were half-coughing, which is only grief before it becomes hysterical mirth.

"Confess?" she said. "So that is what you think, all you fools? Well, I do not care. Confess! Confess to murder?"

"No," said Dr. Fell.

His voice, in that one quiet monosyllable, had a heavy note across the room. And now she stared at him, and now for the first time she began to stare with fright as he moved across towards her.

"No," said Dr. Fell. "You are not the murderer. Let me tell you what you are."

Now he towered over her, black against the candle-light, but he still spoke gently.

"Yesterday, you see, a man named O'Rourke told us several things. Among them was the fact that most illusions either on or off the stage are worked with the aid of a confederate. This was no exception. You were the confederate of the illusionist and murderer."

"The hollow man," said Ernestine Dumont, and suddenly began to laugh hysterically.

"The hollow man," said Dr. Fell, and turned quietly to Hadley, "in a real sense. The hollow man whose naming was a terrible and an ironic jest, even if we did not know it, because it was the exact truth. That is the horror and in a way the shame. Do you want to see the murderer you have been hunting all through this case?—The murderer lies *there*," said Dr. Fell, "but God forbid that we should judge him now."

And with a slow gesture he pointed to the white, dead, tight-lipped face of Dr. Charles Grimaud.

## XX

### *The Two Bullets*

DR. FELL continued to look steadily at the woman, who had again shrunk against the side of the coffin as though to defend it.

"Ma'am," he went on, "the man you loved is dead. He is beyond the reach of the law now, and, whatever he has done, he has paid for it. Our immediate problem, yours and mine, is to hush this thing up so that the living may not be hurt. But, you see, you are implicated, even though you took no actual hand in the murder. Believe me, ma'am, if I could have explained the whole thing without bringing you into it at all, I should have done so. I know have suffered. But you will see for yourself that such a course was impossible if I were to explain the entire problem. So we must persuade Superintendent Hadley that this affair must be hushed up."

Something in his voice, something of the unweary, unchanging, limitless compassion that was Gideon Fell, seemed to touch her as gently as sleep after tears. Her hysteria had gone.

"Do you know?" she asked him, after a pause, and almost eagerly. "Do not fool me! Do you really know?"

"Yes, I really know."

"Go upstairs. Go to *his* room," she said in a dull voice, "and I will join you presently. I—I cannot face you just now. I must think, and— But please do not speak to anybody until I come. Please! No, I will not run away."

Dr. Fell's fierce gesture silenced Hadley as they went out. Still in silence they tramped up the gloomy stairs to the top floor. They passed no one, they saw no one. Once more they came into the study, where it was so dark that Hadley switched on the mosaic lamp at the desk. After he had made sure the door was closed, Hadley turned round rather wildly.

"Are you trying to tell me that Grimaud killed Fley?" he demanded.

"Yes."

"While he was lying unconscious and dying under the eyes of witnesses in a nursing-home, he went to Cagliostro Street and—!"

"Not then," said Dr. Fell quietly. "You see, that's what you don't understand. That's what's led you wrong. That's what I meant by saying that the case had been turned not upside down, but *the wrong way round*. Fley was killed before Grimaud. And, worst of all, Grimaud was trying to tell us the exact, literal truth. He did tell us the exact truth, when he knew he was dying beyond hope—it's one of the good gleams in him—but we chose to misinterpret it. Sit down, and I'll see if I can explain it. Once you have grasped the three essential points, you will need no deduction and very little elucidation from me. The thing will explain itself."

He lowered himself, wheezing, into the chair behind the desk. For a little time he remained staring vacantly at the lamp. Then he went on:

"The three essential points, then, are these. (1) There is no brother Henri; there are only two brothers. (2) Both these brothers were speaking the truth. (3) A question of time has turned the case wrong way round.

"Many things in this case have turned on a matter of brief spaces of time, and how brief they are. It's a part of the same irony which described our murderer as the hollow man that the crux of the case should be a matter of mistaken time. You can easily spot it if you think back.

"Now remember yesterday morning! I already had some occasion to believe there was something queer about that business in Cagliostro Street. The shooting there, we were told by three (truthful) witnesses who agreed precisely and to a second, took place at just ten twenty-five. I wondered, in an idle sort of way, why they corroborated each other with such startling exactitude. In the case of the usual street accident, even the most cool witnesses don't usually take such notice, or are careful to consult their watches, or (even if they do) agree about the time with such uncanny precision. But they were truthful people, and there must have been some reason for their exactitude. The time must have been thrust on them.

"Of course there was a reason. Just across from where the murdered man fell there was a lighted show-window—the only lighted window thereabouts —of a jeweller's shop. It was the most noticeable thing in the foreground. It illuminated the murdered man; it was the first place to which the constable rushed in search of the murderer; it quite naturally focussed their attention. And, facing them from that window, there was an enormous clock of such unusual design that it immediately took the eye. It was inevitable that the constable should look for the time, and natural that the others should also. Hence their agreement.

"But one thing, not apparently important at that time, bothered me a little. After Grimaud was shot, Hadley summoned his men to this house, and instantly despatched one of them to pick up Fley as a suspect. Now, then, those men arrived here . . . about what time?"

"About ten-forty," said Rampole, "according to a rough calculation. I've got it in my time-table."

"And," said Dr. Fell, "a man was sent immediately to get Fley. This man must have arrived in Cagliostro Street—when? Between fifteen and twenty minutes after Fley was presumed to have been killed. But in the space of that brief time what has happened? An incredible number of things! Fley has been carried down to the doctor's house, he has died, an examination has been made, a fruitless effort undertaken to identify Fley; and then, 'after some delay' in the words of the newspaper account, the van is sent for and Fley removed to the mortuary. All this! For, when Hadley's detective arrived in Cagliostro Street to pick up Fley, he found the whole business finished—and the constable back making inquiries from door to door. The entire excitement had died down. Which seemed incredible.

"Unfortunately, I was so dense that I didn't see the significance of this even yesterday morning when I saw the clock in the jeweller's window.

"Think back once more. Yesterday morning we had breakfast at my house; Pettis dropped in, and we talked to him—until what time?"

There was a pause.

"Until exactly ten o'clock," Hadley answered, suddenly, and snapped his fingers. "Yes! I remember, because Big Ben was striking just as he got up to go."

"Quite right. He left us, and afterwards we put on our hats and coats and drove *straight* to Cagliostro Street. Now, allow any reasonable margin of time you like for our putting on our hats, going downstairs, driving a short distance on deserted roads Sunday morning—a drive that took us only ten minutes when there was Saturday-night traffic. I think you'll say the whole process can hardly have taken twenty minutes in all. . . . But in Cagliostro Street you showed me the jeweller's shop, and that fancy clock was just striking *eleven*.

"Even then in my musing density it never occurred to me to look at that clock and wonder, just as in their excitement it never occurred to the three witnesses last night. Just afterwards, you recall, Somers and O'Rourke summoned us up to Burnaby's flat. We made quite a long investigation, and then had a talk with O'Rourke. And while O'Rourke was speaking, I noticed that the earlier dead quiet of the day—the quiet when in the street we heard only the wind—had a new sound. I heard church bells.

"Well, what time *do* church bells begin to ring? Not after eleven o'clock; the service has begun. Usually before eleven, for a preparatory bell. But, if I accepted the evidence of that German clock, it must then be a very long time past eleven o'clock. Then my dull mind woke up. I remembered Big Ben and our drive to Cagliostro Street. The combination of those bells and Big Ben—against (hem!) a trumpery foreign clock. Church and State, so to speak, couldn't both be wrong. . . . In other words, *the clock in that jeweller's window was more than forty minutes fast. Hence the shooting in Cagliostro Street the night before could not have taken place at twenty-five minutes past ten. Actually it must have taken place a short time previous to a quarter to ten. Say, roughly, at nine-forty.*

"Now, sooner or later somebody would have noticed this; maybe somebody has noticed it already. A thing like that would be bound to come out in a coroner's court. Somebody would come forward to dispute the right time. Whether you'd have instantly seen the truth then (as I hope), or whether it would have confused you even more, I don't know. . . . But the solid fact remains that the affair in Cagliostro Street took place some minutes before the man in the false face rang the bell of this house at nine forty-five."

"But I still don't see—!" protested Hadley.

"The impossible situation? No; but I have a clear course now to tell you the whole story from the beginning."

"Yes, but let me get this straightened out. If Grimaud, as you say, shot Fley in Cagliostro Street just before nine forty-five—"

"I didn't say that," said Dr. Fell.

"*What?*"

"You'll understand if you follow my patient elucidation from the beginning. On Wednesday night of last week—when Fley first appeared out of the past, apparently out of his grave, to confront his brother with rather a terrible threat at the Warwick Tavern—Grimaud resolved to kill him. In the whole case, you see, Grimaud was the only person with a motive for killing Fley. And, my God! Hadley, but he did have a motive! He was safe, he was rich, he was respected; the past was buried. And then, all of a sudden, a door blows open to admit this thin grinning stranger who is his brother Pierre. Grimaud, in escaping from prison, had murdered one of his brothers by leav-

ing him buried alive; he would have murdered the other except for an accident. He could still be extradited and hanged—and Pierre Fley had traced
him.

"Now, bear in mind exactly what Fley said when he suddenly flew in to
confront Grimaud that night at the tavern. Study *why* he said and did certain
things, and you will see that even shaky-minded Fley was very far from being
as mad as he liked to pretend. Why, if he were intent merely on private
vengeance, did he choose to confront Grimaud in the presence of a circle of
friends and speak in just the innuendoes he used? He used his *dead* brother
as a threat; and it was the only time he did speak of that *dead* brother. Why
did he say, 'He can be much more dangerous to you than I can'? Because
the dead brother could hang Grimaud! Why did he say, 'I don't want your
life; he does'? Why did he say, 'Shall I have him call on you'? And then why,
just afterwards, did he hand Grimaud his card on which his own address was
carefully written? The giving of that card, combined with his words and later
actions, is significant. What Fley really meant, veiled so that he could throw
a scare into Grimaud before witnesses, was just this: 'You, my brother, are
fat and rich on the proceeds of a robbery we both committed when we were
young. I am poor—and I hate my work. Now will you come and call on me at
my address, so that we can arrange this matter, or shall I set the police on
you?' "

"Blackmail," said Hadley, softly.

"Yes. Fley had a bee in his bonnet, but Fley was far from being a fool.
Now mark how he twisted round his meaning in his last threatening words
to Grimaud. 'I *also* am in danger when I associate with my brother, but I am
prepared to run that risk.' And in that case, as always afterwards, he was referring in strict truth to *Grimaud*. 'You, my brother, might also kill me as
you killed the other, but I will risk it. So shall I call on you amiably, or will
my other dead brother come to hang you?'

"For think of his behaviour afterwards, on the night of his murder. Remember the glee he had of smashing up and getting rid of his illusion-prop-
erties? And what words did he use to O'Rourke? Words which, if you look at
them squarely in the light of what we now know, can have only one explanation. He said:

" 'I shall not need them again. My work is finished. Didn't I tell you? I am
    going to see my brother. He will do something that will settle an old
    affair for both of us.'

"Meaning, of course, that Grimaud had agreed to come to terms. Fley
meant that he was leaving his old life for good; going back to his grave as a
dead man with plenty of money; but he couldn't be more specific without
blowing the gaff. Still, he knew that his brother was tricky; he'd had good
reason in the past to know it. He couldn't leave behind him a big warning

when he spoke with O'Rourke, in case Grimaud really meant to pay; but he threw out a hint:

> " 'In case anything happens to me, you will find my brother in the same street where I myself live. That is not where he really resides, but he has a room there.'

"I'll explain that last statement in just a moment. But go back to Grimaud. Now, Grimaud never had any intention of coming to terms with Fley. Fley was going to die. That wily, shrewd, theatrical mind of Grimaud's (who, as you know, was more interested in magical illusions than anybody else we have met) was determined not to suffer any nonsense from this inconvenient brother of his. Fley must die—but this was more difficult than it looked.

"If Fley had come to him in private, without anybody in the world ever being able to associate Fley's name with his, it would have been simple. But Fley had been too shrewd for that. He had blazoned forth his own name and address, and hinted at mysterious secrets concerning Grimaud, before a group of Grimaud's friends. Awkward! Now if Fley is found obviously murdered, somebody is likely to say, 'Hullo! Isn't that the same chap who—?' And then presently there may be dangerous enquiries; because Lord knows what Fley may have told *other* people about Grimaud. The only thing he isn't likely to have confided to somebody else is his last deadly hold over Grimaud; and that is the thing about which he must be silenced. Whatever happens to Fley, however he dies, there are likely to be enquiries concerning Grimaud. The only thing to do is frankly to pretend that Fley is after his life; to send himself threatening letters (not too obviously); to stir up the household in an ingenious way; finally, to inform everybody that Fley has threatened to call on him on the night he himself intends to call on Fley. You will see very shortly just how he planned to work out a very brilliant murder.

"The effect he intended to produce was this: The murderous Fley should be seen calling on him on Saturday night. There should be witnesses to this. The two should be together alone when Fley goes into his study. A row is heard, the sound of a fight, a shot, and a fall. The door being opened, Grimaud should be found alone—a nasty-looking but superficial wound from a bullet scratched along his side. No weapon is there. Out of the window hangs a rope belonging to Fley, by which Fley is assumed to have escaped. (Remember, it had been predicted that there would be *no* snow that night, so it would have been impossible to trace footprints.) Grimaud says: 'He thought he killed me; I pretended to be dead; and he escaped. No, don't set the police on him, poor devil. I'm not hurt.'—And the next morning Fley would have been found dead in his own room. He would have been found, a suicide, having pressed his own gun against his chest and pulled the trigger. The gun is beside him. A suicide note lies on the table. In despair at thinking he has killed Grimaud, he has shot himself. . . . That, gentlemen, was the illusion Grimaud intended to produce."

"But how did he do it?" demanded Hadley. "And, anyway, it didn't turn out like that!"

"No. You see, the plan miscarried badly. The latter part of the illusion of Fley calling on him in his study when actually Fley would already have been dead in the Cagliostro Street house—I'll deal with in its proper place. Grimaud, with the aid of Madame Dumont, had already made certain preparations.

"He had told Fley to meet him at Fley's room on the top floor over the tobacconist's. He had told Fley to meet him there at nine o'clock on the Saturday night, for a cash settlement. (You recall that Fley, gleefully throwing up his job and burning his properties, left the theatre in Limehouse at about eight-fifteen.)

"Grimaud had chosen Saturday night because that night, by inviolable custom, he remained alone all evening in his study without anyone being allowed to disturb him for any reason whatsoever. He chose that night because he needed to use the areaway door, and go and come by way of the basement; and Saturday night was the night out for Annie, who had her quarters there. You'll remember that, after he went up to his study at seven-thirty, nobody *did* see him until, according to the evidence, he opened the study door to admit the visitor at nine-fifty. Madame Dumont claimed to have spoken to him in the study at nine-thirty, when she gathered up the coffee things. I'll tell you shortly why I disbelieved that statement—the fact is, he was not in the study at all: he was in Cagliostro Street. Madame Dumont had been told to lurk round the study door at nine-thirty, and to come out for some excuse. Why? Because Grimaud had ordered Mills to come upstairs at nine-thirty, you see, and watch the study door from the room down the hall. Mills was to be the dupe of the illusion Grimaud meant to work. But if—as he came upstairs near the study door—Mills had for any reason taken it into his head to try to speak with Grimaud, or see him, Dumont was there to head him off. Dumont was to wait in the archway, and keep Mills away from that door if he showed any curiosity.

"Mills was chosen as the dupe of the illusion: why? Because, although he was so meticulously conscientious that he would carry out his instructions to the tick, he was so afraid of 'Fley' that he would not interfere when the hollow man came stalking up those stairs. It was not only that he must not attack the man in the false face in those dangerous few moments before the man got into the study (as, for instance, Mangan or even Drayman might have done), but also that he must not even venture out of his room. He had been told to stay in that room, and he would. Finally, he had been chosen because he was a very short man, a fact which will presently become clear.

"Now, he was told to go upstairs and watch at nine-thirty. This was because the hollow man was timed to make his appearance only a little after-wards; although, in fact, the hollow man was late. Mark one discrepancy. Mills was told nine-thirty—but Mangan was told ten o'clock! The reason is obvious. There was to be somebody downstairs to testify that a visitor had really arrived by the front door, confirming Dumont. But Mangan might be inclined towards curiosity about this visitor; he might be inclined to chal-lenge the hollow man . . . unless he had first been jokingly told by Grimaud that the visitor would probably not arrive at all, or, if he did arrive, it could not possibly be before ten o'clock. All that was necessary was to throw his mind off, and make him hesitate long enough, for the hollow man to get upstairs past that dangerous door. And, if the worst came to the worst, Man-gan and Rosette could always be locked in.

"For everybody else: Annie was out, Drayman had been supplied with a ticket to a concert, Burnaby was unquestionably playing cards, and Pettis at the theatre. The field was clear.

"At some time before nine o'clock (probably about ten minutes) Grimaud slipped out of the house, using the area door up to the street. Trouble had already started. It had been snowing heavily for some time, contrary to rules. But Grimaud did not regard it as serious trouble. He believed he could do the business and return by half-past nine, and that it would still be snowing heavily enough to gloss over any footprints that he would make, and cause no comment on the absence of any footprints the visitor later *should* have made when the visitor would be supposed to have swung down from his window. In any case, his plans had been carried too far for him to back out.

"When he left the house he was carrying an old and untraceable Colt re-volver, loaded with just two bullets. The sort of hat he wore I don't know, but his overcoat was a light yellow, glaring tweed with chicken-pox spots. He bought this coat several sizes too large. He bought it because it was the sort of coat he had never been known to wear and because nobody would recog-nize him in it if he were to be seen. He—"

Hadley intervened.

"Stop a bit! What about that business of the overcoats changing colour? That would come earlier in the evening. What had happened there?"

"Again I've got to ask you to wait until we get to the last illusion he worked; that's a part of it.

"Well, Grimaud's purpose was to call on Fley. There he would speak with Fley amiably for a time. He would say something like: 'You must leave this hovel, brother! You will be comfortably off now; I will see to that. Why not leave these useless possessions behind and come to my house? Let your land-lord have the damned things in place of notice!'—Any sort of speech, you see, the purpose being to make Fley write one of his ambiguous notes for the landlord. 'I am leaving for good.' 'I am going back to my grave.' Anything *that could be understood as a suicide note when Fley was found dead with a gun in his hand."*

Dr. Fell leaned forward. "And then Grimaud would take out his Colt, jam it against Fley's chest, and smilingly pull the trigger.

"It was the top floor of an empty house. As you have seen, the walls are astonishingly thick and solid. The landlord lived far down in the basement, and was the most incurious man in Cagliostro Street. No shot, especially a muffled shot with the gun held against Fley, could have been heard. It might be some time before the body was discovered; it would certainly not be before morning. And in the meantime, what will Grimaud do? After killing Fley he will turn the same gun on himself to give himself a slight wound, even if he has to imbed the bullet—he had, as we know from that little episode of the three coffins years before, the constitution of an ox and the nerve of hell. Then he would leave the gun lying beside Fley. He would quite coolly clap a handkerchief or cotton wool across this wound, which must be *inside* the coat and across the shirt; bind it with adhesive tape until the time came to rip it open—and go back home to work his illusion, which should prove that Fley came to see him. That Fley shot him, and then returned to Cagliostro Street and used the same gun for suicide, no coroner's jury would afterwards doubt. Do I make it clear so far? It was crime turned the wrong way round.

"That, as I say, was what Grimaud *intended* to do. Had he performed it as he intended, it would have been an ingenious murder; and I doubt whether we should ever have questioned Fley's suicide.

"Now, there was only one difficulty about accomplishing this plan. If anybody—not anybody recognizable as himself, but anybody at all—were seen visiting Fley's house, the fat would be in the fire. It might not appear so easily as suicide. There was only one entrance from the street—the door beside the tobacconist's. And he was wearing a conspicuous coat, in which he had reconnoitred the ground before. (By the way, Dolberman, the tobacconist, had seen him hanging about previously.) He found the solution of his difficulty in Burnaby's secret flat.

"You see, of course, that Grimaud was the likeliest person of all to have known of Burnaby's flat in Cagliostro Street? Burnaby himself told us that, some months before when Grimaud suspected him of having an ulterior motive in painting that picture, Grimaud had not only questioned him—he had *watched* him. From a man who was in such fancied danger, it would have been real watching. He knew of the flat. He knew from spying that Rosette had a key. And so, when the time came and the idea occurred to him, he stole Rosette's key.

"The house in which Burnaby had his flat was on the same side of the street as the house where Fley lived. All those houses are built side by side, with flat roofs; so that you have only to step over a low dividing wall to walk on the roofs from one end of the street to the other. Both men, remember, lived on the top floor. You recall what we saw when we went up to look at Burnaby's flat—just beside the door to the flat?"

Hadley nodded. "Yes, of course. A short ladder going to a trap-door in the roof."

"Exactly. And, on the landing just outside Fley's room, there is a low skylight also communicating with the roof. Grimaud had only to go to Cagliostro Street by the back way, never appearing in the street itself, but going up the alley which we saw from Burnaby's window. He came in the back door (as we saw Burnaby and Rosette do later), he went up to the top floor and thence to the roof. Then he followed the roofs to Fley's lodgings, descended from the skylight to the landing, and could both enter and leave the place without a soul seeing him. Moreover, he knew absolutely that that night Burnaby would be playing cards elsewhere.

"And then everything went wrong.

"He must have got to Fley's lodgings before Fley arrived there himself; it wouldn't do to make Fley suspicious by being seen coming from the roof. But we know that Fley had some suspicions already. This may have been caused by Grimaud's request for Fley to bring along one of his long conjuring-ropes. . . . Grimaud wanted that rope as a piece of evidence to use later against Fley. Or it may have been caused by Fley's knowledge that Grimaud had been hanging about in Cagliostro Street for the past couple of days; possibly seeing him duck across the roofs towards Burnaby's after one reconnoitring, and thereby making Fley believe he had taken a room in the street.

"The two brothers met in that gaslit room at nine. What they talked about we don't know. We may never know. But evidently Grimaud lulled Fley's suspicions; they became pleasant and amiable and forgot old scores; Grimaud jocularly persuaded him to write that note for the landlord. Then—"

"I'm not disputing all this," said Hadley, quietly, "but how do you happen to know it?"

"Grimaud told us," said Dr. Fell.

Hadley stared.

"Oh yes. Once I had tumbled to that terrible mistake in times, I could understand. You'll see. But to continue:

"Fley had written his note. He had got into his hat and coat for departure —because Grimaud wished it to be assumed that he had killed himself just after having returned from a journey *outdoors*: his return from the phantom visit to Grimaud, in other words. They were all ready to go. And then Grimaud leaped.

"Whether Fley was subconsciously on his guard; whether he twitched round to run for the door, since he was no match for the powerful Grimaud; whether it happened in the twisting and scuffle—this we do not know. But Grimaud, with the gun against Fley's coat as Fley wrenched round from him, made a hellish mistake. He fired. And he put the bullet in the wrong place.

Instead of getting his victim through the heart, he got him under the left shoulder blade: a wound of almost the same sort, although at the back, as the one from which Grimaud later died himself. It was a fatal wound, but far from instantly fatal. The poetic ironies were working to kill these brothers, with interchangeable methods, in precisely the same way.

"Of course Fley went down. He could do nothing else; and it was the wisest course, or Grimaud might have finished him. But Grimaud, for a second, must have lost his nerve in sheer terror. This might have wrecked his whole plan. *Could* a man shoot himself in that spot? If not, God help the murderer. And worse—Fley, not caught quickly enough, had screamed out before the bullet went home, and Grimaud thought he heard pursuers.

"He had sense enough, and guts enough, even in that hellish moment, to keep his head. He jammed the pistol into the hand of the motionless Fley, lying on his face. He picked up the coil of rope. Somehow, in spite of crash and fuddlement, the plan must go on. But he had more sense than to risk the noise of another shot to be heard by people possibly listening, or to waste more time. He darted out of the room.

"The roof, do you see! The roof was his only chance. He heard imaginary pursuers everywhere; maybe some grisly recollection came back to him of three graves in a storm below the Hungarian mountains. He imagined that they would hear him and track him across those roofs. So he dashed for the trap-door at Burnaby's, and down into the dark of Burnaby's flat.

"It was only then that his wits began to recover themselves. . . .

"And, meantime, what has happened? Pierre Fley is fatally hurt. But he still has the ribs of that iron frame which once enabled him to survive being buried alive. The murderer has gone. And Fley will *not* give in. He must get help. He must get to—

"*To a doctor,* Hadley. You asked yesterday why Fley was walking towards the other end of the street, towards the end of a blind alley. Because (as you saw in the newspaper) a doctor lived there: the doctor to whose office he later was carried. He is mortally hurt and he knows it; but he will not be beaten! He gets up, still in his hat and overcoat. The gun has been put into his hand; he rams it in his pocket, for it may be useful. Down he goes, downstairs as steadily as he can, to a silent street where no alarm has been raised. He walks on. . . .

"Have you asked yourself why he was walking in the middle of the street and kept looking so sharply round? The most reasonable explanation is not that he was going to visit anybody; but that he knew the murderer to be lurking somewhere, and he expected another attack. He thinks he is safe. Ahead of him, two men are walking rapidly. He passes a lighted jeweller's, he sees a street lamp ahead on the right. . . .

"But what has happened to Grimaud? Grimaud has heard no pursuit, but he is half-insane with wondering. He does not dare go back to the roof and

risk investigation. But stop a moment! If there has been any discovery, he will
be able to know by looking for a second out into the street. He can go down
to the front door, look out, and peer up the street, can't he? No danger in
that, since the house where Burnaby lives is deserted.

"He goes softly downstairs. He opens the door softly, having unbuttoned
his coat to wind the coil of rope round him inside that overcoat. He opens
the door—full in the glow of a street lamp just beyond the door—and facing
him, walking slowly in the middle of the street, is the man he left for dead
in the other house less than ten minutes ago.

"And for the last time those brothers come face to face.

"Grimaud's shirt is a target under that street lamp. And Fley, driven mad
with pain and hysteria, does not hesitate. He screams. *He* cries the words,
'The second bullet is for *you!*'—just before he whips up the same pistol
and fires.

"That last effort is too much. The hemorrhage has got him, and he knows
it. He screams again, lets go of the gun as he tries to throw it (now empty) at
Grimaud; and then he pitches forward on his face. That, my lads, is the shot
which the three witnesses heard in Cagliostro Street. It was the shot which
struck Grimaud in the chest just before he had time to close the door."


## XXI

### The Unravelling

"AND then?" prompted Hadley, as Dr. Fell paused and lowered his head.

"The three witnesses did not see Grimaud, of course," said Dr. Fell,
wheezing, after a long pause, "because he was never outside the door; never
on the steps at all; never within twenty feet of the man who *seemed* to have
been murdered in the middle of a snow desert. Of course Fley already had
the wound, which jetted blood from the last convulsion. Of course any deduction from the direction of the wound was useless. Of course there were
no fingerprints on the gun, since it landed in snow and in a literal sense had
been washed clean."

"By God!" said Hadley, so quietly that he seemed to be making a statement. "It fulfills every condition of the facts, and yet I never thought of it.
. . . But go on. Grimaud?"

"Grimaud is inside the door. He knows he's got it in his chest; but he
doesn't think it's very serious. He's survived worse things than bullets, and
other things (he thinks) *are* more serious.

"After all, he's only got what he was going to give himself—a wound. He
could bark out that chuckle of his at such a thing. But his plan has crashed
to hell! (How is he to know, by the way, that the clock at the jeweller's will

be fast? He doesn't even know that Fley is dead, for there is Fley walking in the street with fire and sting still in him. Luck—by reason of the jeweller's clock—is with him when he thought it had deserted him, but how is he to know it?) All he is sure of is that Fley will never now be found, a suicide, up in that little room. Fley—probably dangerously wounded, yes, but still able to talk—is out in that street with a policeman running towards him. Grimaud is undone. Unless he can use his wits, he's on his way to the hangman, for Fley will not keep silent now.

"All this comes an instant after the shot, the rush of fancies crowding in. He can't stay here in this dark hall. He'd better have a look at that wound, though, and make sure he doesn't leave a trail of blood. Where? Burnaby's flat upstairs, of course. Up he goes, gets the door open, and switches on the lights. Here's the rope wound round him . . . no use for *that* thing now; he can't pretend Fley came to call on him when Fley may now be talking with the police. He flings the rope off and leaves it.

"A look at the wound next. There's blood all over the inside of that light tweed overcoat, and blood on his inner clothes. But the wound is of small consequence. He's got his handkerchief and his adhesive tape, and he can plug himself up like a horse gored in the bull-ring. Károly Horváth, whom nothing can kill, can afford to chuckle at this. He feels as steady and fresh as ever. But he patches himself up—hence the blood in the bathroom of Burnaby's flat—and tries to collect his wits. What time is it? Good God! he's late; it's just on a quarter to ten. Got to get out of here and hurry home before they catch him. . . .

"And he leaves the lights on. When they burnt up a shilling's worth and went out in the later course of the night, we don't know. They were on three-quarters of an hour afterwards, anyhow, when Rosette saw them.

"But I think that his sanity returns as he hurries home. *Is* he caught? It seems inevitable. Yet is there any loophole, any ghost of a fighting chance, however thin? You see, whatever else Grimaud is, he's a fighter. He's a shrewd, theatrical, imaginative, sneering, common-sense blackguard: but don't forget that he's also a fighter. He wasn't all of a black colour, you know. He would murder a brother, but I question whether he would murder a friend or a woman who loved him. In any case, *is* there some way out? There's one chance, so thin that it's almost useless; but the only one. That's to carry through his original scheme and pretend that Fley has called on him and given him that wound *in his own house*. Fley still has the gun. It will be Grimaud's word, and his witnesses' word, that he never left the house all evening! Whereas they can swear that Fley did come to see him—and then let the damned police try to prove anything! Why not? The snow? It's stopped snowing, and Fley won't have left a track. Grimaud has thrown away the rope Fley was supposed to have used. But it's a toss-up, a last daring of the devil, the only course in an extremity. . . .

"Fley shot him at about twenty minutes to ten. He gets back here at a quarter to ten or a little after. Getting into the house without leaving a footprint? Easy! for a man with a constitution like an ox, and only slightly wounded. (By the way, I believe he was really wounded only slightly, and that he'd live now to hang, if he hadn't done certain things; you'll see.) He'll return by way of the steps down to the areaway, and the area door, as arranged. —How? Well, there is a coating of snow on the areaway steps, of course. But the entrance to the areaway steps is beside the next house, isn't it? Yes. And, at the foot of the area steps, the basement door is protected from snow by a projection: the projection of the main front steps overhanging. So that there is no snow exactly in front of the area door. If he can get down there without leaving a mark—

"He can. He can approach from the other direction, as though he were going to the house next door, and then simply jump down the area steps to the cleared patch below. . . . Don't I seem to remember a *thud*, as of some one falling, which some one heard just before the front-door bell rang?"

"But he didn't ring the front-door bell!"

"Oh yes, he did—but from inside. After he'd gone into the house by way of the area door, and up to where Ernestine Dumont was waiting for him. Then they were ready to perform their illusion."

"Yes," said Hadley. "Now we come to the illusion. How was it done, and how do you know how it was done?"

Dr. Fell sat back and tapped his finger tips together as though he were marshalling facts.

"How do I know? Well, I think my first suggestion was the weight of that picture." He pointed sleepily at the big slashed canvas leaning against the wall. "Yes, it was the weight of the picture. That wasn't very helpful, until I remembered something else. . . ."

"Weight of the picture? Yes, the picture," growled Hadley. "I'd forgotten that. How does *it* figure in the blasted business, anyhow? What did Grimaud mean to do with that?"

"H'mf, ha, yes. That's what I wondered, you see."

"But the weight of the picture, man! It doesn't weigh very much. You yourself picked it up with one hand and turned it round in the air."

Dr. Fell sat up with an air of some excitement. "Exactly. You've hit it. I picked it up with one hand and swung it round. . . . Then why should it take two husky men, the cabman and one extra, to carry it upstairs?"

"What?"

"It did, you know. That was twice pointed out to us. Grimaud, when he took it from Burnaby's studio, easily carried it downstairs. Yet, when he returned here with that same painting late in the afternoon, two people had a job carting it up. Where had it picked up so much weight all of a sudden? He didn't have glass put in it—you can see that for yourself. Where was Grimaud all that time, the morning when he bought the picture and the afternoon when he returned with it? It's much too big a thing to carry about with you for pleasure. Why was Grimaud so insistent on having the picture all wrapped up?

"It wasn't a very far-fetched deduction to think that he used that picture as a blind to hide something that the men were carrying up, unintentionally, along with it. Something in the same parcel. Something very big . . . seven feet by four . . . h'm. . . ."

"But there couldn't have been anything," objected Hadley, "or we'd have found it in this room, wouldn't we? Besides, in any case the thing must have been almost absolutely flat, or it would have been noticed in the wrappings of the picture. What sort of object is it that's as big as seven feet by four, and yet thin enough not to be noticed inside the wrappings of a picture; what's as huge a business as that picture, which can nevertheless be spirited out of sight whenever you wish?"

"A mirror," said Dr. Fell.

After a sort of thunderous silence, while Hadley rose from his chair, Dr. Fell went on sleepily: "And it can be spirited out of sight, as you put it, merely by being pushed up the flue of that very broad chimney—where we've all tried to get our fists, by the way—and propped up on the ledge inside where the chimney turns. You don't need magic. You only need to be damnably strong in the arms and shoulders."

"You mean," cried Hadley, "that damned stage trick . . ."

"A new version of the stage trick," said Dr. Fell, "and a very good one which is practical if you care to try it. Now, look round this room. You see the door? What do you see in the wall directly opposite the door?"

"Nothing," said Hadley. "I mean, he's had the bookcases cleared away in a big space on either side. There's blank panelled wall, that's all."

"Exactly. And do you see any furniture in a line between the door and that wall?"

"No. It's cleared."

"So if you were out in that hall looking in, you would see only black carpet, no furniture, and to the rear an expanse of blank oak-panelled wall?"

"Yes."

"Now, Ted, open the door and look out into the hall," said Dr. Fell. "What about the walls and carpet out there?"

Rampole made a feint of looking, although he knew. "They're just the same," he said. "The floor is one solid carpet running to the baseboards, like this one, and the panelling is the same."

"Right! By the way, Hadley," pursued Dr. Fell, still drowsily, "you might drag out that mirror from behind the bookcase over there. It's been behind the bookcase since yesterday afternoon, when Drayman found it in the chimney. It was lifting it down that brought on his stroke. We'll try a little experiment. I don't think any of the household will interrupt us up here, but we can head off anybody who does. I want you to take that mirror, Hadley, and set it up just inside the door—so that when you open the door (it opens inwards and to the right, you see, as you come in from the hall) the edge of the door at its outermost swing is a few inches away from the mirror."

The superintendent with some difficulty trundled out the object he found behind the bookcase. It was bigger than a tailor's swinging mirror; several inches, in fact, higher and wider than the door. Its base rested flat on the carpet, and it was supported upright by a heavy swing-base on the right-hand side as you faced it. Hadley regarded it curiously.

"Set it up inside the door?"

"Yes. The door will only swing open a short distance; you'll see an aperture only a couple of feet wide at the most. . . . Try it!"

"I know, but if you do that . . . well, somebody sitting in the room down at the end of the hall, where Mills was, would see his own reflection smack in the middle of the mirror."

"Not at all. Not at the angle—a slight angle, but enough; a poor thing, but mine own—not at the angle to which I'm going to tilt it. You'll see. The two of you go down there where Mills was while I adjust it. Keep your eyes off until I sing out."

Hadley, muttering that it was damned foolishness, but highly interested in spite of that, tramped down after Rampole. They kept their eyes off until they heard the doctor's hail, and then turned round.

The hallway was gloomy and high enough. Its black-carpeted length ran down to a closed door. Dr. Fell stood outside that door, like an overfat master of ceremonies about to unveil a statue. He stood a little to the right of the door, well back from it against the wall, and had his hand stretched out across to the knob.

"Here she goes!" he grunted, and quickly opened the door—hesitated—and closed it. "Well? What did you see?"

"I saw the room inside," returned Hadley. "Or at least I thought I did. I saw the carpet, and the rear wall. It seemed a very big room."

"You didn't see that," said Dr. Fell. "As a matter of fact, you saw the reflection of the panelled wall immediately to the right of the door where you're standing, and the carpet going up to it. That's why it seemed so big a room: you were looking at a double length of reflection. This mirror is bigger than the door, you know. And you didn't see a reflection of the door itself because it opens inwards to the right. If you looked carefully, you might have seen a line of what looks like shadow just along the top edge of the door. That's where the top edge of the mirror inevitably reflects, being taller, an inch or so of the *inner* top edge of the door. But your attention would be concentrated on any figures you saw. . . . Did you see me, by the way?"

# DIAGRAM TO ILLUSTRATE ILLUSION

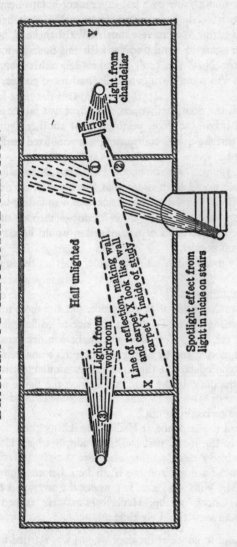

Light from chandelier

Mirror

Hall unlighted

Light from workroom

Line of reflection, making wall look like wall and carpet X inside of study and carpet Y inside of study

X

Spotlight effect from light in niche on stairs

1. Man whose own reflection is seen by watcher, but appearing three inches taller than reflection because watcher, thirty feet away, is sitting down on a much lower level of observation.

2. Confederate who opens and shuts door.

3. Watcher.

In testing this illusion, one important point must be observed. No light must fall directly on the mirror, else there will be a reflected dazzle to betray its presence. It will be seen that a spotlight from the niche on the stairs has been caused to fall across the line of the door, but not in a position to catch any reflection. No light is in the hall, and the workroom light does not penetrate far. In the study itself, the light comes from the chandelier in a very high ceiling, thus coming almost directly over the top of the mirror. It will throw, therefore, very little shadow of this mirror into the hall; and such shadow as it does throw will be obscured by the counter-shadow of the man standing before the door.

"No; you were too far over. You had your arm across the door to the knob, and kept back."

"Yes. As Dumont was standing. Now try a last experiment before I explain how the whole mechanism worked. Ted, you sit down in the chair behind that desk—where Mills was sitting. You're very much taller than he is, but it will illustrate the idea. I'm going to stand outside, with this door open, and look at myself in the mirror. Now, you can't mistake ME, either from the front or the rear; but then I'm more distinguishable than some people. Just tell me what you see."

In the ghostly light, with the door partly open, the effect was rather eerie. A figure of Dr. Fell stood inside the door, peering out at another figure of Dr. Fell standing on the threshold and confronting himself—fixed and motionless, with a startled look.

"I don't touch the door, you see," a voice boomed at them. By the illusion of the moving lips Rampole would have sworn that the Dr. Fell inside the door was speaking. The mirror threw the voice back like a sounding-board. "Somebody obligingly opens and closes the door for me—somebody standing at my right. I don't touch the door, or my reflection would have to do likewise. Quick, what do you notice?"

"Why—one of you is very much taller," said Rampole, studying the images.

"Which one?"

"You yourself: the figure in the hall."

"Exactly. First because you're seeing it at a distance, but the most important thing is that you're sitting down. To a man the size of Mills I should look like a giant. Hey? H'mf. Hah. Yes. Now if I make a quick move to dodge in at that door (supposing me to be capable of such a manœuvre), and at the same time my confederate at the right makes a quick confusing move with me and slams the door, in the muddled illusion the figure inside seems to be—?"

"Jumping in front of you to keep you out."

"Yes. Now come and read the evidence, if Hadley has it."

When they were again in the room, past the tilted mirror which Hadley moved back, Dr. Fell sank into a chair, sighing wheezily.

"I'm sorry, gents. I should have realized the truth long before, from the careful, methodical, exact Mr. Mills' evidence. Let me see if I can repeat from memory his exact words. Check me up, Hadley. H'm." He rapped his knuckles against his head and scowled. "Like this:

"'She [Dumont] was about to knock at the door when I was startled to see the tall man come upstairs directly after us. She turned round and saw him. She exclaimed certain words. . . . The tall man made no reply. He walked to the door, and without haste turned down the collar of his coat and removed his cap, which he placed in his overcoat pocket. . . .'

"You see, gents? He had to do that, because the reflection couldn't show a cap and couldn't show a collar turned up when the figure inside must appear to be wearing a dressing-gown. But I wondered *why* he was so methodical about that, since apparently he didn't remove the mask—"

"Yes, what about that mask? Mills says he didn't—"

"Mills didn't see him take it off; I'll show you why as soon as we go on with Mills:

"'Madame Dumont cried out something, shrank back against the wall, and hurried to open the door. Dr. Grimaud appeared on the threshold—'

"Appeared! That's precisely what he did do. Our methodical witness is uncomfortably exact. But Dumont? There was the first flaw. A frightened woman, looking up at a terrifying figure while she's standing before the door of a room in which there's a man who will protect her, doesn't *shrink back*. She rushes towards the door to get protection. Anyhow, follow Mills' testimony. He says Grimaud was not wearing his eye-glasses (they wouldn't have fitted behind that mask). But the natural movement of a man inside, I thought, would have been to raise his glasses. Grimaud—according to Mills—stands *stockstill* the whole time; like the stranger, with his hands in his pockets. Now for the damning part. Mills says: 'I am under the impression that Madame Dumont, although she was shrinking back against the wall, closed the door after him. I recall that she had her hand on the knob.' Not a natural action for her, either! She contradicted him—but Mills was right."

Dr. Fell gestured.

"No use going on with all this. But here was my difficulty: if Grimaud was alone in that room, if he simply walked in on his own reflection, what became of his clothes? What about that long black overcoat, the brown peaked cap, even the false face? They weren't in the room. Then I remembered that Ernestine Dumont's profession had been the making of costumes for the opera and ballet; I remembered a story O'Rourke had told us; and I knew—"

"Well?"

"That Grimaud had burnt them," said Dr. Fell. "He had burnt them because they were made of paper, like the uniform of the Vanishing Horseman described by O'Rourke. He couldn't risk the long and dangerous business of burning real clothes in that fire; he had to work too fast. They had to be torn up and burnt. And bundles of loose, blank sheets of writing-paper—perfectly blank!—had to be burned on top of them to hide the fact that some of it was coloured paper. Dangerous letters! Oh, Bacchus, I could murder myself for thinking such a thing!" He shook his fist. "When there was no blood-trail, no blood-stain at all, going to the drawer in his desk where he did keep his important papers! And there was another reason for burning papers . . . they had to conceal the fragments of the 'shot.'"

"Shot?"

"Don't forget that a pistol was supposed to have been fired in that room. Of course, what the witnesses really heard was the noise of a heavy firecracker —pinched from the hoard Drayman always keeps, as you know, for Guy Fawkes night. Drayman discovered the missing thunderbolt; I think that's how he tumbled to the scheme, and why he kept muttering about 'fireworks.' Well, the fragments of an exploding firecracker fly wide. They're heavy reënforced cardboard, hard to burn, and they had to be destroyed in the fire or hidden in that drift of papers. I found some of them. Of course, we should have realized no bullet had really been fired. Modern cartridges—such as you informed me were used in that Colt revolver—have smokeless powder. You can smell it, but you can't see it. And yet there was a *haze* in this room (left by the firecracker) even after the window was up.

"Ah, well, let's recapitulate! Grimaud's heavy crêpe-paper uniform consisted of a black coat—black like a dressing-gown, long like a dressing-gown, and having at the front shiny lapels which would show like a dressing-gown when you turned down the collar to face your own image. It consisted of a paper cap, to which the false face was attached—so that in sweeping off the cap you simply folded both together and shoved 'em into your pocket. (The real dressing-gown, by the way, was already in this room while Grimaud was out.) And the black 'uniform,' early last evening, had been incautiously hung up in the closet downstairs.

"Mangan, unfortunately, spotted it. The watchful Dumont knew that he spotted it, and whisked it out of that cupboard to a safer place as soon as he went away. She, naturally, never saw a yellow tweed coat hanging there at all. Grimaud had it upstairs here with him, ready for his expedition. But it was found in the closet yesterday afternoon, and she had to pretend it had been there all the time. Hence the chameleon overcoat.

"You can now make a reconstruction of just what happened when Grimaud, after killing Fley and getting a bullet himself, returned to the house on Saturday night. Right at the start of the illusion he and his confederate were in dangerous trouble. You see, Grimaud was late. He'd expected to be back by nine-thirty—and he didn't get there until a quarter to ten. The longer he delayed, the nearer it got to the time he had told *Mangan* to expect a visitor, and now Mangan would be expecting the visitor he had been told to watch. It was touch-and-go, and I rather imagine the cool Grimaud was fairly close to insane. He got up through the basement entrance, where his confederate was waiting. The tweed coat, with the blood inside it, went into the hall closet to be disposed of presently—and it never was, because he died. Dumont eased open the door, rang the bell by putting her hand out, and then went to 'answer' it while Grimaud was getting ready with his uniform.

"But they delayed too long. Mangan called out. Grimaud, with his wits still not functioning well, grew a little panicky and made a blunder to ward off immediate detection. He'd got so far; he didn't want to fail then from the nosiness of a damned penniless kid. So he said that he was Pettis, and locked them in. (You notice that Pettis is the only one with a voice of the same bass quality as Grimaud's?) Yes, it was a spur-of-the-moment error, but his only wish was to writhe like a footballer down a field and *somehow* escape those hands for the moment.

"The illusion was performed; he was alone in his room. His jacket, probably with blood on that, had been taken in charge by Dumont; he wore the uniform over his shirt-sleeves, open shirt, and bandaged wound. He had only to lock the door behind him, put on his real dressing-gown, destroy the paper uniform, and get that mirror up into the chimney. . . .

"That, I say again, was the finish. The blood had begun to flow again, you see. No ordinary man, wounded, could have stood the strain under which he had already been. He wasn't killed by Fley's bullet. He ripped his own lung like a rotted piece of rubber when he tried to—and superhumanly did—lift that mirror into its hiding-place. That was when he knew. Then was when he began to bleed from the mouth like a slashed artery; when he staggered against the couch, knocked away the chair, and reeled forward in his last successful effort to ignite the firecracker. After all the hates and dodgings and plans, the world was not spinning in front of him: it was only slowly going black. He tried to scream out, and he could not, for the blood was welling in his throat. And at that moment Charles Grimaud suddenly knew what he would never have believed possible, the breaking of the last and most shattering mirror-illusion in his bitter life. . . ."

"Well?"

"He knew that he was dying," said Dr. Fell. "And, stranger than any of his dreams, he was glad."

The heavy leaden light had begun to darken again with snow. Dr. Fell's voice sounded weirdly in the chill room. Then they saw that the door was opening and that in it stood the figure of a woman with a damned face. A damned face and a black dress, but round her shoulders was still drawn a red-and-yellow shawl for love of the dead.

"You see, he confessed," Dr. Fell said in the same low, monotonous tone, "he tried to tell us the truth about his killing of Fley, and Fley's killing of him. Only we did not choose to understand, and I didn't understand until I knew from the clock what must have happened in Cagliostro Street. Man, man, don't you see? Take first his final statement, the statement made just before he died:

"'It was my brother who did it. I never thought he would shoot. God knows how he got out of that room—'"

"You mean Fley's room in Cagliostro Street, after Fley had been left for dead?" demanded Hadley.

"Yes. And the horrible shock of coming on him suddenly, as Grimaud opened the door under the street light. You see:

> " 'One second he was there, and the next he wasn't. . . . I want to tell you who my brother is, so you won't think I'm raving. . . .'

"For, of course, he did not think anybody knew about Fley. Now, in the light of that, examine the tangled, muddled, half-choked words with which—when he heard the statement that he was sinking—he tried to explain the whole puzzle to us.

"First he tried to tell us about the Horváths and the salt-mine. But he went on to the killing of Fley, and what Fley had done to him. *'Not suicide.'* When he'd seen Fley in the street, he couldn't make Fley's death the suicide he pretended. *'He couldn't use rope.'* Fley couldn't, after that, be supposed to use the rope that Grimaud had discarded as useless. *'Roof.'* Grimaud did not mean this roof; but the other roof which he crossed when he left Fley's room. *'Snow.'* The snow had stopped and wrecked his plans. *'Too much light.'* There's the crux, Hadley! When he looked out into the street, there was too much light from the street lamp; Fley recognized him, and fired. *'Got gun.'* Naturally, Fley had got the gun then. *'Fox.'* The mask, the Guy Fawkes charade he tried to work. But finally, *'Don't blame poor—'* Not Drayman; he didn't mean Drayman. But it was a last apology for the one thing, I think, of which he was ashamed; the one piece of imposture he would never have done. 'Don't blame poor Pettis; I didn't mean to implicate him.' "

For a long time nobody spoke.

"Yes," Hadley agreed, dully. "Yes. All except one thing. What about the slashing of that picture, and where did the knife go?"

"The slashing of the picture, I think, was an extra touch of the picturesque to help the illusion; Grimaud did it—or so I imagine. As for the knife, I frankly don't know. Grimaud probably had it here, and put it up the chimney beside the mirror so that the invisible man should seem to be doubly armed. But it isn't on the chimney ledge now. I should suppose that Drayman found it yesterday, and took it away—"

"That is the one point," said a voice, "on which you are wrong."

Ernestine Dumont remained in the doorway, her hands folded across the shawl at her breast. But she was smiling.

"I have heard everything you said," she went on. "Perhaps you can hang me, or perhaps not. That is not important. I do know that after so many years it is not quite worth while going on without Charles. . . . I took the knife, my friend. I had another use for it."

She was still smiling, and there was a blaze of pride in her eyes. Rampole saw what her hands were hiding. He saw her totter suddenly, but he was too late to catch her when she pitched forward on her face. Dr. Fell lumbered out of his chair and remained staring at her with a face as white as her own.

"I have committed another crime, Hadley," he said. "I have guessed the truth again."

THE END

# THE CROOKED HINGE

# I

## THE DEATH OF A MAN

The first rule to be borne in mind by the aspirant is this: Never tell your audience beforehand what you are going to do. If you do so, you at once give their vigilance the direction which it is most necessary to avoid, and increase tenfold the chances of detection. We will give an illustration.
—PROFESSOR HOFFMANN, *Modern Magic*

## CHAPTER I

AT A window overlooking a garden in Kent, Brian Page sat amid a clutter of open books at the writing-table, and felt a strong distaste for work. Through both windows the late July sunlight turned the floor of the room to gold. The somnolent heat brought out an odour of old wood and old books. A wasp hovered in from the apple-orchard behind the garden; and Page waved it out without much animation.

Beyond his garden wall, past the inn of the *Bull and Butcher*, the road wound for some quarter of a mile between orchards. It passed the gates of Farnleigh Close, whose thin clusters of chimneys Page could see above rifts in the trees, and then ascended past the wood poetically known as Hanging Chart.

The pale green and brown of the flat Kentish lands, which rarely acquired a harsh colour, now blazed. Page imagined that there was even colour in the brick chimneys of the Close. And along the road from the Close Mr. Nathaniel Burrows's car was moving with a noise audible for some distance, even if it was not moving fast.

There was, Brian Page thought lazily, almost too much excitement in Mallingford village. If the statement sounded too wild for belief, it could be proved. Only last summer there had been the murder of buxom Miss Daly, strangled by a tramp who had been dramatically killed while trying to get away across the railway-line. Then, in this last week of July, there had been two strangers putting up at the *Bull and Butcher* on successive days: one stranger who was an artist and the other who might be—nobody knew how this whisper got started—a detective.

Finally, there had been today the mysterious running to and fro of Page's friend Nathaniel Burrows, the solicitor from Maidstone. There seemed to be some general excitement or uneasiness at Farnleigh Close, though nobody knew what it meant. It was Brian Page's custom to knock off work at noon, and go over to the *Bull and Butcher* for a pint of beer before lunch; but it was an ominous sign that there had been no gossip at the inn that morning.

Yawning, Page pushed a few books aside. He wondered idly what could stir up Farnleigh Close, which had seldom been stirred up since Inigo Jones built it for the first baronet in the reign of James the First. It had known a long line of Farnleighs: a stringy, hardy line still. Sir John Farnleigh, the present holder of the baronetcy of Mallingford and Soane, had inherited a substantial fortune as well as a sound demesne.

Page liked both the dark, rather jumpy John Farnleigh and his forthright wife, Molly. The life here suited Farnleigh well; he fitted; he was a born squire, in spite of having been so long away from his home. For Farnleigh's story was another of those romantic tales which interested Page and which now seemed so difficult to reconcile with the solid, almost commonplace baronet at Farnleigh Close. From his first voyage out to his marriage to Molly Bishop little more than a year ago, it was (thought Page) another advertisement for the excitements of Mallingford village.

Grinning and yawning again, Page took up his pen. Got to get to work. Oh, Lord.

He considered the pamphlet at his elbow. His "Lives of the Chief Justices of England"—which he was trying to make both scholarly and popular—was going as well as might be expected. He was now dealing with Sir Matthew Hale. All sorts of external matters were always creeping in, because they had to creep in and because Brian Page had no wish to keep them out.

To tell the truth, he never really expected to finish the "Lives of the Chief Justices," any more than he had finished his original law-studies. He was too indolent for real scholarship, yet too restless-minded and intellectually alert to let it alone. It did not matter whether he ever finished the Chief Justices. But he could tell himself sternly that he ought to be working, and then with a sense of relief go wandering down all sorts of fascinating bypaths of the subject.

The pamphlet beside him read, A *Tryal of Witches at the Assizes Held at Bury St. Edmonds for the County of Suffolk, on the Tenth Day of March, 1664, before Sir Matthew Hale, K*., then Lord Chief Baron of his Majesty's Court of Exchequer: printed for D. Brown, J. Walthoe, and M. Wotton, 1718.*

There was a bypath down which he had wandered before. Sir Matthew Hale's connection with witches, of course, was of the slightest. But it would not prevent Brian Page from writing a superfluous half-chapter on any subject which happened to interest him. With a breath of pleasure he took down a well-worn Glanvill from one of the shelves. He was just beginning to muse over it when he heard footsteps in the garden, and somebody "oi'd" at him from outside the window.

It was Nathaniel Burrows, swinging a briefcase with unsolicitor-like gestures.

"Busy?" demanded Burrows.

"We-el," Page admitted, and yawned. He put down Glanvill. "Come in and have a cigarette."

Burrows opened the glass door giving on the garden and stepped into the dim, comfortable room. Though he held himself well in hand, he was excited enough to look chilly and rather pale on a hot afternoon. His father, grandfather, and great-grandfather had handled the legal affairs of the Farnleighs. Sometimes it might have been doubted whether Nathaniel Burrows, with his enthusiasms and occasional explosive speech, was the proper person for a family lawyer. Also, he was young. But as a rule he had all these things under control; and managed, Page thought, to look more frozen-faced than a halibut on a slab.

Burrows's dark hair had a wide parting, and was smoothed round his head with great nicety. He wore shell-rimmed spectacles on a long nose; he was peering over the spectacles, and his face at the moment seemed to have more than the usual number of muscles. He was dressed in black with great nicety and discomfort; his gloved hands were clasped on the briefcase.

"Brian," he said, "are you dining in tonight?"

"Yes. I——"

"Don't," said Burrows abruptly.

Page blinked.

"You're dining with the Farnleighs," Burrows went on. "At least, I don't care whether you dine there; but I should prefer that you were there when a certain thing happens." Something of his official manner came back to him, and swelled his thin chest. "I am authorized to tell you what I am going to tell you. Fortunately. Tell me: did you ever have reason to think that Sir John Farnleigh was not what he seemed?"

"Not what he seemed?"

"That Sir John Farnleigh," explained Burrows carefully, "was an impostor and a masquerader, not Sir John Farnleigh at all?"

"Have you got sunstroke?" asked the other, sitting up. He felt startled and irritated and unwarrantably stirred up. It was not the sort of thing to spring on a person at the laziest period of a hot day. "Certainly I never had reason to think any such thing. Why should I? What the devil are you getting at?"

Nathaniel Burrows got up from the chair, depositing the briefcase there.

"I say that," he answered, "because a man has turned up who claims to be the real John Farnleigh. This isn't a new thing. It's been going on for several months, and now it's come to a head. Er—" He hesitated, and looked round. "Is there anybody else here? Mrs. What's-her-name—you know, the woman who does for you—or anyone?"

"No."

Burrows spoke as though entirely through the front of his mouth and teeth. "I shouldn't be telling you this. But I know I can trust you; and (between ourselves) I am in a delicate position. This is going to make trouble. The Tichborne case won't be a patch on it. Of course—er—officially, as yet, I have no reason to believe that the man whose affairs I administer isn't Sir John Farnleigh. I am supposed to serve Sir John Farnleigh: the proper one. But that is the point. Here are two men. One is the real baronet and the other is a masquerading fraud. The two men are not alike; they don't even *look* alike. And yet may I be damned if I can decide which is which." He paused, and then added: "Fortunately, though, the affair may be settled tonight."

Page had to adjust his thoughts. Pushing the cigarette-box across to his guest, he lit a cigarette for himself and studied Burrows.

"This is one clap of thunder after another," he said. "What started it, anyhow? When has there been any reason to suppose that an impostor stepped in? Has the question ever come up before now?"

"Never. And you'll see why." Burrows got out a handkerchief, mopped his face all over with great care, and settled down calmly. "I only hope it's a mare's nest. I like John and Molly—sorry, Sir John and Lady Farnleigh—I like them enormously. If this claimant is an impostor, I'll dance on the village green—well, maybe not that, perhaps—but I shall make it my business to see that he gets a prison sentence for perjury longer than Arthur Orton's was. In the meantime, since you're going to hear about it tonight, you'd better know the background of the whole thing, and why the infernal mess has come up. Do you know Sir John's story?"

"In a vague general way."

"You should know nothing in a vague general way," retorted Burrows, shaking his head disapprovingly. "Is that the way you write your history? I hope not. Listen to me; and keep these simple facts firmly fixed in your mind.

"We are going back twenty-five years, when the present Sir John Farnleigh was fifteen. He was born in 1898, the second son of old Sir Dudley and Lady Farnleigh. There was no question then of his inheriting the title: the elder son, Dudley, was his parents' pride and joy.

"And they required something noble in the way of sons. Old Sir Dudley (I knew him all my life) was a late-Victorian of the most rigid sort. He wasn't as bad as the romances paint such types nowadays; but I remember as a kid that it always surprised me when he gave me a sixpence.

"Young Dudley was a good boy. John wasn't. He was a dark, quiet, wild sort of boy, but with so much sullenness that nobody could pardon the least offensive things he did. There was no real harm in him; it was merely that he didn't fit and wanted to be treated as a grown-up before he had grown up. In nineteen-twelve, when he was fifteen, he had a fully-grown-up affair with a barmaid in Maidstone——"

Page whistled. He glanced out of the window, as though he expected to see Farnleigh himself.

"At fifteen?" Page said. "Here, he must have been a lad!"

"He was."

Page hesitated. "And yet, you know, I'd always thought from what I've seen of him that Farnleigh was——"

"A bit of a Puritan?" supplied Burrows. "Yes. Anyhow, we're talking about a boy aged fifteen. His studying occult matters, including witchcraft and Satanism, was bad enough. His being expelled from Eton was worse. But the public scandal with the barmaid, who thought she was going to have a child, finished it. Sir Dudley Farnleigh simply decided that the boy was bad clean through, some throwback to the Satanist Farnleighs: that nothing would ever change him: and that he did not care to see him again. The usual course was adopted. Lady Farnleigh had a cousin in America, who was doing well there, and John was packed off to the States.

"The only person who seemed able to manage him at all was a tutor named Kennet Murray. The tutor, then a young fellow of twenty-two or three, had come to Farnleigh Close after John left school. Kennet Murray's hobby, it is important to mention, was scientific criminology: which was what drew the boy to Murray from the beginning. It wasn't a genteel hobby in those days; but old Sir Dudley liked and approved of Murray, so not much more was said.

"Now at this time, it happened, Murray had just been offered a good position as assistant headmaster of a school in Hamilton, Bermuda—provided he cared to go so far away from home. He accepted; his services were no longer required at the Close, anyway. It was arranged that Murray should travel out with the boy to New York, to see that he kept out of trouble. He should hand over the boy to Lady Farnleigh's cousin, and then take another ship down to Bermuda."

Nathaniel Burrows paused, considering the past.

"I don't remember much about those days, speaking personally," he added. "We younger children were kept away from the wicked John. But little Molly Bishop, who was then only six or seven years old, was frantically devoted to him. She wouldn't hear a word against him; and it may be significant that she has since married him. It seems to me I vaguely remember the day John was driven to the railway-station, in a phaeton, wearing a flat straw hat, with Kennet Murray beside him. They were sailing next day, which was a gala day for more reasons than one. I don't need to tell you that the ship they took was the *Titanic*."

Both Burrows and Page now looked at the past. The latter remembered it as a confused time of shoutings, and newspaper-bills at the corners, and legends without foundation.

"The unsinkable *Titanic* rammed an iceberg and sank on the night of April 15th, nineteen-twelve," Burrows went on. "In the confusion Murray and the boy were separated. Murray drifted for eighteen hours in icy water, holding to a wooden grating with two or three others. They were presently picked up by a cargo-boat, the *Colophon*—bound for Bermuda. Murray was taken to the place he meant to go. But he did not worry any longer when he heard by wireless that John Farnleigh was safe, and later got a letter confirming it.

"John Farnleigh, or a boy purporting to be John, was picked up by the *Etrusca*, bound for New York. There Lady Farnleigh's cousin, a Westerner, met him. The situation was exactly as it had been before. Beyond making sure the boy was alive, Sir Dudley was still quit of him. And old Sir Dudley wasn't any more bitter than the boy himself.

"He grew up in America, and lived there for nearly twenty-five years. He wouldn't write a line to his people; he would see them dead before he sent a photograph or a birthday message. Fortunately he took an immediate liking to the American cousin, a man named Renwick, and that supplied the need of parents. He—er—seemed to change. He lived quietly as a farmer on broad acres, just as he might have lived here. During the latter years of the war he served with the American army, but he never once set foot in England or met any of the people he had known. He never even saw Murray again. Murray was existing, though not prospering, in Bermuda. Neither could afford a journey to visit the other, especially as John Farnleigh lived in Colorado.

"Back here at home nothing was disturbed. The boy had been practically forgotten; and, after his mother died in nineteen twenty-six, he was completely forgotten. The father followed her four years later. Young Dudley—he was not so young now—inherited the title and all the estate. He had never married; he said there was time enough for that. But there wasn't. The new Sir Dudley died of ptomaine poisoning in August, nineteen thirty-five."

Brian Page reflected.

"That was just before I came here," Page observed. "But look here! Didn't Dudley try to get in touch with his brother at any time?"

"Yes. The letters were returned unopened. Dudley had been—well, rather a prig in the old days. By this time they had grown so far apart that apparently John didn't feel any family relationship. However, when it became a question of John's inheriting the title and the estate at Dudley's death——"

"John accepted."

"He accepted. Yes. That's the point," said Burrows explosively. "You know him and you understand. Nothing seemed so *right* as his coming back here. It didn't even seem strange to him, though he'd been away for nearly twenty-five years. He didn't seem strange: he still thought and acted and to a certain extent talked like the heir of Farnleigh. He came here at the begin-ning of nineteen thirty-six. As an additional romantic touch, he met a grown-up Molly Bishop and married her in May of the same year. He settles in for a little over a year; and now this happens. This happens."

"I suppose the suggestion is," said Page with some uncertainty, "that there was a substitution of identities at the time of the *Titanic* disaster? That the wrong boy was picked up at sea, and for some reason pretended to be John Farnleigh?"

Burrows had been walking up and down with measured slowness, wagging his finger at any piece of furniture he passed. But he did not look comic. There was about him an intellectual strength which soothed or even hypno-tized clients. He had a trick of turning his head sideways and peering at a companion past the sides of his big spectacles, as he did now.

"That's exactly it. Exactly. If the present John Farnleigh has been playing an imposture, don't you see, he has been playing it since nineteen-twelve—while the real heir lay low? He has grown into it. When he was rescued from the lifeboat after the wreck he wore Farnleigh's clothes and ring; he carried Farnleigh's diary. He has been exposed to the reminiscences of his Uncle Renwick in America. He has come back and settled into old ways. And twenty-five years! Handwritings change; faces and marks alter; even memories become uncertain. Do you see the difficulty? If sometimes he makes a slip, if there are gaps or clouds anywhere, that's only natural. Isn't it?"

Page shook his head.

"All the same, my lad, this claimant has got to have a thundering good case to gain any credence. You know what the courts are like. What sort of case *has* he got?"

"The claimant," answered Burrows, folding his arms, "offers absolute proof that he is the real Sir John Farnleigh."

"Have you seen this proof?"

"We are to see it—or not to see it—tonight. The claimant asks for an opportunity to meet the present holder. No, Brian: I am not in the least simple-minded, although I have nearly gone mad over this affair. It is not merely that the claimant's story is convincing, and that he offers all the minor proofs. It is not merely that he walked into my office (with, I regret to tell you, a bounder who is his legal representative) and told me things which only John Farnleigh could have known. *Only* John Farnleigh, I say. But he has proposed that he and the present holder shall submit to a certain test, which should be conclusive."

"What test?"

"You will see. Oh, yes. You will see." Nathaniel Burrows picked up his briefcase. "There has been only one gleam of comfort in the whole cursed mess. That is, so far there has been no publicity. The claimant is at least a gentleman—both of 'em are—bah—and he isn't anxious for a row. But there is going to be a remarkable row when I get my fingers on the truth. I'm glad my father isn't alive to see this. In the meantime, you be at Farnleigh Close at seven o'clock. Don't bother to dress for dinner. Nobody else will. It's only a pretext and there probably won't even be any dinner."

"And how is Sir John taking all this?"

"Which Sir John?"

"For the sake of clearness and convenience," retorted Page, "the man we have always known as Sir John Farnleigh. But this is interesting. Does it mean you believe the claimant is the real thing?"

"No. Not actually. Certainly not!" said Burrows. He caught himself up and spoke with dignity. "Farnleigh is only—sputtering. And I think that's a good sign."

"Does Molly know?"

"Yes; he told her today. Well, there you are. I've talked to you as no solicitor should and few ever do; but if I can't trust you I can't trust anybody, and I've been a bit uneasy about my conduct of things since my father died. Now get into the swim. Try my spiritual difficulties for yourself. Come up to Farnleigh Close at seven o'clock; we want you as a witness. Inspect the two candidates. Exercise your intelligence. And then, before we get down to business," said Burrows, banging the edge of his briefcase on the desk, "kindly tell me which is which."

## Chapter II

SHADOWS were gathering on the lower slopes of the wood called Hanging Chart, but the flat lands to the left of it were still clear and warm. Set back from the road behind a wall and a screen of trees, the house had those colours of dark-red brick which seem to come from an old painting. It was as smoothed, as arranged, as its own clipped lawns. The windows were tall and narrow, with panes set into a pattern of stone oblongs; and a straight gravel drive led up to the door. Its chimneys stood up thin and close-set against the last light.

No ivy had been allowed to grow against its face. But there was a line of beech trees set close against the house at the rear. Here a newer wing had been built out from the centre—like the body of an inverted letter T—and it divided the Dutch garden into two gardens. On one side of the house the garden was overlooked by the back windows of the library; on the other by the windows of the room in which Sir John Farnleigh and Molly Farnleigh were waiting now.

A clock ticked in this room. It was what might have been called in the eighteenth century a Music Room or Ladies' Withdrawing Room, and it

eemed to indicate the place of the house in this world. A pianoforte stood
ere, of that wood which in old age seems to resemble polished tortoise-
hell. There was silver of age and grace, and a view of the Hanging Chart
rom its north windows; Molly Farnleigh used it as a sitting-room. It was
ery warm and quiet here, except for the ticking of the clock.

Molly Farnleigh sat by the window in the shadow of a great "octopus"
>eech-tree. She was what is called an outdoor girl, with a sturdy and well-
haped body, and a square but very attractive face. Her dark brown hair
vas uncompromisingly bobbed. She had light hazel eyes in a tanned, earnest
ace; and a directness of look which was as good as a handclasp. Her mouth
night have been too broad, but she showed fine teeth when she laughed.
f she was not exactly pretty, health and vigour gave her a strong attractive-
iess which was better than that.

But she was not laughing now. Her eyes never left her husband, who was
>acing the room with short, sharp steps.

"You're not worried?" she asked.

Sir John Farnleigh stopped short. Then he fiddled with his dark wrists,
ind resumed his pacing.

"Worried? No. Oh, no. It's not that. It's only—oh, damn it all!"

He seemed an ideal partner for her. It would convey the wrong impression
o say that he looked in his element as a country squire, for the word has
ome to be associated with beefy roisterers of a hundred years ago. Yet there
s a truer type. Farnleigh was of middle height, of a stringy, active leanness
vhich somehow suggested the lines of a plough: the bright metal, the com-
>actness, the crisp blade that cuts the furrow.

His age might have been forty. He was of darkish complexion, with a thick
>ut close-cropped moustache. He had dark hair in which there were thin lines
>f grey, and sharp dark eyes with growing wrinkles at the corners. You would
iave said that at the moment he was at the top of his mental and physical
orm, a man of enormous repressed energies. Striding back and forth in the
ittle room, he seemed less angry or upset than uncomfortable and embar-
.assed.

Molly started to rise. She cried:

"Oh, my dear, why didn't you *tell* me?"

"No use worrying you with it," the other said. "It's my affair. I'll manage."

"How long have you known about it?"

"A month or so. Thereabouts."

"And that's what's been worrying you all this time?" she asked, with a
>hade of different worry in her eyes.

"Partly," he grunted, and looked at her quickly.

"Partly? What do you mean by that?"

"What I say, my dear: partly."

"John . . . it hasn't got anything to do with Madeline Dane, has it?"

He stopped. "Good God, no! Certainly not. I don't know why you ask
questions like that. You don't like Madeline, really, do you?"

"I don't like her eyes. They're queer eyes," said Molly, and checked her
self out of a certain pride or another feeling she refused to name. "I'm
sorry. I shouldn't have said anything like that, with all these other things
coming up. It's not very pleasant; but there's nothing to it, is there? Of
course the man hasn't got a case?"

"He hasn't got a right. I don't know whether he's got a case."

He spoke brusquely, and she studied him.

"But why is there so much fuss and mystery? If he's an impostor, couldn'
you sling him out and let the matter drop?"

"Burrows says it wouldn't be wise. Not yet, anyway, until we've—er—heard
what he has to say. Then we can take action. And real action. Besides—"

Molly Farnleigh's face grew expressionless.

"I wish you'd let me help you," she said. "Not that I could do anything
I suppose, but I should just like to know what it's all *about*. I know this man
challenges you to let him prove he's really you. Of course that's all non
sense. I knew you years ago; and I knew you when I saw you again; you
would be surprised how easily I knew. But I know you're having this fellow
here at the house, with Nat Burrows and another solicitor, and being hor
ribly mysterious. What are you going to do?"

"Do you remember my old tutor, Kennet Murray?"

"Faintly," said Molly, wrinkling her forehead. "Largish, pleasant man with
a little cropped beard like a naval man or an artist. I suppose he was really
young then, but he seemed ages old. Told wonderful stories——"

"His ambition was always to be a great detective," answered the other
curtly. "Well, the Opposition have brought him from Bermuda. He says he
can absolutely identify the real John Farnleigh. He's at the *Bull and Butcher*
now."

"Wait a bit!" said Molly. "There's a man staying there who 'looks like an
artist.' The village is full of it. Is that Murray?"

"That's old Murray. I wanted to go down and see him; but it wouldn't be
—well, it wouldn't be sporting," said her husband, with a kind of inner struggle and writhing. "It might look as though I were trying to influence him
Or something. He's coming up here to see us both, and identify—me."

"How?"

"He's the one person in the world who really knew me well. The family
has pretty well died out; you know that. The old servants have died out with
my parents: except Nannie, and she's in New Zealand. Even Knowles has
been here for only ten years. There are plenty of people that I knew vaguely,
but you know I was an unsociable cuss and I didn't make friends. Poor old
criminal-investigating Murray is undoubtedly it. He's remaining neutral and

not having anything to do with either side; but, if he wants to have the one shot of his life at playing the great detective——"

Molly drew a deep breath. The health of her tanned face, the health of her whole body, animated the directness with which she spoke.

"John, I don't understand this. I do not understand it. You talk as though this were a wager or a game of some kind. 'Wouldn't be sporting.' 'Not having anything to do with either side.' Do you realize that this man—whoever he is—has coolly announced that he owns everything you own? That he's John Farnleigh? That he's the heir to a baronetcy and thirty thousand pounds a year? And that he means to have it from you?"

"Yes, I realize that."

"But doesn't it mean anything to you?" cried Molly. "You're treating him with as great care and consideration as though it didn't."

"It means everything to me."

"Well, then! If anybody had come to you and said, 'I am John Farnleigh,' I should have thought you would have said, 'Oh, really?' and merely kicked him out without thinking anything more about it, unless you sent for the police. That's what I should have done."

"You don't understand these things, my dear. And Burrows says——"

He looked slowly round the room. He seemed to be listening to the quiet ticking of the clock, to be savouring the odours of scrubbed floors and fresh curtains, to be reaching out in the sunlight over all the rich and quiet acres he now owned. At that moment, oddly enough, he looked most like a Puritan; and also he looked dangerous.

"It would be rather rotten," he said slowly, "to lose all this now."

He caught himself up, altering the quiet violence of his manner, as the door opened. Knowles, the old and bald-headed butler, ushered in Nathaniel Burrows and Brian Page.

Burrows, as Page had observed during their walk up here, wore now his most buttoned-up and halibut-like look. Page would not have known him for the human being of that afternoon. But Page supposed it was necessary because of the awkward atmosphere: he felt it at its worst. Glancing at his host and hostess, he began to wish he hadn't come.

The solicitor greeted his host and hostess with almost painful formality; and Farnleigh had drawn himself up stiffly, as though he were going to fight a duel.

"I think," Burrows added, "we shall be able to proceed to business soon. Mr. Page has kindly consented to act as the witness we desired——"

"Oh, look here," protested Page, with an effort. "We're not being besieged in a citadel, you know. You're one of the largest and most respected landowners in Kent. To hear what I've just heard from Burrows," he looked at Farnleigh, and could not discuss the matter, "is like hearing that grass is red or water runs uphill. It's about as reasonable, in the eyes of most people. Have you got to be so much on the defensive?"

Farnleigh spoke slowly.

"That's true," he admitted. "I suppose I'm being a fool."

"You are," agreed Molly. "Thanks, Brian."

"Old Murray—" said Farnleigh, with a far-away look. "Have you seen him, Burrows?"

"Only for a short time, Sir John. Not officially. Neither have the Other Side. His position is, plainly, that he has a test to apply; and in the meantime he says nothing."

"Has he changed much?"

Burrows became more human. "Not much. He's older and stiffer and sourer, and his beard is grey. Old days——"

"Old days," said Farnleigh. "My God, yes!" He turned something over in his mind. "There's just one question I want to ask you. Have you got any reason to suspect that Murray isn't straight? Wait! I know it's a rotten thing to say. Old Murray always was too honest: transparently. But we haven't seen him for twenty-five years. It's a long time. I've changed. No possibility of crooked work, is there?"

"You can rest assured there is not," said Burrows grimly. "I think we have discussed that before. It was the first thing that occurred to me, of course; and, considering the steps we have taken, you yourself have been satisfied of Mr. Murray's *bona fides*. Have you not?"\*

"Yes, I suppose so."

"Then may I ask why you bring it up now?"

"You will oblige me," retorted Farnleigh, suddenly freezing up in a very passable imitation of Burrows's own manner, "by not looking as though you thought I were the impostor and the crook. You're all doing it. Don't deny it! That's exactly what you're doing. Peace, peace, peace: I've been looking all over the world for peace, and where am I going to get it? But I'll tell you why I ask about Murray. If you don't think there is anything crooked about Murray, why have you got a private detective watching him?"

Behind the big spectacles Burrows's eyes opened in obvious astonishment.

"I beg your pardon, Sir John. I have had no private detective watching Mr. Murray or anybody else."

Farnleigh pulled himself up. "Then who's the other fellow down at the

---

\* Newspaper-readers may remember, in the bitter debate which followed tragedy in the Farnleigh case, that this point was often brought up by amateurs. Having myself once wasted time on many futile theories in an attempt to solve the mystery, I feel that I had better clear it up here. The honesty and good faith of Kennet Murray may be accepted as a fact. The evidence he possessed, with regard to establishing the identity of the real heir, was genuine evidence; and, it may be recalled, was later used to establish the truth.—J. D. C.

*Bull and Butcher?* You know: youngish, hard-faced chap with all the sly sides and questions? Everybody in the village says he's a private detective. He says he's interested in 'folklore,' and writing a book. Folklore my foot. He's sticking to Murray like a limpet."

They all looked at each other.

"Yes," Burrows observed thoughtfully. "I have heard of the folklorist and his interest in people. He may have been sent by Welkyn——"

"Welkyn?"

"The claimant's solicitor. Or he may have nothing to do with the case, s is most probable."

"I doubt it," said Farnleigh, and the blood seemed to come up under his yes, making his face darker. "Not all he's interested in. The private detective chap, I mean. He's been asking all kinds of questions, from what I hear, bout poor Victoria Daly."

To Brian Page it seemed that values had shifted slightly, and all familiar things were becoming unfamiliar. In the midst of a debate about his right o an estate worth thirty thousand pounds a year, Farnleigh seemed more preoccupied with the commonplace—if sordid—tragedy of the previous summer. Well? Victoria Daly, an inoffensive spinster of thirty-five, strangled in her cottage by a tramp who professed to sell boot-laces and collar-studs? Strangled, curiously enough, with a boot-lace; and her purse found in the tramp's pocket when he was killed on the railway-line?

In the midst of a silence, while Page and Molly Farnleigh looked at each other, the door of the room opened. Knowles came in with an air of equal uncertainty.

"There are two gentlemen to see you, sir," Knowles said. "One is a Mr. Welkyn, a solicitor. The other——"

"Well? The other?"

"The other asks me to say that he is Sir John Farnleigh."

"Does he? Oh. Well——"

Molly got up quietly, but muscles had tightened at the corners of her jaws.

"Take back this message from Sir John Farnleigh," she instructed Knowles. "Sir John Farnleigh presents his compliments; and, if the caller has no name o give other than that, he may go round and wait in the servants' hall until Sir John finds time to see him."

"No, come, come!" stuttered Burrows, in a kind of legal agony. "Trying circumstances—necessary to be tactful—freeze him all you like, but don't——"

The shadow of a smile crossed Farnleigh's dark face.

"Very well, Knowles. Take that message."

"Impudence," said Molly, breathing hard.

When Knowles returned he had less the air of a courier than of a sensitive tennis-ball being driven to different corners of the court.

"The gentleman says, sir, that he deeply apologizes for his message, which was premature, and hopes there will be no ill-feeling in the matter. He says he has chosen for some years to be known as Mr. Patrick Gore."

"I see," said Farnleigh. "Show Mr. Gore and Mr. Welkyn into the library."

## Chapter III

THE claimant got up from his chair. Despite the fact that one wall of the library was built of windows, multitudinous panes set in a pattern of stone oblongs, the daylight was going; and the trees threw heavy shadows. On the stone-flagged floor there was insufficient carpeting. The heavy book-shelves were built up like tiers in a crypt, scrolled along the top. Green-shadowed light through the windows drew across the floor a silhouette of a hundred panes, stretching almost to the man who rose to his feet beside the table.

Molly has since confessed that her heart was in her mouth when the door opened, and that she wondered whether a living counterpart of her husband might not appear from behind it, as in a mirror. Yet there was no great resemblance between these two.

The man in the library was no heavier than Farnleigh, yet less wiry. His dark, fine hair had no grey in it, but he was going a little thin on top. Though dark of complexion, he was clean-shaven and his face was comparatively unfurrowed. Any wrinkles in his forehead or round his eyes were those of amusement rather than doggedness. For the claimant's whole expression was one of ease, irony, and amusement, with very dark grey eyes, and eyebrows wisped up a little at the outer corners. He was well dressed, in town clothes as opposed to Farnleigh's old tweeds.

"I beg your pardon," he said.

Even his voice was a baritone, in contrast to Farnleigh's harsh and rasping tenor. His walk was not exactly limping, but a bit clumsy.

"I beg your pardon," he said with grave courtesy, but with a certain oblique look of amusement, "for seeming so insistent about returning to my old home. But you will, I hope, appreciate my motives. Er—let me present my legal representative, Mr. Welkyn."

A fat man with somewhat protuberant eyes had got up from a chair at the other side of the table. But they hardly saw him. The claimant was not only studying them with interest; he was glancing round the room as though he were recognizing and drinking in every detail.

"Let's get down to business," said Farnleigh abruptly. "I think you've met Burrows. This is Mr. Page. This is my wife."

"I have met—" said the claimant, hesitating and then looking full at Molly —"your wife. Forgive me if I do not know quite how to address her. I can't call her Lady Farnleigh. And I can't call her Molly, as I used to do when she wore hair-ribbons."

Neither of the Farnleighs commented. Molly was calm but flushed, and there was a dry strain about her eyes.

"Also," went on the claimant, "I should like to thank you for taking this very awkward and unpleasant business in such good part——"

"I don't," snapped Farnleigh. "I take it in devilish damned bad part, and you might as well understand that. The only reason why I don't throw you out of the house is because my own solicitor seems to think we ought to be tactful. All right: speak up. What have you got to say?"

Mr. Welkyn moved out from the table, clearing his throat.

"My client, Sir John Farnleigh—" he began.

"One moment," interposed Burrows, with equal suavity. Page seemed to hear a faint hiss as legal axes began to grind; as forensic sleeves were rolled up; as the conversation was being geared to the pace these gentlemen would have it take. "May I request, for the sake of convenience, that we refer to your client by some other name? He chose to give the name of 'Patrick Gore.'"

"I should prefer," said Welkyn, "to refer to him simply as 'my client.' Will that be satisfactory?"

"Perfectly."

"Thank you. I have here," pursued Welkyn, opening his briefcase, "a proposal which my client is prepared to submit. My client wishes to be fair. While under the necessity of pointing out that the present holder has no claim to the title and estates, nevertheless my client remembers the circumstances under which the imposture was begun. He also recognizes the present holder's able stewardship and the fact that nothing but credit has been reflected on the family name.

"Therefore, if the present holder will at once withdraw without making it necessary to take the matter into the courts, there will be, of course, no question of prosecution. To the contrary, my client is willing to make some financial compensation to the present holder: let us say an annuity of one thousand pounds a year for life. My client has ascertained that the present holder's wife—née Miss Mary Bishop—has inherited a fortune in her own right; and the question of straitened finances should not, therefore, arise. Of course, I confess that should the present holder's wife care to question the validity of the marriage on the grounds of fraudulent——"

Again the blood had come up under Farnleigh's eyes.

"God!" he said. "Of all the brazen, bare-faced——"

Nathaniel Burrows made a noise which was too polite to be called shushing, but it restrained Farnleigh.

"May I suggest, Mr. Welkyn," Burrows replied, "that we are here at the moment to determine whether your client has a claim? Until that is determined, any other considerations do not arise."

"As you please. My client," said Welkyn, with a disdainful movement of his shoulders, "merely wished to avoid unpleasantness. Mr. Kennet Murray should be with us in a few minutes. After that I fear the result will be no longer in doubt. If the present holder persists in his attitude, then I am afraid the consequences will be——"

"Look here," Farnleigh interposed again, "let's cut the cackle and get down to the horses."

The claimant smiled, which seemed to turn his eyes inwards with some secret joke. "You see?" he remarked. "His pseudo-gentility is so grafted on him that he cannot bring himself to say 'osses."

"It doesn't bring him to giving cheap insults, in any case," said Molly; and now it was the claimant who showed a slight flush.

"I beg your pardon. I should not have said that. But you must remember," said the claimant, his tone again changing a little, "that I have dwelt among wicked ways, and hardly by the springs of Dove. Have I leave to present my own case in my own way?"

"Yes," said Farnleigh. "Shut up," he added to both lawyers. "This is a personal matter now."

As though by common consent they all moved towards the table and took chairs. The claimant sat with his back to the great window. For a time he remained thoughtful, absently patting the slight thinning patch that showed in the crown of his dark hair. Then he looked up, with the edge of mockery showing in the wrinkles round his eyes.

"I am John Farnleigh," he began with great simplicity and apparent earnestness. "Kindly do not interrupt me with legal quibbles at this time; I am presenting my case, and am entitled to call myself the Cham of Tartary if I feel so inclined. However, I really do happen to be John Farnleigh, and I will tell you what happened to me.

"As a boy I may have been something of a young swine; though even now I am not certain I did not have the right attitude. My late father, Dudley Farnleigh, would put up my hackles just as much if he were alive now. No, I cannot say I was wrong, except that I should have learned more give-and-take. I quarreled with my elders for pointing out that I was young, I quarreled with my tutors because I despised every subject in which I was not interested.

"To get down to business, you know why I left here. I sailed with Murray in the *Titanic*. And, from the first, I spent as much time as I could with the steerage passengers. Not, you understand, because I felt any particular liking for the steerage passengers, but simply because I hated my own crowd in first-class. This is not a defence, you know: it is a psychological account which I think you will find convincing.

"In the steerage I met a Rumanian-English boy, about my own age, who was going out alone to the States. He interested me. His father—who could never afterwards be found—he said was an English gentleman. His mother was a Rumanian girl, a snake-dancer at a travelling circus in England during the times when she was not drinking. There came a time when real snakes would not mix with imaginary ones, and the woman was reduced to the position of part-time cook in the circus mess-tent. The boy became a nuisance. An old admirer of hers was doing well in a small way with a circus in America, and so she was sending the boy out to him.

"He would be taught to ride a bicycle on the tight-rope, he would be taught—and how I envied him. Lord of saints and snakes, HOW I envied him! Will any right-minded boy or man blame me?"

The claimant shifted a little in his chair. He seemed to be looking back cynically, yet with a certain satisfaction; and none of the others moved. The suave Mr. Welkyn, who seemed about to interpose with a comment or suggestion, looked quickly round at the group of faces and remained silent.

"The odd part of it," continued the speaker, examining his fingernails, "was that this boy envied me. His name (which was something unpronounceable) he had changed to 'Patrick Gore' because he liked the sound of it. He disliked circus life. He disliked the movement and the change and the din and the upset. He hated stakes driven in overnight to be pulled up in the morning, and elbows in your face at the soup-kitchen. I don't know where he got it: he was a reserved, cold-faced, well-mannered little bounder. The first time we met we flew at each other and fought until half the steerage had to drag us apart. I am afraid that I was so enraged I wanted to go at him afterwards with my clasp-knife. He simply bowed to me and walked away; I can see him yet.—I am referring, my friend, to you."

He glanced up at Farnleigh.

"This can't be real," Farnleigh said suddenly, and passed his hand across his forehead, "I don't believe it. It's a nightmare. Are you seriously suggesting——?"

"Yes," agreed the other, with a decisive snap. "We discussed how pleasant it would be if we could swap identities. Only as a wild dream of let's pretend, of course: at that moment. You said it would never work, though you looked as though you would like to murder me to get it. I don't suppose I ever really meant to carry out any such thing; the interesting point is that you did mean it. I used to give you information about myself. I used to tell you, 'Now if you met my Aunt So-and-So or my Cousin This-and-that, this is what you must say to them,' and lord it over you in a way that I do not like to remember: for this is no justification of my behaviour there. I thought you were a prig and I still think so. I also showed you my diary. I always kept a diary, for the simple reason that there was nobody on earth I could talk to. I still keep one." Here the claimant glanced up almost whimsically. "Do you remember me, Patrick? Do you remember the night the *Titanic* went down?"

There was a pause.

On Farnleigh's face there was no expression of anger: only of bewilderment.

"I keep telling you," he said, "that you're mad."

"When we struck that iceberg," the other went on carefully, "I will tell you exactly what I was doing. I was down in the cabin I shared with poor old Murray, while he was in the smoking-room playing bridge. Murray kept a flask of brandy in one of his coats; and I was sampling it because they would not serve me in the bar.

"I scarcely felt it when we struck; I question if anybody did. There was a very slight bump, hardly enough to spill a filled cocktail-glass on a table; and then the stopping of the engines. I only went out into the alleyway because I wondered why the engines had stopped. The first I knew of it came from the noise of voices getting louder and closer; and then a woman suddenly running past screaming with a blue quilt wrapped round her shoulders."

For the first time the claimant hesitated.

"I am not going to bring back old tragedies by saying anything more about that part of it," he said, opening and shutting his hands. "I will say only this, for which God forgive me, even as a boy: I rather enjoyed it. I was not in the least frightened. I was exhilarated. It was something out of the common, something to take away the ordinary sameness of everyday life; and I had always been looking for things like that. And I was so wild with excitement that I agreed to change identities with Patrick Gore. The determination seemed to come to me all at once, though I am wondering if he had thought about it for a long time.

"I met Gore—I met you," amplified the speaker, looking at his host steadily, "on B Deck. You had all your possessions in a little straw suitcase. You told me quite coolly that the ship was going down, and going down fast: if I really wanted to change identities, it might be managed in the confusion, or if either of us survived. I said, what about Murray? You lied, saying that Murray was overboard and dead already. And I was willing enough to become a great circus-performer, so we changed: clothes, papers, rings, everything. You even got my diary."

Farnleigh said nothing.

"Afterwards," added the claimant, without altering the tone of his voice, "you were very neat. We were ready to run for the boats. You waited until my back was turned; then you fished out the steward's wooden mallet you had stolen, you caught me on the back of the skull with it, and you tried with three blows to finish the work."

Farnleigh still said nothing. Molly got up from her chair; but, at a gesture from him, she sat down again.

"Mind you," insisted the claimant, with a movement as though he were flicking dust from the table, "I am not here to bring that up against you. Twenty-five years is a long time, and you were a boy then, though I am wondering into what sort of man you have grown. I was considered a bad lot myself. It is possible that you despised me and believed you had justification. You need not have been so thorough, because I should have assumed your identity in any case. Still—even if I was the black sheep of the family, I was never quite so black as that.

"The rest of it will be clear to you. By what I must insist was a stroke of luck I was found, damaged but alive, and pushed into the last surviving boat. The casualty lists were at first uncertain, and America is a large country, and I was for some time in the world of shadows. Both the names of John Farnleigh and Patrick Gore appeared as missing. I thought you were dead, as you thought I was. When my possessions and papers identified me as Patrick Gore to Mr. Boris Yeldritch, the circus-proprietor—who had never seen you—I was entirely content.

"If I did not like the life, I thought, I could always reveal myself. Perhaps I should have better treatment, I thought, if I miraculously returned from the dead. The prospect pleased me; it was a dramatic card in reserve; and, believe me, it gave me many comforting nights."

"And," said Molly as though with elaborate interest, "did you become the trick bicycle-rider of the circus?"

The claimant turned his head sideways. His dark grey eye was kindled with such strong inner amusement that he resembled a crafty small boy. Again he lifted his hand and rubbed the thinning patch on the crown of his head.

"No. No, although I had my first sensational success with the circus, I became something else. For the moment I should prefer not to tell you what it was. In addition to the fact that it is an excellent secret, I do not wish to bore you with details of my subsequent life.

"Believe me, I had always intended one day to return to my old home and astonish them with the baaing of a black sheep from the grave. For I *have* been successful; by all the prophets I have!—and I felt that this would make my brother Dudley writhe. But this dramatic plum I reserved. I even visited England without being too much tempted. For, mind you, I had no reason to suspect that 'John Farnleigh' was alive. I thought he was supposed to be dead, instead of flourishing in Colorado.

"You will therefore understand my surprise, some six months ago, when quite by chance I picked up an illustrated paper and saw the picture of Sir John and Lady Farnleigh. My brother Dudley, I noted, was dead of a surfeit of lampreys. His 'younger brother' had inherited. At first I thought this must be the mistake of the paper for some distant connection. But a few inquiries uncovered the truth; and after all, you know, I *am* the heir. Still a young man—still vigorous—but not revengeful.

"Such things grow exceedingly dim. A generation has grown up; there are a thousand good memories between me and the small whelp who tried to alter the succession with a seaman's mallet and who, I hear, has become a useful citizen since. All the trees look the same; but my eyes have changed. I feel strange and raw in my own home. I am not sure that I shall make the best possible patron for the local cricket-club or the local Boy Scouts. But I have (as you observe) a strong weakness for making speeches, and I daresay I shall get on well enough. Now, Patrick Gore, you have heard my proposal. It is generous enough. If I take you to court, I warn you I will have your hide. In the meantime, gentlemen, I am open to answer questions from anyone who has ever known me. I have a few questions to put myself, and I will defy Gore to answer them."

For a time after he had spoken, it was quiet in the darkening room. He had an almost hypnotic voice. But they were looking at Farnleigh, who had risen and stood with his knuckles on the table. In Farnleigh's dark face there was quiet, and relief, and a certain curiosity as he examined his guest. He brushed a hand under his cropped moustache; he almost smiled.

Molly saw that smile, and drew a deep breath.

"You have something to say, John?" she prompted.

"Yes. I don't know why he's come here with this story, or what he hopes to get out of it. But what this man says is absolutely false from beginning to end."

"You intend to fight?" asked the claimant with interest.

"Of course I mean to fight, you ass. Or, rather, I'll let you do the fighting."

Mr. Welkyn seemed about to intervene, with a vast throat-clearing, but the claimant stopped him.

"No, no," he said comfortably. "Please stay out of this, Welkyn. You brethren of the law are all very well to put in the 'whereases' and the 'proceed with caution,' but you are out of place in a personal skirmish like this. To tell the truth, I shall enjoy this. Well, let us apply a few tests. I wonder if you would mind calling your butler in here?"

Farnleigh frowned. "But look here: Knowles wasn't——"

"Why not do as he asks, John?" suggested Molly sweetly.

Farnleigh caught her look; and, if there is a paradox which can be called humourless humour, his sharp features showed it. He rang for Knowles, who entered in the same uncertain way. The claimant regarded him musingly.

"I thought I recognized you when we came in here," the claimant said. "You were here in my father's time, were you not?"

"Sir?"

"You were here in my father's, Sir Dudley Farnleigh's, time. Weren't you?"

An expression of disgust went over Farnleigh's face.

"You will do your case no good by this," interposed Nathaniel Burrows sharply. "The butler in Sir Dudley Farnleigh's time was Stenson, who has been dead——"

"Yes. I was aware of that," said the claimant, turning his eyes sideways. Then he contemplated the butler, sitting back and crossing his legs with some effort. "Your name is Knowles. In my father's time you were the butler at old Colonel Mardale's place, over in Frettenden. You used to keep two rabbits that the colonel knew nothing about. You kept them in a corner of the coach-house nearest the orchard. One of the rabbits was named Billy." He looked up. "Ask this gentleman the name of the other."

Knowles had gone slightly pink.

"Ask him, will you?"

"Rot!" snapped Farnleigh, and drew himself back into his dignity again.

"Oh," said the claimant. "You mean you cannot answer?"

"I mean I don't choose to answer." Yet six pairs of eyes were fastened on him, and he seemed to feel the pressure; he shifted and almost stuttered. "Who can be expected to remember the name of a rabbit after twenty-five years? All right, all right: stop a bit! There was some nonsense about their names, I remember. Let me think. Billy and W—no, that's not it. Billy and Silly, that's it? Or was it? I'm not sure."

"That is correct, sir," Knowles told him with an air of relief.

The claimant was not out of countenance.

"Well, let us try again. Now, Knowles. One evening in summer—it was the year before I went away—you were going through that same orchard to take a message to a certain neighbour. You were surprised and rather shocked to find me making love to a certain young lady of twelve or thirteen. Ask your employer the name of that young lady."

Farnleigh was dark and heavy-looking.

"I don't remember any such incident."

"Are you trying to convey the impression," said the claimant, "that your natural chivalry restrains you? No, my friend, that will not do. It was a long time ago and I give you my solemn word that nothing of a compromising nature passed. Knowles, you remember what went on in the apple-orchard, don't you?"

"Sir," said the bedevilled butler, "I——"

"You do. But I thought this man would not remember it, because I do not think I entered the fact in my valuable diary. What was the name of the young lady?"

Farnleigh nodded. "All right," he answered with an attempt at lightness. "It was Miss Dane, Madeline Dane."

"Madeline Dane—" began Molly.

For the first time the claimant seemed a little taken aback. His quick eyes moved round the group, and his quick intuition seemed to move too.

"She must have written to you in America," returned the claimant. "We shall have to cut deeper. But I beg your pardon: I hope I have committed no blunder? I hope the young lady is not still living in the district at a more mature age, and that I have not touched on any inconvenient subject?"

"Damn you," said Farnleigh suddenly, "I've stood about enough of this. I can't keep my temper much longer. Will you kindly get out of here?"

"No," said the other. "I mean to break down your bluff. For it is a bluff, my boy, and you know it. Besides, I think it was agreed that we should wait for Kennet Murray."

"Suppose we do wait for Murray?" Farnleigh spoke with toiling lucidity. "Where will it get us? What will it prove, beyond this fiddle-faddle of questions to which we both apparently know the answers? And yet you don't know the answers, because you're the one who is bluffing. I could ask some myself, just as nonsensical as yours. But that's nothing. How did you ever expect to prove a thing like this. How do you still think you can prove it?"

The claimant sat back, richly enjoying his position.

"By the incontrovertible evidence of fingerprints," he said.


## Chapter IV

IT WAS as though the man had been keeping this in reserve, waiting for the proper moment to say it and savouring triumph in advance. He seemed a little disappointed that he had to produce the trump so early, and under circumstances less dramatic than he might have wished. But the others were not thinking of it in terms of drama.

Brian Page heard Burrows breathe in with a shaky kind of noise. Burrows got to his feet.

"I was not informed of this," the solicitor said fiercely.

"But you guessed it?" smiled fat Mr. Welkyn.

"It is not my business to guess at anything," returned Burrows. "I repeat, sir, I have not been informed of this. I have heard nothing about fingerprints."

"Nor have we, officially. Mr. Murray has kept his own counsel. But," inquired Welkyn, with rich suavity, "does the present holder need to be told? If he is the real Sir John Farnleigh, surely he remembers that Mr. Murray took the fingerprints of the boy as long ago as the year nineteen ten or eleven."

"I repeat, sir——"

"Let *me* repeat, Mr. Burrows: did you need to be informed of it? What does the present holder himself have to say?"

Farnleigh's expression seemed to have retreated, to have become locked up. As usual when he was among mental brambles, he did two things. He began to walk round the room with short, quick steps; and he took a key-ring out of his pocket and twirled it round his forefinger.

"Sir John!"

"Eh?"

"Do you remember," asked Burrows, "any such circumstances as Mr. Welkyn mentions? Did Mr. Murray ever take your fingerprints?"

"Oh, that," said Farnleigh, as though it were of no importance. "Yes, I remember it now. I'd forgotten it. But it occurred to me when I was talking to you and my wife a while ago—you know. I wondered if that could be it, and it made me a whole lot easier in my mind. Yes, old Murray got my fingerprints right enough."

The claimant turned round. He wore an expression not only of mild astonishment, but of sudden and wondering suspicion as well.

"This will not do, you know," the claimant said. "You don't maintain that you will face the test of fingerprints?"

"Face it? Face it?" repeated Farnleigh, with grim pleasure. "Man, it's the best thing that could have happened. You're the impostor, and you know it. Murray's old fingerprint test—by George, now I come to think of it, I can remember every detail of that business!—will settle matters. Then I can throw you out."

And the two rivals looked at each other.

For some time Brian Page had been trying to put weights into a scales which would not remain still. He had been trying, without friendship or prejudice, to see where the imposture lay. The issue was simple. If Patrick Gore (to give him the name by which he had been announced) were the impostor, he was one of the coolest and most smooth-faced crooks who ever walked into another man's house. If the present John Farnleigh were the impostor, he was not only a slippery criminal behind that naive, straightforward mask: he was a would-be murderer as well.

There was a pause.

"You know, my friend," observed the claimant, as though with refreshed interest, "I admire your cheek. One moment, please. I do not say that as a baiting jeer or to start a row. I state, as a matter of simple fact, that I admire an *aes-triplex* cheek which Casanova himself could not have equalled. Now, I am not surprised that you 'forgot' the fingerprints. They were taken at a time before I began to keep my diary. But to say you forgot them: to SAY you forgot them——"

"Well, what's wrong with that?"

"John Farnleigh wouldn't or couldn't have forgotten a detail of that. I, being John Farnleigh, certainly didn't. That is why Kennet Murray was the only person in the world who had any influence with me. Murray on Footprints. Murray on Disguises. Murray on the Disposal of the Body. Wough! And particularly Murray on Fingerprints, which were then the newest scientific craze. I am aware,"—he interrupted himself, raising his voice and looking round the group,—"that fingerprints were discovered by Sir William Herschel in the eighteen-fifties, and re-discovered by Dr. Faulds in the late seventies. But they were not admitted as legal evidence in an English court until nineteen-five, and even then the judge was dubious. It took years of argument to establish them. Yet, as a possible 'test' of Murray's, you say you never thought of fingerprints."

"You're doing a hell of a lot of talking," said Farnleigh, who again looked swollen and dangerous.

"Naturally. Though you never once thought of fingerprints before, it all comes back to you now. Tell me this. When the prints were taken, how were they taken?"

"How?"

"In what form?"

Farnleigh pondered. "On a sheet of glass," he said.

"Nonsense. They were taken in a 'Thumbograph,' a little book which was quite a popular game or toy at the time. A little grey book. Murray had a lot of others, my father's and my mother's and anybody else's he could get."

"Stop a bit. Hold on. I believe there was a book—we sat over in that window——"

"So you profess to remember now."

"Look here," said Farnleigh quietly, "who do you think I am? Do you think I'm that fellow in the music-halls, the one you shoot questions at and he instantly tells you the number of clauses in the Magna Charta or what horse ran second in the Derby in 1882? That's what *you* sound like. There's a lot of rubbish that's better forgotten. People change. They change, I tell you."

"But not their basic characters, as you profess to have changed. That is the point I am making. You cannot turn your whole soul inside out, you know."

During this controversy Mr. Welkyn had been sitting back with a massive gravity but with a certain complacence which beamed forth from his protuberant blue eyes. Now he lifted his hand.

"Gentlemen, gentlemen. Surely this wrangling is not—er—seemly, if you will allow me to say so? The matter, I am glad to say, can be settled within a very short time——"

"I still insist," snapped Nathaniel Burrows, "that, not having been instructed about this matter of the fingerprints, I may, in the interests of Sir John Farnleigh——"

"Mr. Burrows," said the claimant calmly, "you must have guessed it, even if we did not choose to tell you. I suspect you guessed it from the first, and that is why you tolerated this claim. You are trying to save your face on both sides, whether your man should turn out to be a fraud or whether he should not. Well, you had better come over to our side soon."

Farnleigh stopped pacing. He tossed up the key-ring, caught it with a flat smack against his palm, and closed his long fingers round it.

"Is that true?" he asked Burrows.

"If it were true, Sir John, I should have been compelled to take other steps. At the same time, it is my duty to investigate——"

"That's all right," said Farnleigh. "I only wanted to know where my friends stand. I'm not saying much. My memories, pleasant or unpleasant: and some of them have kept me awake at nights: I'll keep to myself. Just bring on your fingerprints, and then we shall see. The point is, where is Murray? Why isn't he here?"

The claimant wore a look of Mephistophelian pleasure, in which he contrived to suggest a sinister frown.

"If events ran according to form," he answered with relish, "Murray would already have been murdered and his body hidden in the pond in the garden. (There is still a pond there, isn't there? I thought so.) As a matter of sober fact, I believe he is on his way here now. Besides, I do not wish to put ideas into anybody's head."

"Ideas?" said Farnleigh.

"Yes. Like your old one. A quick cosh and an easy life."

The way he spoke seemed to put an unpleasant chill in the air. Farnleigh's voice went high and rasping. He lifted his hand, and then rubbed it down the side of his old tweed coat, as though in a nervous gesture of controlling himself. With uncanny skill his opponent seemed to pick out exactly the sentences that would sting him. Farnleigh had rather a long neck, which was now much in evidence.

"Does anybody believe that?" he got out. "Molly—Page—Burrows—do you believe that?"

"Nobody believes it," answered Molly, with level eyes. "You're being foolish to let him put you off balance, which is exactly what he's trying to do."

The claimant turned an interested look on her.

"You too, madam?"

"Me too, what?" asked Molly, and then grew furiously annoyed with herself. "Sorry to sound like a musical scale, but you know what I mean."

"You believe your husband is John Farnleigh?"

"I know it."

"How?"

"I'm afraid I must answer woman's intuition," said Molly coolly. "But I mean something sensible by it: something that in its own way, and within its own limits, is always right. I knew it the moment I saw him again. Of course I am willing to listen to reasons, but they have got to be the right sort of reasons."

"Are you in love with him, may I ask?"

This time Molly flushed under her tan, but she treated the question in her usual way. "Well, let's say that I am rather fond of him, if you like."

"Exactly. Ex-actly. You are 'fond' of him; you will always be 'fond' of him, I think. You get on and you will get on very well together. But you are not in love with him and you did not fall in love with him. You fell in love with me. That is to say, you fell in love with an imaginary projection of me from your childhood, which surrounded the impostor when 'I' returned home——"

"Gentlemen, gentlemen!" said Mr. Welkyn, like a master of ceremonies to a rowdy banquet. He seemed rather shocked.

Brian Page entered the conversation: with broad amusement, to steady their host.

"Now we're being psychoanalytic," Page said. "Look here, Burrows, what are we to do with this flower of something-or-other?"

"I only know that we are putting in an awkward half-hour," returned Burrows coldly. "Also, we are straying from the point again."

"Not at all," the claimant assured him. The claimant seemed genuinely anxious to please. "I hope I haven't said anything to offend anybody again? You should live with a circus; your skins would grow tougher. However, I appeal to you, sir," he looked at Page. "Don't I state a reasonable proposition with regard to this lady? You may make an objection. You may say that, in order to fix her affections on me as a child, she must have been somewhat older—the age, say, of Miss Madeline Dane? Was that your objection?"

Molly laughed.

"No," said Page. "I wasn't thinking of either a support or an objection. I was thinking of your mysterious profession."

"My profession?"

"The unspecified profession you mentioned, the one you first made a success of at the circus. I can't decide whether you are (1) a fortune-teller, (2) a psychoanalyst, (3) a memory-expert, (4) a conjuror, or even a combination of them. There are mannerisms of them all about you, and much more besides. You are a little too suggestive of Mephistopheles in Kent. You don't belong here. You disturb things, somehow, and you give me a pain in the neck."

The claimant seemed pleased.

"Do I? You all need to be stirred up a bit," he declared. "Regarding my profession, I am perhaps a little of all those things. But there is one person I certainly am: I am John Farnleigh."

Across the room the door opened, and Knowles entered.

"Mr. Kennet Murray to see you, sir," he said.

There was a pause. By a trick of the fading light, a last fiery glow of sunset shifted in through the trees and the high window-panes. It kindled the heavy room; then it subsided to a steady, warm light which was just bright enough to make faces and figures a little more than visible.

Kennet Murray himself had been remembering many things in that midsummer dusk. He was a tall, lean, rather shambling man, who, in spite of a first-rate intelligence, had never been cut out to be a particular success at anything. Though he was hardly fifty, his fair moustache and fair beard, so closely cropped that they looked like stubble, were greyish. He had aged, as Burrows had said; he had grown leaner and more sour out of his former easy good-nature. But there was much of that good-nature remaining, and his look showed it as he ambled into the library. His eyes had the slightly squinted-up look of one who lives under hot suns.

Then he stopped, frowning as though at a book, and drawing himself up. And, to one of the contestants for the estate, old days returned with old memories and fierce bitterness against dead people; yet Murray himself did not look a day older.

Murray stood studying the persons before him. He frowned, then he looked quizzical—the eternal tutor—and then grim. He fixed his eyes at a point midway between the holder and the claimant.

"Well, young Johnny?" he said.

## Chapter V

For a second or two neither of the contestants moved or spoke. First it seemed that each was waiting to see what the other would do; and then each went his separate way. Farnleigh moved his shoulder slightly, as though he would not enter this as a debate, but he consented to nod and gesture and even smile stiffly. There had been authority in Murray's voice. But the claimant, after a slight hesitation, showed no such views. He spoke with quiet affability.

"Good evening, Murray," he said; and Brian Page, who knew the ways of students towards their former schoolmasters, suddenly felt the scale-pans dip towards Farnleigh.

Murray looked round.

"Someone—er—had better present me," he said in a pleasant voice.

It was Farnleigh, stung out of apathy, who did this. By tacit consent Murray was the "old man" of the group, though he was a good deal younger than

Welkyn; there was something of the "old man's" manner about him: something brisk and assured, yet wandering. He sat down at the head of the table, with the light behind his back. Then he gravely fitted on a pair of owlish shell-rimmed reading glasses, and surveyed them.

"I should never have recognized Miss Bishop or Mr. Burrows," he went on. "Mr. Welkyn I know slightly. It was through his generosity that I was able to take my first real holiday in a long time."

Welkyn, evidently well satisfied, thought that the time had now come for him to take charge and get down to real business.

"Exactly. Now, Mr. Murray, my client—"

"Oh, tut, tut, tut!" said Murray, rather testily. "Let me get my breath and talk a moment, as old Sir Dudley used to say." It was as though he wanted to get his breath literally, for he breathed deeply several times, looked round the room, and then at the two opponents. "However, I must say you seem to have landed yourself in the middle of a very bad mess. The affair has not become public property, has it?"

"No," said Burrows. "And you, of course, have not said anything about it?"

Murray frowned.

"There I must plead guilty. I have mentioned it to one person. But, when you hear the name of the person, I don't think you will object. It was my old friend Dr. Gideon Fell, a former schoolmaster like myself, of whose connection with detective work you may have heard. I saw him as I was passing through London. And I—er—mention this to give you a word of warning." Despite Murray's benevolence, his squinted grey eyes became bright and hard and interested. "It is possible that Dr. Fell himself may soon be in this part of the world. You know that there is another man staying at the *Bull and Butcher* besides myself, a man of inquisitive habits?"

"The private detective?" Farnleigh asked sharply, and to the ostensible surprise of the claimant.

"So it took you in?" said Murray. "He is an official detective from Scotland Yard. It was Dr. Fell's idea. Dr. Fell maintained that the best way to conceal your identity as an official detective is to act like a private detective." Though Murray seemed hugely delighted, his eyes remained watchful. "Scotland Yard, on the advice of the Chief Constable of Kent, seem to be curious about the death of Miss Victoria Daly here last summer."

Sensation.

Nathaniel Burrows, who looked fussed, made a vague gesture.

"Miss Daly was killed by a tramp," Burrows said, "later killed himself in escaping the police."

"I hope so. However, I heard it in passing when I mentioned my own little problem in mixed identities to Dr. Fell. He was interested." Again

Murray's voice became sharp; and, if the word can be used, opaque. "Now, young Johnny——"

Even the air of the room seemed to be waiting. The claimant nodded. The host also nodded, but Page thought that there was a faint glitter of sweat on his forehead.

"Can't we get on with this?" Farnleigh demanded. "It's no good playing cat and mouse, Mr.—it's no good playing cat and mouse, Murray. It's not decent, and it's not like you. If you've got those fingerprints, trot 'em out and then we shall see."

Murray's eyes opened, and then narrowed. He sounded annoyed.

"So you know about that. I was reserving it. And may I ask," his voice grew professionally poised and sarcastic, "which of you thought that the final test would be fingerprints?"

"I think I can establish that honour," answered the claimant, looking round as though inquiringly. "My friend Patrick Gore here claims to have remembered it afterwards. But he seems to have been under the impression that you took fingerprints on a sheet of glass."

"And so I did," said Murray.

"That's a lie," said the claimant.

It was an unexpected change of voice. Brian Page suddenly realized that, under his mild and Mephistophelian airs, the claimant concealed a violent temper.

"Sir," said Murray, looking him up and down, "I am not in the habit——"

Then it was as though old days returned; the claimant seemed involuntarily about to move back and beg Murray's pardon. But he conquered this. His face smoothed itself out, and the usual mocking expression reappeared.

"Let us say, then, that I have an alternative suggestion. You took my fingerprints in a 'Thumbograph.' You had several such Thumbographs; you bought them in Tunbridge Wells. And you took the fingerprints of myself and my brother Dudley on the same day."

"That," agreed Murray, "is quite true. The Thumbograph with the fingerprints I have here." He touched the inside breast pocket of his sports-coat.

"I smell blood," said the claimant.

It was true that a different atmosphere seemed to surround the group at the table.

"At the same time," Murray went on, as though he had not heard this, "the first experiments I made with fingerprints were on small glass slides." He grew even more inscrutable and sharp. "Now, sir, as the claimant or plaintiff here, you must tell me a few things. If you are Sir John Farnleigh, certain things are known to me which are known to nobody else. In those days you were an omnivorous reader. Sir Dudley, who you will admit was an enlightened man, made out a list of books which you were permitted to read. You never spoke your views on these books to anyone else: Sir Dudley once spoke a word of harmless ridicule to you about your notions, and tortures would not have opened your mouth afterwards. But you expressed yourself to me in no uncertain terms. Do you remember all that?"

"Very well indeed," said the claimant.

"Then kindly tell me which of those books you liked best, and which made the most impression on you."

"With pleasure," answered the claimant, casting up his eyes. "All of Sherlock Holmes. All of Poe. *The Cloister and the Hearth. The Count of Monte Cristo. Kidnapped. A Tale of Two Cities.* All ghost stories. All stories dealing with pirates, murders, ruined castles, or——"

"That will do," said Murray noncommittally. "And the books you intensely disliked?"

"Every deadly line of Jane Austen and George Eliot. All snivelling school-stories about 'the honour of the school' and so on. All 'useful' books telling you how to make mechanical things or run them. All animal-stories. I may add that these, in general, are still my views."

Brian Page was beginning to like the claimant.

"Let us take the younger children who were hereabouts," Murray continued. "For instance, the present Lady Farnleigh, whom I used to know as little Molly Bishop. If you are John Farnleigh, what was your private nickname for her?"

" 'The gipsy,' " answered the claimant instantly.

"Why?"

"Because she was always tanned, and was always playing with the children in the gipsy tribe that used to camp at the other side of the Chart."

He glanced at a furious Molly, smiling a little.

"And Mr. Burrows, there—what was your nickname for *him?*"

"Uncas."

"The reason for that?"

"At any I-Spy games, or things like that, he could slide through the shrubbery without making a sound."

"Thank you. And now for you, sir." Murray turned to Farnleigh, and eyed him as though he were about to tell him to straighten his tie. "I do not wish to convey the impression that I am playing cat-and-mouse. So I have only one question for you before I proceed to take the fingerprints. On this question, actually, will depend my private judgment before I see the proof in the prints. The question is this. What is the Red Book of Appin?"

It was almost dark in the library. The heat was still strong, but a small breeze had begun to stir with sundown. It moved through the one or two opened panes of the windows; and the trees stirred with it. A grim—a rather unpleasant—smile moved across Farnleigh's face. He nodded. Taking a notebook and a little gold pencil from his pocket, he tore out a sheet and wrote some words on it. This he folded up and pushed across to Murray.

"It has never caught *me*," Farnleigh said. And then: "Is that the right answer?"

"That is the right answer," agreed Murray. He looked at the claimant. "You, sir: will you answer the same question?"

For the first time the claimant seemed uncertain. His gaze flashed from Farnleigh to Murray with an expression which Page could not read. Without a word he beckoned flatly for the notebook and pencil, which Farnleigh handed over. The claimant wrote only two or three words before he ripped out the sheet and gave it to Murray.

"And now, gentlemen," said Murray, rising. "I think we can take the fingerprints. Here I have the original Thumbograph: much aged, you see. Here is an ink-pad, and here are two white cards. If you will just—may I have some light, please?"

It was Molly who went across and touched the electric switch beside the door. In the library there was a chandelier in tiers of wrought iron which had once supported crowns of candles; now there were small electric bulbs, not all of which worked, so that the light was not overly bright. But it pushed back the summer night; a hundred little reflections of bulbs were thrown back from the window-panes; and the books on the tall shelves looked more grimy still. On the table Murray had spread out his paraphernalia. The Thumbograph, at which they all looked first, was a rickety little book with grey paper covers grown thin from use: the title in red letters, and a large red print of a thumb underneath.

"An old friend," said Murray, patting it. "Now, gentlemen. 'Rolled' prints are better than flat ones; but I did not bring a roller because I wished to reproduce the original conditions. I want only your left thumbprint; there is only one print to compare. Here is a handkerchief with an end doused in benzoline: it will take away the perspiration. Use it. Next——"

It was done.

During that time Page's heart was in his mouth; he could not have said why. But they were all in unnatural states of agitation. For some reason Farnleigh insisted on rolling up his sleeve before making the print, as though he were going to have a blood-transfusion. The mouths of both solicitors, Page was glad to observe, were open. Even the claimant used the handkerchief briskly before he leaned against the table. But what impressed Page most was the confidence of both contestants. The wild thought occurred to Page: suppose those two thumbprints turn out to be exactly alike?

The chances of this happening, he recalled, were just one in sixty-four thousand millions. All the same, nobody faltered or cried off before the test. Nobody——

Murray had a bad fountain-pen. It scratched as he wrote names and markings at the foot of each white (unglazed) card. Then he blotted them carefully, while the contestants wiped their fingers.

"Well?" demanded Farnleigh.

"Well! Now if you will be good enough to give me a quarter of an hour to myself, I can get down to work. Forgive my unsociability; but I realize the importance of this as much as you do."

Burrows blinked. "But can't you—that is, aren't you going to tell us——?"

"My good sir," said Murray, whose own nerves appeared to be feeling the strain, "are you under the impression that a glance at these prints will be enough to compare them? Especially with the print of a boy done in faded ink twenty-five years ago? They will require many points of agreement. It can be done, but a quarter of an hour is an unnaturally modest estimate. Double that: you will be nearer the truth. Now may I settle down?"

From the claimant came a low chuckle.

"I expected that," he said. "But I warn you, it is unwise. I smell blood. You will have to be murdered. No, don't scowl; twenty-five years ago you would have relished the position and revelled in your own importance."

"I see nothing funny in the matter."

"In point of fact, there is nothing funny in it. Here you sit in a lighted room, with a wall of windows giving on a dark garden and a screen of trees and the devil whispering behind every leaf. Be careful."

"Well," returned Murray, with a faint smile creeping round his moustache and into his beard, "in that case I shall take all care. The more nervous of you can keep an eye on me through the window. Now you must excuse me."

They went out into the hall, and he closed the door on them. Then six persons stood and looked at each other. Lights had already been turned on in the long, pleasant hall; Knowles stood at the door of the dining-room, in the "new" wing which had been built out at the back from the centre of the house, like the body of the letter T with its head as the front. Molly Farnleigh, though flushed and strained, tried to speak coolly.

"Don't you think we had better have something to eat?" she said. "I've ordered a cold buffet prepared. After all, there's no reason why we shouldn't carry on as usual."

"Thank you," said Welkyn, relieved; "I should like a sandwich."

"Thank you," said Burrows; "I am not hungry."

"Thank you," said the claimant, to swell the chorus. "Whether I accepted or refused, it would sound equally bad. I am going somewhere to smoke a long, strong, black cigar; and then I am going to see that no harm comes to Murray in there."

Farnleigh said nothing. Just behind him in the hall there was a door giving on that part of the garden overlooked by the library windows. He studied his guests with a long, careful scrutiny; then he opened the glass door and went out into the garden.

In the same way Page presently found himself deserted. The only person n sight was Welkyn, who stood in the dimly lighted dining-room and ate ısh-paste sandwiches with great steadiness. Page's watch said that it was wenty minutes past nine o'clock. He hesitated, and then followed Farnleigh ›ut into the cool dimness of the garden.

This side of the garden seemed shut off from the world, and formed an ›blong some eighty feet long by forty feet broad. On one side it was closed n by the new wing; on the other by a stretch of high yew hedge. Through he beech trees the library windows spread out a faint and broken wall of ight from the narrow side of the oblong. In the new wing, too, the dining-›om had glass doors opening out into it, with a balcony overlooking it from he bedroom windows above.

Inspired by King William the Third at Hampton Court, a seventeenth-entury Farnleigh had laid out the garden in severe curves and angles of yew ıedge, with broad sanded walks between. The hedges were built waist-high; t was, in fact, very much like the foundation of a maze. Though you had ıo actual difficulty in finding your way about the garden, it would be (Page ıad always thought) a rare place for hiding-games if you kept down below he line of the hedges. In the centre was a large round open space, buttressed vith rose-trees; and this space in turn enclosed an ornamental pool some ›en feet in diameter, with a very low coping. In the uncertainty between the ights, with faint gleams from the house meeting a faint afterglow from the vest, it was a secret and fragrant place. Yet for some reason Page had never iked the *feel* of that garden.

With this thought came another, a more unpleasant one. There was noth-ıg about a mere garden, a handful of hedges, shrubs, flowers, and soil, which :ould inspire disquiet. It may have been that the minds and thoughts of :veryone here were concentrated so fiercely on the library, moving against hat lighted box like moths on the glass. Of course, it was absurd to suppose hat anything could happen to Murray. Things are not managed like that; hey are not so convenient; it was only the claimant's hypnotic personality vhich had been able to worm in the suggestion.

"However," Page almost said aloud, "I think I might just stroll past the vindow and have a look."

He did so, and jerked back with muttered profanity, for someone else had ›een having a look as well. He did not see who the other person was, because he other person drew away from the screen of beeches against the library vindows. But Page saw Kennet Murray inside, sitting at the library table vith his back to the windows, and Murray seemed to be just opening a ›reyish book.

Nonsense.

Page moved away, and walked quickly out into the cool garden. He skirted :he round pool, looking up at a single clear star (Madeline Dane had a poetic ıame for it) which you could see just above a cluster of chimneys in the

new wing. Working his way through the low labyrinth, he reached the far en
in labyrinthine thought.

Well, was Farnleigh the impostor, or the other fellow? Page did not know
and he had changed his mind so many times in the past two hours that h
did not like to guess. Then, too, there had been the persistent, accidenta
introduction at every turn of the name of Madeline Dane——

At the end of this side of the garden there was a laurel hedge whicl
screened a stone bench from the house. He sat down and lighted a cigarette
Tracing his thoughts back as honestly as he could, he admitted to himsel
that a part of his grouse at the universe was the persistent recurrence o
Madeline Dane's name. Madeline Dane, whose blonde and slender goo
looks suggested the origin of her surname, was the person who mixed u
the "Lives of the Chief Justices" and everything else in Page's thoughts. H
was thinking more about her than was good for him. For here he was, gettin
on towards being a crusty bachelor——

Then Brian Page jumped up from the stone bench, thinking neither o
Madeline nor of marriage: only of the sounds he had heard from the garde
behind. They were not loud sounds, but they came with terrifying clarit
out of the dim, low hedges. The choking noise was the worst: then the shuffl
and scrape of feet: then the splash and thrashings.

For a moment he did not want to turn round.

He did not really believe that anything had happened. He never believe
that. But he dropped his cigarette on the grass, set his heel on it, and walke
back towards the house at a pace that was almost a run. He was some dis
tance away from the house; and in the hide-and-seek paths he took two wron
turnings. At first the uncertain place seemed deserted; next he saw Burrows'
tall figure pounding towards him, and the beam of a flashlight flickered ove
the hedges into his face. When he came close enough to see Burrows's fac
behind the light, the coolness and fragrance of the garden were lost.

"Well, it's happened," said Burrows.

What Page felt at that moment was a slight physical nausea.

"I don't know what you mean," he lied, "except that it can't have hap
pened."

"I'm simply telling you, that's all," returned a white-faced Burrows, witl
patient insistence. "Come along quick and help me haul him out. I can'
swear he's dead, but he's lying on his face in that pond and I'm pretty sur
he's dead."

Page stared in the direction he indicated. He could not see the pool, whicl
was hidden by the hedges; but he now had a good view of the back of th
house. From one window of a lighted room over the library, old Knowle
the butler was leaning out; and Molly Farnleigh was on the balcony outsid
her bedroom windows.

"I tell you," Page insisted, "nobody would dare have a go at Murray! It' impossible. It's nonsensical to—and, anyway, what's Murray doing at the pond?"

"Murray?" said the other, staring at him. "Why Murray? Who said anything about Murray? It's *Farnleigh*, man: John Farnleigh. It was all over before I could get there; and I'm afraid it's too late now."

## Chapter VI

"But who the devil," Page asked, "would want to kill Farnleigh?"

He had to adjust his thoughts. Afterwards he has acknowledged that his original notion of murder had been mere suggestion. Yet, even when another suggestion replaced it, he remembered his first thought: *if* this were murder, it had been ingeniously conceived. As though by an effect of sleight-of-hand, every eye and ear had been concentrated on Kennet Murray. No person in the house had a thought in his head for anybody but Murray. No one would know where anybody had been, anybody but Murray. A person who acted in that vacuum could attack unseen, so long as he did not attack Murray.

"Kill Farnleigh?" repeated Burrows in a queer voice. "Here, this won't do. Wake up. Stop. Steady. Come on."

Still talking like a man giving directions for backing a car, he led the way with his lanky stride. The beam from the flashlight was steady. But he switched it off before they reached the pond, either because there was still enough light from the sky or because he did not wish to see things too clearly just then.

Round the pool there was a border of packed sand some five feet wide. Forms, even faces, were still dimly visible. Farnleigh lay prone in the pool, turned a little towards the right as you faced the rear of the garden. The pool was just deep enough so that his body rocked with the water, which still slopped and splashed over the low round edge of the coping, running across packed sand. They also saw a darker dye in the water, curling upwards and spreading round him; but they did not see the full colour of this dye until it touched a patch of white water-lilies close to the body.

The slopping agitation of the water began again when Page started to haul him out; Farnleigh's heel just touched the edge of the low coping. But, after one minute which Page never wished to remember afterwards, Page got up.

"We can't do him any good," Page said. "His throat's been cut."

The shock had not worn off yet, and they both spoke calmly.

"Yes. I was afraid of that. It's——"

"It's murder. Or," said Page abruptly, "suicide."

They looked at each other in the dusk.

"All the same," argued Burrows, trying to be official-mannered and human at the same time, "we've got to get him out of there. That rule about touching nothing and waiting for the police is all very well, but we can't let him lie there. It's not decent. Besides, his position has been disturbed as it is Shall we——?"

"Yes."

The tweed suit, now black and bulging, seemed to have accumulated a ton of water. With difficulty they rolled Farnleigh over the edge, sending a minor tidal wave across themselves. The peaceful evening scent of the garden, espe cially the roses, had never seemed more theatrically romantic than in the midst of this reality. Page kept thinking: this is John Farnleigh, and he's dead. This is impossible. And it was impossible, except for one though which grew clearer every second.

"You mean suicide," said Burrows, wiping his hands. "We've had a hal lucination of murder put on us, but I don't like this any better. You see what it means? It means he was the impostor after all. He bluffed it out as long as he could, and hoped against hope that Murray might not have the fingerprints. When the test was over he couldn't face the consequences. So he came out here, stood on the edge of the pool, and—" Burrows put up a hand to his throat.

It all fitted very well.

"I'm afraid so," admitted Page. Afraid? Afraid? Yes: wasn't that the worst charge you could make against a dead friend, pile the whole burden on him now that he couldn't speak? Resentment rose up in a dull ache, for John Farnleigh had been his friend. "But it's the only thing we can think. For God's sake what happened here? Did you see him do it? What did he do it with?"

"No. That is, I didn't exactly see him. I was just coming out of the door from the hall back there. I'd got this torch,"—Burrows snapped the button on and off, and then held it up,—"out of the drawer of the table in the hall You know how weak my eyes are when I go out in the dark. Just as I was opening the door, I saw Farnleigh standing out here—very dimly, you know— on the edge of the pool, with his back towards me. Then he seemed to be doing something, or moving about a bit: with my eyesight, it's very difficult to tell. You must have heard the noises. After I heard that splash—and the thrashing round, you know, which was worse. There never was a balder, worse story."

"But there wasn't anybody with him?"

"No," said Burrows, spreading out his fingers against his forehead and pressing the tips of them there. "Or at least—not exactly. These hedges are waist-high, and——"

The meaning of the words "not exactly," spoken by the meticulously care ful Nathaniel Burrows, Page did not have time to inquire. Voices and foot steps were stirring from the direction of the house, and he spoke quickly.

"You're the one with authority. They're all coming. Molly mustn't see this. Can't you use your authority and head 'em off?"

Burrows cleared his throat two or three times, like a nervous orator about to begin, and his shoulders straightened. Switching on the flashlight, he walked towards the house with the light pointing in that direction. Its beam picked out Molly, with Kennet Murray following; but it did not shine on their faces.

"I am sorry," began Burrows, in tones of high and unnatural sharpness. "But there has been an accident to Sir John, and you had better not go out there—"

"Don't be a fool," said Molly in a hard voice. With deliberate strength she pushed past him, and came into the gloom beside the pool. Fortunately she could not see the extent of what had been done. Though she tried to give the impression of calmness, Page heard her heel turn in the path. He put an arm round her shoulder to steady her; she leaned against it, and he felt unsteady breathing. But what she said, flung out in a sob, seemed merely cryptic. Molly said:

"D-damn him for being *right!*"

By something in the tone Page knew that she could not be referring to her husband. But for a moment it so startled him that he could not take it in. Then, hiding her face even from the dark, she started in a hurried walk for the house.

"Let her go," said Murray. "It will be better for her."

But Murray did not appear as capable as you might have thought, faced with a thing of this sort. He hesitated. Taking the flashlight from Burrows's hand, he directed its beam on the body beside the pool. Then he let out a whistle, his teeth showing between cropped moustache and beard.

"Did you prove," asked Page, "that Sir John Farnleigh was not Sir John Farnleigh?"

"Eh? I beg your pardon?"

Page repeated his question.

"I have proved," said Murray with heavy gravity, "absolutely nothing. I mean that I had not completed my comparison of the prints; I had barely begun it."

"It would appear,"—Burrows spoke rather weakly,—"that you would not need to finish."

And so it would. There could not be, in all truth and reason, much doubt of Farnleigh's suicide. Page saw that Murray was nodding, in his sometimes vague manner: nodding as though he were not thinking of the matter at all: and stroking the cheek of his beard like a man who tries to place an old memory. It was not a physical wriggling, yet it gave that impression.

"But you can't have much doubt, can you?" Page was prompted to ask. "Which one of them did you think was the fake?"

"I have already informed you—" Murray snapped.

"Yes, I know, but look here. I was only asking, which one of them did you *think* was the impostor? You surely must have had some notion after you'd talked to them. After all, it's the only really important thing either about the imposture or about this; and you can't have any doubt about it? If Farnleigh is the impostor, he had good reason to kill himself and we can certainly agree that he did. But if by any inconceivable chance he were not the impostor—"

"You are assuming——?"

"No, no, only asking. If he were the real Sir John Farnleigh, there would be no reason for him to cut his throat. So he must be the impostor. Isn't he?"

"The tendency to leap to conclusions without even examining the data," began Murray, in a tone between asperity and comfortable discussion, "is one to which the unacademic mind is strongly——"

"Right you are; question withdrawn," said Page.

"No, no, you misunderstand." Here Murray waved his hand like a hypnotist; he seemed uncomfortable and flustered that the balance of argument had been disturbed. "You intimate that this might be murder on the grounds that, if the—er—unfortunate gentleman before us were the real John Farnleigh, he would not kill himself. But, whether he is or is not the real Johnny, why should anyone kill him? If he is a fraud, why murder him? The law will attend to him. If he is real, why murder him? He has done no harm to anyone. You see, I am only taking both sides of it."

Burrows spoke gloomily. "It's all this talk, suddenly produced, about Scotland Yard and poor Victoria Daly. I've always thought I was a sensible sort of fellow; but it's given me all sorts of ideas that I've got to root out of my head. And then I've never liked the feel of this blasted garden."

"You felt that too?" demanded Page.

Murray was regarding them with a blaze of interest.

"Stop," he said. "About the garden: why don't you like it, Mr. Burrows? Have you any memories connected with it?"

"Not exactly memories." The other considered; he seemed uncomfortable. "It was only that, when anyone used to tell a ghost-story, it was twice as effective here as anywhere else. I remember one about—but that doesn't matter. I used to think it would be very easy to raise the devil here; and I don't mean cut up a row, either. However, this is still beside the point. We've got work to do. We can't stand here talking——"

Murray roused himself; he grew almost excited. "Ah, yes. The police," he said. "Yes, there is a great deal to be done, in the—er—practical world. You will, I think, allow me to take charge. Will you come with me, Mr. Burrows? Mr. Page, will you oblige us by remaining with the—er—body until we return?"

"Why?" asked the practical Page.

"It is customary. Oh, yes. Indeed, it is absolutely necessary. Kindly give Mr. Page your flashlight, my friend. And now this way. There was no telephone at the Close when I lived here; but I presume there is one now? Good, good, good. We must also have a doctor."

He bustled off, shepherding Burrows, and Page was left beside the pool with what remained of John Farnleigh.

With the shock wearing off, Page stood in the dark and reflected on the increasing uselessness and complexity of this tragedy. Yet the suicide of an impostor was simple enough. What disturbed him was the realization that he had got absolutely no change out of Murray. It would also have been simple enough for Murray to have said, "Yes, that is undoubtedly the impostor: I knew it from the beginning"; and, in fact, Murray's whole atmosphere had conveyed that this was what he thought. But he had said nothing. Was it, then, merely his own love of mystery?

"Farnleigh!" Page said aloud. "Farnleigh!"

"Did you call me?" asked a voice almost at his elbow.

The effect of that voice in the dark was to make Page jump back so that he almost stumbled over the body. Forms and outlines were now completely lost in night. The stir of a footstep on a sanded path was followed by the rasping of a match. The flame of the match sprang up over its box, cupped in two hands; and showed, in one opening of the yew hedge, the face of the claimant—Patrick Gore, John Farnleigh—looking into the space beside the pool. He came forward at his slightly clumsy walk.

The claimant was carrying a thin black cigar, half-smoked and gone out. He put it into his mouth, lit it carefully, and then peered up.

"Did you call me?" he repeated.

"I didn't," Page said grimly. "But it's a good thing you answered. Do you know what's happened?"

"Yes."

"Where have you been?"

"Wandering."

The match went out; but Page could hear him breathing faintly. That the man was shaken there could be little doubt. He came closer, his fists on his hips and the cigar glowing in a corner of his mouth.

"Poor crook," said the claimant, looking down. "And something about him a good deal to be respected, too. I'm rather sorry I did this. I've no doubt he reverted to the Puritan faith of his fathers and spent a good many years repenting at the same time he kept fast hold on the estate. After all, he could have continued posing and made a better squire than I ever shall. But the wrong Farnleigh stuff was missing, and so he did this."

"Suicide."

"Without a doubt." The claimant took the cigar out of his mouth and blew out a cloud of smoke, which curled in the darkness with the odd effect of a ghost taking form. "I suppose Murray has finished comparing the prints. You were present at that little inquisition by Murray. Tell me: did you notice the exact point at which our—late friend slipped and gave away the fact that he was not John Farnleigh?"

"No."

Then Page suddenly realized that the claimant's shaken air was due as much to relief as to any other emotion.

"Murray would not be Murray," he said with a certain dryness, "if he had not included a catch question. That always was his nature. I was expecting it and even dreading it: in case it should not really be a catch question, but something I had forgotten. But it was a fairly obvious catch when it came. You remember. 'What is the Red Book of Appin?'"

"Yes. Both of you wrote down something—"

"Of course there is no such thing. I should be interested to see what gibberish my late rival wrote down in order to explain it. It was all the more intriguing when Murray, with a face as solemn as an owl, assured him he had written the correct answer; but you observed that the very assurance almost finished my rival. Oh, curse it all," he broke off, and made a gesture with the lighted end of his cigar which was curiously like a question-mark. "Well, let us see what the poor devil did to himself. May I have that electric torch?"

Page handed it over, and moved away while the other squatted down with the light. There was a long silence, with an occasional muttering. Then the claimant got up. Though he moved slowly, he snapped the button of the electric torch on and off.

"My friend," he said in a different voice, "this won't do."

"What won't do?"

"This. I hate what I am going to say. But I will take my oath this man did not kill himself."

(Score one for suggestion, intuition, or the influence of a certain garden at twilight.)

"Why?" said Page.

"Have you looked at him closely? Then come and do it now. Does a man cut his own throat with three separate slashes, all of which sever the jugular vein, and any one of which would have caused death? Can he do it? I don't know, but I doubt it. Remember, I began my self-made career in a circus. I never saw anything like this since Barney Poole, the best animal-trainer west of the Mississippi, was killed by a leopard."

A night breeze moved in the labyrinth, and stirred the roses.

"Where, I wonder, is the weapon?" he went on. He played the beam of his torch over the misted water. "Probably in the pool here, but I don't think we had better go after it. The police may be more necessary in this business han we think. This alters matters in a way that—that worries me," said the claimant, as though making a concession. "Why kill an impostor?"

"Or a real heir, for that matter," said Page.

Then Page could sense that the other was eyeing him sharply. "You do not still believe——?"

They were interrupted by footsteps coming rapidly if pontifically from the direction of the house. The claimant turned the beam of light on Welkyn, the solicitor, whom Page last remembered eating fish-paste sandwiches in the dining-room. Welkyn, now evidently a very scared man, gripped the edge of the white slip inside his waistcoat as though he were going to make a speech. Then he changed his mind.

"You'd better get back to the house, gentlemen," he said. "Mr. Murray would like to see you. I *hope*," he gave the word a sinister emphasis, and looked hard at the claimant, "I hope neither of you gentlemen has been in the house since this thing happened."

"Patrick Gore" whipped round. "Don't tell me anything else has happened?"

"It has," said Welkyn snappishly. "It appears that someone has taken advantage of this confusion. In Mr. Murray's absence, someone went into the library and stole the Thumbograph containing our only evidence."

# II

*Thursday, July 30th*

## THE LIFE OF AN AUTOMATON

Then all was silent, and presently Moxon reappeared and said, with a rather sorry smile:

"Pardon me for leaving you so abruptly. I have a machine in there that lost its temper and cut up rough."

Fixing my eyes steadily upon his left cheek, which was traversed by four parallel excoriations showing blood, I said:

"How would it do to trim its nails?"

—AMBROSE BIERCE, *Moxon's Master*


## Chapter VII

IN EARLY afternoon of the following day, while grey, warm rain darkened the countryside, Page sat again at the desk in his study; but this time with very different thoughts.

Up and down the room, in a way as monotonous as the sound of the rain itself, paced Detective-Inspector Elliot.

And throned in the largest chair sat Dr. Gideon Fell.

The doctor's thunderous chuckles were today subdued. He had arrived in Mallingford that morning, and he did not seem to like the situation he found. Sitting back in the big chair, he wheezed gently. His eyes, behind the eyeglasses on the broad black ribbon, were fixed with singular concentration on a corner of the desk; his bandit's moustache bristled as though ready for argument, and his big mop of grey-streaked hair had fallen over one ear. On a chair beside him lay his shovel-hat and his stick with the ivory crutch-handle. Though there was a pint tankard of beer at his elbow, he did not seem interested even in this. And, though his red face was even more red in the July heat, it hardly expressed his customary joviality. Page found him even larger, both in height and circumference, than he had been described; when he first came into the cottage, wearing his box-pleated cape, he seemed to fill the place and crowd out even the furniture.

Nor did anybody like the situation within the district of Mallingford and Soane. The district retreated within itself; it was not even eloquently silent. Everybody now knew that the stranger known as a "folklore authority" at the *Bull and Butcher* was an inspector of the Criminal Investigation Department. But not a word was said of it. In the taproom of the *Bull and Butcher*, those who came in for their morning pint spoke in a little lower tone, and

rifted away sooner; that was all. Dr. Fell had been unable to get accommo-
ations at the pub—inn by courtesy—since both guest rooms were occupied;
nd Page had been only too glad to offer the hospitality of his cottage.

Page liked Inspector Elliot as well. Andrew MacAndrew Elliot looked out
f place neither as folklore authority nor as Scotland Yard man. He was
oungish, raw-boned, sandy-haired, and serious-minded. He liked argument,
nd he liked subtleties in a way that would have displeased Superintendent
Hadley. His education had been that thorough Scots one which deals with
he minutest details of the minutest subject. Now, pacing the floor of Page's
tudy while the grey rain fell, he tried to make his position clear.

"H'mf, yes," grunted Dr. Fell. "But exactly what has been done so far?"

Elliot considered. "Captain Marchbanks, the Chief Constable, telephoned
o the Yard this morning and washed his hands of the business," he said.
Ordinarily, of course, they'd have sent a chief inspector. But, since I hap-
ened to be on the spot and already investigating something that may be
connected with this——"

(The murder of Victoria Daly, thought Page. But how connected?)

"You got your chance," said Dr. Fell. "Excellent."

"Yes, sir, I got my chance," agreed Elliot, placing a freckled fist carefully
n the table and bracing himself over it. "And I mean to make something of
t, if I can. It's opportunity. It's—you know all that." He expelled his breath.
'But you know the difficulties I'm going to find. People hereabouts have shut
p tighter than windows. You try to see inside, but they won't let you inside.
They'll drink a glass of beer and talk just as usual; but they fall away as
oon as you say anything about it. With what we'll call the gentry of the
whole district"—his tone showed a certain faint contempt for the word—"it's
een even more difficult, even before this thing happened."

"About the other affair, you mean?" inquired Dr. Fell, opening one eye.

"About the other affair. The only one who's been at all helpful is a Miss
Dane, Madeline Dane. There," declared Inspector Elliot, with measured care-
ulness and emphasis, "is a real woman. It's a pleasure to talk to her. *Not*
ne of your hard-boiled misses who blow smoke in your eye and ring up
heir lawyers as soon as you send in a card. No. A real woman; reminds me
f a girl I used to know at home."

Dr. Fell opened both eyes, while Inspector Elliot (so to speak) fidgeted
nder his freckles for having said this. But Brian Page understood and approved. He was even conscious of a twinge of nonsensical jealousy.

"However," the inspector resumed, "you'll want to know about Farnleigh
Close. I've taken a statement from everybody who was there last night: ex-
lusive of servants, as yet. A brief statement. I had to round some of them
p. Mr. Burrows stayed at the Close last night, to be ready for us today.
But the claimant, this Mr. Patrick Gore, and his solicitor (name of Welkyn)
oth went back to Maidstone." He looked round at Page. "I gather, sir, there

was a bit of a row—or, well, say that things got pretty strained after this Thumbograph had been stolen?"

Page admitted it with some fervour.

"Especially after the Thumbograph was stolen," he replied. "The odd part of it was that to everybody except Molly Farnleigh it seemed more important that the evidence had been stolen than that Farnleigh had been murdered—if he was murdered."

A gleam of interest stirred in Dr. Fell's eye. "By the way, what was the general attitude in the question of suicide v. murder?"

"Very cautious. A great lack of attitude, which is surprising. The only one who definitely said he'd been murdered (screamed it, in fact) was Molly—Lady Farnleigh, I mean. Otherwise accusations of crookedness hurtled about in a way I hope won't be remembered today. I'm glad to say I don't remember half of it. I suppose it was only natural. Beforehand we had all been so strainedly and unnaturally on our best behaviour that the reaction was a little too much. Even solicitors, it appears, are human. Murray tried to take charge, and was swept under. Our local police-sergeant wasn't much better."

"I am endeavouring," said Dr. Fell, making a hideous face of emphasis, "to clear the way to the problem. You say, inspector, you don't have much doubt that it is murder?"

Elliot was firm.

"No, sir, I haven't. There were three gashes across the throat, and no weapon I've been able to find so far, either in the pool or anywhere at hand. Mind," he said cautiously, "I haven't had the medical report. I don't say it's impossible for a man to inflict three such wounds on himself. But the absence of a weapon seems to decide it."

For a moment they listened to the rain, and to the doubtful wheezing of Dr. Fell's breath.

"You don't think," suggested the doctor, "I only—harrumph—put it forward as a suggestion: you don't think he might have killed himself and, in the convulsion, flung the weapon away from him, so that you haven't found it? That has happened before, I think."

"It's remotely possible. But he can't have thrown it clear out of the garden; and, if it's there anywhere, Sergeant Burton will find it." There was a curious look on Elliot's hard face. "Look here, sir: do you think this is suicide?"

"No, no, no," said Dr. Fell earnestly, as though this rather shocked him. "But, even believing that this is murder, I still want to know what our problem is."

"Our problem is who killed Sir John Farnleigh."

"Quite. You still don't perceive the double-alley of hell into which that leads us. I am worried about this case, because all rules have been violated. All rules have been violated because the wrong man had been chosen for a victim. If only Murray had been murdered! (I speak academically, you understand.) Hang it all, Murray should have been murdered! In any well-constituted plot he would have been murdered. His presence cries out for it. Here is a man possessing evidence which will decide a vital problem at the outset: here is a man who can probably solve the puzzle of identities even without that evidence: well, he is the certain candidate for the death-blow. Yet he remains untouched, and the problem of identities is merely made more inexplicable by the death of one of the claimants. You follow that?"

"I do," said Inspector Elliot grimly.

"Let's clear away some of the underbrush," insisted Dr. Fell. "Is the whole thing, for instance, an error on the part of the murderer? Was Sir John Farnleigh (to give him his present name) not intended to be the victim at all? Did the murderer kill him in mistake for somebody else?"

"It seems doubtful," said Elliot, and looked at Page.

"It's impossible," said Page. "I'd thought of that too. Well, I repeat: it's impossible. The light was too good. Farnleigh didn't look like anybody else, and wasn't dressed like anybody else. Even from some distance away you could never have mistaken him, let alone at the close quarters of someone who cuts his throat. It was that queerish watery light where details are blurred but all outlines are clear."

"Then Farnleigh was the intended victim," said Dr. Fell, clearing his throat with a long rumbling noise. "Very well. What other possible undergrowths or verbiage can we rake away? For instance, is it possible that this murder has no connection whatever with the battle over the title and estates? Did some person unaffected by this debate—some person who didn't care whether he was John Farnleigh or Patrick Gore—choose just this moment to slide through the screen and kill him for some outside motive we don't know? It is possible. It is possible if the Powers are being coy. But I for one am not going to worry about it. These things are cohesive; they depend on each other. For, you notice, the Thumbograph-evidence was stolen at the same time Farnleigh was murdered.

"Very well. Farnleigh was deliberately murdered, and murdered for some reason connected with the question of the right heir to the estates. But we still haven't decided what our real problem is. The problem is still double-headed, not to say double-faced. Thus. If the murdered man was an impostor, he might have been killed for any one of two or three reasons. You can imagine them. But, if the murdered man was the real heir, he might have been killed for any one of two or three totally different reasons. You can imagine those too. They entail different sides, different eyes, different motives. Therefore, which of those two is the impostor? We have got to know that before we have the remotest idea in which direction we've got to look. Harrumph."

Inspector Elliot's face hardened.

"You mean that the key is this Mr. Murray?"

"I do. I mean my old, enigmatic acquaintance, Kennet Murray."

"You think he knows which is which?"

"I've got no doubt of it," growled Dr. Fell.

"Nor I," said the inspector dryly. "Let's see, now." He got out his notebook and opened it. "Everyone seems to be agreed—remarkable what a lot of agreement there is—that Mr. Murray was left alone in the study at about twenty minutes past nine o'clock. Correct, Mr. Page?"

"Correct."

"The murder (we'll call it that) was committed at about half-past nine. Two persons give a definite time about this: Murray and the solicitor, Harold Welkyn. Now ten minutes may not be a long time. But the comparison of fingerprints, though you've got to be careful about it, isn't the all-night job Murray gave you to understand. You can't tell me he didn't have *some* idea— Do you think he's a wrong 'un, sir?"

"No," said Dr. Fell, frowning heavily at the tankard of ale. "I think he's trying to do a spot of sensational detection. And in just a minute I'll tell you what I think this case is. You say you got a statement from each of them as to what each was doing during that ten minutes?"

"Bald few lines from everybody," said Elliot, suddenly angry. "No comments. They asked what comments they could make. Well, I mean to ask again, and comment too. Queerish crowd, if you ask me. I know things sound pretty shorn in a policeman's report, because you've got to stick little bits of facts together without anything between: and thankful to get what you do. But there's black murder and plain hell in the midst of them, and this is what they say. Listen."

He opened his notebook.

"*Statement of Lady Farnleigh:* When we left the library I was upset, so I went upstairs to my bedroom. My husband and I have adjoining bedrooms on the first floor of the new wing, over the dining-room. I washed my face and hands. I told my maid to lay out another frock, because I felt grubby. I lay down on the bed. There was only a very small light from the bedside lamp. The windows were open on the balcony of my room overlooking the garden. I heard noises like a fight and a scuffling and a kind of cry, and then a splash. I ran to the balcony and saw my husband. He seemed to be lying in the pool and fighting. He was alone then. I could see this clearly. I ran downstairs by the main staircase, and out to him. I did not see or hear anything suspicious in the garden.

"Next we have:

"*Statement of Kennet Murray:* I remained in the library between nine-twenty and nine-thirty. No one entered the room, and I saw no one else. My back was to the window. I heard the sounds (similarly described). I did not think anything serious had happened until I heard someone run downstairs in the hall. I heard Lady Farnleigh's voice calling out to the butler that she was afraid something had happened to Sir John. I looked at my watch; it was then just nine-thirty. I joined Lady Farnleigh in the hall, and we went out into the garden, where we found a man with his throat cut. I have no comment to make at this time on the fingerprints or my comparisons of them.

"Fine and helpful, isn't it? Then we have:

"*Statement of Patrick Gore, claimant:* I wandered. I was out on the front lawn first, smoking. Then I wandered round the south side of the house to this garden. I did not hear any sounds except a splash, and I heard that very faintly. I think I heard this when I had just started round the side of the house. I did not think anything was wrong. When I came into the garden I heard loud voices talking. I did not want any company, so I kept to the side path along the high yew hedge bounding the garden. Then I heard what they were talking about. I listened. I did not go to the pool until all of them except a man named Page had gone back to the house.

"Finally, we come to:

"*Statement of Harold Welkyn:* I remained in the dining-room and did not leave it at any time. I ate five small sandwiches and drank a glass of port. I agree that the dining-room has glass doors opening out into the garden, and that one of these doors is not far from the pool in a straight line. But the lights were full on in the dining-room, and I could not see anything in the garden because of the contrasting lights——

"A witness dead on the scene. Ground floor: hedges only waist-high: not more than twenty feet from where Farnleigh must have been standing," said Elliot, flicking his notebook with finger and thumb. "But he's deaf and blind in his 'contrasting lights.' He concludes:

"At nine thirty-one by the grandfather clock in the dining-room I heard certain noises resembling a scuffle and a stopped cry. This was followed by a series of loud splashings. I also heard a kind of rustling noise in the hedges or shrubbery, and I thought I saw something looking at me through one of the glass panels of the door, one of the panels down nearest the ground. I was afraid that certain things might have happened which were no affair of mine. I sat down and waited until Mr. Burrows came in and told me the fraudulent Sir John Farnleigh had committed suicide. During this time I did not do anything except eat another sandwich."

Dr. Fell, wheezing into a more upright position, reached out after the tankard of ale and took a deep pull. There was a steady, gleaming excitement behind his eyeglasses, a sort of astonished pleasure.

"Oh, Bacchus!" he said in a hollow voice. "'Shorn' statements, hey? Is that your considered opinion? There is something in our Mr. Welkyn's statement which tends to give me a cauld grue. H'mf, ha, stop a bit. Welkyn! Welkyn! Haven't I heard that name somewhere before? I'm certain of it, because it cries aloud for bad puns, and therefore it would stick in my— 'What is mind?' 'No matter.' 'What is matter?' 'Never mind.' I beg your pardon; I was scatter-braining again. Have you got anything else?"

"Well, there were two other guests, Mr. Page here and Mr. Burrows. You've heard Mr. Page's statement, and you've had the gist of Mr. Burrows's."

"Never mind. Read it again, will you?"

Inspector Elliot frowned.

"*Statement of Nathaniel Burrows:* I could have eaten something, but Welkyn was in the dining-room and I did not think it proper for me to talk to him then. I went to the drawing-room at the other side of the house and waited. Then I thought that my proper place was with Sir John Farnleigh, who had gone out into the south garden. I took an electric torch out of the table in the hall. I did this because my eyesight is not good. As I was starting to open the door to the garden I saw Sir John. He was standing on the edge of the pool. He seemed to be doing something, or moving about a little. From the door to the nearer edge of the pool is about thirty-five feet. I heard the scuffling sounds, and then the splash and the churnings in water. I ran down there and found him. I am not able to swear whether or not there was any-body with him. I cannot give an exact description of the movements he made. It was as though something had got hold of his feet."

"And there we are, sir. You notice certain things. Except Mr. Burrows, nobody ever actually saw the victim before he was attacked and fell or was thrown into the pool. Lady Farnleigh didn't see him until he was in the pool; Mr. Gore, Mr. Murray, Mr. Welkyn, and Mr. Page didn't see him until afterwards—or so they say. There are other things," he prodded, "which you'll have noticed?"

"Eh?" said Dr. Fell vaguely.

"I asked what you made of it."

"Why, I'll tell you what I was thinking. 'A garden is a lovesome thing, God wot,'" said Dr. Fell. "But what about the sequel? After the murder, I gather, the Thumbograph was pinched from the library when Murray came out to see what was up. Did you get a statement from the various persons about what they were doing then, or who might have pinched it?"

"I did," said Elliot. "But I won't read it to you, sir. And why? Because it's one great, serene blank. Analyzed and boiled down, it amounts to this: that anybody might have stolen the Thumbograph, and that in the general confusion nobody would have noticed who did."

"Oh, Lord!" Dr. Fell groaned, after a pause. "We've got it at last."

"Got what?"

"What I've been half-dreading for a long time—an almost purely psycho-logical puzzle. There are no discrepancies in the various stories, in the various times given, even in the various possibilities. There are no incongruities to explain, except the thundering psychological incongruity of why the wrong man should have been so carefully murdered. Above all, there is an almost complete absence of material clues: no cuff-links, cigarette-ends, theatre-ticket-stubs, pens, ink, or paper. H'mf. Unless we get our claws into something more tangible, we shall merely fumble with the greased pig called human behaviour. Which person, then, would be most likely to kill the man who was killed? And why? And which person fits best, psychologically, into the pattern of devilry you've drawn round Victoria Daly's murder?"

Elliot began to whistle through his teeth. He said: "Any ideas, sir?"

"Let me see," muttered Dr. Fell, "if I have mastered the essential facts in the case of Victoria Daly. Age 35, spinster, pleasant, not intelligent, lived alone. H'mf. Ha. Yes. Murdered about 11.45 P.M. on July 31st, last. Right, my lad?"

"Right."

"Alarm given by farmer driving home past her cottage. Screams coming from there. Village policeman, passing on bicycle, follows farmer. Both see a man—tramp known in district—climbing out of window, ground-floor, rear. Both follow in quarter-mile chase. Tramp, trying to cut off pursuit by getting over gates and across tracks ahead of Southern Railway goods-train, is eliminated quickly if not neatly. Right?"

"Right."

"Miss Daly found in ground-floor room of cottage: her bedroom. Strangled with bootlace. When attacked, was retiring but had not yet gone to bed. Wore night-dress, quilted dressing-gown, and slippers. Apparently clear case —money and valuables found on tramp—except for one fact. On examination by doctor, body found smeared with dark sooty compound; same compound also found under all finger-nails. Eh? This substance, analyzed by Home Office man, proved to be composed of juice of water parsnip, aconite, cinque-foil, deadly nightshade, and soot."

Page sat up, mentally stuttering. Until the last part of Dr. Fell's statement, he had heard it all a thousand times before.

"Here!" he protested. "That's the first time anybody's mentioned a thing like that. You found smeared on the body a substance containing two deadly poisons?"

"Yes," said Elliot, with a broad and sardonic grin. "The local doctor didn't have it analyzed, of course. The coroner didn't think it was important and didn't even bring it up at the inquest. He probably thought it was some kind of beauty-preparation, which it would be indelicate to mention. But the doctor later passed on a quiet word, and——"

Page was troubled. "Aconite and deadly nightshade! All the same, they weren't swallowed, were they? They wouldn't have killed her if they only touched her externally, would they?"

"Oh, no. All the same, it's a fairly clear case. Don't you think so, sir?"

"An unfortunately clear case," admitted Dr. Fell.

Above the noise of the rain Page heard a rapping at the front door of the cottage. Trying to place an elusive memory, he went out through the short passage and opened the door. It was Sergeant Burton of the local police, wearing a rubber hood and coat, under which he was shielding something wrapped in newspapers. What he said brought Page's thoughts back from Victoria Daly to the closer problem of Farnleigh.

"Might I see Inspector Elliot and Dr. Fell, sir?" Burton said. "I've got the weapon, right enough. And——"

He gestured with his head. Beyond a muddy front garden pricked up into puddles by the rain, a familiar car stood by the front gate. It was an ancient Morris, and there seemed to be two persons behind the side-curtains. Inspector Elliot came to the door hurriedly.

"You said——?"

"I've got the weapon that killed Sir John, Inspector. And something else too." Again Sergeant Burton moved his head in the direction of the car. "It's Miss Madeline Dane and old Mr. Knowles, who works up at the Close. He used to work for Miss Dane's father's best friend. When he wasn't sure what to do he went to Miss Dane, and she sent him to me. He's got something to tell you that'll probably straighten out the whole case."

## Chapter VIII

THEY put down the newspaper-parcel on Page's writing-table, and unfolded it to reveal the weapon. It was a pocket-knife; a boy's pocket-knife of old-fashioned design; and, under the present circumstances, a heavy and murderous-looking pocket-knife.

In addition to the main blade—which was open now—its wooden handle contained two smaller blades, a corkscrew, and an implement once alleged to be useful for removing stones from horses' hoofs. To Page it brought back the days when to possess such a fine knife was the proud mark of almost-manhood: when you were an adventurer, almost a red Indian. It was an old knife. The main blade, well over four inches long, bore two deep triangular nicks, and the steel was ragged in places; but it was not rusty, and it had been kept razor-sharp. There was about it now no suggestion of playing at Indians. From point to handle the heavy blade was discoloured with blood-stains which had recently dried.

A feeling of uneasiness touched them all as they looked at it. Inspector Elliot straightened up.

"Where did you find this?"

"Stuck down deep inside one of those low hedges; about," said Sergeant Burton, half-closing one eye to estimate, "about ten feet away from the lily-pond."

"Away from the pool in which direction?"

"Towards the left, standing with your back to the house. Towards that high hedge that's the south boundary. A bit nearer in to the house than the lily-pond is. You see, sir," explained the sergeant carefully, "it was luck—me finding it. We might have searched for a month and never found it. No more we mightn't, unless we pulled all the hedges to bits. That yew's as thick as sin. It was the rain that did it. I was running my hand along the top of one hedge; not meaning anything, you understand; just wondering where to look. The hedge was wet, and my hand came away with a bit of reddy-brown colour on it. That was where it'd left a bit of blood on the flat top of the hedge when it went through. You couldn't even see the cut in the top where she'd gone through. I dug her out. The hedge kept the rain off, as you see."

"Somebody'd pushed it straight down through the hedge, you think?"

Sergeant Burton considered.

"Yes, it'd be that. I think. She was stuck in there straight, point downwards. Or else—that's a good heavy knife, sir. Blade's as heavy as the handle. If somebody threw her away, or up into the air, she'd have come down blade first and gone through just like that."

There was a certain look on Sergeant Burton's face which no one there failed to interpret. Dr. Fell, who had been sunk in some obscure musing, rolled up his head; Dr. Fell's large under-lip came out in a mutinous way.

"H'm," he said. "'Threw her away?' After suicide, you mean?"

Burton's forehead altered slightly; he said nothing.

"It's the knife we want, right enough," Inspector Elliot conceded. "I didn't like the jagged, crooked look of two of the three wounds on that fellow. They looked more like mauling or tearing. But look here!—look at the notches in this blade. They'll fit or I'm a Dutchman. What do you say?"

"About Miss Dane and old Mr. Knowles, sir——?"

"Yes; ask them if they'll come in. That's good work, sergeant; damned good work. You might go and see whether the doctor has any news for me."

Dr. Fell and the inspector were beginning to argue as Page picked up an umbrella from the passage and went out to bring Madeline in.

Not rain or mud could alter Madeline's trimness, or ruffle her quiet good-temper. She was wearing one of those transparent oilskin waterproofs, with a hood, which made her look as though she were wrapped in cellophane. Her blonde hair was done into something like curls above the ears; she had a pale, healthy face, the nose and mouth a little broad, the eyes a little long; yet the whole of a beauty which grew on you the more you noticed it. For she never gave the impression of wanting to be noticed; she was one of those persons who seem cut out to be good listeners. Her eyes were very dark blue, with a deep glance of sincerity. Though her figure was good—Page always damned himself for noticing her figure—she conveyed an impression of fragility. She put her hand on his arm, and gave him an uncertain smile, as he helped her out of the car under the umbrella.

"I'm terribly glad it's at your house," she said in her soft voice. "It makes things easier, somehow. But I really didn't know what to do, and it seemed the best way——"

She glanced back at stout Knowles, who was getting out of the car. Knowles carried his bowler hat even in the rain, and he was picking his way in a pigeon-toed waddle through the mud.

Page took Madeline into the study, and introduced her proudly. He wanted to show her off to Dr. Fell. Certainly the doctor's response was everything that could be wished. He beamed down on her in a way that threatened to split several waistcoat-buttons, and seemed to turn on lights behind his eye-glasses; he towered up, chuckling, and it was the doctor himself who took her waterproof when she sat down.

Inspector Elliot was at his most brisk and official. He spoke like a shop-assistant behind a counter.

"Yes, Miss Dane? And what can I do for you?"

Madeline regarded her clasped hands, and looked round with a pleasant frown before her candid gaze met the inspector's.

"You see, it's very difficult to explain," she said. "I know I must do it. Someone must do it, after that terrible affair last night. And yet I don't want Knowles to get into trouble. He mustn't, Mr. Elliot——!"

"If anything's bothering you, Miss Dane, just tell me," said Elliot briskly; "and nobody will get into trouble."

She gave him a grateful look.

"Then perhaps— You'd better tell them, Knowles. What you told me."

"Heh-heh-heh," said Dr. Fell. "Sit down, man!"

"No, sir; thank you; I——"

"Sit down!" thundered Dr. Fell.

As an alternative to being pushed down, which from the doctor's gesture seemed imminent, Knowles obeyed. Knowles was an honest man: sometimes a dangerously honest man. He had one of those faces which in moments of mental stress go transparently pink, as though you could see through the face like a shell. He sat on the edge of the chair, turning his bowler hat round in his hands. Dr. Fell tried to give him a cigar, but he declined this.

"I wonder, sir, if I may speak frankly?"

"I should advise it," said Elliot dryly. "Well?"

"Of course, sir, I know I should have gone to Lady Farnleigh straightaway. But I couldn't tell her. I mean quite sincerely that I couldn't make myself do it. You see, it was through Lady Farnleigh that I came to the Close when Colonel Mardale died. I think I can say honestly that I think more of her than anyone else I know. Honest to God," added Knowles, with a sudden and unexpected descent into the human, and a slight surge up out of his chair. Then he relapsed. "She was Miss Molly, the doctor's daughter, from Sutton Chart. I knew——"

Elliot was patient.

"Yes, we appreciate that. But this information you were going to give us?"

"It's about the late Sir John Farnleigh, sir," said Knowles. "He committed suicide. I saw him do it."

The long silence was broken only by the diminishing noise of the rain. Page heard the rustle of his own sleeve as he looked round to see whether they had hidden the stained clasp-knife; he did not want Madeline to see it. It was now concealed under the newspapers on the table. Inspector Elliot, seeming even more hard-boned, was staring steadily at the butler. From Dr. Fell's direction there issued a faint ghost of a noise, like half-humming or half-whistling behind closed teeth; he has a habit of whistling thus at times, to the tune of 'Auprès de ma Blonde,' though he looked half asleep.

"You—saw—him—do it?"

"Yes, sir. I could have told you this morning; only you didn't question me; and, frankly, I'm not sure I should have told you even then. It's like this. I was standing at the window of the Green Room last night, the room just over the library, looking out into the garden, when it all happened. I saw everything."

(This, Page remembered, was true. When he had gone with Burrows to look at the body first, he had seen Knowles standing at the window of the room above the library.)

"Anybody will tell you about my eyesight," Knowles said warmly. Even his shoes squeaked with vehemence. "I'm seventy-four years old, and I can read a motor-car number-plate at sixty yards. You just go out in the garden there, and you take a box or a sign or something with small letters—" He corrected himself, and sat back.

"You saw Sir John Farnleigh cut his own throat?"

"Yes, sir. As good as."

"'As good as?' What do you mean by that?"

"I mean this, sir. I didn't actually see him draw the—you know—because his back was towards me. But I saw him put his hands up. And there wasn't a living soul near him. Remember, I was looking straight down on him and into the garden. I could see into that circular open space all round the pool; and there's a good five-foot border of sand between the pool and the nearest hedge all round. Nobody could have come near him without my seeing. And he was all alone in that open space, I'll tell you to my dying day."

Still the sleepy and tuneless whistling wheezed from Dr. Fell's direction.

"'Tous les oiseaux du monde,'" muttered the doctor, "'viennent y faire leurs nids—'" Then he spoke out. "Why should Sir John Farnleigh kill himself?"

Knowles braced himself.

"Because he wasn't Sir John Farnleigh, sir. The other gentleman is. I knew it as soon as I clapped eyes on him last night."

Inspector Elliot remained impassive.

"What reason have you for saying that?"

"It's hard to tell you so you'll understand, sir," Knowles complained. (For the first time in his life he showed a lack of tact.) "Now, I'm seventy-four. I wasn't any chicken, if you'll excuse me for saying so, when young Mr. Johnny went away from home in nineteen-twelve. You see, to old people like myself the younger ones never change. They always seem just the same, whether they're fifteen or thirty or forty-five. Lord bless you, do you think I wouldn't have recognized the real Mr. Johnny whenever I met him? Mind!" said Knowles, again forgetting himself and raising his finger. "I don't say that when the late gentleman came here and pretended to be the new Sir John— I don't say I twigged it. No. Not at all. I thought, Well, he's different; he's been to America, and you never know them after that; it's only natural, and I'm getting old. So I never really suspected him of not being the right master, though I'm bound to admit that now and again he did say things that——"

"But——"

"Now, you'll say," continued Knowles, in real and blinding earnest, "I wasn't at the Close in the old days. That's true. I've been here only ten years, since Miss Molly asked the late Sir Dudley to offer me the honour. But, when I served Colonel Mardale, young Mr. Johnny used to spend a lot of time in the big orchard between the colonel's and the major's——"

"The major's?"

"Major Dane, sir, Miss Madeline's father; he was the colonel's great friend. Well, young Mr. Johnny liked that orchard, with the wood behind it. That orchard is close to the Hanging Chart, you know—leads into it. He pretended he was a wizard, and a mediaeval knight, and I don't know what; but some things I didn't like at all. Anyway, I knew last night, even before he started asking me about rabbits and the like, that this new gentleman was the real Mr. Johnny. He knew I knew it. That's why he had me called in. But what could I *say*?"

Page remembered that interview only too well. But he remembered other things too, and wondered if Elliot had learned them. He glanced across at Madeline.

Inspector Elliot opened his notebook.

"So he killed himself. Eh?"

"Yes, sir."

"Did you see the weapon he used?"

"No, not properly, I'm afraid."

"I want you to tell me just exactly what you did see. For instance, you say you were in the 'Green Room' when it happened. When and why did you go there?"

Knowles got his wits together.

"Well, sir, it might have been two or three minutes before it happened——"

"Twenty-seven or twenty-eight minutes past nine. Which?" asked Inspector Elliot, with a hard passion for accuracy.

"I can't say, sir. I didn't take any account of the time. One of them. I was in the hall near the dining-room, in case I should be wanted, though there was nobody in the dining-room except Mr. Welkyn. Then Mr. Nathaniel Burrows came out of the drawing-room, and asked me where he could find an electric torch. I said I thought there was one in the Green Room upstairs, which the late—gentleman used as a kind of study, and I said I would go and fetch it for him. I have since learned," Knowles was now giving evidence, as his diction showed, "that Mr. Burrows found one in the drawer of the table in the hall; but I had not known there was one there."

"Go on."

"I went upstairs and I went into the Green Room——"

"Did you turn on the light?"

"Not then," said Knowles, a little flustered. "Not just at that moment. There is no wall-switch in the room. You must turn on the light from the ceiling-fixture. The table where I thought I had seen the electric torch is between the windows. I went towards that table, and when I went past I glanced out of the window."

"Which window?"

"The right-hand one, facing out on the garden."

"Was the window open?"

"Yes, sir. Now, here's how it was. You must have noticed. There are trees all along the back of the library; but they've been pruned down so that they don't cut off the view from the windows of the floor above. The ceilings at the Close are eighteen feet high, most of them—except the new wing, which is a little low doll's house of a place—and that gives you a good height of tree without having them stretch up past the windows of the Green Room. That's why it's called the Green Room, because you look out over tree-tops. So you see I was high over the garden, looking down into it."

Here Knowles got up from his chair and craned himself forward. He had seldom executed this movement before, and it evidently gave him a twinge, but his grimness was such that he held the position while he talked.

"Here I was, you see. Then there were the green leaves, lit up from underneath by the library windows." He moved his hand. "Then there was the garden, with every hedge and path distinct, and the pool in the centre. The light wasn't bad, sir. I've seen them play tennis in worse. Then there was Sir John—or the gentleman who called himself that—standing by it with his hands in his pockets."

At this point Knowles had to leave off play-acting and sit down.

"That's all," he said, with a slightly quicker breath.

"That's *all?*" repeated Inspector Elliot.

"Yes, sir."

Elliot, pulled up at this unexpected conclusion, stared at him.

"But what happened, man? That's what I'm trying to get you to tell me!"

"Just that. I thought I heard a movement down in the trees under me, and I glanced down. When I looked up again——"

"Are you going to tell me," said Elliot very calmly and carefully, "that YOU didn't see what happened either?"

"No, sir. I saw him fall forward in the pool."

"Yes; but what else?"

"Well, sir, there certainly wasn't time for someone—you know what I mean, sir—to cut his throat three times and then run away. There couldn't 'a' been. He was alone every bit of the time, before and after. So he must have killed himself."

"What did he use to kill himself?"

"A kind of knife, I think."

"You think. Did you see the knife?"

"Not properly, no."

"Did you see it in his hand?"

"Not properly. It was too far away to see that plain. Sir," replied Knowles, remembering that he had a position in the world and drawing himself up with dignity, "I am trying to give you a true, so-help-me-God story of what I saw——"

"Well, what did he do with the knife afterwards? Did he drop it? What happened to it?"

"I didn't notice, sir. I honestly didn't. I was paying attention to him; and something seemed to be happening to the front of him."

"Could he have thrown the knife from him?"

"He might. I don't know."

"Would you have seen it if he had thrown it?"

Knowles considered long. "That would depend on the size of the knife. And there are bats in that garden. And sometimes, sir, you can't see a tennis-ball until it's—" He was a very old man. His face grew clouded, and for a moment they were afraid he was going to cry. But he spoke again with dignity. "I am sorry, sir. If you don't believe me, have I your permission to go?"

"Oh, hang it all, it isn't that—!" said Elliot, stung to youthful naturalness, and his ears grew slightly red. Madeline Dane, who had said not a word the whole time, was watching him with a faint smile.

"Just one other point, for the time being," Elliot went on stiffly. "If you had a good view of the whole garden, did you see anybody else in the garden at the time of the—attack?"

"At the time it happened, sir? No. Immediately afterwards, though, I turned on the lights in the Green Room, and by that time there were a number of persons in the garden. But beforehand, at the time of the—*excuse* me, sir; yes, there was!" Again Knowles raised his finger and frowned. "There was somebody there when it happened. I saw him! You remember, I said I heard a noise down in the trees round the library windows?"

"Yes; well?"

"I looked down. That was what took away my attention. There was a gentleman down there, looking into the library windows. I could see plainly; because the branches of the trees, of course, don't quite reach to the windows, and everything was all lighted up between, like a little alley between the trees and the windows. He was standing there looking into the library."

"Who was?"

"The new gentleman, sir. The real Mr. Johnny that I used to know. The one who now calls himself Mr. Patrick Gore."

There was a silence.

Elliot very carefully put down his pencil, and glanced across at Dr. Fell. The doctor had not moved; he would have seemed asleep if one little eye had not gleamed half-open.

"Have I got this clear?" Elliot demanded. "At the same time as the attack, or suicide, or murder, or whatever-we-call-it, Mr. Patrick Gore was standing down there in your sight by the library windows?"

"Yes, sir. Over to the left he stood, towards the south. That's how I could see his face."

"Now, you'll swear to that?"

"Yes, sir, of course," said Knowles, opening his eyes.

"This was at the time of the various scuffling sounds, the splash, the fall, and so on?"

"Yes, sir."

Elliot nodded in a colourless way and leafed back through his notebook. "I should like to read you a part of Mr. Gore's testimony dealing with that same time. Listen. '*I was out on the front lawn first, smoking. Then I wandered round the side of the house to this garden. I did not hear any sounds except a splash, and I heard that very faintly. I think I heard this when I had just started round the side of the house.*' He goes on to say that he kept to the side paths along the south boundary.—Now, you tell us that, when the splash occurred, he was standing down underneath you looking into the library. His statement contradicts it."

"I can't help what he says, sir," answered Knowles helplessly. "I'm sorry, but I can't. That's what he was doing."

"But what did he do after you saw Sir John go into the pool?"

"I can't say that. I was looking towards the pool then."

Elliot hesitated, muttering to himself, and then glanced at Dr. Fell. "Any questions you'd like to ask, doctor?"

"Yes," said Dr. Fell.

He bestirred himself, beaming on Madeline, who smiled back. Then he assumed an argumentative air as he beamed on Knowles.

"There are several troublesome queries following your theory, my boy. Among them, if Patrick Gore is the real heir, the question of who stole the Thumbograph, and why. But let's stick first to the vexed business of suicide *v.* murder." He reflected. "Sir John Farnleigh—the dead man, I mean—he was right-handed, was he?"

"Right-handed? Yes, sir."

"It was your impression that he had this knife in his right hand when he killed himself?"

"Oh, yes, sir."

"H'mf, yes. Now I want you to tell me what he did with his hands after this curious seizure by the pool. Never mind the knife! We'll admit you didn't properly see the knife. Just tell me what he did with his hands."

"Well, sir, he put them up to his throat—like this," said Knowles, illustrating. "Then he moved a little, and then he lifted them up over his head and threw them out, like this." Knowles made a large gesture, spreading his arms wide. "That was just before he went forward into the pool and began to writhe there."

"He didn't cross his arms? He simply lifted them and threw them out one to each side? Is that it?"

"That's right, sir."

Dr. Fell took his crutch-handled stick from the table and hoisted himself to his feet. Lumbering over to the table, he took up the newspaper packet, unfolded it, and showed Knowles the bloodstained clasp-knife inside.

"The point is this," he argued. "Farnleigh has the knife in his right hand, supposing this to be suicide. He makes no gestures except to fling both arms wide. Even if he were helping support the knife with his left hand, his right would have the grip on it. The knife flies from his right hand as the arm is thrown wide. Excellent well. But will someone explain how in blazes that knife completely altered its flight in the air, passed high over the pool, and dropped into the hedge some ten feet to the *left*? And all this, mind you, after he has just inflicted not one, but three fatal wounds on himself? It won't do, you know."

Apparently oblivious to the fact that he was holding the newspaper with its grisly exhibit almost against Madeline's cheek, Dr. Fell frowned at it. Then he looked at the butler.

"On the other hand, how can we doubt this chap's eyesight? He says Farnleigh was alone by the pool; and there is some confirmation. Nathaniel Burrows is inclined to agree that he was alone. Lady Farnleigh, who ran out on the balcony immediately after the splash, saw nobody by the pool or within reach of it. We shall have to take our choice. On the one hand we have a somewhat preposterous suicide; but on the other hand, unfortunately, we have a more than somewhat impossible murder. Will someone kindly oblige me with an idea?"

## Chapter IX

As VIGOROUSLY and even violently as he had spoken, Dr. Fell had been talking to himself. He had not expected an answer, nor did he get one. For a time he remained blinking at the book-shelves. He appeared to wake up when Knowles ventured a frightened cough.

"I beg your pardon, sir; is that the–?" He nodded towards the knife.

"We think so. It was found in a hedge to the left of the pool. How do you think it squares with suicide?"

"I don't know, sir."

"Did you ever see this knife before?"

"Not to my knowledge, sir."

"Or you, Miss Dane?"

Though Madeline seemed startled and a little shocked, she shook her head quietly. Then she leaned forward. Page noted again how the breadth of her face, the slight breadth and bluntness of her nose, did not in the least detract from her beauty, but seemed to add to it. His mind was always searching for comparisons or images when he saw her; and he found in her something mediaeval, something in length of eye or fulness of lip, some inner spring of quietness, which suggested the rose-garden or the turret window. The sentimentality of the comparison must be excused, for he felt it and believed it.

"I'm afraid, you know," Madeline said almost pleadingly, "that I've no right to be here at all, and that I'm talking about things which do not concern me. And yet–well, I suppose I must." She smiled at Knowles. "I wonder if you will wait for me in my car?"

Knowles bowed and was gone–vague and troubled; and still the grey rain fell.

"Yes," said Dr. Fell, sitting down again and folding his hands over the top of his stick. "You were the one I wanted to ask the questions, Miss Dane. What do you think of Knowles's views? About the real heir, I mean?"

"Only that it's much more difficult than you think."

"Do you believe what he says?"

"Oh, he's absolutely and completely sincere; you must have seen that. But he's an old man. And, among the children, he was always most fanatically devoted first to Molly (her father, you know, saved Knowles's mother's life once), and next to young John Farnleigh. I remember he once made a conical wizard's hat for John, out of cardboard painted blue, with silver-paper stars and whatnots. When this affair came up, he simply couldn't tell Molly; he couldn't. So he came to me. They all do–come to me, that is. And I try to do them what good I can."

Dr. Fell's forehead was wrinkled. "Still, I was wondering . . . h'mf . . . you knew John Farnleigh pretty well in the old days? I understand," here he beamed, "that there was a kind of boy-and-girl romance between you?"

She made a wry face.

"You remind me that I'm past my youth. I'm thirty-five. Or thereabouts; you mustn't ask me to be too precise. No, there never was even a boy-and-girl romance between us, really. Not that I should have minded, but it didn't interest him. He—he kissed me once or twice, in the orchard and in the wood. But he used to say that I didn't have enough of the Old Adam—or do I mean Old Eve?—in me. Not enough of the devil, anyhow."

"But you never married?"

"Oh, that's unfair!" cried Madeline, flushing and then laughing. "You talk as though I were sitting with my dim spectacled eyes over a piece of knitting in the chimney-corner——"

"Miss Dane," said Dr. Fell, with thunderous solemnity, "I don't. I mean that I can see suitors standing in droves at your door, stretching away like the Great Wall of China; I can see Nubian slaves bowed down by the weight of great chocolate-boxes; I can—ahem. Let us omit that."

It was a long time since Page had seen a genuine blush; he believed, nowadays, that such mainsprings were dried up and with the dodo; but, all the same, he did not mind seeing Madeline blush. For what she said was:

"If you're thinking that I cherished a romantic passion for John Farnleigh all these years, I'm afraid you're hopelessly wrong." There was a twinkle in her eye. "I was always a little frightened of him, and I'm not even sure I liked him—then."

"Then?"

"Yes. I liked him later, but only liked."

"Miss Dane," said Dr. Fell, growling out of his several chins and moving his head curiously, "some inner Little Bird seems to tell me that you're trying to convey something to me. You still haven't answered my question. Do you think Farnleigh was an impostor?"

She made a slight gesture.

"Dr. Fell, I am not trying to be mysterious. Really and truly I'm not; and I think I can tell you something. But, before I do, will you—or somebody —tell me just what did happen at the Close last night? I mean, before the last horrible business happened? I mean, what those two said and did while each was claiming to be the real one?"

"We might as well have the story again, Mr. Page," said Elliot.

Page told it, with as many shadings and impressions as he could remember. Madeline nodded her head several times in the course of it; she was breathing rapidly.

"Tell me, Brian: what struck you most about the whole interview?"

"The absolute assurance of both claimants," said Page. "Farnleigh faltered once or twice, but over what seemed unimportant points; when any real test was mentioned, he was eager. I only saw him smile and look relieved once. That was when Gore was accusing him of attempted murder with a seaman's mallet aboard the *Titanic*."

"Just one other thing, please," Madeline requested, breathing still more rapidly. "Did either of them say anything about the dummy?"

There was a pause. Dr. Fell, Inspector Elliot, and Brian Page looked at each other blankly.

"The dummy?" repeated Elliot, clearing his throat. "What dummy?"

"Or about bringing it to life? Or anything about the 'Book'?" Then a mask seemed to close over her face. "I'm sorry. I shouldn't have mentioned that, only I should have thought it would be the first thing to be brought up. Please forget it."

An expression of refreshed pleasure animated Dr. Fell's large face.

"My dear Miss Dane," he rumbled, "you demand a miracle. You demand a miracle greater than any that could have happened in that garden. Consider what you demand. You refer to a certain dummy, to the possibility of its being brought to life, and to something you call the 'Book,' all presumably in connection with this mystery. You acknowledge that it is the first thing you would have thought should be brought up. And then you ask us to forget it. Do you think that ordinary human beings of feverish curiosity could——"

Madeline looked stubborn.

"But you ought not to have asked me about it," she protested. "Not that I know anything, really. You ought to have asked them."

" 'The Book,' " mused Dr. Fell. "You don't mean, I suppose, the Red Book of Appin?"

"Yes, I believe I later heard it called that. I read about it somewhere. It's not a book, really; it's a manuscript, or so John once told me."

"Wait a bit," interposed Page. "Murray asked that question, and both of them wrote down answers for it. Gore later told me that it was a catch question, and there was no such thing as 'the Red Book of Appin.' If there is such a thing, it makes Gore out the impostor, doesn't it?"

Dr. Fell seemed about to speak, with some excitement and vehemence; but he drew a long breath through his nose and restrained himself.

"I wish I knew," said Elliot. "I never thought there could be so much doubt and confusion caused by only two persons. Now you're certain it's one of them, again you're just as certain it's the other. And—as Dr. Fell says—we can't get much further until we establish that. I hope, Miss Dane, you're not trying to evade the question. You still haven't answered: do you think the late Farnleigh was an impostor?"

Madeline threw her head back against the back of the chair. It was the

greatest sign of animation, the only sign of spasmodic action, Page had ever
seen her give. She opened and shut her right hand.

"I can't tell you," she said helplessly. "I *can't*. Not until I've seen Molly,
anyhow."

"But what has Lady Farnleigh got to do with us?"

"Only that he—told me things. Things he didn't even confide to her. Oh,
please don't look shocked!" (As a matter of fact, Elliot did not; but he
looked interested.) "Or believe a lot of gossip you may have heard. But I've
got to tell Molly first. You see, she believed in him. Of course, Molly was
only seven years old when he left home. All she hazily remembers is a boy
who took her to a gipsy camp, where they taught her to ride a pony and
throw stones better than any man. Besides, any dispute over the Farnleigh
name or estates wouldn't trouble her at all. Dr. Bishop wasn't a country G.P.;
he died worth nearly half a million, and Molly inherited it all in her own
right. Also, sometimes I've thought she never really liked being mistress of
that house; she doesn't seem to *care* for responsibilities of that sort. She
didn't marry him because of his position or income, and she wouldn't really
have cared—and won't now—whether his name is Farnleigh or Gore or whatever you like. So why should he have told her?"

Elliot looked rather dazed, as he had reason to do.

"Just a moment, Miss Dane. What are you trying to tell us: that he was
or was not an impostor?"

"But I don't know! I don't know which he was!"

"The startling lack of information with which we are provided," said Dr.
Fell sadly, "proceeds from all sources and o'erflows its basin. Well, let's leave
that for the moment. But on one point I insist on having my curiosity satisfied. What's all this about a dummy?"

Madeline hesitated.

"I don't know whether they've still got it," she answered, staring at the
window in a fascinated way. "John's father kept it locked up in an attic room,
along with the—books he didn't like. The old-time Farnleighs were an unpleasant lot, as you may know, and Sir Dudley was always afraid John had
taken after them. Though there certainly didn't seem to have been anything
wrong or unpleasant about this figure.

"I—I only saw it once. John stole the key from his father, and took me up
all those stairs to see it, with a candle in a dark-lantern. He said the door
hadn't been opened for generations. When it was new, they say the figure
was as absolutely life-like and beautiful as a real woman, sitting on a kind
of padded box in Restoration costume. But when I saw it, it was only old and
black and withered-looking, and it frightened me horribly. I suppose it
hadn't been touched for well over a hundred years. But I don't know what
the story was that made people afraid of it."

There was something about her tone which made Page vaguely uneasy, because he could not place the inflection: he had never heard Madeline speak quite like that before. And he had never, certainly, heard of this "figure" or "dummy," whatever it was.

"It may have been very ingenious," Madeline explained, "yet I can't understand why there should have been anything bad about it. Did you ever hear of Kempelen's and Maelzel's mechanical chess-player, or Maskelyne's 'Zoe' or 'Psycho,' the whist-playing figure?"

Elliot shook his head, though he looked interested; and Dr. Fell was so interested that the eyeglasses tumbled off his nose.

"You don't mean—?" he said. "Archons of Athens, this is better than anything I had hoped for! They were among the best of a series of nearly life-size automatons which puzzled Europe for two hundred years. Didn't you ever read of the harpsichord, exhibited before Louis XIV, which played by itself? Or the dummy invented by Kempelen, shown by Maelzel, which was owned by Napoleon and later lost in the museum fire at Philadelphia? For all practical purposes, Maelzel's automaton was alive. It played chess with you; and usually won. There have been several explanations of how it worked —Poe wrote one—but to my own simple mind it still isn't satisfactorily explained. You can see 'Psycho' in the London Museum today. You don't mean there's one at Farnleigh Close?"

"Yes. That's why I should have thought this Mr. Murray would have *asked* about it," said Madeline. "As I say, I don't know the story. This automaton was exhibited in England during the reign of Charles II, and bought by a Farnleigh then. I don't know whether it played cards or chess, but it moved and spoke. When I saw it, as I say, it was old and black and withered-looking."

"But this—harrumph—this business of bringing it alive?"

"Oh, that was only the nonsense John used to talk when he was a silly child. I wasn't trying to talk seriously about that, don't you see? I was only trying to go back and test what could be remembered of him in the old days. The room where they used to keep the figure was full of books with—well, with downright evil in them," again she flushed, "and that was what attracted John. The secret of how to make the figure work had been forgotten; I daresay that was what he meant."

On Page's desk the telephone-bell rang. He had been so engrossed in watching Madeline, the slight turns of her head, the intentness of her dark-blue eyes, that he groped after the 'phone before finding it. But at the sound of Burrows's voice on the wire he became very much alert.

"For God's sake," said Burrows, "come up to the Close straightaway, and bring the inspector and Dr. Fell."

"Steady!" said Page, feeling a certain unpleasant warmth creep round his chest. "What's up?"

"For one thing, we've found the Thumbograph——"

"What! Where?"

They were all looking at him now.

"One of the maids: Betty: do you know her—?" Burrows hesitated.

"Yes; go on."

"Betty disappeared, and nobody knew what had become of her. They looked all over the place for her: that is, they looked in the only places she was likely to be found. No Betty. Everything was a bit disorganized, because for some reason Knowles wasn't here either. Finally Molly's maid found her in the Green Room, where it wasn't Betty's business to go. Betty was lying on the floor with the Thumbograph in her hand. But that isn't all. Her face was such a queer colour, and she was breathing so queerly, that we sent for the doctor. Old King is worried. Betty's still unconscious, and she won't be in any condition to tell us anything for a long time. She's not physically hurt, but King says there's not much doubt about what caused it."

"Well?"

Again Burrows hesitated.

"Fright," he said.

## Chapter X

IN THE library at Farnleigh Close, Patrick Gore sat back in the embrasure of the windows and smoked a black cigar. Ranged near him were Burrows, Welkyn, and a sleepy-looking Kennet Murray. Inspector Elliot, Dr. Fell, and Brian Page sat by the table.

At the Close they had found a frightened and disorganized household, the more frightened because of a completely pointless upset in the middle of an ordinary afternoon, and the more disorganized because of the absence of the butler.

Facts? What did you mean, facts? The group of domestics whom Elliot questioned did not know what he meant. It was only this maid, Betty Harbottle; a nice girl; ordinary. She had not been seen since midday dinner. When it came time for her to wash the windows of two of the upstairs bedrooms with Agnes, another maid, Agnes had gone to look for her. She was not found until four o'clock. At this time Teresa—Lady Farnleigh's maid —had gone into the Green Room, the late Sir John's study, and found her lying on the floor by a window overlooking the garden. She was lying on her side, with the paper-covered book in her hand. Dr. King had been summoned from Mallingford; and neither the expression of his face nor Betty's did anything to reassure the household. Dr. King was with the patient still.

This thing was wrong. Terrors should not be domestic terrors. It was like being told that in your own home you may completely disappear for four hours. It was like being told that in your own home you may open a familiar door, and enter not your own room, but a room you have never seen before, where something is waiting. From the housekeeper, the cook, and the other maids he learned little except domestic details; about Betty he learned little except that she liked apples and wrote letters to Gary Cooper.

Knowles's arrival soothed the staff; and Madeline's arrival, Page hoped, would have a good effect on Molly Farnleigh. Madeline had accompanied her to her sitting-room while the men glared at one another in the library. Page had wondered what would happen at a meeting between Madeline and Patrick Gore; yet there was little on which even the imagination could fasten. They were not introduced. Madeline moved past, softly, with her arm round Molly; she and the claimant looked at each other; and Page thought that an amused look of recognition opened Gore's eyes; but neither spoke.

And it was Gore who put the case to the inspector when the others were gathered in the library, just before Dr. Fell flung a hand-grenade of remarkable explosive power.

"It's no good, inspector," said Gore, re-lighting a black cigar which would not remain lit. "You asked the same kind of questions this morning, and this time I assure you it's no good. This time it is, where were you when the girl was—well, whatever happened to her—and the Thumbograph was put in her hand? I have replied quite simply that I am damned if I know. So have all the others. We were here. You ordered us to be here. But you may be sure we were not courting each other's society, and we have not the remotest idea when the girl collapsed."

"Look here, you know," said Dr. Fell abruptly, "a part of this had better be settled."

"I only hope you can settle it, my friend," answered Gore, who seemed to have taken a sincere liking to him. "But, inspector, you have already had our statements with the servants. We have been over that again and——"

Inspector Elliot was cheerful.

"That's right, sir," he said. "And, if it's necessary, we shall have to go over them again. And again."

"Really—" interposed Welkyn.

The claimant sat on him again. "But, if you're so interested in the wanderings of that Thumbograph, why not pay some slight attention to what is *in* the Thumbograph?" He glanced at the tattered grey book, which now lay on the table between Elliot and Dr. Fell. "Why in the name of sense and sanity don't you settle the matter now? Why don't you decide, between a dead man and myself, which is the real heir?"

"Oh, I can tell you that," said Dr. Fell affably.

There was an abrupt silence, broken only by the scrape of the claimant's foot on the stone floor. Kennet Murray took away the hand with which he had been shading his eyes. The expression of cynicism remained on his ageing face; but his eyes were bright and hard and indulgent, and he used one finger to stroke his beard, as though he were listening to a recitation.

"Yes, doctor?" he prompted, in that tone used exclusively among school-masters.

"Furthermore," continued Dr. Fell, tapping the book on the table, "it's no good getting down to business with *this* Thumbograph. It's a fake. No, no, I don't mean that you haven't got the evidence. I merely say that THIS Thumbograph, the one that was stolen, is a fake. Mr. Gore pointed out last night, they tell me, that you had several Thumbographs in the old days." He beamed on Murray. "My boy, you retain your melodramatic soul of old, for which I am glad. You believed that there might be some attempt to pinch the Thumbograph. So you came to the house last night equipped with two of them——"

"Is this true?" demanded Gore.

Murray seemed at once pleased and annoyed; but he nodded, as though he were following the matter carefully.

"—and," continued Dr. Fell, "the one you showed to these people in the library was bogus. That was why you were so long in getting down to business. Hey? After you had shoved everybody out of the library, you had to get the real Thumbograph (a clumsy kind of book, apt to tear) out of your pocket, and put the valueless one in. But they had said they were going to keep a close watch on you. And, with a wall of windows stretching across the room, you were afraid somebody might see you and cry trickery if you were seen fooling about with the evidence. So you had to make sure there was nobody watching——"

"I was finally obliged," said Murray gravely, "to get into that cupboard and do it." His nod indicated an old book-closet built into the wall on the same side as the windows. "It is somewhat late in life to feel as though I were cheating at an examination."

Inspector Elliot did not say anything. After glancing sharply from one to the other of them, he began to write in his notebook.

"H'mf, yes. You were delayed," said Dr. Fell. "Mr. Page here, passing the windows only a few minutes before the murder, on his way out to the back of the garden, saw that you were just 'opening' the Thumbograph. So you hardly had time to get down to real work——"

"Three or four minutes," corrected Murray.

"Very well. You hardly had time to get down to real work before there were alarums of bloodshed." Dr. Fell looked pained. "My dear young Murray, you are not simple-minded. Such an alarm might be a trick, especially a trick *you* would suspect. You would never on earth have gone thundering out, leaving the Thumbograph open and inviting on that table. I couldn't be-lieve that when I heard it. No, no, no. Back went the real one into your pocket, and out came the dummy one for a honeyed lure. Hey?"

"Confound you," said Murray without heat.

"You therefore decided to lie doggo and exultantly apply your detective faculties when the dummy was stolen. You have probably been sitting up all night writing out a statement about the prints, with the real Thumbograph in front of you, together with your affidavit that the real heir——"

"The real heir is who?" asked Patrick Gore coolly.

"Is *you*, of course," growled Dr. Fell.

Then he looked at Murray.

"Hang it all," he added plaintively, "you must have known that! He was your pupil. You must have known it. I knew it as soon as I heard him open his mouth——"

The claimant, who had got to his feet, now sat down rather awkwardly. The claimant's face expressed an almost simian pleasure; his bright grey eye and even his bald-spot seemed to twinkle.

"Dr. Fell, I thank you," Gore said, with his hand on his heart. "But I must point out that you have asked me not a single question."

"Look here, you fellows," said Dr. Fell. "You had the opportunity to listen to him all last evening. Look at him now. Listen to him. Does he remind you of anybody? I don't mean in appearance; I mean in turn of phrase, in shaping of ideas, in way of expressing himself. Well, of whom does he remind you? Hey?"

And at last the troublesome sense of familiarity fitted into place in Page's mind, while the doctor blinked round at them.

"Of Murray," replied Page, in the midst of a silence.

"Of Murray. Got it in one. Misted by time, of course; pulled round a bit by character; but there and unmistakable. Of Murray, who had him in sole charge during the formative years of his life, and was the only one with influence over him. Study his bearing. Listen to the smooth turn of those sentences, rolling like the Odyssey. It's only superficial, I cheerfully acknowledge; they are no more alike in their natures than I am like Elliot or Hadley. But the echo lingers on. I tell you, the only important question Murray asked last night was what books the real John Farnleigh had enjoyed as a boy, and what books he hated. Look at this fellow!"—he pointed to Gore. "Didn't I hear how his dead eye glowed when he talked about *The Count of Monte Cristo* and *The Cloister and the Hearth*? And of what books he hated and still hates? No impostor would have dared to talk like that before the person to whom he'd poured out his soul years ago. In a case like this, facts are piffle. Anybody can learn facts. You want the inner boy. I say, Murray: honestly, you'd better come off it and give us the truth. It's all very well to be the Great Detective and play 'possum, but this has gone far enough."

A red bar showed across Murray's forehead. He looked snappish and a trifle shamefaced. But his far-away mind caught at something out of this.

"Facts are not piffle," Murray said.

"I tell you," roared Dr. Fell, "that facts are—" He caught himself up. "Harrumph, well. No. Perhaps not. Altogether. But am I correct?"

"He did not recognize the Red Book of Appin. He wrote down that there was no such thing."

"Which he knew only as a manuscript. Oh, I am not his champion. I'm only trying to establish something. And I repeat: am I correct?"

"Confound you, Fell, you do spoil a fellow's pleasure," complained Murray, in a slightly different tone. He glanced across at Gore. "Yes, he's the real Johnny Farnleigh. Hullo, Johnny."

"Hullo," said Gore. And, for the first time since Page had met him, his face did not look hard.

The quiet in that room was of a dwindling and shrinking sort, as though values were being restored and a blurred image had come into focus. Both Gore and Murray looked at the floor, but they looked vaguely, uncomfortably amused. It was Welkyn's rich voice which now arose with authority.

"You are prepared to prove all this, sir?" he asked briskly.

"There goes my holiday," said Murray. He reached into his stuffed inside pocket, and became austere again. "Yes. Here you are. Original Thumbograph, and print—*with* signature of John Newnham Farnleigh as a boy, and date. In case there should be any doubt this is the original one I brought with me, I had photographs of it taken and deposited with the Commissioner of Police at Hamilton. Two letters from John Farnleigh, written to me in 1911: compare signatures with the signature on the thumbprint. Present thumbprint, taken last night, and my analysis of their points of agreement—"

"Good. Good, very good," said Welkyn.

Page looked at Burrows, and he noticed that Burrows's face was white. Nor had Page realized that the breaking of the long tension would have such an effect on their nerves.

But he realized it when he looked round, and saw that Molly Farnleigh was in the room.

She had come in unobserved, with Madeline Dane just behind her; she must have heard all of it. They all got up, with an awkward scraping of chairs.

"They say you're honest," she said to Murray. "Is this true?"

Murray bowed. "Madam, I am sorry."

"He was a cheat?"

"He was a cheat who could have deceived nobody who had really known him."

"And now," interposed Welkyn suavely, "perhaps it would be as well if Mr. Burrows and I were to have a talk—without prejudice, of course—"

"One moment," said Burrows with equal suavity. "This is still most irregular; and I may point out that I have seen nothing yet in the nature of proof. May I be allowed to examine those documents? Thank you. Next, Lady Farnleigh, I should like to speak with you alone."

Molly had a glazed, strained, puzzled look in her eyes.

"Yes, that would be best," she agreed. "Madeline has been telling me things."

Madeline put a hand soothingly on her arm, but she threw it off with a shake of her sturdy body. Madeline's self-effacing blonde beauty was in contrast to the anger which blazed round Molly and seemed to darken everything away from her. Then, between Madeline and Burrows, Molly went out of the room. They heard Burrows's shoes squeak.

"God!" said Patrick Gore. "And now what have we got?"

"If you'll take it easy and listen to me, sir," Elliot suggested grimly, "I'll tell you." His tone made both Gore and Welkyn look at him. "We've got an impostor who was somehow killed by that pool. Why or by whom we don't know. We've got someone who stole a valueless Thumbograph,"—he held up the little book—"and later returned it. Presumably because the person knew it was valueless. We've got a housemaid, Betty, whom nobody had seen since noon; but who was found at four o'clock in the afternoon, half dead of fright, in the room above this library. Who or what frightened her we don't know, or how the Thumbograph got into her hand. By the way, where is Dr. King now?"

"Still with the unfortunate Betty, I believe," said Gore. "But what then?"

"Finally, we have some new evidence," Elliot told him. He paused. "As you say, you have all been patiently repeating the stories you told last night. Now, Mr. Gore. In the account you gave of your movements at the time of the murder, were you telling the truth? Think before you answer. There is someone who contradicts your story."

Page had been waiting for it, wondering how long it would be before Elliot would bring it up.

"Contradicts my story? Who contradicts it?" asked Gore sharply, and took the dead cigar out of his mouth.

"Never mind that, if you please. Where were you when you heard the victim fall into the pool?"

The other comtemplated him with amusement. "I suppose you've got a witness. I was watching this ancient," he indicated Murray, "through the window. It suddenly occurs to me that I have now no reason for keeping back the information any longer. Who saw me?"

"You realize, sir, that if what you say is true this provides you with an alibi?"

"Unfortunately as regards clearing me from suspicion, yes."

"Unfortunately?" Elliot froze up.

"A bad joke, inspector. I beg your pardon."

"May I ask why you didn't tell me this at first?"

"You may. And in doing so you might ask what I saw through the window."

"I don't follow you."

Elliot was always careful to conceal his intelligence. A shade of exasperation passed over Gore's face. "In words of one syllable, inspector, ever since I came into this house last night I suspected the presence of dirty work. This gentleman walked in." He looked at Murray, and did not seem to know how to treat him. "He knew me. I knew he knew me. But he never spoke out."

"Well?"

"What happened? I came round the side of the house—as you have so shrewdly discovered—possibly a minute or so before the murder." He broke off. "By the way, *have* you determined that it was murder?"

"Just one moment, please. Go on."

"I looked in here, and I saw Murray sitting with his back to me like a stuffed dummy, not even moving. Immediately afterwards I heard all the sounds we have so often heard, beginning with the choking noise and ending with the thrashings in water. I moved away from the window, over towards the left, and looked out to see what was happening in the garden. But I did not go nearer. At this time Burrows ran out from the house towards the pool. So I withdrew again, back towards the library windows. The alarm seemed to have gone up inside the house. And this time what did I see? I saw this distinguished, venerable gentleman," again his curt nod indicated Murray, "carefully juggling *two* Thumbographs, guiltily putting one in his pocket and hastily putting the other on the table. . . ."

Murray had been listening with critical interest.

"So, so?" he observed, with an almost Teutonic inflection. "You thought I was working against you?" He seemed pleased.

"Naturally. Working against me! As usual, you understate the case," returned Gore. His face darkened. "So I did not care to tell where I had been. I reserved the knowledge of what I had seen for a shot in the locker in case dirty work had been attempted."

"Have you anything more to add to that?"

"No, inspector, I think not. The rest of what I said was true. But may I ask who saw me?"

"Knowles was standing at the window of the Green Room," said Elliot, and the other began to whistle through his teeth. Then Elliot's gaze moved from Gore to Murray to Welkyn. "Has any of you ever seen this before?"

From his pocket he took a smaller section of newspaper, in which the stained clasp-knife had been carefully wrapped. He opened it and exhibited the knife.

The expressions of Gore and Welkyn showed a general blankness. But Murray sucked in his bearded cheeks; he blinked at the exhibit and hitched his chair closer.

"Where did you find this?" Murray asked briskly.

"Near the scene of the crime. Do you recognize it?"

"H'm. You have tested it for fingerprints? No. Ah, a pity," said Murray, rowing brisker and brisker. "Will you allow me to touch it if I handle it with he greatest circumspection? Correct me if I am wrong. But didn't you, young ohnny"—he glanced at Gore—"use to have a knife exactly like this? Didn't present it to you, in fact? Didn't you carry it for years?"

"I certainly did. I always carry a pocket-knife," admitted Gore, reaching nto his pocket and producing an old knife only slightly smaller and lighter han the one before them. "But——"

"For once," interposed Welkyn, slapping his hand on the table, "for once nd all I must insist on exercising the rights with which you, sir, have seen it to endow me. Such questions are absurd and improper; and as your legal dviser I must tell you to disregard them. Such knives are as common as lackberries. I once had one myself."

"But what is wrong with the question?" asked Gore, puzzled. "I owned a nife like that. It went with the rest of my clothes and effects in the *Titanic*. But it seems absurd to suppose that the one there could be——"

Before anybody could stop him, Murray had whipped a handkerchief out f his pocket, moistened it at his lips (a handkerchief in the mouth is one f the things which always set Page's teeth on edge), and wiped clean a mall section of the blade about halfway down. Into the cleared steel had een roughly cut letters forming the word

*Madeline.*

"It is yours, Johnny," said Murray comfortably. "You put this name there ne day when I took you through the stonecutting works at Ilford."

"Madeline," repeated Gore.

Opening a pane of the window behind him, he threw out his cigar into the odden trees. But Page saw his face reflected momentarily in the gloomy lass: it was a curious, set, indecipherable face, unlike the one of mockery vith which Gore usually pointed out the difference between his moods and he world's. He turned back.

"But what about the knife? Are you suggesting that that poor, tortured, vould-be-honest crook kept it about him all these years, and finally cut his hroat with it by the pool? You seem to have determined that this is a case f murder; and yet—and yet——"

He beat the flat of his hand slowly on his knee.

"I'll tell you what it is, gentlemen," said Elliot, "it's an absolutely im-ossible crime."

He detailed to them Knowles's story. The interest exhibited by both Gore nd Murray was in contrast to the evident disgust and bewilderment of Welkyn. When Elliot described the finding of the knife there was an uneasy novement through the group.

"Alone, and yet murdered," said Gore reflectively. He looked at Murray. 'Magister, this is a matter after your own heart. I don't seem to know you.

Perhaps we have grown too far apart; but in the old days you would have hopped round the inspector, full of strange theories and bearded like the pard——"

"I am no longer a fool, Johnny."

"Still, let us hear a theory. Any theory. So far, you are the only one who has been reticent about the whole affair."

"I second that motion," observed Dr. Fell.

Murray settled himself more comfortably, and began to wag his finger.

"The exercise of pure logic," he began, "is often comparable to working out immense sums in arithmetic and finding at the end that we have somewhere forgotten to carry one or multiply by two. Every one of a thousand figures and factors may be correct except that one; but the difference in the answer to the sum may be disconcerting. Therefore I do not put this forward as pure logic. I make a suggestion.—You know, inspector, that the coroner's inquest is almost certainly going to call this suicide?"

"Can't say that, sir. Not necessarily," declared Elliot. "A Thumbograph was stolen and then returned; a girl was nearly frightened to death——"

"You know as well as I do," said Murray, opening his eyes, "what verdict a coroner's jury will return. It is remotely possible that the victim might have killed himself and flung the knife away; it is impossible that he should have been murdered. But I assume that it is murder."

"Heh," said Dr. Fell, rubbing his hands. "Heh-heh-heh. And the suggestion?"

"Assuming that it is murder," said Murray, "I suggest that the victim was not, in fact, killed with the knife you have there. I suggest that the marks on his throat are more like the marks of fangs or claws."

## Chapter XI

"Claws?" repeated Elliot.

"The term was fanciful," said Murray, now so didactic that Page longed to administer a swift kick. "I do not necessarily mean literal claws. Shall I argue out my suggestion for you?"

Elliot smiled. "Go right ahead. I don't mind. And you may be surprised how much there is to argue."

"Put it like this," said Murray in a startlingly ordinary tone. "Assuming that it was murder, and assuming that this knife was used to do it, one question bothers me badly. It is this. *Why didn't the murderer drop the knife into the pool afterwards?*"

The inspector still looked at him inquiringly.

"Consider the circumstances. The person who killed this man had an almost perfect—er——"

"Set-up?" suggested Gore, as the other groped.

"It is a rotten word, Johnny; but it will do. Well. The murderer had an lmost perfect set-up for suicide. Suppose he had cut this man's throat and lropped the knife into the pool? Not one person would afterwards have loubted that it was suicide. This man, an impostor, was about to be un-nasked: here would have seemed his way out. Even as things are you have lifficulty in believing it was not suicide. With the knife in the pool it would lave been a clear case. It would even take care of the matter of fingerprints: he water would have washed away any fingerprints which the dead man night have been assumed to have left on the knife.

"Now, gentlemen, you can't tell me that the murderer did not *want* this o be thought suicide. You can't tell me any murderer ever wants that. If it an be managed, a fraudulent suicide is the best possible way out. Why vasn't that knife dropped in the pool? The knife incriminates nobody—xcept the dead man, another indication of suicide and probably the reason vhy the murderer chose it. Yet instead the murderer takes it away and (if follow you) thrusts it deep down into a hedge ten feet away from the ool."

"Proving?" said Elliot.

"No, no. Proving nothing." Murray lifted his finger. "But suggesting a reat deal. Now consider this behaviour in relation to the crime. Do you elieve old Knowles's story?"

"You're giving the theories, sir."

"No, that is a fair question," said Murray rather sharply. Page felt that ie only just checked himself from adding, "Come, come, sir!" "Otherwise ve shall get nowhere."

"We shall get nowhere if I say I believe an impossibility, Mr. Murray."

"Then you do believe in suicide?"

"I didn't say that."

"Which do you believe in, then?"

Elliot grinned faintly. "If you get the bit in your teeth, sir, you'll convince ne that I ought to answer you. Knowles's story is supported by—um—con-ributory evidence. For the sake of argument let's say I believe he was telling he truth, or thought he was telling the truth. What happens then?"

"Why, it follows that he did not see anything because there was nothing o see. That can hardly be doubted. This man was alone in the middle of a ircle of sand. Therefore no murderer went near him. Therefore the mur-lerer did not use that notched and suggestively stained knife you have there; ind the knife was, in fact, 'planted' in the hedge afterwards to make you hink it was used for the crime. You follow that? Since the knife could not lave flown out of the air, cut his throat three times, and dropped into the ledge, it is evident that the knife could not have been used at all. That argu-nent is plain?"

"Not exactly plain," objected the inspector. "You say it was some other weapon? Then some other weapon hung in the air, cut his throat three times, and disappeared? No, sir. I don't believe that. Definitely not. That's worse than believing in the knife."

"I appeal to Dr. Fell," said Murray, evidently stung. "What do you say, doctor?"

Dr. Fell sniffed. Mysterious wheezes and noises of internal combustion suggested argument; but he spoke mildly.

"I abide by the knife. Besides, you know, there certainly was something moving in that garden; something of damned bluish cast of countenance, if you'll allow me. I say, inspector. You've taken the statements. But d'you mind if I probe and pry into them a bit? I should very much like to ask a few questions of the most interesting person here."

"The most interesting person here?" repeated Gore, and prepared himself.

"H'mf, yes. I refer, of course," said Dr. Fell, lifting his stick and pointing, "to Mr. Welkyn."

Superintendent Hadley has often wished that he would not do this. Dr. Fell is, possibly, too much concerned with proving that the right thing is always the wrong thing, or at least the unexpected thing; and waving flags with both hands above the ruin of logic. Certainly Page would never have taken Harold Welkyn for the most interesting person there. The fat solicitor, with his long disapproving chin, evidently did not think so either. But, as even Hadley admits, the old beggar is often unfortunately right.

"You spoke to me, sir?" inquired Welkyn.

"I was telling the inspector a while ago," said Dr. Fell, "that your name seemed very familiar. I remember now. Is it a general interest in the occult? Or are you a collector of curious clients? I rather imagine you collected our friend here," he nodded towards Gore, "in the same way you collected that Egyptian some time ago."

"Egyptian?" asked Elliot. "What Egyptian?"

"Think! You'll remember the case. Ledwidge v. Ahriman, before Mr. Justice Rankin. Libel. Mr. Welkyn here was instructed for the defence."

"You mean that ghost-seer or whatever he was?"

"Yes," said Dr. Fell, with great pleasure. "Little bit of a chap; hardly more than a dwarf. But he didn't see ghosts: he saw through people, or so he said. He was the fashion of London; all the women flocked to him. Of course, he could have been prosecuted under the old Witchcraft Act, still in force——"

"A most infamous act, sir," declared Welkyn, slapping the table.

"—but it was a question of a libel suit, and Mr. Welkyn's ingenious defence, combined with Gordon-Bates as counsel, got him off. Then there was Madame Duquesne, the medium, who was up for manslaughter because one of her clients died of fright in her house. (Fascinating point of law, eh?)

Mr. Welkyn was also instructed for the defence there. The trial, as I remember it, was rather grisly. Oh, yes! And another one: a girl, good-looking blonde as I remember her. The charges against her never got past the Grand Jury, because Mr. Welkyn—"

Patrick Gore was looking at his solicitor with quick interest. "Is this true?" he demanded. "Believe me, gentlemen, I did not know it."

"It is true, isn't it?" inquired Dr. Fell. "You're the same chap?"

Welkyn's face was full of cold wonder.

"Of course it is true," he answered. "But what of it? What has it to do with the present case?"

Page could not have said why it seemed so incongruous. Harold Welkyn, examining his pink finger-nails, then glancing up sharply from little eyes, was a model of business decorum; and yet why not? The white slip inside his waistcoat, the glossy wings of his collar, had no connection with the clients he sought or the beliefs he held.

"You see, Mr. Welkyn," rumbled Dr. Fell, "I had another reason for asking. You were the only one who saw or heard anything queer in the garden last night. Will you read out the part of Mr. Welkyn's statement I mean, inspector?"

Elliot nodded, not taking his eyes from Welkyn until he opened the notebook.

" '*I heard a kind of rustling noise in the hedges or shrubbery, and I thought I saw something looking at me through one of the glass panels of the door, one of the panels down nearest the ground. I was afraid that certain things might be happening which were no affair of mine.*' "

"Exactly," said Dr. Fell, and closed his eyes.

Elliot hesitated, debating two courses; but Page had a feeling that the matter was out in the open now, and that both Dr. Fell and the inspector thought it was better so. Elliot's hard, sandy-haired head bent forward a little.

"Now, sir," he said. "I didn't want to ask you too much this morning, until we—knew more. What does that statement mean?"

"What it says."

"You were in the dining-room, only fifteen feet or so away from the pool, yet you didn't once open one of those doors and look out? Even when you heard the sounds you describe?"

"No."

" '*I was afraid that certain things might be happening that were no affair of mine,*' " read Elliot. "Does this refer to the murder? Did you think that a murder was being committed?"

"No, certainly not," said Welkyn, with a slight jump. "And I still have no reason to suspect that one was committed. Inspector, are you mad? Clear evidence of suicide is brought to you; and you all go star-gazing after some thing else——"

"Did you think that suicide was being committed last night, then?"

"No, I had no reason to suspect it."

"Then what were you referring to?" asked Elliot practically.

Welkyn had the palms of his hands flat on the table. By lifting his fingers slightly he conveyed the effect of a shrug; but his bland dumpling countenance betrayed nothing else.

"I'll try to put it in another way. Mr. Welkyn, do you believe in the supernatural?"

"Yes," said Welkyn briefly.

"Do you believe that someone is attempting to produce supernatural phenomena here?"

Welkyn looked at him. "And you from Scotland Yard! *You* say that!"

"Oh, it's not as bad as all that," said Elliot; and he wore a curious, dark expression which his countrymen have understood for centuries. "I said 'attempting,' and there are various ways of doing that. Real and unreal. Believe me, sir, there may be queer doings here—implanted here—growing from one ancestor to another—queerer doings than you think. I came down here because Miss Daly had been murdered; and there may be more behind that than a purse of money stolen by a tramp. All the same, I wasn't the one who suggested there might be something supernatural here. You suggested it."

"I did?"

"Yes. 'I thought I saw something looking at me through one of the glass panels of the door, one of the panels down nearest the ground.' You said 'something.' Why didn't you say 'someone'?"

A small bead of sweat appeared on Welkyn's forehead, up near the large vein by the temple. It was his only change of expression, if it can be called that; at least it was the only moving thing on his face.

"I did not recognize who it was. Had I recognized the person, I should have said 'someone.' I was merely attempting to be accurate."

"It was a person, then? A 'someone'?"

The other nodded.

"But, in order to peep at you through one of the lower panels, this person must have been crouched down to the ground or lying on the ground?"

"Not exactly."

"Not exactly? What do you mean by that, sir?"

"It was moving too quickly—and jumpily. I hardly know how to express what I mean."

"Can't you describe it?"

"No. I only received the impression that it was dead."

Something like horror had got into Brian Page's bones; how it had come there, even when it had come, he could not tell. Almost imperceptibly the conversation had moved into a new element, yet he felt that this had always been in the background of the case, waiting for a touch to be wakened. Harold Welkyn then made a very quick movement. He took a handkerchief out of his breast pocket, wiped the palms of his hands quickly on it, and replaced it. When he spoke again he had recovered something of his old solemn, careful manner.

"One moment, inspector," he put in before Elliot could speak. "I have been trying to tell you truthfully and literally what I saw and felt. You ask me whether I believe in—such things. I do. I tell you frankly I wouldn't go into that garden after dark for a thousand pounds. It seems to surprise you that a man of my profession should have such ideas."

Elliot pondered. "To tell you the truth, it does, somehow. I don't know why it should. After all, I suppose even a lawyer may believe in the supernatural."

The other's tone was dry.

"Even a lawyer may," he agreed; "and be none the worse man of business for doing so."

Madeline had come into the room. Only Page noticed her, for the others were too intent on Welkyn; she was walking on tiptoe, and he wondered whether she had heard what had gone before. Though he tried to give her his chair, she sat down on the arm of it. He could not see her face: only the soft line of chin and cheek: but he saw that the breast of her white silk blouse was rising and falling rapidly.

Kennet Murray's eyebrows were pinched together. He was very polite, but he had the air of a customs-officer about to examine luggage.

"I presume, Mr. Welkyn," Murray said, "you are—er—honest about this. It is certainly extraordinary. That garden has a bad reputation. It has had a bad reputation for centuries. In fact, it was remodelled in the late seventeenth century in the hope of exorcising the shadow by fresh prospects. You remember, young Johnny, how your demonological studies tried to raise up things there?"

"Yes," answered Gore. He was about to add something, but he checked himself.

"And on your homecoming," said Murray, "you are greeted by a crawling legless something in the garden, and a housemaid frightened into a fit. Look here, young Johnny: you're not up to your old tricks of frightening people, are you?"

To Page's surprise, Gore's dusky face had gone pale. Murray, it appeared, was the only person who could sting him or rouse him out of his urbanity.

"No," Gore said. "You know where I was. I was keeping an eye on you in the library. And just one thing more. Just who the hell do you think you are, to talk to me as though I were still a fifteen-year-old child? You kow-towed to my father; and, by God, I'll have decent respect from you or I'll take a cane to you as you used to do to me."

The outburst was so unexpected that even Dr. Fell grunted. Murray got to his feet.

"Is it going to your head already?" he said. "Just as you like. My usefulness is over. You have your proofs. If I am wanted for anything more, inspector, I shall be at the inn."

"That, John," interposed Madeline softly, "was rather a rotten thing to say, don't you think? Forgive me for interrupting."

For the first time both Murray and Gore looked at her fully, and she at them. The latter smiled.

"You are Madeline," he said.

"I am Madeline."

"My old, cold light-of-love," said Gore. The wrinkles deepened round his eyes. He detained Murray, and there was apology in his voice. "It's no good, magister. We can't pick up the past, and now I am quite certain I don't care to. It seems to me that for twenty-five years I have been moving forward, mentally, while you have been standing still. I used to imagine what would happen when I returned to what are poetically known as the halls of my fathers. I used to imagine myself moved by the sight of a picture on a wall or letters cut with a pen-knife into the back of a bench. What I find is a group of alien sticks and stones; I begin to wish I had not intruded. But that is not the point now. Something seems to have gone out of line. Inspector Elliot! Didn't you say a minute ago that you had come down here because 'Miss Daly had been murdered'?"

"That's right, sir."

Murray had sat down again, evidently curious, while Gore turned to the inspector.

"Victoria Daly. That's not by any chance the little girl who used to live with her aunt—Ernestine Daly, was it?—at Rose-Bower Cottage on the other side of the Hanging Chart?"

"I don't know about her aunt," returned Elliot, "but that's where she lived. She was strangled on the night of July 31st, last year."

The claimant was grim. "Then I can at least produce an alibi there. I was happily in America then. All the same, will somebody take us out of this fen? What has the murder of Victoria Daly got to do with this business here?"

Elliot gave an inquiring glance towards Dr. Fell. The doctor nodded sleepily but violently; his great bulk hardly seemed to breathe, and he was watching. Taking up the briefcase from beside his chair, Elliot opened it and drew out a book. It was of quarto size, bound in dark calf-skin at some comparatively recent date (say a hundred years ago), and had on its back the somewhat unexhilarating title of *Admirable History*. The inspector pushed it across to Dr. Fell, who opened it. Then Page saw that it was a much older volume, a translation from the French of Sébastien Michaëlis, published at London in 1613. The paper was brownish and ridged, and across from the title-page there was a very curious book-plate.

"H'mf," said Dr. Fell. "Has anybody here ever seen this book before?"

"Yes," said Gore quietly.

"And this book-plate?"

"Yes. That book-plate has not been used in the family since the eighteenth century."

Dr. Fell's finger traced out the motto. " '*Sanguis eius super nos et super filios nostros,*' Thos. Farnleigh, 1675. 'His blood be upon us and upon our children.'—Was this book ever in the library here at the Close?"

Gore's eye quickened and gleamed as he looked at the book; but he remained puzzled. He spoke sardonically.

"No, it certainly was not. That's one of the books of darkness which my father, and his father before him, kept locked in the little room in the attic. I stole his key once, and had some duplicates made, so that I could go up there and read. Lord, the time I spent there—under pretext, if anyone should find me, of getting an apple from the apple-room next door." He looked round. "Do you remember, Madeline? I took you up there once to give you a glimpse of the Golden Hag? I even gave you a key. But I am afraid you never liked it.—Doctor, where did you get that book? How did it get out of captivity?"

Inspector Elliot got up and rang the bell for Knowles.

"Will you find Lady Farnleigh," he said to a scared butler, "and ask her if she will come in here?"

With great leisureliness Dr. Fell took out pipe and pouch. He filled the pipe, lit it, and inhaled with deep satisfaction before he spoke. Then he made a flourishing gesture and pointed.

"That book? Because of the innocuous title, nobody at the time even glanced into it or thought twice about it. Actually, it contains one of the most unnerving documents in recorded history: the confession of Madeleine de la Palud, at Aix in 1611, or her participation in ceremonies of witchcraft and the worship of Satan. It was found on the table by Miss Daly's bed. She had been reading it not long before she was murdered."

## Chapter XII

IN THE quiet of the library, Page heard very distinctly the footsteps of Molly Farnleigh and Burrows as they came in.

Murray cleared his throat. "Meaning—?" he prompted. "Didn't I understand that Miss Daly was killed by a tramp?"

"Quite possibly she was."

"Well, then?"

It was Molly Farnleigh who spoke. "I came in here to tell you," she said, "that I am going to fight this ridiculous claim, *your* claim," her whole vigorous nature went into the glance of cold dislike she gave Gore, "to the end. Nat Burrows says it will probably take years and we shall all lose our shirts, but I can afford that. In the meantime, the important thing is who killed John. I'll call a truce for the time being, if you will. What did I hear you all talking about when we came in here?"

A certain sense of relief went through the group. But one man was instantly on guard.

"You think you have a case, Lady Farnleigh?" asked Welkyn, all solicitor again. "I am bound to warn you——"

"A better case than you may have any idea of," retorted Molly, with a curious significant look at Madeline. "What did I hear you talking about when we came in?"

Dr. Fell, fiery with interest now, spoke in a kind of apologetic thunder.

"We're on rather an important aspect of it just now, ma'am," he said, "and we should very much appreciate your help. Is there still, in the attic of this house, a little room containing a collection of books on witchcraft and kindred subjects? Eh?"

"Yes, of course. But what has that to do with it?"

"Look at this book, ma'am. Can you tell us positively whether it comes from that collection?"

Molly approached the table. They had all risen, but she made a gesture of impatience at the formality.

"I think so. Yes, I'm almost sure of it. All of them had that book-plate, and none of the other books have: it's a kind of badge. Where on earth did you get the book?"

Dr. Fell told her.

"But that's impossible!"

"Why?"

"Because there was such a terrible fuss and bother and to-do about those books. My husband caused it; I never knew why. We had only been married a little over a year, you know." Her quiet brown eyes looked at the past. She took the chair Burrows set out for her. "When I came here as a—as a bride, he gave me all the household keys except the key to that room. Of course I handed them straight over to Mrs. Apps, the housekeeper; but you know the principle of the thing. It interested me, rather."

"Like Bluebeard?" suggested Gore.

"No controversy, please," said Dr. Fell sharply, as she turned to the claimant in a cold fury.

"Very well," said Molly. "Anyhow, I heard about it. My husband wanted to burn it—the collection, I mean. It seems that when they were valuing the property just before he came into it, they had a man down from London to look at the books. He said that little collection in the attic was worth thousands and thousands of pounds and almost danced with delight, the silly ass. He said there were all kinds of rarities in it, including something unique. I do remember what that was. It was a manuscript book which was supposed to have been lost since the beginning of the nineteenth century. Nobody knew where it had gone, and there it was right in our attic. They called it the Red Book of Appin. He said it was supposed to be the big harum-scarum hocus-pocus of magic, and it was so magical that anybody who read it had to wear a hoop of iron round his head. I jolly well do remember that, because you were all arguing about it last night, and this man"—she looked at Gore—"didn't even know what it was."

"As Dr. Fell suggests, no controversy," said Gore pleasantly. But he addressed Murray. "Fair play, magister. I never knew the sacred volume under that name, you know. But I can tell you what it is, and I can even identify it if it is still upstairs. I'll give you one of its qualities. Anyone who possessed it was said to know what any inquiry would be before the inquirer opened his lips."

"That must have been very useful to you," Molly said sweetly, "last night."

"As proving that I had read the book, yes. It was also said to confer the power of giving life to inanimate objects, which almost suggests that Lady Farnleigh must have read it herself."

Dr. Fell hammered the ferrule of his stick on the floor to call for attention. When the threatened storm had been hammered away, he looked at Molly benevolently.

"Heh," said Dr. Fell. "Heh-heh-heh. I gather, ma'am, that you don't believe in the magical properties of the Red Book of Appin or anything else?"

"Oh, so-and-so!" said Molly, using a short Anglo-Saxon word which made Madeline colour.

"H'mf, yes. Exactly. But you were telling us?"

"Well, anyway, my husband was frightfully upset and concerned about those books. He wanted to burn them. I said not to be absolutely silly: if he had to get rid of them, why not sell them, and in any case what harm were they doing? He said they were full of eroticism and wickedness." Molly hesitated, but she went on in her candid way. "That did interest me a bit, if you must know. I peeped into one or two of them—when he showed me the room—but it certainly wasn't anything like that. You never read such horribly dull stuff in your life. There was nothing low about it. It was a lot of long-winded rubbish about the twin life-lines or something, and all done with those funny 'f's' for 's's' that make it look as though the writer lisped. I couldn't get up *any* interest in it. So, when my husband insisted on keeping the place locked, I never bothered any more about it and I'm sure it hasn't been opened since."

"But this book," Dr. Fell tapped it, "came from there?"

"Ye-es, I'm sure of it."

"And your husband always kept the key to that locked room. Yet somehow it got out of there and into Miss Daly's possession. H'm." Dr. Fell was smoking in short puffs; now he took the pipe out of his mouth and sniffed massively. "Consequently, we have a connection—on a thread like this— through Miss Daly's death to your husband's death. Eh?"

"But what connection?"

"For instance, ma'am, could he have given Miss Daly the book himself?"

"But I've already told you what he thought about those books!"

"That, you know, ma'am," said Dr. Fell apologetically, "was not the question. Could he? After all, we've heard that when he was a boy—if he was the real John Farnleigh, as you claim—he thought very highly of those books."

Molly faced it out.

"You've got me in a cleft stick. If I say he hated such things out of all reason, you can answer that it's too much of a change and proves he wasn't John Farnleigh. If I say he could have given the book to Victoria—well, I don't know what you'll say."

"All we want is an honest answer, ma'am," said Dr. Fell. "Or, rather, an honest impression. Heaven pity the person who tries to tell all the truth. But look here: did you know Victoria Daly well?"

"Pretty well. Poor Victoria was the sort who exulted in Good Works."

"Should you have said," Dr. Fell made a vague gesture with his pipe, "should you have said she was the sort to be deeply interested in the subject of witchcraft?"

Molly clenched her hands.

"But will you tell me, please, how on earth this witchcraft talk comes into it? Granting that's what this book is about—if it comes from the attic it must be—does it prove anything just because she was reading it?"

"There is other evidence, believe me," said Dr. Fell gently. "Your own native intelligence, ma'am, will show you that the important thing is the connection of Miss Daly + a locked library + that book. For instance: did your husband know her well?"

"H'm. I don't know. Not very well, I should have thought."

Dr. Fell's forehead was wrinkled. "And yet consider his behaviour last night, as it has been described to me. Confirm this. A claimant to his estate appears. The possession of this estate, rightfully or wrongfully, is the most important driving force in his life. And now the citadel is attacked. Mr. Gore, Mr. Welkyn, with their convincing stories and their deadly proof of fingerprints, are closing in on him. It is true that he paces the floor; yet, at the very moment the attack is launched, he seems more concerned over the fact that there is a detective in the village investigating the death of Victoria Daly. Is that true?"

It was true. Page remembered it only too well. And Molly was forced to admit it.

"So, we perceive, the thread spins out. Let's try to follow that thread wherever it leads. I am more and more interested in that locked attic room. Is there anything else up there besides books?"

Molly reflected.

"Only that mechanical robot thing. I saw it once when I was a little girl, and I rather loved it. I asked my husband why we couldn't have it down and see whether we couldn't find a way to make it work: I love things that work: but *it* stayed there too."

"Ah, the mechanical robot thing," repeated Dr. Fell, hauling himself up with a wheeze and flash of interest. "What can you tell us about that?"

It was Kennet Murray who answered, when Molly shook her head.

"Now there is a matter, doctor," Murray said comfortably, settling himself in the chair, "you would do well to investigate. *I* tried to investigate it years ago, and so did young Johnny."

"Well?"

"Here are all the *facts* I could unearth." Murray spoke with emphasis. "Sir Dudley never allowed me to look at the figure, and I had to work from outside. It was constructed by M. Raisin, the organist of Troyes, who made the self-playing harpsichord for Louis XIV; and it was exhibited with great success at the court of Charles II in 1676-77. It was a nearly life-sized figure, sitting on a kind of small couch, and it was said to represent one of the king's ladies: there is argument about which one. Its actions delighted the people of that time. It played two or three tunes on a cittern (what we nowadays call a zither); it thumbed its nose at the spectators, and went through a variety of gestures, some undoubtedly indecorous."

There was no doubt that he had caught the immediate interest of his audience.

"It was bought by Sir Thomas Farnleigh, whose book-plate you have there," said Murray. "Whether it was the immodesty of the automaton that later caused a blight to fall on it, or some other cause, I have never been able to find out. But something happened—dead silence of all records as to what. That seems no reason for the horror it inspired in the eighteenth century, though such a contraption wouldn't have recommended itself to Sir Dudley or his father or grandfather. Presumably old Thomas learned the secret of how to make it work; but that secret has never been passed on. Eh, young Jo . . . I beg your pardon. Sir John?"

At the thick and exaggerated courtesy of his tone, Gore showed some contempt. But he was interested in other matters.

"No, it was not passed on," Gore admitted. "And it will never be learned.

I know, gentlemen. In my younger days I racked my brains over the secret of the Golden Hag. I could easily show you why none of the obvious explanations would work. If we—" He looked startled. "By all the gods, why shouldn't we go up and have a look at her? I only just thought of it. I'm inhibited. I was thinking of all sorts of excuses and crooked ways by which I could sneak up there as I used to do. But why not? Why not, in the open light of day?"

He thumped his fist down on the arm of the chair, blinking a little as though he himself had just come into light. Inspector Elliot interposed rather sharply.

"Just one moment, sir," Elliot said. "This is all very interesting; and we can go into it another time; but I don't see that it has any bearing on——"

"Are you sure?" asked Dr. Fell.

"Sir?"

"Are you sure?" repeated the doctor with great intensity. "I say, somebody! What does this automaton look like?"

"It's a good deal decayed, of course; at least, it was twenty-five years ago——"

"It was," agreed Madeline Dane, and shuddered. "Don't go up there. Please say you won't!"

"But why on earth not?" cried Molly.

"I don't know. I'm afraid."

Gore regarded her with indulgence.

"Yes, I hazily remember that it had a powerful effect on you. But you were asking what it looked like, doctor. It must have been uncannily life-like when it was new. The framework is of jointed iron, of course; but the 'flesh' is wax, with glass eyes—one missing—and real hair. The decay has not improved it; it is rather fat, and used to look somewhat unpleasant when you imagined things. It wears, or used to wear, a brocaded gown. The hands and fingers are of painted iron. In order to play the zither and make gestures, the fingers are long and jointed and sharp, almost like . . . It used to smile, but the smile had rotted away when I saw it last."

"And Betty Harbottle," said Dr. Fell abruptly, "Betty Harbottle, like Eve, has a strong fondness for apples."

"I beg your pardon?"

"She has, you know," urged Dr. Fell. "Betty Harbottle, the frightened maid, is fond of apples. That was the first thing which was pointed out to us when we questioned the servants. I suspect our good housekeeper, Mrs. Apps, of conveying a hint. By the darkness of Eleusis, that's exactly what it was! And you"—the doctor's red face shone with concentration as he blinked at Gore—"you told me a minute ago that you used to have a pretext when you wanted to visit the den of the books and the Golden Hag. You went to the apple-room, next door to it in the attic. Will somebody offer me odds as to where Betty Harbottle was when she was frightened, and where the Thumbo-graph was hidden last night?"

Harold Welkyn got up and began to walk round the table; but he was the only one who moved. Afterwards Page was to remember that circle of faces in the gloom of the library, and the brief expression he surprised on one of them.

It was Murray who spoke, smoothing his moustache.

"Ah. Yes. Yes, it is undoubtedly interesting. If I still have my geography straight, the stairs to the attic are at the back of the passage beside the Green Room. You suggest that the girl was carried downstairs and put in the Green Room?"

Dr. Fell wagged his head. "I only suggest that we have got to follow our dim intelligences or go home to bed. Every thread leads back to that little den. It's the core of the labyrinth and the heart of every disturbance, like the little bowl of fluid in *The House and the Brain:* which is an apter title than we may think. We had better pay a visit there."

Inspector Elliot spoke slowly.

"I think we had. Now. Do you mind, Lady Farnleigh?"

"No, not at all, except that I don't know where the key is. Oh, bother that! Break the lock. It's a new padlock my husband had put on; and if you think it will help you can tear—you can t-tear—" Molly brushed her hand across her eyes, held tight to her feelings, and regained control again. "Shall I lead the way?"

"Thank you." Elliot was brisk. "How many of the rest of you have ever been in that room? Only Miss Dane and Mr. Gore? Will you two come with Dr. Fell and me, please? And Mr. Page. The others please remain here."

Elliot and the doctor went ahead, talking in low tones. Molly then put herself in front of them, as though discreetly deaf, placing them between herself and the claimant. Page followed with Madeline.

"If you'd rather not go up—?" he said to Madeline.

She pressed his arm. "No, please. I *want* to go up. I do, really, to see if I can understand what is going on. You know, I'm afraid something I said has upset Molly terribly, but I had to tell her: there was no other way out. Brian. You don't think I'm a cat, do you?"

He was startled. Though her half-smiling mouth made fun of this sugges-tion, the long eyes had a look of great intensity.

"Good Lord, no! What put that idea into your head?"

"Oh, nothing. But she didn't love him, really. She's only doing all this because she thinks she ought to. In spite of all appearances, I tell you they weren't suited to each other. He was idealistic and she is practical. Wait: I know he was an impostor, but you don't know all the circumstances or you'd understand——"

"Then give me the practical," Page snapped.

"Brian!"

"I mean it. Idealistic my eye! If he did what they say he did, and what you yourself admit he did, our late dead friend was a hundred-carat swine and you know it. Were you by any chance in love with him yourself?"

"Brian! You have no right to say that!"

"I know I haven't; but were you?"

"I was not," said Madeline quietly, and looked at the floor. "If you had better eyes, or understood things better, you would know enough not to ask that." She hesitated; it was clear that she wanted to change the subject. "What do Dr. Fell and the inspector think of—all this?"

He opened his mouth to answer, and realized that he had no idea.

He had no idea. Their group had gone up the broad, shallow oak staircase to the floor above, along the gallery, and round the turning of a passage to the left. On the left was the Green Room, its open door showing heavy study-furniture of the last century and walls biliously patterned. On the right were two bedroom doors. The passage ran straight down to a window at the end, overlooking the garden. The stairs up to the attic—Page vaguely remembered—were in the outer thickness of the wall at the end of the passage, the door to them being in the left-hand wall.

But he was not thinking of this. Despite Dr. Fell's thunderous geniality, and the easy-talking frankness of Inspector Elliot, he realized that he knew nothing whatever. Both of them would talk until Doomsday, of course. But what about routine police-work: a fingerprint here, a footprint there, a searching of the garden by Elliot or a clue sealed into an envelope? The finding of the knife, yes; he knew of that because under the circumstances it could hardly have been avoided. What else, even as regarded theories? Certain statements had been taken from certain persons; what were we to think of those statements?

After all, it was their business. Yet it disquieted him. New discoveries were being turned up out of what he had thought was old ground, like skulls at Blenheim, and you had no warning of the skull until it rolled across the table. No, better change the simile. Up ahead towered Dr. Fell's huge back, seeming to fill the passage.

"Which room is she in?" Elliot asked in a low voice.

Molly indicated the farther bedroom door, across the passage from the door to the attic. Elliot knocked very lightly at the door; but from inside came a faint muttered cry.

"Betty," whispered Madeline.

"In there?"

"Yes. They put her in the nearest bedroom. She's not," said Madeline, "she's not in very good shape."

The full implications of this were beginning to creep into Page's mind.

Dr. King opened the bedroom door, glanced behind him, and eased it softly shut as he slipped out into the passage.

"No," he said. "You can't see her yet. Tonight, maybe; tomorrow or next day more likely. I wish the sedatives would take hold. They won't, properly."

Elliot looked puzzled and worried. "Yes, but, doctor, surely it's not—not——?"

"Serious, were you going to say?" asked King, lowering his grizzled head as though he were about to butt with it. "My God! Excuse me."

He opened the door again.

"Has she said anything?"

"Nothing for your notebook, inspector. Delirium, more than half of it. I wish I could find out what she saw."

He was speaking to a very quiet group. Molly, whose expression had altered, seemed to be trying to hold fiercely to accepted rules. Dr. King had been a lifelong friend of her father, and they stood on no ceremony with each other.

"Uncle Ned, I want to know. I'd do anything for Betty, and you know it. But I never realized—that is, it's not really what we can call *serious*, is it? It can't be. People get frightened, but it's not the same thing as being actually ill? It's not dangerous?"

"Oh," said the other, "it's not dangerous. Fine, lusty wench you are; no nerves; surplus energy; see something and biff it one. Yes, you would. Well, maybe it takes people differently. Maybe it was a mouse or wind in the chimney. Only I hope I don't run across it, whatever it was." His tone softened. "No, it'll be all right. No help, thanks; Mrs. Apps and I can manage. But you might have some tea sent up."

The door closed.

"Yes, my good friends," observed Patrick Gore, with his hands deep in his pockets, "I think I am safe in saying that something has happened. Shall we go upstairs?"

He went over and opened the door opposite.

The staircase inside was steep-pitched and had that faint, sour smell which comes from old stone enclosed within walls. It was as though you saw the ribs and bones inside the house, unsmoothed by modern crafts. The servants' quarters, Page knew, were at the other side of the house. There was no window here; and Elliot, who went ahead, had to use an electric torch. Gore followed him, then Dr. Fell, then Molly, with Madeline and Page in the rear.

Nor had any of this part of the attic been altered since Inigo Jones sketched out his small windows and backed his brick with stone. On the landing the floor sloped in such humped fashion towards the stairs that an unwary footstep might send you down. There was a mighty strength of oak beams, too huge for the picturesque, conveying only power to uphold or crush. Faint grey light entered; the air was thick, damp, and hot.

They found the door they wanted at the far end. It was a heavy door, black, suggesting a cellar rather than an attic. The hinges were of the eighteenth century; the knob was gone and a more modern lock disused; a tight chain and padlock now secured it. But it was not at the lock that Elliot first directed his light.

Something had been flung down and partly crushed by the closing of the door.

It was a half-eaten apple.


## Chapter XIII

WITH the edge of a sixpence as a screw-driver, Elliot carefully unscrewed the staple which held the chain of the padlock. It took a long time, but the inspector worked carefully, like a carpenter. When the chain had fallen the door swung open of its own accord.

"The lair of the Golden Hag," said Gore with gusto, and kicked the half-eaten apple out of the way.

"Steady on, sir!" said Elliot sharply.

"What? Do you think the apple is evidence?"

"You never know. When we go in here, please don't touch anything unless I tell you to."

"When we go in" was an optimistic phrase. Page had expected to see a room. What he found was a kind of book-closet hardly six feet square, with a sloping roof in which a small and thick-grimed pane of glass showed opaque. There were many gaps in the shelves, where ragged calfskin mingled with more modern bindings. Over everything was a film of dust; but it was that thin, blackish, gritty dust of attics, in which few decipherable marks are left. An early Victorian armchair was pushed into it—and the hag herself seemed to jump out at them when the light of Elliot's torch fell inside.

Even Elliot jumped back a little. The hag was not a beauty. She might once have been an alluring charmer, but now only one eye looked out of half a face: the other side of the head was ruined, like the remnants of the velvet brocaded gown which might once have been yellow. Her appearance was not improved by the cracks opening out across her face.

Had she been standing up, she would have been something under life-size. She sat on an oblong box, once gilded and painted to resemble a couch, but not much broader or deeper than she was, and set up off the floor on wheels which were evidently of later date than the automaton itself. The hands were partly lifted with burlesque and rather horrible coquetry. The whole squat, ponderous machine must have weighed two or three hundred-weight.

Madeline uttered a kind of giggle, as of nerves or relief. Elliot growled, and Dr. Fell swore. The doctor said:

"Shades of *Udolpho!* Is this anti-climax?"

"Sir?"

"You know what I mean. Did that girl try to get into Bluebeard's room, see this thing for the first time, and—" He paused, blowing out the ends of his moustache. "No. No, that won't do."

"I'm afraid it won't," agreed Elliot soberly. "*If* something happened to her here, that is. How did she get in? And who carried her downstairs? And where did she get the Thumbograph? You can't tell me that the mere sight of this thing would affect her as badly as she seems to have been affected. She might scream, or something of the sort. It might give her a turn. But nothing like this, unless she's a hysterical case. Lady Farnleigh, did the servants know about this dummy?"

"Of course," said Molly. "Nobody has seen it, except Knowles or possibly Mrs. Apps, but they all knew about it."

"Then it wouldn't even come as a surprise?"

"No."

"If, as I say, she was frightened by something in this little two-by-four place—of which we haven't any evidence——"

"Look there," said Dr. Fell, pointing with his stick.

The beam of the torch played on the floor by the base of the automaton. It found a heap of crumpled linen which, when Elliot picked it up, proved to be a maid's frilled apron. Though it had recently been freshly laundered, it was stained with patches of dust and dirt; and, in one place, there were two short jagged rents in it. Dr. Fell took it from the inspector and handed it to Molly.

"Betty's?" he said.

Molly examined a minute tab, with an even more minute name in ink, sewn to the hem of the apron; and Molly nodded.

"Stop a bit!" urged Dr. Fell, shutting his eyes. He began to lumber back and forth by the door, pressing on his eyeglasses as though to keep them from falling off. When he took his hand away again, his face was lowering and grave. "All right. I'll tell you, my lad. I can't prove it, any more than I could prove the part about the apple and the apple-room. But I can tell you what happened in that book-closet as certainly as though I had seen it. It's no longer mere routine: it's the most vital thing in the case that we should know just when, between lunch-time and four o'clock in the afternoon, that girl was frightened, and what the various people here were doing at that time.

"Because, my lad, the murderer was here—in this book-closet. Betty Harbottle found him here. I don't know what the murderer was doing; but it was vital that nobody should know he had been here at all. Something happened. Afterwards he used the girl's apron to remove possible footprints, fingerprints, marks of any kind in this dust. He carried or dragged her down-stairs. He put into her hand the useless Thumbograph he had stolen the night before. And then he went away, as they all do, and left the apron lying neatly in the middle of the floor. Eh?"

Elliot raised his hand.

"Steady on, sir. Not so fast." He thought it over. "There are two bad objections to that, I'm afraid."

"Which are?"

"One. If it was so vital to conceal the fact that he'd been in this little room, doing whatever he was doing, how was he covering his tracks just by moving the unconscious girl from one place to another? He wasn't pre-venting disclosure; he was only postponing it. The girl's alive. She will re-cover. And she'll tell who was here, and what he was doing—if anything."

"Apparently a poser," said Dr. Fell. "Apparently a stinger whang in the gold. And yet, do you know," he spoke with some violence, "I should not be surprised if the answer to that seeming contradiction is the answer to our problem. What's the other objection?"

"Betty Harbottle wasn't hurt. Physically, she wasn't touched. She was put into the shape she was in by plain old-fashioned fright at something she saw. Yet all she could have seen was an ordinary human being doing something he shouldn't. It's not reasonable, sir; girls are pretty tough these days.— What could have put her into that state, then?"

Dr. Fell looked at him.

"Something that the automaton did," he answered. "Suppose it reached out now and took your hand?"

Such is the power of suggestion that every person in the group shied back. Six pairs of eyes turned to the ruined head and the curious hands of the dummy. They would not be pleasant hands to take or touch. Nothing about that figure, from the mildewed gown to the cracked-open wax of the face, would be good to the touch.

Elliot cleared his throat.

"You mean he made the dummy work?"

"He did not make it work," interposed Gore. "I thought of that years ago. That is, he did not make it work unless some electrical system or other trickery has been shoved into it since my time. Damn it all, gentlemen, nine generations of Farnleighs have tried to discover what made it work. And I'll make you a flat offer. I will pay a thousand pounds to the man who can show me how it does work."

"Man or woman?" said Madeline. Page could see that she was forcing a laugh, but Gore spoke in very desperate earnest.

"Man or woman or child or anybody else. To the man or woman who can make it work without modern hocus-pocus, and under the same conditions as it was exhibited two hundred and fifty years ago."

"The offer's generous enough," said Dr. Fell cheerfully. "Well, wheel her out and let's have a look at her."

With some effort Elliot and Page, laying hold of the iron box on which the dummy sat, pulled it out of the book-closet with a bump over the sill. She jerked her head and quivered; Page wondered whether the hair would come off. Yet the wheels moved with surprising ease. With a heavy creaking and a faint rattling noise, they pushed her over into the light from the window near the head of the stairs.

"Go on. Demonstrate," said Dr. Fell.

Gore made a careful examination. "To begin with, you will find that the body of the thing is full of clockwork. I am no mechanical expert, and I can't tell you whether all the wheels and whatnots are genuine, or whether they were put there for effect. I suspect that most of them are dummies even if some are genuine. Anyhow, the point is that the body is completely filled. There's a long window at the back. If it still opens, put your hand through, and—oh, you scratch, do you?"

Gore's face darkened, and he jerked his own hand back. In his absorption he made a gesture too close to the sharp fingers of the automaton; a crooked scratch drew blood on the back of his hand. He put it to his mouth.

"My good old clock-guts!" he said. "My faithful old clock-guts! I ought to knock the rest of your face off."

"Don't!" cried Madeline.

He was amused. "As you wish, little one. In any case, inspector—will you poke about among the works? What I want to establish is that the body is full of them and that nobody could hide in there."

Elliot was as serious as ever. The glass had long gone from the window at the back; with the aid of his flashlight he examined the mechanism and groped inside. Something seemed to startle him, but he only said:

"Yes, that's right, sir. No room for anything here. You mean it was suggested that somebody was hiding in the thing and working it?"

"The only suggestion anybody could hazard. Now, then. That takes care of the automaton itself. The only other part of it, as you can see for yourself, is the couch on which she sits. Watch."

This time he had more difficulty. At the left of the couch's front there was a small knob; Page could see that the whole front opened out like a little door on a hinge. With some manipulation he managed to get the door open. The interior of the box, bare iron badly corroded with rust, was well under three feet long and not more than eighteen inches high.

Gore beamed with pleasure.

"You remember," he said, "the explanation that was advanced for the chess-playing automaton of Maelzel? The figure sat on a series of large boxes, each with its own little door. Before the demonstration, the showman opened these doors to show that there was no hoax. It was said, however, that inside lurked a *small child*, who deftly contorted himself from one compartment to another; and these movements were so synchronized with the shrewd manipulation of doors that the spectators believed they had seen all of an empty inside.

"Something like that was said about the hag here. But spectators have written that this could not be the case. I don't need to point out that, first, it would have to be a very small child; and, second, no exhibitor could possibly travel all over Europe with a child and have nobody aware of that fact.

"But in the hag there is only one small space and one door. Spectators were invited to feel inside the space and make sure there was no deception. Most of them did so. The figure stood by itself, raised well off the ground and on a carpet provided by the host. Yet, in spite of there being no means by which she could come alive, at the word of command our lively lady received a cittern—played any tune whose name was called out by the spectators—returned the cittern—conversed with the spectators by dumb-show, and performed other antics of a nature suited to the time. Do you wonder that my respected ancestor was delighted? But I have always wondered what made him change his mind when he learned the secret."

Gore dropped his lofty manner.

"Now tell me how it worked," he added.

"You little—ape!" said Molly Farnleigh. She spoke in her sweetest manner, but her hands were clenched at her sides. "Will you always prance, no matter what happens? Aren't you satisfied? Would you like to play trains or toy soldiers? My God, Brian, come here; I can't stick this. And you too—and you, a police-officer—fiddling with a dummy—crawling round it like a lot of children, when—don't you realize a man was killed last night?"

"Very well," said Gore. "Let us change the subject. Then, for a change, tell me how *that* was worked."

"I suppose you will say it was suicide, of course."

"Madam," said Gore, with a gesture of despair, "it makes no difference what I say. Somebody invariably jumps down my throat in any case. If I say it was suicide, I am assaulted by A, B, and C. If I say it was murder, I am assaulted by D, E, and F. I have not suggested that it was accident, if only to avoid incurring the wrath of G, H, and I."

"That's very clever, no doubt. What do you say, Mr. Elliot?"

Elliot spoke out of a personal honesty.

"Lady Farnleigh, I'm only trying to do the best I can in the most difficult business I was ever put into, which isn't helped by the attitude of any of you. You must see that. If you'll think for just a minute, you must see this machine has something very much to do with the case. I only ask you not to talk out of plain temper. For there's something else to do with the machine as well."

He put his hand on its shoulder.

"I don't know whether the clockwork inside this is dummy clockwork or not, as Mr. Gore says. I'd like to have a go at it in my workshop and find out. I don't know whether the mechanism might still be expected to work after two hundred years; though, if clocks still go after that time, why shouldn't it? But this much I did find out when I looked into the back. The mechanism in this has been recently oiled."

Molly frowned.

"Well?"

"I was wondering, Dr. Fell, whether you—" Elliot turned round. "Here! Where are you, sir?"

Page's conviction that anything might happen was strengthened by the disappearance of so very tangible a bulk as the doctor. He was not yet used to Dr. Fell's trick of fading from the scene and reappearing somewhere else, usually engaged in some meaningless occupation. This time Elliot was answered by a flicker of light from the book-closet. Dr. Fell had been striking a series of matches and blinking with fierce absorption at the lower shelves.

"Eh? I beg your pardon?"

"Haven't you been listening to this demonstration?"

"Oh, that? Harrumph, yes. I can hardly claim to succeed off-hand where so many generations of the family have failed, but I should rather like to know how the original exhibitor was dressed."

"Dressed?"

"Yes. The traditional magician's costume, I daresay, which has always seemed to me singularly unimpressive but suggestive of possibilities. However, I have been pouncing and poking in that cupboard, with or without results—"

"The books?"

"The books are the usual orthodox collection of the unorthodox though there are several witch-trials that are new to me. I did find what seems to be an account of how the automaton was exhibited, which I hope I may borrow? Thank you. But particularly there's this."

While Gore watched him with bright, wicked eyes of amusement, he lumbered out of the closet carrying a decrepit wooden box. And at the same time it seemed to Page that the attic was filling with people.

It was only that Kennet Murray and Nathaniel Burrows, evidently having grown restive, had insisted on following them upstairs. Burrows's big spectacles, and Murray's towering calm face, appeared over the attic stairs as though out of a trapdoor. For the moment they did not come nearer. Dr. Fell rattled the wooden box. He balanced it as well as he could on the narrow ledge of couch round the automaton.

"Here, steady the machine!" said the doctor sharply. "This floor's got a bad canter, and we don't want her rolling downstairs on us. Now have a look. An odd collection of the dust of years, don't you think?"

In the box they saw a number of child's glass marbles, a rusty knife with a painted handle, some fishing-flies, a small heavy ball of lead into which four large hooks had been welded like a bouquet, and (incongruously) a woman's garter of many years ago. But they did not look at these things. They looked at what lay on top: a double false-face or mask made of parchment on wire, and forming a kind of head with a face back and front like the images of Janus. It was blackish, shrivelled, and without features. Dr. Fell did not touch it.

"It's beastly to look at," whispered Madeline. "But what on earth is it?"

"The mask of the god," said Dr. Fell.

"The what?"

"The mask worn by the master of ceremonies presiding at witch-gatherings. Most of those who read about it, and even some of those who write about it, have no idea what witchcraft really was. I firmly do not mean to lecture. But we have an example here. Satanism was an unholy parody of Christian ritual; but it had its old roots in Paganism. Two of its deities were Janus the double-headed, patron of fertility and of the cross-roads; and Diana, patron both of fertility and virginity. The master (or mistress) wore either the goat-mask of Satan or a mask such as we have here. Bah!"

He ticked his forefinger and thumb against the mask.

"You have been hinting at something like that for a long time," said Madeline quietly. "Perhaps I shouldn't ask, but will you please answer a straight question? It seems ridiculous even to ask it. Are you saying that there is a Satanist group somewhere hereabouts?"

"That's the joke," declared Dr. Fell, with an expression of heavy enlightenment. "The answer is, NO."

There was a pause. Inspector Elliot turned round. He was so surprised that he forgot they were talking in front of witnesses.

"Steady on, sir! You can't mean that. Our evidence——"

"I do mean it. Our evidence isn't worth *that*."

"But——"

"Oh, Lord, why didn't I think of it before!" said Dr. Fell vehemently. "A case after my own heart, and I have only just thought of the solution. Elliot, my boy: there have been no sinister gatherings in the Hanging Chart. There have been no goat-pipes or revels by night. A whole group of solid Kentish people have not been snared into any such mad tomfoolery. It was one of the things that stuck in my gullet when you began collecting your evidence, and I see the grimy truth now. Elliot, there is one crooked soul in this whole affair, and only one. Everything, from mental cruelty to murder, is the work of one person. I give you all the truth gratis."

Murray and Burrows joined the group, their footsteps creaking.

"You seem excited," Murray said dryly.

The doctor looked apologetic.

"Well, I am, a bit. I haven't got it all worked out yet. But I see the beginnings of it, and I shall have something to say presently. It's—er—a matter of motives." He stared far off, and a faint twinkle appeared in his eye. "Besides, it's rather novel. I never heard of the trick before. I tell you frankly, Satanism itself is an honest and straightforward business compared to the intellectual pleasures a certain person has invented. Excuse me, gents—and ladies. There's something I should rather like to look at in the garden. Carry on, inspector."

He had stumped towards the stairs before Elliot woke up. Elliot ignored everything, and became brisk.

"Now, then.— Yes? You wanted something, Mr. Murray?"

"I wanted to see the automaton," returned the other with asperity. "I've been rather left out of it, I notice, since I produced my proofs-of-identity and ceased to be of any value. So this is the hag. And this: do you mind if I look at it?"

He picked up the wooden box, rattling it, and moved it closer to the faint dust-grimed light from the window. Elliot studied him.

"Have you ever seen any of those things before, sir?"

Murray shook his head. "I have heard of this parchment-mask. But I have never seen it. I was wondering——"

And that was when the automaton moved.

To this day Page swears that nobody pushed it. This may or may not be true. Seven persons were jostling round it on a creaking, crackling floor which ran down in a smooth hump towards the stairs. But the light from the window was very uncertain, and Murray, his back to the hag, was fixing their attention with the exhibit he held in his right hand. If a hand moved, if a foot moved, if a shoulder moved, nobody knew. What they did not see was the rotted dummy jerking forward with the stealthy suddenness of a motor-car slipping its brakes. What they did see was three-hundredweight of rattling iron darting out of reach and driving like a gun-carriage for the well of the stairs. What they heard was the screech of the wheels, the tap of Dr. Fell's stick on the stairs, and Elliot's scream:

*"For God's sake, look out below!"*

Then the crash as it went over.

Page reached it. He had his fingers round the iron box, and he might just as well have tried to stop a runaway gun; but he kept it upright when it might have gone head-over-heels-side-to-side, sweeping the whole staircase in crazy descent and crushing anything in its way. The black weight kept to its wheels. Sprawling down the first steps, Page saw Dr. Fell peering upwards —half-way down. He saw the daylight from the open door at the foot of the stairs. He saw Dr. Fell, unable to move an inch in that enclosed space, throw up one hand as though to ward off a blow. He saw, out of an inferno of crashings, the black shape plunge past within a hair's clearance.

But he saw more; more which no one could have foreseen. He saw the automaton clear the open door, and land in the passage below. One of its wheels snapped off as it struck, but its momentum was too great. Lurching once, it hurtled against the door directly opposite across the passage; and the door came open.

Page stumbled down the stairs. He did not need to hear the cry from the room across that passage. He remembered who was in that room, and why Betty Harbottle was there, and what had just gone in to visit her now. In the cessation of noise after the automaton had been stopped, small sounds crept out. After a time he heard distinctly the squeak of the hinges as Dr. King opened the bedroom door, and the physician had a face like white paper. He said:

"You devil up there, what have you done?"

*Friday, July 31st*

## THE RISE OF A WITCH

Car, au fond, c'est cela le Satanisme, se disait-il; la question agitée depuis que le monde existe, des visions extérieures, est subsidiare, quand on y songe; le Démon n'a pas besoin de s'exhiber sous des traits humains ou bestiaux afin d'attester sa présence; il suffit, pour qu'il s'affirme, qu'il élise domicile en des âmes qu'il exulcère et incite à d'inexplicables crimes.

—J.-K. Huysmans, *Là-Bas*

### *Chapter XIV*

THE coroner's inquest on Sir John Farnleigh was held the following day, and produced a sensation that blew off every journalistic roof in Great Britain.

Inspector Elliot, like most policemen, is not fond of inquests. This is for practical reasons. Brian Page is not fond of them for artistic reasons: because you never learn anything you did not know before, because there is seldom anything of a sensational nature, and because the verdict, whatever it is, brings you no nearer to a solution than before.

But this inquest—held on the morning of Friday, July 31st—he admitted did not go according to pattern. A suicide verdict, of course, was a foregone conclusion. Yet it was spectacular enough to produce a first-class row before the first witness had said ten words, and it ended in a way that left Inspector Elliot dazed.

Page, drinking very black coffee at breakfast, offered up profane thanks that they had not another inquest on their hands from the business of the previous afternoon. Betty Harbottle was not dead. But she had gone through a narrow graze of it after seeing the hag for the second time, and she was still in no condition to speak. Afterwards Elliot's endless questioning ran in a dismal circle. "Did you push it?" "I swear I didn't; I don't know who did; we were tramping on an uneven floor and maybe nobody did."

Elliot summed it up when he and Dr. Fell talked late over pipes and beer. Page, after taking Madeline home, forcing her to have something to eat, quieting threatened hysterics, and trying to think of a thousand things at once, heard the conclusion of the inspector's views.

"We're licked," he said briefly. "Not a single ruddy thing we can prove, and yet look at the string of events we've got! Victoria Daly is murdered: maybe by a tramp, maybe not: but with the indications of other dirty work that we needn't discuss now. That's a year ago. Sir John Farnleigh dies with his throat cut. Betty Harbottle is in some way 'attacked' and brought down from the attic; and her torn apron is found in the book-closet upstairs. The Thumbograph disappears and returns. Finally, a deliberate attempt is made to kill you by pushing that machinery downstairs, an attempt which you only escaped by one whistle and the grace of God."

"Believe me, I appreciate that," muttered Dr. Fell uncomfortably. "It was one of the worst moments of my life when I looked round and saw that juggernaut coming down. It was my own fault. I talked too much. And yet——"

Elliot regarded him with sharp inquiry.

"All the same, sir, it showed you were on the right track. The murderer knew you knew too much. As to just what that track is, if you've got any ideas now is the time to tell me. I shall be recalled to town, you know, unless something is done."

"Oh, I'll tell you fast enough," growled Dr. Fell. "I'm not making mysteries. Even when I do tell you, though, and even in the event I happen to be right, it still doesn't prove anything. Besides, I'm not sure about another thing. I am very flattered, of course. But I'm not sure the automaton was pushed downstairs with the purpose of what is poetically known as rubbing me out."

"For what purpose, then? It couldn't be just to frighten the girl again, sir. The murderer couldn't have known it would land smack against that bedroom door."

"I know," said Dr. Fell stubbornly, and ruffled his hands through his big mop of grey-streaked hair. "And yet—and yet—proof——"

"That's exactly what I mean. Here are all these points, a connected series of events, and not one blasted one of 'em I can prove! Not one thing I can take to my superintendent and say, 'Here; grab this.' Not one bit of evidence that isn't capable of another interpretation. I can't even show that the events are in any way connected, which is the real snag. Now take this inquest to-morrow. Even the police evidence must plump for a suicide verdict——"

"Can't you get the inquest adjourned?"

"Of course. Ordinarily that's what I should do, and keep on adjourning it until we either had evidence of murder or had to drop the case altogether. But there's the last and greatest snag. What have I got to hope for by more investigation, as matters stand? My superintendent is just about convinced that Sir John Farnleigh's death is suicide, and so is the A.C. When they learned that there are traces of the dead man's fingerprints on that clasp-knife Sergeant Burton found in the hedge——"

(Here was news to Page, the final nail in a suicide's coffin.)

"—that finished it," Elliot corroborated him. "What else can I look for?"

"Betty Harbottle?" suggested Page.

"All right: suppose she does recover and tell her story? Suppose she says she saw somebody in that book-closet? Doing what? And what of it? What connection has it got with a suicide in the garden? Where's your proof, laddie? Anything about the Thumbograph? Well, it's never been suggested that the Thumbograph was in the possession of the dead man, so where do you get with that line of argument? No. Don't look at it sensibly, sir; look at it legally. It's a hundred to one they'll recall me at the end of today, and the case will be shelved. You and I know that there's a murderer here, worming so neatly that he or she can keep right on in the same old way unless somebody stops it. And apparently nobody can stop it."

"What are you going to do?"

Elliot gulped down half a pint of beer before he answered.

"There's just one chance, as I say: a full-dress inquest. Most of our suspects will give evidence. It's remotely possible that somebody, under oath, will make a slip. Not much hope, I admit—but it's happened before (remember the Nurse Waddington case?), and it may happen again. It's the last hope of the police when nothing else works."

"Will the coroner play your game?"

"I wonder," said Elliot thoughtfully. "This chap Burrows is up to something; I know that. But he won't come to me and I can't get any change out of him. He's gone to the coroner about something. I gather that the coroner doesn't particularly like Burrows, didn't particularly like the late alleged 'Farnleigh,' and himself thinks it's suicide. But he'll play fair, and they'll all stand together against the outsider—meaning me. The ironical part is that Burrows himself would like to prove murder, because a suicide verdict more or less proves his client was an impostor. The whole thing is going to be just one hilarious field-day about lost heirs, with only one possible verdict: suicide, my recall, and the end of the case."

"Now, now," said Dr. Fell soothingly. "By the way, where is the automaton now?"

"Sir?"

Elliot roused himself out of grievances and stared at the other.

"The automaton?" he repeated. "I pushed it into a cupboard. After the whacking it took, it's not good for much now except scrap-iron. I was going to have a look at it, but I doubt if a master-mechanic could make sense of the works now."

"Yes," said Dr. Fell, taking up his bedroom candle with a sigh. "That, you see, was why the murderer pushed it downstairs."

Page spent a troubled night. There were many things for the next day besides the inquest. Nat Burrows, he reflected, was not the man his father had been; even matters like funeral arrangements had to be turned over to Page. It appeared that Burrows was busying himself over some other aspect of the difficulty. There was also the question of leaving Molly "alone" in a house of questionable atmosphere, and the disquieting news that the servants were threatening to leave almost in a body.

These things churned through sleep into a day of brilliant sunshine and heat. The riot of motor-cars began by nine o'clock. He had never seen so many cars in Mallingford; the Press and the outside world poured in to an extent that made him realize the immense noise this case was making outside their gates. It angered him. It was, he thought, nobody else's damned business. Why didn't they put up swings and roundabouts, and sell hot dogs? They swamped the *Bull and Butcher*, in whose "hall"—a sort of long shed built for the jollifications of hop-pickers—the inquest was to be held. Sunlight winked on many camera-lenses in the road. There were women. Old Mr. Rowntree's dog chased somebody clear up the road to Major Chambers's, and had a hysteria of barking all morning, and couldn't be quieted.

In this the people of the district moved without comment. They did not take sides. In country life each person depends on the other for something, giving and receiving; in a case like this you had to wait and see what happened, so that matters could be reasonably comfortable whichever way verdicts went. But from the outside world came the tumult of LOST HEIR SLAIN OR LOST HEIR FRAUD?; and at eleven o'clock in the hot morning they opened the inquest.

The long, low, gloomy shed was packed. Page felt the appropriateness of a starched collar. The coroner, a forthright solicitor who was determined to stand no nonsense from the Farnleighs, sat behind a heap of papers at a broad table, with a witness-chair at his left.

First of all, evidence of identification of the body was given by Lady Farnleigh, the widow. Even this—as a rule the merest of formalities—was questioned. Molly had hardly begun to speak when up rose Mr. Harold Welkyn, in frock-coat and gardenia, on behalf of his client. Mr. Welkyn said that he must protest against this identification in the matter of a technicality, since the dead man was not, in fact, Sir John Farnleigh; and, since the matter was of the utmost importance in determining whether the deceased took his own life or was murdered, he respectfully begged leave to bring it to the coroner's attention.

There ensued a long argument in which the coroner, aided by a frigid and indignant Burrows, quite properly sat on Mr. Welkyn. But Welkyn, relapsing, perspired with satisfaction. He had made the point. He had set the pace. He had outlined the real terms of the battle, and everybody knew it.

It also compelled Molly to discuss the matter in reply to the coroner's questions as to the deceased's state of mind. He treated her well, but he was determined to thrash the matter out and Molly looked badly rattled. Page began to realize the state of affairs when the coroner, instead of next calling evidence as to the finding of the body, called Kennet Murray. The whole tory came out; and, under Murray's gentle firmness, the imposture of the deceased stood out as clear and black as a fingerprint. Burrows fought every step of the way, but only succeeded in angering the coroner.

Evidence of finding the body was given by Burrows and Page. (The latter's own voice sounded wrong to him.) Then the medical testimony was called. Dr. Theophilus King testified that on the night of Wednesday, July 9th, he had gone to Farnleigh Close in response to a telephone-call from Detective-Sergeant Burton. He had made a preliminary examination and ascertained that the man was dead. The next day, the body having been removed to the mortuary, he had on the instructions of the coroner performed post-mortem examination, verifying the cause of death.

*The coroner:* Now, Dr. King, will you describe the wounds on the throat of the deceased?

*The doctor:* There were three fairly shallow wounds, beginning at the left side of the throat and ending under the angle of the right jaw in a slightly upward direction. Two of the wounds crossed each other.

*Q:* The weapon was passed across the throat from left to right?

*A:* That is so.

*Q:* Would this have been the course taken by a weapon held in the hand of a man taking his own life?

*A:* If the man were right-handed, yes.

*Q:* Was the deceased right-handed?

*A:* To the best of my knowledge, he was.

*Q:* Should you say it was impossible for the deceased to have inflicted such wounds on himself?

*A:* Not at all.

*Q:* From the nature of the wounds, doctor, what sort of weapon should you say had been used to inflict them?

*A:* I should say a ragged or uneven blade some four or five inches long. There was much laceration of tissue. It is a matter in which it is difficult to speak precisely.

*Q:* We quite appreciate that, doctor. I shall presently call evidence to show that there was found in a hedge some ten feet to the left of the deceased a knife with a blade such as you describe. Have you seen the knife to which I refer?

*A:* I have.

*Q:* In your opinion, could the knife in question have inflicted wounds such as you describe on the throat of the deceased?

*A:* In my opinion, it could.

*Q:* Finally, doctor, I come to a point which must be put with some care. Mr. Nathaniel Burrows has testified that a moment before the deceased's fall the deceased was standing at the edge of the pool with his back to the house. Mr. Burrows is unable to say definitely whether or not the deceased was alone at this time, though I have pressed him to do so. Now, in the event—I say in

the event—that the deceased was alone, could he have flung a weapon awa
from him to a distance of say ten feet?

A: It is well within the physical possibilities.

Q: Let us suppose that he had a weapon in his right hand. Could thi
weapon instead have been thrown towards the left?

A: I cannot venture on a guess as to the convulsions of a dying man. I cai
only say that such a thing is physically possible.

After this high-handed carrying of matters, the story of Ernest Wilbertsor
Knowles left no doubt. Everybody knew Knowles. Everybody knew his likes
his dislikes, his nature. Everybody had seen for decades that there was nc
guile in him. He told of the view from the window, the man alone in a
closed circle of sand, the impossibility of murder.

Q: But are you satisfied in your own mind that what you saw was the
deceased taking his own life?

A: I am afraid so, sir.

Q: Then how do you account for the fact that a knife held in the righ
hand was thrown to the left rather than the right?

A: I am not sure I can properly describe the gestures the late gentlemar
made, sir. I thought I could at first, but I have been thinking it over and I an
not sure. It was all so rapid that his gestures might have been anything.

Q: But you did not actually see the knife thrown from him?

A: Yes, sir, I am under the impression that I did.

"WOW!" said a voice among the spectators. It sounded rather like Tony
Weller speaking out from the gallery. And it was, in fact, Dr. Fell, whc
throughout the proceedings had remained wheezily asleep with his red face
smoking in the heat.

"I will have silence in this room," shouted the coroner.

Cross-examined by Burrows as counsel for the widow, Knowles said tha
he would not swear to having seen the deceased throw the knife. He hac
good eyesight, but not such good eyesight as that. And his patent sincerity
of manner kept the sympathies of the jury. Knowles admitted that he spoke
only from an impression and admitted the (remote) possibility of an error
with which Burrows had to be content.

There followed to an inevitable end the police evidence, the evidence o.
the deceased's movements, to a rounding-up. In that hot shed, with row
of pencils going like spiders' legs, there was determined for practical purpose
the imposture of the dead man. Glances were being cast at Patrick Gore
the real hêir. Quick glances. Appraising glances. Hesitant glances. Ever
friendly glances, under which he remained bland and impassive.

"Members of the jury," said the coroner, "there is one more witness tc
whom I shall ask you to listen, though I am unacquainted with the nature
of the witness's testimony. At the request of Mr. Burrows and at her owr
request, the witness comes here to make a statement of importance, which

I trust will be of assistance to you in your painful duty. I therefore call Miss
Madeline Dane."

Page sat up.

There was a puzzled stir in the court, the reporters quickening with interest at Madeline's very real beauty. What she was doing here Page himself
had no idea, but it disturbed him. Way was made for her to come to the
witness-chair, where the coroner handed her the Book and she took the oath
in a nervous but clear voice. As though for a kind of distant-mourning, she
wore dark blue, with a dark blue hat the colour of her eyes. Something of
the corrugated-iron feeling was removed. The corrugated-iron self-consciousness of the men on the jury relaxed. They did not actually beam on her,
but Page felt it was not far off. Even the coroner fussed with consideration.
Among the males of the population Madeline was a favourite who had few
competitors. A handsome feeling went through the inquest.

"Again I must insist on silence in this room!" said the coroner. "Now
will you give your name, please?"

"Madeline Elspeth Dane."

"Your age?"

"Th-thirty-five."

"Your address, Miss Dane?"

"Monplaisir, near Frettenden."

"Now, Miss Dane," said the coroner, brisk but gentle, "I believe you
wished to make a statement regarding the deceased? What is the nature of
the evidence you wish to give?"

"Yes, I must tell you. Only it's so difficult to know where to begin."

"Perhaps I can help Miss Dane out," said Burrows, on his feet with perspiring dignity. "Miss Dane, was it——"

"Mr. Burrows," snapped the coroner, losing all control of his temper, "you
have constantly interrupted these proceedings with a lack of respect for your
rights and mine which I cannot and will not tolerate. You are entitled to
question the witness when I have done questioning her, and not until then.
In the meantime you will remain silent or leave this court. Hrrrr! Ahem.
Now, Miss Dane?"

"Please don't quarrel."

"We are not quarrelling, madam. I am indicating the respect due to this
court, a court gathered to determine how the deceased met his death, and a
respect which, whatever may be said of it from some sources"—here his eye
sought out the reporters—"I have every intention of upholding. Now, Miss
Dane?"

"It's about Sir John Farnleigh," said Madeline earnestly, "and whether he
was or was not Sir John Farnleigh. I want to explain why he was so anxious
to receive the claimant and the claimant's solicitor; and why he didn't show
them out of the house; and why he was so eager to have the fingerprint

taken; oh, and all the things that may help you decide about his death."

"Miss Dane, if you merely wish to give an opinion as to whether the deceased was Sir John Farnleigh, I am afraid I must inform you——"

"No, no, no. I don't know whether he was. But that's the whole dreadful thing. You see, *he didn't know himself.*"

## Chapter XV

BY THE stir in the dim shed, it was beginning to be felt that this might be the sensation of the day, even if nobody knew what it meant. The coroner cleared his throat, his head turning like an alert marionette's.

"Miss Dane, this is not a court of law; it is an inquiry; and therefore I can allow you to give what testimony you like, provided only it has some bearing which will help us. Will you be so good as to explain what you mean?"

Madeline drew a deep breath.

"Yes, if you let me explain you'll see how important it is, Mr. Whitehouse. What is hard to say in front of all of you is how he came to tell me about it. But he had to confide in somebody, you know. He was too fond of Lady Farnleigh to tell *her*; that was a part of the trouble; and sometimes it worried him so horribly that you may have noticed how ill he looked. And I suppose I'm a safe person to confide in"—she wrinkled her forehead half wryly and half smilingly—"so that's how it was."

"Yes, yes? How what was, Miss Dane?"

"You've let them tell all about the meeting the night before last, to argue over the estate and take the fingerprints," resumed Madeline, with a probably unconscious thrust. "I was not there, but I heard all about it from a friend of mine who was there. He said what impressed him most was the absolute assurance of both claimants, right up to the taking of the fingerprints and afterwards. He said that the only time poor John—I beg your pardon: Sir John—smiled at all or looked relieved was when the claimant was talking about that terrible affair on the *Titanic*, and about being hit with a seaman's mallet."

"Yes; well?"

"Here is what Sir John told me months ago. After the wreck of the *Titanic*, as a boy, he woke up in a hospital in New York. But he didn't know it was New York or about the *Titanic*. He didn't know where he was, or how he had got there, or even who he was. He had had concussion of the brain, after getting some knocks on the head accidentally or deliberately in the wreck of the ship, and he was suffering from what they call amnesia. Do you understand what I mean?"

"Perfectly, Miss Dane. Continue."

"They told him his clothes and papers had identified him as John Farn-
eigh. There was a man standing over the bed in the hospital, a man who
aid he was his mother's cousin—oh, that's badly put, but you know what I
nean—and told him to go to sleep and get well.

"But you know what boys of that age are. He was very frightened and
orribly worried. For he didn't know anything about himself. And worst of
ll, like boys of that age, he didn't dare tell anybody for fear he might be
aad or there might be something wrong with him or they might put him in
aol.

"That's how it seemed to him. He hadn't any reason to think he *wasn't*
his John Farnleigh. He hadn't any reason to believe they weren't telling
he truth in all they told him about himself. He had a hazy recollection of
houting or confusion, something to do with open air or cold; but that was
ll he could remember. So he never spoke a word about it to anybody. He
retended to his cousin—a Mr. Renwick from Colorado—that he remem-
ered everything. Mr. Renwick never suspected.

"He nursed that little secret for years. He kept reading his diary, and
rying to bring things back. He told me that sometimes he would sit for
ours with his hands pressed to his head, concentrating. Sometimes he would
hink he remembered a face or an event faintly, like something you see
nder water. Then again it would seem to him that there was something
rong. The only thing he ever brought out of it, as a phrase rather than an
mage, had to do with a hinge: a crooked hinge."

Under the iron roof the spectators sat like dummies. No papers rustled.
Nobody whispered. Page felt his collar damp and his heart ticking like a
vatch. Smoky sunlight came through the windows, and Madeline winked
he corner of her eye in it.

"A crooked hinge, Miss Dane?"

"Yes. I don't know what he meant. Neither did he."

"Go on, please."

"In those early years in Colorado he was afraid they would put him in gaol
f there should be anything wrong and they found out about it. Handwriting
vas no good, because two of his fingers were nearly crushed in the wreck and
ae could never hold a pen properly. He was afraid to write home; that's why
ae never did. He was even afraid to go to a doctor and ask if he might be
aad, for fear the doctor should tell on him.

"Of course, in time it got fainter. He convinced himself that it was an
infortunate thing which happens to some people, and so on. There was the
Var and all that. He consulted a mental specialist who told him after a lot
f psychological tests that he really was John Farnleigh, and that he had
aothing to worry about. But he never lost the horror of those years, and even
vhen he thought he had forgotten it he dreamed about it.

"Then it was all revived when poor Dudley died and he inherited the title and estate. He had to come to England. He was—how can I say this?—academically interested. He thought at long last he *must* remember. And he didn't. You all know how he used to go wandering round like a ghost a poor old ghost who didn't even know whether he was a ghost. You know how jumpy he was. He loved it here. He loved every acre and yard of it Mind you, he didn't honestly doubt he was John Farnleigh. But he had to KNOW."

Madeline bit her lip.

Her luminous, now rather hard eyes wandered among the spectators.

"I used to talk to him and try to make him quiet. I would ask him not to think too much; then perhaps he would remember. I used to arrange it so that I reminded him of things, and made him think he had remembered them for himself. Maybe it would be a gramophone playing, 'To thee, beautiful lady,' far away in the evening; and he would remember how we danced to it as children. Maybe it would be a detail of the house. In the library there's a kind of cupboard with shelves of books—built into the wall by the windows, you know—and instead of being just a cupboard, it's got a door that used to open out into the garden. It still will open if you find the right catch. I persuaded him to find the right catch. He said he slept well for nights after that.

"But he still had to know. He said he wouldn't mind so much if he could only know, even if it turned out he was not John Farnleigh. He said he wasn't a wild adolescent boy any longer. He said he could face it quietly and it would be the greatest thing in the world just to know the truth

"He went to London and saw two more doctors; I know that. You can see how worried he was when he even went to a person who was supposed to have psychic powers—a horrible little man called Ahriman, in Half-Moon Street—who was all the rage then. He took a crowd of us along under pretext of having our fortunes told, and pretended to laugh at it. But he told this fortune-teller all about himself.

"Still he kept wandering about the place. He used to say, 'Well, I am a good steward'; and you know he was. He used to go into the church a lot, too he liked the hymns best; and sometimes, when they played, 'Abide with Me'—anyway, when he was near the church, and looking up at the walls he used to say that if ever he were in a position to——"

Madeline paused.

Her breast rose with a deep breath. Her eyes were fixed on the front rows and her fingers opened wide on the arms of the chair. All passion and mysticism seemed in her then, as deep as roots and as strong as hearts yet she was, after all, only a woman making what defence she could in a hot and stuffy shed.

"I'm so sorry," she blurted. "Perhaps it is better not to talk about that; it does not concern us, anyhow. I'm sorry if I'm taking up your time with things that don't matter—"

"I will have silence in here," said the coroner, flinging round his head at the rustle that grew. "I am not sure I think you are taking up our time with things that do not matter. Have you anything else to tell the jury?"

"Yes," said Madeline, turning and looking at them. "One other thing."

"Which is?"

"When I heard about the claimant to the estate and his lawyer, I knew what John had been thinking. You know now what was in his mind all along. You can follow every step of his thoughts and every word he said. You now now why he smiled, and why the relief was almost too much, when he heard the claimant's story about the seaman's mallet and the blows on the head in the wreck of the *Titanic*. For *he* was the one who suffered from concussion of the brain and a loss of memory that lasted for twenty-five years.

"Please wait! I don't say the claimant's story isn't true. I don't know, or profess to decide. But Sir John—the one you call the deceased as though he had never been alive—must have felt a mighty relief when he heard something that in his eyes couldn't possibly have been true. He saw his dream being fulfilled at last, that his identity should be proved. You know now why he welcomed that fingerprint test. You know why he was the most eager of all. You know why he could hardly wait, why he was all wire and nerves, to learn the result."

Madeline grasped the arms of the chair.

"Please. Perhaps I'm putting all this stupidly, but I hope you understand me. To prove things one way or the other was the one end of his life. If he were Sir John Farnleigh, he would be happy to the end of his life. If he were not, it wouldn't matter so much once he really knew. Like winning a football pool, you know. You put your sixpence on it. You think perhaps you've won thousands and thousands of pounds. You're almost sure of it, you could swear it's true. But you can't be sure until the telegram comes. If it doesn't come, you think, 'Well, that's that,' and let it go. Well, that's John Farnleigh. This was his football pool. Acres and acres of things he loved: they were his football pool. Respect and honour and sound sleep at night forever: they were his football pool. The end of torture and the beginning of the future: they were his football pool. He believed now that he had won it. And now people are trying to tell you he killed himself. Don't you think it for a minute. You know better. Can you believe, dare you believe, that he'd have deliberately cut his throat half an hour before he could learn the result?"

She put her hand over her eyes.

There was a genuine uproar, which the coroner put down. Mr. Harold Welkyn was on his feet. Page saw that his shiny face was slightly pale, and he spoke as though he had been running.

"Mr. Coroner. As a piece of special pleading, all this is no doubt very

interesting," he said acidly. "I shall not be impertinent enough to remind
you of your duties. I shall not be impertinent enough to point out that n
question has been asked in the last ten minutes. But if this lady has com
pletely finished her remarkable statement, which if true tends to show tha
the deceased was an even greater impostor than we believed, I shall leave
as counsel for the real Sir John Farnleigh, to cross-examine."

"Mr. Welkyn," said the coroner, flinging round his head again, "you wil
ask questions when I give you leave and you will remain silent until then
Now, Miss Dane——"

"Please let him ask questions," said Madeline. "I remember seeing hin
at the house of that horrible little Egyptian, Ahriman, in Half-Moon Street.

Mr. Welkyn got out a handkerchief and mopped his forehead.

And the questions were asked. And the coroner summed up. And In
spector Elliot went into another room and privately danced the saraband
And the jury, throwing the case straight to the police to handle, brough
in a verdict of murder by a person or persons unknown.


## Chapter XVI

ANDREW MACANDREW ELLIOT lifted a glass of very passable hock and in
spected that.

"Miss Dane," he declared, "you're a born politician. No, I'll say diploma
it sounds better; I don't know why. That touch about the football pools wa
sheer genius. It brought things home to the jury as certainly as sixpenc
and two wrong. How did you come to think of it?"

In the long, warm afterglow of sunset, Elliot, Dr. Fell, and Page wer
having dinner with Madeline at the unfortunately named but comfortabl
Monplaisir. The table stood by the French windows of the dining-room
and the French windows opened on a deep garden of laurels. At the en
of it were two acres of apple-orchard. In one direction a footpath wen
through the orchard to what used to be Colonel Mardale's. In another i
wound across a brook and up through the Hanging Chart, whose slope o
trees showed dark against the evening sky to the left of the orchard. If yo
followed the latter path up through the Chart, over its shoulder, and dow
again, you came to the back gardens of Farnleigh Close.

Madeline lived alone, having a woman who came in by day to cook an
"do." It was a trim little house, bright with military prints that were a
heritage from her father, full of brass and bustling clocks. It stood rathe
isolated, the nearest house being that of the unfortunate Victoria Daly; bu
Madeline had never minded the isolation.

She sat now at the head of the table beside the open windows, beyond
polished wood and silver in a dusk which was not quite dark enough for th

ighting of the dinner-table candles. She wore white. The great, low oak
beams of the dining-room, the pewter and the busy clocks, all were a background for her. Dinner over, Dr. Fell had lit a Gargantuan cigar; Page had
it a cigarette for Madeline; and, at Elliot's question, Madeline laughed in
he light of the match.

"About the football pools?" she repeated. She flushed a little as well. "As
a matter of fact, I didn't think of it. It was Nat Burrows. He wrote it out and
made me get it word-perfect like a recitation. Oh, every word I said was true.
I felt it terribly. It was the most awful cheek of me to carry on like that
before all those people; and every second I was afraid poor Mr. Whitehouse
was going to stop me; but Nat said it was absolutely the only way. Afterwards I went upstairs at the *Bull and Butcher* and had hysterics and cried
and felt better. Was it very awful of me?"

They were certainly staring at her.

"No," said Dr. Fell quite seriously, "it was a remarkable performance.
But, oh, Lord! Burrows coached you? Wow!"

"Yes, he was here half of last night doing it."

"Burrows? But when was he here?" asked Page, surprised. "I brought you
home."

"He came here after you left. He was full of what I had just told Molly,
and terribly excited."

"You know, gents," rumbled Dr. Fell, taking a meditative pull at the large
cigar, "we mustn't underestimate our friend Burrows. Page here told us long
ago that he was an unco' intelligent chap. Welkyn seemed to run rings
ound him at the beginning of this circus; but all the time, psychologically
—confound that word—he had the inquest exactly where he wanted it. He'll
be fighting, naturally. It will naturally make a big difference to the firm of
Burrows & Burrows whether they keep the management of the Farnleigh
estate. And he's a fighter. When, as, and if the case of Farnleigh *v.* Gore ever
comes to trial, it ought to be a sizzler."

Elliot faced something else.

"Look here, Miss Dane," he said stubbornly. "I'm not denying you did us
a good turn. It's a victory, if only an outward and newspaper victory. Now
the case won't be closed officially, even if the A.C. tears his hair and swears
the jury were a pack of thick-witted yokels under the spell of a good-looking
—er—female. But what I want to know is why you didn't come to *me* with
all this information in the first place. I'm not a twister. I'm not—er—a half
bad fellow, if you can put it like that. Why didn't you tell me?"

The odd and almost comic part of it was, Page thought, that he sounded
personally hurt.

"I wanted to," said Madeline. "Honestly I did. But I had to tell Molly
first. Then Nat Burrows made me swear all kinds of horrid oaths I wouldn't
breathe a word of it to the police until after the inquest. He says he doesn't

trust the police. Also, he's working on a theory to prove—" She checked her self, biting her lip, and made an apologetic gesture with her cigarette. "You know how some people are."

"Still, where do we stand?" asked Page. "After this morning, have we gone round in the old circle to wondering which of them is the real heir? I Murray swears Gore is, and if they don't upset that fingerprint evidence that seems to end it. Or so I thought. This morning, once or twice, I wasn' quite so sure. Certain hints and innuendoes—you made them yourself—seemed to centre round good old Welkyn."

"Really, Brian! I only said what Nat told me to say. What do you mean?"

"Well, possibly that the whole claim to the estate might have been en gineered by Welkyn himself. Welkyn, the spooks' solicitor and spiritualists advocate. Welkyn, who collects some rather rummy friends, and may have collected Gore as he collected Ahriman and Madame Duquesne and the res of them. I said when we met Gore he was some kind of showman. Welkyn who said he saw a ghost in the garden at the time of the murder. Welkyn who at the time of the murder was only fifteen feet away from the victim and with only a sheet of glass between. Welkyn——"

"But surely, Brian, you don't suspect Mr. Welkyn of the murder?"

"Why not? Dr. Fell said——"

"I said," interposed the doctor, frowning at his cigar, "that he was the mos interesting person in the group."

"It usually amounts to the same thing," said Page gloomily. "What's you real opinion, Madeline, about the real heir? You told me yesterday you thought the late Farnleigh was an impostor. Do you?"

"Yes, I do. But I don't see how anybody could keep from feeling sorry for him. He didn't want to be an impostor, don't you see? He only wanted to know who he was. As for Mr. Welkyn, he couldn't possibly be the mur derer. He was the only one of us who wasn't in the attic when—well, it seems horrible to talk about after dinner and on a nice evening, but who wasn' in the attic when that machine fell."

"Sinister," said the doctor. "Very sinister."

"You must be terribly brave," said Madeline with the utmost seriousness "to laugh about that iron idol tumbling down——"

"My dear young lady, I am not brave. The wind was blowing violently and I felt ill. Afterwards I began, like St. Peter, to curse and swear. Then I made jokes. Harrumph. Fortunately I began thinking about that girl in the other room, who hasn't my padding to sustain her. And I swore a mighty oath myself—" His fist hovered over the table, huge in the twilight. They had the impression of a dangerous force behind jokes and absence of mind, a force that could fall and bind. But he did not bring the fist down. He looked out into the darkening garden, and continued to smoke mildly.

"Then where do we stand, sir?" asked Page. "Have you found you can trust us by now?"

It was Elliot who answered him. Elliot took a cigarette out of the box on the table. He lit it with careful movings of the match. In the light of the match his expression was again brisk, impassive, but as though conveying a hint Page could not interpret.

"We must be moving along soon," the inspector said. "Burton is driving us to Paddock Wood, and Dr. Fell and I are catching the ten o'clock train for town. We have a conference with Mr. Bellchester at the Yard. Dr. Fell has an idea."

"About—what to do here?" Madeline asked eagerly.

"Yes," said Dr. Fell. For a time he continued to smoke with a sleepy air. "I was wondering. Perhaps it would be as well if I gave a few hollow subterranean whispers. For example, that inquest today served a double-barrelled purpose. We hoped for a murder verdict and we hoped that one of the witnesses would make a slip. We got the murder verdict; and somebody blundered."

"Was that where you said 'wow' out loud?"

"I said 'wow' many times," answered the doctor gravely. "To myself. At a price, the inspector and I will tell you what caused both of us to say 'wow,' or at least a hint of it. I say: at a price. After all, you ought to do for us what you did for Mr. Burrows, and under the same pledge of secrecy. A minute ago you said he was working on a theory to prove something. What theory? And what does he want to prove?"

Madeline stirred, and crushed out her cigarette. In the semi-darkness she looked cool and clean in white, her short throat swelling above the low-necked dress. Page always remembered her at that moment: the blonde hair done into something like curls above the ears, the broad face even more softened and etherealized by twilight, the slow closing of her eyes. Outside a faint wind stirred in the laurels. Towards the west over the garden the low sky was thin yellow-orange, like brittle glass; but over the mass of the Hanging Chart there was a star. The room seemed to have retreated, as though it were waiting. Madeline put her hands on the table and seemed to push herself back.

"I don't know," she said. "People come and tell me these things. They think I can keep a secret; I look the sort of person who can keep a secret; and I can. Now it seems as though all the secrets were being dragged out of me, and I feel as though I had done something indecent by all that talking today."

"And?" prompted Dr. Fell.

"All the same, you ought to know this. You really and truly ought to know it. Nat Burrows suspects someone of the murder, and hopes he can prove it."

"And he suspects——?"

"He suspects Kennet Murray," said Madeline.

The glowing end of Elliot's cigarette stopped in the air. Then Elliot struck the table with the flat of his hand.

"Murray! Murray?"

"Why, Mr. Elliot?" asked Madeline, opening her eyes. "Does it surprise you?"

The inspector's voice remained impersonal. "Murray is the last person who should be suspected, both in the real sense and in what the doctor here calls the detective-story sense. He was the person everyone was watching. Even if it might have been only a joke, he was the person they were all thinking of as the victim. Burrows is a damned sight too clever by half —I beg your pardon, Miss Dane: 'ware language. No. And again no. Has Burrows got any reason to think this, except the idea of being clever? Why the man's got an alibi as big as a house!"

"I don't understand part of it," said Madeline, wrinkling her forehead, "because he didn't tell me. But that's the point. Has he got an alibi, really? I'm only telling you what Nat told me. Nat says that if you go by the evidence there wasn't anybody actually watching him except this Mr. Gore standing down by the library windows."

The inspector and Dr. Fell exchanged a glance. They did not comment. "Go on, please."

"You remember my mentioning at the inquest today the little cupboard or book-closet built into the wall of the library—like the one in the attic? The one that's got a door opening into the garden if you find the spring?"

"I do," said Dr. Fell rather grimly. "Humph. Murray mentioned that place to us himself, when he said he went in there during his vigil to change the bogus Thumbograph for the real one so that he shouldn't be seen from the windows. I begin to understand."

"Yes. I told that to Nat, and he was terribly interested. He said to be sure to mention it so that it could go into the records. If I understood him at all, he says you're concentrating your attention on the wrong man. He says all this is a trumped-up conspiracy against poor John. He says that because this 'Patrick Gore' has a clever tongue and an interesting way with him, you've mistaken him for the leader of the group. But Nat maintains that Mr. Murray is the real—what's that horrid word they use in thrillers——?"

"Master-mind?"

"That's it. Of the gang. Of a gang composed of Gore and Welkyn and Murray; Gore and Welkyn being puppets who wouldn't have the courage for any real crime."

"Go on," said Dr. Fell in a curious voice.

"Nat was wildly excited when he explained it. He points to the rather odd behaviour of Mr. Murray all through this. Well, of course I—I wouldn't know about that. I haven't seen enough of him. He does seem a bit different from the old days, but then I know we all must be.

"Poor Nat has even got a theory of how the scheme might have been worked. Mr. Murray was in touch with a shady lawyer (Mr. Welkyn). Mr. Welkyn was in a position to tell him, through one of the fortune-tellers of his clientele, that Sir John Farnleigh was suffering from loss of memory and mental trouble over you know what. So Murray, the old tutor, thought of presenting an impostor with forged credentials. Through Welkyn he found a suitable impostor (Gore) among Welkyn's clients. Murray drilled him for six months in every particular. Nat says that's why Gore's way of speaking and conducting himself is so much like Murray's: the thing Nat says you noticed, Dr. Fell."

The doctor stared across the table at her.

He put his elbows on the table and his head in his hands, so that Page could not tell what he was thinking. The air stirring through the open windows was very warm and full of fragrance; yet it is a fact that Dr. Fell shivered.

"Go on," Elliot prompted again.

"Nat's idea of what happened is—is horrible," replied Madeline, closing her eyes again. "I could see it, even if I didn't want to see it. Poor John, who had never done anybody any harm, had to be killed so that there would be nobody to fight their claim, and so that it should be believed he had killed himself. Just as most people do believe, you know."

"Yes," said Elliot. "Just as most people do believe."

"Welkyn and Gore, the sawdust-men without the courage, had their parts to play. They had the two sides of the house guarded, you see. Welkyn was in the dining-room. Gore was to watch the library windows for two reasons: first, to swear to Mr. Murray's alibi; and, second, to keep any other person away from looking in the window while Mr. Murray was out of the library.

"They stalked poor John like a—oh, you know. He never had a chance. When they knew he was in the garden, Mr. Murray came out ever so softly. He's a big man. He caught John and killed him. He didn't do it until the last moment. That is, they hoped that John might break down and confess he had lost his memory and might *not* be the real heir. Then they mightn't have had to kill him. But he didn't. And so they did. But Mr. Murray had to explain why he had been so unnecessarily long in 'comparing fingerprints.' So he invented the story of juggling with Thumbographs, and stole one and later returned it. And Nat says"—she concluded rather breathlessly, looking at Dr. Fell—"he says you tumbled straight into their trap, as Mr. Murray planned you should."

Inspector Elliot carefully put out his cigarette.

"That's it, eh? Does this Mr. Burrows explain how Murray committed a murder unseen under the eyes of Knowles and practically under the eyes of Burrows himself?"

She shook her head.

"He wouldn't tell me that. Either he didn't want to, or he hasn't got it worked out yet."

"He hasn't got it worked out yet," said Dr. Fell in a hollow voice. "A slight slowness of cerebral activity. A little late with the homework. Oh, my ancient hat. This is awful."

Once again that day Madeline had talked herself into a state of quickened breathing. It was as though she herself, at the end of a great nervous strain, had been touched by that wind from the garden or the sense of expectancy and waiting from the house.

"What do you think of it?" she asked.

Dr. Fell reflected.

"There are flaws in it. Bad flaws."

"That doesn't matter," said Madeline, looking straight at him. "I don't think I believe it myself. But I've told you what you wanted to know. What were the hints you were going to give us, about what really happened?"

He regarded her in a curious way, as though he wondered.

"Have you told us everything, ma'am?"

"Everything I—I can or dare to. Don't ask me any more. Please."

"Still," argued Dr. Fell, "at risk of seeming to make more mysteries, I'm going to ask you another question. You knew the late Farnleigh very well. Now, the point is nebulous and psychological again; but find the answer to the following question and you come near the truth. Why did Farnleigh worry for twenty-five years? Why was he weighed down and oppressed in the blindness of his memory? Most men would have been troubled for a while; yet it should not have left such a terrifying scar in his mind. Was he, for instance, tortured by a memory of crime or evil?"

She nodded. "Yes, I believe he was. I've always thought of him as being like those old Puritans in books, brought up to date."

"But he couldn't remember what it concerned?"

"No—except this image of the crooked hinge."

Page found the words themselves disturbing and bothersome. It seemed as though they ought to convey something or suggest something. What was a crooked hinge? Or, for that matter, a straight hinge?

"Sort of polite version of a screw loose?" he asked.

"N-no, I don't think so. I mean, it wasn't a figure of speech. Sometimes he seemed to see a hinge; a hinge on a door; a *white* hinge. It would become crooked as he looked, and droop or crack somehow. He said it stuck in his mind in the way you notice the pattern of a wall-paper when you are ill."

"A white hinge," said Dr. Fell. He looked at Elliot. "That rather tears it, my lad. Eh?"

"Yes, sir."

A long sniff rumbled in the doctor's nose.

"Very well. Now let's see if there are any suggestions of the truth in all this. I will give you a few.

"First. There has been much talk from the beginning about who was or wasn't battered on the head with what has been described as a 'seaman's wooden mallet.' There has been a great amount of curiosity about the fact, but very little about the mallet. Where did anybody get such an implement? How was it obtainable at all? Such an article wouldn't be of much use to sailors aboard modern mechanized ships. I can think of only one thing answering the description.

"You have probably seen such mallets if you have crossed the Atlantic. One of them hangs by each of the steel doors which are set at intervals along the passages below decks in a modern liner. These steel doors are, or are supposed to be, water-tight. In the event of disaster they can be closed, to form a series of bulkheads or compartments against water flooding in. And the mallet by each door—a sombre reminder—is for use as a weapon by the steward in case of panic and a stampede on the part of passengers. The *Titanic*, you remember, was famous for its water-tight compartments."

"Well?" prompted Page, as the doctor paused. "What of it?"

"It doesn't suggest anything to you?"

"No."

"Second point," said Dr. Fell. "That interesting automaton, the Golden Hag. Find out what made the automaton work in the seventeenth century, and you will have the essential secret of this case."

"But it doesn't make *any* sense!" cried Madeline. "At least, I mean, it doesn't have any connection with what I was thinking. I thought you were thinking just the same things as I was, and now——"

Inspector Elliot looked at his watch. "We shall have to be moving, sir," he said in a flat voice, "if we want to catch that train and still stop in at the Close on our way."

"Don't go," said Madeline abruptly. "Don't go. Please. You won't, will you, Brian?"

"I thought we should come to it, ma'am," Dr. Fell told her in a very quiet voice. "Just what is wrong?"

"I'm afraid," said Madeline. "I suppose that's why I've been talking so much, really."

The realization of something different about her, and the reason for it, came to Brian Page with a kind of shock.

Dr. Fell laid his cigar in the saucer of his coffee-cup. Striking a match with great care, he leaned across and lit the candles on the table. Four golden flames curled and then drew up steadily in the warm, still air; they seemed to hover as though disembodied above the candles. The twilight was pushed back into the garden. In the snug little nook on the edge of it, Madeline's eyes reflected the candlelight; they were steady but dilated. It was as though in the fear there showed a measure of expectancy.

The doctor seemed uneasy. "I'm afraid we can't stay, Miss Dane. We shall be back tomorrow, but there are some ends of the case we've got to gather up in town. All the same, if Page could——?"

"You won't leave me, will you, Brian? I'm sorry to be such a fool and to bother you——"

"Good Lord, of course I won't leave you!" roared Page, feeling such a fierce protectiveness as he had never known before. "I'll cause a scandal. I won't let you beyond arm's length until morning. Not that there's anything to be afraid of."

"Aren't you forgetting the date?"

"The date?"

"The anniversary. July 31st. Victoria Daly died a year ago tonight."

"It is also," supplied Dr. Fell, looking curiously at both of them, "it is also Lammas Eve. A good Scot like Elliot will tell you what that is. It's the night of one of the Great Sabbaths and the powers from down under are exalted. H'mf. Hah. Well. I'm a cheerful blighter, eh?"

Page found himself puzzled and nervy and angry.

"You are," he said. "What's the good of putting nonsense into people's heads? Madeline is upset enough as it is. She's played other people's games and done things for other people until she's worn out. What the devil do you mean by trying to make it worse? There's no danger here. If I see anything hanging about I'll wring its ruddy neck and ask permission from the police afterwards."

"Sorry," said Dr. Fell. For a moment he stood looking down from his great height with tired, kindly, vaguely troubled eyes. Then he took his cloak, his shovel-hat, and his crutch-handled stick from a chair.

"Good night, sir," said Elliot. "If I've got the geography of the neighbourhood right, we can go up that path to the left from the garden here, and through the wood, and down to Farnleigh Close on the other side? Is that right?"

"Yes."

"Well—er—good night, then. Thank you again for everything, Miss Dane, for a very pleasant and instructive evening. And just—keep your eye out, you know, Mr. Page."

"Yes. And watch out for bogles in the wood," Page shouted after them.

He stood in the French window and watched them go down the garden among the laurels. It was a very warm night, and the scents of the garden were thick and enervating. In the east stars were brightening against a slope of sky, but they winked dimly as though distorted by heat-waves. Page's irrational anger grew.

"Bunch of old women," he said. "Trying to——"

He turned round and saw the fleeting of Madeline's smile. She was calm again; but she looked flushed.

"I'm sorry to make such an exhibition of myself, Brian," she said gently. "I know there's no danger of any kind." She got up. "Will you excuse me for a moment? I want to go upstairs and powder my nose. Shan't be a second."

"Bunch of old women. Trying to——"

Alone, he lit a cigarette with care. After a very brief time he was able to laugh at his own annoyance, and he felt better. On the contrary, an evening alone with Madeline was one of the pleasantest things he could imagine. A brown moth flashed through the window and dived in a long sweep towards one flame; he brushed it away, and shifted as it passed his face.

This little core of candlelight was very soothing and pleasant, but they might as well have more light. He went to the electric switch. Subdued wall lamps brought out the grace of the room and the pattern of chintzes. It was odd, he thought, how clear and sharply defined the ticking of a clock could be. There were two of them in the room; they did not vie with each other, but each filled up the beats the other lacked, and produced a kind of quick rustling. The tiny pendulum of one switched backwards and forwards in a way that drew the eye.

He went back to the table, where he poured himself some almost cold coffee. The noise of his own footsteps on the floor, the rattle of the cup in the saucer, the clink of the china coffee-pot on the edge of the cup: all these made sounds as clearly defined as those of the clocks. For the first time he became aware of mere emptiness as a positive quality. His thoughts ran progressively: this room is absolutely empty: I am alone: what of it?

The emptiness of the place was emphasized by the clearness of the lights. To one subject he kept his mind closed, though he had guessed a certain secret that afternoon and confirmed it from a book in his library. Something cheerful was indicated—for Madeline, of course. This house, neat as it might be, was too isolated. Round it was a wall of darkness stretching for half a mile.

Madeline was taking rather a long time to powder her nose. Another moth zig-zagged through the open window and flapped on the table. Curtains and candle-flames stirred a little. Better close the windows. He went across the bright, hard room, stood in one French window looking out into the garden, and then stood very still.

In the garden, in the darkness just beyond the thin edge of light from the windows, sat the automaton from Farnleigh Close.

## Chapter XVII

FOR the space of perhaps eight seconds he stood looking at it, as motionless as the automaton itself.

The light from the windows was faint yellow. It stretched out ten or a dozen feet across the grass, just touching the once-painted base of the figure. Even wider cracks gaped across her wax face; she leaned a little sideways from her fall downstairs, and half of her clockwork insides were gone. Some effort had been made to mend this by pulling the decayed gown across the wounds. Old and smashed and half-blind, she looked at him malignantly from the shadow of the laurels.

He had to force himself to do what he did. He walked out slowly towards her, feeling that his steps took him farther than need be from the lighted windows. She was alone, or seemed alone. Her wheels had been mended, he noticed. But the ground was so baked from long July drought that the wheels left hardly a trace in the grass. Not far to the left was a gravel drive which would leave no traces.

Then he hurried back to the house, for he heard Madeline coming downstairs.

Carefully he closed all the French windows. Then he picked up the heavy oak table and carried it to the middle of the room. Two of the candlesticks rocked. Madeline, appearing in the doorway, found him steadying one of them as he set down the table.

"Moths getting in," he explained.

"But won't it be awfully stuffy? Hadn't you better leave one——"

"I'll do it." He set the middle window open about a foot.

"Brian! There's nothing wrong, is there?"

Again he became aware, with intense clarity, of the ticking of the clocks; but most of all of the sympathetic presence of Madeline, exuding the wish to be protected. Uneasiness takes people in strange ways. She did not now seem so remote or self-effacing. The aura of her—there is no other word for it —filled the room.

He said:

"Good Lord, no; of course there's nothing wrong. It's just that moths are a nuisance, that's all. That's why I closed the windows."

"Shall we go into the other room?"

Better not be out of touch with it. Better not have it free to go where it liked.

"Oh, let's stay here and smoke another cigarette."

"Of course. What about some more coffee?"

"Don't trouble."

"It's no trouble. It's all prepared on the stove."

She smiled, the bright smile of one strung up by nerves, and went across to the kitchen. While she was gone he did not look out of the window. She seemed to be in the kitchen a long time, and he went in search of her. He met her in the doorway, carrying a fresh pot of coffee. She spoke quietly.

"Brian, there *is* something wrong. The back door is open. I know I left it shut, and Maria always closes it when she goes home."

"Maria forgot it."

"Yes. If you say so. Oh, I'm being silly. I know I am. Let's have something cheerful."

She seemed to wake up, with an apologetic and yet defiant laugh, and a brighter complexion. In one corner of the room, unobtrusive like Madeline herself, there was a radio. She switched it on. It took a few seconds to grow warm; then the resulting volume of noise startled them both.

She toned it down, but the flooding jingles of a dance-orchestra filled the rooms like surf on a beach. The tunes seemed as usual; the words rather worse than usual. Madeline listened to it for a moment. Then she returned to the table, sat down, and poured out their coffee. They were sitting at right angles to each other, so close he could have touched her hand. Her back was to the windows. All the while he was conscious of something outside, waiting. He wondered what his feelings would be if a cracked face were poked against the glass.

Yet, at the same time his nerves were touched, his brain stirred as well. It seemed to him that he woke up. It seemed to him that he was rationally reasoning for the first time; that bonds fell apart and the brain emerged from iron bands.

Now what were the facts about that dummy? It was dead iron and wheels and wax. It was no more dangerous of itself than a kitchen boiler. They had examined it, and they knew. Its only purpose was to *terrify*, a human purpose managed by a solid hand.

It had not pushed itself across the path from Farnleigh Close, like a malignant old woman in a wheel-chair. It had been brought here to terrify, again the solid purpose managed by the solid hand. And it seemed to him that this automaton was fitting itself into a pattern which the case had taken since the beginning, and which from the beginning he should have seen. . . .

"Yes," said Madeline, into his thoughts. "Let's talk about it. That would be better, really."

"It?"

"This whole thing," said Madeline, clenching her hands. "I—I may know rather more about it than you think."

She swam into his vision again. Again she had put the palms of her hands flat on the table, as though she were going to push herself back. The faint, frightened smile still lingered about her eyes and mouth. But she was quiet, almost coquettish; and she had never been more persuasive.

"I wonder if you know," he said, "what I've guessed?"

"I wonder."

He kept his eyes fixed on the partly open window. It seemed to him that he was talking less to Madeline than to something out there, something waiting, whose presence surrounded the house.

"It'll probably be best to get this out of my system," he went on with his eye still on the window. "Let me ask you something. Had *you* ever heard of a—a witch-cult hereabouts?"

Hesitation.

"Yes. I've heard rumours. Why?"

"It's about Victoria Daly. I had the essential facts yesterday from Dr. Fell and Inspector Elliot; I even had the information to interpret them; but I hadn't the wits to put the whole thing together. It's come to daylight now. Did you know that after Victoria's murder her body was found smeared with a substance composed of the juice of water parsnip, aconite, cinquefoil, deadly nightshade, and soot?"

"But whatever for? What have all those beastly things got to do with it?"

"A great deal. That is one of the formulas for the famous ointment—you've heard of it right enough—with which Satanists bedaubed themselves before going off to the Sabbath.* It lacks one of the original ingredients: the flesh of a child: but I suppose there are limits even to a murderer's efforts at realism."

"Brian!"

For it seemed to him that the picture which was emerging from these sly and tangled events was less that of a Satanist than that of a murderer.

"Oh, yes, it's true. I know something about that subject, and I can't imagine why I didn't remember it from the first. Now, I want you to think of the obvious deductions we can draw from that fact, the deductions Dr. Fell and the inspector made long ago. I don't mean about Victoria's indulgence, or pretended indulgence, in Satanist practices. That's clear enough without any deduction."

"Why?"

"Follow it out. She uses this ointment on Lammas Eve, the night of one of the great Satanist meetings. She is murdered at 11.45, and the Sabbath begins at midnight. It's clear that she had applied this ointment some minutes before the murderer caught her. She is murdered in her ground-floor

* For a medical analysis of these ointments, see Margaret Alice Murray, *The Witch-Cult in Western Europe* (Oxford University Press, 1921), Appendix V, 279-280; and J. W. Wickwar, *Witchcraft and the Black Art* (Herbert Jenkins, 1925), 36-40. See also Montague Summers, *History of Witchcraft and Demonology* (Kegan Paul, 1926).

bedroom, the window of which is set wide open: traditionally the way in which Satanists left, or thought they left, for their gatherings."

Though he was not looking directly at her, he thought that a slight frown had gathered on Madeline's forehead.

"I think I see what you're getting at, Brian. You say 'thought they left' because——"

"I'm coming to that. But, first, what deductions can we make about her murderer? Most important, this: Whether or not the tramp killed Victoria Daly, *there was a third person in that house at the time of the murder or just afterwards.*"

Madeline sprang to her feet. He was not looking at her, yet he felt that her large blue eyes were fixed on his face.

"How so, Brian? I still don't follow that."

"Because of the nature of the ointment. Do you realize what a substance like that would do?"

"Yes, I think I see that. But tell me."

"For six hundred years," he went on, "there's been a vast mass of testimony from those who claim to have gone to Witches' Sabbaths and seen the presence of Satan. What impresses you as you read it is the absolute sincerity, the careful detail, with which people have described things that couldn't possibly be true. We can't deny, as a matter of history, that the Satanist cult really existed and was a powerful force from the Middle Ages to the seventeenth century. It had an organization as carefully arranged and managed as the Church itself. But what about these miraculous journeys in the air, these wonders and ghosts, these demons and familiars, these incubi and succubi? They can't be accepted as facts (not by my practical mind, anyhow); and yet they are firmly presented as facts by a great number of people who weren't demented and weren't hysterical and weren't tortured. —Well, what would make a person believe them to be facts?"

Madeline said quietly: "Aconite and belladonna, or deadly nightshade."

They looked at each other.

"I believe that's the explanation," he told her, still with his attention on the window. "It's been argued, and I think reasonably, that in a great number of cases the 'witch' never left her own house or even her own room. She thought she had attended the Sabbath in the grove. She thought she had been conveyed by magic to the defiled altar and found a demon lover there. She thought so because the two chief ingredients of the ointment were aconite and belladonna. Do you know anything about the effects of poisons like that, rubbed into the skin externally?"

"My father had a *Medical Jurisprudence* here," said Madeline. "I was wondering——"

"Belladonna, absorbed through the pores of the skin—and under the quicks of the nails—would rapidly produce excitement, then violent hallucinations and delirium, and finally unconsciousness. Add to this the symptoms produced by aconite: mental confusion, dizziness, impaired movement, irregular heart-action, and an end in unconsciousness. A mind steeped in descriptions of Satanist revels (there was a book dealing with them on the table by Victoria Daly's bed) would do the rest. Yes, that's it. I think we know now how she 'attended the Sabbath' on Lammas Eve."

Madeline walked her fingers along the edge of the table. She studied them. Then she nodded.

"Ye-es. But even suppose that were true, Brian? How does it prove there was anybody else in the house the night she died? Anybody, I mean, aside from Victoria and the vagabond who killed her?"

"Do you remember how she was dressed when the body was found?"

"Of course. Night-gown, dressing-gown, and slippers."

"Yes—when the body was found. That's the point. A careful new night-gown, to say nothing of the extra flourish of a dressing-gown, over that sticky, oily, soot-coloured ointment? Acute discomfort and unusual marks afterwards? A dressing-gown for the Sabbath? The costume for the Sabbath consisted of the merest rags, which would not impede movement or get in the way of the ointment, when it consisted of any costume at all.

"Don't you see what happened? The woman was falling from delirium into unconsciousness in a dark house. A poor devil of a derelict, seeing a dark house and an open window, thought he had found an easy crib to crack. What he met was a woman roused and screaming in delirium: and it must have been rather an unnerving apparition which rose up at him from the bed or the floor. He lost his head and killed her.

"Anyone suffering delirium from that ointment couldn't have and wouldn't have put on the night-dress, dressing-gown, and slippers. The murderer wouldn't have put them on her. He was interrupted and chased before he had finished his work.

"But there was somebody else in the dark house. Victoria Daly was lying there dead with the ointment on her body and in a queer kind of costume which would cause a furious scandal when her body was found. Some wiseacre might even guess what had happened. To avert discovery, this third person crept into the bedroom before the body had been seen by anybody. (Remember? The two men who heard the screams saw the murderer escaping from the window, and gave chase; they didn't return until some time afterwards.) This third person then removed whatever 'witch's' clothes Victoria wore, and decorously dressed the body in night-gown, dressing-gown, and slippers. That's it. That's got it. That's what really happened."

His heart was thumping. The mental images, hidden for so long, were of such clarity that he knew he was right. He nodded towards Madeline.

"You know that's true, don't you?"

"Brian! How could I know it?"

"No, no, you don't understand. I mean you're as certain as I am, aren't you? That's the assumption on which Elliot has been working all this time."

She took a long time before she replied.

"Yes," she admitted, "I'd thought that. At least, I'd thought so until tonight, when those hints Dr. Fell gave didn't seem in the least to square with my ideas—and I told him so. Besides, it doesn't even seem to fit in with what they think either. You remember, he said yesterday there was no witch-cult hereabouts?"

"And so there isn't."

"But you've just explained——"

"I've explained what one person did. One person, and only one. Remember, Dr. Fell told us that yesterday. 'Everything, from mental cruelty to murder, is the work of one person.' And, 'I tell you frankly, Satanism itself is an honest and straightforward business compared to the intellectual pleasures a certain person has invented.' Put all these words together; put them into a pattern. Mental cruelty, plus intellectual pleasures, plus the death of Victoria Daly, plus a vague and undefined rumour of witchcraft among—what did Elliot tell me?—the gentry of the neighbourhood.

"I wonder what prompted this person to take it up? Pure boredom? Boredom with life, utter and simple, coming from an inability to take an interest in ordinary things? Or a tendency inherited from childhood, under the surface, but always growing up and feeding on secret things?"

"To take what up?" cried Madeline. "That's what I'm trying to get at. To take what up?"

Behind her a hand rapped on the glass of the window, with a malevolent tearing sound like a scratch.

Madeline screamed. That knock or blow had almost closed the partly open window, which rattled with a small noise against the frame. Page hesitated. The jingle of the dance-orchestra still filled the room. Then he went to the window and pushed it open.

## Chapter XVIII

DR. FELL and Inspector Elliot did not catch the train. They did not catch it because, when they arrived at Farnleigh Close, they were told that Betty Harbottle was awake and could speak to them.

They did not talk much on their way through the orchard and up through the wood. What they said, too, might have seemed cryptic to a listener. But it had a very deadly bearing on events which were to take place only an hour or two later, when one of the most cunning murderers in Dr. Fell's experience was (perhaps prematurely) snared into the open.

It was close and dark in the wood. Leaves made a heavy pattern against the starlight; Elliot's flashlight threw a beam ahead on a path of bare earth, making the green spectral. From the gloom behind it sounded two voices, the harsh tenor of the inspector and the wheezing bass of Dr. Fell.

"Still, sir, are we any nearer to proving it?"

"I think so. I hope so. If I've read one person's character correctly, he'll give us all the proof we need."

"And if your explanation works?"

"H'mf, yes. If it works. Of sticks and stones and rags and bones I made it; but it ought to serve."

"Do you think there's any danger," Elliot seemed to jerk his head over his shoulder in the direction of Madeline's house, "back there?"

There was a pause before Dr. Fell answered, while their footsteps swished among ferns.

"Dammit, I wish I knew! I hardly think so, though. Consider the character of the murderer. A sly, cracked head—like the dummy's; under that pleasant exterior—just as the dummy used to have. But emphatically not a fabled monster, intent on strewing the place with corpses. Not a monster at all. A moderate murderer, my lad. When I think of the number of persons who, by all the laws of progressive homicide, SHOULD have been murdered in this case, I have a tendency towards goose-flesh.

"We've known cases in which the murderer, after taking careful pains about his original crime, then goes berserk and begins to eliminate people all over the place. It seems to be like getting olives out of a bottle: you have infinite trouble with the first one, and the rest roll out all over the table. Without, indeed, anybody seeming to pay much attention to them. This murderer is human, my lad. I'm not, you understand, praising the murderer for this sporting restraint and good manners in refraining from killing people. But, my God, Elliot, the people who have gone in danger from the first! Betty Harbottle might have been killed. A certain lady we know of might have been killed. For a certain man's safety I've had apprehensions from the start. And not one of 'em has been touched. Is it vanity? Or what?"

In silence they came out of the wood and down the hill. Only a few lights burned at Farnleigh Close. They went through the part of the garden on the opposite side from the place where the murder had been committed, and round to the front door. A subdued Knowles admitted them.

"Lady Farnleigh has retired, sir," he said. "But Dr. King asks me to say that he wishes you gentlemen would join him upstairs, if you will."

"Is Betty Harbottle—?" Elliot stopped.

"Yes, sir. I think so."

Elliot whistled through his teeth as they went upstairs and into the dimly lighted passage between the Green Room and the bedroom where the girl lay. Dr. King held them off a moment before they entered.

"Now, look here," King said in his abrupt fashion. "Five minutes, ten minutes maybe: no more. I want to warn you. You'll find her as quiet and easy-spoken as though she were talking about a bus-ride. But don't let that deceive you. It's a part of the reaction, and she's got a dose of morphia in her. You'll also find her quick with her eyes and tolerably intelligent—curiosity was always Betty's chief feature—so don't start her going with too many suggestions and general fol-de-rol. Is that understood? Right, then. In you go."

Mrs. Apps, the housekeeper, slipped out as they entered. It was a large room in which every globe was illuminated in the old-fashioned chandelier. Not an impressive room: large old-fashioned photographs of Farnleighs were framed on the walls, and the dressing-table held a menagerie of china animals. The bed was black, square, and uncompromising. From it Betty regarded them with vague interest.

She had one of those faces called "bright," with very straight bobbed hair. Her pallor, and the slightly sunken look of the eyes, were the only signs of illness. She seemed pleased to see them rather than otherwise; and the only thing or person that seemed to make her uncomfortable was Dr. King. Her hands slowly smoothed the counterpane.

Dr. Fell beamed on her. His vast presence made the whole room comfortable.

"Hullo," he said.

"Hullo, sir," said Betty with an effort at brightness.

"Do you know who we are, my dear? And why we're here?"

"Oh, yes. You want me to tell you what happened to me."

"And can you?"

"I don't mind," she conceded.

She fixed her eyes on the foot of the bed. Dr. King took out his watch and put it on the dressing-table.

"Well—I don't know how to tell you, hardly. I went upstairs there to get an apple—" Betty abruptly seemed to change her mind. She shifted in bed. "No, I didn't!" she added.

"You didn't?"

"I didn't go up to get an apple. When I get well my sister's taking me away from here (I'm going to have a holiday at Hastings, too), so that's why I'll tell you. I *didn't* go up there to get an apple. I went up often to see if I could get a peep at what's in the cupboard there, the locked cupboard."

Her tone was not in the least defiant: she was too listless to be defiant: she was merely speaking out truth as though she were under the influence less of morphia than of scopolamine.

Dr. Fell looked heavily puzzled. "But why should you be interested in the locked cupboard?"

"Oh, everybody knows about it, sir. Somebody'd been using it."

"Using it?"

"Sitting up there with a light. There's a little window in the roof, like a skylight. At night, if you're a little way off from the house, and there's a light inside, you can see it against the roof. Everybody knows about it, though we're not supposed to. Even Miss Dane knows about it. I was over at Miss Dane's house one evening, taking her a parcel from Sir John, and I was going back through the Chart. Miss Dane asked me whether I wasn't afraid to go through the Chart after dark. I said, Oh, no; perhaps I should see the light in the roof, and that would be worth it. I only said it as a joke, because the light was always on the south side, and the path through the Chart takes you to the north side. Miss Dane laughed and put her arm round my shoulder and asked whether I was the only one who had seen it. I said, Oh, no, everybody had; because we had. Besides, we were all interested about that machine like a gramophone, that dummy——"

The look in her eyes altered slightly.

There was a pause.

"But who was 'using' the room?"

"Well, mostly they said it was Sir John. Agnes saw him come down from the attic one afternoon, with his face all perspiring and something like a dog-whip in his hand. I said, So would you be perspiring, too, if you sat in a little bit of a place like that with the door shut. But Agnes said he didn't look quite like that."

"Anyway, my dear, will you tell us what happened yesterday? Hey?"

Dr. King interposed sharply. "Two minutes, my lads."

Betty looked surprised.

"I don't mind," she responded. "I went up there to get an apple. But this time, when I went past the door of the little room, I saw the padlock wasn't fastened. The padlock was open, hanging on the staple. The door was closed, but with something stuck in between the door and the frame to hold it shut."

"What did you do?"

"I went and got an apple. After that I came back and looked at the door and started to eat the apple. Then I went to the apple-room again, and finally I came back and thought I would see what was inside after all. But I didn't want to, as much as usually."

"Why not?"

"Because there was a noise in there, or I thought so. A rattly kind of noise, like winding a grandfather clock; but not very loud."

"Do you remember what time this was, Betty?"

"No, sir. Not properly. It was past one o'clock, maybe a quarter past or more than that."

"What did you do then?"

"I went over ever so quickly, before I should decide not to do it, and opened the door. The thing that was keeping it shut was a glove. Stuck into the door, you know, sir."

"A man's glove or a woman's glove?"

"A man's, I think. It had oil on it; or it smelt like oil. It dropped on the floor. I went inside. I could see the old machine-thing there, a bit sideways to me, like. I didn't want one more look at it: not that you could see very well in there. But I no sooner stepped inside than the door closed ever so softly; and somebody put up the chain across the door and I heard the padlock close together outside; so I was locked in, you see."

"Steady!" said the physician sharply. He took up his watch from the dressing-table.

Betty was twisting the fringe of the counterpane. Dr. Fell and the inspector looked at each other; Dr. Fell's red face was heavy and grave.

"But—are you still all right, Betty?—who was in there? Who was in the little room?"

"Nobody. Nobody except the old machine-thing. Nobody at all."

"You're sure of that?"

"Oh, yes."

"What did you do?"

"I didn't do anything. I was afraid to call out and ask to be let out. I was afraid I should get the sack. It wasn't quite dark. I stood there and didn't do anything for, oh, maybe it was a quarter of an hour. And nobody else did anything either: I mean the machine-thing didn't. Presently I started to move away from it, and got back as far as I could, because it started to put its arms around me."

If, at that moment, so much as the ash of a cigar had fallen into an ashtray, Dr. Fell swears it would have been heard. Elliot heard the breath drawn through his own nostrils. Elliot said:

"It moved, Betty? The machine moved?"

"Yes, sir. It moved its arms. They didn't move fast, and neither did the body, the way it sort of ducked forward towards me; and it made a noise when it moved. But that wasn't what I minded so much. I didn't seem to feel anything, because I had been standing in there with it for a quarter of an hour already. What I minded was the eyes it had. It didn't have eyes in the proper place. It had eyes in the skirt, right by the knees of the old dummy thing; and they looked up at me. I could see them move round. I don't mind even them so much. I expect I shall get used to them. At that time I don't remember anything more about it; I must have fainted or something; but it's outside the door now," continued Betty, with absolutely no change of expression or tone while she nodded at the door.

"I should like to go to sleep," she added in a plaintive tone.

Dr. King swore under his breath.

"That's done it," he said. "Out you go, now. No, she'll be all right; but—out you go."

"Yes," agreed Elliot, looking at Betty's closed eyes, "I think we had better."

They went out with guilty quietness, and King made a pantomime of slamming the door after them. "I hope," he muttered, "hearing common delirium helps you." Still without speaking, Dr. Fell and the inspector went across to the dark Green Room. It was furnished as a study in heavy antique style; and the windows were rectangles of starlight. They went across and stood by one window.

"That settles it, sir? Even aside from the—er—answer to the inquiries——?"

"Yes. That settles it."

"Then we'd better get on to town, and——"

"No," said Dr. Fell after a long pause. "I don't think it'll be necessary. I think we'd better try the experiment now, while the metal is hot. Look there!"

The garden below showed in clear etching-lines against the dark. They saw the maze of hedges veined with whitish paths, the clear space round the pool, and the white smears of the water-lilies. But they were not looking at this. Someone, carrying an object recognizable even in that light, slipped past under the library windows and round the south corner of the house.

Dr. Fell expelled his breath. Lumbering across the room to the central light-fixture, he turned on the lamp and swung round with a vast billow of his cape.

"Psychologically, as we've come to say," he told Elliot with sardonic dryness, "tonight is the night. Now's the time, man. Now, or we may lose the whole advantage. Get 'em together, I tell you! I should like to do a little explaining as to how a man can be murdered when alone in a circle of sand; and then we can pray Old Nick will come and get his own. Hey?"

A small cough interrupted them as Knowles came into the room.

"I beg your pardon, sir," he said to Dr. Fell. "Mr. Murray is here, and asking to see you gentlemen. He says he's been looking for you for some time."

"Has he, now?" inquired Dr. Fell, with ferocious affability. The doctor beamed and shook his cape. "Did he say what he wanted?"

Knowles hesitated. "No, sir. That is—" Knowles hesitated again. "He says he's disturbed about something, sir. He also wishes to see Mr. Burrows. And, as regards that——"

"Speak up, man! What's on your mind?"

"Well, sir, may I ask whether Miss Dane received the automaton?"

Inspector Elliot whirled round from the window.

"Whether Miss Dane received the automaton? What automaton? What about it?"

"You know the one, sir," returned Knowles, with a guilty expression which (less smoothly done) might have been a leer. "Miss Dane rang up this after-noon, and asked whether she might have the automaton sent over to her home this evening. We—er—we thought it was an odd request; but Miss Dane said a gentleman was coming there, an expert on such things, and she wished him to have a good look at it."

"So," observed Dr. Fell without inflection. "She wished him to have a good look at it."

"Yes, sir. Macneile (that's the gardener) mended the wheel, and I had it sent over in a cart. Macneile and Parsons said there was nobody at home at Miss Dane's at the time, so they put it into the coal-house. Then—er—Mr. Burrows arrived here, and expressed annoyance that it had gone. He also knows of a gentleman who is an expert on such things."

"How popular the hag is becoming in her old age," rumbled Dr. Fell, with a wheeze of what might or might not have been pleasure. "How excellent to eke out her days among throngs of admirers. By thunder, how excellent! A perfect woman, nobly planned, to warn, to comfort, and command. Cold eyelids that hide like a jewel hard eyes that grow soft for an hour—waugh!" He stopped. "And is Mr. Murray also interested in the automaton?"

"No, sir. Not that I know of."

"A pity. Well, shoot him into the library. He is remarkably at home there. One of us will be down in a moment. And what," he added to Elliot, when Knowles had gone, "do you make of this little move?"

Elliot rubbed his chin. "I don't know. But it doesn't seem to fit in with what we saw. In any case, it mightn't be a bad idea for me to get back to Monplaisir as fast as I can."

"I agree. Profoundly."

"Burton ought to be here with the car. If he is, I can make it by the road in three minutes. If he isn't——"

He wasn't. What adjustment had gone wrong with the scales or the night Elliot did not know. Nor could he get a car from the garage at the Close, whose doors were (revealingly) locked. Elliot set off for Monplaisir by the path through the wood. The last thing he saw before he left the house was Dr. Fell descending the main staircase, lowering himself step by step on his crutch-handled stick; and on Dr. Fell's face was an expression that is very seldom seen there.

Inspector Elliot told himself that he had no reason to hurry. But, as he mounted the hill through the Hanging Chart, he found himself walking fast. Nor did he particularly like his surroundings. He knew that they were the victims, no longer gullible, of a series of ingenious hoaxes no more to be feared than the black Janus-face in the attic. The hoax at best was unpleas-ant and at worst was murderous; but it was no more than a hoax.

And yet, even as he increased his step, he kept the beam of his electric torch playing from side to side. Something stirred in him that was rooted in his blood and race. Out of his boyhood he sought a word to describe the present doings, and found it. The word was "heathenish."

He did not expect anything to happen. He knew that he would not be needed.

It was not until he was almost out of the wood that he heard a shot fired.

## Chapter XIX

BRIAN PAGE stood in the open French window and looked out into the garden. After that knock he had been prepared, in the usual fashion, for anything except nothing. And there was nothing—or so it seemed.

The automaton had gone. The quiet light, almost draining the grass of its colour, barely showed the wheel-marks where iron had rested. But the presence or absence of that dead metal meant nothing; someone or something had rapped on the window. He took one step across the sill.

"Brian," said Madeline quietly, "where are you going?"

"Just to see who called on us, or started to call on us."

"Brian, don't go out there. Please." She came closer, and her voice was full of urgency. "I've never asked you to do anything for me before, have I? Well, I ask you to do something now. Don't go out there. If you do I'll—well, I don't know what I will do, exactly, except that it will be something you won't like. Please! Come in and close the window, won't you? You see, I know."

"Know?"

She nodded towards the garden. "What was sitting out there a moment ago, and isn't there now. I saw it from the back door when I was in the kitchen. I didn't want to worry you in case you hadn't seen it, though I—I was pretty sure you had." She slid her hands up the lapels of his coat. "Don't go out there. Don't go after it. That's what it wants you to do."

He looked down at her, at the pleading eyes and the curve of the short throat upturned. In spite of what he was thinking and feeling just then, he spoke with a kind of impassioned detachment.

He said:

"Of all the extraordinary places to say what I am going to say, this is the most extraordinary. Of all the inappropriate times to say what I am going to say, this is the most inappropriate. I maintain this because I have got to use superlatives somehow in getting my feelings off my chest, and what I mean is that I love you."

"Then there's some good in Lammas Eve," said Madeline, and lifted her mouth.

It is a problem how far, in accounts of violence, there may be expressed the things he thought and said then. Yet, without a violence that moved round the edges of a lighted window, it is possible that he would never have learned or heard the things he learned and heard then. He was not concerned with this. He was concerned with other matters: the paradox of how remote and mysterious a loved face looks by very reason of being closer: the strange chemistry of kissing Madeline, which altered his life and in whose actuality he could not even yet believe. He wanted to utter a mighty shout of pure joy; and, after many minutes at that window, he did.

"Oh, God, Brian, why didn't you ever tell me so before?" said Madeline, who was half-laughing and half-crying. "I mustn't swear! My moral character is falling deplorably. But why didn't you ever tell me so before?"

"Because I didn't see how you could possibly be interested in me. I didn't want you to laugh."

"Did you think I would laugh?"

"Frankly—yes."

She held to his shoulders and studied him with her face upturned. Her eyes were shining curiously.

"Brian, you do love me, don't you?"

"For some minutes I have been trying to make that clear. But I haven't got the slightest objection to beginning all over again. If——"

"A spinster like me——"

"Madeline," he said, "whatever else you do, don't use that word 'spinster.' It is one of the ugliest-sounding words in the language. It suggests something between 'spindle' and 'vinegar.' To describe you properly, it is necessary to——"

Again he noticed the curious shining in her eyes.

"Brian, if you really do love me (you do?) then I may show you something, mayn't I?"

Out in the garden there was a noise of a footstep in the grass. Her tone had been odd, so odd as to make him wonder; but there was no time to reflect on this. At that swishing of the footstep they stood apart quickly. Among the laurels a figure was taking shape and coming closer. It was a lean, narrow-shouldered figure, with a walk between a brisk stride and a shamble; after which Page saw, with relief, that it was only Nathaniel Burrows.

Burrows did not seem to know whether to keep his halibut-faced expression or to smile. Between the two he appeared to struggle: producing something of an amiable contortion. His large shell-rimmed spectacles were grave. His long face, which had a very genuine charm when he chose to exercise it, now showed only a part of that charm. His very correct bowler hat was set at a somewhat rakish angle.

"Tsk! Tsk!" was his only comment, with a smile. "I've come," he added pleasantly, "for the automaton."

"The—?" Madeline blinked at him. "The automaton?"

"You should not stand in windows," said Burrows severely. "It upsets your mental equilibrium when you have visitors afterwards. You shouldn't stand in windows either," he added, looking at Page. "The dummy, Madeline. The dummy you borrowed from Farnleigh Close this afternoon."

Page turned to look at her. She was staring at Burrows, her colour heightening.

"Nat, what on earth are you talking about? The dummy I borrowed? I never did any such thing."

"My dear Madeline," returned Burrows, putting his gloved hands wide apart and bringing them together again. "I've not yet properly thanked you for all the good work you have done for me—at the inquest. But hang it!" Here he looked at her sideways past his spectacles. "You rang up and asked for that dummy this afternoon. Macneile and Parsons brought it over. It's in the coal-house now."

"You must be absolutely mad," said Madeline, in a high and wondering voice.

Burrows, as usual, was reasonable. "Well, it's there. That's the supreme answer. I couldn't make anyone hear at the front of the house. I came round here, and I—er—still couldn't make anyone hear. My car's out in the main road. I drove over to get the automaton. Why you should want it I can't imagine; but would you mind very much if I took it along? I can't quite see, as yet, how it fits into the picture. However, after my expert has a look at it, it may give me an idea."

The coal-house was built into the wall a little to the left of the kitchen. Page went over and opened the door. The automaton was there. He could make out its outlines faintly.

"You see?" said Burrows.

"Brian," said Madeline rather frantically, "will you believe I never did anything of the kind? I never asked for the thing to be sent here, or thought of it, or anything of the sort. Why on earth should I?"

"Of course I know you didn't," Page told her. "Somebody seems to have gone completely mad."

"Why not go inside?" suggested Burrows. "I should like to have a little talk with both of you about this. Just wait a moment until I put on the side-lights of my car."

The other two went inside, where they looked at each other. The music from the radio had stopped; somebody was talking instead, about a subject Page does not remember, and Madeline shut off the set. Madeline seemed to be in the grip of a reaction.

"This isn't real," she said. "It's all illusion. We're dreaming it. At least—all but a part of it, I hope." And she smiled at him. "Have you any idea what's happening?"

As for what happened in the few seconds after that, Page is still confused in his mind. He remembers that he had taken her hand, and opened his mouth to assure her that he did not particularly give a curse what had happened, provided those minutes by the window were not illusion. They both heard the detonation from the direction of the garden or the orchard behind. It had a flat and bursting noise. It was loud enough to make them jump. Yet it seemed to have no connection with them, to be remote from them, in spite of the fact that a wiry sound sang close to their ears—and one of the clocks stopped.

One of the clocks stopped. Page's ears took note of that at the same time his eyes noted the small round hole, starred with a faint web of cracks, in the glass of the window. It then became clear that the clock had stopped because there was a bullet buried in it.

The other clock ticked on.

"Get back from the window," Page said. "This can't be: I don't believe it: but there's somebody firing at us from the garden. Where the devil has Nat got to?"

He went over and switched out the lights. The candles remained; and he blew them out just as a sweating Burrows, his hat crushed down on his head, ducked low through the window as though for safety.

"There's somebody—" Burrows began in a strange voice.

"Yes. We had noticed that."

Page moved Madeline across the room. He was calculating, by the position of the bullet in the clock, that two inches to the left would have sent it through Madeline's head, just above the small curls there.

No other shot was fired. He heard Madeline's frightened breathing, and the slow, sharp breathing of Burrows from across the room. Burrows stood inside the last of the windows: only his polished shoe was visible as he braced himself there.

"Do you know what I think happened?" Burrows asked.

"Well?"

"Do you want me to show you what I think happened?"

"Go on!"

"Wait," whispered Madeline. "Whoever it is—listen!"

Burrows, startled, poked his head out like a turtle's past the line of the window. Page heard the hail from the garden and answered it. It was Elliot's voice. He hurried out and met the inspector, whose run through the grass from the orchard was easy to follow. Elliot's face was inscrutable in the gloom as he listened to Page's story; also, his manner was at its most heavily official.

"Yes, sir," he said. "But I think you can put on those lights now. I don't think you will be troubled again."

"Inspector, are you going to do nothing?" demanded Burrows in a wiry voice of remonstrance. "Or are you accustomed to this sort of thing in London? I assure you we're not." He mopped his forehead with the back of a gloved hand. "Aren't you going to search the garden? Or the orchard? Or wherever the shot was fired from?"

"I said, sir," repeated Elliot woodenly, "that I don't think you will be troubled again."

"But who did it? What was the point of it?"

"The point is, sir," said Elliot, "that this nonsense is going to stop. For good. We've had a bit of a change in plans. I think, if you don't mind, I'd like to have you all come back to the Close with me—just in case, you understand. I'm afraid I've got to make the request something like an order."

"Oh, nobody's got any objection," said Page cheerfully; "though it would almost seem that we'd had enough excitement for one evening."

The inspector smiled in a way that was not reassuring.

"I think you're wrong," he said. "You haven't seen anything like excitement tonight. But you will, Mr. Page. I promise you you will. Has anybody got a car?"

That uneasy suggestion remained with them while Burrows drove them all to Farnleigh Close. All efforts to question the inspector were useless. To Burrow's insistence that the automaton should be removed with them, Elliot only answered that there was not time and that it was not necessary.

A worried-looking Knowles admitted them to the Close. The center of tension was in the library. There, as two nights ago, the gaping crown of electric-bulbs from the ceiling was reflected in a wall of windows. In the chair formerly occupied by Murray sat Dr. Fell, with Murray across from him. Dr. Fell's hand was supported on his stick, and his lower lip outthrust above the chins. The echo of emotion came to them as soon as the library door was opened. For Dr. Fell had just finished talking, and Murray shaded his eyes with an unsteady hand.

"Ah," said the doctor with dubious affability. "Good evening, good evening, good evening! Miss Dane. Mr. Burrows. Mr. Page. Good. I'm afraid we have commandeered the house in a reprehensible way; but something has made it necessary. It is very necessary to have a gathering for a little conference. Couriers have been despatched for Mr. Welkyn and Mr. Gore. Knowles: will you ask Lady Farnleigh to join us? No: don't go yourself; send a maid; I should prefer that you remain here. In the meantime, certain matters can be discussed."

The tone of his voice was such that Nathaniel Burrows hesitated before sitting down. Burrows raised a hand sharply. He did not look at Murray.

"We cannot go as fast as that," Burrows returned. "Stop! Is there anything in this discussion that is likely to be of a—er—a controversial nature?"

"There is."

Again Burrows hesitated. He had not glanced in Murray's direction; but Page, studying them, felt a twinge of pity for Murray without knowing why. The tutor looked worn and old.

"Oh! And what are we going to discuss, doctor?"

"The character of a certain person," said Dr. Fell. "You will guess who it is."

"Yes," agreed Page, hardly conscious that he had spoken aloud. "The person who initiated Victoria Daly into the pleasantries of witchcraft."

It was remarkable, he thought, the effect that name had. You had only to introduce the words "Victoria Daly," like a talisman, and everybody shied away from it; the prospect seemed to open into new vistas which were not liked. Dr. Fell, vaguely surprised but interested, turned round and blinked at him.

"Ah!" said the doctor, wheezing with approval. "So you guessed that."

"I tried to work it out. Is that person the murderer?"

"That person is the murderer." Dr. Fell pointed his stick. "It will help us, you know, if the view is also shared by you. Let's hear what you think. And speak out, my lad. There will be worse things said in this room before any of us leaves it."

With some care, and a vividness of image which he hardly sought to use, Page repeated the story he had already told to Madeline. Dr. Fell's sharp little eyes never left his face, nor did Inspector Elliot miss a word. The body smeared with ointment, the dark house with the open window, the panic-mad vagabond, the third person waiting: these images seemed to be enacted in the library like pictures on a screen.

At the end of it Madeline spoke. "Is this true? Is it what you and the inspector think?"

Dr. Fell merely nodded.

"Then I ask you what I was trying to ask Brian. If there is no witch-cult—as he says—if the whole affair was a dream, what was this 'third person' doing or trying to do? What about the *evidences* of witchcraft?"

"Ah, the evidences," said Dr. Fell.

After a pause he went on:

"I will try to explain. You have among you somebody whose mind and heart have been steeped for years in a secret love of these things and what they stand for. Not a belief in them! That I hasten to point out. That I emphasize. Nobody could be more cynical as regards the powers of darkness and the lords of the four-went-ways. But a surpassing love of them, made all the more powerful and urgent by an (altogether prudish) necessity for never letting it show. This person, you understand, figures before you in a very different character. This person will never admit before you to even an interest in such matters, an interest such as you and I might have. So that secret interest—the desire to share it—the desire, above all, to experiment on other people—grew so strong that it had to burst its bonds somehow.

"Now what was this person's position? What could this person do? Found a new witch-cult in Kent, such as existed here in previous centuries? It must have been a fascinating idea; but this person knew that it was as wild as wind. This person is, essentially, very practical.

"The smallest group in the organization for the worship of Satan was (may I say?) the coven. The coven consisted of thirteen persons, twelve members and a masked leader. To be the Janus-masked leader of such a cotillion must have appealed to our person as a fine dream; but no more than a dream. It was not only that the practical difficulties were too great to be overcome. It was also that for the thing to be interesting—to be shared with a few others—the number of persons concerned must be very small. As the interest was secret, so it must be narrow and personal and individual.

"This, I emphasize, was no measured affiliation with the powers of evil, supposing any such powers to exist. It had no such high ambition; or, to put it more properly, no such high-falutin. It was not carefully planned. It was not managed by a person of any great intelligence. It was not a cult as we know cults seriously developed. It was simply an idle and greedy liking for such things, a kind of hobby. Lord love you, I don't suppose any great harm would have been done—if the person had kept away from poisonous drugs to produce hallucinations. If people choose merely to act the fool, if they don't violate any laws or even any conventions, then it's no concern of the police. But, when a woman just outside Tunbridge Wells dies from the application of belladonna to the skin (which is exactly what happened eighteen months ago, though we've never been able to prove it), then, by thunder, it *is* a concern of the police! Why do you think Elliot was sent here to begin with? Why do you think he's been so much concerned with the story of Victoria Daly? Hey?

"Do you begin to see what somebody has been doing?

"This person chose a few suitable and sympathetic friends to confide in. There were not many: two or three or four, perhaps. We shall probably never know who they are. This person had many talks with them. Many books were given or loaned. Then, when the friend's mind was sufficiently stuffed and excited with wild lore, it was time. It was time to inform the friend that there really was a Satanist cult hereabouts, to which the candidate could now be admitted."

There was a sharp noise as Dr. Fell struck the ferrule of his stick on the floor. He was impatient and he was annoyed.

"Of course there never was any such thing. Of course the neophyte never left the house or stirred from one room on the night of the gatherings. Of course it was all a matter of an ointment whose two chief ingredients were aconite and belladonna.

"And of course, as a rule, the person who instigated this never went near the friend, much less joined any gathering, on the night of an alleged 'meeting.' That might have been too dangerous, if the poisonous effects of the ointment were too great. The pleasure lay in spreading this gospel: in sharing accounts of (mythical) adventures: in watching the decay of minds under the effects of the drug and under the effects of what they thought they had seen at the Sabbaths: in short, of combining a degree of rather heavy-witted mental cruelty with the pleasure of letting loose this interest in a safe and narrow circle."

Dr. Fell paused. And in the silence that followed Kennet Murray spoke thoughtfully.

"It reminds me," he said, "of the mentality which writes poison-pen letters."

"You've got it," said Dr. Fell, nodding. "It is almost exactly the same, turned to different and more harmful outlets."

"But if you can't prove the other woman died of poison—the one near Tunbridge Wells, whom I hadn't heard of—where are you? Has the 'person' done anything which is concretely illegal? Victoria Daly didn't die of poison."

"That depends, sir," observed Inspector Elliot suavely. "You seem to think that poisons aren't poisons unless they are taken internally. I can tell you different. But that's not the point now. Dr. Fell was only telling you the secret."

"The secret?"

"This person's secret," said Dr. Fell. "In order to preserve that secret, a man was murdered beside the pool in the garden two nights ago."

There was another silence, this time of an eerie quality as though everyone had drawn back a little.

Nathaniel Burrows put one finger inside his collar.

"This is interesting," he said. "Very interesting. But at the same time I feel I've been brought here under false pretences. I'm a solicitor, not a student of heathen religions. I don't see that the heathen religions have anything to do with the only thing that matters to me. In the story you outline, there is no connection whatever with the proper succession to the Farnleigh estates—"

"Oh, yes, there is," said Dr. Fell.

He went on:

"It is, in fact, at the root of the whole matter, as I hope to make you understand in about two seconds.

"But you," he looked argumentatively at Page, "you, my friend, asked a little while ago what caused this person to take up such practices. Was it sheer boredom? Was it a kink inherited from childhood, never lost, and increasing from year to year? I'm inclined to suspect that it was a little of both. In this case all things grow up together, like the poison *Atropa belladonna* plant in the hedgerow. They are entwined and inseparable.

"Who might be a person with these instincts, always obliged to repress them? Who is there in whom we can trace the kink, with all the evidence be-

fore us? Who can be shown to be the one person, and the only one, wit
direct access to the toys of both witchcraft and murder? Who did undoub
edly suffer from the boredom of a loveless and miserable marriage, and at th
same time suffered from the super-abundant vitality which——"

Burrows sprang to his feet with a ringing oath of enlightenment.

And at the same time, in the open door of the library, there was a whi
pered conference between Knowles and someone outside.

Knowles's face was white when he spoke.

"Excuse me, sir, but they—they tell me her ladyship is not in her room
They say she packed a bag some time ago, and took a car from the garage
and——"

Dr. Fell nodded.

"Exactly," he said. "That's why we don't have to hurry to London. He
flight has blown the gaff. And we shall have no difficulty now in obtaining
warrant for the arrest of Lady Farnleigh on a charge of murder."


## Chapter XX


"OH, COME!" said Dr. Fell, rapping his stick on the floor and peering roun
the group with an air of benevolent expostulation. He was both amused an
exasperated. "Don't tell me it surprises you. Don't tell me it shocks you
You, Miss Dane! Didn't you know about her all along? Didn't you know hov
she hated you?"

Madeline passed the back of her hand across her forehead. Then sh
reached out and took Page's arm.

"I didn't know about her," Madeline said. "I guessed. But I could hardl
tell you that outright, could I? I'm afraid you've thought me enough of
cat as it is."

For Page some readjustment of thought was necessary. So, it appeared, wa
it necessary for the others. Yet a new notion caught and held in Page's brai
even as he tried to assimilate the first. The thought was:

This case is not finished.

Whether it was a slight expression flickering in Dr. Fell's eyes, a turn o
his hand on the stick, a slight quiver even in that mountain, he could no
tell. But the impression was there, and Dr. Fell still held the room as thoug
he had not ended with revelation. Somewhere there was an ambush. Some
where there were guns to be fired on the brain.

"Go on," said Murray quietly. "I don't doubt you; but go on."

"Yes," said Burrows in a vacant way—and sat down.

The doctor's big voice sounded sleepily in the quiet library.

"From the physical evidences," he continued, "there could hardly hav
been much doubt about it from the first. The centre of all disturbances

psychic and otherwise, was always *here*. The centre of all disturbances was that locked book-closet in the attic. Somebody had been haunting it. Somebody had been juggling with its contents, removing and replacing its books, playing with its trinkets. Somebody, always distinguished for exuberance of action, had made it into a kind of lair.

"Now, the notion that some outsider had done this—that some neighbour had crept into the nest—was so fantastic as not to be worth serious consideration. Such a course of action would have been impossible, both psychologically and practically. You do not make a sort of one-man club in the attic of someone else's house, particularly under the eyes of a staff of curious servants. You do not come and go through that house at night, unseen by servants or anybody else. You do not so casually treat a new padlock watched by the master of the house. For it will be observed that though Miss Dane, for instance"—here there was a broad and cherubic beam on Dr. Fell's face —"though Miss Dane had once possessed a key to that little room, it was the key to a lock no longer in use.

"Next question: what ailed Sir John Farnleigh?

"Just reflect on that, ladies and gentlemen.

"Why did that restless Puritan, already be-dazed with troubles of his own, never find any solace at home? What else was on his mind? Why does he, on the very night his great inheritance is to be challenged, do nothing but pace the floor and talk of Victoria Daly? Why is he so uneasily concerned with detectives asking 'folklore' questions in the vicinity? What is the meaning of his cryptic hints to Miss Dane? In moments of emotion he used to look up at the church, and say that if he were in a position to——'

"To do what? Speak out against the defamers of the church? Why does he once visit that attic with a dog-whip in his hand; but come down white and sweating, unable to use the whip on the person he finds there?

"The points in this case are mental ones, as revealing as the physical clues with which I shall deal in a moment; and I can't do better than to trace them."

Dr. Fell paused. He stared heavily and rather sadly at the table. Then he got out his pipe.

"Let's take the history of this girl, Molly Bishop: a resolute woman and a fine actress. Patrick Gore said one true thing about her two nights ago. He appears to have shocked most of you by saying that she had never fallen in love with the Farnleigh you knew. He said that she had seized upon and married a 'projected image' of the boy she had known all those years before. And so she had. Whereupon she discovered, with what fury we may never know, that it was not the same boy or even the same person.

"What was the origin of that obsession or kink, even in the brain of a child of seven?

"It's not difficult. That's the age at which our essential tastes begin to be stamped on us by outside impressions. They are never eradicated, even when we think we have forgotten them. To my dying day I shall like pictures of fat old Dutchmen playing chess and smoking churchwarden pipes, because I remember one hanging on the wall of my father's study when I was a small child. You may like ducks or ghost-stories or motor-mechanisms for the same reason.

"Well, who was the only person who had idolized the boy John Farnleigh? Who was the only one to defend him? Whom did John Farnleigh take to gipsy-camps (I call the gipsy-camps to your attention as significant), and take with him into the wood? What manner of Satanist lessons did she hear him recite, before she understood them or even before she understood the lessons she learned at Sunday School?

"And the intervening years? We don't know how the taste grew and developed in her brain. Except this: that she spent much time among the Farnleighs, for she had enough influence with old and young Sir Dudley to get Knowles his position as butler here.—Didn't she, Knowles?"

He peered round.

From the moment he had made that announcement Knowles had not moved. He was seventy-four. The transparent colour of his face, which seemed to show every emotion there, now showed nothing at all. He opened and shut his mouth and nodded in pantomime of reply; but he did not say anything. About him there was only a look of horror.

"It is probable," continued Dr. Fell, "that she was borrowing books from that sealed library a long time ago. When she first instituted her private Satanist-cult Elliot has not been able to trace; but it was several years before her marriage. The number of men in the district who have been her lovers is large enough to surprise you. But they cannot or will not say anything about the Satanist business. And that, after all, is the only thing with which we are concerned. It is the thing with which *she* was most concerned, and it brought about the tragedy. For what happened?

"After a long and romantic absence, the supposed 'John Farnleigh' returned to the supposed home of his fathers. For a short time Molly Bishop was transfigured. Here was her ideal. Here was her preceptor. Him she was determined to marry in spite of hell and himself. And something over a year ago—to be exact, a year and three months—they were married.

"Oh, Lord, was there ever a worse match?

"I ask that quite solemnly. You know who and what she thought she was marrying. You know instead the sort of person she did marry. You can guess the silent, cold contempt he had for her; and the frigid politeness he had for her when he learned. You can imagine what she felt for him, and the mask of concerned wifeliness she had to adopt, knowing always that he knew. And between them lay always the polite fiction that neither was aware of the other's knowledge. For, just as he knew about her, so she as certainly knew after a very short time that he was not the real John Farnleigh. So there together they shared each other's secret, in unadmitted hate.

"Why didn't he ever give her away? It wasn't merely that she was what he in his Puritan soul condemned first to the pit. It wasn't merely that he would have taken a whip to her if he had dared. But she was a criminal (make no mistake about that, gentlemen) as well. She was a supplier of more dangerous drugs than heroin or cocaine; and he knew it. She was accessory after the fact in Victoria Daly's murder; and he knew it. You have heard of his outbursts. You know his thoughts. Why, then, didn't he ever give her away as he longed to do?

"Because he was not in a position to do so. Because they held each other's secret. He didn't *know* he was not Sir John Farnleigh; but he feared it. He didn't *know* she could prove he was not, and might do so if he provoked her; but he feared it. He didn't *know* whether she might suspect; but he feared it. He had not quite the character of sweetness and light which Miss Dane gave him. No, he was not a conscious impostor. His memory was blind and he groped there. Very often he was sure he must be the real Farnleigh. But he would not, in the depths of a natural human soul, challenge fate too far, unless it pinned him in a corner and he had to face it out. For he might be a criminal as well."

Nathaniel Burrows jumped to his feet.

"I cannot put up with this," he said in a shrill voice. "I refuse to put up with this. Inspector, I call on you to stop this man! He has no right to prejudice an issue not yet decided. As a representative of the law, you have no right to say that my client——"

"Better sit down, sir," said Elliot quietly.

"But——"

"I said sit down, sir."

Madeline was speaking to Dr. Fell.

"You said something like that earlier tonight," she reminded him. "Something about his 'labouring under a sense of crime,' even though he did not know what it was. His 'sense of crime,' that made him a worse Puritan, seems to run all through this; and yet, really and truly, I can't see what that has to do with it. What's the explanation?"

Dr. Fell put the empty pipe in his mouth and drew at it.

"The explanation," he answered, "is a crooked hinge, and the white door the hinge supported. It's the secret of this case. We shall come to it presently.

"So these two, each having a secret like a dagger in the sleeve, mopped and mowed and pretended in front of the world: even in front of themselves. Victoria Daly died, a victim of the secret witch-cult, only three months after they had been married. We know what Farnleigh must have felt by that time. *If I were ever in a position to*—had become with him a fetish and a refrain. So long as he was never in a position to speak out, she was safe. For over a year she was safe.

"But then occurred the thunderclap that a claimant to the estate had appeared. Whereupon certain eventualities presented themselves to her as flat and clear and inevitable as a, b, c. Thus:

"He was not the real heir, as she knew.

"It seemed probable that the claimant would prove to be the real heir.

"If the claimant were proved to be the real heir, her husband would be dispossessed.

"If he were dispossessed, he would no longer have a reason for not speaking out about her, and he would speak out.

"Therefore he had to die.

"As simple and certain as that, ladies and gentlemen."

Kennet Murray shifted in his chair, taking away the hand with which he had been shading his eyes.

"One moment, doctor. This was a long-planned crime, then?"

"No!" said Dr. Fell with great earnestness. "No, no, no! That's what I want to stress. It was brilliantly planned and executed in desperation on the spur of the moment two nights ago. It was as quickly flung out as the automaton was pushed downstairs.

"Let me explain. As she believed from the time she had first heard of the claimant (farther back, I suspect, than she would admit), she had nothing to fear *just yet*. Her husband would fight the claim; she must make him fight, and, ironically, fight for him. Far from wishing to see the hated one ousted, she must clasp him even more tightly than before. It was quite possible that he would win his claim, the law being what it is and the courts being very wary of claimants to an established estate. At all events the law's delays would give her breathing-space to think.

"What she did not know, what had been carefully concealed by the other side until two nights ago, was the existence of the fingerprints. Here was solid proof. Here was certainty. With that deadly fingerprint, the whole question could be settled in half an hour. Knowing her husband's mind, she knew he was coldly honest enough to admit the imposture as soon as it had been proved to him: as soon as he knew in his own soul that he was not John Farnleigh.

"When this hand-grenade exploded, she saw imminent peril. You recall Farnleigh's mood that night? If you have described it correctly to me, through every word he said and every move he made runs one strong and reckless flavour: 'Well, here's the test. If I survive it, well and good. If I don't, there is one compensation which almost reconciles me to everything else: I can speak out about the woman to whom I am married.'—Harrumph, yes. Have I interpreted the mood correctly?"

"Yes," admitted Page.

"So she took desperate measures. She must act at once. At once, at once! She must act before the fingerprint-comparison had been completed. She took these measures—just as yesterday, in the attic, she struck back at me before the words were out of my mouth—she acted magnificently; and she killed her husband."

Burrows, white-faced and sweating, had been vainly hammering on the table to call for order. Now there was a gleam of hope in his manner.

"There seems to be no way of stopping you," Burrows said. "If the police won't do it, I can't do more than protest. But now, I think, you are at a place where these glib theories won't do. I say nothing of the fact that you have no evidence. But until you can show how Sir John was murdered—alone, mind you, with nobody near him—until you can show that—" His words choked him; he only stuttered, and made a broad gesture. "And that, doctor, that you cannot show."

"Oh, yes, I can," said Dr. Fell.

"Our first real lead came at the inquest yesterday," he went on reflectively. "It's good that the testimony is in the records. After that we had only to pick up certain pieces of evidence which had been lying under our noses from the first. Behold a miracle dropped into our laps. We are given hanging evidence by word of mouth. We apply it. We arrange the bits in order. We hand them to the prosecuting counsel. And"—he made a gesture—"we draw the bolt of the gallows-trap."

"You got your evidence at the inquest?" repeated Murray, staring at him. "Evidence from whom?"

"From Knowles," said Dr. Fell.

A whimpering kind of cry came from the butler. He took a step forward, and put his hand up to his face. But he did not speak.

Dr. Fell contemplated him.

"Oh, I know," the doctor growled. "It's sour medicine. But there you are. It's an ironical turn of the screw. But there you are. Knowles, my lad, you love that woman. She's your petted child. And by your testimony at the inquest, in all innocence, in all desire to tell the truth, you have hanged her as surely as though you drew the bolt yourself."

Still he kept his eyes fixed on the butler.

"Now, I daresay," he continued comfortably, "that some people thought you lied. I knew you didn't lie. You said that Sir John Farnleigh had committed suicide. You clinched your story by saying—something you had remembered in your subconscious mind—that you saw him fling away the knife. You said you saw the knife in the air.

"I knew you weren't lying, because you had had exactly the same trouble with that point when you talked to Elliot and me the day before. You had hesitated. You had groped after an uncertain memory. When Elliot pressed you about it, you puzzled and shook. 'It would depend on the size of the knife,' you said. 'And there are bats in that garden. And sometimes you can't see a tennis-ball until it's—' The choice of words is significant. In other words: *at about the time of the crime you had seen something flying in the air.* What puzzled your subconscious mind was that you saw it just before the murder rather than just afterwards."

He spread out his hands.

"A very remarkable bat," said Burrows, with shrill sarcasm. "A still more remarkable tennis-ball."

"Something very like a tennis-ball," agreed Dr. Fell seriously, "though much smaller, of course. Very much smaller.

"We will return to that. Let's go on and consider the nature of the wounds. Already we have heard much astonished and feeling comment about those wounds. Mr. Murray here maintained that they were like the marks of fangs or claws; he maintained that the blood-stained clasp-knife found in the hedge could not have produced them. Even Patrick Gore, if you have correctly quoted him to me, made a very similar comment. And what did he say? 'I never saw anything like this since Barney Poole, the best animal-trainer west of the Mississippi, was killed by a leopard.'

"The claw-mark motif runs all through the case. We find it coming out with curious guardedness and in a strikingly suggestive way in Dr. King's medical evidence at the inquest. I have some notes here of his testimony. Harrumph! Hah! Let me see:

" 'There were three fairly shallow wounds,' says the physician." Here Dr. Fell looked very hard at his audience. " 'Three fairly shallow wounds, beginning at the left side of the throat and ending under the angle of the right jaw in a slightly upward direction. Two of the wounds crossed each other.' And presently this still more damning statement: 'There was much laceration of tissue.'

"Laceration of tissue, eh? Surely that is odd, gents, if the weapon were that exceedingly sharp (if notched) knife which Inspector Elliot is showing you now. Laceration of the throat suggests——

"Well, let's see. Let's return to the claw-mark motif and examine it. What are the characteristics of wounds made by claws, and how are they fulfilled in the death of Sir John Farnleigh? The characteristics of marks left by claws are these:

"1. They are shallow.

"2. They are made by sharp points which tear and scratch and lacerate rather than cut.

"3. They are not separate cuts, but are all made at the same time.

"Every one of these qualifications, we find, is fulfilled by the description of the wounds in Farnleigh's throat. I call your attention to the somewhat odd testimony given by Dr. King at the inquest. He does not tell a direct lie; but he is obviously working like blazes and talking wildly in order to make Farnleigh's death a suicide! Why? Observe—he too, like Knowles, has a petted child in Molly Farnleigh, the daughter of his oldest friend, who calls him 'Uncle Ned' and whose traits of character are probably known to him. But, unlike Knowles, he screens her; he does not send her out to have her neck cracked in two at the end of a rope."

Knowles put out his hands as though in supplication. His forehead was smeary with perspiration; but he still did not speak.

Dr. Fell went on.

"Mr. Murray suggested the basis of our case to us some time ago, when he spoke of something flying in the air and pertinently asked why the knife had not been dropped in the pool if it were really the weapon. But what have we got now? We've got something that flew at Farnleigh in the dusk, something smaller than a tennis-ball. We've got something equipped with claws or points which would make marks like claws——"

Nathaniel Burrows uttered a ghost of a chuckle.

"The episode of the flying claws," he jeered. "Really, doctor! And can you tell us what the flying claws were?"

"I'll do better than that," said Dr. Fell. "I'll show them to you. You saw them yesterday."

From his capacious side-pocket he took out something wrapped in a large red bandana handkerchief. Unfolding it so that the needle-sharp points should not catch in the handkerchief, he disclosed an object which Page recognized with a shock, even though it was a puzzled shock. It was one of the objects which Dr. Fell had unearthed from the wooden box put away in the book-closet. It was (to be precise) a small but heavy leaden ball into which at intervals had been set four very large hooks of the sort used to catch fighting deep-sea fish.

"Did you wonder at the purpose of this singular instrument?" asked the doctor amiably. "Did you wonder what earthly use it could be to anybody? But among the Middle-European gipsies—among the gipsies, I repeat—it has a very effective and dangerous use. Let me have Gross: will you, inspector?"

Elliot opened his briefcase and took out a large flat book in a grey jacket.

"Here," pursued Dr. Fell, juggling the book, "we have the most complete text-book on crime ever compiled.* I sent to town for it last night to verify a reference. You'll find a full description of this leaden ball on pages 249-50.

"It is used by the gipsies as a throwing weapon, and accounts for some of their mysterious and almost supernatural thefts. Into the other end of this

* *Criminal Investigation:* A Practical Textbook for Magistrates, Police Officers, and Lawyers, Adapted from the System der Kriminalistik of Dr. Hans Gross, Professor of Criminology in the University of Prague, by John Adam, M.A., Barrister-at-Law, and J. Collyer Adam, Barrister-at-Law; edited by Normal Kendal, Assistant Commissioner, Criminal Investigation Dept., Metropolitan Police. (London, Sweet & Maxwell, 1934.)

ball is fastened a long length of very light but very strong fishing-line. The ball is thrown; and, at whatever it is thrown, the hooks lightly catch no matter in what direction they fall—like a ship's anchor. The leaden ball lends the necessary weight for throwing, and the fishing-line draws it back with the booty. Hear Gross on the use of it:

" 'As regards the throwing, gipsies, especially the children, are remarkably skilful. Among all races children amuse themselves by throwing stones, but their particular object in doing so is to throw them as far as possible. Not so the young gipsy; he gathers together a heap of stones about the size of a nut and then chooses a target, such as a fairly large stone, a small plank, or an old cloth, at a distance of about ten to twenty paces; he then launches his stock of projectiles. . . . He keeps going for hours and soon acquires such skill at this exercise that he never misses anything larger than one's hand. When he reaches this stage he is given a throwing hook. . . .

" 'The young gipsy comes out of his apprenticeship when he is able to strike and carry off a piece of rag thrown upon the branches of a tree among which he has to cast his hook.'

"Into a tree, mind you! This is how, with amazing skill, he is able to carry off linen, clothes, and so on, through barred windows or in enclosed yards. But as a throwing weapon you can imagine its horrible effectiveness. It will tear the throat from a man, and back it goes——"

Murray uttered a kind of groan. Burrows did not speak.

"H'mf, yes. Now, we've heard of Molly Farnleigh's uncanny and amazing ability at throwing, a trick she learned among the gipsies. Miss Dane told us of it. We know of her deadly snap-judgments, and the suddenness with which she could strike.

"Where, then, was Molly Farnleigh at the time of the murder? I hardly need to tell you: she was on the balcony of her bedroom overlooking the pool. My eye, *directly* above the pool; and her bedroom, as we know, is built over the dining-room. Like Welkyn in the room below, she was much less than twenty feet away from the pool, and raised above it. Very high up? Not at all. As Knowles here—invaluable at giving us hints on how to hang her—as Knowles told us, the new wing of the house is 'a little low doll's house of a place,' the balcony hardly eight or nine feet above the garden.

"So there she is in the dusk, facing her husband below, and raised up high enough to give purchase to her arm. The room behind her is dark—as she admitted. Her maid was in the next room. What brought her to that deadly snap-decision? Did she whisper something to make her husband look up? Or was it because he was already looking at a star, with his long throat upturned?"

With an expression of growing horror in her eyes, Madeline repeated: "Looking at a star?"

"Your star, Miss Dane," said Dr. Fell sombrely. "I've talked a good deal with the various persons in this case; and I think it was your star."

Again memory returned to Page. He himself had thought of "Madeline's star" when he walked through the garden beside the pool on the night of the murder: the single eastern star to which she had given a poetic name, and which from the pool you could just see by craning your neck to look over the farther chimney-tops of the new wing . . .

"Yes, she hated you. Her husband's attentions to you had done that. It may have been the sight of him looking up, staring at your star and facing her blindly, that brought out murder in a flood. With the line in one hand and the leaden ball in the other, she lifted her arm and struck.

"Gents, I call your attention to the curious, the weird behaviour of that poor devil when something caught him. It has vaguely troubled everybody who has tried to describe it. The shufflings, the chokings, the jerkings of the body before he was yanked forward into the pool—what has it reminded you of? Ah! Got it, have you? Shows clearly, does it? Of a hooked fish on a line; and that is what it was. The hooks did not penetrate deeply: she saw to that. There was a good deal of mauling, on which everybody commented. The direction of the wounds, obviously, was from left to right, running upwards, as he was pulled off balance; and he went into the pool (you recall?) with his head slightly towards the new wing. When he was in the pool she jerked back the weapon."

With a heavy grimness of expression Dr. Fell held up the leaden ball.

"And this little beauty?

"Obviously, of course, it left no blood-trail or any traces when it was pulled back. It had landed in the pool and had been washed clean. You recall that the water in the pool had been so agitated (naturally, by his strugglings) that it was slopped over the sand for some feet round. But the ball did leave one trace—it rustled in the shrubbery.

"Reflect. Who was the only person who heard that curious rustling? Welkyn, in the dining-room below: the only person who was near enough to hear it. That rustling was an intriguing point. Clearly it had not been made by any *person*. If you will try the experiment of attempting to slip through yew hedges as thick as a wide screen (as Sergeant Burton noticed when he later found the knife 'planted' there, with the dead man's fingerprints conveniently on it), you will realize what I mean.

"I spare you details. But that, in essence, is how she planned and carried out one of the wickedest murders in my experience. It was all flash and hate; and it succeeded. She fished for men as she has always done; and she caught her victim. She won't get away, naturally. She will be nabbed by the first policeman she passes. Then she will hang. And all, happily for the cause of justice, because of Knowles's happy inspiration in telling us about the flight of a tennis-ball at dusk."

Knowles made a slight waggling gesture of his hand as though he were trying to stop a bus. His face was like oiled paper, and Page was afraid he was going to faint. But still he could not speak.

Burrows, with his eyes gleaming, seemed inspired.

"It's ingenious," Burrows said. "It's clever. But it's a lie, and I'll beat you in court with it. It's all false and you know it. For other people have sworn things too. There's Welkyn! You can't explain away what *he* said! Welkyn saw somebody in the garden! He said he did! And what have you got to say to that?"

Page noted with alarm that Dr. Fell himself was looking somewhat pale. Very slowly Dr. Fell pushed himself to his feet. He stood towering over them, and he made a gesture towards the door.

"There's Mr. Welkyn now," he replied. "Standing just behind you. Ask him. Ask him if he's now so sure of what he saw in the garden."

They all looked round. How long Welkyn had been standing in the doorway they could not tell. Immaculate, brushed as ever, the overgrown cherubic countenance was uneasy, and Welkyn pulled at his lower lip.

"Er—" he said, clearing at his throat.

"Well, speak up!" thundered Dr. Fell. "You've heard my say. Now tell us: ARE you sure you saw something looking at you? ARE you sure there was anything there to see?"

"I have been reflecting," said Welkyn.

"Yes?"

"I—er—gentlemen." He paused. "I wish you would cast your minds back to yesterday. You all went up to the attic, and I am given to understand that you investigated certain curious articles you found there. Unhappily I did not go along with you. I did not see any of those articles until today, when Dr. Fell called them to my attention. I—er—refer to the black Janus-faced mask which you seem to have found in a wooden box there." Again he cleared his throat.

"This is a plot," said Burrows, looking rapidly right and left like a man hesitating before wild traffic in a road. "You can't get away with this. It's all a deliberate conspiracy, and you're all in it—"

"Kindly allow me to finish, sir," retorted Welkyn with asperity. "I said I saw a face looking at me through the lower panel of the glass door. I know what it was now. It was that Janus mask. I recognized it as soon as I saw it. It occurs to me, as Dr. Fell suggests, that the unhappy Lady Farnleigh—in order to prove to me the presence of someone actually in the garden—merely let down that mask on another length of fishing-line; and unfortunately sent it too low against the window, so that . . ."

Then Knowles spoke at last.

He came up to the table and put his hands on it. He was crying; and for a moment the tears would not let him speak coherently. When the words did come out, they shocked his listeners as though a piece of furniture had spoken.

"It's a bloody *lie*," said Knowles.

Old and muddled and pitiful, he began to beat with his hand on the table.

"It's like Mr. Burrows said. It's all lies and lies and lies and lies. You're all in it." His voice grew frantic, rising to a quaver, and his hand beat frantically on the table. "You're all against her, that's what you are. You none of you will give her a chance. What if she did carry on a bit? What if she did read them books and maybe carry on with a lad or two? What difference is it, much, from the games they used to play when they were kids? They're all kids. She didn't mean any harm. She never meant any harm. And you shan't hang her. By Christ, you shan't. I'll see nobody harms my little lady, that's what I'll do."

His voice grew to a scream through the tears, and he waggled his finger at them.

"I'll fool you, with all your grand ideas and your grand guesses. She didn't kill that crazy silly beggar that came here pretending to be Master Johnny. Master Johnny my foot! That beggar a Farnleigh? *That* beggar? He got just exactly what he deserved, and I'm sorry he can't be killed all over again. Came out of a pig-sty, that's where he came from. But I don't care about him. I tell you you're not going to hurt my little lady. She never killed him; she never did; and I can prove it."

In the vast silence they heard the tap of Dr. Fell's stick on the floor, and the wheezing of his breath, as he walked over to Knowles and put his hand on Knowles's shoulder.

"I know she didn't," he said gently.

Knowles stared at him with blurred frenzy.

"Do you mean," shouted Burrows, "that you've been sitting here telling us a pack of fairy-tales just because——"

"And do you think I like what I'm doing?" asked Dr. Fell. "Do you think I like one word I've said or one move I've had to make? Everything I told you about the woman and her private witch-cult and her relations with Farnleigh was true. Everything. She inspired the murderer and directed the murder. The only difference is that she did not kill her husband. She did not make the automaton work and she was not the person in the garden. But"—his hand tightened on Knowles's shoulder—"you know the law. You know how it moves and how it crushes. I've set it in motion. And Lady Farnleigh will hang higher than Haman unless you tell us the truth. Do you know who committed the murder?"

"Of course I know it," snarled Knowles. "Yah!"

"And who was the murderer?"

"That's an easy one," said Knowles. "And that silly beggar got everything that was coming to him. The murderer was——"

# IV

## THE FALL OF A HINGE

There was one thing which Flambeau, with all his dexterity of disguise, could not cover, and that was his singular height. If Valentin's quick eye had caught a tall apple-woman, a tall grenadier, or even a tolerably tall duchess, he might have arrested them on the spot. But all along his train there was nobody who could be a disguised Flambeau, any more than a cat could be a disguised giraffe.

—G. K. Chesterton, *The Blue Cross*

### Chapter XXI

*Being a letter from Patrick Gore (born John Farnleigh) to Dr. Gideon Fell.*

Outward bound,

At a certain date.

My dear doctor:

Yes, I am the culprit. I alone killed that impostor, and produced all the manifestations which seem to have alarmed you.

I write you this letter for a number of reasons. First: I retain (however foolishly) a genuine liking and respect for you. Second: You have never done anything better. The way in which you forced me step by step through every room, through every door, and out of the house into flight, rouses my admiration to such an extent that I should like to see whether I have correctly followed your deductions. I pay you the compliment of saying that you are the only person who has ever outwitted me; but then I have never been at my best against schoolmasters. Third: I believe I have found the one really perfect disguise, and, now that it is no longer of use to me, I should rather like to brag about it.

I shall expect an answer to this letter. By the time you receive it, I and my adored Molly will be in a country which has no extradition-treaty with Great Britain. It is rather a hot country, but then both Molly and I are fond of hot countries. I will drop you a line as to the address when we are settled in our new home.

One request I should like to make. In the *débâcle* of horrified talk which will follow our flight, I shall doubtless be presented by newspapers, judges, and other distorters of the public eyesight as a Fiend, a Monster, a Werewolf, and so on. Now, you are quite well aware that I am nothing of the sort. I have no liking for murder; and if I cannot feel any repentance over the death of that swine it is, I hope, because I am not a hypocrite. Certain people are constituted in certain ways, like Molly and myself. If we prefer to make the world a more exciting place with our studies and our day-dreams, I should think it would be an inspiration to Suburbia and a hint towards better things. When, therefore, you hear someone indulging in maudlin speech about the Fiend and his Witch-bride, kindly inform the person that you have had tea with both of us, and perceived no sign of horns or stigmata.

But now I must tell you my secret, which is also the secret of the case you have been so earnestly investigating. It is a very simple secret, and can be expressed in four words:

I have no legs.

I have no legs. Both of them were amputated in April, 1912, after being crushed by that swine in a little affair aboard the *Titanic*, which I shall describe in a moment. The admirable sets of artificial legs I have since worn have not altogether, I fear, disguised this disability. I saw that you noticed my walk—which is not exactly a limp, but is always clumsy and sometimes awkward enough to betray me if I attempt to move rapidly. I cannot, in fact, move rapidly; and with this also I shall deal in a moment.

Have you ever thought of the remarkable opportunity presented by artificial legs for the purposes of disguise? We have had mummeries of wig and beard and grease-paint; we have had faces altered with clay and figures with padding; we have had the subtlest turns to the subtlest illusion. But, astonishing to state, we have never had the eyes deceived in the simplest way, and there has always been the statement, "This and that a man can do, but there is one thing he cannot disguise: his height." I beg leave to state that I can make my height anything I please, and that I have been doing so for quite a number of years.

I am not a tall man. That is, to be strictly accurate, I believe that I should not be a tall man had I any means of estimating what my height would have been. Let us say that, without the interference of my small friend on the *Titanic*, I should have been about five feet five inches tall. The removal of underpinning (observe my delicacy) leaves my actual body less than three feet high. Should you doubt this, measure your own height against a wall and observe the proportion taken up by these mysterious appendages we call legs.

With several sets of limbs made to order—this was first done in the circus —and a good deal of painful practice in the harness, I can make my height what I choose. It is interesting to discover how easily the eye is deceived. Imagine, for example, a small and slender friend of yours appearing before you as a six-footer; your brain would refuse to take it in, and the smallest dexterity in other branches of disguise would render him completely unrecognizable.

I have been several heights. I have been six-feet-one. And again, in my famous role as "Ahriman," the fortune-teller, I was almost a dwarf: with such success as completely to deceive the good Mr. Harold Welkyn, when I later appeared before him as Patrick Gore.

Perhaps it would be best to start with the business aboard the *Titanic*. Now, when I returned to claim my inheritance the other day, the story I told to the assembled gapers in the library was true—with one slight distortion and one notable omission.

We changed identities, as I said. The gentle-hearted lad did in reality try to kill me, as I said. But he attempted to do it by strangling, since he was at that time the stronger. This little tragic-comedy was played among the pillars of high tragedy; and you have guessed its background. Its background was one of the great white-painted steel doors, bulkhead doors, which shut a liner into compartments and can swing several hundredweight of ponderous metal against the creeping water. The crumpling and dissolving of its hinges as the ship lurched was, I think, as terrifying a spectacle as I have ever seen; it was like the breaking of all ordered things or the fall of the gates of Gath.

My friend's purpose was of no great complexity. After squeezing my windpipe until I was unconscious, he meant to shut me into the flooding compartment and make his escape. I fought back with anything within reach—in this case, a wooden mallet hanging beside the door. How many times I hit him I cannot remember, but the snake-dancer's son did not even seem to mind it. I was able to dodge, unfortunately for myself, to the outer side of the door; the snake-dancer's son threw himself against it, and, with the settling of the ship, the hinges gave. All of me, I need scarcely say, got out of the way of it except my legs.

It was a time of heroisms, doctor: heroisms never set to music or told afterwards except stammeringly. Who rescued me—whether it was a passenger or one of the crew—I do not know. I recall being picked up like a puppy and carried out to a boat. The snake-dancer's son, with his blood-stained head and wandering eye, I thought had been left behind to die. That I did not die myself I suppose I must attribute to the salt-water, but it was not a pleasant time for me and I remember nothing of what happened until a week later.

In my story to the group at Farnleigh Close some nights ago, I told of my reception as "Patrick Gore" by old Boris Yeldritch, since dead, the proprietor of the circus. I explained something of my state of mind. If I did not explain my entire state of mind, you know the reason. Boris easily found a use for me with the circus, since I was (not to put too fine a point on it) a freak with a knack for telling fortunes gained from my studies back home. It was a painful and humiliating time, especially in learning to "walk" by using my hands. I do not dwell on this part of it, for I would not have you think I am asking for pity or sympathy: the notion angers me furiously. I feel like the man in the play. Your liking I will have if I can. Your respect I will have or kill you. But your pity? Damn your impudence!

It occurs to me, too, that I have been posturing like a tragedian over something which, after all, I had almost forgotten. Let us take matters more amiably and be amused at what we cannot correct. You know my profession: I have been a fortune-teller, a bogus spiritualist and occultist, and an illusionist. I somewhat imprudently hinted at this when I came to Farnleigh Close the other night. Yet I have been so many different persons, and served under so many different aliases as He Who Knows All, that I did not greatly fear detection.

I cheerfully assure you that the absence of legs has been, in fact, a boon to me in my business. I would not have it otherwise. But the artificial ones always hampered me; and I fear I have never learned to manage them properly. I early learned to move myself about by the use of my hands: with, I venture to think, incredible speed and agility. I need hardly tell you in how many ways this was useful to me in my business as a fraudulent spiritist medium, and what remarkable effects I was able to produce for my sitters. Reflect on it a while; you will understand.

Whenever I am up to such tricks, I am in the habit of wearing under my artificial limbs and ordinary trousers close-fitting breeches equipped with leather pads, which serve as my limbs and leave no traces on any sort of ground. Since speed in change has often been of the utmost necessity, I have learned to remove or put back my artificial harness in exactly thirty-five seconds.

And this, of course, is the painfully simple secret of how I worked the automaton.

A word concerning it, since history has repeated itself. It not only could have happened before; it did happen before. Are you aware, doctor, that this was how the automaton chess-player of Kempelen and Maelzel was run?* With the simple assistance of a man like myself inside the box on which the figure sat, they baffled Europe and America for fifty years. When the hoax deceived men of such different temperaments as Napoleon Bonaparte and Phineas Barnum, you need not feel cast down if it deceived you. But it did not, in fact, deceive you; and this you gave me clearly to understand by your hints in the attic.

* Mr. Gore is telling the truth. I first came across this explanation in an old edition of the *Encyclopaedia Britannica* (ninth edition, published in 1883). The writer, J. A. Clarke, says: "The first player was a Polish patriot, Worousky, who had lost both legs in a campaign; as he was furnished with artificial limbs when in public, his appearance, together with the fact that no dwarf or child travelled in Kempelen's company, dispelled the suspicion that any person could be employed inside the machine. This automaton, which made more than one tour to the capitals and courts of Europe, was owned for a short time by Napoleon I, was exhibited by Maelzel after the death of Kempelen in 1819, and ultimately perished in a fire at Philadelphia in 1854."—Vol. XV, p. 210.

I have no doubt that this was the original secret of the Golden Hag in the seventeenth century. Do you see now why the automaton fell into such disrepute when my respected ancestor Thomas Farnleigh, after buying it for a whacking price, learned the truth? He had been told the inner mystery; and, like many others who have learned inner mysteries, he was furious. He thought to get a miracle. Instead he paid for an ingenious trick with which he could not hoax his friends unless he kept a special kind of operator on the premises.

This is how the whole effect was originally managed: The space inside is big enough, as you have observed, for a person like myself. Once you are inside the box or "couch," and the door closed, the shutting of the door opens a small panel in the top of the box communicating with the works of the figure. Here—worked by simple mechanical weights—are a dozen rods communicating with the hands and body. Concealed holes by the knees of the automaton, which can be opened from inside, allow the operator to see. That was how Maelzel's dummy played chess; and how the Golden Hag played the cittern over a hundred years before.

But, in the case of the hag, one of the best features of the illusion was the device by which the operator was conveyed inside the box unseen. There, I think, is where the inventor of the hag outdid Kempelen. At the beginning of the performance the magician in charge opened the box and let everybody inspect the inside to show that it was empty. How, then, was the operator spirited in?

I don't need to tell *you*. By your remarks in the attic the day after the murder—carefully aimed at me—about the costume worn by the exhibitor, you demonstrated that you knew; and I knew that my goose was done to a cinder.

The traditional wizard's costume, as everybody knows, consists of a huge flowing robe covered with hieroglyphics. And the original inventor merely applied a principle later used by the somewhat clumsy Indian fakirs. That is, the robe was used to cover something: in the case of the fakir, a child who climbs into a basket unseen; in the case of the exhibitor of the hag, the operator who slid into the machine while the magician in his great robe fussed with it at the dimming of the lights. I have made use of the trick successfully in many of my own entertainments.

To which history of my life I must return.

My most successful rôle was in London as "Ahriman," if you can forgive the name of a Zoroastrian devil as applied to an Egyptian. Poor Welkyn, whom you must not suspect of any part in my dirty work, does not know to this day that I was the bearded dwarf of whom he took such good care. He defended me nobly in that libel suit; he believed in my psychic powers; and, when I reappeared as the missing heir, I thought it only fair to make him my legal representative.

(Magister, that libel suit still tickles my fancy. I hoped fervently that I should be able to give some demonstration of my psychic powers in court. You see, my father had been at school with the judge; and I was prepared to go into a trance in the witness-box and tell his Lordship some realistic things about himself. My father, indeed, had been well-known socially in London during the nineties: which fact is less a tribute to Ahriman's awesome insight into his sitters' hearts than to the power of information on which he had to draw. But a weakness for spectacular effect has always been one of my characteristics.)

It is as Ahriman, then, that my story properly begins.

I had no notion that "John Farnleigh" was supposed to be alive, much less that he was now Sir John Farnleigh, baronet—until he walked one day into my consulting-room in Half-Moon Street, and told me his troubles. That I did not laugh in the man's face I simply state as a fact. Monte Cristo himself never dreamed of such a situation. But I think, I say I *think*, that in applying balm to his fevered mind I contrived to give him some unpleasant days and nights.

However, the matter of importance is less that I met him than that I met Molly.

On this subject my views are too fervent to be fashioned into smooth prose. Don't you see that we are two of a kind? Don't you see that, once having found each other, Molly and I would have come together from the ends of the earth? It was a love-affair sudden, complete, and blinding; there was burning pitch in it; it was, in the terms of an American pastime called Red Dog, "high, low, jack, and the goddam game." I must laugh at this, or I shall find myself fashioning incoherence into poetry and curses into endearments. She did not think (when she learned) my crippled body either funny or repulsive. I had not, before her, to sing the refrain of Quasimodo or He Who Gets Slapped. Do not, I urge you, make light of love-affairs whose inspiration is infernal rather than of celestial gentleness. Pluto was as true a lover as the lord of Olympus, and helped to fertilize the earth; whereas Jove, poor wretch, could go about only as a swan or a shower of gold; and I thank you for your kind attention on this subject.

Molly and I planned the whole thing, of course. (Didn't it strike you that in our thrust-and-parry at the Close we were just a little too much at each other's throats? That she was a little too quick with flat insults and I with elaborate barbs?)

The ironical part was that I was the real heir, yet there was nothing we could do about it except what we did. The swine back there had found out about what you call her private witch-cult; he was using it against her as pure, sharp-clawed blackmail to cling to his place; and if he were dislodged he would dislodge her. If I were to regain the estate—as I was resolved to do— and if I were to regain her for my lawful wife so that we could live without

furtiveness in our mutual interests—as I was also resolved to do—I had to
kill him and make it look like suicide.

There you have it. Molly could not bring herself to murder: whereas I,
with the proper concentration, can bring myself to anything. I say no word
of the fact that I owed him something, and when I saw what he had grown
into after his pious beginnings I knew what makes Puritans and why they
have been wiped from the earth.

The crime was timed to take place at some time on the night it did: I
could not lay my plans any more closely than that. It could not take place
before then, because I must not *appear* at the Close or risk showing myself
prematurely; and the fellow could hardly be expected to commit suicide
until he knew the weight of evidence against him. You know the admirable
opportunity afforded me when he walked into that garden during the comparison of the fingerprints.

Now, my friend, a word of congratulation to you. You took an impossible
crime; and, in order to make Knowles confess, you spun out of sticks and
stones and rags and bones a perfectly logical and reasonable explanation of
the impossible. Artistically I am glad you did so; your hearers would have
felt cheated and outraged without it.

Yet the fact is—as you very well know—that there never was an impossible
crime.

I simply went up to the fellow; I pulled him down; I killed him by the
pool with the clasp-knife you later found in the hedge; and that is all.

Knowles, by either bad or good luck, saw the whole affair from the window
of the Green Room. Even then, had I not bungled the whole affair with
my one great error, the scheme would have been doubly secure. Knowles
not only swore to the world that it was suicide: he went out of his way to
give me a gratuitous alibi which astonished me not a little. For he, as you
have observed, always disliked and distrusted the late incumbent; he never
really believed the man was a Farnleigh; and he would have gone to the
gallows rather than admit that the real John Farnleigh had killed the fraudulent one who had stolen his patrimony.

I killed the fellow, of course, minus my artificial legs. That was only common sense, since I can move with rapidity and ease only on my leather pads;
and in the artificial legs I could not have bent down so as not to be seen by
anybody behind those waist-high hedges. The hedges afforded an admirable
screen, as well as innumerable alleys of escape in case of danger. In the event
that anybody should see me, I took along under my coat the sinister-looking
Janus-mask from the attic.

I came on him, actually, from the north side of the house: that is, from the
direction of the new wing. I must, I think, have been a sufficiently unnerving
sight. It so paralyzed our impostor that I pulled him down before he could

move or speak. The strength developed in my arms and shoulders through these years, doctor, is not negligible.

Afterwards, regarding this part of it—the attack on him—the testimony of Nathaniel Burrows gave me a few uneasy moments. Burrows was standing at the garden door some thirty-odd feet away; and, as he himself admits, his eyesight is not good in semi-darkness. He saw unusual occurrences which he could not explain even in his own mind. He could not see me, since waist-high hedges intervened; yet the victim's behaviour worried him. Read over his testimony again and you will see what I mean. He concludes: "I cannot give an exact description of the movements he made. It was as though something had got hold of his feet."

And something had.

Nevertheless, this danger was negligible compared to what Welkyn almost saw from the dining-room a few seconds after the killing. Doubtless it has been apparent to you that what Welkyn saw, through one of the lower glass panels of the French window, was your obedient servant. It was foolhardy of me to let anyone get so much as a fleeting glimpse of me, but at that time (as you shall see) I was upset over the ruin of my plan; and, fortunately, I had my mask on.

His actual glimpse of me was not so dangerous as the interpretation of a shade of words—an impression—put on this incident when it came to be discussed next day. Here my old tutor Murray, that eternal trafficker in words, was the offender. In Welkyn's description of the incident Murray caught an echo of what Welkyn was (gropingly and uncertainly) trying to convey. And Murray said to me: "On your homecoming you are greeted by a crawling *legless* something in the garden——"

That was disaster fine and full. It was the one thing which nobody must suspect, the one suggestion which must not be implanted. I felt my face contract, and I know that I lost colour like a spilled jug, and I saw you looking at me. I was foolish enough to flare out at poor old Murray and call him names for a reason which must have been inexplicable to everybody but you.

All the same, I feared that by this time I was finished in any case. I have referred to the colossal blunder I made at the outset, which ruined the case I was attempting to build up. It was this:

I used the wrong knife.

What I had intended to use was a common clasp-knife I had bought for the purpose. (I took this one out of my pocket and showed it to you next day, pretending it was my own knife.) I then intended to press his hand on it and leave it by the pool, completing the picture of suicide.

What I actually found in my hand, when it was too late to draw back, was my own clasp-knife—the knife I have owned since I was a boy—the knife a thousand people have seen in my hand in America, with Madeline Dane's name cut into the blade. You remember that your most diligent efforts could not trace that knife to the impostor. But you would have traced it to me fast enough.

It was all the worse because, on the very night of the murder, I had gone so far as to mention this same knife to the group in the library. In telling my story of the affair aboard the *Titanic*, I told how I had met the real Patrick Gore, how we had fought at sight, and how I had been with difficulty prevented from going for him with my clasp-knife. A surer indication of character and weapon it would be difficult to beat. It came of trying to make too artistic a lie, and of telling all the truth except the part you mean to suppress. I warn you against the practice.

So here was I, with the infernal thing in my gloved hand by the pool, after pressing his fingerprints on it; and people running towards me. I was compelled to make a snap-decision. I dared not leave the knife. So I wrapped it in my handkerchief and put it into my pocket.

Welkyn saw me when I went to regain my harness at the north side of the house. I therefore thought it best to say I had been at the south side. I didn't dare carry the knife about with me, so I had to hide it until I could find an opportunity to get it away undetected. And I maintain that, theoretically, I chose an undetectable hiding-place. Your Sergeant Burton acknowledges that except for one chance in a million he would never have found the knife in the hedge without systematically rooting up every foot of hedge in the whole garden.

Were the Parcae, do you say, giving me some particularly nasty breaks? Oh, I don't know. It is true that I was obliged to alter my whole plan at the outset and express a belief in murder. Yet Knowles, with noble instincts of sacrifice, straightway provided me with an alibi; he conveyed a hint before I had left the house that night; and I was ready for you next day.

The rest of it is simply indicated. Molly insisted on trying to make our case better by stealing the Thumbograph, once I had privately made it clear that this must be murder: for, you observe, *I* could not be accused of stealing a Thumbograph with evidence of my own identity. We were going to return it anyway, and with double quickness when it was discovered to be a dummy.

Molly acted well all the way through, don't you think? That little scene in the garden just after the discovery of the body ("Damn him for being right!") had been carefully rehearsed beforehand. Interpreted, it was meant to convey that I had been right when I said before all the company she had never been really in love with her husband (another rehearsed scene), and that she had always been in love with an image of me. We could not have the widow *too* inconsolable, you know. We could not have her so prostrated with grief that she might be expected to retain an enmity towards me forever. It was a far-sighted plan, directed towards bringing us together when animosities had been smoothed down in the future—and yet how we wrecked it!

For there was that final unfortunate business next day, when Betty Harbottle caught me tinkering with the automaton in the attic. I must mutter *mea culpa* again. As a matter of strict fact, I had gone up to the attic to get the Thumbograph. But it suddenly occurred to me, when I saw the hag, that I could bring her to life at last. As a boy I knew her secret; but at that time I had not been small enough to get inside the box. So nothing would do but that I must tinker about with it, like a respectable husband with a respectable clock in a respectable attic.

Molly, finding me gone an unconscionable time, came upstairs. She was just in time to find Betty Harbottle investigating the book-closet. And at this time I was actually inside the automaton.

Molly, I honestly believe, thought that I would deal with the little girl as I had dealt with another person. Molly saw that Betty was inside and locked the door. But I had no wish to hurt her. The girl could not, of course, see me: yet I was most badly afraid she would see my harness, propped into the corner behind the machine. I think you know what happened. Fortunately it was not necessary to hurt her; a few movements sufficed; though I could have sworn she saw my eyes through the peep-holes in the automaton. Afterwards Molly and I were in no vast danger. Had you pressed us too hard as to our whereabouts at the time, we should simply have provided each other with a reluctant and grudging alibi. Still, it was a mistake to forget that girl's apron—the hag's claws tore it off as part of the pantomime—and leave it behind when we cleared out.

Well, I had been foolish; and there you are. I saw as soon as the day after the murder that I was, in the simple phrase, for it. You found the knife. Though I made light of it as one the impostor had taken from me years ago, and though Murray assisted me with some unconsciously helpful suggestions designed to make you suspicious of the knife as a real weapon, I was following you and I knew that you had seen through the absence of legs.

You brought up the subject of Ahriman the Egyptian. Inspector Elliot followed with his questioning of Welkyn about the hopping thing in the garden. You returned with some pressing questions on the subject of witchcraft, and neatly brought Molly into it. I questioned in reply; and you conveyed some suggestive hints. Next you stressed the connection between all these points, beginning with Victoria Daly, passing to the late Patrick Gore's behaviour on the night of his murder, and going on to trace Betty Harbottle to the book-closet in the attic.

Your remarks when you saw the automaton were the penultimate giveaway. You intimated that the murderer had been doing something here with the automaton which would betray him; and yet at the same time Betty Harbottle had not seen him at all—in the sense that it was not necessary for the murderer to silence her. I then challenged you to show how the automaton worked. You paid little attention, merely remarking that you supposed the original exhibitor wore the traditional magician's costume. And you concluded with a few words designed to show Molly's private witch-cult was about to be discovered if it had not already been discovered. That was when I pushed the automaton downstairs. Believe me, my friend, I had no thought of damage to your person. But I did definitely want to damage the automaton beyond repair, so that one guess as to how it worked would be as good as another.

The inquest showed two more points next day. Knowles was obviously lying, and you knew it. Madeline Dane knew much more about Molly's doings than we could afford.

I am afraid Molly does not like Madeline. Her scheme was to ensure silence on the latter's part by terrorization, followed by real trouble if it became necessary. Hence Molly's not altogether inspired device of the faked telephone-call purporting to come from Madeline, and asking for the automaton at Monplaisir: she knew Madeline's rooted horror of the machine, and made me promise to bring it to life again for Madeline's edification. I did not do that; I had better fish to fry.

Fortunately for Molly and myself, I was in the garden at Monplaisir when you and the inspector had dinner there with Madeline and Page. I overheard your conversation; and I knew that it was all over as regards your knowing everything—the question was what you could prove. When you and the inspector left the house, I thought it much more profitable to follow you through the wood and listen.

After contenting myself merely with pushing out the harmless old hag by the windows, I went after you. Your conversation, properly interpreted, showed me that what I had feared about your manner of proceeding was correct. I now know fully what you did, though I had more than a glimmer then. I knew your objective: Knowles. I knew my weak link: Knowles. I knew where there was a witness who could hang me: Knowles. I knew that he would be tortured rather than admit under mere ordinary pressure who had committed the crime. But there was one person he could not see touched or even breathed upon: Molly. There was only one way to make him speak. That was to make a garrotte for her neck and tighten the screw by degrees until he could not stand the sight of it any longer. That was what you were going to do; I was intelligent enough to read evidence as well as you; and it occurred to me with some realism that we were done for.

Only one thing was left to us, which was to get away. Had I been the bowelless and altogether unbelievable person you will probably hear described, I should without doubt have decided to kill Knowles as casually as paring an onion. But who could kill Knowles? Who could kill Madeline Dane? Who could kill Betty Harbottle? These are real persons I have known, ot dummies to pad out a chapter; and they are not to be treated like stuffed ats at a fair. I was tired and a little ill, to tell you the truth, as though I ad got into a maze and could not get out again.

Following you and the inspector, I came to the Close and saw Molly. I old her our only course was to get away. Remember, we believed we had mple time; you and the inspector had intended to go to London that night, nd we did not fear disclosure for some hours. Molly agreed it was the only hing to do—I am given to understand that you saw her leaving the Close, vith a suitcase in her hand, when you looked down from the windows of he Green Room. I think it was unwise, though, deliberately to let us get way so that we should damn ourselves by quick flight. Such a course is vise, doctor, only if you are certain of nailing the quarry when you want im.

In one respect, to conclude this account, I had difficulty with Molly. She lid not find it easy to go without a final word to Madeline. When we were lriving away in the car she was filled with fantastic notions (I can say this because the lady knows I love her) for getting back at the "cat" at Monplaisir.

I could not prevent her. We arrived there within a very few minutes, eaving the car in a back lane by Colonel Mardale's old house. We arrived, n short—and stopped to listen. For we were being treated to a very lucid iccount, heard through the half-open window of the dining-room, of the leath of Victoria Daly and the probable character of the witch-mistress responsible for it: it was being delivered by Mr. Page. The automaton was till there; and I pushed it back into the coal-house only because Molly vanted to smash it through the windows at Madeline. Such behaviour is childish, no doubt; yet my lady's quarrel with Madeline is of a personal iature—as mine was with the late Patrick Gore; and I tell you that nothing vhich had occurred so far in the case infuriated her as much as that talk n the dining-room.

I did not know, at the time, that she had brought a pistol with her from Farnleigh Close. I realized this only when she took it out of her handbag ind rapped it against the window. Whereupon I realized, doctor, that immediate action was necessary for two reasons: first, that we wanted no vomen's flaming row at this moment; and, second, that a car (Burrows's) iad just stopped at the front of the house. I put Molly under one of my irms and I urged her away with some haste. Fortunately a wireless was going nside and we escaped detection. It was, I am convinced, only a subsequent ove-scene of outstanding incoherence—a scene taking place in the window— vhich caused her to escape my vigilance and fire into the dining-room as ve were about to leave. My lady is a good shot and she had no intention vhatever of hitting anyone; she wishes me to say that she meant it merely is a comment on poor Madeline's morals, and that she would jolly well do t again.

I stress these unimportant and even ludicrous goings-on, in conclusion, fo
one very good reason: the reason with which I began. I do not want you to
think that we went away in an atmosphere of high tragedy under the darl
mutterings of the gods. I do not want you to think that nature held it
breath at the evil of our passing. For I think, doctor—I rather think—tha
in order to make Knowles confess you must have deliberately painted Molly'
character as much more stiff with wicked impulse than it really is.

She is not crafty; she is the reverse of crafty. Her private witch-cult wa
not the coldly intellectual effort of a woman interested in watching mind
writhe; she is the reverse of coldly intellectual, and well you know it. She
did what she did because she liked it. She will, I trust, continue to like it
To speak of her as though she killed Victoria Daly is nonsense; and anythin
concerning the woman near Tunbridge Wells is so cloudy as to be beyonc
proof or even accusation. That she has much of the Lower Plane in he
nature I concede, as I have in mine; but what else? Our departure from
Kent and from England was not, as I have tried to indicate, a curtain to ɑ
Morality Play. It was very much like the jumbled rush of the ordinary famil
to the seaside, where father cannot remember what he did with the ticket
and mother is certain she left the light burning in the bathroom. A simila
haste and overset, I suspect, attended the departure of Mr. and Mrs. Adam
from a more spacious garden; and this, the king may say without denia
from Alice, is the oldest rule in the book.

> Yours sincerely,
> John Farnleigh (whilom Patrick Gore)

THE END.

# THE CASE OF THE
# CONSTANT SUICIDES

# I

THE 9:15 train for Glasgow pulled out of Euston half an hour late that night, and forty minutes after the sirens had sounded.

When the sirens went, even the dim blue lights along the platform were extinguished.

A milling, jostling, swearing crowd, mainly in khaki, groped about the platform, its shins and knuckles barked by kit and luggage, its hearing deadened by the iron coughing of engines. Lost in it was a youngish professor of history, who was trying to find his sleeping compartment on the Glasgow train.

Not that anyone had cause for apprehension. It was only the first of September, and the heavy raiding of London had not yet begun. We were very young in those days. An air-raid alert meant merely inconvenience, with perhaps one lone raider droning somewhere, and no barrage.

But the professor of history, Alan Campbell (M.A., Oxon.; Ph.D., Harvard) bumped along with unacademic profanity. The first-class sleepers appeared to be at the head of a long train. He could see a porter, with much luggage, striking matches at the open door of a carriage, where names were posted on a board opposite the numbers of the compartments assigned to them.

Striking a match in his turn, Alan Campbell discovered that the train appeared to be full and that his own compartment was number four.

He climbed in. Dim little lighted numerals over each door in the corridor showed him the way. When he opened the door of his compartment, he felt distinctly better.

This, he thought, was really first-rate in the way of comfort. The compartment was a tiny metal room, green-painted, with a single berth, nickel washbasin, and a long mirror on the door communicating with the next compartment. Its blackout consisted of a sliding shutter which sealed the window. Though it was intensely hot and close, he saw over the berth a metal ventilator which you could twist to let in air.

Pushing his suitcase under the berth, Alan sat down to get his breath. His reading matter, a Penguin novel and a copy of the *Sunday Watchman,* lay beside him. He eyed the newspaper, and his soul grew dark with bile.

"May he perish in the everlasting bonfire!" Alan said aloud, referring to his only enemy in this world. "May he——"

Then he checked himself, remembering that he ought to remain in a good temper. After all, he had a week's leave; and, though no doubt his mission was sad enough in a formal way, still it was in the nature of a holiday.

Alan Campbell was a Scot who had never in his life set foot in Scotland.

341

For that matter, except for his years at the American Cambridge and a fe visits to the Continent, he had never been out of England. He was thirty-fiv bookish, serious-minded though not without humor, well-enough looking b perhaps already inclined toward stodginess.

His notions of Scotland were drawn from the novels of Sir Walter Sco or, if he felt in a frivolous mood, John Buchan. Added to this was a vagu idea of granite and heather and Scottish jokes—which last he rather resente showing himself no true Scot in spirit. Now he was at last going to see f himself. And if only——

The sleeping-car attendant knocked at the door, and put his head in.

"Mr. Campbell?" he inquired, consulting the little imitation ivory ca on the door, on which names could be written with a pencil and rubbed ou

"Dr. Campbell," said Alan, not without stateliness. He was still youn enough to get a thrill at the newness and unexpectedness of the title.

"What time would you like to be called in the morning, sir?"

"What time do we get to Glasgow?"

"Well, sir, we're *due* in at six-thirty."

"Better call me at six, then."

The attendant coughed. Alan correctly interpreted this.

"Call me half an hour before we do get in, then."

"Yes, sir. Would you like tea and biscuits in the morning?"

"Can I get a proper breakfast on the train?"

"No, sir. Only tea and biscuits."

Alan's heart sank along with his stomach. He had been in such a hur to pack that he had eaten no dinner, and his inside now felt squeezed u like a concertina. The attendant understood his look.

"If I was you, sir, I should nip out and get something at the buffet now

"But the train's due to start in less than five minutes!"

"I shouldn't let that worry you, sir. We'll not be starting as soon as tha to my way of thinking."

Yes: he'd better do it.

Ruffled, he left the train. Ruffled, he groped along a noisy and crowde platform in the dark, back through the barrier. When he stood at the buffe with a slopped cup of tea and some dry sandwiches containing ham cut s thin as to have achieved a degree of transparency, his eye fell again on th *Sunday Watchman.* And bile rose again in his soul.

It has been stated that Alan Campbell had only one enemy in the worl Indeed, except for a fight in his school days in which he had exchanged blac eyes and a bloody nose with the boy who later became his best friend, h could not even remember disliking anyone very much.

The man in question was also named Campbell: though he was not, Ala hoped and believed, any relation. The other Campbell lived in a siniste air at Harpenden, Herts. Alan had never set eyes on him, and did not even know who he was. Yet he disliked him very cordially indeed.

Mr. Belloc has pointed out that no controversy can grow more heated, more bitter (or, to a detached observer, more funny) than a controversy between two learned dons over some obscure point that nobody cares twopence about.

We have all, with glee, seen the thing happen. Somebody writes in a dignified newspaper or literary weekly that Hannibal, when crossing the Alps, passed close to the village of Viginum. Some other erudite reader then writes in to say that the name of the village was not Viginum, but Biginium. On the following week, the first writer mildly but acidly deplores your correspondent's ignorance, and begs leave to present the following evidence that it was Viginum. The second writer then says he regrets that an acrimonious note seems to have crept into the discussion, which is no doubt what makes Mr. So-and-So forget his manners; but is under the necessity of pointing out——

And that tears it. The row is sometimes good for two or three months.

Something of a similar nature had dropped with a splosh into Alan Campbell's placid life.

Alan, a kindly soul, had meant no offence. He sometimes reviewed historical works for the *Sunday Watchman*, a newspaper very similar to the *Sunday Times* or the *Observer*.

In the middle of June this paper had sent him a book called, *The Last Days of Charles the Second*, a weighty study of political events between 1680 and 1685, by K. I. Campbell (M.A., Oxon.). Alan's review of this appeared on the following Sunday, and his sin lay in the following words, toward the end of the notice.

"It cannot be said that Mr. Campbell's book throws any fresh light on the subject; and it is not, indeed, free from minor blemishes. Mr. Campbell surely cannot believe that Lord William Russell was ignorant of the Rye House Plot. Barbara Villiers, Lady Castlemaine, was created Duchess of Cleveland in 1670: not, as the printer has it, 1680. And what is the reason for Mr. Campbell's extraordinary notion that this lady was 'small and auburn-haired'?"

Alan sent in his copy on Friday, and forgot the matter. But in the issue nine days later appeared a letter from the author dated at Harpenden, Herts. It concluded:

"May I say that my authority for what your reviewer considers this 'extraordinary' notion is Steinmann, the lady's only biographer. If your reviewer is unfamiliar with this work, I suggest that a visit to the British Museum might repay his trouble."

This riled Alan considerably.

"While I must apologize for drawing attention to so trivial a matter (he

wrote), and thank Mr. Campbell for his courtesy in drawing my attention to
a book with which I am already familiar, nevertheless, I think a visit to the
British Museum would be less profitable than a visit to the National Portrait
Gallery. There Mr. Campbell will find a portrait, by Lely, of this handsome
termagent. The hair is shown as jet-black, the proportions as ample. It might
be thought that a painter would flatter his subject. But it cannot be thought
that he would turn a blonde into a brunette, or depict any court lady a
fatter than she actually was."

That, Alan thought, was rather neat. And not far from devastating either
But the snake from Harpenden now began to hit below the belt. After a
discussion of known portraits, he concluded:

"Your reviewer, incidentally, is good enough to refer to this lady as a
'termagent.' What are his reasons for this? They appear to be that she had
a temper and that she liked to spend money. When any man exhibit
astounded horror over these two qualities in a woman, it is permissible to
inquire whether he has ever been married."

This sent Alan clear up in the air. It was not the slur on his historical
knowledge that he minded: it was the implication that he knew nothing
about women—which, as a matter of fact, was true.

K. I. Campbell, he thought, was in the wrong; and knew it; and was now
as usual, trying to cloud the matter with side issues. His reply blistered the
paper, the more so as the controversy caught on with other readers.

Letters poured in. A major wrote from Cheltenham that his family had
for generations been in possession of a painting, said to be that of the Duch
ess of Cleveland, which showed the hair as medium brown. A savant from the
Athenaeum wanted them to define their terms, saying what proportions they
meant by "ample," and in what parts of the body, according to the standards
of the present day.

"Bejasus," said the editor of the Sunday Watchman, "it's the best thing
we've had since Nelson's glass eye. Leave 'em to it."

Throughout July and August the row continued. The unfortunate mistress
of Charles the Second came in for almost as much notoriety as she had known
in the days of Samuel Pepys. Her anatomy was discussed in some detail
The controversy was entered, though not clarified, by another savant named
Dr. Gideon Fell, who seemed to take a malicious delight in confusing the
two Campbells, and mixing everybody up.

The editor himself finally called a halt to it. First, because the anatomical
detail now verged on the indelicate; and, second, because the parties to the
dispute had grown so confused that nobody knew who was calling whom
what.

But it left Alan feeling that he would like to boil K. I. Campbell in oil
For K. I. Campbell appeared every week, dodging like a sharpshooter and
always stinging Alan. Alan began to acquire a vague but definite reputation

or ungallant conduct, as one who has traduced a dead woman and might raduce any lady of his acquaintance. K. I. Campbell's last letter more than inted at this.

His fellow members of the faculty joked about it. The undergraduates, he uspected, joked about it. "Rip" was one term; "rounder" another.

He had breathed a prayer of relief when the debate ended. But even now, rinking slopped tea and eating dry sandwiches in a steamy station buffet, Jan stiffened as he turned over the pages of the *Sunday Watchman*. He eared that his eye might light on some reference to the Duchess of Cleveand, and that K. I. Campbell might have sneaked into the columns again.

No. Nothing. Well, at least that was a good omen to start the journey. The hands of the clock over the buffet stood at twenty minutes to ten.

In sudden agitation Alan remembered his train. Gulping down his tea when you are in a hurry there always seems to be about a quart of it, boiling ot), he hurried out into the blackout again. For the second time he took ome minutes to find his ticket at the barrier, searching through every pocket efore he found it in the first one. He wormed through crowds and luggage rucks, spotted the right platform after some difficulty, and arrived back at he door of his carriage just as doors were slamming all along the train, and he whistle blew.

Smoothly gliding, the train moved out.

Off on the great adventure, then. Alan, pleased with life again, stood in he dim corridor and got his breath. Through his mind moved some words ut of the letter he had received from Scotland: "The Castle of Shira, at nveraray, on Loch Fyne." It had a musical, magical sound. He savored it. Then he walked down to his compartment, threw open the door, and stopped hort.

An open suitcase, not his own, lay on the berth. It contained female wearng apparel. Bending over it and rummaging in it stood a brown-haired girl f twenty-seven or twenty-eight. She had been almost knocked sprawling by he opening of the door, and she straightened up to stare at him.

"Wow!" said Alan inaudibly.

His first thought was that he must have got the wrong compartment, or he wrong carriage. But a quick glance at the door reassured him. There was is name, Campbell, written in pencil on the imitation ivory strip.

"I beg your pardon," he said. "But haven't you—er—made a mistake?"

"No, I don't think so," replied the girl, rubbing her arm and staring back t him with increasing coolness.

Even then he noticed how attractive she was, though she wore very little owder or lipstick, and there was a look of determined severity about her ounded face. She was five feet two inches tall, and pleasantly shaped. She ad blue eyes, spaced rather wide apart, a good forehead, and full lips which

she tried to keep firmly compressed. She wore tweeds, a blue jumper, and ta\
stockings with flat-heeled shoes.

"But this," he pointed out, "is compartment number four."

"Yes. I know that."

"Madam, what I am trying to indicate is that it's my compartment. M\
name is Campbell. Here it is on the door."

"And my name," retorted the girl, "happens to be Campbell too. And \
must insist that it's *my* compartment. Will you be good enough to leave\
please?"

She was pointing to the suitcase.

Alan looked, and looked again. The train rattled and clicked over point\
swaying and gathering speed. But what he could not assimilate easily wa\
the meaning of the words painted in tiny white letters on the side of th\
suitcase.

*K. I. Campbell. Harpenden.*

## II

IN ALAN'S mind and emotions, incredulity was gradually giving way to some\
thing very different.

He cleared his throat.

"May I ask," he said sternly, "what the initials 'K.I.' stand for?"

"Kathryn Irene, of course. My first names. But will you *please*——?"

"So!" said Alan. He held up the newspaper. "May I further ask whether yo\
have recently taken part in a disgraceful correspondence in the *Sunda\
Watchman?*"

Miss K. I. Campbell put up a hand to her forehead as though to shad\
her eyes. She put the other hand behind her to steady herself on the rim\
of the washbasin. The train rattled and jerked. A sudden suspicion, and the\
comprehension, began to grow in the blue eyes.

"Yes," said Alan. "I am A. D. Campbell, of University College, Highgate.\

By his proud and darkly sinister bearing, he might have been saying, "And\
Saxon, I am Roderick Dhu." It occurred to him that there was somethin\
vaguely ridiculous in his position as he inclined his head sternly, threw th\
paper on the berth, and folded his arms. But the girl did not take it lik\
this.

"You beast! You weasel! You worm!" she cried passionately.

"Considering, madam, that I have not had the honour of being formall\
introduced to you, such terms indicate a degree of intimacy which——"

"Nonsense," said K. I. Campbell. "We're second cousins twice removed\
But you haven't got a beard!"

Alan instinctively put a hand to his chin.

"Certainly I have not got a beard. Why should you suppose that I had a beard?"

"We all thought you had. We all thought you had a beard this long," cried the girl, putting her hand at about the level of her waist. "And big double-lensed spectacles. And a nasty, dry, sneering way of talking. You've got that, though. On top of which, you come bursting in here and knock me about——"

Belatedly, she began to rub her arm again.

"Of all the nasty, sneering, patronizing book reviews that were ever written," she went on, "that one of yours——"

"There, madam, you show a want of understanding. It was my duty, as a professional historian, to point out certain errors, glaring errors——"

"Errors!" said the girl. "Glaring errors, eh?"

"Exactly. I do not refer to the trivial and meaningless point about the Duchess of Cleveland's hair. I refer to matters of real moment. Your treatment of the elections of 1680, if you will excuse my plain speaking, would make a cat laugh. Your treatment of Lord William Russell was downright dishonest. I do not say that he was as big a crook as your hero Shaftesbury. Russell was merely a muttonhead: 'of,' as it was put at the trial, 'imperfect understanding'; to be pitied, if you like, but not to be pictured as anything except the traitor he was."

"You're nothing," said K. I. Campbell furiously, "but a beastly *Tory!*"

"In reply, I quote no less an authority than Dr. Johnson. 'Madam, I perceive that you are a vile Whig.'"

Then they stood and looked at each other.

Alan didn't ordinarily talk like this, you understand. But he was so mad and so much on his dignity that he could have given points and a beating to Edmund Burke.

"Who are you, anyway?" he asked in a more normal tone, after a pause.

This had the effect of putting Kathryn Campbell again on her dignity. She compressed her lips. She drew herself up to the full majesty of five feet two.

"Though I consider myself under no obligation to answer that question," she replied, putting on a pair of shell-rimmed glasses which only increased her prettiness, "I don't mind telling you that I am a member of the department of history at the Harpenden College for Women——"

"Oh."

"Yes. And as perfectly capable as any man, more so, of dealing with the period in question. Now will you *please* have the elementary decency to get out of my compartment?"

"No, I'm damned if I do. It's not your compartment!"

"I say it is my compartment."

"And I say it's not your compartment."

"If you don't get out of here, Dr. Campbell, I'll ring the bell for the at
tendant."

"Please do. If you don't, I'll ring it myself."

The attendant, brought running by two peals on the bell each made by
different hand, found two stately but almost gibbering professors attemptin
to tell their stories.

"I'm sorry, ma'am," said the attendant, worriedly consulting his list, "I'n
sorry, sir: but there seems to have been a mistake somewhere. There's onl
one Campbell down here, without even a 'Miss' or a 'Mr.' I don't know wha
to say."

Alan drew himself up.

"Never mind. Not for the world," he declared loftily, "would I disturl
this lady in possession of her ill-gotten bed. Take me to another compart
ment."

Kathryn gritted her teeth.

"No, you don't, Dr. Campbell. I am not accepting any favors on th
grounds of my sex, thank you. Take me to another compartment."

The attendant spread out his hands.

"I'm sorry, miss. I'm sorry, sir. But I can't do that. There's not a sleepe
to be had on the whole train. Nor a seat either, if it comes to that. They'r
even standing in third class."

"Never mind," snapped Alan, after a slight pause. "Just let me get m
bag from under there, and I'll stand up in the corridor all night."

"Oh, don't be silly," said the girl in a different voice. "You can't do that.

"I repeat, madam——"

"All the way to Glasgow? You can't do that. Don't be silly."

She sat down on the edge of the berth.

"There's only one thing we can possibly do," she added. "We'll share thi
compartment, and sit up all night."

A powerful shade of relief went over the attendant.

"Now, miss, that's very kind of you! And I know this gentleman appreci
ates it. Don't you, sir? If you wouldn't mind, I'm sure the company'll mak
it right with you at the other end. It's very kind of the lady, isn't it, sir?

"No, it is not. I refuse——"

"What's the matter, Dr. Campbell?" asked Kathryn, with icy sweetness
"Are you afraid of me? Or is it that you just daren't face historical fact whe
it is presented to you?"

Alan turned to the attendant. Had there been room, he would have pointe
to the door with a gesture as dramatic as that of a father turning out hi
child into the storm in an old-fashioned melodrama. As it was, he merel
banged his hand on the ventilator. But the attendant understood.

"Then that's all right, sir. Good night." He smiled. "It shouldn't be s•
unpleasant, should it?"

"What do you mean by that?" Kathryn demanded sharply.

"Nothing, miss. Good night. Sleep—I mean, good night."

Again they stood and looked at each other. They sat down, with mutual suddenness, at opposite ends of the berth. Though they had been fluent enough before, now that the door was closed they were both covered with pouring self-consciousness.

The train was moving slowly: steadily, yet with a suggestion of a jerk, which probably meant a raider somewhere overhead. It was less hot now that air gushed down the ventilator.

It was Kathryn who broke the tension of self-consciousness. Her expression began as a superior smile, turned into a giggle, and presently dissolved in helpless laughter. Presently Alan joined in.

"Sh-h!" she urged in a whisper. "We'll disturb the person in the next compartment. But we have been rather ridiculous, haven't we?"

"I deny that. At the same time——"

Kathryn removed her spectacles and wrinkled up her smooth forehead. "Why are you going north, Dr. Campbell? Or should I say Cousin Alan?"

"For the same reason, I suppose, that you are. I got a letter from a man named Duncan, who bears the impressive title of Writer to the Signet."

"In Scotland," said Kathryn, with cutting condescension, "a Writer to the Signet is a lawyer. Really, Dr. Campbell! Such ignorance! Haven't you ever been in Scotland?"

"No. Have you?"

"Well—not since I was a little girl. But I do take the trouble to keep myself informed, especially about my own flesh and blood. Did the letter say anything else?"

"Only that old Angus Campbell had died a week ago; that such few members of the family as could be found were being informed; and could I find it convenient to come up to the Castle of Shira, at Inveraray, for a family conference? He made it clear that there was no question of inheritance, but not quite so clear what he meant by 'family conference.' I used it as a good excuse to get leave for a much-needed holiday."

Kathryn sniffed. "Really, Dr. Campbell! Your own flesh and blood!"

And Alan found his exasperation rising again.

"Oh, look here! I'd never even heard of Angus Campbell. I looked him up, through a very complicated genealogy, and found that he's a cousin of my father. But I never knew him, or anybody near him. Did you?"

"Well . . ."

"In fact, I'd never even heard of the Castle of Shira. How do we get there, by the way?"

"At Glasgow, you take a train to Gourock. At Gourock you get a boat across to Dunoon. At Dunoon you hire a car and drive out round Loch Fyne to Inveraray. You used to be able to go from Dunoon to Inveraray by water but they've stopped that part of the steamer service since the war."

"And what is that in? The Highlands or the Lowlands?"

This time Kathryn's glance was withering.

Alan would not pursue the matter further. He had a hazy idea that in estimating the Lowlands or the Highlands, you just drew a line across the map of Scotland about the middle; that the upper part would be the Highlands, the lower part the Lowlands: and there you were. But now he felt somehow that it could not be quite as simple as this.

"Really, Dr. Campbell! It's in the Western Highlands, of course."

"This Castle of Shira," he pursued, allowing (though with reluctance) his imagination some play. "It's a moated-grange sort of place, I suppose?"

"In Scotland," said Kathryn, "a castle can be almost anything. No: it's not a big place like the Duke of Argyll's castle. Or at least I shouldn't think so from photographs. It stands at the entrance to Glen Shira, a little way off from Inveraray by the edge of the loch. It's rather a slatternly-looking stone building with a high tower.

"But it's got a history. You, as a historian, of course wouldn't know anything about that. That's what makes it all so interesting: the way Angus Campbell died."

"So? How did he die?"

"He committed suicide," returned Kathryn calmly. "Or he was murdered."

The Penguin novel which Alan had brought along was bound in green for a crime thriller. He did not read such things often, but he considered it his duty, sometimes, in the way of relaxation. He stared from this back to Kathryn's face.

"He was—*what?*" Alan almost yelped.

"Murdered. Of course you hadn't heard about that either? Dear me! Angus Campbell jumped or was thrown from a window at the top of the tower."

Alan searched his wits.

"But wasn't there an inquest?"

"They don't have inquests in Scotland. In the event of a suspicious death, they have what is called a 'public inquiry,' under the direction of a man named the Procurator Fiscal. But if they think it's murder, they don't hold the public inquiry at all. That's why I've been watching the Glasgow *Herald* all week, and there's been no report of an inquiry. It doesn't necessarily mean anything, of course."

The compartment was almost cool. Alan reached out and twisted the mouth of the ventilator, which was hissing beside his ear. He fished in his pocket.

"Cigarette?" he offered, producing a packet.

"Thanks. I didn't know you smoked. I thought you used snuff."

"And why," said Alan with austerity, "should you imagine that I used snuff?"

"It got into your beard," explained Kathryn, making motions of intense disgust. "And dropped all over everywhere. It was horrid.—Big-breasted hussy, anyway!"

"Big-breasted hussy? Who?"

"The Duchess of Cleveland."

He blinked at her. "But I understood, Miss Campbell, that you were the lady's particular champion. For nearly two and a half months you've been vilifying my character because you said I vilified hers."

"Oh, well. You seemed to have a down on her. So I had to take the other side, hadn't I?"

He stared at her.

"And this," he said, whacking his knee, "*this* is intellectual honesty!"

"Do you call it intellectual honesty when you deliberately sneered at and patronized a book because you knew it had been written by a woman?"

"But I didn't know it had been written by a woman. I specifically referred to you as 'Mr. Campbell,' and——"

"That was only to throw people off the track."

"See here," pursued Alan, lighting her cigarette with a somewhat shaky hand, and lighting his own. "Let us get this straight. I have no down on women scholars. Some of the finest scholars I've ever known have been women."

"Listen to the patronizing way he says *that!*"

"The point is, Miss Campbell, that it would have made no difference to my notice whether the writer of the book had been a man or a woman. Errors are errors, whoever writes them."

"Indeed?"

"Yes. And for the sake of truth will you now admit to me, strictly in private and between ourselves, that you were all wrong about the Duchess of Cleveland being small and auburn-haired?"

"I most certainly will not!" cried Kathryn, putting on her spectacles again and setting her face into its severest lines.

"Listen!" he said desperately. "Consider the evidence! Let me quote to you for example, an instance I could hardly have used in the newspaper. I refer to Pepys's story——"

Kathryn looked shocked.

"Oh, come, Dr. Campbell! You, who pretend to be a serious historian, actually give any credit to a story which Pepys received at third hand from his hairdresser?"

"No, no, no, madam. You persist in missing the point. The point is not whether the story is true or apocryphal. The point is that Pepys, who saw the lady so often, could have believed it. Very well! He writes that Charles the Second and the Duchess of Cleveland (who was then Lady Castlemaine) weighed each other; 'and she, being with child, was the heavier.' When we remember that Charles, though lean, was six feet tall and on the muscular side, this makes out the lady to be rather a fine figure of a woman.

"Then there is the account of her mock marriage with Frances Stewart, in which she acted the part of the bridegroom. Frances Stewart was herself no flyweight. But is it reasonable to suppose that the part of the bridegroom was enacted by the smaller and lighter woman?"

"Pure inference."

"An inference, I submit, warranted by the facts. Next we have Reresby's statement——"

"Steinmann says——"

"Reresby makes quite clear——"

"*Hey!*" interrupted an exasperated voice from the next compartment, followed by a rapping on the metal door. "*Oi!*"

Both disputants instantly piped down. For a long time there was a guilty silence, broken only by the flying click and rattle of the wheels.

"Let's turn out the light," whispered Kathryn, "and draw the blackout, and see what's going on outside."

"Right."

The click of the light switch appeared to satisfy the disturbed occupant of the next compartment.

Pushing aside Kathryn's suitcase in the dark, Alan pulled back the sliding metal shutter over the window.

They were rushing through a dead world, pitch-black except where, along a purple horizon, moved a maze of searchlights. Jack's beanstalk went no higher than these white beams. The white lines shuttled back and forth, in unison, like dancers. They heard no noise except the click of the wheels: not even the waspish, coughing drone of *war-war, war-war,* which marks the cruising bomber.

"Do you think he's following the train?"

"I don't know."

A sense of intimacy, uneasy and yet exhilarating, went through Alan Campbell. They were both crowded close to the window. The two cigarette ends made glowing red cores, reflected in the glass, pulsing and dimming. He could dimly see Kathryn's face.

The same powerful self-consciousness suddenly overcame them again. They both spoke at the same time, in a whisper.

"The Duchess of Cleveland——"

"Lord William Russell——"

The train sped on.

### III

At three o'clock on the following afternoon, a mellow day of Scotland's most golden weather, Kathryn and Alan Campbell were walking up the hill comprising the one main street in Dunoon, Argyllshire.

The train, due to reach Glasgow at half past six in the morning, actually got there toward one o'clock in the afternoon. By this time they were ravenously, ragingly hungry, but they still got no lunch.

An amiable porter, whose conversation was all but unintelligible to both Campbells, informed them that the train for Gourock left in five minutes. So they piled into this, and were borne lunchless along Clydeside to the coast.

To Alan Campbell it had been a considerable shock when he woke in the morning, tousled and unshaven, to find himself hunched back against the cushions of a railway carriage, and a good-looking girl asleep with her head on his shoulder.

But, once he had collected his scattered wits, he decided that he loved it. A sense of adventure was winging straight into his stodgy soul, and making him drunk. There is nothing like spending the night with a girl, even platonically, to remove a sense of constraint. Alan was surprised and somewhat disappointed, on looking out of the window, to see that the scenery was still the same as it was in England: no granite cliffs or heather yet. For he wanted an excuse to quote Burns.

They washed and dressed, these two roaring innocents, to the accompaniment of a stern debate—carried on through a closed door and above the splash of running water—about the Earl of Danby's financial reconstruction policy of 1679. They concealed their hunger well, even in the train to Gourock. But when they discovered, aboard the squat tan-funneled steamer which carried them across the bay to Dunoon, that there was food to be had below, they pitched into Scotch broth and roast lamb with silence and voracity.

Dunoon, white and grey and dun-roofed, lay along the steel-grey water in the shelter of low-lying, purple hills. It looked like a good version of all the bad paintings of Scottish scenery which hang in so many houses: except that these usually include a stag, and this did not.

"I now understand," Alan declared, "why there are so many of these daubs. The bad painter cannot resist Scotland. It gives him the opportunity to smear in his purples and yellows, and contrast 'em with water."

Kathryn said that this was nonsense. She also said, as the steamer churned in and butted the pier sideways, that if he did not stop whistling "Loch Lomond" she would go crazy.

Leaving their suitcases at the pier, they crossed the road to a deserted tourist agency and arranged for a car to take them to Shira.

"Shira, eh?" observed the dispirited-looking clerk, who talked like an Englishman. "Getting to be quite a popular place." He gave them a queer look which Alan was afterwards to remember. "There's another party going to Shira this afternoon. If you wouldn't mind sharing the car, it 'ud come less expensive."

"Hang the expense," said Alan, his first words in Dunoon; and it is merely to be recorded that the advertising posters did not drop off the wall. "Still, we don't want to seem uppish. It's another Campbell, I imagine?"

"No," said the clerk, consulting a pad, "this gentleman's name is Swan. Charles E. Swan. He was in here not five minutes ago."

"Never heard of him." Alan looked at Kathryn. "That's not the heir to the estate, by any chance?"

"Nonsense!" said Kathryn. "The heir is Dr. Colin Campbell, Angus's first brother."

The clerk looked still more odd. "Yes. We drove him out there yesterday. Very positive sort of gentleman. Well, sir, will you share Mr. Swan's car, or have one of your own?"

Kathryn intervened.

"We'll share Mr. Swan's car, of course, if he doesn't mind. The idea! Flinging good money about like that! When will it be ready?"

"Half past three. Come back here in about half an hour, and you'll find it waiting. Good day, ma'am. Good day, sir. Thank you."

They wandered out into the mellow sunshine, happily, and up the main street looking into shop windows. These appeared to be mainly souvenir shops, and everywhere the eye was dazzled by the display of tartans. There were tartan ties, tartan mufflers, tartan-bound books, tartan-painted tea sets, tartans on the dolls and tartans on the ash trays—usually the Royal Stewart, as being the brightest.

Alan began to be afflicted with that passion for buying things which overcomes the stoutest traveller. In this he was discouraged by Kathryn, until they reached a haberdasher's some distance up on the right, which displayed in its windows tartan shields (Campbell of Argyll, Macleod, Gordon, MacIntosh, MacQueen) which you hung on the wall. These conquered even Kathryn.

"They're lovely," she admitted. "Let's go in."

The shop bell pinged, but went unheard in the argument which was going on at the counter. Behind the counter stood a stern-looking little woman with her hands folded. In front of the counter stood a tallish, leathery-faced young man in his late thirties, with a soft hat pushed back on his forehead. He was surrounded by a huge assortment of tartan neckties.

"They're very nice," he was saying courteously, "but they're not what I want. I want to see a necktie with the tartan of the Clan MacHolster. Don't you understand? MacHolster. M-a-c, H-o-l-s-t-e-r, MacHolster. Can't you show me the tartan of the Clan MacHolster?"

"There isna any Clan MacHolster," said the proprietress.

"Now look," said the young man, leaning one elbow on the counter and holding up a lean forefinger in her face. "I'm a Canadian; but I've got Scottish blood in my veins and I'm proud of it. Ever since I was a kid, my father's said to me, 'Charley, if you ever go to Scotland, if you ever get to Argyllshire, you look up the Clan MacHolster. We're descended from the Clan MacHolster, as I've heard your granddad say many a time.'"

"I keep telling ye: there isna any Clan MacHolster."

"But there's *got* to be a Clan MacHolster!" pleaded the young man, stretching out his hands. "There could be a Clan MacHolster, couldn't there? With all the clans and people in Scotland? There *could* be a Clan MacHolster?"

"There could be a Clan MacHitler. But there isna."

His bewildered dejection was so evident that the proprietress took pity on him.

"What wad your name be, now?"

"Swan. Charles E. Swan."

The proprietress cast up her eyes and reflected.

"Swan. That'd be the MacQueens."

Mr. Swan seized eagerly at this. "You mean I'm related to the clan of the MacQueens?"

"I dinna ken. Ye may be. Ye may not be. Some Swans are."

"Have you got their tartan here?"

The proprietress showed it to him in a necktie. It was undoubtedly striking, its predominating color being a rich scarlet, and took Mr. Swan's fancy at once.

"Now that's what I call something like it!" he announced fervently, and turned round and appealed to Alan. "Don't you think so, sir?"

"Admirable. Bit on the loud side for a necktie, though, isn't it?"

"Yes, I like it myself," agreed Mr. Swan musingly, holding the tie at arm's length like a painter studying perspective. "Yes. This is the tie for me. I'll take a dozen of 'em."

The proprietress reeled.

"A *dozen?*"

"Sure. Why not?"

The proprietress felt compelled to sound a note of warning.

"They're three-and-saxpence each?"

"That's all right. Wrap 'em up. I'll take 'em."

As the proprietress bustled off through a door at the back of the shop,

Swan turned round with a confidential air. He removed his hat out of defer-
ence to Kathryn, revealing a mop of wiry mahogany-coloured hair.

"You know," he confided in a low voice, "I've travelled a lot in my time;
but this is the queerest damn country I ever got into."

"Yes?"

"Yes. All they seem to do is run around telling each other Scotch jokes.
I dropped into the bar of the hotel down there, and the local comedian was
bringing the house down with nothing but Scotch jokes. And there's another
thing. I've only been in this country a few hours—got in by the London train
this morning—but on four different occasions I've been buttonholed with the
same joke."

"We haven't had that experience so far."

"But I have. They hear me talk, see? Then they say, 'You're an American,
eh?' I say, 'No, Canadian.' But that doesn't stop 'em. They say, 'Have you
heard about my brother Angus, who wouldn't even give the bloodhounds a
cent?' "

He paused expectantly.

The faces of his listeners remained impassive.

"Don't you get it?" demanded Swan. 'Wouldn't even give the bloodhounds
a cent. C-e-n-t, s-c-e-n-t."

"The point of the story," replied Kathryn, "is fairly obvious; but——"

"Oh, I didn't say it was *funny*," Swan hastened to assure them. "I'm just
telling you how queer it sounds. You don't find mothers-in-law running
around telling each other the latest mother-in-law joke. You don't find the
English telling each other stories about the Englishman getting the point of
the joke wrong."

"Are the English," inquired Alan with interest, "popularly supposed to do
that?"

Swan flushed a little.

"Well, they are in the stories told in Canada and the States. No offence.
You know the kind of thing. 'You cannot drive a nail with a sponge no matter how hard you soak it,' rendered as, 'You cannot drive a nail with a sponge
no matter how wet it is.' Now, wait! I didn't say *that* was funny either. I
only——"

"Never mind," said Alan. "What I really wanted to ask: are you the Mr.
Swan who's hired a car to go out to Shira this afternoon?"

A curiously evasive look went over Swan's leathery face, with the fine wrinkles round eyes and mouth. He seemed on the defensive.

"Yes. That's right. Why?"

"We're going out there ourselves, and we were wondering whether you'd
mind if we shared the car. My name is Campbell, Dr. Campbell. This is my
cousin, Miss Kathryn Campbell."

Swan acknowledged the introductions with a bow. His expression changed, and lit up with good nature.

"Not the least little bit in the world! Only too pleased to have you!" he declared heartily. His light grey eyes quickened and shifted. "Members of the family, eh?"

"Distant ones. And you?"

The evasive look returned.

"Well, since you know what my name is, and that I'm related to the Mac-Holsters or the MacQueens, I couldn't very well pretend to be a member of the family, could I? Tell me, though." He grew more confidential. "What can you tell me about a Miss or Mrs. Elspat Campbell?"

Alan shook his head, but Kathryn came to the rescue.

"Aunt Elspat, you mean?"

"I'm afraid I don't know anything about her, Miss Campbell."

"Aunt Elspat," replied Kathryn, "isn't really an aunt, and her name isn't Campbell, though they all call her that. Nobody quite knows who she is or where she came from. She just walked in one day, forty years or so ago, and she's been there ever since. Sort of female head of Shira. She must be nearly ninety, and she's supposed to be rather a terror. I've never met her, though."

"Oh," said Swan, but volunteered no more. The proprietress brought him his parcel of neckties, and he paid for it.

"Which reminds me," he went on, "that we'd better get going, if we want to be in time for that car."

After bidding an elaborate farewell to the proprietress, Swan held open the shop door for them.

"It must be a good way out there, and I want to get back before dark; I'm not staying. I suppose they have the blackout up here too? I want a decent night's rest tonight for once. I sure didn't get one on the train last night."

"Can't you sleep on trains?"

"It wasn't that. There was a married couple in the next compartment, having a hell of a row about some dame from Cleveland, and I hardly closed my eyes all night."

Alan and Kathryn cast a quick, uneasy glance at each other, but Swan was preoccupied with his grievance.

"I've lived in Ohio myself; know it well; that's why I listened. But I couldn't get this thing straight. There was some guy named Russell, and another one called Charles. But whether the dame from Cleveland was running around with Russell, or with Charles, or with this woman's husband, I never did make out. You just heard enough so that you couldn't understand anything. I knocked on the wall, but even after they'd turned out the light——"

"Dr. Campbell!" cried Kathryn warningly.

But the murder was out.

"I'm afraid," said Alan, "that that must have been us."

"You?" said Swan. He stopped short in the hot, bright, drowsy street. His eyes travelled to Kathryn's ringless left hand. They seemed to be registering something, as though writing it down.

Then he continued, with such a jerking and obvious change of subjects that even his smooth voice added to the obviousness of it.

"They certainly don't seem to be feeling any shortage of food up here, anyway. Look in these grocery-store windows! That stuff over there is haggis. It——"

Kathryn's face was scarlet.

"Mr. Swan," she said curtly, "may I assure you that you are making a mistake? I am a member of the department of history at the Harpenden College for Women——"

"It's the first time I ever saw haggis, but I can't say I like the look of it. It can manage to look nakeder than any meat I ever did see. That stuff that looks like slices of boloney is called Ulster fry. It——"

"Mr. Swan, will you *please* give me your attention? This gentleman is Dr. Campbell, of University College, Highgate. We can both assure you——"

Again Swan stopped short. He peered round as though to make sure they were not overheard, and then spoke in a low, rapid, earnest voice.

"Look, Miss Campbell," he said, "I'm broadminded. I know how these things are. And I'm sorry I ever brought the subject up."

"But——!"

"All that business about my losing sleep was a lot of bunk. I went to sleep just as soon as you turned the light out, and didn't hear a thing afterwards. So let's just forget I ever spoke about it, shall we?"

"Perhaps that would be best," agreed Alan.

"Alan Campbell, do you *dare* . . ."

Swan, his manner soothing, pointed ahead. A comfortable blue five-seater car was drawn up before the tourist office, with a chauffeur in cap, uniform, and leggings leaning against it.

"There's the golden chariot," Swan added. "And I've got a guidebook. Come on. Let's enjoy ourselves."

## IV

Past the tiny shipyard, past the Holy Loch, under heavy timbre-furred hills, up the rise past Heath Jock, and into the long, straight stretch beside deep Loch Eck, the car sped on.

They took to the driver at once.

He was a burly, red-faced, garrulous man with a singularly bright blue eye and a vast fund of secret inner amusement. Swan sat in front with him, while Alan and Kathryn sat in the rear. Swan began by being fascinated with the driver's accent, and ended by trying to imitate it.

Pointing to a trickle of water down the hillside, the driver said that this was a "wee burn." Swan seized on the words as a good thing. Henceforward water in any form, even a mountain torrent which would have carried away a house, became a wee burn: Swan calling attention to it and experimentally giving the letter "r" a sound like a death rattle or a singularly sustained gargle.

He did this to Alan's intense discomfort, but Alan need not have minded. The driver did not mind. It was as though (say) Sir Cedric Hardwicke were to hear the purity of his English commented on with amusement by Mr. Schnozzle Durante.

Those who regarded Scotsmen as dour or uncommunicative, Alan thought, should have listened to this one. It was impossible to stop him talking. He gave details of every place they passed; and, surprisingly, as it turned out from Swan's guidebook later, with accuracy.

His usual work, he said, was driving a hearse. He entertained them with a description of the many fine funerals, to which he referred with modest pride, where he had had the honour of conducting the corpse. And this gave Swan an opportunity.

"You didn't happen to drive the hearse at a funeral about a week ago, did you?"

To their left, Loch Eck lay like an old tarnished mirror among the hills. No splash or ripple stirred it. Nothing moved on the slopes of fir and pine, stretching up to a pate of outcropping rock, which closed it in. What deadened the mind was the quality of utter silence here, of barriers against the world, and yet of awareness behind it: as though these hills still hid the shaggy shields.

The driver was silent for so long a time, his big red hands gripped round the wheel, that they thought he could not have heard or understood. Then he spoke.

"That'd be auld Campbell of Shira," he stated.

"Aye," said Swan, with perfect seriousness. The thing was infectious: Alan had several times been on the point of saying this himself.

"And ye'll be Campbells tu, I'm thinkin'?"

"Those two are," said Swan, jerking his head toward the two in the rear. "I'm a MacHolster, sometimes called MacQueen."

The driver turned round and looked very hard at him. But Swan was perfectly sincere.

"I drove one of 'em yesterday," said the driver grudgingly. "Colin Campbell it was; and as guid a Scot as masel', for a' he talked like an Englishman."

His face darkened.

"Such bletherin' and blusterin' ye niver heard! An atheist forbye, and thocht nae shame tae admit it! Cau'd me ivery name he caud lay his tongue tu," glowered the driver, "for sayin' Shira is no' a canny place. And it isna either."

Again there was a heavy silence, while the tires sang.

"Canny, I suppose," observed Alan, "being the opposite of uncanny?"

"Aye."

"But if Shira isn't a canny place, what's wrong with it? Ghosts?"

The driver whacked the steering wheel with a slow and dogged hand, as though he were setting a stamp on it.

"I'm no' sayin' it's ghaists, I'm no' sayin' *wha* it is. I'm sayin' it isna a canny place, and it isna."

Swan, after whistling between his teeth, opened the guidebook. While the car jolted, and the long afternoon light grew less golden, he turned to the section devoted to Inveraray. He read aloud:

"Before entering the town by the main road, the traveller should look (left) at the *Castle of Shira*.

"This building contains no features of architectural interest. It was built toward the end of the sixteenth century, but has since been added to. It will be recognized by its round tower, with a conical slate roof, at the south-eastern corner. This tower, sixty-two feet high, is thought to have been the first effort in an ambitious scheme of building which was later abandoned.

"Tradition has it that in 1692, following the massacre of Glencoe in February of that year——"

Swan interrupted himself.

"Hold on!" he said, rubbing his jaw. "I've heard about the massacre of Glencoe. I remember, when I was at school in Detroit . . . What the devil's the matter with *him*? Hoy!"

The driver, his good humour now restored, was bending back and forth over the wheel in paroxysms of silent inner amusement, so that tears stood in his eyes.

"What is it, governor?" demanded Swan. "What's wrong?"

The driver choked. His inner mirth seemed like torture.

"I *thocht* ye were an American," he declared. "Tell me, noo. Hae ye heard aboot ma brither Angus, who wadna e'en gie the bluid-hoonds a cent?"

Swan smote his forehead.

"Man, dinna ye see it? Hae ye no sense o' humour? C-e-n-t, cent; s-c-e-n-t, scent."

"Curiously enough," said Swan, "I do see it. And I'm not an American; I'm a Canadian, even if I did go to school in Detroit. If anybody Brother-Anguses me again today, I'll slaughter him. Which reminds me. (Stop chortling, can't you? Preserve a proper Scottish gravity!)

"But about this massacre of Glencoe. We acted it out in a play at school long ago. Somebody massacred somebody. What I can't remember is whether the MacDonalds killed the Campbells, or the Campbells killed the MacDonalds."

It was Kathryn who answered him.

"The Campbells killed the MacDonalds, of course," she returned. "I say: they're not still touchy about it in these parts, are they?"

The driver, wiping the tears out of his eyes and becoming stern again, assured her that they weren't.

Swan opened the book again.

"Tradition has it that in 1692, following the massacre of Glencoe in February of that year, Ian Campbell, a soldier in the troop of Campbell of Glenlyon, was so embittered by remorse that he committed suicide by leaping from the topmost window of the tower, dashing out his brains on the pavingstones below."

Swan looked up.

"That isn't what happened to the old man the other day?"

"Aye."

"Another tradition is that this suicide was not caused by remorse, but by the 'presence' of one of his victims, whose mangled body pursued him from room to room, until he had no alternative to keep it from touching him except to—"

Swan shut up the book with a snap. "I think that's enough," he added. His eyes narrowed, and his voice grew soft. "What happened, by the way? The old man didn't sleep up at the top of the tower, did he?"

But the driver was not to be drawn. Ask no questions, his bearing intimated, and you will be told no lies.

"Ye'll be seein' Loch Fyne i' a moment, and then Shira," he said. "Ah! Luke, now!"

Reaching a crossroads, they turned to the right at Strachar. A glimmer of water spread out before them. And not a person there but uttered an exclamation of sheer appreciation.

The loch seemed long, wide, and southwards, to their left, endless. Southwards it curved in sun-silvered widening, between heavy banks, for miles to join the Firth of Clyde.

But northwards it lay landlocked—narrower, timelessly placid, its glimmering water slate-coloured—and ran in the shape of a wedge to its end some three miles away. The smooth-moulded hills, black or dark purple except where stray sunlight caught a splashing of pale purple heather or the dark green of pine and fir, closed round it as though patted into shape with a tone of underlying brown.

Far across the loch, along the water's edge, they could dimly see the low-lying white houses of a town, partly screened behind a belt of trees. They saw a church steeple; and, on the dominating hill above, a dot that looked like a watch tower. So clear was the air that even at this distance Alan could have sworn he saw the white houses mirrored in the motionless water.

The driver pointed.

"Inveraray," he said.

Their car swept on. Swan was evidently so fascinated that he even forgot to point out wee burns.

The road—a very good one, like all the roads they had seen so far—ran straight along the bank of the loch parallel with its length toward the north. Thus to reach Inveraray, which was on the opposite bank, they would have to drive to the head of the loch, circle round it, and come back on a parallel course to a point opposite where they were now.

This, at least, was what Alan thought. Inveraray looked very close now, just across the gleaming water at its narrowest. Alan was leaning back expansively, taking comfort from the vast, strong hills, when the car stopped with a jerk and the driver climbed out.

"Ge' out," he beamed. "Donald MacLeish'll have a boat here, I'm thinkin'."

They stared at him.

"Did you say boat?" exploded Swan.

"Aye."

"But what in Satan's name do you want a boat for?"

"Tae row ye across."

"But the road goes there, doesn't it? Can't you just drive 'way up there, and come round into Inveraray on the other side?"

"Waste petrol when I've got ma arms?" demanded the driver, not without horror. "No si' a fule! Ge' out. It's five, sax miles by the road."

"Well," smiled Kathryn, who seemed to be preserving her gravity only with considerable effort, "I'm sure I don't mind a turn on the water."

"Nor me," conceded Swan, "provided somebody else does the rowing. But, my God, man!" He searched the air with gestures. "What's the big idea? It's not your petrol, is it? It belongs to the company, doesn't it?"

"Aye. But the preenciple's the same. Ge' in."

An almost extravagantly solemn trio, with the driver very cheerful at the oars, was ferried across the loch in the hush of early evening.

Kathryn and Alan, their suitcases at their feet, sat in the stern of the boat facing toward Inveraray. It was that hour when the water seems lighter and more luminous than the sky, and there are shadows.

"Brr!" said Kathryn presently.

"Cold?"

"A little. But it's not that." She looked at the driver, now the ferryman. "That's the place, isn't it? Over there, where there's a little landing stage?"

"That's it," agreed the other, craning round to peer over his shoulder. The rowlocks creaked painfully. "It isna much tae luke at; but they do say, mind, that auld Angus Campbell left mair siller than ye caud shake a stick at."

Silently they watched the Castle of Shira grow up and out at them.

It was some distance away from the town, and faced the loch. Built of ancient stone and brick painted grey, with a steep-pitched slate roof, it straggled along the water side; Kathryn's word "slatternly" occurred to Alan in connection with it.

Most of all you noticed the tower. Round, and of moss-patched grey stone, it reared up to a conical slate roof at the southeastern angle of the house. On the side facing the loch it appeared to have only one window. This was a latticed window, with two lights, set close up near the roof; and from there to the uneven flagstones which paved the ground in front of the house must have been close to sixty feet.

Alan thought of the sickening plunge from that window, and moved uneasily.

"I suppose," Kathryn hesitated, "it's rather—well, primitive?"

"Hoots!" said the driver, with rich scorn. "They hae the electric light."

"Electric light?"

"Aye. And a bathroom tu, though I'm no' sae sure of that." Again he craned over his shoulder, and his face darkened. "D'ye see the man standin' by the wee pier and lukin' at us? That'll be the Dr. Colin Campbell I was tellin' ye aboot. Practices medicine in Manchester, or some sic heathen place."

The figure by the pier partly blended with the grey and brown of the landscape. It was that of a man short in stature, but very broad and burly, with a dogged, truculent lift to the shoulders. He wore an old shooting coat, with corduroy breeches and leggings, and had his hands thrust into his pockets.

It was the first time in many years that Alan had seen a doctor with a beard and moustache. These, though close-cropped, were untidy and gave an impression of shagginess together with the shaggy hair. Its colour was an indeterminate brown, touched with what might have been yellow or more probably grey. Colin Campbell, the first of Angus's two younger brothers, was in his middle or late sixties, but looked younger.

He watched them critically as Alan assisted Kathryn out of the boat, and Swan scrambled after them. Though his manner was not unamiable, there was always a suggestion of a bristle about it.

"And who," he said in a heavy bass voice, "might you be?"

Alan performed introductions. Colin took his hands out of his pockets, but did not offer to shake hands.

"Well," he said, "you might as well come in. Why not? They're all here: the Fiscal, and the law agent, and the man from the insurance company, and Uncle Tom Cobleigh and all. This is Alistair Duncan's doing, I suppose?"

"That's the solicitor?"

"Law agent," corrected Colin, with a ferocious grin which Alan rather liked. "Law agent, when you're in Scotland. Yes. That's what I meant."

He turned to Swan, and his shaggy eyebrows drew together over a pair of leonine eyes.

"What did you say *your* name was? Swan? Swan? I don't know any Swans."

"I'm here," said Swan, as though bracing himself, "at the request of Miss Elspat Campbell."

Colin stared at him.

"Elspat sent for you?" he roared. "*Elspat?* God's wounds! I don't believe it!"

"Why not?"

"Because, barring a doctor or a minister, Aunt Elspat never sent for anything or anybody in her life. The only person or thing she ever wanted to see was my brother Angus and the London *Daily Floodlight*. God's wounds! The old girl's more cracked than ever. Reads the *Daily Floodlight* from cover to cover; knows the names of all the contributors; talks about jitterbugs and God knows what."

"The *Daily Floodlight?*" said Kathryn, with virtuous contempt. "That filthy scandal sheet?"

"Here! Oi! Go easy!" protested Swan. "You're talking about my paper."

It was the turn of all of them to stare at him.

"You're not a reporter?" breathed Kathryn.

Swan was soothing. "Now look," he said with great earnestness. "It's all right. I'm not going to use that bit about you and Doc Campbell sleeping in the same compartment on the train: that is, unless I have to. I only——"

Colin interrupted him with a sudden and unexpected deep-throated bellow of laughter. Colin smote his knee, squared himself, and seemed to be addressing the whole universe.

"A reporter? Why not? Come in and welcome! Why not spread the story all over Manchester and London too? Do us good! And what's this about the two scholars of the family being up to hanky-panky on the train?"

"I tell you——"

"Not another word. I like you for it. God's wounds! I like to see a bit of spirit in the younger generation, the kind *we* used to have. God's wounds!"

He clapped Alan on the back, and put a heavy arm round Alan's shoulders, shaking him. His amiability was as overpowering as his truculence. Then, after roaring all this into the evening air, he lowered his voice conspiratorially.

"We can't put you in the same room here, I'm afraid. Got to keep up some of the proprieties. Let you have adjoining rooms, though. But mind you don't mention this to Aunt Elspat."

"*Listen! For the love of——*"

"She's a great stickler for the conventions, in spite of being Angus's mistress for forty years; and anyway, in Scotland, she's now got the status of a common-law wife. Come in! Don't stand there making funny faces! Come in! (Throw up those suitcases, Jock, and look sharp about it!)"

"Ma name's not Jock," said the oarsman, jumping up precariously in the boat.

Colin stuck out his bearded chin.

"It's Jock," he retorted, "if I say it's Jock. Just get that through your head, my lad. Do you want any money?"

"Not from you. Ma name——"

"Then that's just as well," said Colin, taking a suitcase under each arm as though they were parcels; "because damn me if I know whether I've got any to give you."

He turned to the others.

"That's the situation. If Angus was murdered, by Alec Forbes or anybody else, or if he fell out of that window by accident, then Elspat and I are rich. Elspat and a hard-working, stony broke G.P. are both rich. But if Angus committed suicide, I tell you straight we haven't got a penny to bless our names."

## V

"But I understood—" Alan began.

"You understood the old skinflint was rich? Yes! So did everybody else. But it's the same old story." Colin's next remarks were darkly mysterious. "Ice cream!" he said. "Tractors! Drake's gold! Trust a skinflint to be a simpleton when he thinks he can get richer.

"Not that Angus was exactly a skinflint, mind. He was a swine, but a decent sort of swine, if you know what I mean. He helped me when I needed it, and he'd have helped our other brother too, if anybody'd known where to find the bounder after he got into trouble.

"Well, what are we all standing here for? Get on into the house! You—where's *your* suitcase?"

Swan, who had been vainly attempting to get in a word edgeways throughout this, gave it up for the moment as a bad job.

"I'm not staying, thanks very much," Swan replied. He turned to the driver. "You'll wait for me?"

"Aye. I'll wait."

"Then that's settled," roared Colin. "Here—you—Jock. Get round to the kitchen and tell 'em to give you a half. Angus's best whisky, mind. The rest of you, follow me."

Leaving behind them a man passionately announcing to the air that his name was not Jock, they followed Colin to the arched doorway. Swan, who appeared to have something on his mind, touched Colin's arm.

"Look," he said. "It's none of my business, but are you sure you know what you're doing?"

"Know what I'm doing? How?"

"Well," said Swan, pushing his soft grey hat to the back of his head, "I've heard the Scotch were booze-histers, of course; but this beats anything I ever expected. Is half a pint of whisky at one shot your usual tipple in these parts? He won't be able to see the road on the way back, will he?"

"A half, you ruddy Sassenach, is a small whisky. And you!" Colin now got behind Kathryn and Alan, and shooed them ahead of him. "You must have something to eat. Got to keep your strength up."

The hall into which he led them was spacious, but rather musty; and it smelt of old stone. They could make out little in the semi-gloom. Colin opened the door of a room on the left.

"Wait in there, you two," he ordered. "Swan, my lad, you come with me. I'll dig out Elspat. Elspat! *Elspat!* Where the devil are you, Elspat? Oh: and if you hear anybody arguing in the back room, that's only Duncan, the law agent, and Walter Chapman from the Hercules Insurance Company."

Alone, Alan and Kathryn found themselves in a long but rather low-ceilinged room with a faintly pervading odour of damp oilcloth. A wood fire had been lighted in the grate against the evening chill. By the light of the 'fire, and the fainter one which struggled in through the two windows facing the loch, they saw that the furniture was horsehair, the pictures large, numerous, and running to broad gilt frames, and the carpet red but faded.

On a side table lay an immense family Bible. A photograph, draped in black crepe, stood on the red tasselled cloth of the overmantel. The resemblance of the man in the photograph to Colin, despite the fact that he was smooth-shaven and had clear white hair, left no doubt who this was.

No clock ticked. They spoke, instinctively, in whispers.

"Alan Campbell," whispered Kathryn, whose face was as pink as confectionery, "you beast!"

"Why?"

"In heaven's name, don't you realize what they're *thinking* about us? And that dreadful *Daily Floodlight* will print anything. Don't you mind at all?"

Alan considered this.

"Candidly," he startled even himself by replying, "I don't. My only regret is that it isn't true."

Kathryn fell back a little, putting her hand on the table which held the family Bible as though to support herself. He observed, however, that her colour was deeper than ever.

"*Dr.* Campbell! What on earth has come over you?"

"I don't know," he was honest enough to admit. "I don't know whether Scotland usually affects people like this——"

"I should hope not!"

"But I feel like taking down a claymore and stalking about with it. Also, I feel no end of an old rip and I am enjoying it. Has anyone ever told you, by the way, that you are an exceedingly attractive wench?"

"Wench! You called me a wench?"

"It is classical seventeenth-century terminology."

"But nothing like your precious Duchess of Cleveland, of course," said Kathryn.

"I acknowledge," said Alan, measuring her with an appraising eye, "a lack of proportions which would have aroused enthusiasm in Rubens. At the same time——"

"Sh-h!"

At the end of the room opposite the windows there was a partly open door. From the room beyond two voices suddenly spoke together, as though after a long silence. One voice was dry and elderly, the other voice was younger, brisker, and more suave. The voices apologized to each other. It was the younger voice which continued.

"My dear Mr. Duncan," it said, "you don't seem to appreciate my position in this matter. I am merely the representative of the Hercules Insurance Company. It is my duty to investigate this claim——"

"And investigate it fairly."

"Of course. To investigate, and advise my firm whether to pay or contest the claim. There's nothing personal in it! I would do anything I could to help. I knew the late Mr. Angus Campbell, and liked him."

"You knew him personally?"

"I did."

The elderly voice, which was always preceded by a strong inhalation through the nose, now spoke as with the effect of a pounce.

"Then let me put a question to you, Mr. Chapman."

"Yes?"

"You would have called Mr. Campbell a sane man?"

"Yes, certainly."

"A man sensible, shall we say," the voice sniffed, and became even more dry before it pounced, "to the value of money?"

"Very much so."

"Yes. Good. Very well. Now, Mr. Chapman, besides his life-insurance policies with your company, my client had two policies with other companies."

"I would know nothing of that."

"But I tell you so, sir!" snapped the elderly voice, and there was a little rap as of knuckles on wood. "He held large policies with the Gibraltar Insurance Company and the Planet Insurance Company."

"Well?"

"Well! Life insurance now constitutes the whole of his assets, Mr. Chapman. The *whole* of them, sir. It was the sole one of his possessions which he was sensible enough not to throw into these mad financial ventures of his. Each one of those policies contains a suicide clause . . ."

"Naturally."

"I quite agree. Naturally! But attend to me. Three days before he died, Mr. Campbell took out still another policy, with your company again, for three thousand pounds. I should—ah—imagine that the premiums, at his age, would be enormous?"

"They are naturally high. But our doctor considered Mr. Campbell a first-class risk, good for fifteen years more."

"Very well. Now that," pursued Mr. Alistair Duncan, law agent and Writer to the Signet, "made a grand total of some thirty-five thousand pounds in insurance."

"Indeed?"

"And each policy contained a suicide clause. Now, my good sir! My very good sir! Can you, as a man of the world, for one moment imagine that three days after he has taken out this additional policy, Angus Campbell would deliberately commit suicide and invalidate everything?"

There was a silence.

Alan and Kathryn, listening without scruple, heard someone begin slowly to walk about the floor. They could imagine the lawyer's bleak smile.

"Come, sir! Come! You are English. But I am a Scotsman, and so is the Procurator Fiscal."

"I acknowledge——"

"You *must* acknowledge it, Mr. Chapman."

"But what do you suggest?"

"Murder," replied the law agent promptly. "And probably by Alec Forbes. You have heard about their quarrel. You have heard about Forbes's calling here on the night of Mr. Campbell's death. You have heard about the mysterious suitcase (or dog carrier, whatever the term is), and the missing diary."

There was another silence. The slow footsteps paced up and down, carrying an atmosphere of worry. Mr. Walter Chapman, of the Hercules Insurance Company, spoke in a different voice.

"But, hang it all, Mr. Duncan! We just can't go on things like that!"

"No?"

"No. It's all very well to say, 'Would he have done this or that?' But, by the evidence, he *did* do it. Would you mind letting me talk for a minute?"

"Not at all."

"Right! Now, Mr. Campbell usually slept in that room at the top of the tower. Correct?"

"Yes."

"On the night of his death, he was seen to retire as usual at ten o'clock, locking and bolting the door on the inside. Admitted?"

"Admitted."

"His body was found early the following morning, at the foot of the tower. He had died of a broken back and multiple injuries caused by the fall."

"Yes."

"He was not," pursued Chapman, "drugged, or overcome in any way, as the post-mortem examination showed. So an accidental fall from the window can be ruled out."

"I rule out nothing, my dear sir. But continue."

"Now as to murder. In the morning, the door was still locked and bolted on the inside. The window (you can't deny this, Mr. Duncan) is absolutely inaccessible. We had a professional steeple jack over from Glasgow to look at it.

"That window is fifty-eight and a quarter feet up from the ground. There are no other windows on that side of the tower. Below is a fall of smooth stone to the pavement. Above is a conical roof of slippery slate.

"The steeple jack is willing to swear that nobody, with whatever ropes or tackle, could get up to that window or down from it again. I'll go into details, if you like——"

"That won't be necessary, my dear sir."

"But the question of somebody climbing up to that window, pushing Mr. Campbell out, and climbing down again; or even hiding in the room (which nobody was) and climbing down afterwards: both these are out of the question."

He paused.

But Mr. Alistair Duncan was neither impressed nor abashed.

"In that case," the law agent said, "how did that dog carrier get into the room?"

"I beg your pardon?"

The bleak voice rolled on.

"Mr. Chapman, allow *me* to refresh *your* memory. At half past nine that night, there had been a violent quarrel with Alec Forbes, who forced himself into the house and even into Mr. Campbell's bedroom. He was—ah—ejected with difficulty."

"All right!"

"Later, both Miss Elspat Campbell and the maid-servant, Kirstie Mac-Tavish, were alarmed for fear Forbes had come back, and might have hidden himself with the intention of doing Mr. Campbell some injury.

"Miss Campbell and Kirstie searched Mr. Campbell's bedroom. They looked in the press, and so on. They even (as I am, ah, told is a woman's habit) looked under the bed. As you say, nobody was hiding there. But mark the fact, sir. Mark it.

"When the door of Mr. Campbell's room was broken open the following morning, there was found under the bed a leather and metal object like a large suitcase, with a wire grating at one end. The sort of case which is used to contain dogs when they are taken on journeys. *Both women swear that this case was not under the bed when they looked there the night before, just before Mr. Campbell locked and bolted the door on the inside.*"

The voice made an elaborate pause.

"I merely ask, Mr. Chapman: how did that case get there?"

The man from the insurance company groaned.

"I repeat, sir: I merely put the question. If you will come with me, and have a word with Mr. MacIntyre, the Fiscal——"

There were steps on the floor beyond. A figure came into the dim front room, ducking to avoid the rather low door top, and touched a light switch beside the door.

Kathryn and Alan were caught, guiltily, as the light went on. A large, brassy-stemmed chandelier, which could have contained six electric bulbs and did contain one, glowed out over their heads.

Alan's mental picture of Alistair Duncan and Walter Chapman was more or less correct, except that the law agent was rather taller and leaner, and the insurance man rather shorter and broader, than he had expected.

The lawyer was stoop-shouldered and somewhat nearsighted, with a large Adam's apple and grizzled hair round a pale bald spot. His collar was too large for him, but his black coat and striped trousers remained impressive.

Chapman, a fresh-faced young-looking man in a fashionably cut double-breasted suit, had a suave but very worried manner. His fair hair, smoothly brushed, shone in the light. He was the sort who, in Angus Campbell's youth, would have grown a beard at twenty-one and lived up to it ever afterwards.

"Oh, ah," said Duncan, blinking vaguely at Alan and Kathryn. "Have you —er—seen Mr. MacIntyre about?"

"No, I don't think so," replied Alan, and began introductions. "Mr. Duncan, we are . . ."

The law agent's eyes wandered over to another door, one facing the door to the hall.

"I should imagine, my dear sir," he continued, addressing Chapman, "that he's gone up into the tower. Will you be good enough to follow me, please?" For the last time Duncan looked back to the two newcomers. "How do you do?" he added courteously. "Good day."

And with no more words he held open the other door for Chapman to precede him. They passed through, and the door closed.

Kathryn stood staring after them.

"Well!" she began explosively. "Well!"

"Yes," admitted Alan, "he does look as though he might be a bit vague, *except* when he's talking business. But that, I submit, is the sort of lawyer you want. I'd back that gentleman any time."

"But, Dr. Campbell——"

"Will you kindly stop calling me 'Dr. Campbell'?"

"All right, if you insist: Alan." Kathryn's eyes were shining with a light
of interest and fascination. "This situation is dreadful, and yet . . . Did
you hear what they said?"

"Naturally."

"He wouldn't have committed suicide, and yet he couldn't have been
murdered. It——"

She got no further, for they were interested by the entrance of Charles
Swan from the hall. But this was a Swan with his journalistic blood up.
Though usually punctilious about his manners, he had still neglected to
remove his hat, which clung in some mysterious fashion to the back of his
head. He walked as though on eggshells.

"Is this a story?" he demanded: a purely rhetorical question. "Is this a
*story?* Holy, jumping . . . look. I didn't think there was anything in it. But
my city editor—sorry; you call 'em news editors over here—thought there
might be good stuff in it; and was he right?"

"Where have you been?"

"Talking to the maid. Always go for maids first, if you can corner 'em.
Now look."

Opening and shutting his hands, Swan peered round the room to make
sure they were alone, and lowered his voice.

"Dr. Campbell, Colin I mean, has just dug out the old lady. They're
bringing her in here to put me on view."

"You haven't seen her yet?"

"No! But I've got to make a good impression if it's the last thing I ever do
in my life. It ought to be a snip, because the old lady has a proper opinion
of the *Daily Floodlight,* which other people," here he looked very hard at
them—"don't seem to share. But this may be good for a daily story. Cripes,
the old dame might even invite me to stay at the house! What do you
think?"

"I think she might. But——"

"So get set, Charley Swan, and do your stuff!" breathed Swan in the nature
of a minor prayer. "We've got to keep in with her anyway, because it seems
she's the autocrat of the place. So get set, you people. Dr. Campbell's
bringing her along here now."


# VI


It was unnecessary for Swan to point this out, since the voice of Aunt
Elspat could already be heard outside the partly open door.

Colin Campbell spoke in a low-voiced bass rumble, of which no words
were audible, evidently urging something under his breath. But Aunt Elspat,
who had a particularly penetrating voice, took no trouble to lower it.

She said:

"Adjoinin' rooms! Indeed and I'll no' gie 'em adjoinin' rooms!"

The bass rumble grew more blurred, as though in protest or warning. But Aunt Elspat would have none of it.

"This is a decent, God-fearin' hoose, Colin Campbell; and a' yere sinfu' Manchester ways canna mak' it any different! Adjoinin' rooms! *Who's burnin' ma guid electric light at this time o' the day?*"

This last was delivered, in a tone of extraordinary ferocity, the moment Aunt Elspat appeared at the door.

She was a middle-sized, angular woman in a dark dress, who somehow contrived to appear larger than her actual size. Kathryn had suggested her age as "nearly ninety"; but this, Alan knew, was an error. Aunt Elspat was seventy, and a well-preserved seventy at that. She had very sharp, very restless and penetrating black eyes. She carried a copy of the *Daily Floodlight* under her arm, and her dress rustled as she walked.

Swan hastened over to extinguish the light, almost upsetting her as he did so. Aunt Elspat eyed him without favour.

"Swi' on that light again," she said curtly. "It's sae dark a body canna see. Where's Alan Campbell and Kathryn Campbell?"

Colin, now as amiable as a sportive Newfoundland, pointed them out. Aunt Elspat subjected them to a long, silent, and uncomfortable scrutiny, her eyelids hardly moving. Then she nodded.

"Aye," she said. "Ye're Campbells. *Our* Campbells." She went across to the horsehair sofa beside the table which held the family Bible, and sat down. She was wearing, evidently, boots; and not small ones.

"Him that's gone," she continued, her eyes moving to the black-draped photograph, "caud tell a Campbell, our Campbells, i' ten thousand. Aye, if he blacked his face and spoke wi' a strange tongue, Angus wad speir him."

Again she was silent for an interminable time, her eyes never leaving her visitors.

"Alan Campbell," she said abruptly, "what's yere releegion?"

"Well—Church of England, I suppose."

"Ye suppause? Dinna ye ken?"

"All right, then. It *is* Church of England."

"And that'd be your releegion tu?" Aunt Elspat demanded of Kathryn.

"Yes, it is!"

Aunt Elspat nodded as though her darkest suspicions were confirmed.

"Ye dinna gang tae the kirk. I kenned it." She said this in a shivering kind of voice, and suddenly got steam up. "Rags o' Popery!" she said. "Think shame tae yereself, Alan Campbell, think shame and sorrow tae yere ain kith and kin, that wad dally wi' sin and lechery i' the hoose of the Scairlet Woman!"

Swan was shocked at such language.

"Now, ma'am, I'm sure he never goes to places like that," Swan protested, defending Alan. "And, besides, you could hardly call this young lady a——"

Aunt Elspat turned round.

"Who's yon," she asked, pointing her finger at Swan, "wha' burns ma guid electric light at this time o' the day?"

"Ma'am, I didn't——"

"Who's yon?"

Taking a deep breath, Swan assumed his most winning smile and stepped in front of her.

"Miss Campbell, I represent the London *Floodlight*, that paper you've got there. My editor was very pleased to get your letter; pleased that we've got appreciative readers all over this broad country. Now, Miss Campbell, you said in your letter that you had some sensational disclosures to make about a crime that was committed here——"

"Eh?" roared Colin Campbell, turning to stare at her.

"And my editor sent me all the way from London to interview you. I'd be very pleased to hear anything you'd like to tell me, either on or off the record."

Cupping one hand behind her ear, Aunt Elspat listened with the same unwinking, beady stare. At length she spoke.

"So ye're an American, eh?" she said, and her eye began to gleam. "Hae ye heard——"

This was much to bear, but Swan braced himself and smiled.

"Yes, Miss Campbell," he said patiently. "You don't need to tell me. I know. I've heard all about your brother Angus, who wouldn't even give the bloodhounds a penny."

Swan stopped abruptly.

He seemed to realize, in a vague kind of way, that he had made a slip somewhere and that his version of the anecdote was not quite correct.

"I mean—" he began.

Both Alan and Kathryn were looking at him not without interested curiosity. But the most pronounced effect was on Aunt Elspat. She merely sat and stared at Swan. He must have realized that she was staring fixedly at the hat still on his head, for he snatched it off.

Presently Elspat spoke. Her words, slow and weighty as a judge's summing up, fell with measured consideration.

"And why should Angus Campbell gie the bluidhoonds a penny?"

"I mean——"

"It wadna be muckle use tae them, wad it?"

"I mean, *cent!*"

"Sent wha'?"

"C-e-n-t, cent."

"In ma opeenion, young man," said Aunt Elspat, after a long pause, "ye'r a bug-hoose. Gie'in' siller tae bluidhoonds!"

"I'm sorry, Miss Campbell! Skip it! It was a joke." Of all the unfortunat words he could have used in front of Aunt Elspat, this was the worst. Eve: Colin was now glaring at him.

"Joke, is it?" said Elspat, gradually getting steam up again. "Angus Camp bell scarce cauld in his coffin, and ye'd come insultin' a hoose o' mournir wi' yere godless *jokes?* I'll no' stand it! In ma opeenion, ye skellum, ye didn come fra the *Daily Floodlight* at all. Who's Pip Emma?" she flung at him

"Pardon?"

"Who's Pip Emma? Ah! Ye dinna ken that either, du ye?" cried Aun Elspat, flourishing the paper. "Ye dinna ken the lass wha' writes the colum i' ye're ain paper! Dinna fash yeresel' tae mak' excuses!—What's yere name?"

"MacHolster."

"Wha'?"

"MacHolster," said the scion of that improbable clan, now so rattled b Aunt Elspat that his usually nimble wits had deserted him. "I mean, Mac Queen. What I mean is: it's really Swan, Charles Evans Swan, but I'm de scended from the MacHolsters or the MacQueens, and——"

Aunt Elspat did not even comment on this. She merely pointed to th door.

"But I tell you, Miss Campbell——"

"Gang your ways," said Aunt Elspat. "I'll no' tell ye twice."

"You heard what she said, young fellow," interposed Colin, putting hi thumbs in the armholes of his waistcoat and turning a fierce gaze on th visitor. "God's wounds! I wanted to be hospitable, but there are some thing we don't joke about in this house."

"But I swear to you——"

"Now will you go by the door," inquired Colin, lowering his hands, "o will you go by the window?"

For a second Alan thought Colin was really going to take the visitor by th collar and the slack of the trousers, and run him through the house like chucker-out at a pub.

Swan, breathing maledictions, reached the door two seconds before Colin They heard him make a speedy exit. The whole thing was over so quickl that Alan could hardly realize what had happened. But the effect on Kathry was to reduce her almost to the verge of tears.

"What a family!" she cried, clenching her fists and stamping her foot o the floor. "Oh, good heavens, what a family!"

"And wha' ails *you,* Kathryn Campbell?"

Kathryn was a fighter.

"Do you want to know what I really think, Aunt Elspat?"

"Weel?"

"I think you're a very silly old woman, that's what I think. Now throw me out too."

To Alan's surprise, Aunt Elspat smiled.

"Maybe no' sae daft, ma dear," she said complacently, and smoothed her skirt. "Maybe no' sae daft!"

"What do you think, Alan?"

"I certainly don't think you should have chucked him out like that. At least, without asking to see his press card. The fellow's perfectly genuine. But he's like the man in Shaw's *The Doctor's Dilemma:* congenitally incapable of reporting accurately anything he sees or hears. He may be able to make a lot of trouble."

"Trouble?" demanded Colin. "How?"

"I don't know, but I have my suspicions."

Colin's bark was, obviously, very much worse than his bite. He ran a hand through his shaggy mane of hair, glared, and ended by scratching his nose.

"Look here," he growled. "Do you think I ought to go out and fetch the fellow back? Got some eighty-year-old whisky here, that'd make a donkey sing. We'll tap it tonight, Alan my lad. If we fed him that——"

Aunt Elspat put her foot down with a calm, implacable arrogance that was like granite.

"I'll no' hae the skellum in ma hoose."

"I know, old girl; but——"

"I'm tellin' ye: I'll no' hae the skellum in ma hoose. That's all. I'll write tae the editor again——"

Colin glared at her. "Yes, but that's what I wanted to ask you. What's all this tommyrot about mysterious secrets you will tell the newspapers but won't tell us?"

Elspat shut her lips mulishly.

"Come on!" said Colin. "Come clean!"

"Colin Campbell," said Elspat, with slow and measured vindictiveness, "du as I tell ye. Tak' Alan Campbell up tae the tower, and let him see how Angus Campbell met a bad end. Let him think o' Holy Writ. You, Kathryn Campbell, sit by me." She patted the sofa. "Du ye gang tae the godless dance halls o' London, noo?"

"Certainly not!" said Kathryn.

"Then ye hae never seen a jitterbug?"

What might have come of this improving conversation Alan never learned. Colin impelled him toward the door across the room, where Duncan and Chapman had disappeared a while ago.

It opened, Alan saw, directly into the ground-floor of the tower. It was a big, round, gloomy room, with stone walls whitewashed on the inside, and an earth floor. You might have suspected that at one time it had been used

for stabling. Wooden double doors, with a chain and padlock, opened o
into the court on the south side.

These now stood open, letting in what light there was. In the wall was
low-arched door, giving on a spiral stone stair which climbed up inside th
tower.

"Somebody's always leaving these doors open," growled Colin. "Padloc
on the outside, too, if you can believe that! Anybody who got a duplica
key could . . .

"Look here, my lad. The old girl knows something. God's wounds! She
not daft; you saw that. But she knows something. And yet she keeps her li
buttoned, in spite of the fact that thirty-five thousand pounds in insuranc
may hang on it."

"Can't she even tell the police?"

Colin snorted.

"Police? Man, she can't even be civil to the Procurator Fiscal, let alon
the regular police! She had some row with 'em a long time ago—about a cow
or I don't know what—and she's convinced they're all thieves and villain
That's the reason for this newspaper business, I imagine."

From his pocket Colin fished out a briar pipe and an oilskin pouch. H
filled the pipe and lit it. The glow of the match illumined his shaggy bear
and moustache, and the fierce eyes which acquired a cross-eyed expression a
he stared at the burning tobacco.

"As for me . . . well, that doesn't matter so much. I'm an old war hors
I've got my debts; and Angus knew it; but I can pull through somehow. C
at least I hope I can. But Elspat! Not a farthing! God's wounds!"

"How is the money divided?"

"Provided we get it, you mean?"

"Yes."

"That's simple. Half to me, and half to Elspat."

"Under her status as his common-law wife?"

"Sh-h!" thundered the quiet Colin, and looked round quickly, and wave
the shrivelled match end at his companion. "Slip of the tongue. She'll neve
put in a claim to be his common-law wife: you can bet your boots on tha
The old girl's passion for respectability verges on the morbid. I told yo
that."

"I should have gathered it, somehow."

"She'll never admit she was more than his 'relative,' not in thirty year
Even Angus, who was a free-spoken devil, never alluded to it in public. N
no, no. The money is a straight bequest. Which we're never likely to get.

He flung away the spent match. He squared his shoulders, and nodde
towards the staircase.

"Well! Come on. That is, if you feel up to it. There's five floors abov his, and a hundred and four steps to the top. But come on. Mind your head."

Alan was too fascinated to bother about the number of steps.

But they seemed interminable, as a winding stair always does. The staircase was lighted at intervals along the west side—that is, the side away from the loch—by windows which had been hacked out to larger size. It had a musty, stably smell, not improved by the savour of Colin's pipe tobacco.

In daylight that was almost gone, making walking difficult on the uneven stone humps, they groped up along the outer face of the wall.

"But your brother didn't always sleep clear up at the top, did he?" Alan inquired.

"Yes, indeed. Every night for years. Liked the view out over the loch. Said the air was purer too, though that's all my eye. God's wounds! I'm out of condition!"

"Does anybody occupy any of these other rooms?"

"No. Just full of junk. Relics of Angus's get-rich-quick-and-be-happy schemes."

Colin paused, puffing, at a window on the last landing but one.

And Alan looked out. Remnants of red sunset lay still ghostly among the trees. Though they could not have been so very high up, yet the height seemed immense.

Below them, westwards, lay the main road to Inveraray. Up the Glen of Shira, and, farther on, the fork where Glen Aray ascended in deep hills towards Dalmally, were tangled stretches where the fallen timbre now rotted and turned grey. It marked the track, Colin said, of the great storm which had swept Argyllshire a few years back. It was a wood of the dead, even of dead trees.

Southwards, above spiky pines, you could see far away the great castle of Argyll, with the four great towers whose roofs change colour when it rains. Beyond would be the estate office, once the courthouse, where James Stewart, guardian of Alan Breck Stewart, had been tried and condemned for the Appin murder. All the earth was rich and breathing with names, with songs, with traditions, with superstitions——

"Dr. Campbell," said Alan, very quietly, "how did the old man die?"

Sparks flew from Colin's pipe.

"You ask me? I don't know. Except that he never committed suicide. Angus kill himself? Hoots!"

More sparks flew from the pipe.

"I don't want to see Alec Forbes hang," he added querulously; "but he's ruddy well got to hang. Alec 'ud have cut Angus's heart out and never thought twice about it."

"Who is this Alec Forbes?"

"Oh, some bloke who came and settled here, and drinks too much, and

thinks he's an inventor too, in a small way. He and Angus collaborated o■
one idea. With the result usual to collaboration: bust-up. He said Angu■
cheated him. Probably Angus did."

"So Forbes came in here and cut up a row on the night of the—murder?"

"Yes. Came clear up to Angus's bedroom here, and wanted to have it ou■
Drunk, as like as not."

"But they cleared him out, didn't they?"

"They did. Or rather Angus did. Angus was no soft 'un, for all his yea■
and weight. Then the womenfolk joined in, and *they* had to search the bec
room and even the other rooms to make sure Alec hadn't sneaked back.

"Which, evidently, he hadn't."

"Right. Then Angus locks his door—*and* bolts it. In the night, somethin■
happens."

If his fingernails had been longer, Colin would have gnawed at them.

"The police surgeon put the time of death as not earlier than ten o'cloc
and not later than one. What the hell good is that? Eh? We know he didn
die before ten o'clock anyway, because that's the last time he was seen aliv■
But the police surgeon wouldn't be more definite. He said Angus's injurie
wouldn't have killed him instantly, so he might have been unconscious bu
alive for some time before death.

"Anyway, we do know that Angus had gone to bed when all this happened.

"How do we know that?"

Colin made a gesture of exasperation.

"Because he was in his nightshirt when they found him. And the bed wa
rumpled. And he'd put out the light and taken down the blackout from th
window."

Alan was brought up with something of a start.

"Do you know," Alan muttered, "I'd almost forgotten there was a wa
going on, and even the question of the blackout? But look here!" He swep
his hand toward the window. "*These* windows aren't blacked out?"

"No. Angus could go up and down here in the dark. He said blackouts fo
'em were a waste of money. But a light showing up in that room could hav
been seen for miles, as even Angus had to admit. God's wounds, don't as
me so many questions! Come and see the room for yourself."

He knocked out his pipe and ran like an ungainly baboon up the remainin■
stairs.


# VII

ALISTAIR DUNCAN and Walter Chapman were still arguing.

"My dear sir," said the tall, stoop-shouldered lawyer, waving a pince-ne in the air as though he were conducting an orchestra, "surely it is now obvious that this is a case of murder?"

"No."

"But the suitcase, sir! The suitcase, or dog carrier, which was found under the bed after the murder?"

"After the death."

"For the sake of clearness, shall we say murder?"

"All right: without prejudice. But what I want to know, Mr. Duncan, is: what *about* that dog carrier? It was empty. It didn't contain a dog. Microscopic examination by the police showed that it hadn't contained *anything*. What is it supposed to prove anyway?"

Both of them broke off at the entrance of Alan and Colin.

The room at the top of the tower was round and spacious, though somewhat low of ceiling in comparison to its diameter. Its one door, which opened in from a little landing, had its lock torn out from the frame; and the staple of the bolt, still rustily embedded round the bolt, was also wrenched loose.

The one window, opposite the door, exerted over Alan an ugly fascination.

It was larger than it had seemed from the ground. It consisted of two leaves, opening out like little doors after the fashion of windows in France, and of leaded-glass panes in diamond shapes. It was clearly a modern addition, the original window having been enlarged; and was, Alan thought, dangerously low.

Seen thus in the gloaming, a luminous shape in a cluttered room, it took the eye with a kind of hypnosis. But it was the only modern thing here, except for the electric bulb over the desk and the electric heater beside the desk.

A huge uncompromising oak bedstead, with a double feather bed and a crazy-quilt cover, stood against one rounded wall. There was an oak press nearly as high as the room. Some effort had been made toward cheerfulness by plastering the walls and papering them with blue cabbages in yellow joinings.

There were pictures, mainly family photographs going back as far as the fifties or sixties. The stone floor was covered with straw matting. A marble-topped dressing table, with a gaunt mirror, had been crowded in beside a big roll-top desk bristling with papers. More correspondence, bales of it, lined the walls and set the rocking chairs at odd angles. Though there were many trade magazines, you saw no books except a Bible and a postcard album.

It was an old man's room. A pair of Angus's button boots, out of shape from bunions, still stood under the bed.

And Colin seemed to feel the reminder.

"Evening," he said, half bristling again. "This is Alan Campbell, from London. Where's the Fiscal?"

Alistair Duncan put on his pince-nez.

"Gone, I fear, home," he replied. "I suspect him of avoiding Aunt Elspat.

Our young friend here,"—smiling bleakly, he reached out and tapped Chapman on the shoulder—"avoids her like the plague and won't go near her."

"Well, you never know where you are with her. I deeply sympathize with her, and all that; but hang it all!"

The law agent drew together his stooped shoulders, and gloomed down on Alan.

"Haven't we met before, sir?"

"Yes. A little while ago."

"Ah! Yes. Did we—exchange words?"

"Yes. You said, 'How do you do?' and, 'Good-by.'"

"Would," said the law agent, shaking his head, "would that all our social relations were so uncomplicated! How do you do?" He shook hands, with a bony palm and a limp grasp.

"Of course," he went on. "I remember now. I wrote to you. It was very good of you to come."

"May I ask, Mr. Duncan, why you wrote to me?"

"Pardon?"

"I'm very glad to be here. I know I should have made my acquaintance with our branch of the family long before this. But neither Kathryn Campbell nor I can seem to serve any very useful purpose. What did you mean, precisely, by a 'family conference'?"

"I will tell you," Duncan spoke promptly, and (for him) almost cheerfully. "Let me first present Mr. Chapman, of the Hercules Life Insurance Company. A stubborn fellow."

"Mr. Duncan's a bit stubborn himself," smiled Chapman.

"We have here a clear case of accident or murder," pursued the lawyer. "Have you heard the details of your unfortunate relative's death?"

"Some of them," Alan answered. "But——"

He walked forward to the window.

The two leaves were partly open. There was no upright bar or support between them: making, when the leaves were pushed open, an open space some three feet wide by four feet high. A magnificent view stretched out over the darkling water and the purple-brown hills, but Alan did not look at it.

"May I ask a question?" he said.

Chapman cast up his eyes with the expression of one who says, "Another one!" But Chapman made a courteous gesture.

"By all means."

Beside the window on the floor stood its blackout: a sheet of oilcloth nailed to a light wooden frame, which fitted flat against the window.

"Well," continued Alan, indicating this, "could he have fallen out accidentally while he was taking down the blackout?

"You know what we all do. Before climbing into bed, we turn out the light, and then grope across to take down the blackout and open the window.

"If you accidentally leaned too hard on this window while you were open-ing the catch, you might pitch straight forward out of it. There's no bar between."

To his surprise Duncan looked annoyed and Chapman smiled.

"Look at the thickness of the wall," suggested the man from the insurance company. "It's three feet thick: good old feudal wall. No. He couldn't pos-sibly have done that unless he were staggering drunk or drugged or overcome in some way; and the post-mortem examination proved, as even Mr. Duncan will admit—"

He glanced inquiringly at the lawyer, who grunted.

"—proved that he was none of these things. He was a sharp-eyed, sure-footed old man in full possession of his senses."

Chapman paused.

"Now, gentlemen, while we're all here, I may as well make clear to all of you why I don't see how this can be anything but suicide. I should like to ask Mr. Campbell's brother a question."

"Well?" said Colin sharply.

"It's true, isn't it, that Mr. Angus Campbell was what we'll call a gentle-man of the old school? That is, he always slept with the windows closed?"

"Yes, that's true," admitted Colin, and shoved his hands into the pockets of his shooting coat.

"I can't understand it myself," said the man from the insurance company, puffing out his lips. "I should have a head like a balloon if I ever did that. But my grandfather always did; wouldn't let in a breath of night air.

"And Mr. Campbell did too. The only reason he ever took the blackout down at night was so that he should know when it was morning.

"Gentlemen, I ask you now! When Mr. Campbell went to bed that night, this window was closed and its catch locked as usual. Miss Campbell and Kirstie MacTavish admit that. Later the police found Mr. Campbell's finger-prints, *and only Mr. Campbell's fingerprints, on the catch of the window.*

"What he did is pretty clear. At some time after ten he undressed, put on his nightshirt, took down the blackout, and went to bed as usual." Chap-man pointed to the bed. "The bed is made now, but it was rumpled then."

Alistair Duncan sniffed.

"That," he said, "is Aunt Elspat's doing. She said she thought it was only decent to redd up the room."

Chapman's gesture called for silence.

"At some time between then and one o'clock in the morning he got up, walked to the window, opened it, and deliberately threw himself out.

"Hang it all, I appeal to Mr. Campbell's brother! My firm want to do the right thing. I want to do the right thing. As I was telling Mr. Duncan, I knew the late Mr. Campbell personally. He came in to see me at our Glasgow office, and took out his last policy. After all, you know, it's not *my* money. I'm not paying it out. If I could see my way clear to advise my firm to honour this claim, I'd do it like a shot. But can you honestly say the evidence warrants that?"

There was a silence.

Chapman finished almost on a note of eloquence. Then he picked up his brief case and bowler hat from the desk.

"The dog carrier—" began Duncan.

Chapman's colour went up.

"Oh, damn the dog carrier!" he said, with unprofessional impatience. "Can you, sir—can any of you—suggest any reason for the dog carrier to figure in this business at all?"

Colin Campbell, bristling, went across to the bed. He reached underneath and fished out the object in question, which he regarded as though he were about to give it a swift kick.

It was about the size of a large suitcase, though somewhat wider in box shape. Made of dark-brown leather, it had a handle like a suitcase, but two metal clasps on the upper side. An oblong grating of wire at one end had been inset for the purpose of giving air to whatever pet might be carried.

To whatever pet might be carried. . . .

In the mind of Alan Campbell there stirred a fancy so grotesque and ugly, even if unformed, as to come with a flavour of definite evil in the old tower room.

"You don't suppose," Alan heard himself saying, "he might have been frightened into doing what he did?"

His three companions whirled round.

"Frightened?" repeated the lawyer.

Alan stared at the leather box.

"I don't know anything about this man Alec Forbes," he went on, "but he seems to be a pretty ugly customer."

"Well, my dear sir?"

"Suppose Alec Forbes brought that box along with him when he came here. It'd look like an ordinary suitcase. Suppose he came here deliberately, pretending to want to 'have it out' with Angus, but really to leave the box behind. He distracts Angus's attention, and shoves the box under the bed. In the row Angus doesn't remember the suitcase afterwards. But in the middle of the night something gets out of the box . . ."

Even Alistair Duncan had begun to look a trifle uncomfortable.

And Chapman was eying Alan with an interest which all his skeptical and smiling incredulity could not conceal.

"Oh, see here!" he protested. "What are you suggesting, exactly?"

Alan stuck it out.

"I don't want you to laugh. But what I was actually thinking about was—

well, a big spider, or a poisonous snake of some kind. It would have been bright moonlight that night, remember."

Again the silence stretched out interminably. It was now so dark that they could barely see.

"It is an extraordinary thing," murmured the lawyer in his thin, dry voice. "Just one moment."

He felt in the inside breast pocket of his coat. From this he took a worn leather notebook. Carrying it to the window, and adjusting his pince-nez, he cocked his head at an angle to examine one page of the notebook.

"'Extracts from the statement of Kirstie MacTavish, maidservant,'" he read, and cleared his throat. "Translated from the Doric and rendered into English, listen to this:

"'Mr. Campbell said to me and Miss Campbell, "Go to bed and let's have no more nonsense. I have got rid of the blellum. Did you see that suitcase he had with him, though?" We said we had not, as we did not arrive until Mr. Campbell had put Mr. Forbes out of the house. Mr. Campbell said: "I will bet you he is leaving the country to get away from his creditors. But I wonder what he did with the suitcase? He was using two hands to try to hit me when he left."'"

Duncan peered up over his pince-nez.

"Any comments on that, my dear sir?" he inquired.

The insurance agent was not amused.

"Aren't you forgetting what you pointed out to me yourself? When Miss Campbell and the maid searched this room just before Mr. Campbell retired, they saw no suitcase under the bed."

Duncan rubbed his jaw. In that light he had a corpselike, cadaverous pallour, and his grizzled hair looked like wire.

"True," he admitted. "True. At the same time——"

He shook his head.

"Snakes!" snorted the insurance agent. "Spiders! Dr. Fu Manchu! Look here! Do you know of any snake or spider that would climb out of its box, and then carefully close the clasps of the box afterwards? Both clasps on that thing were found fastened on the following morning."

"That would certainly appear to be a stumbling block," conceded Duncan. "At the same time——"

"And what happened to the thing afterwards?"

"It wouldn't be very pleasant," grinned Colin Campbell, "if the thing were still here in the room somewhere."

Mr. Walter Chapman hurriedly put on his bowler hat.

"I must go," he said. "Sorry, gentlemen, but I'm very late as it is and I've got to get back to Dunoon. Can I give you a lift, Mr. Duncan?"

"Nonsense!" roared Colin. "You're staying to tea. Both of you."

Chapman blinked at him.

"Tea? Great Scott, what time do you have your dinner?"

"You'll get no dinner, my lad. But the tea will be bigger than most dinners you ever ate. And I've got some very potent whisky I've been aching to try out on somebody, beginning with a ruddy Englishman. What do you say?"

"Sorry. Decent of you, but I must go." Chapman slapped at the sleeves of his coat. Exasperation radiated from him. "What with snakes and spiders— *and* the supernatural on top of it——"

If the scion of the MacHolsters could have chosen no more unfortunate word than "joke" in addressing Elspat Campbell, Chapman himself in addressing Colin could have chosen no more unfortunate word than "supernatural."

Colin's big head hunched down into his big shoulders.

"And who says this was supernatural?" he inquired in a soft voice.

Chapman laughed.

"I don't, naturally. That's a bit outside my firm's line. But the people hereabouts seem to have an idea that this place is haunted; or at least that there's something not quite right about it."

"Oh?"

"And, if I may say so without offence,"—the insurance agent's eye twinkled—"they seem not to have a very high opinion of you people here. They mutter, 'a bad lot,' or something of the sort."

"We are a bad lot. God's wounds!" cried the atheistical doctor, not without pride. "Who's ever denied it? Not me. But haunted! Of all the . . . look here. You don't think Alec Forbes went about carrying a bogle in a dog box?"

"I don't think, frankly," retorted Chapman, "that anybody carried anything in any box." His worried look returned. "All the same, I should feel better if we could have a word with this Mr. Forbes."

"Where is he, by the way?" asked Alan.

The law agent, who had shut up his notebook and was listening with a dry, quiet smile, struck in again.

"That, too, is an extraordinary thing. Even Mr. Chapman would admit something suspicious—something just a trifle suspicious—about Alec Forbes's conduct. For, you see, Alec Forbes can't be found."

## VIII

"You mean," asked Alan, "he did go away to escape his creditors?"

Duncan waved the pince-nez.

"Slander. No: I merely state the fact. Or he may be on a spree, which is possible. All the same, it is curious. Eh, my dear Chapman? It is *curious*."

The insurance agent drew a deep breath.

"Gentlemen," he said, "I'm afraid I can't argue the matter any further now. I'm going to get out of here before I break my neck on those stairs in the dark.

"Here is all I am able to tell you now. I'll have a word with the Fiscal tomorrow. He must have decided by now whether he thinks this is suicide, accident, or murder. On what he does must necessarily depend what *we* do. Can I say any fairer than that?"

"Thank you. No, that will suit us. All we ask is a little time."

"But if you're sure this is murder," interposed Alan, "why doesn't your Fiscal take some real steps about it? For instance, why doesn't he call in Scotland Yard?"

Duncan regarded him with real horror.

"Summon Scotland Yard to Scotland?" he expostulated. "My dear sir!"

"I should have thought this would have been the very place for 'em," said Alan. "Why not?"

"My dear sir, it is never done! Scots law has a procedure all its own."

"By George, it has!" declared Chapman, slapping his brief case against his leg. "I've only been up here a couple of months, but I've found that out already."

"Then what are you going to do?"

"While all the rest of you," observed Colin, throwing out his barrel chest, "have been doing nothing but fiddle-faddling about and talking, other people haven't been idle. I won't tell you what I'm going to do. I'll tell you what I *have* done." His eye dared them to say it wasn't a good idea. "I've sent for Gideon Fell."

Duncan clucked his tongue thoughtfully.

"That's the man who——?"

"It is. And a good friend of mine."

"Have you thought of the—ah—expense?"

"God's wounds, can't you stop thinking about money for five seconds? Just five seconds? Anyway, it won't cost you a penny. He's coming up here as my guest, that's all. You offer him money and there'll be trouble."

The lawyer spoke stiffly.

"We all know, my dear Colin, that your own contempt for the monetary side has not failed to prove embarrassing to you at times." His glance was charged with meaning. "You must allow *me*, however, to think of the pounds, shillings and pence. A while ago this gentleman,"—he nodded toward Alan—"asked why this 'family conference' had been summoned. I'll tell you. If the insurance companies refuse to pay up, proceedings must be instituted. Those proceedings may be expensive."

"Do you mean to say," said Colin, his eyes starting out of their sockets, "that you brought those two kids clear up from London just in the hope they'd contribute to the basket? God's wounds, do you want your ruddy neck wrung?"

Duncan was very white.

"I am not in the habit of being talked to like that, Colin Campbell."

"Well, you're *being* talked to like that, Alistair Duncan. What do you think of it?"

For the first time a personal note crept into the law agent's voice.

"Colin Campbell, for forty-two years I've been at the beck and call of your family——"

"Ha ha ha!"

"Colin Campbell——"

"Here! I say!" protested Chapman, so uncomfortable that he shifted from one foot to the other.

Alan also intervened by putting his hand on Colin's shivering shoulder. In another moment, he was afraid, Colin might be running a second person out of the house by the collar and the slack of the trousers.

"Excuse me," Alan said, "but my father left me pretty well off, and if there *is* anything I can do . . ."

"So? Your father left you pretty well off," said Colin. "And well you knew it, didn't you, Alistair Duncan?"

The lawyer sputtered. What he attempted to say, so far as Alan could gather, was 'Do you wish me to wash my hands of this matter?' What he actually said was something like, 'Do you wash me to wish my hands of this matter?' But both he and Colin were so angry that neither noticed it.

"Yes, I do," said Colin. "That's just what I smacking well do. Now shall we go downstairs?"

In silence, with aching dignity, the quartet stumbled and blundered and groped down some very treacherous stairs. Chapman attempted to lighten matters by asking Duncan if he would care for a lift in the former's car, an offer which was accepted, and a few observations about the weather.

These fell flat.

Still in silence, they went through into the sitting room on the ground floor, now deserted, and to the front door. As Colin and the law agent said good night, they could not have been more on their dignity had they been going to fight a duel in the morning. The door closed.

"Elspat and little Kate," said Colin, moodily smouldering, "will be having their tea. Come on."

Alan liked the dining room, and would have liked it still more if he had not felt so ruffled.

Under a low-hanging lamp which threw bright light on the white tablecloth, with a roaring fire in the chimney, Aunt Elspat and Kathryn sat at a meal composed of sausages, Ulster fry, eggs, potatoes, tea, and enormous quantities of buttered toast.

"Elspat," said Colin, moodily drawing out a chair, "Alistair Duncan's given notice again."

Aunt Elspat helped herself to butter.

"A'weel," she said philosophically, "it's no' the fairst time, and it'll no' be the last. He gie'd me notice tu, a week syne."

Alan's intense discomfort began to lighten.

"Do you mean to say," Alan demanded, "that that business wasn't—wasn't serious?"

"Oh, no. He'll be all right in the morning," said Colin. Stirring uncomfortably, he glowered at the well-filled table. "You know, Elspat, I've got a bloody temper. I wish I could control it."

Aunt Elspat then flew out at him.

She said she would not have such profane language used in her house, and especially in front of the child: by which she presumably meant Kathryn. She further rated them for being late for tea, in terms which would have been violent had they missed two meals in a row and emptied the soup over her at the fourth.

Alan only half listened. He was beginning to understand Aunt Elspat a little better now, and to realize that her outbursts were almost perfunctory. Long ago Aunt Elspat had been compelled to fight and fight to get her own way in all things; and continued it, as a matter of habit, long after it had ceased to be necessary. It was not even bad temper: it was automatic.

The walls of the dining room were ornamented with withered stags' heads, and there were two crossed claymores over the chimneypiece. They attracted Alan. A sense of well-being stole into him as he devoured his food, washing it down with strong black tea.

"Ah!" said Colin, with an expiring sigh. He pushed back his chair, stretched, and patted his stomach. His face glowed out of the beard and shaggy hair. "Now that's better. That's very much better. Rot me if I don't feel like ringing up the old weasel and apologizing to him!"

"Did you," said Kathryn hesitantly, "did you find out anything? Up there in the tower? Or decide on anything?"

Colin inserted a toothpick into his beard.

"No, Kitty-kat, we didn't."

"And please don't call me Kitty-kat! You all treat me as though I weren't grown up!"

"Hoots!" said Aunt Elspat, giving her a withering look. "Ye're *not* grown up."

"We didn't decide on anything," pursued Colin, continuing to pat his stomach. "But then we didn't need to. Gideon Fell'll be here tomorrow. In fact, I thought it was Fell coming when I saw your boat tonight. And when *he* gets here——"

"Did you say Fell?" cried Kathryn. "Not Dr. Fell?"

"That's the chap."

"Not that horrible man who writes letters to the newspapers? *You* know, Alan."

"He's a very distinguished scholar, Kitty-kat," said Colin; "and as such you ought to take off your wee bonnet to him. But his main claims to notoriety lie along the line of detecting crime."

Aunt Elspat wanted to know what his religion was.

Colin said he didn't know, but that it didn't matter a damn *what* his religion was.

Aunt Elspat intimated, on the contrary, that it mattered very much indeed, adding remarks which left her listeners in no doubt about her views touching Colin's destination in the afterlife. This, to Alan, was the hardest part of Elspat's discourse to put up with. Her notions of theology were childish. Her knowledge of Church history would have been considered inaccurate even by the late Bishop Burnet. But good manners kept him silent, until he could get in a relevant question.

"The only part I haven't got quite clear," he said, "is about the diary."

Aunt Elspat stopped hurling damnation right and left, and applied herself to her tea.

"Diary?" repeated Colin.

"Yes. I'm not even sure if I heard properly; it might refer to something else. But, when Mr. Duncan and the insurance fellow were talking in the next room, we heard Mr. Duncan say something about a 'missing diary.' At least, that's how I understood it."

"And so did I," agreed Kathryn.

Colin scowled.

"As far as I can gather,"—he put a finger on his napkin ring, sending it spinning out on the table to roll back to him—"somebody pinched it, that's all."

"What diary?"

"*Angus's* diary, dammit! He carefully kept one every year, and at the end of the year burned it so that nobody should ever find it and know what he was really thinking."

"Prudent habit."

"Yes. Well, he wrote it up every night just before he went to bed. Never knew him to miss. It should have been on the desk next morning. But—at least, so they tell me—it wasn't. Eh, Elspat?"

"Drink your tea and dinna be sae daft."

Colin sat up.

"What the devil's daft about that? The diary wasn't there, was it?"

Carefully, with a ladylike daintiness which showed she knew her manners, Elspat poured tea into the saucer, blew on it, and drank.

"The trouble is," Colin continued, "that nobody even noticed the absence of the diary until a good many hours afterwards. So anybody who saw it lying there could have pinched it in the meantime. I mean, there's no proof that the phantom murderer got it. It might have been anybody. Eh, Elspat?"

Aunt Elspat regarded the empty saucer for a moment, and then sighed. "I suppause," she said resignedly, "you'll be wantin' the whisky, noo?" Colin's face lit up.

"Now there," he boomed, with fervency, "there, in the midst of this mess, is the idea that the world's been waiting for!" He turned to Alan. "Lad, would you like to taste some mountain dew that'll take the top of your head off? Would you?"

The dining room was snug and warm, though the wind rose outside. As always in the presence of Kathryn, Alan felt expansive and on his mettle.

"It would be very interesting," he replied, settling back, "to find any whisky that could take the top of my head off."

"Oho? You think so, do you?"

"You must remember," said Alan, not without reason on his side, "that I spent three years in the United States during prohibition days. Anybody who can survive *that* experience has nothing to fear from any liquor that ever came out of a still—or didn't."

"You think so, eh?" mused Colin. "Do you, now? Well, well, well! Elspat, this calls for heroic measures. Bring out the Doom of the Campbells."

Elspat rose without protest.

"A'weel," she said, "I've seen it happen befair. It'll happen again when I'm gone. I caud du wi' a wee nip masel', the nicht bein' cauld."

She creaked out of the room, and returned bearing a decanter nearly full of a darkish brown liquid filled with gold where the light struck it. Colin placed it tenderly on the table. For Elspat and Kathryn he poured out an infinitesimal amount. For himself and Alan he poured out about a qaurter of a tumblerful.

"How will you have it, lad?"

"American style. Neat, with water on the side."

"Good! Damn good!" roared Colin. "You don't want to spoil it. Now drink up. Go on. Drink it."

They—or at least Colin and Elspat—were regarding him with intense interest. Kathryn sniffed suspiciously at the liquid in her glass, but evidently decided that she liked it. Colin's face was red and of a violent eagerness, his eyes wide open and mirth lurking in his soul.

"To happier days," said Alan.

He lifted the glass, drained it, and almost literally reeled.

It did not take the top of his head off; but for a second he thought it was going to. The stuff was strong enough to make a battleship alter its course. The veins of his temples felt bursting; his eyesight dimmed; and he decided that he must be strangling to death. Then, after innumerable seconds, he opened swimming eyes to find Colin regarding him with proud glee.

Next, something else happened.

Once that spiritous bomb had exploded, and he could recover breath and eyesight, a fey sense of exhilaration and well-being crawled along his veins. The original buzzing in the head was succeeded by a sense of crystal clearness, the feeling which Newton or Einstein must have felt at the approaching solution of a complex mathematical problem.

He had kept himself from coughing, and the moment passed.

"Well?" demanded Colin.

"Aaah!" said his guest.

"Here's to happier days too!" thundered Colin, and drained his own glass. The effects here were marked as well, though Colin recovered himself a shade more quickly. Then Colin beamed on him. "Like it?"

"I do!"

"Not too strong for you?"

"No."

"Care for another?"

"Thanks. I don't mind if I do."

"A'weel!" said Elspat resignedly. "A'weel!"

## IX

ALAN CAMPBELL opened one eye.

From somewhere in remote distances, muffled beyond sight or sound, his soul crawled back painfully, through subterranean corridors, up into his body again. Toward the last it moved to a cacophony of hammers and lights.

Then he was awake.

The first eye was bad enough. But, when he opened the second eye, such a rush of anguish flowed through his brain that he hastily closed them again.

He observed—at first without curiosity—that he was lying in bed in a room he had never seen before; that he wore pajamas; and that there was sunlight in the room.

But his original concerns were purely physical. His head felt as though it were rising toward the ceiling with long, spiralling motions; his stomach was an inferno, his voice a croak out of a dry throat, his whole being composed of fine wriggling wires. Thus Alan Campbell, waking at twelve midday with the king of all hangovers, for the moment merely lay and suffered.

Presently he tried to climb out of bed. But dizziness overcame him, and he lay down again. It was here that his wits began to work, however. Feverishly he tried to remember what had happened last night.

And he could not remember a single thing.

Alan was galvanized.

Possible enormities stretched out behind him, whole vistas of enormities which he might have said or done, but which he could not remember now. There is perhaps not in the world any anguish to compare to this. He knew, or presumed, that he was still at the Castle of Shira; and that he had been lured into quaffing the Doom of the Campbells with Colin; but this was all he knew.

The door of the room opened, and Kathryn came in.

On a tray she carried a cup of black coffee and a revolting-looking mixture in a glass eggcup. She was fully dressed. But the wan expression of her face and eyes strangely comforted him.

Kathryn came over and put down the tray on the bedside table.

"Well, Dr. Campbell," were her first unencouraging words, "don't you feel ashamed of yourself?"

All Alan's emotion found vent in one lingering, passionate groan.

"Heaven knows *I've* no right to blame you," said Kathryn, putting her hands to her head. "I was almost as bad as you were. Oh, God, I feel *awful!*" she breathed, and tottered on her feet. "But at least I didn't——"

"Didn't what?" croaked Alan.

"Don't you remember?"

He waited for enormity to sweep him like the sea.

"At the moment—no. Nothing."

She pointed to the tray. "Drink that prairie oyster. I know it looks foul; but it'll do you good."

"No: tell me. What did I do? Was I very bad?"

Kathryn eyed him wanly.

"Not as bad as Colin, of course. But when *I* tried to leave the party, you and Colin were fencing with claymores."

"Were what?"

"Fencing with real swords. All over the dining room and out in the hall and up the stairs. You had kitchen tablecloths slung on for plaids. Colin was talking in Gaelic, and you were quoting *Marmion*, and *The Lady of the Lake*. Only you couldn't seem to decide whether you were Roderick Dhu or Douglas Fairbanks."

Alan shut his eyes tightly.

He breathed a prayer himself. Faint glimmers, like chinks of light in a blind, touched old-world scenes which swam at him and then receded in hopeless confusion. All lights splintered; all voices dimmed.

"Stop a bit!" he said, pressing his hands to his forehead. "There's nothing about Elspat in this, is there? I didn't insult Elspat, did I? I seem to remember . . ."

Again he shut his eyes.

"My dear Alan, that's the one good feature of the whole night. You're

Aunt Elspat's white-haired boy. She thinks that you, next to the late Angus, are the finest member of the whole family."

"*What?*"

"Don't you remember giving her a lecture, at least half an hour long, about the Solemn League and Covenant and the history of the Church of Scotland?"

"Wait! I do seem vaguely to——"

"She didn't understand it; but you had her spellbound. She said that anybody who knew the names of so many ministers couldn't be as godless as she'd thought. Then you insisted on her having half a tumbler of that wretched stuff, and she walked off to bed like Lady Macbeth. This was before the fencing episode, of course. And then—don't you remember what Colin did to that poor man Swan?"

"Swan? Not the MacHolster Swan?"

"Yes."

"But what was *he* doing here?"

"Well, it was something like this: though it's rather dim in my own mind. After you'd fenced all over the place, Colin wanted to go out. He said, 'Alan Oig, there is dirty work to be done this night. Let us hence and look for Stewarts.' You thought that would be a perfectly splendid idea.

"We went out the back, on the road. The first thing we saw, in the bright moonlight, was Mr. Swan standing and looking at the house. Don't ask me what he was doing there! Colin whooped out, 'There's a bluidy Stewart!' and went for him with the claymore.

"Mr. Swan took one look at him, and shot off down the road harder than I've ever seen any man run before. Colin went tearing after him, and you after Colin. I didn't interfere: I'd reached the stage where all I could do was stand and giggle. Colin couldn't quite manage to overtake Mr. Swan, but he did manage to stick him several times in the—in the——"

"Yes."

"—before Colin fell flat and Mr. Swan got away. Then you two came back singing."

There was obviously something on Kathryn's mind. She kept her eyes on the floor.

"I suppose you don't remember," she added, "that I spent the night in here?"

"*You spent the night in here?*"

"Yes. Colin wouldn't hear of anything else. He locked us in."

"But we didn't . . . I mean . . . ?"

"Didn't what?"

"You know what I mean."

Kathryn evidently did, to judge by her colour.

"Well—no. We were both too far gone anyway. I was so dizzy and weak that I didn't even protest. You recited something about,

> " 'Here dies in my bosom
> The secret of heather ale.'

"Then you courteously said, 'Excuse me,' and lay down on the floor and went to sleep."

He became conscious of his pajamas. "But how did I get into these?"

"I don't know. You must have waked up in the night and put them on. I woke up about six o'clock, feeling like death, and managed to push the key in the door out, so it fell on the outside and I dragged it under the sill on a piece of paper. I got off to my own room, and I don't think Elspat knows anything about it. But when I woke up and found you there . . ."

Her voice rose almost to a wail.

"Alan Campbell, what on earth has come over us? Both of us? Don't you think we'd better get out of Scotland before it corrupts us altogether?"

Alan reached out for the prairie oyster. How he managed to swallow it he does not now remember; but he did, and felt better. The hot black coffee helped.

"So help me," he declared, "I will never touch another drop as long as I live! And Colin. I hope he's suffering the tortures of the inferno. I hope he's got such a hangover as will——"

"Well, he hasn't."

"No?"

"He's as bright as a cricket. He says good whisky never gave any man a headache. That dreadful Dr. Fell has arrived, too. Can you come downstairs and get some breakfast?"

Alan gritted his teeth.

"I'll have a try," he said, "if you can overcome your lack of decency and get out of here while I dress."

Half an hour later, after shaving and bathing in the somewhat primitive bathroom, he was on his way downstairs feeling much better. From the partly open door of the sitting room came the sound of two powerful voices, those of Colin and Dr. Fell, which sent sharp pains through his skull. Toast was all he could manage in the way of breakfast. Afterwards he and Kathryn crept guiltily into the sitting room.

Dr. Fell, his hands folded over his crutch-handled stick, sat on the sofa. The broad black ribbon of his eyeglasses blew out as he chuckled. His big mop of grey-streaked hair lay over one eye, and many more chins appeared as his amusement increased. He seemed to fill the room: at first Alan could hardly believe him.

"Good morning!" he thundered.

"Good morning!" thundered Colin.

"Good morning," murmured Alan. "Must you shout like that?"

"Nonsense. We weren't shouting," said Colin. "How are you feeling this morning?"

"Terrible."

Colin stared at him. "You haven't got a head?"

"No?"

"Nonsense!" snorted Colin, fiercely and dogmatically. "Good whisky never gave any man a head."

This fallacy, by the way, is held almost as a gospel in the North. Alan did not attempt to dispute it. Dr. Fell hoisted himself ponderously to his feet and made something in the nature of a bow.

"Your servant, sir," said Dr. Fell. He bowed to Kathryn. "And yours, madam." A twinkle appeared in his eye. "I trust that you have now managed to settle between you the vexed question of the Duchess of Cleveland's hair? Or may I infer that at the moment you are more interested in the hair of the dog?"

"That's not a bad idea, you know," said Colin.

"No!" roared Alan, and made his own head ache. "I will never touch that damned stuff again under any circumstances. That is final."

"That's what you think now," Colin grinned comfortably. "I'm going to give Fell here a nip of it tonight. I say, my boy: would you like to taste some mountain dew that'll take the top of your head off?"

Dr. Fell chuckled.

"It would be very interesting," he replied, "to find any whisky that could take the top of my head off."

"Don't say that," warned Alan. "Let me urge you in advance: don't say it. *I* said it. It's fatal."

"And must we talk about this, anyway?" inquired Kathryn, who had been eying Dr. Fell with a deep suspicion which he returned by beaming like the Ghost of Christmas Present.

Rather to their surprise, Dr. Fell grew grave.

"Oddly enough, I think it would be advisable to talk of it. Archons of Athens! It's quite possible the matter may have some bearing on——"

He hesitated.

"On what?"

"On Angus Campbell's murder," said Dr. Fell.

Colin whistled, and then there was a silence. Muttering to himself, Dr. Fell appeared to be trying to chew at the end of his bandit's moustache.

"Perhaps," he went on, "I had better explain. I was very happy to get my friend Colin Campbell's invitation. I was much intrigued by the full details of the case as he wrote them. Putting in my pocket my Boswell and my toothbrush, I took a train for the North. I beguiled my time rereading the great Doctor Johnson's views on this country. You are no doubt familiar with his stern reply when told that he should not be so hard on Scotland since, after all, God had made Scotland? 'Sir, comparisons are invidious; but God made hell.' "

Colin gestured impatiently. "Never mind that. What were you saying?"

"I arrived in Dunoon," said Dr. Fell, "early yesterday evening. I tried to get a car at the tourist agency——"

"We know it," said Kathryn.

"But was informed that the only car then available had already taken a batch of people to Shira. I asked when the car would be back. The clerk said it would not be back. He said he had just that moment received a telephone call from Inveraray from the driver, a man named Fleming——"

"Jock," Colin explained to the others.

"The driver said that one of his passengers, a gentleman called Swan, had decided to stay the night in Inveraray, and wanted to keep car and driver to take him back to Dunoon in the morning. This, with suitable costs, was arranged."

"Infernal snooper," roared Colin.

"One moment. The clerk said, however, that if I would come to the agency at half past nine in the morning—this morning—the car would be back and would take me to Shira.

"I spent the night at the hotel, and was there on time. I then observed the somewhat unusual spectacle of a motorcar coming along the main street with its one passenger, a man in a grey hat and a very violent tartan necktie, standing up in the back seat."

Colin Campbell glowered at the floor.

A vast, dreamy expression of pleasure went over Dr. Fell's face. His eye was on a corner of the ceiling. He cleared his throat.

"Intrigued as to why this man should be standing up, I made inquiries. He replied (somewhat curtly) that he found the sitting position painful. It required little subtlety to get the story out of him. Indeed, he was boiling with it. Harrumph."

Alan groaned.

Dr. Fell peered over his eyeglasses, first at Alan and then at Kathryn. He wheezed. His expression was one of gargantuan delicacy.

"May I inquire," he said, "whether you two are engaged to be married?"

"Certainly not!" cried Kathryn.

"Then," Dr. Fell urged warmly, "in heaven's name *get* married. Do it in a hurry. You both hold responsible positions. But what you are likely to read about yourselves in today's *Daily Floodlight*, at risk of libel or no, is not likely to find favour with either Highgate University or the Harpenden College for Women. That thrilling story of the moonlight chase with claymores, with the lady shouting encouragement while the two cutthroats pursued him, really did put the tin hat on it."

"I never shouted encouragement!" said Kathryn.

Dr. Fell blinked at her.

"Are you sure you didn't, ma'am?"

"Well . . ."

"I'm afraid you did, Kitty-kat," observed Colin, glaring at the floor. "But it was my fault. I——"

Dr. Fell made a gesture.

"No matter," he said. "That was not what I wanted to tell you. Intrigued and inspired by this revival of old Highland customs, I spoke with the driver, Mr. Fleming."

"Yes?"

"Now here is what I most seriously want to ask. Did any of you, last night, at any time go up into the tower? *Any of you, at any time?*"

There was a silence. The windows facing the loch were open to a clear, cool, pleasant day. They all looked at each other.

"No," returned Kathryn.

"No," stated Colin.

"You're quite sure of that, now?"

"Definitely."

"Mr. Swan," Dr. Fell went on, with a curious insistence which Alan found disturbing, "says that the two men were 'dressed up' in some way."

"Oh, it's silly and horrible!" said Kathryn. "And it's all Alan's fault. They weren't exactly 'dressed up.' They had checkered tablecloths draped over their shoulders for plaids, that's all."

"Nothing else?"

"No."

Dr. Fell drew in his breath. His expression remained so grave, his colour so high, that nobody spoke.

"I repeat," Dr. Fell continued, "that I questioned the driver. Getting information out of him was rather more difficult than drawing teeth. But on one point he did give some information. He says that this place is not 'canny'——"

Colin interrupted with a fierce grunt of impatience, but Dr. Fell silenced him.

"And now he says he's in a position to swear to it."

"How?"

"Last night, after they had put up at Inveraray, Swan asked him to drive back here. Swan was going to have another try at getting in to see Miss Elspat Campbell. Now let's see if I've got the geography straight. The road to Inveraray runs along the back of the house, doesn't it?"

"Yes."

"And the front door faces the loch, as we see. Swan asked the driver to walk round and knock at the front door, as a sort of messenger, while

Swan remained at the back. The driver did so. It was bright moonlight, remember."

"Well?"

"He was just about to knock at the door, when he happened to look up at the window of the tower room. And he saw somebody or something at that window."

"But that's impossible!" cried Kathryn. "We were——"

Dr. Fell examined his hands, which were folded on the handle of his stick.

Then Dr. Fell looked up.

"Fleming," he went on, "swears he saw something in Highland costume, with half its face shot away, looking down at him."

## X

IT IS all very well to be hardheaded. Most of us are, even with headaches and shaky nerves. But to find a breath of superstitious terror is far from difficult here.

"Were you thinking," asked Kathryn, "of that story of what happened after the massacre of Glencoe? That the ghost of one of the victims pursued a man called Ian Campbell, who——"

Despairing of words, she made a gesture as of one who jumps.

Colin's face was fiery.

"Ghosts!" he said. "Ghosts! Look here. In the first place, there never was any such tradition as that. It was put into a lying guidebook because it sounded pretty. Professional soldiers in those days weren't so thin-skinned about executing orders.

"In the second place, that room's not haunted. Angus slept there every night for years, and *he* never saw a bogle. You don't believe such rubbish, do you, Fell?"

Dr. Fell remained unruffled.

"I am merely," he answered mildly, "stating what the driver told me."

"Rubbish. Jock was pulling your leg."

"And yet, d'ye know,"—Dr. Fell screwed up his face—"he hardly struck me as a man addicted to that form of gammon. I have usually found that Gaels will joke about anything except ghosts. Besides, I think you miss the real point of the story."

He was silent for a moment.

"But when did this happen?" asked Alan.

"Ah, yes. It was just before the two cutthroats with their lady came out of the back door and set on Swan. Fleming didn't knock at the front door after all. Hearing the shouts, he went to the back. He started up his car and eventually picked up Swan on the road. But he says he wasn't feeling too well. He says he stood in the moonlight for several minutes after he'd seen the thing at the window, and didn't feel too well at all. I can't say I blame him."

Kathryn hesitated. "What did it look like?"

"Bonnet and plaid and face caved in. That's all he could tell with any distinctness."

"Not a kilt too?"

"He wouldn't have been able to see a kilt. He only saw the upper half of the figure. He says it looked decayed, as though the moths had got at it, and it had only one eye." Again the doctor cleared his throat, rumblingly. "The point, however, is this. Who, besides you three, was in the house last night?"

"Nobody," replied Kathryn, "except Aunt Elspat and Kirstie, the maid. And they'd gone to bed."

"I tell you it's rubbish!" snarled Colin.

"Well, you can speak to Jock himself, if you like. He's out in the kitchen now."

Colin rose to find Jock and end this nonsense; but he did not do so. Alistair Duncan, followed by a patient but weary-looking Walter Chapman, was ushered in by the maid Kirstie—a scared-eyed, soft-voiced girl whose self-effacing habits rendered her almost invisible.

The lawyer made no reference to last night's rumpus with Colin. He stood very stiffly.

"Colin Campbell—" he began.

"Look here," grumbled Colin, shoving his hands into his pockets, lowering his neck into his collar, and looking like a Newfoundland dog which has been at the larder. "I owe you an apology, dammit. I apologize. I was wrong. There."

Duncan expelled his breath.

"I am glad, sir, that you have the decency to acknowledge it. Only my long friendship with your family enables me to overlook a piece of ill manners so uncalled-for and so flagrant."

"Hoy! Now wait a bit! Wait a bit! I didn't say——"

"So let us think no more about it," concluded the lawyer, as Colin's eye began to gleam again. Duncan coughed, indicating that he had left personal matters and now dealt with business.

"I thought I had better inform you," he went on, "that they think they may have found Alec Forbes."

"Wow! Where?"

"He's been reported to have been seen at a crofter's cottage near Glencoe."

Chapman intervened.

"Can't we settle it?" the insurance man suggested. "Glencoe's no great distance from here, as I understand it. You could drive there and back easily in an afternoon. Why not hop in my car and run up and see him?"

The lawyer's manner had a sort of corpselike benevolence.

"Patience, my dear fellow. Patience, patience, patience! First let the police find out if it *is* Alec. He has been reported before, you remember. Once in Edinburgh and once in Ayr."

"Alec Forbes," struck in Dr. Fell, "being the sinister figure who called on Mr. Campbell the night the latter died?"

They all swung round. Colin hastily performed an introduction.

"I have heard of you, Doctor," said Duncan, scrutinizing Dr. Fell through his pince-nez. "In fact, I—ah—confess I came here partly in the hope of seeing you. We have here, of course," he smiled, "a clear case of murder. But we are still rather confused about it. Can you unriddle it for us?"

For a moment Dr. Fell did not reply.

He frowned at the floor, drawing a design on the carpet with the end of his stick.

"H'mf," he said, and gave the ferrule of the stick a rap on the floor. "I sincerely trust it is murder. If it is not, I have no interest in it. But—Alec Forbes! Alec Forbes! Alec Forbes!"

"What about him?"

"Well, who is Alec Forbes? What is he? I could bear to know much more of him. For instance: what was the cause of his quarrel with Mr. Campbell?"

"Ice cream," replied Colin.

"*What?*"

"Ice cream. They were going to make it by a new process, in great quantity. And it was to be coloured in different tartan patterns. No, I'm perfectly serious! That's the sort of idea Angus was always getting. They built a laboratory, and used artificial ice—that chemical stuff that's so expensive—and ran up bills and raised merry blazes. Another of Angus's ideas was a new kind of tractor that would both sow and reap. And he also financed those people who were going to find Drake's gold and make all the subscribers millionaires."

"What sort of person is Forbes? Labouring man? Something of that sort?"

"Oh, no. Bloke of some education. But scatty in the money line, like Angus. Lean, dark-faced chap. Moody. Fond of the bottle. Great cyclist."

"H'mf. I see." Dr. Fell pointed with his stick. "That's Angus Campbell's photograph on the mantelpiece there, I take it?"

"Yes."

Dr. Fell got up from the sofa and lumbered across. He carried the crepe-draped picture to the light, adjusted his eyeglasses, and puffed gently as he studied it.

"Not the face, you know," he said, "of a man who commits suicide."

"Definitely not," smiled the lawyer.

"But we can't—" Chapman began.

"Which Campbell are you, sir?" Dr. Fell asked politely.

Chapman threw up his arms in despair.

"I'm not a Campbell at all. I represent the Hercules Insurance Company, and I've got to get back to my office in Glasgow or business will go to blazes. See here, Dr. Fell. I've heard of you too. They say you're fair-minded. And I put it to you: how can we go by what a person 'would' or 'wouldn't' have done, when the evidence shows he *did* do it."

"All evidence," said Dr. Fell, "points two ways. Like the ends of a stick. That is the trouble with it."

Absent-mindedly he stumped back to the mantelpiece, and put the photograph down. He seemed very much disturbed. While his eyeglasses came askew on his nose, he made what was (for him) the great exertion of feeling through all his pockets. He produced a sheet of paper scrawled with notes.

"From the admirably clear letter written by Colin Campbell," he went on, "and from facts he has given me this morning, I have been trying to construct a précis of what we know, or think we know."

"Well?" prompted the lawyer.

"With your permission,"—Dr. Fell scowled hideously—"I should like to read out these points. One or two things may appear a little clearer, or at least more suggestive, if they are heard in skeleton form. Correct me if I am wrong in any of them.

"1. Angus Campbell always went to bed at ten o'clock.
"2. It was his habit to lock and bolt the door on the inside.
"3. It was his habit to sleep with the window shut.
"4. It was his habit to write up his diary each night before going to bed."

Dr. Fell blinked up.

"No misstatement there, I trust?"

"No," admitted Colin.

"Then we pass on to the simple circumstances surrounding the crime.

"5. Alec Forbes called on A. Campbell at nine-thirty on the night of the crime.
"6. He forced his way into the house, and went up to Angus's bedroom.
"7. Neither of the two women saw him at this time."

Dr. Fell rubbed his nose.

"Query," he added, "how did Forbes get in, then? Presumably he didn't just break down the front door?"

"If you'd like to step out of that door there," responded Colin, pointing, "you can see. It leads to the ground-floor of the tower. In the ground-floor room there are wooden double-doors leading out to the court. They're supposed to be padlocked, but half the time they're not. That's how Forbes came—without disturbing anybody else."

Dr. Fell made a note.

"That seems to be clear enough. Very well. We now take arms against a sea of troubles.

"8. At this time Forbes was carrying an object like a 'suitcase.'

"9. He had a row with Angus, who evicted him.

"10. Forbes was empty-handed when he left.

"11. Elspat Campbell and Kirstie MacTavish arrived in time to see the eviction.

"12. They were afraid Forbes might have come back. This becomes more understandable when we learn of the isolated tower with its outside entrance and its five empty floors.

"13. They searched the empty rooms, and also Angus's room.

"14. There was nothing under the bed in Angus's bedroom at this time.

"Still correct?" inquired Dr. Fell, raising his head.

"No, it isna," announced a high, sharp, positive voice which made them all jump.

Nobody had seen Aunt Elspat come in. She stood sternly on her dignity, her hands folded.

Dr. Fell blinked at her. "What isn't true, ma'am?"

"It isna true tae say the box tae carry the dog wasna under the bed when Kirstie and I luked. It was."

Her six auditors regarded her with consternation. Most of them began to speak at once, a frantic babble which was only stilled by Duncan's stern assertion of legal authority.

"Elspat Campbell, listen to me. You said there was nothing there."

"I said there was nae *suitcase* there. I didna say aboot the ither thing."

"Are you telling us that the dog carrier was under the bed before Angus locked and bolted his door?"

"Aye."

"Elspat," said Colin, with a sudden gleam of certainty in his eye, "you're lying. God's wounds, you're lying! You said there was *nothing* under that bed. I heard you myself."

"I'm tellin' ye the gospel truth, and Kirstie will tu." She favoured them all with an equally malignant look. "Dinner's on its way, and I'm no' settin' places for the parcel o' ye."

Inflexible, making this very clear, she walked out of the room and closed the door.

The question is, thought Alan, does this alter matters or doesn't it? He shared Colin Campbell's evident conviction that Elspat was lying. But she had one of those faces so used to household deceit, so experienced in lying

for what she believed a good purpose, that it was difficult to distinguis◖
between truth and falsehood in anything.

This time it was Dr. Fell who stilled the babble of argument.

"We will query the point," he said, "and continue. The next points defin◖
our problem squarely and simply.

"15. Angus locked and bolted his door on the inside.

"16. His dead body was found by the milkman at six o'clock on the fol◖
lowing morning, at the foot of the tower.

"17. He had died of multiple injuries caused by the fall.

"18. Death took place between ten p.m. and one a.m.

"19. He had not been drugged or overcome in any way.

"20. The door was still locked and bolted on the inside. Since the bolt wa◖
rusty, difficult to draw and firmly shot in its socket, this rules out any pos◖
sibility of tampering with it."

In Alan's mind rose the image of the shattered door as he had seen i◖
last night.

He remembered the rustiness of the bolt, and the stubborn lock torn from
its frame. Jiggery-pokery with string or any similar device must clearly be pu◖
aside. The image faded as Dr. Fell continued.

"21. The window was inaccessible. We have this from a steeple jack◖

"22. There was no person hiding in the room.

"23. The bed had been occupied."

Dr. Fell puffed out his cheeks, frowned, and tapped a pencil on the notes◖

"Which," he said, "brings us to a point where I must interpose anothe◖
query. Your letter didn't say. When his body was found in the morning◖
was he wearing slippers or a dressing gown?"

"No," said Colin. "Just his wool nightshirt."

Dr. Fell made another note.

"24. His diary was missing. This, however, might have been taken at som◖
subsequent time.

"25. Angus's fingerprints, and only his, were found on the catch of th◖
window.

"26. Under the bed was a case of the sort used to carry dogs. It did no◖
belong in the house; had presumably been brought by Forbes; but was i◖
any case not there the night before.

"27. This box was empty.

"We are therefore forced to the conclusion——"

Dr. Fell paused.

"Go on!" Alistair Duncan prompted in a sharp voice. "To what con◖
clusion?"

Dr. Fell sniffed.

"Gentlemen, we can't escape it. It's inevitable. We are forced to the con◖

clusion that either (a) Angus Campbell deliberately committed suicide, or (b) there was in that box something which made him run for his life to escape it, and crash through the window to his death in doing so."

Kathryn shivered a little. But Chapman was not impressed.

"I know," he said. "Snakes. Spiders. Fu Manchu. We were all over that last night. And it gets us nowhere."

"Can you dispute my facts?" inquired Dr. Fell, tapping the notes.

"No. But can you dispute *mine*? Snakes! Spiders——"

"And now," grinned Colin, "ghosts."

"Eh?"

"A rattlebrain by the name of Jock Fleming," explained Colin, "claims to have seen somebody in Highland dress, with no face, gibbering at the window last night."

Chapman's face lost some of its colour.

"I don't know anything about that," he said. "But I could almost as soon believe in a ghost as in a dexterous spider or snake that could close up the clasps of a suitcase afterwards. I'm English. I'm practical. But this is a funny country and a funny house; and I tell you I shouldn't care to spend a night up in that room."

Colin got up from his chair and did a little dance round the room.

"That's done it," he roared, when he could get his breath. "*That's torn it!*"

Dr. Fell blinked at him with mild expostulation. Colin's face was suffused and the veins stood out on his thick neck.

"Listen," he went on, swallowing with powerful restraint. "Ever since I got here, everybody has been ghosting me. And I'm sick of it. This tomfoolery has got to be blown sky-high and I'm the jasper to do it. I'll tell you what I'm going to do. I'm going to move my things into that tower this very afternoon, and I'm going to sleep there henceforward. If so much as a ghost of a ghost shows its ugly head there, if anybody tries to make *me* jump out of a window . . ."

His eye fell on the family Bible. The atheistical Colin ran across to it and put his hand on it.

"Then I hereby swear that I'll go to the kirk every Sunday for the next twelve months. Yes, and prayer meeting too!"

He darted across to the door to the hall, which he set open.

"Do you hear that, Elspat?" he roared, coming back and putting his hand on the Bible again. "Every Sunday, and prayer meeting on Wednesdays. Ghosts! Bogles! Warlocks! Isn't there a sane person left in this world?"

His voice reverberated through the house. You might have imagined that it drew back echoes. But Kathryn's attempt to shush him was unnecessary. Colin already felt better. It was Kirstie MacTavish who supplied the distraction, by thrusting her head in at the doorway and speaking in a tone not far removed from real awe.

"That reporter's back again," she said.

## XI

COLIN opened his eyes. "Not the chap from the *Daily Floodlight?*"

"It's him."

"Tell him I'll see him," said Colin, straightening his collar and drawing a deep breath.

"No!" said Alan. "In your present state of mind you'd probably cut his heart out and eat it. Let *me* see him."

"Yes, please!" cried Kathryn. She turned a fervent face. "If he's dared to come back here, he can't have said anything very awful about us in the paper. Don't you see: this is our chance to apologize and put everything right again? Please let Alan see him!"

"All right," Colin agreed. "After all, you didn't stick him in the seat of his pants with a claymore. You may be able to smooth him down."

Alan hurried out into the hall. Just outside the front door, clearly of two minds on how to approach this interview, stood Swan. Alan went outside, and carefully closed the front door.

"Look here," he began, "I honestly am terribly sorry about last night. I can't think what came over us. We'd had one over the eight . . ."

"You're telling *me?*" inquired Swan. He looked at Alan, and anger seemed less predominant than real curiosity. "What were you drinking, for God's sake? T.N.T. and monkey glands? I used to be a track man myself, but I never saw anybody cover ground like that thick-set old buster since Nurmi retired to Finland."

"Something like that."

Swan's expression, as he saw that he was dealing with a chastened man, grew increasingly more stern.

"Now look," he said impressively. "You know, don't you, that I could sue you all for heavy damages?"

"Yes; but——"

"And that I've got enough on you to make your name mud in the press, if I was the sort of a fellow who bears malice?"

"Yes, but——"

"You can just thank your lucky stars, Dr. Campbell, that I'm *not* the sort of a fellow who bears malice: that's all I say." Swan gave a significant nod. He was wearing a new light-grey suit and tartan tie. Again his gloomy sternness was moved by curiosity. "What kind of a professor are you, anyway?

.unning around with women professors from other colleges—always going
o houses of ill fame——"

"Here! For the love of——"

"Now don't deny it," said Swan, pointing a lean finger in his face. "I
eard Miss Campbell herself say, in front of witnesses, that that's exactly
hat you were always doing."

"She was talking about the Roman Catholic Church! That's what the old-
imers called it."

"It's not what the old-timers called it where I come from. On top of that,
ou get all ginned up and chase respectable people along a public road with
roadswords. Do you carry on like that at Highgate, Doc? Or just in vaca-
ions? I really want to know."

"I swear to you, it's all a mistake! And here's the point. I don't care what
ou say about me. But will you promise not to say anything about Miss
Campbell?"

Swan considered this.

"Well, I don't know," he said, with another darkly significant shake of his
.ead, and a suggestion that, if he did this, it would be only from the kindness
f his heart. "I've got a duty to the public, you know."

"Rubbish."

"But I tell you what I'll do," Swan suggested, as though suddenly coming
o a decision. "Just to show you I'm a sport, I'll make a deal with you."

"Deal?"

The other lowered his voice.

"That fellow in there, the great big fat fellow, is Dr. Gideon Fell: isn't
t?"

"Yes."

"I only discovered it when he'd slipped away from me. And, when I phoned
ny paper, they were pretty wild. They say that wherever *he* goes, a story
reaks with a wallop. They say to stick to him. Look, Doc. I've *got* to get a
tory! I've incurred a lot of expense over this thing; I've got another car that's
ating its head off. If I fall down on this story I won't get the expenses O.K.'d,
nd I may even get the air."

"So?"

"So here's what I want you to do. Just keep me posted, that's all. Let me
now everything that goes on. In return for that——"

He paused, shying back a little, as Colin Campbell came out of the front
loor. But Colin was trying to be affable: too affable, massively affable, with
. guilty grin.

"In return for that, just keeping me posted," resumed Swan, "I'll agree to
orget all I know about you and Miss Campbell, and,"—he looked at Colin—
what you did as well, which might have caused me a serious injury. I'll do
hat just to be a sport and show there are no hard feelings. What do you say?"

Colin's face had lightened with relief.

"I say it's fair enough," Colin returned, with a bellow of pleasure. "Now that's damned decent of you, young fellow! Damned decent! I was tight and I apologize. What do you say, Alan Oig?"

Alan's voice was fervent.

"I say it's fair enough too. You keep to that bargain, Mr. Swan, and you'll have nothing to complain about. If there are any stories going, you shall have them."

He could almost forget that he had a hangover. A beautiful sense of well-being, a sense of the world set right again, crept into Alan Campbell and glowed in his veins.

Swan raised his eyebrows.

"Then it's a deal?"

"It is," said Colin.

"It is," agreed the other miscreant.

"All right, then!" said Swan, drawing a deep breath but still speaking darkly. "Only just remember that I'm straining my duty to my public to oblige you. So remember where we all stand and don't try any——"

Above their heads, a window creaked open. The contents of a large bucket of water, aimed with deadly and scientific accuracy, descended in a solid, glistening sheet over Swan's head. In fact, Swan might be said momentarily to have disappeared.

At the window appeared the malignant face of Aunt Elspat.

"Can ye no' tak' a hint?" she inquired. "I tauld ye to gang your ways, and I'll no' tell ye again. Here's for guid measure."

With the same accuracy, but almost with leisureliness, she lifted a second bucket and emptied it over Swan's head. Then the window closed with a bang.

Swan did not say anything. He stood motionless, and merely looked. His new suit was slowly turning black. His hat resembled a piece of sodden blotting paper from beneath whose down-turned brim there looked out the eyes of a man gradually being bereft of his reason.

"My dear chap!" bellowed Colin in real consternation. "The old witch! I'll wring her neck; so help me, I will! My dear chap, you're not hurt, are you?"

Colin bounded down the steps. Swan began slowly, but with increasing haste, to back away from him.

"My dear chap, wait! Stop! You must have some dry clothes!"

Swan continued to back away.

"Come into the house, my dear fellow. Come——"

Then Swan found his voice.

"Come into the house," he shrilled, backing away still farther, "so you can steal my clothes and turn me out again? No, you don't! Keep away from me!"

"Look out!" screamed Colin. "One more step and you'll be in the loch! Look——"

Alan glanced round wildly. At the windows of the sitting room observed an interested group of watchers composed of Duncan, Chapman, and Dr. Fell. But most of all he was conscious of Kathryn's horror-stricken countenance.

Swan saved himself by some miracle on the edge of the pier.

"Think I'll go into that booby hatch, do you?" Swan was raving. "You're a bunch of criminal lunatics, that's what you are, and I'm going to expose you. I'm going to——"

"Man, you can't walk about like that! You'll catch your death of cold! Come on in. Besides," argued Colin, "you'll be on the scene of it, won't you? Smack in the middle of things alongside Dr. Fell?"

This appeared to make Swan pause. He hesitated. Still streaming like an enthusiastic fountain, he wiped the water from his eyes with a shaky hand, and looked back at Colin with real entreaty.

"Can I depend on that?"

"I swear you can! The old hag has got it in for you, but I'll take care of her. Come on."

Swan seemed to be debating courses. At length he allowed himself to be taken by the arm and urged toward the door. He ducked quickly when he passed the window, as though wondering whether to expect boiling lead.

A scene of some embarrassment ensued inside. The lawyer and the insurance man took a hasty leave. Colin, clucking to his charge, escorted him upstairs to change his clothes. In the sitting room a dejected Alan found Kathryn and Dr. Fell.

"I trust, sir," observed Dr. Fell, with stately courtesy, "you know your own business best. But, candidly, do you really think it's wise to antagonize the press quite so much as that? What did you do to the fellow this time? Duck him in the water butt?"

"We didn't do anything. It was Elspat. She poured two buckets of water on him from the window."

"But is he going to—" cried Kathryn.

"He promises that if we keep him posted about what's going on here, he won't say a word. At least, that's what he *did* promise. I can't say how he's feeling now."

"Keep him posted?" asked Dr. Fell sharply.

"Presumably about what's going on here, and whether this is suicide or murder, and what you think of it." Alan paused. "What do you think, by the way?"

Dr. Fell's gaze moved to the door to the hall, making sure it was firmly closed. He puffed out his cheeks, shook his head, and finally sat down on the sofa again.

"If only the facts," he growled, "weren't so infernally simple! I distrust their simplicity. I have a feeling that there's a trap in them. I should also like to know why Miss Elspat Campbell now wants to change her testimony, and swears that the dog carrier *was* under the bed before the room was locked up."

"Do you think the second version is true?"

"No, by thunder, I don't!" said Dr. Fell, rapping his stick on the floor. "I think the first is true. But that only makes our locked-room problem the worse. Unless——"

"Unless what?"

Dr. Fell disregarded this.

"It apparently does no good merely to repeat those twenty-seven points over and over. I repeat: it's too simple. A man double locks his door. He goes to bed. He gets up in the middle of the night without his slippers (mark that), and jumps from the window to instant death. He——"

"That's not quite accurate, by the way."

Dr. Fell lifted his head, his underlip outthrust.

"Hey? What isn't?"

"Well, if you insist on a shade of accuracy, Angus didn't meet an instant death. At least, so Colin told me. The police surgeon wouldn't be definite about the time of death. He said Angus hadn't died instantly, but had probably been alive though unconscious for a little while before he died."

Dr. Fell's little eyes narrowed. The wheezing breaths, which ran down over the ridges of his waistcoat, were almost stilled. He seemed about to say something, but checked himself.

"I further," he said, "don't like Colin's insistence on spending the night in that tower room."

"You don't think there's any more danger?" Kathryn asked.

"My dear child! Of course there's danger!" said Dr. Fell. "There's always danger when some agency we don't understand killed a man. Pry the secret out of it, and you're all right. But so long as you don't understand it . . ."

He brooded.

"You have probably observed that the very things we try hardest to avoid happening are always the things that do happen. V*ide* the saga of Swan. But here, in an uglier way, we have the same wheel revolving and the same danger returning. Archons of Athens! What COULD have been in that dog carrier? Something that left *no* trace, nothing whatever? And why the open end? Obviously so that something could breathe through the wire and get air. But what?"

Distorted pictures, all without form, floated in Alan's mind.

"You don't think the box may be a red herring?"

"It may be. But, unless it does mean something, the whole case collapses and we may as well go home to bed. It has got to mean something."

"Some kind of animal?" suggested Kathryn.

"Which closed the clasps of the box after it got out?" inquired Dr. Fell.

"That may not be so difficult," Alan pointed out, "if it were thin enough to get out through the wire. No, hang it, that won't do!" He remembered the box itself, and the mesh. "That wire is so close-meshed that the smallest snake in existence could hardly wriggle out through it."

"Then," pursued Dr. Fell, "there is the episode of the Highlander with the caved-in face."

"You don't believe that story?"

"I believe that Jock Fleming saw what he says he saw. I do not necessarily believe in a ghost. After all, such a piece of trickery, in the moonlight and from a distance of sixty feet up in a tower, wouldn't be very difficult. An old bonnet and plaid, a little make-up——"

"But why?"

Dr. Fell's eyes opened wide. His breath laboured with ghoulish eagerness as he seemed to seize on the point.

"Exactly. That's it. Why? We mustn't miss the importance of the tale: which is not whether it was supernatural, but why it was done at all. That is, if it had any reason at all in the way we mean." He became very thoughtful. "Find the contents of that box, and we're on the view halloo. That's our problem. Some parts of the business, of course, are easy. You will already have guessed who stole the missing diary?"

"Of course," replied Kathryn instantly. "*Elspat* stole it, of course."

Alan stared at her.

Dr. Fell, with a vast and gratified beam, regarded her as though she were a more refreshing person than even he had expected, and nodded.

"Admirable!" he chuckled. "The talent for deduction developed by judicious historical research can just as well be applied to detective work. Never forget that, my dear. I learned it at an early age. Bull's-eye. It was Elspat for a fiver."

"But why?" demanded Alan.

Kathryn set her face into its severest lines, as though they had again returned to the debate of two nights ago. Her tone was withering.

"My *dear* Dr. Campbell!" she said. "Consider what we know. For many, many years she was rather more than a housekeeper to Angus Campbell?"

"Well?"

"But she's horribly, morbidly respectable, and doesn't even believe anybody's guessed her real thoughts?"

(Alan was tempted to say, "Something like you," but he restrained himself.)

"Yes."

"Angus Campbell was a free-spoken person who kept a diary where he could record his intimate—well, you know!"

"Yes?"

"All right. Three days before his death, Angus takes out still another insurance policy, to take care of his old-time love in the event of his death. It's almost certain, isn't it, that in writing down that he did take out an insurance policy he'll make some reference to *why* he did it?"

She paused, raising her eyebrows.

"So, of course, Elspat stole the diary out of some horrid fear of having people learn what she did years and years ago.

"Don't you remember what happened last night, Alan? How she acted when you and Colin began talking about the diary? When you did begin to discuss it, she first said everybody was daft and finally headed you off by suggesting that wretched whisky? And, of course, it did head you off. That's all."

Alan whistled.

"By gad, I believe you're right!"

"Thank you so much, dear. If you were to apply a little of that brain of yours," remarked Kathryn, wrinkling up her pretty nose, "to observing and drawing the inferences you're always telling everyone else to draw——"

Alan treated this with cold scorn. He had half a mind to make some reference to the Duchess of Cleveland, and the paucity of inference K. I. Campbell had been able to draw there, but he decided to give that unfortunate court lady a rest.

"Then the diary hasn't really anything to do with the case?"

"I wonder," said Dr. Fell.

"Obviously," Kathryn pointed out, "Aunt Elspat knows *something*. And probably from the diary. Otherwise why all this business of writing to the *Daily Floodlight?*"

"Yes."

"And since she did write to them, it seems fairly clear that there wasn't anything in the diary to compromise her reputation. Then why on earth doesn't she speak out? What's the matter with her? If the diary gives some indication that Angus was murdered, why doesn't she say so?"

"Unless, of course," said Alan, "the diary says that he meant to commit suicide."

"Alan, Alan, Alan! To say nothing of all the other policies, Angus takes out a last policy, pays the premium, and then writes down that he's going to kill himself? It's just—against nature, that's all!"

Alan gloomily admitted this.

"Thirty-five thousand pounds in the balance," breathed Kathryn, "and she won't claim it. Why doesn't somebody tackle her about it? Why don't you tackle her, Dr. Fell? Everybody else seems to be afraid of her."

"I shall be most happy," beamed Dr. Fell.

Ponderously, like a man-o'-war easing into a dock, he turned round on the sofa. He adjusted his eyeglasses, and blinked at Elspat Campbell, who was standing in the doorway with an expression between wrath, pain, uncertainty, and the fear of damnation. They caught only the tail of this expression, which was gone in a flash, to be replaced by a tightening of the jaws and a determination of granite inflexibility.

Dr. Fell was not impressed.

"Well, ma'am?" he inquired offhandedly. "You really did pinch that diary, didn't you?"


## XII

Twilight was deepening over Loch Fyne as they descended through the grey ghostly wood of fallen trees, and turned northwards along the main road to Shira.

Alan felt healthily and pleasantly tired after an afternoon in the open. Kathryn, in tweeds and flat-heeled shoes, had colour in her cheeks and her blue eyes glowed. She had not once put on her spectacles for argument, even when she had been clucked at for being unfamiliar with the murder of the Red Fox, Colin Campbell of 1752, who had been shot by nobody knows whose hand, but for which James Stewart was tried at Inveraray courthouse.

"The trouble is," Alan was declaring, as they tramped down the hill, "Stevenson has so cast the glamour over us that we tend to forget what this 'hero,' this famous Alan Breck—one 'l,' please—was actually like. I've often wished somebody would take the side of the Campbells, for a change."

"Intellectual honesty again?"

"No. Just for fun. But the weirdest version of the incident was in the film version of *Kidnapped*. Alan Breck, and David Balfour, and a totally unnecessary female, are fleeing from the redcoats. Disguised up to the ears, they are driving in a cart along a troop-infested road, singing 'Loch Lomond'; and Alan Breck hisses, 'They'll never suspect us now.'

"I felt like arising and addressing the screen, saying: 'They damn well will if you insist on singing a Jacobite song.' That's about as sensible as though a group of British secret service agents, disguised as Gestapo, were to swagger down Unter den Linden singing, *There'll Always Be an England*."

Kathryn seized on the essential part of this.

"So the female was totally unnecessary, eh?"

"What's that?"

"The female, says he in all his majesty, was totally unnecessary. Of course!"

"I only mean that she wasn't in the original version, and she spoiled what little story was left. Can't you forget this sex war for five minutes?"

"It's you who are always dragging it in."

"Me?"

"Yes, you. I don't know what to make of you. You—you *can* be rather nice, you know, when you try." She kicked the fallen leaves out of her path, and suddenly began to giggle. "I was thinking about last night."

"Don't remind me!"

"But that's when you were nicest, really. Don't you remember what you said to me?"

He had thought the incident buried in merciful oblivion. It was not.

"What did I say?"

"Never mind. We're terribly late for tea again, and Aunt Elspat will carry on again, just as she did last night."

"Aunt Elspat," he said sternly, "Aunt Elspat, as you very well know, won't be down to tea. She's confined to her room with a violent and hysterical fit of the sulks."

Kathryn stopped and made a hopeless gesture.

"You know, I can't decide whether I like that old woman or whether I'd like to murder her. Dr. Fell tackles her about the diary, and all she does is go clear up in the air, and scream that it's her house, and she won't be bullied, and the dog carrier *was* under the bed——"

"Yes; but——"

"I think she just wants her own way. I think she won't tell anybody anything just because they want her to, and she's determined to be the boss. Just as she finished off in real sulks because Colin insisted on having that poor inoffensive Swan man in the house."

"Young lady, don't evade the question. What was it I said to you last night?"

The little vixen, he thought, was deliberately doing this. He wanted not to give her the satisfaction of showing curiosity. But he could not help it. They had come out into the main road only half a dozen yards from the Castle of Shira. Kathryn turned a demure but wicked-looking countenance in the twilight.

"If you can't remember," she told him innocently, "I can't repeat it to you. But I can tell you what my answer would have been, if I had made any answer."

"Well?"

"Oh, I should probably have said something like, 'In that case, why don't you?'"

Then she ran from him.

He caught up with her only in the hall, and there was no time to say anything more. The thunder of voices from the dining room would have warned them of what was in progress, even had they not caught sight of Colin through the partly open door.

The bright light shone over a snug table. Colin, Dr. Fell, and Charlie Swan had finished a very large meal. Their plates were pushed to one side

d in the center of the table stood a decanter bearing a rich brown liquid.
n the faces of Dr. Fell and Swan, before whom stood empty glasses, was
ie expression of men who have just passed through a great spiritual experi-
ice. Colin twinkled at them.

"Come in!" he cried to Kathryn and Alan. "Sit down. Eat before it gets
ld. I've just been giving our friends their first taste of the Doom of the
ampbells."

Swan's expression, preternaturally solemn, was now marred by a slight
ccup. But he remained solemn, and seemed to be meditating a profound
perience.

His costume, too, was curious. He had been fitted out with one of Colin's
irts, which was too big in the shoulders and body, but much too short in
ie sleeves. Below this, since no pair of trousers in the house would fit him,
e wore a kilt. It was the very dark green and blue of the Campbells, with
in transversing stripes of yellow and crossed white.

"Cripes!" Swan muttered, contemplating the empty glass. "Cripes!"

"The observation," said Dr. Fell, passing his hand across a pink forehead,
s not unwarranted."

"Like it?"

"Well—" said Swan.

"Have another? What about you, Alan? And you, Kitty-kat?"

"No." Alan was very firm about this. "I want some food. Maybe a little
f that alcoholic tabasco sauce later, but a very little and not now."

Colin rubbed his hands.

"Oh, you will! They all do. What do you think of our friend Swan's getup?
eat, eh? I fished it out of a chest in the best bedroom. The original tartan
f the Clan MacHolster."

Swan's face darkened.

"Are you kidding me?"

"As I believe in heaven," swore Colin, lifting his hand, "that's the Mac-
olster tartan as sure as I believe in heaven."

Swan was mollified. In fact, he seemed to be enjoying himself.

"It's a funny feeling," he said, eying the kilt. "Like walking around in
ublic without your pants. Cripes, though! To think that I, Charley Swan
f Toronto, should be wearing a real kilt in a real Scotch castle, and drinking
ld dew of the mountain like a clansman! I must write to my father about
is. It's decent of you to let me stay all night."

"Nonsense! Your clothes won't be ready until morning, anyway. Have an-
ther?"

"Thanks. I don't mind if I do."

"You, Fell?"

"Harrumph," said Dr. Fell. "That is an offer (or, in this case, challenge)
very seldom refuse. Thank'ee. But——"

"But what?"

"I was just wondering," said Dr. Fell, crossing his knees with considerable effort, "whether the *nunc bibendum est* is to be followed by a reasonable *sat prata hiberunt*. In more elegant language, you're not thinking of another binge? Or have you given up the idea of sleeping in the tower tonight?"

Colin stiffened.

A vague qualm of uneasiness brushed the old room.

"And why should I give up the idea of sleeping in the tower?"

"It's just because I don't know why you shouldn't," returned Dr. Fell frankly, "that I wish you wouldn't."

"Rubbish! I've spent half the afternoon repairing the lock and bolt of that door. I've carried my duds up there. You don't think *I'm* going to commit suicide?"

"Well," said Dr. Fell, "suppose you did?"

The sense of uneasiness had grown greater. Even Swan seemed to feel it. Colin was about to break out into hollow incredulity, but Dr. Fell stopped him.

"One moment. Merely suppose that. Or, to be more exact, suppose that tomorrow morning we find you dead at the foot of the tower under just such circumstances as Angus. Er—do you mind if I smoke while you're eating, Miss Campbell?"

"No, of course not," said Kathryn.

Dr. Fell took out a large meerschaum pipe with a curved stem, which he filled from an obese pouch, and lighted. He sat back in his chair, argumentatively. With a somewhat cross-eyed expression behind his eyeglasses, he watched the smoke curl up into the bright bowl of the lamp.

"You believe," he went on, "you believe that your brother's death was murder: don't you?"

"I do! And I thundering well hope it was! If it was, and we can prove it, I inherit seventeen thousand five hundred pounds."

"Yes. But if Angus's death *was* murder, then the same force which killed Angus can kill you. Had you thought of that?"

"I'd like to see the force that could do it: God's wounds, I would!" snapped Colin.

But the calmness of Dr. Fell's voice had its effect. Colin's tone was considerably more subdued.

"Now, if anything should by any chance happen to you," pursued Dr. Fell, while Colin stirred, "what becomes of your share of the thirty-five thousand pounds? Does it revert to Elspat Campbell, for instance?"

"No, certainly not. It's kept in the family. It goes to Robert. Or to Robert's heirs if he's not alive."

"Robert?"

"Our third brother. He got into trouble and skipped the country years

go. We don't even know where he is, though Angus was always trying to
find him. We do know he married and had children, the only one of us three
who did marry. Robert would be—about sixty-four now. A year younger than
am."

Dr. Fell continued to smoke meditatively, his eye on the lamp.

"You see," he wheezed, "assuming this to be murder, we have got to look
or a motive. And a motive, on the financial side at least, is very difficult to
ind. Suppose Angus was murdered for his life-insurance money. By you. (Tut,
now, don't jump down my throat!) Or by Elspat. Or by Robert or his heirs.
Yet no murderer in his senses, under those circumstances, is going to plan a
crime which will be taken for suicide. Thereby depriving himself of the
money which was the whole motive for the crime.

"So we come back to the personal. This man Alec Forbes now. I suppose
he was capable of killing Angus?"

"Oh, Lord, yes!"

"H'm. Tell me. Has he got any grudge against you?"

Colin swelled with a kind of obscure satisfaction.

"Alec Forbes," Colin replied, "hates my guts almost as much as he hated
Angus's. I ridiculed his schemes. And if there's one thing one of these moody
chaps can't stand, it's ridicule. I never disliked the fellow myself, though."

"Yet you admit that the thing which killed Angus could kill you?"

Colin's neck hunched down into his shoulders. He stretched out his hand
or the decanter of whisky. He poured out very large portions of it for Dr.
Fell, for Swan, for Alan, and for himself.

"If you're trying to persuade me not to sleep in the tower——"

"I am."

"Then be hanged to you. Because I'm going to." Colin scanned the faces
ound him with fiery eyes. "What's the matter with all of you?" he roared.
"Are you all dead tonight? We had things better last night. Drink up! I'm
not going to commit suicide; I promise you that. So drink up, and let's have
no more of this tomfoolery now."

When they separated to go to bed at shortly past ten o'clock, not a man in
hat room was cold sober.

In gradations of sobriety they ranged from Swan, who had taken the stuff
indiscreetly and could barely stand, to Dr. Fell, whom nothing seemed to
hake. Colin Campbell was definitely drunk, though his footstep was firm
and only his reddish eyes betrayed him. But he was not drunk with the
grinning, whooping abandon of the night before.

Nobody was. It had become one of those evenings when even the tobacco
smoke turns stale and sour; and men, perversely, keep taking the final one
which they don't need. When Kathryn slipped away before ten, no one at-
empted to stop her.

On Alan the liquor was having a wrong effect. Counteracting the weariness

of his relaxed muscles, it stung him to tired but intense wakefulness.
Thoughts scratched in his mind like pencils on slate; they would not go away
or be still.

His bedroom was up on the first floor, overlooking the loch. His legs felt
light as he ascended the stairs, saying good night to Dr. Fell, who went to
his own room (surprisingly) with magazines under his arm.

A lightness in the legs, a buzzing head, an intense discomfort, are no
tonics for sleep. Alan groped into his room. Either out of economy or
because of the sketchiness of the blackout, the chandelier contained no electric
bulbs and only a candle could be used for illumination.

Alan lit the candle on the bureau. The meager little flame intensified the
surrounding darkness, and made his face in the mirror look white. It seemed
to him that he was tottering; that he was a fool to have touched that stuff
again, since this time it brought neither exhilaration nor surcease.

Round and round whirled his thoughts, jumping from one point to another
like clumsy mountain goats. People used to study by candlelight. It was a
wonder they hadn't all gone blind. Maybe most of them had. He thought of
Mr. Pickwick in the Great White Horse at Ipswich. He thought of Scott
ruining his eyesight by working under "a broad star of gas." He thought
of . . .

It was no good. He *couldn't* sleep.

He undressed, stumbling, in the dark. He put on slippers and a dressing
gown.

His watch ticked on. Ten-thirty. A quarter to eleven. The hour itself.
Eleven-fifteen . . .

Alan sat down in a chair, put his head in his hands, and wished passionately for something to read. He had noticed very few books at Shira. Dr
Fell, the doctor had informed him that day, had brought a Boswell along.

What a solace, what a soothing and comfort, Boswell would be now! To
turn over those pages, to talk with Doctor Johnson until you drifted into a
doze, must be the acme of all pleasure on this night. The more he thought
of it, the more he wished he had it. Would Dr. Fell lend it to him, for instance?

He got up, opened the door, and padded down a chilly hall to the doctor's
room. He could have shouted for joy when he saw a thin line of light under
the sill of the door. He knocked, and was told to come in in a voice which
he hardly recognized as that of Dr. Fell.

Alan, strung to a fey state of awareness, felt his scalp stir with terror as
he saw the expression on Dr. Fell's face.

Dr. Fell sat by the chest of drawers, on top of which a candle was burning
in its holder. He wore an old purple dressing gown as big as a tent. The
meerschaum pipe hung from one corner of his mouth. Round him was scattered a heap of magazines, letters, and what looked like bills. Through a

mist of tobacco smoke in the airless room, Alan saw the startled, faraway expression of Dr. Fell's eyes, the open mouth which barely supported the pipe.

"Thank God you're here!" rumbled Dr. Fell, suddenly coming to life. "I was just going to fetch you."

"Why?"

"I know what was in that box," said Dr. Fell. "I know how the trick was worked. I know what set on Angus Campbell."

The candle flame wavered slightly among shadows. Dr. Fell reached out for his crutch-handled stick, and groped wildly before he found it.

"We've got to get Colin out of that room," he added. "There may not be any danger; there probably isn't; but, by thunder, we can't afford to take any chances! I can show him now what did it, and he's got to listen to reason. See here."

Puffing and wheezing, he impelled himself to his feet.

"I underwent the martyrdom of climbing up those tower stairs once before today, but I can't do it again. Will you go up there and rout Colin out?"

"Of course."

"We needn't rouse anybody else. Just bang on the door until he lets you in; don't take no for an answer. Here. I've got a small torch. Keep it shielded when you go up the stairs, or you'll have the wardens after us. Hurry!"

"But what——"

"I haven't time to explain now. Hurry!"

Alan took the torch. Its thin, pale beam explored ahead of him. He went out in the hall, which smelt of old umbrellas, and down the stairs. A chilly draught touched his ankles. He crossed the lower hall, and went into the living room.

Across the room, on the mantelpiece, the face of Angus Campbell looked back at him as the beam of his torch rested on the photograph. Angus's white, fleshy-jowled countenance seemed to stare back with the knowledge of a secret.

The door leading to the ground-floor of the tower was locked on the inside. When Alan turned the squeaky key and opened the door, his fingers were shaking.

Now the earthen floor under him felt icy. A very faint mist had crept in from the loch. The arch leading to the tower stairs, a gloomy hole, repelled and somewhat unnerved him. Though he started to take the stairs at a run, both the dangerous footing and the exertion of the climb forced him to slow down.

First floor. Second floor, more of a pull. Third floor, and he was breathing hard. Fourth floor, and the distance up seemed endless. The little pencil of light intensified the coldness and close claustrophobia brought on by that enclosed space. It would not be pleasant to meet suddenly, on the stairs, a man in Highland costume with half his face shot away.

Or have the thing come out of one of the tower rooms, for instance, and touch him on the shoulder from behind.

You could not get away from anything that chose to pursue you here.

Alan reached the airless, windowless landing on which was the door to the topmost room. The oak door, its wood rather rotted by damp, was closed. Alan tried the knob, and found that it was locked and bolted on the inside.

He lifted his fist and pounded heavily on the door.

"Colin!" he shouted. "Colin!"

There was no reply.

The thunder of the knocking, the noise of his own voice, rebounded with infernal and intolerable racket in that confined space. He felt it must wake everybody in the house; everybody in Inveraray, for that matter. But he continued to knock and shout, still with no reply.

He set his shoulder to the door, and pushed. He got down on his knees, and tried to peer under the sill of the door, but he could see nothing except an edge of moonlight.

As he got to his feet again, feeling lightheaded after that exertion, the suspicion which had already struck him grew and grew with ugly effect. Colin *might* be only heavily asleep, of course, after all that whisky. On the other hand——

Alan turned round, and plunged down the treacherous stairs. The breath in his lungs felt like a rasping saw, and several times he had to pull up. He had even forgotten the Highlander. It seemed half an hour, and was actually two or three minutes, before he again reached the bottom of the stairs.

The double doors leading out into the court were closed, but the padlock was not caught. Alan threw them open—creaking, quivering frames of wood which bent like bow shafts as they scraped the flagstones.

He ran out into the court, and circled round the tower to the side facing the loch. There he stopped short. He knew what he would find, and he found it.

The sickening plunge had been taken again.

Colin Campbell—or a bundle of red-and-white striped pajamas which might once have been Colin—lay face downwards on the flagstones. Sixty feet above his head the leaves of the window stood open, and glinted by the light of the waning moon. A thin white mist, which seemed to hang above the water rather than rise from it, had made beads of dew settle on Colin's shaggy hair.

## XIII

Dawn—warm gold and white kindling from smoky purple, yet of a soap-bubble luminousness which tinged the whole sky—dawn was clothing the valley when Alan again climbed the tower stairs. You could almost taste the early autumn air.

But Alan was in no mood to enjoy it.

He carried a chisel, an auger, and a saw. Behind him strode a nervous, wiry-looking Swan in a now-dry grey suit which had once been fashionable but which at present resembled sackcloth.

"But are you sure you want to go in there?" insisted Swan. "I'm not keen on it myself."

"Why not?" said Alan. "It's daylight. The Occupant of the box can't hurt us now."

"What occupant?"

Alan did not reply. He thought of saying that Dr. Fell now knew the truth, though he had not divulged it yet; and that Dr. Fell said there was no danger. But he decided such matters were best kept from the papers as yet.

"Hold the torch," he requested. "I can't see why they didn't put a window on this landing. Colin repaired this door yesterday afternoon, you remember. We're now going to arrange matters so that it can't be repaired again in a hurry."

While Swan held the light, he set to work. It was slow work, boring a line of holes touching each other in a square round the lock, and Alan's hands were clumsy on the auger.

When he had finished them, and splintered the result with a chisel, he got purchase for the saw and slowly sawed along the line of the holes.

"Colin Campbell," observed Swan, suddenly and tensely, "was a good guy. A real good guy."

"What do you mean, 'was'?"

"Now that he's dead——"

"But he's not dead."

There was an appreciable silence.

"Not dead?"

The saw rasped and bumped. All the violence of Alan's relief, all the sick reaction after what he had seen, went into his attack on the door. He hoped Swan would shut up. He had liked Colin Campbell immensely, too much to want to hear any sickly sentimentalities.

"Colin," he went on, without looking round to see Swan's expression, "has got two broken legs and a broken hipbone. And, for a man of his age, that's no joke. Also, there's something else Dr. Grant is very much excited about. But he's not dead and he's unlikely to die."

"A fall like that——"

"It happens sometimes. You've probably heard of people falling from heights greater than that and sometimes not even being hurt at all. And if they're tight, as Colin was, that helps too."

"Yet he deliberately jumped from the window?"

"Yes."

In a fine powdering of sawdust, the last tendon of wood fell free. Alan pushed the square panel inwards, and it fell on the floor. He reached through, finding the key still securely turned and the rusty bolt shot home immovably in its socket. He turned the key, pulled back the bolt; and, not without a qualm of apprehension, opened the door.

In the clear, fresh light of dawn, the room appeared tousled and faintly sinister. Colin's clothes, as he had untidily undressed, lay flung over the chairs and over the floor. His watch ticked on the chest of drawers. The bed had been slept in; its clothes were now flung back, and the pillows punched into a heap which still held the impression of a head.

The wide-open leaves of the window creaked gently as an air touched them.

"What are you going to do?" asked Swan, putting his head round the edge of the door and at last deciding to come in.

"What Dr. Fell asked me to do."

Though he spoke easily enough, he had to get a grip on himself before he knelt down and felt under the bed. He drew out the leather dog carrier which had contained the Occupant.

"You're not going to fool around with the thing?" asked Swan.

"Dr. Fell said to open it. He said there wouldn't be any fingerprints, so not to bother about them."

"You're taking a lot for granted on that old boy's word. But if you know what you're doing—open it."

This part was the hardest. Alan flicked back the catches with his thumbs, and lifted the lid.

As he had expected, the box was empty. Yet his imagination could have pictured, and was picturing, all sorts of unpleasant things he might have seen.

"What did the old boy tell you to do?" inquired Swan.

"Just open it, and make sure it was empty."

"But what *could* have been in it?" roared Swan. "I tell you, I'm going nuts trying to figure this thing out! I—" Swan paused. His eyes widened, and then narrowed. He extended a finger to point to the roll-top desk.

On the edge of the desk, half hidden by papers but in a place where it certainly had not been the day before, lay a small leather book of pocket size, on whose cover was stamped, in gilt letters, *Diary, 1940.*

"That wouldn't be what you've been looking for, would it?"

Both of them made a dart for the diary, but Alan got there first.

The name Angus Campbell was written on the flyleaf in a small but stiff and schoolboyish kind of hand which made Alan suspect arthritis in the fingers. Angus had carefully filled out the chart for all the miscellaneous information, such as the size of his collar and the size of his shoes (why the makers of these diaries think we are likely to forget the size of our collars remains a mystery); and after "motorcar licence number" he had written "none."

But Alan did not bother with this. The diary was full of entries all crammed together and crammed downhill. The last entry was made on the night of Angus's death, Saturday the twenty-fourth of August. Alan Campbell became conscious of tightened throat muscles, and a heavy thumping in his chest, as his eye encountered the item.

"*Saturday*. Check cleared by bank. O.K. Elspat poorly again. Memo: syrup of figs. Wrote to Colin. A. Forbes here tonight. Claims I cheated him. Ha ha ha. Said not to come back. He said he wouldn't, wasn't necessary. Funny musty smell in room tonight. Memo: write to War Office about tractor. Use for army. Do this tomorrow."

Then there was the blank which indicated the end of the writer's span of life.

Alan flicked back over the pages. He did not read any more, though he noticed that at one point a whole leaf had been torn out. He was thinking of the short, heavy, bulbous-nosed old man with the white hair, writing these words while something waited for him.

"H'm," said Swan. "That isn't much help, is it?"

"I don't know."

"Well," said Swan, "if you've seen what you came to see, or rather what you didn't see, let's get downstairs again, shall we? There may be nothing wrong with this place, but it gives me the willies."

Slipping the diary into his pocket, Alan gathered up the tools and followed. In the sitting room downstairs they found Dr. Fell, fully dressed in an old black alpaca suit and string tie. Alan noticed with surprise that his box-pleated cape and shovel hat lay across the sofa, whereas last night they had hung in the hall.

But Dr. Fell appeared to be violently interested in a very bad landscape hung above the piano. He turned round a guileless face at their entrance, and addressed Swan.

"I say. Would you mind nipping up to—harrumph—what we'll call the sickroom, and finding out how the patient is? Don't let Dr. Grant bully you. I want to find out whether Colin's conscious yet, and whether he's said anything."

"So do I," agreed Swan with some vehemence, and was off with such celerity as to make the pictures rattle.

Dr. Fell hastily picked up his box-pleated cape, swung it round his shoulders with evident effort, and fastened the little chain at the neck.

"Get your hat, my lad," he said. "We're off on a little expedition. The presence of the press is no doubt stimulating; but there are times when it is definitely an encumbrance. We may be able to sneak out without our friend Swan seeing us."

"Where are we going?"

"Glencoe."

Alan stared at him.

"Glencoe! At seven o'clock in the morning?"

"I regret," sighed Dr. Fell, sniffing the odour of frying bacon and eggs which had begun to seep through the house, "that we shall not be able to wait for breakfast. But better miss breakfast than spoil the whole broth."

"Yes, but how in blazes are we going to get to Glencoe at this hour?"

"I've phoned through to Inveraray for a car. They haven't your slothful habits in this part of the country, my lad. Do you remember Duncan telling us yesterday that Alec Forbes had been found, or they thought he had been found, at a cottage near Glencoe?"

"Yes?"

Dr. Fell made a face and flourished his crutch-handled stick.

"It may not be true. And we may not even be able to find the cottage: though I got a description of its location from Duncan, and habitations out there are few and far between. But, by thunder, we've got to take the chance! If I'm to be any good to Colin Campbell at all, I've GOT to reach Alec Forbes before anybody else—even the police—can get to him. Get your hat."

Kathryn Campbell, pulling on her tweed jacket, moved swiftly into the room.

"Oh, no, you don't!" she said.

"Don't what?"

"You don't go without me," Kathryn informed them. "I heard you ringing up for that car. Aunt Elspat is bossy enough anywhere, but Aunt Elspat in a sickroom is simply bossy past all endurance. Eee!" She clenched her hands. "There's nothing more I can do anyhow. *Please* let me come!"

Dr. Fell waved a gallant assent. Tiptoeing like conspirators, they moved out to the back of the house. A brightly polished four-seater car was waiting beyond the hedge which screened Shira from the main road.

Alan did not want a loquacious chauffeur that morning, and he did not get one. The driver was a gnarled little man, dressed like a garage mechanic, who grudgingly held open the door for them. They were past Dalmally before they discovered that he was, in fact, an English cockney.

But Alan was too full of his latest discovery to mind the presence of a witness. He produced Angus's diary, and handed it to Dr. Fell.

Even on an empty stomach, Dr. Fell had filled and lighted his meerschaum. It was an open car, and, as it climbed the mighty hill under a somewhat damp-looking sky, the breeze gave Dr. Fell considerable trouble in its attentions to his hat and the tobacco smoke. But he read carefully through the diary, giving at least a glance at every page of it.

"H'mf, yes," he said, and scowled. "It fits. Everything fits! Your deductions, Miss Campbell, were to the point. It *was* Elspat who stole this."

"But——"

"Look here." He pointed to the place where a page had been torn out. "The entry before that, at the foot of the preceding page, reads, 'Elspat says Janet G.'—whoever she may be—'godless and lecherous. In Elspat's younger days—' There it breaks off.

"It probably went on to recount gleefully an anecdote of Elspat's younger and less moral days. So the evidence was removed from the record. Elspat found nothing more in the diary to reflect on her. After giving it a careful reading, probably several readings to make sure, she returned the diary to a place where it could easily be found."

Alan was not impressed.

"Still, what about these sensational revelations? Why get in touch with the press, as Elspat did? The last entry in the diary may be suggestive, but it certainly doesn't tell us very much."

"No?"

"Well, does it?"

Dr. Fell eyed him curiously.

"I should say, on the contrary, that it tells us a good deal. But you hardly expected the sensational revelation (if any) to be in the last entry, did you? After all, Angus had gone happily and thoughtlessly to bed. Whatever attacked him, it attacked him after he had finished writing and put out his light. Why, therefore, should we expect anything of great interest in the last entry?"

Alan was brought up with something of a bump.

"That," he admitted, "is true enough. All the same——"

"No, my boy. The real meat of the thing is *here*." Dr. Fell made the pages riffle like a pack of cards. "In the body of the diary. In the account of his activities for the past year."

He frowned at the book, and slipped it into his pocket. His expression of gargantuan distress had grown along with his fever of certainty.

"Hang it all!" he said, and smote his hand on his knee. "The thing is inescapable! Elspat steals the diary. She reads it. Being no fool, she guesses——"

"Guesses what?"

"How Angus Campbell really died. She hates and distrusts the police to the very depths of her soul. So she writes to her favourite newspaper and plans to explode a bomb. And suddenly, when it is too late, she realizes with horror——"

Again Dr. Fell paused. The expression on his face smoothed itself out. He sat back with a gusty sigh against the upholstery of the tonneau, and shook his head.

"You know, that tears it," he added blankly. "That really does tear it."

"I personally," Kathryn said through her teeth, "will be in a condition to tear something if this mystification goes on."

Dr. Fell appeared still more distressed.

"Allow me," he suggested, "to counter your very natural curiosity with just one more question." He looked at Alan. "A moment ago you said that you thought the last entry in Angus's diary was 'suggestive.' What did you mean by that?"

"I meant that it certainly wasn't a passage which could have been written by anyone who meant to kill himself."

Dr. Fell nodded.

"Yes," he agreed. "Then what would you say if I were to tell you that Angus Campbell really committed suicide after all?"


XIV


"I SHOULD reply," said Kathryn, "that I felt absolutely cheated! Oh, I know I shouldn't say that; but it's true. You've got us looking so hard for a murderer that we can't concentrate on anything else."

Dr. Fell nodded as though he saw the aesthetic validity of the point.

"And yet," he went on, "for the sake of argument, I ask you to consider this explanation. I ask you to observe how it is borne out by every one of our facts."

He was silent for a moment, puffing at the meerschaum.

"Let us first consider Angus Campbell. Here is a shrewd, embittered, worn-out old man with a tinkering brain and an intense love of family. He is now broke, stony broke. His great dreams will never come true. He knows it. His brother Colin, of whom he is very fond, is overwhelmed with debts. His ex-mistress Elspat, of whom he is fonder still, is penniless and will remain penniless.

"Angus might well consider himself, in the hard-headed Northern fashion, a useless encumbrance. Good to nobody—except dead. But he is a hale old body to whom the insurance company's doctor gives fifteen more years of life. And in the meantime how (in God's name, how) are they to live?

"Of course, if he were to die now . . ."

Dr. Fell made a slight gesture.

"But, if he dies now, it must be established as certain, absolutely *certain*, that his death is not a suicide. And that will take a bit of doing. The sum involved is huge: thirty-five thousand pounds, distributed among intelligent insurance companies with nasty suspicious minds.

"Mere accident won't do. He can't go out and stumble off a cliff, hoping it will be read as accident. They might think that; but it is too chancy, and nothing must be left to chance. His death must be murder, cold-blooded murder, proved beyond any shadow of a doubt."

Again Dr. Fell paused. Alan improved the occasion to utter a derisive laugh which was not very convincing.

"In that case, sir," Alan said, "I turn your own guns on you."

"So? How?"

"You asked last night why any person intending to commit a murder for the insurance money should commit a murder which looked exactly like suicide. Well, for the same reason, why should Angus (of all people) plan a suicide which looked exactly like suicide?"

"He didn't," answered Dr. Fell.

"Pardon?"

Dr. Fell leaned forward to tap Alan, who occupied the front seat, very decisively on the shoulder. The doctor's manner was compounded of eagerness and absent-mindedness.

"That's the whole point. He didn't. You see, you haven't yet realized what was in that dog carrier. You haven't yet realized what Angus deliberately put there.

"And I say to you,"—Dr. Fell lifted his hand solemnly—"I say to you that but for one little unforeseeable accident, a misfortune so unlikely that the mathematical chances were a million to one against it, there would never have been the least doubt that Angus was murdered! I say to you that Alec Forbes would be in jail at this moment, and that the insurance companies would have been compelled to pay up."

They were approaching Loch Awe, a gem of beauty in a deep, mountainous valley. But none of them looked at it.

"Are you saying," breathed Kathryn, "that Angus was going to kill himself, and deliberately frame Alec Forbes for the job?"

"I am. Do you consider it unlikely?"

After a silence Dr. Fell went on:

"In the light of this theory, consider our evidence.

"Here is Forbes, a man with a genuine, bitter grudge. Ideal for the purposes of a scapegoat.

"Forbes calls—for which we may read, 'is summoned'—to see Angus that night. He goes upstairs to the tower room. There is a row, which Angus can arrange to make audible all over the place. Now, was Forbes at this time carrying a 'suitcase'?

"The women, we observe, don't know. They didn't see him until he was ejected. Who is the only witness to the suitcase? Angus himself. He carefully calls their attention to the fact that Forbes was supposed to have one, *and* says pointedly that Forbes must have left it behind.

"You follow that? The picture Angus intended to present was that Forbes had distracted his attention and shoved the suitcase under the bed, where Angus never noticed it, but where the thing inside it could later do its deadly work."

Alan reflected.

"It's a curious thing," Alan said, "that the day before yesterday I myself suggested just that explanation, with Forbes as the murderer. But nobody would listen to it."

"Yet I repeat," asserted Dr. Fell, "that except for a totally unpredictable accident, Forbes would have been nailed as the murderer straightaway."

Kathryn put her hands to her temples.

"You mean," she cried, "that Elspat looked under the bed before the door was locked, and saw there was no box there?"

But to their surprise Dr. Fell shook his head.

"No, no, no, no! That was another point, of course. But it wasn't serious. Angus probably never even thought her glance under the bed noticed anything one way or the other. No, no, no! I refer to the contents of the box."

Alan closed his eyes.

"I suppose," he said in a restrained voice, "it would be asking too much if we were to ask you just to *tell* us what was in the box?"

Dr. Fell grew still more solemn, even dogged.

"In a very short time we are (I hope) going to see Alec Forbes. I am going to put the question to him. In the meantime, I ask you to think about it; think about the facts we know; think about the trade magazines in Angus's room; think about his activities of the past year; and see if you can't reach the solution for yourselves.

"For the moment let us return to the great scheme. Alec Forbes, of course, had carried no suitcase or anything else. The box (already prepared by Angus himself) was downstairs in one of the lower rooms. Angus got rid of the women at ten o'clock, slipped downstairs, procured the box, and put it under the bed, after which he re-locked and re-bolted his door. This, I submit, is the only possible explanation of how that box got into a hermetically sealed room.

"Finally, Angus wrote up his diary. He put in those significant words that he had told Forbes not to come back, and Forbes said it wouldn't be necessary. Other significant words too: so many more nails in Forbes's coffin. Then

Angus undressed, turned out the light, climbed into bed, and with real grim fortitude prepared for what had to come.

"Now follow what happens next day. Angus has left his diary in plain sight, for the police to find. Elspat finds it herself, and appropriates it.

"She thinks Alec Forbes killed Angus. On reading through the bulk of the diary, she realizes—as Angus meant everybody to realize—exactly what killed Angus. She has got Alec Forbes, the murderer. She will hang the sinful higher than Haman. She sits down and writes to the *Daily Floodlight*.

"Only after the letter is posted does she suddenly see the flaw. If Forbes did that, he must have pushed the box under the bed before he was kicked out. But Forbes can't have done that! For she herself looked under the bed, and saw no box; and, most horrifying of all, she has already told the police so."

Dr. Fell made a gesture.

"This woman has lived with Angus Campbell for forty years. She knows him inside out. She sees through him with that almost morbid clarity our womenfolk exhibit in dealing with our vagaries and our stupidities. It doesn't take her long to understand where the hanky-panky lies. It wasn't Alec Forbes; it was Angus himself who did this. And so——

"Do I have to explain further? Think over her behaviour. Think of her sudden change of mind about the box. Think of her searching for excuses to fly into a tantrum and throw out of the house the newspaperman she has summoned herself. Think, above all, of her position. If she speaks out with the truth, she loses every penny. If she denounces Alec Forbes, on the other hand, she condemns her soul to hell-fire and eternal burning. Think of that, my children; and don't be too hard on Elspat Campbell when her temper seems to wear thin."

The figure of one whom Kathryn had called a silly old woman was undergoing, in their minds, a curious transformation.

Thinking back to eyes and words and gestures, thinking of the core under that black taffeta, Alan experienced a revulsion of feeling as well as a revulsion of ideas.

"And so—?" he prompted.

"Well! She won't make the decision," replied Dr. Fell. "She returns the diary to the tower room, and lets us decide what we like."

The car had climbed to higher, bleaker regions. Uplands of waste, spiked with ugly posts against possible invasion by air, showed brown against the granite ribs of the mountains. The day was clouding over, and a damp breeze blew in their faces.

"May I submit," Dr. Fell added after a pause, "that this is the only explanation which fits all the facts?"

"Then if we're not looking for a murderer——"

"Oh, my dear sir!" expostulated Dr. Fell. "We *are* looking for a murderer!"

They whirled round on him.

"Ask yourselves other questions," said Dr. Fell. "Who impersonated the ghostly Highlander, and why? Who sought the death of Colin Campbell, and why? For remember: except for lucky chance, Colin would be dead at this minute."

He brooded, chewing the stem of a pipe that had gone out, and making a gesture as though he were pursuing something which just eluded him.

"Pictures," he added, "sometimes give extraordinary ideas."

Then he seemed to realize for the first time that he was talking in front of an outsider. He caught, in the driving mirror, the eye of the gnarled little chauffeur who for miles had not spoken or moved. Dr. Fell rumbled and snorted, brushing fallen ash off his cape. He woke up out of a mazy dream, and blinked round.

"H'mf. Hah. Yes. So. I say, when do we get to Glencoe?"

The driver spoke out of the side of his mouth.

"This *is* Glen Coe," he answered.

All of them woke up.

And here, Alan thought, were the wild mountains as he had always imagined them. The only adjective which occurred in connection with the place was Godforsaken: not as an idle word, but as a literal fact.

The glen of Coe was immensely long and immensely wide, whereas Alan had always pictured it as a cramped, narrow place. Through it the black road ran arrow-straight. On either side rose the lines of mountain ridges, granite-grey and dull purple, looking as smooth as stone. No edge of kindliness touched them: it was as though nature had dried up, and even sullenness had long petrified to hostility.

Burns twisting down the mountainside were so far off that you could not even be sure if the water moved, and only were sure when you saw it gleam. Utter silence emphasized the bleakness and desolation of the glen. Sometimes you saw a tiny whitewashed cottage, which appeared empty.

Dr. Fell pointed to one of them.

"We are looking," he said, "for a cottage on the left-hand side of the road, down a slope among some fir trees, just past the Falls of Coe. You don't happen to know it?"

The driver was silent for a time, and then said he thought he knew it.

"Not far off now," he added. "Be at the Falls in a minute or two."

The road rose, and, after its interminable straightness, curved round the slaty shoulder of a hill. The hollow, tumbling roar of a waterfall shook the damp air as they turned into a narrow road, shut in on the right by a cliff.

Driving them some distance down this road, the chauffeur stopped the car, sat back, and pointed without a word.

They climbed out on the breezy road, under a darkening sky. The tumult of the waterfall still splashed in their ears. Dr. Fell was assisted down a slope on which they all slithered. He was assisted, with more effort, across a stream; and in the bed of the stream the stones were polished black, as though they had met the very heart of the soil.

The cottage, of dirty whitewashed stone with a thatched roof, stood beyond. It was tiny, appearing to consist of only one room. The door stood closed. No smoke went up from the chimney. Far beyond it the mountains rose up light purple and curiously pink.

Nothing moved—except a mongrel dog.

The dog saw them, and began to run round in circles. It darted to the cottage, and scratched with its paws on the closed door. The scratching sound rose thinly, above the distant mutter of the falls. It set a seal on the heart, of loneliness and depression in the evil loneliness of Glencoe.

The dog sat back on its haunches, and began to howl.

"All right, old boy!" said Dr. Fell.

That reassuring voice seemed to have some effect on the animal. It scratched frantically at the door again, after which it ran to Dr. Fell and capered round him, leaping up to scrape at his cloak. What frightened Alan was the fright in the eyes of the dog.

Dr. Fell knocked at the door, without response. He tried the latch, but something held the door on the inside. There was no window in the front of the cottage.

"Mr. Forbes!" he called thunderously. "Mr. Forbes!"

Their footsteps scraped amidst little flinty stones. The shape of the cottage was roughly square. Muttering to himself, Dr. Fell lumbered round to the side of the house, and Alan followed him.

Here they found a smallish window. A rusty metal grating, like a mesh of heavy wire, had been nailed up over the window on the inside. Beyond this its grimy windowpane, set on hinges to swing open and shut like a door, stood partly open.

Cupping their hands round their eyes, they pressed against the grating and tried to peer inside. A frowsty smell, compounded of stale air, stale whisky, paraffin oil, and sardines out of a tin, crept out of the room. Gradually, as their eyes grew accustomed to the gloom, outlines emerged.

The table, with its greasy mess of dishes, had been pushed to one side. In the center of the ceiling was set a stout iron hook, presumably for a lamp. Alan saw what was hanging from that hook now, and swaying gently each time the dog pawed at the door.

He dropped his hands. He turned away from the window, putting one hand against the wall to steady himself. He walked round the side of the cottage to the front, where Kathryn was standing.

"What is it?" He heard her voice distantly, though it was almost a scream. "What's wrong?"

"You'd better come away from here," he said.

"What is it?"

Dr. Fell, much less ruddy of face, followed Alan round to the front door. The doctor breathed heavily and wheezily for a moment before he spoke.

"That's rather a flimsy door," he said, pointing with his stick. "You could kick it in. And I think you better had."

On the inside was a small, new, tight bolt. Alan tore the staple loose from the wood with three vicious kicks into which he put his whole muscle and the whole state of his mind.

Though he was not anxious to go inside, the face of the dead man was now turned away from them, and it was not so bad as that first look through the window. The smell of food and whisky and paraffin grew overpowering.

The dead man wore a long, grimy dressing gown. The rope, which had formed the plaited cord of his dressing gown, had been shaped at one end into a running noose, and the other tied tightly round the hook in the ceiling. His heels swung some two feet off the floor as he hung there. An empty keg, evidently of whisky, had rolled away from under him.

Whining frenziedly, the mongrel dog shot past them, whirled round the dead man, and set him swinging again in frantic attempts to spring up.

Dr. Fell inspected the broken bolt. He glanced across at the grated window. His voice sounded heavy in the evil-smelling room.

"Oh, yes," he said. "Another suicide."

## XV

"I suppose," Alan muttered, "it *is* Alec Forbes?"

Dr. Fell pointed with his stick to the camp bed pushed against one wall. On it an open suitcase full of soiled linen bore the painted initials, "A.G.F." Then he walked round to the front of the hanging figure where he could examine the face. Alan did not follow him.

"And the description fits, too. A week's growth of beard on his face. And, in all probability, ten years' growth of depression in his heart."

Dr. Fell went to the door, barring it against Kathryn, who stood white-faced under the overcast sky a few feet away.

"There must be a telephone somewhere. If I remember my map, there's a village with a hotel a mile or two beyond here. Get through to Inspector Donaldson at Dunoon police station, and tell him Mr. Forbes has hanged himself. Can you do that?"

Kathryn gave a quick, unsteady nod.

"He did kill himself, did he?" she asked in a voice barely above a whisper. "It isn't—anything else?"

Dr. Fell did not reply to this. Kathryn, after another quick nod, turned and made her way back.

The hut was some dozen feet square, thick-walled, with a primitive fireplace and a stone floor. It was no crofter's cottage, but had evidently been used by Forbes as a sort of retreat. Its furniture consisted of the camp bed, the table, two kitchen chairs, a washstand with bowl and pitcher, and a stand of mildewed books.

The mongrel had now ceased its frantic whimpering, for which Alan felt grateful. The dog lay down close to the silent figure, where he could raise adoring eyes to that altered face; and, from time to time, he shivered.

"I ask what Kathryn asked," said Alan. "Is this suicide, or not?"

Dr. Fell walked forward and touched Forbes's arm. The dog stiffened. A menacing growl began in its throat and quivered through its whole body.

"Easy, boy!" said Dr. Fell. "Easy!"

He stood back. He took out his watch and studied it. Grunting and muttering, he lumbered over to the table, on whose edge stood a hurricane lantern with a hook and chain by which it could be slung from the roof. With the tips of his fingers Dr. Fell picked up the lantern and shook it. A tin of oil stood beside it.

"Empty," he said. "Burnt out, but obviously used." He pointed to the body. "Rigor is not complete. This undoubtedly happened during the early hours of the morning: two or three o'clock, perhaps. The hour of suicides. And look there."

He was now pointing to the plaited dressing-gown cord round the dead man's neck.

"It's a curious thing," he went on, scowling. "The genuine suicide invariably takes the most elaborate pains to guard himself against the least discomfort. If he hangs himself, for instance, he will never use a wire or chain: something that is likely to cut or chafe his neck. If he uses a rope, he will often pad it against chafing. Look there! Alec Forbes has used a soft rope, and padded that with handkerchiefs. The authentic touch of suicide, or——"

"Or what?"

"Real genius in murder," said Dr. Fell.

He bent down to inspect the empty whisky keg. He went across to the one window. Thrusting one finger through the mesh of the grating, he shook it and found it solidly nailed up on the inside. Back he went, with fussed and fussy gestures, to the bolt of the door, which he examined carefully without touching it.

Then he peered round the room, stamping his foot on the floor. His voice had taken on a hollow sound like wind along an underground tunnel.

"Hang it all!" he said. "This *is* suicide. It's got to be suicide. The keg is just the right height for him to have stepped off, and just the right distance away. Nobody could have got in or out through that nailed window or that solidly bolted door."

He regarded Alan with some anxiety.

"You see, for my sins I know something about hocussing doors or windows. I have been—ahem—haunted and pursued by such matters."

"So I've heard."

"But I can't," pursued Dr. Fell, pushing back his shovel hat, "I can't tell you any way of hocussing a bolt when there's no keyhole and when the door is so close-fitting that its sill scrapes the floor. Like that one."

He pointed.

"And I can't tell you any way of hocussing a window when it is covered with a steel meshwork nailed up on the inside. Again, like that one there. If Alec Forbes—hullo!"

The bookstand was placed cater-cornered in the angle beside the fireplace. Dr. Fell discovered it as he went to inspect the fireplace, finding to his disgust that the flue was too narrow and soot-choked to admit any person. Dusting his fingers, he turned to the bookstand.

On the top row of books stood a portable typewriter, its cover missing and a sheet of paper projecting from the carriage. On it a few words were typed in pale blue ink.

To any jackal who finds this:
      I killed Angus and Colin Campbell with the same thing they used to swindle me. What are you going to do about it now?

"Even, you see," Dr. Fell said fiercely, "the suicide note. The final touch. The brush stroke of the master. I repeat, sir: this must be suicide. And yet—well, if it is, I mean to retire to Bedlam."

The smell of the room, the black-faced occupant, the yearning dog, all these things were commencing to turn Alan Campbell's stomach. He felt he could not stand the air of the place much longer. Yet he fought back.

"I don't see why you say that," he declared. "After all, Doctor, can't you admit you may be wrong?"

"Wrong?"

"About Angus's death being suicide." Certainty, dead certainty, took root in Alan Campbell's brain. "Forbes *did* kill Angus and tried to kill Colin. Everything goes to show it. Nobody could have got in or out of this room, as you yourself admit; and there's Forbes's confession to clinch matters.

"He brooded out here until his brain cracked, as I know mine would in these parts unless I took to religion. He disposed of both brothers, or thought he had. When his work was finished, he killed himself. Here's the evidence. What more do you want?"

"The truth," insisted Dr. Fell stubbornly. "I am old fashioned. I want the truth."

Alan hesitated.

"I'm old fashioned too. And I seem to remember," Alan told him, "that you came North with the express purpose of helping Colin. Is it going to help Colin, or Aunt Elspat either, if the detective they brought in to show Angus was murdered goes about shouting that it was suicide—even after we've got Alec Forbes's confession?"

Dr. Fell blinked at him.

"My dear sir," he said in pained astonishment, and adjusted his eyeglasses and blinked at Alan through them, "you surely don't imagine that I mean to confide any of my beliefs to the police?"

"Isn't that the idea?"

Dr. Fell peered about to make sure they were not overheard.

"My record," he confided, "is an extremely black one. Harrumph. I have on several occasions flummoxed the evidence so that a murderer should go free. Not many years ago I outdid myself by setting a house on fire. My present purpose (between ourselves) is to swindle the insurance companies so that Colin Campbell can bask in good cigars and fire water for the rest of his life . . ."

"What?"

Dr. Fell regarded him anxiously.

"That shocks you? Tut, tut! All this (I say) I mean to do. But, dammit, man!" He spread out his hands. "For my own private information, I like to know the truth."

He turned back to the bookstand. Still without touching it, he examined the typewriter. On top of the row of books below it stood an angler's creel and some salmon flies. On top of the third row of books lay a bicycle spanner, a bicycle lamp, and a screwdriver.

Dr. Fell next ran a professional eye over the books. There were works on physics and chemistry, on Diesel engines, on practical building, and on astronomy. There were catalogues and trade journals. There was a dictionary, a six-volume encyclopaedia, and (surprisingly) two or three boys' books by G. A. Henty. Dr. Fell eyed these last with some interest.

"Wow!" he said. "Does anybody read Henty nowadays, I wonder? If they knew what they were missing, they would run back to him. I am proud to say that I still read him with delight. Who would suspect Alec Forbes of having a romantic soul?" He scratched his nose. "Still——"

"Look here," Alan persisted. "What makes you so sure this isn't suicide?"

"My theory. My mule-headedness, if you prefer it."

"And your theory still holds that Angus committed suicide?"

"Yes."

"But that Forbes here was murdered?"

"Exactly."

Dr. Fell wandered back to the centre of the room. He eyed the untidy camp bed with the suitcase on it. He eyed a pair of gum boots under the bed.

"My lad, I don't trust that suicide note. I don't trust it one little bit. And there are solid reasons why I don't trust it. Come out of here. Let's get some clean air."

Alan was glad enough to go. The dog raised its head from its paws, and gave them a wild, dazed sort of look; then it lowered its head again, growling, and settled down with ineffable patience under the dead.

Distantly, they could hear the rushing of the waterfall. Alan breathed the cool, damp air, and felt a shudder go over him. Dr. Fell, a huge bandit shape in his cloak, leaned his hands on his stick.

"Whoever wrote that note," he went on, "whether Alec Forbes or another, knew the trick that had been employed in Angus Campbell's death. That's the first fact to freeze to. Well! Have you guessed yet what the trick was?"

"No, I have not."

"Not even after seeing the alleged suicide note? Oh, man! Think!"

"You can ask me to think all you like. I may be dense; but if you can credit it, I still don't know what makes people jump up out of bed in the middle of the night and fall out of windows to their death."

"Let us begin," pursued Dr. Fell, "with the fact that Angus's diary records his activities for the past year, as diaries sometimes do. Well, what in Satan's name *have* been Angus's principal activities for the past year?"

"Mixing himself up in various wildcat schemes to try to make money."

"True. But only one scheme in which Alec Forbes was concerned, I think?"

"Yes."

"Good. What was that scheme?"

"An idea to manufacture some kind of ice cream with tartan patterns on it. At least, so Colin said."

"And in making their ice cream," said Dr. Fell, "what kind of freezing agent did they employ in large quantities? Colin told us that too."

"He said they used artificial ice, which he described as 'that chemical stuff that's so expen——' "

Alan paused abruptly.

Half-forgotten memories flowed back into his mind. With a shock he recalled a laboratory of his school days, and words being spoken from a platform. The faint echo of them came back now.

"And do you know," inquired Dr. Fell, "what this artificial ice, or 'dry' ice, really is?"

"It's whitish stuff to look at; something like real ice, only opaque. It——"

"To be exact," said Dr. Fell, "it is nothing more or less than liquefied gas. And do you know the name of the gas which is turned into a solid 'snow' block, and can be cut and handled and moved about? What is the name of that gas?"

"Carbon dioxide," said Alan.

Though the spell remained on his wits, it was suddenly as though a blind had flown up with a snap, and he saw.

"Now suppose," argued Dr. Fell, "you removed a block of that stuff from its own airtight cylinders. A big block, say one big enough to fit into a large suitcase—or, better still, some box with an open end, so that the air can reach it better. What would happen?"

"It would slowly melt."

"And in melting, of course, it would release into the room . . . what would it release?"

Alan found himself almost shouting.

"Carbonic acid gas. One of the deadliest and quickest-acting gases there is."

"Suppose you placed your artificial ice, in its container, under the bed in a room where the window is always kept closed at night. What would happen?

"With your permission, I will now drop the Socratic method and tell you. You have planted one of the surest murder traps ever devised. One of two things will happen. Either the victim, asleep or drowsy, will breathe in that concentrated gas as it is released into the room; and he will die in his bed.

"Or else the victim will notice the faint, acrid odour as it gets into his lungs. He will not breathe it long, mind you. Once the stuff takes hold, it will make the strongest man totter and fall like a fly. He will want air—air at any cost. As he is overcome, he will get out of bed and try to make for the window.

"He may not make it at all. If he does make it, he will be so weak on the legs that he can't hold up. And if this window is a low window, catching him just above the knees; if it consists of two leaves, opening outwards, so that he falls against it——"

Dr. Fell pushed his hands outwards, a rapid gesture.

Alan could almost see the limp, unwieldy body in the nightshirt plunge outwards and downwards.

"Of course, the artificial ice will melt away and leave no trace in the box. With the window now open, the gas will presently clear away.

"You now perceive, I hope, why Angus's suicide scheme was so foolproof. Who but Alec Forbes would have used artificial ice to kill his partner in the venture?

"Angus, as I read it, never once intended to jump or fall from the window. No, no, no! He intended to be found dead in bed, of poisoning by carbonic acid gas. There would be a post-mortem. The 'band' of this gas would be found in his blood as plain as print. The diary would be read and interpreted. All the circumstances against Alec Forbes would be recalled, as I outlined them to you a while ago. And the insurance money would be collected as certainly as the sun will rise tomorrow."

Alan, staring at the stream, nodded.

"But at the last moment, I suppose——?"

"At the last moment," agreed Dr. Fell, "like many suicides, Angus couldn't face it. He had to have *air*. He felt himself going under. And in a panic he leaped for the window.

"Therein, my boy, lies the million-to-one chance I spoke of. It was a million to one that either (a) the gas would kill him, or (b) the fall would kill him instantly as he plunged out face forwards. But neither of these things happened. He was mortally injured; yet he did not immediately die. Remember?"

Again Alan nodded.

"Yes. We've come across that point several times."

"Before he died, his lungs and blood were freed of the gas. Hence no trace remained for the post-mortem. Had he died instantly or even quickly, those traces would have been there. But they were not. So we had only the meaningless spectacle of an old gentleman who leaps from his bed in order to throw himself out of the window."

Dr. Fell's big voice grew fiery. He struck the ferrule of his stick on the ground.

"I say to you—" he began.

"Stop a bit!" said Alan, with sudden recollection.

"Yes?"

"Last night, when I went up to the tower room to rout out Colin, I bent down and tried to look under the sill of the door. When I straightened up, I remember feeling lightheaded. In fact, I staggered when I went down the stairs. Did *I* get a whiff of the stuff?"

"Of course. The room was full of it. Only a very faint whiff, fortunately for yourself.

"Which brings us to the final point. Angus carefully wrote in his diary that there was a 'faint musty smell in the room.' Now, that's rubbish on the face of it. If he had already begun to notice the presence of the gas, he could never have completed his diary and gone to bed. No: that was only another artistic touch designed to hang Alec Forbes."

"And misinterpreted by me," growled Alan. "I was thinking about some kind of animal."

"But you see where all this leads us?"

"No, I don't. Into the soup, of course; but aside from that——"

"The only possible explanation of the foregoing facts," insisted Dr. Fell, "is that Angus killed himself. If Angus killed himself, then Alec Forbes didn't kill him. And if Alec Forbes didn't kill him, Alec had no reason to say he did. Therefore the suicide note is a fake.

"Up to this time, d'ye see, we have had a suicide which everybody thought was murder. Now we have a murder which everybody is going to take for suicide. We are going places and seeing things. All roads lead to the lunatic asylum. Can you by any chance oblige me with an idea?"

## XVI

ALAN shook his head.

"No ideas. I presume that the 'extra' thing which ailed Colin, and exercised Dr. Grant so much, was carbon-dioxide poisoning?"

Dr. Fell grunted assent. Fishing out the meerschaum pipe again, he filled and lighted it.

"Which," he assented, speaking between puffs like the Spirit of the Volcano, "leads us at full tide into our troubles. We can't blame Angus for that. The death box didn't load itself again with artificial ice.

"Somebody—who knew Colin was going to sleep there—set the trap again in a box already conveniently left under the bed. Somebody, who knew Colin's every movement, could nip up there ahead of him. He was drunk and wouldn't bother to investigate the box. All that saved his life was the fact that he slept with the window open, and roused himself in time. Query: who did that, and why?

"Final query: who killed Alec Forbes, and how, and why?"

Alan continued to shake his head doubtfully.

"You're still not convinced that Forbes's death was murder, my lad?"

"Frankly, I'm not. I still don't see why Forbes couldn't have killed both the others, or thought he had, and then killed himself."

"Logic? Or wishful thinking?"

Alan was honest. "A little of both, maybe. Aside from the money question, I should hate to think that Angus was such an old swine as to try to get an innocent man hanged."

"Angus," returned Dr. Fell, "was neither an old swine nor an honest Christian gentleman. He was a realist who saw only one way to provide for those he was fond of. I do not defend it. But can you dare say you don't understand it?"

"It isn't that. I can't understand, either, why he took the blackout down from the window if he wanted to be sure of smothering himself with the . . ."

Alan paused, for the sudden expression which had come over Dr. Fell's face was remarkable for its sheer idiocy. Dr. Fell stared, and his eyes rolled. The pipe almost dropped from his mouth.

"O Lord! O Bacchus! O my ancient hat!" he breathed. "Blackout!"

"What is it?"

"The murderer's first mistake," said Dr. Fell. "Come with me."

Hurriedly he swung round and blundered back into the hut again. Alan followed him, not without an effort. Dr. Fell began a hurried search of the room. With an exclamation of triumph he found on the floor near the bed a piece of tar paper nailed to a light wooden frame. He held this up to the window, and it fitted.

"We ourselves can testify," he went on, with extraordinary intensity, "that when we arrived here there was no blackout on this window. Hey?"

"That's right."

"Yet the lamp,"—he pointed—"had obviously been burning for a long time, far into the night. We can smell the odour of burned paraffin oil strongly even yet?"

"Yes."

Dr. Fell stared into vacancy.

"Every inch of this neighbourhood is patrolled all night by the Home Guard. A hurricane lantern gives a strong light. There wasn't even so much as a curtain, let alone a blackout, on this window when we arrived. How is it that nobody noticed that light?"

There was a pause.

"Maybe they just didn't see it."

"My dear chap! So much as a chink of light in these hills would draw down the Home Guard for miles round. No, no, no! That won't do."

"Well, maybe Forbes—before he hanged himself—blew out the lantern and took down the blackout. The window's open, we notice. Though I don't see why he should have done that."

Again Dr. Fell shook his head with vehemence.

"I quote you again the habits of suicides. A suicide will never take his own life in darkness if there is any means of providing light. I do not analyze the psychology: I merely state the fact. Besides, Forbes wouldn't have been able to see to make all his preparations in the dark. No, no, no! It's fantastic!"

"What do you suggest, then?"

Dr. Fell put his hands to his forehead. For a time he remained motionless, wheezing gently.

"I suggest," he replied, lowering his hands after an interval, "that, after Forbes had been murdered and strung up, the murderer himself extinguished the lantern. He poured out the oil remaining in it so that it should later seem to have burned itself out. Then he took down the blackout."

"But why in blazes bother to do that? Why not leave the blackout where it was, and go away, and leave the lantern to burn itself out?"

"Obviously because he had to make use of the window in making his escape."

This was the last straw.

"Look here," Alan said, with a sort of wild patience. He strode across. "Look at the damned window! It's covered by a steel grating nailed up solidly on the inside! Can you suggest any way, any way at all, by which a murderer could slide out through that?"

"Well—no. Not at the moment. And yet it was done."

They looked at each other.

From some distance away they heard the sound of a man's voice earnestly allooing, and scraps of distant talk. They hurried to the door.

Charles Swan and Alistair Duncan were striding toward them. The lawyer, n a raincoat and bowler hat, appeared more cadaverous than ever; but his vhole personality was suffused with a kind of dry triumph.

"I think you're a good deal of a cheapskate," Swan accused Alan, "to run way like that after you'd promised me all the news there was. If I hadn't had ny car I'd have been stranded."

Duncan silenced him. Duncan's mouth had a grim, pleased curve. He owed slightly to Dr. Fell.

"Gentlemen," he said, taking up a position like a schoolmaster, "we have ust learned from Dr. Grant that Colin Campbell is suffering from the effects f carbonic acid gas."

"True," agreed Dr. Fell.

"Administered probably from artificial ice taken from Angus Campbell's aboratory."

Again Dr. Fell nodded.

"Can we therefore," pursued Duncan, putting his hands together and rubing them softly, "have any doubt of how Angus died? Or of who adminstered the gas to him?"

"We cannot. If you'd care to glance in that cottage there," said Dr. Fell, odding toward it, "you will see the final proof which completes your case."

Duncan stepped quickly to the door, and just as quickly stepped back gain. Swan, more determined or more callous, uttered an exclamation and vent in.

There was a long silence while the lawyer seemed to be screwing up his ourage. His Adam's apple worked in his long throat above the too-large ollar. He removed his bowler hat and wiped his forehead with a handkerhief. Then, replacing the hat and straightening his shoulders, he forced imself to follow Swan into the cottage.

Both of them reappeared, hastily and without dignity, pursued by a series f savage growls which rose to a yelping snarl. The dog, red-eyed, watched hem from the doorway.

"Nice doggie!" crooned Duncan, with a leer of such patent hypocrisy that he dog snarled again.

"You shouldn't have touched him," said Swan. "The pooch naturally got ore. I want a telephone. Cripes, what a scoop!"

Duncan readjusted his ruffled dignity.

"So it *was* Alec Forbes," he said.

Dr. Fell inclined his head.

"My dear sir," continued the lawyer, coming over to wring Dr. Fell's hand vith some animation, "I—we—can't thank you too much! I daresay you guessed, from the trade magazines and bills you borrowed from Angus's room, what had been used to kill him?"

"Yes."

"I cannot imagine," said Duncan, "why it was not apparent to all of us from the first. Though, of course, the effects of the gas had cleared away when Angus was found. No wonder the clasps of the dog carrier were closed! When I think how we imagined snakes and spiders and heaven knows what, I am almost amused. The whole thing is so extraordinarily simple, once you have grasped the design behind it."

"I agree," said Dr. Fell. "By thunder, but I agree!"

"You—ah—observed the suicide note?"

"I did."

Duncan nodded with satisfaction.

"The insurance companies will have to eat their words now. There can be no question as to their paying in full."

Yet Duncan hesitated. Honesty evidently compelled him to worry at another point.

"There is just one thing, however, that I cannot quite understand. If Forbes placed the dog carrier under the bed before being ejected, as this gentleman," —he looked at Alan—"so intelligently suggested on Monday, how is it that Elspat and Kirstie did not observe it when they looked there?"

"Haven't you forgotten?" asked Dr. Fell. "She *did* see it, as she has since told us. Miss Elspat Campbell's mind is as literal as a German's. You asked her whether there was a suitcase there, and she said no. That is all."

It would not be true to say that the worry cleared away altogether from Duncan's face. But he cheered up, although he gave Dr. Fell a very curious look.

"You think the insurance companies will accept that correction?"

"I know the police will accept it. So the insurance companies will have to, whether they like it or not."

"A plain case?"

"A plain case."

"So it seems to me." Duncan cheered up still more. "Well, we must finish up this sad business as soon as we can. Have you informed the police about—this?"

"Miss Kathryn Campbell has gone to do so. She should be back at any minute. We had to break the door in, as you see, but we haven't touched anything else. After all, we don't want to be held as accessories after the fact."

Duncan laughed.

"You could hardly be held for that in any case. In Scots law, there is no such thing as an accessory after the fact."

"Is that so, now?" mused Dr. Fell. He took the pipe out of his mouth and

added abruptly: "Mr. Duncan, were you ever acquainted with Robert Campbell?"

There was something in his words so arresting, even if so inexplicable,
that everyone turned to look at him. The faint thunder of the Falls of Coe
appeared loud in the hush that followed.

"Robert?" repeated Duncan. "The third of the brothers?"

"Yes."

An expression of fastidious distaste crossed the lawyer's face.

"Really, sir, to rake up old scandals——"

"Did you know him?" insisted Dr. Fell.

"I did."

"What can you tell me about him? All I've learned so far is that he got
into trouble and had to leave the country. What did he do? Where did he go?
Above all, what was he like?"

Duncan grudgingly considered this.

"I knew him as a young man." He shot Dr. Fell a quick glance. "Robert,
if I may say so, was by far the cleverest and brainiest of his family. But he had
a streak of bad blood: which, fortunately, missed both Angus and Colin.
He had trouble at the bank where he worked. Then there was a shooting
affray over a barmaid.

"As to where he is now, I can't say. He went abroad—the colonies, America
—I don't know where, because he slipped aboard a ship at Glasgow. You
surely cannot consider that the matter is of any importance now?"

"No. I daresay not."

His attention was diverted. Kathryn Campbell scrambled down the bank,
crossed the stream, and came toward them.

"I've got in touch with the police," she reported breathlessly, after a sharp
glance at Duncan and Swan. "There's a hotel, the Glencoe Hotel, at the village of Glencoe about two miles farther on. The telephone number is
Ballachulish—pronounced Ballahoolish—four-five."

"Did you talk to Inspector Donaldson?"

"Yes. He says he's always known Alec Forbes would do something like this.
He says we needn't wait here, if we don't want to."

Her eyes strayed toward the cottage, and moved away uneasily.

"Please. *Must* you stay here? Couldn't we go on to the hotel and have
something to eat? I ask because the proprietress knew Mr. Forbes very well."

Dr. Fell stirred with interest.

"So?"

"Yes. She says he was a famous cyclist. She says he could cover incredible
distances at incredible speeds, in spite of the amount he drank."

Duncan uttered a soft exclamation. With a significant gesture to the others,
he went round the side of the cottage, and they instinctively followed him.

Behind the cottage was an outhouse, against which leaned a racing bicycle fitted out with a luggage grid at the back. Duncan pointed to it.

"The last link, gentlemen. It explains how Forbes could have got from here to Inveraray and back whenever he liked. Did your informant add anything else, Miss Campbell?"

"Not much. She said he came up here to drink and fish and work out schemes for perpetual motion, and things of that sort. She said the last time she saw him was yesterday, in the bar of the hotel. They practically had to throw him out at closing time in the afternoon. She says he was a bad man, who hated everything and everybody but animals."

Dr. Fell slowly walked forward and put his hand on the handle bar of the bicycle. Alan saw, with uneasiness, there was again on his face the startled expression, the wandering blankness of idiocy, which he had seen there once before. This time it was deeper and more explosive.

"O Lord!" thundered Dr. Fell, whirling round as though galvanized. "What a turnip I've been! What a remarkable donkey! What a thundering dunce!"

"Without," observed Duncan, "without sharing the views you express, may I ask why you express them?"

Dr. Fell turned to Kathryn.

"You're quite right," he said seriously, after reflecting for a time. "We must get on to that hotel. Not only to refresh the inner man; though I, to be candid, am ravenous. But I want to use a telephone. I want to use a telephone like billy-o. There's a million-to-one chance against it, of course; but the million-to-one chance came off before and it may happen again."

"What million-to-one chance?" asked Duncan, not without exasperation. "To whom do you want to telephone?"

"To the local commandant of the Home Guard," answered Dr. Fell, and lumbered round the side of the cottage with his cloak flying out behind him.

## XVII

"ALAN," Kathryn asked, "Alec Forbes didn't really kill himself, did he?"

It was late at night, and raining. They had drawn up their chairs before a brightly burning wood fire in the sitting room at Shira.

Alan was turning over the pages of a family album, with thick padded covers and gilt-topped leaves. For some time Kathryn had been silent, her elbows on the arm of the chair and her chin in her hand, staring into the fire. She dropped the question out of nowhere: flatly, as her habit was.

He did not raise his eyes.

"Why is it," he said, "that photographs taken some years ago are always

o hilariously funny? You can take down anybody's family album and split
our sides. If it happens to contain pictures of somebody you know, the
effect is even more pronounced. Why? Is it the clothes, or the expression, or
what? We weren't really as funny as that, were we?"

Disregarding her, he turned over a page or two.

"The women, as a rule, come out better than the men. Here is one of
Colin as a young man, which looks as though he'd drunk about a quart of
he Doom of the Campbells before leering at the photographer. Aunt Elspat,
on the other hand, was a really fine-looking woman. Bold-eyed brunette; Mrs.
Siddons touch. Here she is in a man's Highland costume: bonnet, feather,
plaid, and all."

"Alan Campbell!"

"Angus, on the other hand, always tried to look so dignified and pensive
that——"

"Alan darling."

He sat up with a snap. The rain pattered against the windows.

"What did you say?" he demanded.

"It was only a manner of speaking." She elevated her chin. "Or at least—
well, anyway, I *had* to get your attention somehow. Alec Forbes didn't really
kill himself, did he?"

"What makes you think that?"

"I can see it in the way you look," returned Kathryn; and he had an uncomfortable feeling that she would always be able to do this, which would
provide some critical moments in the future.

"Besides," she went on peering round to make sure they were not overheard, and lowering her voice, "why should he? He certainly couldn't have
been the one who tried to kill poor Colin."

Reluctantly Alan closed the album.

The memory of the day stretched out behind him: the meal at the Glencoe
Hotel, the endless repetitions by Alistair Duncan of how Alec Forbes had
committed his crimes and then hanged himself, all the while that Dr. Fell
said nothing, and Kathryn brooded, and Swan sent off to the *Daily Floodlight*
a story which he described as a honey.

"And why," he asked, "couldn't Forbes have tried to kill Colin?"

"Because he couldn't have known Colin was sleeping in the tower room."

(Damn! So she's spotted that!)

"Didn't you hear what the proprietress of the hotel said?" Kathryn insisted. "Forbes was in the bar of the hotel until closing time yesterday afternoon. Well, it was early in the afternoon here that Colin swore his great
oath to sleep in the tower. How on earth could Forbes have known that? It
was a snap decision which Colin made on the spur of the moment, and
couldn't have been known outside the house."

Alan hesitated.

Kathryn lowered her voice still further.

"Oh, I'm not going to broadcast it! Alan, I know what Dr. Fell thinks. A
he told us going out to the car, he thinks Angus committed suicide. Which i
horrible, and yet I believe it. I believe it still more now that we've hear
about the artificial ice."

She shivered.

"At least, we do know it isn't—supernatural. When we were thinking abou
snakes and spiders and ghosts and whatnots, I tell you I was frightened ou
of my wits. And all the while it was nothing but a lump of dry ice!"

"Most terrors are like that."

"Are they? Who played ghost, then? And who killed Forbes?"

Alan brooded. "*If* Forbes was murdered," he said, half-conceding this fo
the first time, "the motive for it is clear. It was to prove Angus's death wa
murder after all, like the attempt on Colin; to saddle Forbes with bot
crimes; and to clean up the whole business."

"To get the insurance money?"

"That's what it looks like."

The rain pattered steadily. Kathryn gave a quick glance at the door to th
hall.

"But, Alan! In that case . . . ?"

"Yes. I know what you're thinking."

"And, in any case, how *could* Forbes have been murdered?"

"Your guess is as good as mine. Dr. Fell thinks the murderer got out b
way of the window. Yes, I know the window was covered with an untouche
grating! But so was the end of the dog carrier, if you remember. Twenty-fou
hours ago I would have sworn nothing could have got out of the dog carrie
grating, either. And yet something did."

He broke off, with an air of elaborate casualness and a warning glance t
Kathryn, as they heard footsteps in the hall. He was again turning over th
pages of the album when Swan came into the sitting room.

Swan was almost as wet as he had been after Elspat's two pails of water
He stamped up to the fire, and let his hands drip into it.

"If I don't catch pneumonia one way or the other, before this thing i
over," he announced, shifting from one foot to the other, "the reason won'
be for want of bad luck. I've been obeying orders and trying to stick to Dr
Fell. You'd think that would be easy, wouldn't you?"

"Yes."

Swan's face was bitter.

"Well, it isn't. He's ditched me twice today. He's doing something wit
the Home Guard. Or at least he was before this rain started in. But wha
it is I can't find out and Sherlock Holmes himself couldn't guess. Anythin
up?"

"No. We were just looking at family portraits." Alan turned over pages

Ie passed one photograph, started to turn the page, and then, with sudden tterest, went back to it. "Hullo," he said. "I've seen *that* face somewhere!"

It was a full-face view of a light-haired man with a heavy down-curved toustache, *circa* 1906, a handsome face with washed-out eyes. This impreson, however, may have come from the faded brown color of the photograph. .cross the lower right-hand corner was written in faded ink, with curlicues, Best of luck!"

"Of course you've seen it," said Kathryn. "It's a Campbell. There's a remblance, more or less, in every one of our particular crowd."

"No, no. I mean——"

He detached the photograph from the four slits in the cardboard, and irned it over. Across the back was written, in the same handwriting, "Robert Campbell, July, '05."

"So that's the brainy Robert!"

Swan, who had been peering over his shoulder, was clearly interested in mething else.

"Wait a minute!" Swan urged, fitting back the photograph again and turn-ig back a page quickly. "Cripes, what a beauty! Who's the good-looking oman?"

"That's Aunt Elspat."

"*Who?*"

"Elspat Campbell."

Swan winked his eyes. "Not the old hag who—who—" Wordlessly, his hands ent to his new suit, and his face became distorted.

"Yes. The same one who baptized you. Look at this other one of her in Iighland costume, where she shows her legs. If I may mention the subject, ley are very fine legs; though maybe on the heavy and muscular side for opular taste nowadays."

Kathryn could not restrain herself.

"But nothing, of course," she sneered, "to compare to the legs of your recious Duchess of Cleveland."

Swan begged their attention.

"Look," he said impressively, "I don't want to seem inquisitive. But—" is voice acquired a note of passion—"who *is* this dame from Cleveland, nyhow? Who is Charles? Who is Russell? And how did you get tangled p with her? I know I oughtn't to ask; but I can't sleep nights for thinking bout it."

"The Duchess of Cleveland," said Alan, "was Charles's mistress."

"Yes, I gathered that. But is she your mistress too?"

"No. And she didn't come from Cleveland, Ohio, because she's been dead or more than two hundred years."

Swan stared at him.

"You're kidding me."

"I am not. We were having a historical argument, and——"

"I tell you, you're kidding me!" repeated Swan, with something like in credulous horror in his voice. "There's *got* to be a real Cleveland woman in it! As I said about you in my first story to the *Floodlight*——"

He paused. He opened his mouth, and shut it again. He seemed to fee that he had made a slip; as, in fact, he had. Two pairs of eyes fastened on him during an ominous silence.

"What," Kathryn asked very clearly, "what did you say about us in you first story to the *Floodlight?*"

"Nothing at all. Word of honour, I didn't! Just a little joke, nothing libe ous in it at all——"

"Alan," murmured Kathryn, with her eye on a corner of the ceiling, "don you think you'd better get down the claymores again?"

Swan had instinctively moved away until his back was shielded again the wall. He spoke in deep earnest.

"After all, you're going to get married! I overheard Dr. Fell himself sa you had to get married. So what's wrong? I didn't mean any harm." (An clearly, thought Alan, he hadn't.) "I only said——"

"What a pity," continued Kathryn, still with her eye on the ceiling, "wha a pity Colin hasn't got the use of his legs. But I hear he's a rare hand wit a shotgun. And, since his bedroom windows face the main road——"

She paused, significantly musing, as Kirstie MacTavish flung open the doo

"Colin Campbell wants tae see you," she announced in her soft, swee voice.

Swan changed colour.

"He wants to see who?"

"He wants tae see all o' you."

"But he isn't allowed visitors, is he?" cried Kathryn.

"I dinna ken. He's drinkin' whusky in bed, annahoo."

"Well, Mr. Swan," said Kathryn, folding her arms, "after giving us a solem promise, which you promptly broke and intended to break; after acceptin hospitality here under false pretenses; after being handed on a plate prob bly the only good story you ever got in your life; and hoping to get some mor —have you the courage to go up and face Colin now?"

"But you've got to look at my side of it, Miss Campbell!"

"Oh?"

"Colin Campbell'll understand! He's a good egg! He . . ." As an ide evidently occurred to him, Swan turned to the maid. "Look. He's not pickle is he?"

"Wha'?"

"Pickled. Soused," said Swan apprehensively, "cockeyed. Plastered. Full.

Kirstie was enlightened. She assured him that Colin was not full. Thoug the effectiveness of this assurance was somewhat modified by Kirstie's exper

enced belief that no man is full until he can fall down two successive flights
of stairs without injury, Swan did not know this and it served its purpose.

"I'll put it up to him," Swan argued with great earnestness. "And in the
meantime I'll put it up to both of you. I come up here; and what happens
to me?"

"Not a patch," said Kathryn, "on what's going to happen. But go on."
Swan did not hear her.

"I get chased along a road," he continued, "and get a serious injury that
might have given me blood poisoning. All right. I come round the next day,
in a brand-new suit that cost ten guineas at Austin Reed's, and that mad
woman empties two buckets of water over me. Not *one* bucket, mind you.
*Two.*"

"Alan Campbell," said Kathryn fiercely, "do you find anything so very
funny in this?"

Alan could not help himself. He was leaning back and roaring.

"Alan Campbell!"

"I can't help it," protested Alan, wiping the tears out of his eyes. "It just
occurs to me that you'll have to marry me after all."

"Can I announce that?" asked Swan instantly.

"Alan Campbell, what on earth do you mean? I'll do no such thing! The
deal!"

"You can't help yourself, my wench. It's the only solution to our difficulties. I have not yet read the *Daily Floodlight*, but I have my suspicions as
to the nature of the hints that will have appeared there."

Swan seized on this.

"I knew you wouldn't be sore," he said, his face lighting up. "There's
nothing anybody could object to, I swear! I never said a word about your
always going to bawdy houses. That's really libelous anyway——"

"What's this," inquired Kathryn, breaking off with some quickness, "about
you going to bawdy houses?"

"I'm sorry I said that," interposed Swan, with equal quickness. "I wouldn't
have said it for the world in front of you, Miss Campbell, only it slipped
out. It probably isn't true anyway, so just forget it. All I wanted to say was
that I've got to play the game straight both with you and the public."

"Are ye comin'?" asked Kirstie, still waiting patiently in the doorway.

Swan straightened his tie.

"Yes, we are. And I know Colin Campbell, who's as good an egg as ever
walked, will understand my position."

"I hope he does," breathed Kathryn. "Oh, good heavens, I hope he does!
You did say he'd got some whisky up there, didn't you Kirstie?"

It was, in a sense, unnecessary to answer this question. As the three of them
followed Kirstie up the stairs, and along the hall to the back of the house,
it was answered by Colin himself. The doors at Shira were good thick doors,

and very little in the nature of noise could penetrate far through them. The voice they heard, therefore, was not very loud. But it carried distinctly to the head of the stairs.

> "*I love a lassie, a boh-ny, boh-ny lassie;*
> *She's as puir as the li-ly in the dell!*
> *She's as sweet as the heather, the boh-ny pur-ple*
> *heath-er—*"

The singing stopped abruptly as Kirstie opened the door. In a spacious back bedroom with oak furniture, Colin Campbell lay on what should have been and undoubtedly was, a bed of pain. But you would never have guessed this from the demeanour of the tough old sinner.

His body was bandaged from the waist down, one leg supported a little above the level of the bed by a portable iron framework and supports. But his back was hunched into pillows in such a way that he could just raise his head.

Though his hair, beard, and moustache had been trimmed, he managed to look shaggier than ever. Out of this, fiercely affable eyes peered from a flushed face. The airless room smelt like a distillery.

Colin had insisted, as an invalid, on having plenty of light, and the chandelier glowed with bulbs. They illuminated his truculent grin, his gaudy pajama tops, and the untidy litter of articles on the bedside table. His bed was drawn up by one blacked-out window.

"Come in!" he shouted. "Come in, and keep the old crock company. Filthy position to be in. Kirstie, go and fetch three more glasses and another decanter. You! The rest of you! Pull up your chairs. Here, where I can see you. I've got nothing to do but this."

He was dividing his attention between the decanter, somewhat depleted and a very light 20-bore shotgun, which he was attempting to clean and oil.


## XVIII

"KITTY-KAT my dear, it's a pleasure to see your face," he continued, holding up the gun so that he could look at her through one of the barrels. "What have you been up to now? I say. Would you like to point out something to me, so that I could have a shot at it?"

Swan took one look at him, turned round, and made a beeline for the door.

Kathryn instantly turned the key in the lock, and held tightly to it as she backed away.

"Indeed I would, Uncle Colin," said Kathryn sweetly.

"That's my Kitty-kat. And how are you, Alan? And you, Horace Greeley how are *you?* I'm filthy, I don't mind telling you. Swaddled up like a blooming Chinese woman, though they've got more of me than just my feet. God's wounds! If they'd only give me a *chair,* I could at least move about."

He reflected.

Snapping shut the breech of the shotgun, he lowered it to stand against the side of the bed.

"I'm happy," he added abruptly. "Maybe I shouldn't be, but I am. You've heard, haven't you, about what happened to me? Artificial ice. Same as Angus. It was murder, after all. It's a pity about poor old Alec Forbes, though. I never did dislike the fellow. Stop a bit. Where's Fell? Why isn't Fell here? What have you done with Fell?"

Kathryn was grimly determined.

"He's out with the Home Guard, Uncle Colin. Listen. There's something we've got to tell you. This wretch of a reporter, after promising——"

"What the devil does he want to go joining the Home Guard for, at *his* age and weight? They may not pot him for a parachutist; but if they see him against the sky line they'll ruddy well pot him for a parachute. It's crazy. It's worse than that: it's downright dangerous."

"Uncle Colin, *will* you listen to me, please?"

"Yes, my dear, of course. Joining the Home Guard! Never heard such nonsense in my life!"

"This reporter——"

"He didn't say anything about it when he was in here a while ago. All he wanted to do was ask a lot of questions about poor old Rabbie; and what we'd all been saying up in the tower room on Monday. Besides, how could he get into the Home Guard in Scotland? Are you pulling my leg?"

Kathryn's expression was by this time so desperate that even Colin noticed it. He broke off, peering shaggily at her.

"Nothing wrong, is there, Kitty-kat?"

"Yes, there is. That is, if you'd just listen to me for a moment! Do you remember that Mr. Swan promised not to say a word about anything that happened here, if we let him get what stories he wanted?"

Colin's eyebrows drew together.

"God's wounds! You didn't print in that rag of yours that we stuck you in the seat of the pants with a claymore?"

"No, so help me I didn't!" returned Swan, instantly and with patent truth. "I didn't say a word about it. I've got the paper, and I can prove it."

"Then what's biting you, Kitty-kat?"

"He's said, or intimated, dreadful things about Alan and me. I don't know exactly what; and Alan doesn't even seem to care; but it's something about Alan and me being immoral together——"

Colin stared at her. Then he leaned back and bellowed with laughter. The mirth brought tears into his eyes.

"Well, aren't you?"

"No! Just because of a dreadful accident, just because we *had* to spend the night in the same compartment on the train from London——"

"You didn't have to spend the night in the same room here on Monday,' Colin pointed out. "But you ruddy well did. Eh?"

"They spent the night in the same room here?" Swan demanded quickly.

"Of course they did," roared Colin. "Come on, Kitty-kat! Be a man! I mean, be a woman! Admit it! Have the courage of your convictions. What were you doing, then, if you weren't improving your time? Nonsense!"

"You see, Miss Campbell," pleaded Swan, "I had to get the sex angle into the story somehow, and that was the only way to do it. *He* understands. Your boy friend understands. There's nothing at all to worry about, not the least little thing."

Kathryn looked from one to the other of them. An expression of hopeless despair went over her pink face. Tears came into her eyes, and she sat down in a chair and put her face in her hands.

"Here! Easy!" said Alan. "I've just been pointing out to her, Colin, that her reputation is hopelessly compromised unless she marries me now. I asked her to marry me——"

"You never did."

"Well, I do so now, in front of witnesses. Miss Campbell: will you do me the honour of becoming my wife?"

Kathryn raised a tear-stained face of exasperation.

"Of course I will, you idiot!" she stormed at him. "But why couldn't you do it decently, as I've given you a hundred opportunities to, instead of black-mailing me into it? Or saying I blackmailed you into it?"

Colin's eyes opened wide.

"Do you mean," he bellowed delightedly, "there's going to be a wedding?"

"Can I print that?"

"Yes to both questions," replied Alan.

"My dear Kitty-kat! My dear fellow! By George!" said Colin, rubbing his hands. "This calls for such a celebration as these walls haven't seen since the night Elspat's virtue fell in 1900. Where's Kirstie with that decanter? God's wounds! I wonder if there are any bagpipes in the house? I haven't tried 'em for years, but what I could do once would warm the cockles of your heart."

"You're not mad at *me*?" asked Swan anxiously.

"At you? Great Scott, no! Why should I be? Come over here, old chap, and sit down!"

"Then what," persisted Swan, "did you want that toy shotgun for?"

" 'Toy' shotgun, is it? 'Toy' shotgun?" Colin snatched up the 20-bore. "Do you know it takes a devil of a lot more skill and accuracy to use this than it does a 12-bore? Don't believe that, eh? Like me to show you?"

"No, no, no. I'll take your word for it!"

"That's better. Come and have a drink. No, we haven't got any glasses. Where's Kirstie? And Elspat! We've got to have Elspat here. Elspat!"

Kathryn was compelled to unlock the door. Swan, with an expiring sigh of relief, sat down and stretched his legs like one completely at home. He sprang up again with deep suspicion when Elspat appeared.

Elspat, however, ignored him with such icy pointedness that he backed away. Elspat gave them each in turn, except Swan, an unfathomable glance. Her eyelids were puffed and reddish, and her mouth was a straight line. Alan tried to see in her some resemblance to the handsome woman of the old photograph; but it was gone, all gone.

"Look here, old girl," said Colin. He stretched out his hand to her. "I've got great news. Glorious news. These two,"—he pointed—"are going to get married."

Elspat did not say anything. Her eyes rested on Alan, studying him. Then they moved to Kathryn, studying her for a long time. She went over to Kathryn, and quickly kissed her on the cheek. Two tears, amazing tears, overflowed Elspat's eyes.

"Here, I say!" Colin stirred uncomfortably. Then he glared. "It's the same old family custom," he complained in a querulous voice. "Always turn on the waterworks when there's going to be a wedding. This is a *happy* occasion, hang it! Stop that!"

Elspat still remained motionless. Her face worked.

"If you don't stop that, I'm going to throw something," yelled Colin. "Can't you say, 'Congratulations,' or anything like that? Have we got any pipes in the house, by the way?"

"Ye'll hae no godless merriment here, Colin Campbell," snapped Elspat, choking out the words despite her working face. She fought back by instinct, while Alan's discomfort increased.

"Aye, I'll gie ye ma blessing," she said, looking first at Kathryn and then at Alan. "If the blessin' of an auld snaggletooth body's worth a groat tae ye."

"Well, then," said Colin sulkily, "we can at least have the whisky. You'll drink their health, I hope?"

"Aye. I caud du wi' that tonight. The de'il's walkin' on ma grave." She shivered.

"I never saw such a lot of killjoys in all my born days," grumbled Colin. But he brightened as Kirstie brought in the glasses and a decanter. "One more glass, my wench. Stop a bit. Maybe we'd better have a third decanter, eh?"

"Just a moment!" said Alan. He looked round at them and, in some uneasiness, at the shotgun. "You're not proposing another binge tonight, are you?"

"Binge! Nonsense!" said Colin, pouring himself a short one evidently to give him strength to pour for the others, and gulping it down. "Who said anything about a binge? We're drinking health and happiness to the bride, that's all. You can't object to that, can you?"

"*I* can't," smiled Kathryn.

"Nor me," observed Swan. "I feel grand!" Swan added. "I forgive everybody. I even forgive madam,"—he hesitated, for he was clearly frightened of Elspat—"for ruining a suit that cost me ten guineas."

Colin spoke persuasively.

"See here, Elspat. I'm sorry about Angus. But there it is. And it's turned out for the best. If he had to die, I don't mind admitting it's got me out of a bad financial hole.

"Do you know what I'm going to do? No more doctoring in Manchester, for the moment. I'm going to get a ketch and go for a cruise in the South Seas. And you, Elspat. You can get a dozen big pictures painted of Angus, and look at 'em all day. Or you can go to London and see the jitterbugs. You're safe, old girl."

Elspat's face was white.

"Aye," she blazed at him. "*And d'ye ken why we're safe?*"

"Steady!" cried Alan.

Even in his mist of good will and exhilaration, he knew what was coming. Kathryn knew too. They both made a move toward Elspat, but she paid no attention.

"I'll hae ma conscience nae mair damned wi' lees. D'ye ken why we're safe?"

She whirled round to Swan. Addressing him for the first time, she announced calmly that Angus had killed himself; she poured out the entire story, with her reasons for believing it. And every word of it was true.

"Now that's very interesting, ma'am," said Swan, who had taken one glass of whisky and was holding out his tumbler for a second. He appeared flattered by her attention. "Then you're not mad at me any longer either?"

Elspat stared at him.

"Mad at ye? Hoots! D'ye hear what I'm saying?"

"Yes, of course, ma'am," Swan replied soothingly. "And of course I understand how this thing has upset you——"

"Mon, dinna ye believe me?"

Swan threw back his head and laughed.

"I hate to contradict a lady, ma'am. But if you'll just have a word with the police, or with Dr. Fell, or with these people here, you'll see that either somebody has been kidding you or you've been kidding yourself. I ought to know, oughtn't I? Hasn't anybody told you that Alec Forbes killed himself, and left a note admitting he killed Mr. Campbell?"

Elspat drew in her breath. Her face wrinkled up. She turned and looked at Colin, who nodded.

"It's true, Elspat. Come abreast of the times! Where have you been all day?"

It stabbed Alan to the heart to see her. She groped over to a chair and sat down. A human being, a sentient, living, hurt human being, emerged from behind the angry clay in which Elspat set her face to the world.

"Ye're no' deceivin' me?" she insisted. "Ye swear to the Guid Man——!"

Then she began to swing back and forth in the rocking chair. She began to laugh, showing that she had fine teeth; and it kindled and illumined her face. Her whole being seemed to breathe a prayer.

Angus had not died in the sin of suicide. He had not gone to the bad place. And Elspat, this Elspat whose real surname nobody knew, rocked back and forth and laughed and was happy.

Colin Campbell, serenely missing all this, was still acting as barman.

"You understand," he beamed, "neither Fell nor I ever for a minute thought it *was* suicide. Still, it's just as well to get the whole thing tidied up. I never for a second thought you didn't know, or I'd have crawled off this bed to tell you. Now be a good sport. I know this is still officially a house of mourning. But, under the circumstances, what about getting me those pipes?"

Elspat got to her feet and went out of the room.

"By Jupiter," breathed Colin, "she's gone to get 'em! . . . What ails you, Kitty-kat?"

Kathryn regarded the door with uncertain, curiously shining eyes. She bit her lip. Her eyes moved over toward Alan.

"I don't know," she answered. "I'm happy,"—here she glared at Alan—"and yet I feel all sort of funny and mixed up."

"Your English grammar," said Alan, "is abominable. But your sentiments are correct. That's what she believes now; and that's what Elspat has got to go on believing. Because, of course, it's true."

"Of course," agreed Kathryn quickly. "I wonder, Uncle Colin, whether you would do me a big favour?"

"Anything in the world, my dear."

"Well," said Kathryn, hesitantly extending the tumbler, "it isn't very much, perhaps; but would you mind making my drink just a *little* stronger?"

"Now that's my Kitty-kat!" roared Colin. "Here you are . . . Enough?"

"A little more, please."

"A little *more?*"

"Yes, please."

"Cripes," muttered Swan, on whom the first smashing, shuddering effect of the Doom of the Campbells had now passed to a quickened speech and excitement, "you two professors are teamed up right. I don't understand how you do it. Does anybody (maybe, now?) feel like a song?"

Beatific with his head among the pillows, as though enthroned in state,

Colin lifted the shotgun and waved it in the air as though conducting an orchestra. His bass voice beat against the windows.

*"I love a lassie, a boh-ny, boh-ny las-sie—"*

Swan, drawing his chin far into his collar, assumed an air of solemn portentousness. Finding the right pitch after a preliminary cough, he moved his glass gently in time and joined in.

*"She's as pure as the li-ly in the dell—!"*

To Alan, lifting his glass in a toast to Kathryn, there came a feeling that all things happened for the best; and that tomorrow could take care of itself. The exhilaration of being in love, the exhilaration of merely watching Kathryn, joined with the exhilaration of the potent brew in his hand. He smiled at Kathryn; she smiled back; and they both joined in.

*"She's as sweet as the heath-er, the boh-ny pur-ple heather—"*

He had a good loud baritone, and Kathryn a fairly audible soprano. Their quartet made the room ring. To Aunt Elspat, returning with a set of bagpipes—which she grimly handed to Colin, and which he eagerly seized without breaking off the song—it must have seemed that old days had returned.

"A'weel," said Aunt Elspat resignedly. "A'weel!"


## XIX

ALAN CAMPBELL opened one eye.

From somewhere in remote distances, muffled beyond sight or sound, his soul crawled back painfully, through subterranean corridors, up into his body again. Toward the last it moved to the conviction that he was looking at a family photograph album, from which there stared back at him a face he had seen, somewhere, only today . . .

Then he was awake.

The first eye was bad enough. But, when he opened the second eye, such a rush of anguish flowed through his brain that he knew what was wrong with him, and realized fairly that he had done it again.

He lay back and stared at the cracks on the ceiling. There was sunlight in the room.

He had a violent headache, and his throat was dry. But it occurred to him in a startled sort of way that he did not feel nearly as bad as he had felt the first time. This prompted an uneasy flash of doubt. Did the infernal stuff take hold of you? Was it (as the temperance tracts said) an insidious poison whose effects seemed to grow less day by day?

Then another feeling, heartening or disheartening according to how you viewed the stuff, took possession of him.

When he searched his memory he could recall nothing except blurred scenes which seemed to be dominated by the noise of bagpipes, and a vision of Elspat swinging back and forth beatifically in a rocking chair amidst it.

Yet no sense of sin oppressed him, no sense of guilt or enormity. He *knew* that his conduct had been such as becomes a gentleman, even *en pantoufles.* It was a strange conviction, but a real one. He did not even quail when Kathryn opened the door.

On the contrary, this morning it was Kathryn who appeared guilty and hunted. On the tray she carried not one cup of black coffee, but two. She put the tray on the bedside table, and looked at him.

"It ought to be you," she said, after clearing her throat, "who brought this to me this morning. But I knew you'd be disgusting and sleep past noon. I suppose you don't remember anything about last night either?"

He tried to sit up, easing the throb in his head.

"Well, no. Er—I wasn't——?"

"No, you were not. Alan Campbell, there never was such a stuffed shirt as you who ever lived. You just sat and beamed as though you owned the earth. But you *will* quote poetry. When you began on Tennyson, I feared the worst. You recited the whole of 'The Princess,' and nearly all of 'Maud.' When you actually had the face to quote that bit about 'Put thy sweet hand in mine and trust in me,' and patted my hand as you did it—well, really!"

Averting his eyes, he reached after the coffee.

"I wasn't aware I knew so much Tennyson."

"You didn't, really. But when you couldn't remember, you just thought for a moment, and then said, 'Umble-bumble, umble-bumble,' and went on."

"Never mind. At least, we were all right?"

Kathryn lowered the cup she had raised to her lips. The cup rattled and clicked on its saucer.

"All right?" she repeated with widening eyes. "When that wretch Swan is probably in hospital now?"

Alan's head gave a violent throb.

"We didn't——?"

"No, not you. Uncle Colin."

"My God, he didn't assault Swan again? But they're great pals! He couldn't have assaulted Swan again! What happened?"

"Well, it was all right until Colin had about his fifteenth Doom; and Swan, who was also what he called 'canned' and a little too cocksure, brought out the newspaper article he wrote yesterday. He'd smuggled the paper in in case we didn't like it."

"Yes?"

"It wasn't so bad, really. I admit that. Everything was all right until Swan described how Colin had decided to sleep in the tower room."

"Yes?"

"Swan's version of the incident ran something like this. You remember, he was hanging about outside the sitting-room windows? His story said: 'Dr. Colin Campbell, a deeply religious man, placed his hand on the Bible and swore an oath that he would not enter the church again until the family ghost had ceased to walk in the melancholy Castle of Shira.' For about ten seconds Colin just looked at him. Then he pointed to the door and said, 'Out.' Swan didn't understand until Colin turned completely purple and said, 'Out of this house and stay out.' Colin grabbed his shotgun, and——'

"He didn't——?"

"Not just then. But when Swan leaped downstairs, Colin said, 'Turn out the light and take down the blackout. I want to get him from the window as he goes up the road.' His bed is by the window, you remember."

"You don't mean to say Colin shot Swan in the seat of the pants as he ran for Inveraray?"

"No," answered Kathryn. "Colin didn't. I did."

Her voice became a wail.

"Alan darling, we've *got* to get out of this insidious country. First you, and now me. I don't know what's come over me; I honestly don't!"

Alan's head was aching still harder.

"But wait a minute! Where was I? Didn't I interfere?"

"You didn't even notice. You were reciting 'Sir Galahad' to Elspat. The rain had cleared off—it was four o'clock in the morning—and the moon was up. I was boiling angry with Swan, you see. And there he was in the road.

"He must have heard the window go up, and seen the moonlight on the shotgun. Because he gave one look, and never ran so fast even on the Monday night. I said, 'Uncle Colin, let *me* have a go.' He said, 'All right; but let him get a sporting distance away; we don't want to hurt him.' Ordinarily I'm frightened of guns, and I couldn't have hit the side of a barn door. But that wretched stuff made everything different. I loosed off blindly, and got a bull's-eye with the second barrel.

"Alan, do you think he'll have me arrested? And don't you *dare* laugh, either!"

"'Pompilia, will you let them murder me?'" murmured Alan. He finished his coffee, propped himself upright, and steadied a swimming world. "Never mind," he said. "I'll go and smooth him down."

"But suppose I——?"

Alan studied the forlorn figure.

"You couldn't have hurt him much. Not at a distance, with a twenty-bore and a light load. He didn't fall down, did he?"

"No; he only ran harder."

"Then it's all right."

"But what am I to *do*?"

" 'Put thy sweet hand in mine and trust in me.' "

"Alan Campbell!"

"Well, isn't it the proper course?"

Kathryn sighed. She walked to the window, and looked down over the loch. Its waters were peaceful, a-gleam in sunshine.

"And that," she told him, after a pause, "isn't all."

"Not more——!"

"No, no, no! Not more trouble of that kind, anyway. I got the letter this morning. Alan, I've been recalled."

"Recalled?"

"From my holiday. By the college. A.R.P. I also saw this morning's Scottish *Daily Express*. It looks as though the real bombing is going to begin."

The sunlight was as fair, the hills as golden and purple, as ever. Alan took a packet of cigarettes from the bedside table. He lit one and inhaled smoke. Though it made his head swim, he sat contemplating the loch and smoking steadily.

"So our holiday," he said, "is a kind of entr'acte."

"Yes," said Kathryn, without turning round. "Alan, *do* you love me?"

"You know I do."

"Then do we care?"

"No."

There was a silence.

"When have you got to go?" he asked presently.

"Tonight, I'm afraid. That's what the letter says."

"Then," he declared briskly, "we can't waste any more time. The sooner I get my own things packed, the better. I hope we can get adjoining sleepers on the train. We've done all we can do here anyway, which wasn't much to start with. The case, officially, is closed. All the same—I should have liked to see the real end of it, if there is an end."

"You may see the end of it yet," Kathryn told him, and turned round from the window.

"Meaning what?"

She wrinkled up her forehead, and her nervous manner was not entirely due to her apprehensions about the night before.

"You see," she went on, "Dr. Fell is here. When I told him I had to go back tonight, he said he had every reason to believe he would be going as well. I said, 'But what about you-know?' He said, 'You-know will, I think, take care of itself.' But he said it in a queer way that made me think there's something going on. Something—rather terrible. He didn't come back here until nearly dawn this morning. He wants to see you, by the way."

"I'll be dressed in half a tick. Where is everybody else this morning?"

"Colin's still asleep. Elspat, even Kirstie, are out. There's nobody here but you and me and Dr. Fell. Alan, it isn't hangover and it isn't Swan and it isn't nerves. But—I'm frightened. Please come downstairs as quick as you can."

He told himself, when he nicked his face in shaving, that this was due to the brew of the night before. He told himself that his own apprehensions were caused by an upset stomach and the misadventures of Swan.

Shira was intensely quiet. Only the sun entered. When you turned on a tap, or turned it off, ghostly clankings went down through the house and shivered away. And, as Alan went down to get his breakfast, he saw Dr. Fell in the sitting room.

Dr. Fell, in his old black alpaca suit and string tie, occupied the sofa. He was sitting in the warm, golden sunlight, the meerschaum pipe between his teeth, and his expression far away. He had the air of a man who meditates a dangerous business and is not quite sure of his course. The ridges of his waistcoat rose and fell with slow, gentle wheezings. His big mop of grey-streaked hair had fallen over one eye.

Alan and Kathryn shared buttered toast and more coffee. They did not speak much. Neither knew quite what to do. It was like the feeling of not knowing whether you had been summoned to the headmaster's study, or hadn't.

But the question was solved for them.

"Good morning!" called a voice.

They hurried out into the hall.

Alistair Duncan, in an almost summery and skittish-looking brown suit, was standing at the open front door. He wore a soft hat and carried a brief case. He raised his hand to the knocker of the open door, as though by way of illustration.

"There did not seem to be anybody about," he said. His voice, though meant to be pleasant, had a faint irritated undertone.

Alan glanced to the right. Through the open door of the sitting room he could see Dr. Fell stir, grunt, and lift his head as though roused out of sleep. Alan looked back to the tall, stoop-shouldered figure of the lawyer, framed against the shimmering loch outside.

"*May* I come in?" inquired Duncan politely.

"P-please do," stammered Kathryn.

"Thank you." Duncan stepped in gingerly, removing his hat. He went to the door of the sitting room, glanced in, and uttered an exclamation which might have been satisfaction or annoyance.

"Please come in here," rumbled Dr. Fell. "All of you, if you will. And close the door."

The usual odour as of damp oilcloth, of old wood and stone, was brought out by the sun in that stuffy room. Angus's photograph, still draped in crepe, faced them from the overmantel. Sun made tawdry the dark, bad daubs of the pictures in their gilt frames, and picked out worn places in the carpet.

"My dear sir," said the lawyer, putting down his hat and brief case on the table which held the Bible. He spoke the words as though he were beginning a letter.

"Sit down, please," said Dr. Fell.

A slight frown creased Duncan's high, semi-bald skull.

"In response to your telephone call," he replied, "here I am." He made a humorous gesture. "But may I point out, sir, that I am a busy man? I have been at this house, for one cause or another, nearly every day for the past week. And, grave as the issue has been, since it is now settled——"

"It is not settled," said Dr. Fell.

"But——!"

"Sit down, all of you," said Dr. Fell.

Blowing a film of ash off his pipe, he settled back, returned the pipe to his mouth, and drew at it. The ash settled down across his waistcoat, but he did not brush it off. He eyed them for a long time, and Alan's uneasiness had grown to something like a breath of fear.

"Gentlemen, and Miss Campbell," continued Dr. Fell, drawing a long sniff through his nose. "Yesterday afternoon, if you remember, I spoke of a million-to-one chance. I did not dare to hope for much from it. Still, it had come off in Angus's case and I hoped it might come off in Forbes's. It did."

He paused, and added in the same ordinary tone:

"I now have the instrument with which, in a sense, Alec Forbes was murdered."

The deathlike stillness of the room, while tobacco smoke curled up past starched lace curtains in the sunlight, lasted only a few seconds.

"Murdered?" the lawyer exploded.

"Exactly."

"You will pardon me if I suggest that——"

"Sir," interrupted Dr. Fell, taking the pipe out of his mouth, "in your heart of hearts you know that Alec Forbes was murdered, just as you know that Angus Campbell committed suicide. Now don't you?"

Duncan took a quick look round him.

"It's quite all right," the doctor assured him. "We four are all alone here— as yet. I have seen to that. You are at liberty to speak freely."

"I have no intention of speaking, either freely or otherwise." Duncan's voice was curt. "Did you bring me all the way out here just to tell me that? Your suggestion is preposterous!"

Dr. Fell sighed.

"I wonder whether you will think it is so preposterous," he said, "if I tell you the proposal I mean to make."

"Proposal?"

"Bargain. Deal, if you like."

"There is no question of a bargain, my dear sir. You told me yourself that this is an open-and-shut case, a plain case. The police believe as much. I saw Mr. MacIntyre, the Procurator Fiscal, this morning."

"Yes. That is a part of my bargain."

Duncan was almost on the edge of losing his temper.

"Will you kindly tell me, Doctor, what it is you wish of me: if anything? And particularly where you got this wicked and indeed dangerous notion that Alec Forbes was murdered?"

Dr. Fell's expression was vacant.

"I got it first," he responded, puffing out his cheeks, "from a piece of blackout material—tar paper on a wooden frame—which should have been up at the window in Forbes's cottage, and yet wasn't.

"The blackout *had been* up at the window during the night, else the lantern light would have been seen by the Home Guard. And the lantern (if you remember the evidence) *had been* burning. Yet for some reason it was necessary to extinguish the lantern and take down the blackout from the window.

"Why? That was the problem. As was suggested to me at the time, why didn't the murderer simply leave the lantern burning, and leave the blackout in its place, when he made his exit? At first sight it seemed rather a formidable problem.

"The obvious line of attack was to say that the murderer had to take down the blackout in order to make his escape; and, once having made it, he couldn't put the blackout back up again. That is a very suggestive line, if you follow it up. Could he, for instance, somehow have got through a steel-mesh grating, and somehow replace it afterwards?"

Duncan snorted.

"The grating being nailed up on the inside?"

Dr. Fell nodded very gravely.

"Yes. Nailed up. So the murderer couldn't very well have done *that*, could he?"

Duncan got to his feet.

"I am sorry, sir, that I cannot remain to listen to these preposterous notions any longer. Doctor, you shock me. The very idea that Forbes——"

"Don't you want to hear what my proposal is?" suggested Dr. Fell. He paused. "It will be much to your advantage." He paused again. "Very much to your advantage."

In the act of taking his hat and brief case from the little table, Duncan dropped his hands and straightened up. He looked back at Dr. Fell. His face was white.

"God in heaven!" he whispered. "You do not suggest—ah—that I am the murderer, do you?"

"Oh, no," replied Dr. Fell. "Tut, tut! Certainly not."

Alan breathed easier.

It was the same idea which had occurred to him, all the more sinister for the overtones in Dr. Fell's voice. Duncan ran a finger round inside his loose collar.

"I am glad," he said, with an attempt at humorous dryness, "I am glad, at least to hear that. Now, come, sir! Let's have the cards on the table. What sort of proposition have you which could possibly interest me?"

"One which concerns the welfare of your clients. In short, the Campbell family." Again Dr. Fell leisurely blew a film of ash off his pipe. "You see, I am in a position to *prove* that Alec Forbes was murdered."

Duncan dropped hat and brief case on the table as though they had burnt him.

"Prove it? How?"

"Because I have the instrument which was, in a sense, used to murder him."

"But Forbes was hanged with a dressing-gown cord!"

"Mr. Duncan, if you will study the best criminological authorities, you will find them agreed on one thing. Nothing is more difficult to determine than the question of whether a man has been hanged, or whether he has first been strangled and then hung up afterwards to simulate hanging. That is what happened to Forbes.

"Forbes was taken from behind and strangled. With what, I don't know. A necktie. Perhaps a scarf. Then those artistic trappings were all arranged by a murderer who knew his business well. If such things are done with care, the result cannot be told from a genuine suicide. This murderer made only one mistake, which was unavoidable. But it was fatal.

"Ask yourself again, with regard to that grated window——"

Duncan stretched out his hands as though in supplication.

"But what is this mysterious 'evidence'? And who is this mysterious 'murderer'?" His eye grew sharp. "You know who it is?"

"Oh, yes," said Dr. Fell.

"You are not in a position," said the lawyer, rapping his knuckles on the table, "to prove Angus Campbell committed suicide."

"No. Yet if Forbes's death is proved to be murder, that surely invalidates the false confession left behind? A confession conveniently written on a typewriter, which could have been written by anybody and was actually written by the murderer. What will the police think then?"

"What are you suggesting to me, exactly?"

"Then you will hear my proposition?"

"I will hear anything," returned the lawyer, going across to a chair and sitting down with his big-knuckled hands clasped together, "if you give me some line of direction. Who is this murderer?"

Dr. Fell eyed him.

"You have no idea?"

"None, I swear! And I—ah—still retain the right to disbelieve every word you say. Who is this murderer?"

"As a matter of fact," replied Dr. Fell, "I think the murderer is in the house now, and should be with us at any minute."

Kathryn glanced rather wildly at Alan.

It was very warm in the room. A late fly buzzed against one bright window-pane behind the starched curtains. In the stillness they could distinctly hear the noise of footsteps as someone walked along the hall toward the front.

"That should be our friend," continued Dr. Fell in the same unemotional tone. Then he raised his voice and shouted. "We're in the sitting room! Come and join us!"

The footsteps hesitated, turned and came toward the door of the room.

Duncan got to his feet, spasmodically. His hands were clasped together, and Alan could hear the knuckle joints crack as he pressed them.

Between the time they first heard the footsteps, and the time that the knob turned and the door opened, was perhaps five or six seconds. Alan has since computed it as the longest interval of his life. Every board in the room seemed to have a separate creak and crack; everything seemed alive and aware and insistent like the droning fly against the windowpane.

The door opened, and a certain person came in.

"That's the murderer," said Dr. Fell.

He was pointing to Mr. Walter Chapman, of the Hercules Insurance Company.

## XX

EVERY detail of Chapman's appearance was picked out by the sunlight. The short, broad figure clad in a dark blue suit. The fair hair, the fresh complexion, the curiously pale eyes. One hand held his bowler hat, the other was at his necktie, fingering it. He had moved his head to one side as though dodging.

"I beg your pardon?" he said in a somewhat shrill voice.

"I said, come in, Mr. Chapman," answered Dr. Fell. "Or should I say Mr. Campbell? Your real name is Campbell, isn't it?"

"What the devil are you talking about? I don't understand you."

"Two days ago," said Dr. Fell, "when I first set eyes on you, you were standing in much the same place as now. I was standing over by that window there (remember?), making an intense study of a full-face photograph of Angus Campbell.

"We had not been introduced. I lifted my eyes from studying the photograph; and I was confronted by such a startling, momentary family likeness that I said to you, 'Which Campbell are you?' "

Alan remembered it.

In his imagination, the short, broad figure before him became the short, broad figure of Colin or Angus Campbell. The fair hair and washed-out eyes became (got it!) the fair hair and washed-out eyes of that photograph of Robert Campbell in the family album. All these things wavered and changed and were distorted like images in water, yet folded together to form a composite whole in the solid person before them.

"Does he remind you of anyone *now*, Mr. Duncan?" inquired Dr. Fell.

The lawyer weakly subsided into his chair. Or, rather, his long lean limbs seemed to collapse like a clothes horse as he groped for and found the arms of the chair.

"Rabbie Campbell," he said. It was not an exclamation, or a question, or any form of words associated with emotion; it was the statement of a fact. "You're Rabbie Campbell's son," he said.

"I must insist—" the alleged Chapman began, but Dr. Fell cut him short.

"The sudden juxtaposition of Angus's photograph and this man's face," pursued the doctor, "brought a suggestion which may have been overlooked by some of you. Let me refresh your memory on another point."

He looked at Alan and Kathryn.

"Elspat told you, I think, that Angus Campbell had an uncanny flair for spotting family resemblances; so that he could tell one of his own branch even if the person 'blacked his face and spoke with a strange tongue.' This same flair is shared, though in less degree, by Elspat herself."

This time Dr. Fell looked at Duncan.

"Therefore it seemed to me very curious and interesting that, as you yourself are reported to have said, Mr. 'Chapman' always kept out of Elspat's way and would never under any circumstances go near her. It seemed to me worth investigating.

"The Scottish police can't use the resources of Scotland Yard. But I, through my friend Superintendent Hadley, can. It took only a few hours to discover the truth about Mr. Walter Chapman, though the transatlantic telephone call (official) Hadley put through afterwards did not get me a reply until the early hours of this morning."

Taking a scribbled envelope from his pocket, Dr. Fell blinked at it, and then adjusted his eyeglasses to stare at Chapman.

"Your real name is Walter Chapman Campbell. You hold, or held, passport number 609348 on the Union of South Africa. Eight years ago you came to England from Port Elizabeth, where your father, Robert Campbell, is still alive: though very ill and infirm. You dropped the Campbell part of your name because your father's name had unpleasant associations with the Hercules Insurance Company, for which you worked.

"Two months ago (as you yourself are reported to have said) you were moved from England to be head of one of the several branches of your firm in Glasgow.

"There, of course, Angus Campbell spotted you."

Walter Chapman moistened his lips.

On his face was printed a fixed, skeptical smile. Yet his eyes moved swiftly to Duncan, as though wondering how the lawyer took this, and back again.

"Don't be absurd," Chapman said.

"You deny these facts, sir?"

"Granting," said the other, whose collar seemed inordinately tight, "granting that for reasons of my own I used only a part of my name, what for God's sake am I supposed to have done?"

He pounced a little, a gesture which reminded the watchers of Colin.

"I could also bear to know, Dr. Fell, why you and two Army officers woke me up at my hotel in Dunoon in the middle of last night, merely to ask some tomfool questions about insurance. But let that go. I repeat: what for God's sake am I supposed to have done?"

"You assisted Angus Campbell in planning his suicide," replied Dr. Fell; "you attempted the murder of Colin Campbell, and you murdered Alec Forbes."

The colour drained out of Chapman's face.

"Absurd."

"You were not acquainted with Alec Forbes?"

"Certainly not."

"You have never been near his cottage by the Falls of Coe?"

"Never."

Dr. Fell's eyes closed. "In that case, you won't mind if I tell you what I think you did.

"As you said yourself, Angus came to see you at your office in Glasgow when he took out his final insurance policy. My belief is that he had seen you before. That he taxed you with being his brother's son; that you denied it, but were ultimately compelled to admit it.

"And this, of course, gave Angus the final triple security for his scheme. Angus left *nothing* to chance. He knew your father for a thorough bad hat; and he was a good enough judge of men to diagnose you as a thorough bad hat too. So, when he took out that final, rather unnecessary policy as an excuse to hang about with you, he explained to you exactly what he meant to do. You would come to investigate a curious death. If there were *any* slip-up, any at all, you could always cover this up and point out that the death was murder because you knew what had really happened.

"There was every inducement for you to help Angus. He could point out to you that you were only helping your own family. That, with himself dead, only a sixty-five-year-old Colin stood between an inheritance of nearly eighteen thousand pounds to your own father; and ultimately, of course, to you.

He could appeal to your family loyalty, which was Angus's only blind fetish.

"But it was not a fetish with you, Mr. Chapman Campbell. For you suddenly saw how you could play your own game.

"With Angus dead, and Colin dead as well . . ."

Dr. Fell paused.

"You see," he added, turning to the others, "the attempted murder of Colin made it fairly certain that our friend here must be the guilty person. Don't you recall that *it was Mr. Chapman, and nobody else, who drove Colin to sleep in the tower?*"

Alistair Duncan got to his feet, but sat down again.

The room was hot, and a small bead of sweat appeared on Chapman's forehead.

"Think back, if you will, to two conversations. One took place in the tower room on Monday evening, and has been reported to me. The other took place in this room on Tuesday afternoon, and I was here myself.

"Who was the first person to introduce the word 'supernatural' into this affair? That word which always acts on Colin as a matador's cape acts on a bull? It was Mr. Chapman, if you recall. In the tower on Monday evening he deliberately—even irrelevantly—dragged it into the conversation, when nobody had suggested any such thing before.

"Colin swore there was no ghost. So, of course, our ingenious friend had to give him a ghost. I asked before: what was the reason for the mummery of the phantom Highlander with the caved-in face, appearing in the tower room on Monday night? The answer is easy. It was to act as the final, goading spur on Colin Campbell.

"The Masquerade wasn't difficult to carry out. This tower here is an isolated part of the house. It has a ground-floor entrance to the outside court, so that an outsider can come and go at will. That entrance is usually open; and, even if it isn't, an ordinary padlock key will do the trick. With the assistance of a plaid, a bonnet, a little wax and paint, the ghost 'appeared' to Jock Fleming. If Jock hadn't been there, anybody else would have done as well.

"And then?

"Bright and early on Wednesday, Mr. Chapman was ready. The ghost story was flying. He came here and (don't you remember?) pushed poor Colin clear over the edge by his remarks on the subject of ghosts.

"What was the remark which made Colin go off the deep end? What was the remark which made Colin say, 'That's torn it,' and swear his oath to sleep in the tower? It was Mr. Chapman's shy, sly little series of observations ending, 'This is a funny country and a funny house; and I tell you I shouldn't care to spend a night up in that room.'"

In Alan's memory the scene took form again.

Chapman's expression now, too, was much the same as it had been. But now there appeared behind it an edge of desperation.

"It was absolutely necessary," pursued Dr. Fell, "to get Colin to sleep in the tower. True, the artificial-ice trick could have been worked anywhere. But it couldn't have been worked anywhere by *Chapman*.

"He couldn't go prowling through this house. The thing had to be done in that isolated tower, with an outside entrance for him to come and go. Just before Colin roared good night and staggered up all those stairs, Chapman could plant the box containing the ice and slip away.

"Let me recapitulate. Up to this time, of course, Chapman couldn't for a second pretend he had any glimmering of knowledge as to how Angus might have died. He had to pretend to be as puzzled as anybody else. He had to keep saying he thought it must be suicide; and rather a neat piece of acting it was.

"Naturally, no mention of artificial ice must creep in *yet*. Not yet. Otherwise the gaff would be blown and he couldn't lure Colin by bogey threats into sleeping in the tower. So he kept on saying that Angus must deliberately have committed suicide, thrown himself out of the window for no cause at all—as our friend did insist in some detail, over and over—or, if there were any cause, it was something damnable in the line of horrors.

"This was his game *up to the time Colin was disposed of*. Then everything would change.

"Then the apparent truth would come out with a roar. Colin would be found dead of carbon-dioxide poisoning. The artificial ice would be remembered. If it wasn't, our ingenious friend was prepared to remember it himself. Smiting his forehead, he would say that of course this was murder; and of course the insurance must be paid; and where was that fiend Alec Forbes, who had undoubtedly done it all?

"Therefore it was necessary *instantly*, on the same night when Colin had been disposed of, to dispose of Alec Forbes."

Dr. Fell's pipe had gone out. He put it in his pocket, hooked his thumbs in the pockets of his waistcoat, and surveyed Chapman with dispassionate appraisal.

Alistair Duncan swallowed once or twice, the Adam's apple moving in his long throat.

"Can you—can you prove all this?" the lawyer asked in a thin voice.

"I don't have to prove it," said Dr. Fell, "since I can prove the murder of Forbes. To be hanged by the neck until you are dead, and may God have mercy upon your soul, is just as effective for one murder as for two. Isn't it, Mr. Chapman?"

Chapman had backed away.

"I—I may have spoken to Forbes once or twice—" he began, hoarsely and incautiously.

"Spoken to him!" said Dr. Fell. "You struck up quite an acquaintance with him, didn't you? You even warned him to keep out of the way. Afterwards it was too late.

"Up to this time your whole scheme had been triple foolproof. For, d'ye see, Angus Campbell really *had* committed suicide. When murder came to be suspected, the one person they couldn't possibly suspect was you; because you weren't guilty. I am willing to bet that for the night of Angus's death you have an alibi which stands and shines before all men.

"But you committed a bad howler when you didn't stay to make sure Colin was really dead after falling from the tower window on Tuesday night. And you made a still worse howler when you climbed into your car afterwards and drove out to the Falls of Coe for your last interview with Alec Forbes. What is the licence number of your car, Mr. Chapman?"

Chapman winked both eyes at him, those curious light eyes which were the most disturbing feature of his face.

"Eh?"

"What is the licence number of your car? It is,"—he consulted the back of the envelope—"MGM 1911, isn't it?"

"I—I don't know. Yes, I suppose it is."

"A car bearing the number MGM 1911 was seen parked by the side of the road opposite Forbes's cottage between the hours of two and three o'clock in the morning. It was seen by a member of the Home Guard who is willing to testify to this. You should have remembered, sir, that these lonely roads are no longer lonely. You should have remembered how they are patrolled late at night."

Alistair Duncan's face was whiter yet.

"And that's the sum of your evidence?" the lawyer demanded.

"Oh, no," said Dr. Fell. "That's the least of it."

Wrinkling up his nose, he contemplated a corner of the ceiling.

"We now come to the problem of Forbes's murder," he went on, "and how the murderer managed to leave behind him a room locked up on the inside. Mr. Duncan, do you know anything about geometry?"

"Geometry?"

"I hasten to say," explained Dr. Fell, "that I know little of what I was once compelled to learn, and wish to know less. It belongs to the limbo of school days, along with algebra and economics and other dismal things. Beyond being unable to forget that the square of the hypotenuse is equal to the sum of the squares of the other two sides, I have happily been able to rid my mind of this gibberish.

"At the same time it might be of value (for once in its life) if you were to think of Forbes's cottage in its geometrical shape." He took a pencil from his pocket and drew a design in the air with it. "The cottage is a square, twelve feet by twelve feet. Imagine, in the middle of the wall facing you, the door. Imagine, in the middle of the wall to your right, the window.

"I stood in the cottage yesterday; and I racked my brains over that infernal, tantalizing window.

"*Why* had it been necessary to take down the blackout? It could not have been, as I indicated to you some minutes ago, because the murderer had in some way managed to get his corporeal body through the grated window. This, as the geometricians are so fond of saying (rather ill-manneredly, it always seemed to me) was absurd.

"The only other explanation was that the window had to be used in some way. I had examined the steel-wire grating closely, if you remember?" Dr. Fell turned to Alan.

"I remember."

"In order to test its solidity, I put my finger through one of the openings in the mesh and shook it. Still no glimmer of intelligence penetrated the thick fog of wool and mist which beclouded me. I remained bogged and sunk until you,"—here he turned to Kathryn—"passed on a piece of information which even to a dullard like myself gave a prod and a hint."

"I did?" cried Kathryn.

"Yes. You said the proprietress of the Glencoe Hotel told you Forbes often came out there to fish."

Dr. Fell spread out his hands. His thunderous voice was apologetic.

"Of course, all the evidences were there. The hut, so to speak, reeked of fishiness. Forbes's angler's creel was there. His flies were there. His gum boots were there. Yet it was only then, only then, when the fact occurred to me that in all that cottage I had seen no sign of a fishing *rod*.

"No rod, for instance, such as this."

Impelling himself to his feet with the aid of his stick, Dr. Fell reached round to the back of the sofa. He produced a large suitcase, and opened it.

Inside lay, piecemeal, the disjointed sections of a fishing rod, black metal with a nickel-and-cork grip into which were cut the initials, 'A.M.F.' But no line was wound round the reel. Instead, to the metal eyelet on what would have been the end or tip of the joined rod, had been fastened tightly with wire a small fishing hook.

"A neat instrument," explained Dr. Fell.

"The murderer strangled Forbes, catching him from behind. He then strung Forbes up with those artistic indications of suicide. He turned out the lamp and poured away the remaining oil so that it should seem to have burned itself out. He took down the blackout.

"Then the murderer, carrying this fishing rod, walked out of the hut by the door. He closed the door, leaving the knob of the bolt turned uppermost.

"He went round to the window. Pushing the rod through the mesh of the grating—there was plenty of room for it, since I myself could easily get my forefinger through those meshes—he stretched out the rod in a *diagonal* line, from the window to the door.

"With this hook fastened to the tip of the rod, he caught the knob of the bolt, and pulled toward him. It was a bright, *new* bolt (remember?) so that it would shine by (remember?) the moonlight, and he could easily see it. Thus, with the greatest ease and simplicity, he pulled the bolt toward him and fastened the door."

Dr. Fell put the suitcase carefully down on the sofa.

"Of course he had to take the blackout down from the window, and, you see, could not now replace it. Also, it was vitally necessary to take the rod away with him. The handle and reel wouldn't go through the window in any case; and, if he were to pitch the other parts in, his game would be given away to the first spectator who arrived and saw them.

"He then left the premises. He was seen and identified, on getting into his car——"

Chapman let out a strangled cry.

"—by the same Home Guard who had first been curious about that car. On the way back, he took the rod apart and threw away its pieces at intervals into the bracken. It seemed too much to hope for a recovery of the rod; but, at the request of Inspector Donaldson of the Argyllshire County Constabulary, a search was made by the local unit of the Home Guard."

Dr. Fell looked at Chapman.

"They're covered with your fingerprints, those pieces," he said, "as you probably remember. When I visited you at your hotel in the middle of the night, with the purpose of getting your prints on a cigarette case, you were at the same time identified as the man seen driving away from Forbes's cottage just after the time of the murder. Do you know what'll happen to you, my friend? You'll hang."

Walter Chapman Campbell stood with his fingers still twisting his necktie. His expression was like that of a small boy caught in the jam cupboard.

His fingers moved up, and touched his neck, and he flinched. In that hot room the perspiration was moving down his cheeks after the fashion of side whiskers.

"You're bluffing," he said, first clearing his throat for a voice that would not be steady. "It's not true, any of it, and you're bluffing!"

"You know I'm not bluffing. Your crime, I admit, was worthy of the son of the cleverest member of this family. With Angus and Colin dead, and Forbes blamed for it, you could go back quietly to Port Elizabeth. Your father is very ill and infirm. He would not last long as heir to nearly eighteen thousand pounds. You could then claim it without ever coming to England or Scotland at all, or being seen by anyone.

"But you won't claim it now, my lad. Do you think you've got a dog's chance of escaping the rope?"

Walter Chapman Campbell's hands went to his face.

"I didn't mean any harm," he said. "My God, I didn't mean any harm!" His voice broke. "You're not going to give me up to the police, are you?"

"No," said Dr. Fell calmly. "Not if you sign the document I propose to dictate to you."

The other's hands flew away from his face, and he stared with foggy hope. Alistair Duncan intervened.

"What, sir, is the meaning of this?" he asked harshly.

Dr. Fell rapped his open hand on the arm of the sofa.

"The meaning and purpose of this," he returned, "is to let Elspat Campbell live out her years and die happily without the conviction that Angus's soul is burning in hell. The purpose is to provide for Elspat and Colin to the end of their lives as Angus wanted them provided for. That is all.

"You will copy out this document"—Dr. Fell took several sheets of paper from his pocket—"or else write at my dictation, the following confession. You will say that you deliberately murdered Angus Campbell . . ."

"What?"

"That you tried to murder Colin, and that you murdered Alec Forbes. That, with the evidence I shall present, will satisfy the insurance companies and the money will be paid. No, I know you didn't kill Angus! But you're going to say you did; and you have every motive for having done so.

"I can't cover you up, even if I wanted to. And I don't want, or mean to. But this much I can do. I can withhold that confession from the police for forty-eight hours, in time for you to make a getaway. Ordinarily you would have to get an exit permit to leave the country. But you're close to Clydeside; and I think you could find an obliging skipper to take you aboard an outgoing ship. If you do that, rest assured that in these evil days they won't bring you back.

"Do that, and I'll give you the leeway. Refuse to do it, and my evidence goes to the police within the next half-hour. What do you say?"

The other stared back.

Terror, befuddlement, and uncertainty merged into suspicious skepticism.

"I don't believe you!" shrilled Chapman. "How do I know you wouldn't take the confession and hand me over to the police straight away?"

"Because, if I were foolish enough to do that, you could upset the whole apple cart by telling the truth about Angus's death. You could deprive those two of the money and tell Elspat exactly what her cherished Angus actually did. You could prevent me from achieving the very thing I'm trying to achieve. If you depend on me, remember that I depend on you."

Again Chapman fingered his necktie. Dr. Fell took out a large gold watch and consulted it.

"This," Alistair Duncan said out of a dry throat, "is the most completely illegal, fraudulent——"

"That's it," stormed Chapman. "You wouldn't dare let me get away anyway! It's a trick! If you have that evidence and held up the confession, they'd have you as accessory after the fact!"

"I think not," said Dr. Fell, politely. "If you consult Mr. Duncan there, he will inform you that in Scots law there is no such thing as an accessory after the fact."

Duncan opened his mouth, and shut it again.

"Rest assured," pursued Dr. Fell, "that every aspect of my fraudulent villainy has been considered. I further propose that the real truth shall be known to us in this room, and to nobody else. That here and now we swear an oath of secrecy which shall last to the end of our days. Is that acceptable to everyone?"

"It is to me!" cried Kathryn.

"And to me," agreed Alan.

Duncan was standing in the middle of the room, waving his hands. If, thought Alan, you could imagine any such thing as a sputtering which was not funny, not even ludicrous, but only anguished and almost deathlike, that was his expression.

"I ask you," he said, "I ask you, sir, before it is too late, to stop and consider what you propose! It goes beyond all bounds! Can I, as a reputable professional man, sanction or even listen to this?"

Dr. Fell remained unimpressed.

"I hope so," he answered calmly. "Because it is precisely what I mean to carry out. I hope you of all people, Mr. Duncan, won't upset the apple cart you have pushed for so long and kept steady with such evident pain. Can't you, as a Scotsman, be persuaded to be sensible? Must you learn practicality from an Englishman?"

Duncan moaned in his throat.

"Then," said Dr. Fell, "I take it that you have given up these romantic ideas of legal justice, and will row in the same boat with us. The question of life or death now lies entirely with Mr. Walter Chapman Campbell. I am not going on with this offer all day, my friend. Well, what do you say? Will you confess to two murders, and get away? Or will you deny both, and hang for one?"

The other shut his eyes, and opened them again.

He looked round the room as though he were seeing it for the first time. He looked out of the windows at the shimmering waters of the loch; at all the domain which was slipping away from him; but at a house cleansed and at peace.

"I'll do it," he said.

.    .    .    .    .    .

The 9:15 train from Glasgow to Euston slid into Euston only four hours late, on a golden sunshiny morning which dimmed even the cavernous grime of the station.

The train settled in and stopped amid a sigh of steam. Doors banged. A porter, thrusting his head into a first-class sleeping compartment, was depressed by the sight of two of the most prim, respectable (and probably low-tipping) stuffed shirts he had ever beheld.

One was a young lady, stern of mouth and lofty of expression, who wore shell-rimmed spectacles severely. The other was a professorial-looking man with an even more lofty expression.

"Porter, ma'am? Porter, sir?"

The young lady broke off to eye him.

"*If* you please," she said. "It will surely be evident to you, *Dr.* Campbell, that the Earl of Danby's memorandum, addressed to the French king and endorsed, 'I approve of this; C.R.,' by the king himself, can have been inspired by no such patriotic considerations as your unfortunate Tory interpretation suggests."

"This 'ere shotgun don't belong to you, ma'am, does it? Or to you, sir?"

The gentleman eyed him vaguely.

"Er—yes," he said. "We are removing the evidence out of range of the ballistics authorities."

"Sir?"

But the gentleman was not listening.

"If you will cast your mind back, madam, to the speech made by Danby in the Commons in December, 1680, I feel that certain considerations of reason contained therein must penetrate even the cloud of prejudice with which you appear to have surrounded yourself. For example . . ."

Laden with the luggage, the porter trudged dispiritedly along the platform after them. *Floreat scientia!* The wheel had swung round again.

THE END